# FINAL WITNESS

WANG HONGJIA

*Translated by*
James Trapp

SINOIST

University House
11-13 Lower Grosvenor Place,
London SW1W 0EX, UK
Tel: +44 (0)20 7834 7676
Fax: +44 (0)20 7973 0076
E-mail: info@alaincharlesasia.com
Web: www.alaincharlesasia.com

Beijing Office
Tel: +86(0)10 8472 1250
Fax: +86(0)10 5885 0639

Author: Wang Hongjia
Translator: James Trapp
Editor: David Lammie
Cover art: Daniel Li

Published by Sinoist Books (an imprint of ACA Publishing Ltd) in association with China Translation and Publishing House

Chinese text © 2016, China Translation and Publishing House, Beijing, China

ALL RIGHTS RESERVED. NO PART OF THIS PUBLICATION MAY BE REPRODUCED IN MATERIAL FORM, BY ANY MEANS, WHETHER GRAPHIC, ELECTRONIC, MECHANICAL OR OTHER, INCLUDING PHOTOCOPYING OR INFORMATION STORAGE, IN WHOLE OR IN PART, AND MAY NOT BE USED TO PREPARE OTHER PUBLICATIONS WITHOUT WRITTEN PERMISSION FROM THE PUBLISHER.

The greatest care has been taken to ensure accuracy but the publisher can accept no responsibility for errors or omissions, or for any liability occasioned by relying on its content.

Paperback ISBN: 978-1-910760-96-3
Hardback ISBN: 978-1-83890-502-6
eBook ISBN: 978-1-910760-97-0

A catalogue record for *Final Witness: The Story of China's First Crime Scene Investigator* is available from the National Bibliographic Service of the British Library.

# FINAL WITNESS

## THE STORY OF CHINA'S FIRST CRIME SCENE INVESTIGATOR

### WANG HONGJIA

Translated by
**JAMES TRAPP**

SINOIST BOOKS

# PREFACE TO THE ENGLISH EDITION

As I write this, an extraordinarily vivid memory is summoned.

It's midday, and I am a young man of eighteen or nineteen. In the 1960s and 1970s, more than two million young people like me left the city to go and live and work in the countryside. We had a name: we were called – 知青 the 'educated youths'. That day, an 'educated youth' from elsewhere came to our village for a short while. He brought with him a tattered book, missing both its front and back covers. When I leafed through it, I was riveted.

Actually, it would be more accurate to say, I was thunderstruck.

I discovered, for the first time, that there was a branch of learning called abductive reasoning.

It was also the first time I heard the name of Sherlock Holmes.

That day, I read two and a half detective stories; the half was because the owner of the book had to leave. There were many other stories in the book that I didn't get to read, as he took them away with him. I was rather depressed at the realisation he was departing with something that could have opened my eyes and changed my life.

As it was, the change that did occur was almost mystical. As I read those two and a half stories, I had a kind of out-of-body experience. I forgot my surroundings completely, and as the plots unfolded, I found myself immersed, instead, in the streets and alleys of Victorian London. From this I learned the power of writing, even in a short space of time, to open the gates of understanding.

Many years later, I discovered that these stories were the work of the British writer Sir Arthur Conan Doyle and came from his book *The Casebook of*

*Sherlock Holmes*. Even more years have passed, and I have written a book of my own about the investigations of China's famous judge, Song Ci, which is being published in the United Kingdom in a translation by James Trapp. Now, as I write this preface to the English edition, the vivid memory of that midday in a village courtyard is still with me, and I think, with gratitude, of what a fine thing it is that reading can allow people to share the wisdom of scholars of far distant countries.

Of course, there are major differences between Song Ci and Sherlock Holmes. Holmes is a fictional character, while Song Ci was a real person. In Holmes's time, there was electricity, and the whistles of steamships could be heard on the River Thames. Song Ci lived when the Song dynasty ruled over only half its territory, and Genghis Khan was uniting all the tribes north of the Gobi desert. Soon, the Mongol horde would leave its indelible mark on the whole of China and much of Europe.

I chanced on Song Ci because we share the same hometown. Even though he has been dead for more than 700 years, I experienced a sudden spiritual meeting of minds that resulted in a vivid and permanent connection.

Song Ci's story is extraordinary enough in its own right. The book he wrote in the Song dynasty, *Collected Cases of Injustice Righted*, also known as *The Washing Away of Wrongs*, is recognised by later generations as the first work, anywhere in the world, on forensic medicine. Song Ci is regarded as the founder of this particular branch of science. Yet he is not mentioned in the official *History of the Song Dynasty*. The Qing dynasty's *Complete Library of the Four Treasuries* purports to include every aspect of Chinese culture and civilisation, but its table of contents contains only a 'summary' of *Collected Cases of Injustice Righted*, and of Song Ci himself, it just says "full details uncertain".

Why has he been so neglected? His theories have been carried across the world by visitors to China from Korea, Japan, France, the UK, the Netherlands, Germany and many other countries, and have had a deep and lasting influence on the development of forensic science. But in none of those translations and interpretations of his work was his name even mentioned, and the world remained in ignorance of his existence. Again, I ask, why is that? It is the literary and scientific equivalent of the mystery of the Flying Dutchman.

It was in 1978, when I was twenty-five years old, that I was first drawn to this mystery. I heard an inner voice asking me: can you not bring Song Ci to the world's attention in literary form? At first my stomach lurched at this thought, but then my excitement mounted. Why not give it a go?

But how was I to set about this task?

Reading... I had to read the book! But the Song dynasty edition of

*Collected Cases of Injustice Righted* has long ago been lost, and only a tiny number of Yuan dynasty versions survive. The first thing I found, when I started searching, was a manuscript copy, from which I could see that the work did not contain any mention of specific cases. This was like a medical text book failing to refer to actual patients. But the observations on investigation and examination contain profound wisdom. What medium would be best to spread an understanding of Song Ci and what he stood for? That was when I thought of a novel, and remembered Sherlock Holmes.

It has always been a challenge to draw out the hidden, inner truth of things and make it patent to human understanding. Morning to evening I pondered over all this, and as the sound of insects chirruping in the lush vegetation filled the night air of my hometown, time and time again a voice asked me: How was Song Ci able to write the world's first textbook of forensic medicine? I began to realise that, in tracking down the real Song Ci, I could not rely solely on the traces of him to be found in the historical record. I also had to consider the circumstances of his upbringing and his youthful experiences. From then on, images began to unroll before my eyes of our hometown of Jianyang in the Song dynasty, and of the world, both inside and outside China, as the Song was superseded by the Liao and the Yuan.

I also recalled the assassination of Julius Caesar in 44 BCE, and how the autopsy performed by the physician Antistius has long been regarded by Westerners as the first ever performed in the history of forensic medicine. But this is not the case. The *Feng Zhen Shi*, excavated from the Qin tomb in Hubei province, is a book on criminal investigation, written on bamboo slips, in which many different types of examination and investigation are recorded.

To take one example: Woman A was six months pregnant when she quarrelled with Woman B, who knocked her to the ground. Woman A suffered a miscarriage and took the foetus, wrapped in a bundle, with her when she went to lay charges against Woman B. When the presiding magistrate ordered the bundle to be cut open, all he could see was a bloody lump, about the size of a man's hand, which was not clearly distinguishable as a foetus. He called for a basin of water, into which he put the bloody lump, and then swished the water around it. As the blood gradually cleared away, a foetus appeared on which the head, torso, arms, hands, fingers, legs, feet, right down to the toes, were all clearly visible. Only the eyes, ears and mouth could not be distinguished. The magistrate then ordered one of his concubines to examine the woman's private parts. The concubine reported that there was dried blood on both sides of the woman's vulva, and that there was fresh blood flow that was not consistent with the woman's menses. Thereupon, the magistrate sent his men to arrest Woman B. Thus, this case involved not just the 'autopsy' of a premature foetus, but also the examination of a woman who had recently suffered a miscarriage. The tomb from which the *Feng Zhen Shi* was excavated has been established by archaeological investigation to date from the Warring States to Qin dynasty period. Qin Shihuang reunified China in 221 BCE. We can be certain, therefore, that the cases of examination and investigation recorded in the *Feng Zhen Shi*, however you look at it, predate the autopsy of Julius Caesar by at least 200 years.

But the investigations recorded in the *Feng Zhen Shi* are not the earliest in Chinese history. We know from the *Book of Rites* that there were specialist investigating officials in Zhou dynasty prisons who conducted differential examinations of injuries to skin, flesh, bone and combined trauma to both flesh and bone. And that was 3,000 years ago. *Collected Cases of Injustice Righted* shows us that Song Ci was not only the repository of a long tradition of forensic investigation by judges in the past, he also added to that tradition with discoveries made in the course of the cases he himself presided over.

From the Yuan and Ming dynasties onwards, there have been many editions of *Collected Cases of Injustice Righted*, with both additions and deletions, some of which have been translated into other languages. The earliest European edition is a translation into French of the Qing dynasty text known as *The Washing Away of Wrongs* published in Paris in 1779, in the periodical *The History of Arts and Science in China*. This was three years after Great Britain recognised the independence of America, and twenty years before the Napoleonic Code was promulgated in France. In 1853, the *Report of the Royal Asiatic Society* in England published a review of an essay entitled 'Evidence for the Washing Away of Wrongs'; in 1873 the Professor of Chinese at Cambridge University, HA Giles, published his translation in instalments in the periodical *The China Review*, and the complete work was published in 1924 in the bulletin of the Royal Society of Medicine, and also as a single volume abstract.

In the course of my voyage of discovery of Song Ci in China and abroad, I came to feel that, on the one hand, I was quite capable of producing my own work of literature, but, on the other, I lacked the necessary discrimination to accurately depict the multi-faceted and intricate nature of the subject. It is always said that the human spirit is the most difficult thing to write about, and that success in this depends very much on the psychology of the writer himself.

One source of inspiration did come quietly and naturally to my pen, when I understood that I could strive to fuse together literary skill and historical accuracy. Thus, when you read in this book of Song Ci's birth, his education, his growth to maturity and his dedicated official service, all of this is historically accurate; the details of the main judicial examinations and their basis all come from *Collected Cases of Injustice Righted*, and even the particulars of the sentences handed down are all in accordance with the Song penal code. I came to understand that the novel could remain within the limits of historical accuracy, and still express a fundamental truth – one might even say a higher truth.

There are many novels out there, and many biographies. This book is a marriage of the two genres. The combination can have an even deeper effect on the critical reader. It is said that Conan Doyle's Sherlock Holmes has genuinely stimulated English people's analytical ability. I would like to tell my readers that when, many years ago, I first strove to use the literary form to achieve this task, it proved to be an extraordinary beginning to my own journey of self-discovery. You might say that every line written for public consumption was also a brick in the construction of my own identity. I believe that this book will help young readers to develop their analytical skills and advance their intellectual ability; and I hope that it may also inspire in them the determination to achieve great things themselves.

5 December 2017

*History records Song Ci's tour of inspection to the interior, or, as it also is described, 'his wheel tracks stopped wherever there was injustice'. That is to say, he saw the scope of his responsibilities as extending to the most hazardous places and poorest of villages, and he carried out inspections in every one. This is not some fiction added for dramatic effect. There is no record of a contemporary, high-ranking official acting in such a way in any Western country, so he may truly be called a model judge for all mankind and the father of forensic medicine.*

**Wang Hongjia**

# CHAPTER I

## HOOFBEATS ON THE ANCIENT ROAD

I started out on this history because Song Ci's hometown of Jianyang was also my own. In 111 BCE, when the Yumen Pass marked one of the north-west limits of the Han empire, the city of Jianyang was one of its most far-flung fortifications in the south-east. By the Song dynasty, the ancient road from the southern states of Wu and Yue into Fujian had been transformed by commercial traffic into a major highway. In the tenth year of the Jiading period (1217), when Song Ci passed the exams for imperial service with close to top marks, his father Song Gong fell ill, and Song Ci hurried home from the capital. Soon afterwards, his father died, and Song Ci was unable to take up an official post as he had to remain at home to observe the mourning period. In the winter of the same year, unable to defend against the attacks of the ferocious Mongol horsemen, the Jin army turned its attentions to swallowing up the Southern Song in order to strengthen its defensive positions against the Mongols. They crossed the Huai River, and launched a large-scale assault on the south...

# CHAPTER I

## ROME IS ON THE ANCIENT ROAD

# 1

# STORMY WEATHER

The dawn wind blowing in from the wilderness carried a damp chill that scoured the face. A few lonely villages, scattered across the landscape like stars, emerged fleetingly from the swirling mist. No sound of cocks crowing or dogs barking came from these villages, and the only noise was of hoofbeats clattering like raindrops, steady and continuous on the trail of the morning stars.

The trunk road ran from the capital, Lin'an (Hangzhou), across southern Zhejiang Province to Fujian. The dawn light silhouetted two horses galloping along this road at breakneck speed. They carried two men, Song Ci and Song Xie. This was their second day in the saddle, and the previous night they had taken only the briefest of rests before continuing their journey. Since receiving the news of his father's illness, Song Ci had seemingly lost all desire to sleep.

The Song family descended over several generations down a single line, and Song Ci himself was an only child. His father had great hopes for him, and chose for him the given name Ci (compassionate) and the courtesy name[1] Huifu (benevolent official). This underlined the expectation that he would reach the highest rank in imperial service and become a paragon of official virtue whose care for the people would stand as an example for future generations.

But reaching the highest rank is much easier said than done.

Song Ci was born in the thirteenth year of the Chunxi period of the Song emperor, Xiaozong (1186) and he entered the Imperial Academy in Lin'an at the age of twenty. At that time, the academy was still following the 'three colleges' system introduced by Wang Anshi during the Xining period of

Emperor Shenzong (1068-1077), which divided students into the three colleges: Outer, Inner and Superior. Because of his extensive knowledge of the classics and his ability as a poet, Song Ci was enrolled in the Superior College. Students in this college could by-pass the lesser examinations at prefectural and provincial levels, and enter directly into the imperial examinations. However, Song Ci, twice running, failed to find a place on the list of successful candidates.

"The system is rigged," Song Ci complained bitterly.

"That is not a constructive attitude," his father replied.

Fathers take responsibility for their sons and it's hard for them to accept that their offspring's failings might actually be attributed to another individual, or, indeed, to a corrupt system.

In fact, the Song civil service examinations used a succession of tactics to combat fraud. In the third year of the Chunhua period of Emperor Taizong (993 CE), the 'locked room' system was implemented. This was followed by the 'sealed copy' system and subsequently the 'transcription' system. In this last system, officials made fair copies of the candidates' scripts so that examiners had no opportunity either to see the names or even to recognise the handwriting.

Song Ci's father was an upright official of the old school, and although he loved his son deeply, it was a stern and upright love, so his words were like a thorn in the young man's side. From then on, as he laboured over his books late into the night, Song Ci felt he was tasting the bitterest gall a life of study had to offer. In the end, however, in the tenth year of the Jiading period (1217), having passed the examinations for the Ministry of Rites, Song Ci entered the palace examinations for the imperial court of Emperor Ningzong. This time he succeeded brilliantly, coming third out of the whole cohort. In the top three in the imperial examinations! His first thoughts on this long-awaited day were of his father and how to get the joyous news to him so far away in Guangzhou. And then, out of nowhere, came word of his father's potentially terminal illness.

The horses' hooves clattered continually along the deserted trunk road until around noon when Song Ci and Song Xie stopped at a small wayside inn, dismounted, snatched a bite to eat, watered the horses and then resumed their journey.

Song Ci's father, Song Gong, who had taken up a post as a prefectural judge in Guangzhou, was approaching his sixtieth birthday and for many years had enjoyed generally good health. But a succession of colds and flu had undermined this irreparably. The most recent illness had struck at the end of summer and had begun with a slight swelling of the abdomen, a stomach-ache and some problems with elimination. But it had not really worried Song Gong, and he had thought it would pass of its own accord. As the days turned into months with no improvement, however, he became aware of a lump growing in his side and which was causing some discomfort. He grew more and more easily tired until he reached the point where he could no longer attend to his official duties. By the following spring, his skin had begun to darken, and he was losing weight constantly though his swollen abdomen gave him the appearance of being pregnant. He looked weak and strained and his blood vessels stood out, thumping like a drum and then occasionally fluttering like a hummingbird's wings. None of the many doctors in Guangzhou offered any hope of a cure, so Song Gong resolved to return home to Jianyang.

Song Gong's ancestral home was not originally in Jianyang, in the south-eastern province of Fujian. In the time of the Tang Chancellor, the Duke of Wenzhen (Wei Zheng 580-643 CE), his forebears moved from Xingtai in Hebei Province in north-eastern China, where they had lived for four generations, to Jiande in Zhejiang Province. Only after a further three generations did they move to Jianyang. The Song family ancestral official who settled in Jianyang was called Song Shitang. He was county deputy there, and the family records describe him as "an incorruptible guardian of the law, wise in all matters". He ended his period of office in Jianyang, and on his death-bed exhorted his wife and son to settle there. From then on, Jianyang became the Song family ancestral home.

Song Shitang's son was Song Xiang, who, according to the family annals, was an accomplished poet at the age of seven. Later, he became an officer in the records department of the Ministry of Education, and he developed a reputation as a talented, scholarly and influential official in the capital city. After he retired back to Jianyang, he funded the building of the Tongyou Bridge. Generation by generation, the Song family ancestors grew in the esteem of the people of Jianyang. Song Shitang's courtesy name was Shiqing (noble official) while Song Gong's was Zhiqing (upright official), which show the importance each generation placed on their descendants continuing the tradition of government service. So, when Song Gong realised he was nearing his end, he was desperate to know how his son had fared in the examinations. One day he said to his faithful old retainer, Song Xie: "Quickly, pack everything we need. We're going home."

Seeing the strain in Song Gong, Song Xie couldn't help himself remonstrating: "But Master, think of your health. How will you cope with such a rough and arduous journey?"

"Not another word! Go and pack."

"There would be no harm in waiting a while…"

"No more delay! If we return now, I can consult Dr Haiting."

At the mention of Dr Haiting, back in Jianyang, Song Xie remained silent. He had thought of this, too, but had hoped to wait until his master's health had improved a little before making the journey. Considering it now, he began to feel there was little point in waiting any longer, adding to Song Gong's anxiety over his son. So perhaps the sooner they left, the better. He packed their belongings carefully, and they set out on the road home. With Song Xie tending to his master's every need, the two of them left Guangdong and made their way to Fujian, soon reaching Jianyang.

As they arrived, one of the servants in their retinue hurried ahead to announce them, and, in a state of great excitement, all the members of the Song family rushed out to meet the travellers.

By this time Song Gong was very weak, barely able even to recognise his own family. Song Xie gently lifted him down from his bed in the palanquin and took him straight to the bed in his wife's chamber.

The mistress of the household was already past fifty, and not in good health herself, but her serene and imperturbable nature gave all who met her the impression of a woman of great beauty and high intelligence.

Her daughter-in-law, Song Ci's wife, came from the Lian clan and was a model of womanly grace, charm and elegance. She immediately ordered a maid to bring a bowl of hot water, and herself wrung out a wet towel to wipe her father-in-law's face. Her daughter, Song Qi, stood beside the old man's bed holding onto her mother's skirts, unaware of the gravity of the situation.

"Kang Liang, go at once to Anshan and see if Dr Haiting is at home," the old lady ordered one of the family retainers.

"I'll go myself," said Song Xie, sweating profusely.

"No!" Song Gong ordered, opening his eyes and looking at Song Xie as he shook his head slightly.

Song Xie realised the old man had something to tell him, so he stooped to listen. "Go straight to Lin'an," Song Gong said urgently.

Seeing the old man's serious expression, Song Xie's eyes suddenly filled with tears, and he replied immediately that he would set out at once.

It was the time of the spring floods in the regions south of the Yangtze, and the river in front of the two men had washed away a wooden bridge. But the waters had already receded, and although the bridge had not been repaired, when the men stopped on the banks they could see that the water was, in fact, quite shallow. They urged their horses into the river, hooves splashing…

There were two men close to Song Ci's heart: his father and Dr Haiting. Dr

Haiting was the most famous doctor for many miles around his home town and had long had a reputation for miraculous cures. Some years before, Song Ci's wife was undergoing a difficult labour but Dr Haiting ensured both mother and daughter survived what had seemed a hopeless situation. The trouble was that the good doctor would often go off on his wanderings, never for less than two or three weeks and often for months on end, so there was no way of knowing if he was currently in Jianyang.

Dusk was falling, and the hoofbeats startled the birds roosting in the trees beside the road. The red orb of the sun slid slowly behind the mountains to be replaced by a crescent moon, and the hoofbeats pounded on…

2

# A NIGHT VISIT TO DR HAITING

Jianyang is an ancient city in Zhi County in the northern reaches of Bamin (the old name for Fujian Province). The first city was built by Zou Wuzhu, King of Minyue in the Han dynasty. He was descended over thirteen generations from King Goujian of Yue, and is the first recorded ruler in the written records of Fujian. In 111 BCE, as the Yumen Pass became the most westerly pass of the Western Han empire, Datan City, as Jianyang was then known, represented the south-eastern extreme of its territory. It also marked the principal access route into Fujian.

By the Song dynasty, more than a thousand years later, the feet, hooves and wheels of countless merchants and their horses and carriages had pounded this route between Wu Yue and Min into a bustling trunk road. And now along it hurried the two travellers, stopping briefly only to satisfy their hunger before continuing directly to Jianyang.

Jianyang nestles between the river and the mountains, and beyond its eastern Yongan Gate, across the river, is the ancient township of Tongyou where the Song family home was to be found.

At dusk, the ancient city walls came into view, and as the hoofbeats stopped outside the door, Song Ci's wife hurried out to greet her husband.

"How is my father?" Song Ci asked urgently as he dismounted and handed the reins to Song Xie.

"He's dozing," his wife Song Yulan replied tensely.

Song Ci stepped over the threshold and entered the house. As soon as Song Ci's mother saw her son, her remaining self-possession deserted her, and she could not speak as she choked back tears. After greeting his mother, Song Ci hurried over to his father's bedside.

The maid, Qiu Juan, brought a lamp and Song Ci could see that his father was looking pale and haggard, and was clearly disoriented. Song Ci fell to his knees beside the bed and wept uncontrollably.

"Has Dr Haiting examined him?" he asked.

Song Yulan turned to look at her mother-in-law, and the old woman nodded her head and choked out: "Yes, he has."

"Well?" he exclaimed, and when no one replied, continued: "Speak up!"

Still nobody spoke, and Song Ci was puzzled. Finally, Song Yulan said: "Dr Haiting would not prescribe anything."

"Why not?"

His mother let out a sob, and the whole family fell to weeping.

The fact was that Dr Haiting's first consideration was always to ascertain if the condition was curable. No matter how intractable the illness, if there was a possibility of a cure he would go through fire and water to effect it. But if it was terminal, he never prescribed. Song Ci had long known this, but now, for the first time, he understood for himself.

"No, no!" he cried, turning to his mother. "I'll go and consult him myself."

Night had fallen and all was deathly quiet when Song Ci set out from the town, with Song Xie again by his side. As he rode through the darkness, all he could think of was his helplessness in the face of his father's illness and his desperation at leaving him in this condition. As for Dr Haiting, whom he revered, and his refusal to treat the patient, that he simply could not comprehend. As he considered what lay ahead, he realised it all hung on whether or not he could change Dr Haiting's mind. The doctor had, after all, already refused treatment, but begging him to reconsider was his only option.

"In the end, Dr Haiting is Dr Haiting, and that's all there is to it."

Dr Haiting's family name was Xiong, his given name Yu and his courtesy name Yunxuan. He was a native of Jianyang and came from a long line of respected scholars. One of his ancestors, Xiong Mi, had been a government minister in the Tang dynasty, and he established an academy of classical learning in his home town that catered only for the children of aristocratic families. When he was young, Xiong Yu contracted a strange disease; multi-coloured sores the size of cherries appeared on the top of his head and they ulcerated and spread down his body. His family thought there was no hope for him, but then, out of nowhere, he was cured by an anonymous, itinerant doctor who had come to the door asking for a drink of water. When he had recovered, Xiong Yu left home to follow this doctor on his wanderings across the country.

In fact, this itinerant doctor was a famous medical man from the Northern Song capital of Dongjing (Kaifeng). After the fall of the capital to the Jin (Jurchen Tartars), his entire family had been slaughtered by the invaders, leaving him all alone. Thereafter, he took to the roads as a travelling doctor, wandering where the heavens led him. Xiong Yu followed the doctor to Zhongdu (Beijing) which the Jin had already established as their capital, and from there to Zhongxingfu (Yinchuan in Ningxia), which was the capital of the Western Xia.

It was not long after this that the old doctor died. Observing all due ceremony, Xiong Yu arranged his burial and then headed southwards on his solitary travels. After reaching the border town of Jianchangfu in the Kingdom of Dali (Xichang in Sichuan), he set off on the Tongzhoufu road within the borders of the Southern Song. It was not long before he reached the banks of the Yangtze where he took the river back east until once again he was approaching his home town, the hair on his temples by now as white as heavy frost. His fellow townsfolk didn't recognise him and had no idea of his real name, so, because he had called himself Haiting on his travels, that's what they called him, too, adding the title Doctor.

The gloom of the night was deepening, and the bad weather hid the moon and brought a damp chill to the air. As he sped along, Song Ci couldn't help thinking of the year when Dr Haiting had brought his wife and daughter back from the dead.

Song Yulan, whose courtesy name was Lianshi, was born into a literary family of long-standing, and was the maternal niece of Song Ci's childhood teacher, Wu Zhi. Yulan's father had been involved in a disastrous lawsuit, the stress of which drove both her mother and father into the grave, so she was raised in her maternal uncle's household. As childhood playmates, Song Ci and Yulan grew up like brother and sister, and remained deeply attached to each other as they became adults. They married when Yulan was eighteen, but by the time she was twenty-four she was still childless. On several occasions, Song Ci's parents thought of urging him to take another consort, but Song Ci was unwilling. Song Gong always remembered that he had been married for quite a number of years before his own son was born, so he did not press the matter. When she was twenty-five, Yulan became pregnant, but her appetite immediately waned, and six months in, she was suffering from frequent bouts of vomiting and profuse sweating. With great difficulty, she made it into her eighth month and then began to feel a bit more herself. But only a few days later she developed a crippling pain in her abdomen and went into labour.

It was the time of the New Year's Eve feast in the third year of the Jiading period (1210). The midwife had been summoned and the whole household was running in circles. The next day, Yulan was suffering stabbing pains in her abdomen and her lower back was going into spasms. It seemed the baby was on its way, come what may. Yulan was in a terrible state, her long black hair soaked in sweat, her face white as paper. Her hands had been clutching the quilt, but they gradually relaxed and she fell into a swoon.

"Mistress," the midwife said timidly to Song Ci's mother, "the lady is already very weak from her pregnancy, and with the shock of this breech delivery, I'm afraid…"

Song Ci's father was away, and the young man had never had to deal with a crisis like this before. He was totally at a loss, so his mother took control: "Son, go and fetch Dr Haiting at once."

It was highly unseemly in such circumstances to summon the doctor, who was a lifelong bachelor, and besides there was no certainty that he would come. But desperate times call for desperate measures. Song Ci turned to go, and when he was at the door, his mother urged him: "No matter how much he tries to refuse, you have to make him come."

Song Ci went.

Dr Haiting came.

It seemed as though a spring wind had swept into the Song household. As long as there was the slightest hope for the patient, male and female were all the same to Dr Haiting. Through the bed's gauze canopy, the doctor looked at Lianshi and then ordered the midwife: "Quick, cut the excess hair from the crown of her head."

Urgently, he took a handful of castor beans and mashed them to a paste, then he cracked four eggs, discarding the whites and keeping the yolks. Along with these, he added a measure from a packet of yellow-coloured medicine and mixed it all into the castor bean paste. This he then spread onto the crown of Lianshi's head. Instantly, Lianshi felt some rhythmic contractions starting in her womb, just as though something was lifting up the foetus inside.

Dr Haiting then removed the bean paste from the patient's head, mixed some wine into it and re-applied it to the gushing spring acupuncture point on both her feet. Presently, Lianshi had a similar sensation to the one before in her womb, but this time it felt as though something was drawing the foetus downwards. However, by now Lianshi was completely exhausted and nothing more happened. This time the doctor took some Tongguansan powder and blew it up Lianshi's nostrils, making her sneeze. She sneezed violently several times, and little by little, miraculously, the baby was born.

But the baby was still, neither moving nor crying, and everyone thought there was no hope for it. Unhurriedly, Dr Haiting picked up the baby, held it upside down by its feet and smacked it three times on the buttocks. With a single loud "Wah!", the baby came to life, crying and wriggling. Of course, this baby was none other than Song Qi. Indeed, the girl owed her name, in part, to the *huangqi* medicine that Dr Haiting used at her birth. *Huangqi* is a tonifying and invigorating medicine that acts to replenish *qi* and strengthen the core.

As they reached the foot of Anshan, which is situated about twenty *li* east of Jianyang Prefecture, the dark shadow of the mountain enveloped the road ahead. By the start of the path up the mountain, there was a homestead that served as a stabling place for the horses and carriages of pilgrims going to burn incense in the temple at the summit. Song Ci and Song Xie went in to light tapers and then set off up the mountain.

After Dr Haiting returned from his wanderings, he had made his home on Anshan. The mountain got its name in the Later Tang dynasty (923-37 CE) and the story goes that, in the time of Emperor Mingzong, there was a celebrated hermit called Shihu who built the Lingquan Shrine on the mountain, and it was this shrine that gave it its name. Anshan is the highest mountain in the eastern part of Jianyang Prefecture, an area of many towering peaks. Three thousand vertiginous steps snake their way to the top in a series of ninety-nine turns. Its slopes are covered in luxuriant bamboo forests, rich green all year round, interspersed with flowering trees and bushes that seem to be perpetually in bloom. The Lingquan shrine perches on the mountainside like a sky-pavilion, and people say it is "lofty and imposing as Mount Wuyi, dominating the region". On Lion Ridge on the northern peak of the mountain there is a spring from which the waters, clear as transparent jade, gush ceaselessly, never drying up. One mouthful of water from this spring refreshes the heart and purifies the spirit, and so it became known as Ling Quan, the Magic Fountain. Dr Haiting had found a spot under the cliffs near the spring, sheltered from wind and rain, to build himself a grass hut to live in. From there, he gathered all kinds of dew-watered medicinal mountain plants and herbs to make his pills and potions.

Living on the mountain top had two advantages for Haiting as a doctor: first, it was very convenient for his preparation of medicines, and second it meant that his ability to make a living wasn't being hindered by people constantly wanting to consult him about every kind of illness, big or small.

Because of this second reason, he had, for many years, stuck firmly to his guiding principle – take no notice of minor ailments, concentrate only on the serious. Thus, with Song Gong's critical illness, Haiting was deeply concerned, and when the old family retainer came to summon him, he left the mountain immediately. But at the same time he was equally worried that, in this instance another of his guiding principles might apply – if the illness is terminal, do not prescribe.

As they climbed, the wind grew stronger, making their torches flicker and almost go out. As they came to the fortieth hairpin, a thousand or more steps up, the wind, which was swirling remorselessly through the mountains and valleys, screamed around them and finally extinguished the torches. Fortunately, Song Xie had some knowledge and experience of night travel, so he went first, and with Song Ci tight behind him, they made their way on up. The going was hard and it was midnight before they reached the summit.

The wind was getting wilder, making the trees and shrubs shudder and crash into each other with a noise like ocean waves. In all his thirty-one years, Song Ci had never experienced anything like this, and it sent a chill down his spine. The night sky was starless, and as the two men looked around, the only light they could see was the glowing halo of a lantern to the north of them, seemingly immune to the gusting wind.

They made their way towards it and quite soon could hear the faint sound of a wind chime that hung from the eaves of the Lingquan shrine. A little further on and there, indeed, they could make out through the darkness the even darker silhouette of the ancient building. The lamp they could see, under the cliffs to the left of the shrine, marked Dr Haiting's hut.

The wind began to drop as they skirted the shrine and made their way towards the lamp. Encouraged by the proximity of the light, the two men strode on, finding themselves in a spot that was sheltered from the wind. Now they could see it more clearly, the lamp revealed itself as an ordinary cloth-covered lantern, hanging above the single plank door of a grass hut. And on that door hung a wooden tablet inscribed with the words "Haiting lives here". The doctor had placed the lantern there specifically as a beacon for any patients climbing the mountain at night to consult him.

When Song Ci and Song Xie reached the hut door, there was no sound inside. They guessed Haiting had already retired to bed, so there was no alternative but to rouse him. Song Xie knocked on the door. As the knock died away, they heard the sound of footsteps. "Hello?" said a nervous voice, and there, standing in the lamplight as he opened the door was a young apprentice.

"Is Dr Haiting at home?" Song Ci asked excitedly.

"Yes, sir. Please come in, gentlemen," said the apprentice, opening the door wider.

"Is the doctor asleep?" Song Ci asked, following the boy into the hut.

"No, sir." The boy pointed. "He's over there."

While talking, they reached the entrance to the main room of the hut, and Song Xie looked inside to see Dr Haiting. Clothed in a hemp robe with a black sash and wearing wooden clogs, he was sitting under a lamp, writing.

"Come in," he said, not looking up and writing a few more characters before laying down his brush.

It had been a good few years since Song Ci had last seen the doctor, and he was suddenly aware that time had taken its toll on the old man. He looked thin and shrivelled, and his face was carved with deep wrinkles. The silver whiskers on his chin were sparse and straggling, and only his eyes glinting in the candlelight were a sign of the extraordinary spirit within.

"You are Song Gong's son, are you not?" said Haiting, recognising Song Ci.

"Yes, I am. Master, my father…"

"Honoured Song Ci," Haiting interrupted gently, "I have already examined your noble father and it is not a case of my being unwilling to make every effort for him. It is simply that he is beyond the help of any medicine, and I hope that you will consider carefully before you say any more."

When Song Ci heard these words, he forgot his carefully prepared urgings, and abandoning all niceties and proper salutations, blurted out: "How can you say he is beyond the help of medicine when you haven't prescribed any yet?"

"Honoured Son, your father's life has run its course, and no human power can overrule heaven's decree."

"No, Doctor!" Song Ci pleaded, his words flooding out as though from the very depths of his heart. "All this posturing about not overruling heaven's decree is just a way of protecting your reputation for infallibility."

Dr Haiting looked up.

"Master," Song Ci continued, "you have travelled the world and met with countless hardships. Your medical skill is truly hard-earned. You are admired as a doctor by all your countrymen. So how can you now think of giving up at the first hurdle…"

"Honoured Son, it is not seemly for you to pit praise and censure against each other like this. I am an old man…"

Song Ci dropped to his knees, tears streaming from his eyes onto the ground: "That was not my intention, master. You have spent a lifetime gathering medical knowledge from far and wide and surely should dare to try things our ancestors could not. Even if you don't succeed, you are at least gathering personal experience that could benefit future generations. The ancients have said that a man of integrity never forgets he can use his own corpse to plug a hole in a dam. Master, what is the point of circumscribing your actions just to preserve a reputation? If you are indeed a man of integrity, you cannot let vanity lead you astray. Surely, Master, during our brief time on earth, it is better to employ your wisdom and renown in the cause of the higher virtue of selflessness."

As he spoke, Song Ci's tears were bedewing the top of his gown. He and Song Xie were kneeling in front of Dr Haiting, and the apprentice was standing just outside the room. The doctor looked grave. After a long pause, he looked up, thoughtfully taking the measure of the young man who knelt in front of the desk waiting with self-possession for a reply, as though it was the first time he had met him.

He saw a pale oval face, with a wide forehead and long, slanting eyebrows. The short moustache was soft and appealing, but the bridge of the nose was straight as a brush, with a slightly hooked tip that gave the whole a solemn and earnest look. The sharply drawn lips were upturned, not exactly in a smile, but silently pursed to suggest that nothing unexpected could disturb his self-possession. The glint in the dark, purple-black pupils indicated a lively spirit and a sharp mind. Fine lines were etched on the skin at the corners of the eyes that didn't quite match the rest of the smooth, pale face, leading the observer to guess that they were the reminders of long hours of over-zealous study. Completing this careful appraisal of Song Ci, Dr Haiting stood up and, without a word, made his way into the inner chamber.

There was silence, disturbed only by the sound of the wind still swirling around the mountain outside.

Parting a curtain across a cupboard, Dr Haiting took out ten large packets of medicine and a sheet of notepaper bearing his seal, on which were carefully described the different usages of the medicines. Handing these objects over to the still-kneeling Song Ci, he said softly: "Take these and hurry down the mountain. But remember, there are no guarantees."

Song Ci thanked him with the utmost respect.

Haiting helped him to his feet, and gesturing to the door, whispered urgently: "Go!"

3

# AN UNEXPECTED DEATH

Song Ci and Song Xie hurried down the mountain, reaching home before daybreak.

The whole household roused themselves. The first priority was to seek out the active ingredients Dr Haiting had written on the notepaper. None of these were easy to find: for example, thirty live toads were required, but the house could not provide them and they had to be procured from farmers in the surrounding fields and hills. Then, once they had the live toads, the method of preparation was most unusual: they had to be cut open and disembowelled and the cavity stuffed with *wu ling zhi* (flying squirrel droppings) and salted *sha ren* (cardamom seed). The body was then sewn back up with silk thread, sealed in oil-paper, gently dry roasted, ground to a powder and added to the decoction. Another example involved procuring ten live red earthworms, boiled in aromatic vinegar and the vinegar added to the medicine, and so on and so on. Song Ci busied himself assiduously in all the preparations, and when the medicines were ready, fed them spoonful by spoonful to his father.

After this, Song Ci spent his time shuttling between Tongyou and Anshan, reporting to Dr Haiting any changes in his father's condition after each dose of medicine, and bringing back new medicines to try. All this hard work seemed to be rewarded, as under these conscientious ministrations, Song Gong's condition took a turn for the better.

All this time, Song Ci was also seeking out and reading medical books such as the *Nan Jing* (*Canon of Eighty Difficult Issues*), and discussing his father's condition with Dr Haiting. These conversations helped him to understand the doctor better. And on Haiting's part, he was full of admiration for Song Ci's ability to absorb and understand all this obscure knowledge, and he gradually came to respect his courage and perseverance in seeking the unknown.

Song Ci began to look on Haiting as his master, and Haiting treated Song Ci as a disciple. Come summer, Song Gong was gradually able to get out of bed and walk around, so Song Ci's visits to Anshan became less frequent. Each time he did make the trip, Haiting insisted on his staying the night, and the two of them shared both a meal and a bed, where they talked medicine through the night until dawn.

With autumn, Song Gong had almost completely recovered, and Song Ci decided that he would celebrate the mid-autumn festival with his family and then take up his official duties. Before that, he would have to return to Anshan to take formal leave of Dr Haiting.

So, on the tenth day of the eighth lunar month, Song Ci decided to climb Anshan. Knowing the early autumn heat was usually quite oppressive, he got up particularly early, and with the first glimmerings of dawn showing faint blue on the horizon, set out on his journey. He made his way to Anshan along the main road, which was flanked on both sides by well-irrigated fields. The crops were glistening with dew and ripe for harvest, moist and clear like a canopy of green muslin. The bright, sweet smell of rice paddies enveloped Song Ci, gladdening his heart and lightening his spirit. He thought about the past few months and the labours undertaken by him and Dr Haiting that had brought about such a miraculous cure. And he thought about his official post and the duties he was soon to take up. Song Ci rejoiced in it all. Some skylarks were singing lustily in the slowly brightening dawn sky, and he joined them in serenading the heavens.

When he was halfway up the long flights of dark green steps, the sun emerged, bursting gloriously through the morning mists that swirled among the valleys and gorges. Song Ci could not help stopping to look as the massed peaks surged out of their escort of clouds like an ocean wave rushing into the far reaches of the sky; and the steps he was climbing, weaving in and out of sight, finally disappeared into the sea of clouds. Song Ci thought about his future career, and it seemed to him as unfathomable as the flight of steps melting into the mists. If he could only persevere, he too would burst through to the grandeur and mystery of the summit. After a brief pause, as he continued his climb, he heard the sound of bells spiralling out of the depths of the clouds. At first, he paid it little heed, but as he listened he began to think it rather strange. Why was the bell of the Lingquan shrine ringing out continuously, apparently with no intention of stopping? In that tranquil morning, each peal seemed more solemn. Then, as Song Ci reached the end of the narrow path at the top of the mountain, the seemingly infinite ringing finally stopped. He hurried on towards the north peak, and in the distance he could see a long banner flying from the cliff under which Dr Haiting lived.

"That looks ominous," Song Ci thought to himself. "Could it be that the doctor…"

As he hurried towards the doctor's hut, he could see that all the monks from the shrine had assembled there, chanting sutras in unison, and the rhythmic beating of the accompanying drum filled the dwelling. Instantly, Song Ci understood. Without asking, he knew that Dr Haiting was dead, and the monks were there to mourn him and praise his life of virtue and good deeds. He went into the main room of the hut, the very room where he had so often in the past sat and talked with the good doctor long into the night. He parted the funerary curtain, and behind it saw all the members of the Xiong clan, kneeling. Dr Haiting's body, already clothed in a fine gown and turban, was laid out on a stone table, still looking slender and elegant. His eyes were closed and there was a peaceful smile on his lips, content in death just as he had been in life. Song Ci knelt silently and wept before the doctor's corpse.

After a little while, somebody touched him lightly on the shoulder, and he looked up to see the young apprentice, his head covered in a mourning shawl. In his hands was an old pine book-box, and gesturing with it he said: "My master was taken from us suddenly yesterday. As he lay on his deathbed, with his last breath he ordered me to give this to Your Worship."

Still kneeling in front of the body, Song Ci took the box and opened it. Inside, six large characters in the doctor's *kaishu* (regular script) calligraphy leapt out at him: "*Yi nan bing an shou zha*" – "A personal record of the diagnosis of intractable disease". Song Ci removed from the box six thick manuscript volumes also written in *kaishu*, and as he leafed through them he saw that every page was covered in densely packed characters, no bigger than a fly's head. They were the doctor's daily observations on the treatment of the serious conditions he had encountered. Song Ci immediately realised the true importance of these documents.

Although he had never set out to study medicine, and even now had no pretence to any skill, he recognised what huge benefit the doctor's records would be to him henceforward, representing as they did the hard-earned and deep learning of a lifetime's study and experience. Song Ci's eyes filled with tears as he respectfully raised the documents in both hands.

He stayed on the mountain for three days, but then, realising it was almost the fifteenth day of the month, he took his leave and descended. The sun had already set behind the mountain, but, loth to go completely, was still leaving its blood-red hue on the slopes. As he followed the stone steps down, Song Ci could not help turning back for one last look at Anshan.

At the end of the path stood a stone stele, hard by the monastery gate that perched between cliff and valley. The whole scene had a supernatural air and the towering rocks by the gate looked as though they had been hewn by a demon's axe. An ancient pine tree was perched at the very top, wreathed in clouds, which, as he looked at it, reminded Song Ci irresistibly of Dr Haiting in its stillness and poise. He stopped to look at the couplet carved on the stone stele:

*Through this gate you may reach the Palace of Heaven,*
*And come to the islands of the immortals far from the world of men.*

As he read the couplet, Song Ci thought of the doctor's life, and how he had indeed, in dying, reached the Palace of Heaven.

It was the night of the mid-autumn festival, and all the households had hung red lanterns from their eaves. Young and old in Song Ci's house, even down to the servants and maids, were sitting at a large round table feasting together. After the food, everyone went out into the courtyard to offer fresh fruit to the Moon Goddess Chang E, eat mooncakes and celebrate the full moon. It had been quite an accomplishment for the whole Song family to gather for the festival, but Song Ci knew it was not to last for long, as next morning he would have to leave to take up his post far away. This knowledge cast something of a shadow over the family.

Song Gong had been taciturn over the last few days. For one thing, the death of Dr Haiting had robbed him of sleep for many days. His own miraculous recovery from near death had been solely down to the doctor's unique medical skill. He had never imagined that such a shining light would be extinguished and that the doctor would die before him. How could Song Gong be anything but grief-stricken? And now his son was leaving for distant parts. Of course, this was indeed at his own constant urging, as he believed his son should go to carve out an illustrious career. But even so, on reflection, he couldn't help wondering if this would be the last time he would see his son. He could not stop the tears coming to his eyes.

"Father, I know I must go." Song Ci stood beside his father, realising the old man had something to tell him.

Looking at his son, Song Gong said: "You remember Confucius' instruction to his students always to display respect, tolerance, honesty, diligence and benevolence?"

Song Ci replied: "Respect avoids dishonour, tolerance gains the support of the people, honesty brings advancement, diligence is the foundation of a meritorious career and benevolence earns people's respect."

"Book learning alone accomplishes nothing," his father said. "Over the centuries, loyal ministers have come to grief, while the crafty and obsequious flourish. Many able and virtuous men have met with misfortune through incautious words. Since you were a child you have always been honest and straightforward, but now in your official career you need to be especially prudent."

"Your son will remember this."

"I don't want you to be over-cautious and punctilious. The guiding principle in life should be to be true to one's parents and courageous before the world."

Song Ci listened, nodding, and at that moment the little girl Song Qi came over, asking for a hug from her father. But Lianshi intercepted her, saying: "Come here. Mummy will give you a hug."

Song Qi wasn't happy with this and tried to clamber up onto her father, but the maid Qiu Juan came across and whispered something in the little girl's ear. She frowned and let go of her father, then happily clasped her arms around Qiu Juan's neck and went off with her to play.

Song Gong continued: "All I want is that from now on you are serious and prudent in pursuit of your duties – that you are modest and open-minded, always conscientious and erudite, and that you give great thought to your planning so that, if you receive advancement at some time in the future and have to deal with corrupt officials, or reorganise a department, you will be able to take it all in your stride."

Father and son talked long into the night until the bright moon had moved to the western quadrant, but Song Gong then remembered that his daughter-in-law would also have much she wanted to say to her husband. So he brought the conversation to an end and urged his son to go to bed at once.

Who could have known that, later that night, just as day dawned and as Song Gong rose from bed to empty his bowels, he would suddenly feel dizzy and pitch headlong to the ground? It was only when his wife, hearing a thud, called out several times and got no reply, that she leapt out of bed and discovered Song Gong stretched out on the floor, a large pool of blood forming around his head.

Song Gong's old illness had returned and Song Ci could not possibly leave. In the course of two days, Song Gong's whole body turned yellow, his scrotum swelled, there was blood in his urine and stools, and sweat poured off him ceaselessly. This time, despite three months of constant care, Song Ci finally lost his father.

"Ci, my son... remember... your name..." Song Gong had spoken these words just before he died, and they were carved deep on Song Ci's heart.

In that one sentence were distilled all Song Gong's hopes and aspirations for his son. He had called his son Ci Huifu, which means compassionate benevolent official, hoping that this would inspire him to live up to these attributes in his duties. But now, although he had received his appointment, he could not even travel to take it up, as he had to remain at home to observe the necessary period of mourning.

Following Song Gong's death, his faithful retainer for half a lifetime, Song Xie, took his leave of the Song household to become a Buddhist monk.

At this time in history, the country was in a state of violent and tumultuous change. Eleven years before, in 1206 CE, one of the greatest events in world history took place when the Mongol clan led by Genghis Khan succeeded in uniting all the other tribes of the great steppe area under his banner, and established the Mongol khanate along the banks of the Onon River. Before this, the Mongols had been just one small tribe among the many that inhabited the steppes. But from 1206 onwards, all the peoples of the grasslands were known as Mongols. No one could have imagined that, not only would these people invade the central plain and unite China under their rule, but they would also advance through central and west Asia into Europe. In 1214, the Jin dynasty could no longer resist Genghis Khan's assault and they retreated from their capital city of Zhongdu and moved to their southern capital Nanjing (present day Kaifeng). Soon, Zhongdu and more than 830 cities in Liaodong, Hebei and Shandong were under the control of the Great Khan's Mongol horde.

The Jin government developed two different strategies: one was to ally themselves with the Song dynasty to resist the Mongols; and the other was simply to swallow up the Southern Song so as to increase the area of resistance. In the end, they chose the latter and in the winter of the tenth year of the Jiading period, the Jin army crossed the river and launched a major offensive to the south.

# CHAPTER II

## A LOCAL MURDER

Song Ci is at home in mourning for his father, and is immersed in his books. Then, from nowhere, successive murders are committed at his doorstep, which cause him to take a serious look at himself: years of bitter toil over his studies might bring him the reputation of a classical scholar and recognition as a rhetorician, but what difference would these rarefied skills make to ordinary people and their affairs? In a moment of shattering clarity, he realises how futile it would be to wait until completing his studies to make his mark, when under his nose there are things of real importance to be done.

## CHAPTER II

### A LOCAL MURDER

1

# THE MAID QIU JUAN

In the twelfth month of the tenth year of the Jiading period of the Song dynasty (1217), the Jin army invaded Sichuan, and the Song commander, Huang Yansun, put up no resistance and fled. The Jin then advanced on the Sanguan Pass, and once again the commander, Liu Xiong, relinquished his post without a fight. The invaders put the Sanguan area to the torch and moved on to capture the garrison fort at Zaojiao. There followed further news of defeat after defeat.

At the time, Song Ci was still at home in mourning for his father, and he seldom went out. Occasionally, his thoughts turned to his old student friends, of whom some had already taken up official posts elsewhere, some were teaching in the countryside, and there were even some who had been executed for immoral behaviour. Occasionally, he would get up early to join a group of them to study in Dr Wu Zhi's Tanxi library. There were many more he thought of from his days at the Imperial Academy in Zhongdu, and he particularly missed his great friend Liu Kezhuang.

At dusk, he was often to be found alone on the banks of the Tongyou River, where the evening sun splintered off the water in a myriad of colours. A supple evening mist drifted across the river and in the distance the sound of the evening bell from the Sansheng Temple pierced the twilight colours. Here and there, wisps of smoke from kitchen fires drifted up and out across dilapidated roofs. The distant evening bell reminded him of the solemn sound of the bell for the imperial examinations the year before. It also reminded him of a luxurious tower thirty *li* away beside the lake at Xizi. In the fiery evening light, his memories were swept along like a river in spate, washing away many emotional events from the past. He was thirty-one when he passed the examinations, and now at thirty-two, he had accomplished nothing in life beyond his studies. How was he going to achieve anything in the years to come?

He remembered his old teacher at the academy, Zhen Dexiu. After Master Zhen received his *jinshi* degree in his year's metropolitan examinations, he carried on working hard, and through diligent study he went on to pass the specialist examination for erudite literati that led directly to prime-ministerial rank. So, in the future, events beyond his control notwithstanding, could he too not undertake a further three years study and sit the literati exam... And so, at the time of which we write, continuing home-study of the imperial administrative system became the focus of his existence. He was not to know that, that very autumn, something would occur in his own backyard that would scupper this plan.

In the autumn of the eleventh year of Jiading (1218), a cold wind was gusting through the mountain districts of northern Fujian Province. It was the harvest season; most of the crop had already been gathered, leaving the fields with a melancholy air. Over the next few days, announcements from the local government about the collection of the autumn taxes appeared on the street in front of the *yamen*,[1] casting an immediate winter-like gloom on the place. Bailiffs toured the townships and countryside, banging gongs and chanting repeatedly: "All pay heed to the imperial command. War is coming and everyone is reminded of their duty. Prepare all monies owing for the next five years – fees for exemption from military service, interest on grain-handling charges, taxes on house and land transactions..." These words put fear into the hearts of all who heard them.

At the start of the Northern Song, imperial tax revenue was more than sixteen million strings of cash (one thousand coins to a string) and reached a high-point of sixty million under Emperor Shenzong (1048-1085). The Southern Song's territory was considerably smaller and initially its revenue dropped below ten million, but within thirty years had increased again dramatically to sixty million, roughly the same as in the Northern Song at its height. After another thirty years, it had grown to eighty million and thirty-one years after that, in the eleventh year of Jiading, it was continuing to grow apparently without limit. Even so, the court was still levying taxes in advance. Under Emperor Gaozong, it was only one or two years ahead, under Xiaozong it increased to three or four years, and from the time of Guangzong until the point we have now reached in the story under Emperor Ningzong, a golden rice bowl area such as Jianyang was expected to pay five years in advance. The people had great difficulty in meeting these tax demands, and the *yamen* had to send out troops around the four districts to enforce collection. Every day, the chief of the metropolitan police in the area, Liang E, led several dozen archers and a similar number of horse-drawn carriages flying banners bearing the word 'Tax', out of the city. If any of the countryfolk were even a little late in paying up, they were immediately flogged; if they defaulted, they were carted off to the county jail or locked up in the courthouse. Those arrested and brought in along the western road passed right in front of Song Ci's door, and wept as the archers lashed them with whips and beat them with truncheons. However, Song Ci was ensconced in his library at the back of the house and knew little of what was going on outside.

It was dusk on this particular day, the sun had already set behind the mountain, and the evening gloom was beginning to invade the library where Song Ci was reading in the last of the light. Suddenly, he heard the sound of hurrying footsteps outside the door, which banged open to reveal his wife, Lianshi.

"Why are you so flustered?" he asked.

"Qiu Juan's father couldn't pay his advance taxes and argued with Chief of Police Liang. He was arrested and taken to the county jail..."

"What of it?"

"He has starved to death in there."

"He's dead?" said Song Ci, jumping to his feet. "How can that be?"

"Why not? We are at war and money is short, local officials are under orders to collect the taxes by any means they see fit, so anything can happen. Yesterday, one of the tenant farmers picked a fight with an archer. He was held under the water-powered threshing hammer and pounded into meat-paste in the mortar."

Song Ci couldn't believe what he was hearing. His wife continued: "And Qiu Juan's mother was stamped on by Police Chief Liang until she vomited blood. She may not survive."

Song Ci was astounded. How could so many bloody deeds take place in such a short space of time?

"How is Qiu Juan?" he asked.

"She's crying in the kitchen."

Song Ci hurried off towards the kitchen.

Qiu Juan was a country girl who had joined the Song household as a maid to earn her living. At first, she didn't have a name, so Lianshi called her Qiu Juan, which means Autumn Grace, because of the season of her birth. She was ten when she arrived, and, now sixteen, had grown into a beautiful young woman.

Leaving the library, Lianshi went to her bedroom to fetch some silver coins and then joined Song Ci on the way to the kitchen. There, they found Qiu

Juan's younger brother, who had brought the news, standing beside his sister. Song Ci's mother and the old family servant Kang Liang were also there.

"Qiu Juan!" Song Ci called out.

Qiu Juan turned towards him, and he could see that her face was wet with tears. He was at a loss how best to console her, so in the end he handed her some of the silver his wife had brought, saying: "Go and look after your mother, and give her this money to get some treatment for her injuries."

Qiu Juan didn't dare accept at first, so Lianshi stuffed the coins in the bosom of her gown and said: "You have been with the family a long time, so you mustn't refuse it."

They all escorted Qiu Juan and her brother to the front gate, where the young girl dropped to her knees. Lianshi hastily raised her up, saying: "Quickly, go now."

In the growing dusk, the two young people turned to go, when little Song Qi suddenly piped up: "Qiu Juan, are you coming back?"

Qiu Juan's face glistened with tears in the gloom. Lianshi hugged her daughter and said: "The sooner she goes, the sooner she will come back."

So Qiu Juan left, carrying a cloth bundle over her shoulder and, looking back from time to time, disappeared into the twilight.

Dusk, a few days later, and footsteps once again were heard approaching Song Ci's library. The door opened and there, as before, was Lianshi, her eyes brimming with tears. She didn't enter, nor did she speak.

"What is it?" Song Ci asked

"Qiu Juan is dead!"

"What?"

"Qiu Juan is dead!"

Lianshi wept: "Kang Liang went out today, and saw with his own eyes Qiu Juan's brother and some villagers carrying Qiu Juan's body out of Chai Wanlong's mansion."

"Is that true?"

"I told you, he saw it with his own eyes," said Lianshi. "Qiu Juan's family were tenants of the Chai family. When her father died, Chai Wanlong knew they wouldn't be able to pay the rent, so he sent the Tian brothers to repossess the buildings from her mother. When they saw Qiu Juan, they dragged her off."

"Who are the Tian brothers?"

"They are the Chai family's hired muscle. The elder brother is called Tian Huai and the younger one Tian Ju. They are martial arts experts and the whole countryside is afraid of them."

"What happened next?"

"That night, they claim Qiu Juan ran away, and then a few days later she was found floating in the Chai family pond."

"How come?"

"They must have been molesting her."

"Someone must go to the *yamen* to lay information against them."

"Who is going to go?" Lianshi asked. "Qiu Juan's brother took their sister's body home, and as soon as her mother saw it, she started coughing up blood and died. The neighbours helped out with the funeral for Qiu Juan and her mother, and told her brother that it wasn't safe for him to stay in the area, and that he should run for his life to somewhere far away. So, the brother fled and no one knows where he has gone."

"Why did he run? Why didn't he come and find us?"

"People are more afraid of evil men than they have faith in honest ones. The Chai family have relatives in office in the capital. They themselves are quite low-ranking, but it is said they have connections high up in the Ministry of Appointments and the Ministry of Justice. Even the county magistrate here is afraid of them. With only Qiu Juan's little brother left of the family, they may be afraid he will try to take revenge. If he didn't, in fact, flee, wouldn't they think he was a threat to them?"

As Song Ci listened, he couldn't tell whether he was shocked, disbelieving or angry. All he could hear was his wife's voice, over and over, saying: "Qiu Juan is dead... Qiu Juan is dead..."

The evening wind blew in through the window, swishing open the curtain. Looking out into the courtyard, Song Ci could see a melon frame bursting with ripe fruit – the very fruit that Qiu Juan had tended so carefully every day. The pear trees in the yard had begun to shed their leaves, and some birds returning to their nests had perched in the crooks of the branches, calling dolefully. Beside the perimeter wall some seasonal vegetables were growing, and Song Ci could still see Qiu Juan watering them, her apron overflowing with the blue-green leaves she had picked. "Big sister, come and help me catch the dragonflies." It was little Qi's voice that he had heard one day in the library when, his eyes tired from reading, he had jumped up and stood by the window. Again, he could see Qiu Juan, who was watering the plants, look up and smile, then make her way over to Song Qi.

And now Qiu Juan was dead – only sixteen and suddenly dead, for no reason. All that was left was the wind sighing through the deserted melon frame and its ripe melons, and the bright yellow-green cauliflowers bursting through their leaves.

2

# THE STRANGE GRIEVANCE OF THE TONG FAMILY

The moon was just coming up, spreading its mournful reflection on the Tongyou River. The rushing waters were breaking in white crests against the rocky banks, and the autumn wind blowing across the surface brought a stinging chill to Song Ci's cheeks.

He was still having trouble believing Kang Liang's report of the tragedy that had befallen Qiu Juan. The young girl's family lived in a village called Wulijiang.[1] He felt he had no choice but to go himself and check whether the version of events given by Kang Liang matched that of the villagers. So far, he knew that the neighbours had helped out by burying all three family members in the same grave, and that no one knew the whereabouts of Qiu Juan's little brother. These pitiful circumstances tugged at his heartstrings.

The track from Tongyou to Wulijiang followed the course of the river, and Song Ci hadn't gone far along it when he heard a loud barking. Continuing just a little further on his way, he heard more noise. This time it was the crashing of overturned furniture coming from inside a bamboo hut beside the river, and a voice shouting: "Knife! Knife!"

Startled by the commotion, Song Ci could clearly make out that it was coming from the hut, which had a sign advertising basket staves hanging over its doorway. He made his way over and pushed open the door.

Inside he saw six or seven men wrestling for control of a stave-shaving knife in the hand of a young lad. Suddenly, with one great wrench, the lad tore the hand holding the knife free of his assailants and made a rush for the door. One of the men managed to grasp his trailing leg, and the youth fell to the ground with all the others piling in on top of him. Somehow, he wriggled free and, springing up, gave a great shout, grasped the knife in his mouth, raised his fists, knocked several of the men to the ground and once again rushed for the door.

Song Ci was standing four-square in the doorway, and the young man stared blankly at him for a second before snatching the knife from his mouth and trying to force his way out. Song Ci struck him a lightning blow with the point of his elbow. The knife fell to the ground with a clatter, and the lad tried once again to muscle his way out of the hut. Song Ci shot out a fist and the lad tumbled back inside.

Now, you may wonder how it was that Song Ci could deal such devastating blows. The answer is that, as a child, his father had not just supervised his book-learning, but had also made sure he was well versed in martial arts. The old man reckoned that, in such troubled times and with the country in turmoil, a man needed to know how to look after himself. So he made Song Ci read books on martial arts on the basis that, even if he didn't attain the level of Yue Fei, a famous generals known for smashing through enemy lines, even a little knowledge could come in useful in a tight spot. In fact, Song Ci had been more diligent in his conventional studies than in his fighting ones, and was rather surprised by the effectiveness of his blows. As it was, the men caught the lad as he fell back into the hut and, looking in amazement towards the door, recognised Song Ci.

"Master Song!" they exclaimed.

Song Ci entered the hut and, seeing the bamboo furniture scattered about the floor, looked across at the men. They were all locals of Tongyouzhen, but because he had been away from the area for a long time, and even on his return seldom went out and about, Song Ci recognised only one of them. That was the pharmacist from the apothecary shop in town whom he had often consulted to make up medicines for his father. The other men he did not know.

"What's going on here?" he asked.

The men looked at each other, but no one replied.

"I asked, what is going on here?" he repeated, looking at the pharmacist.

Now the pharmacist was a clever fellow who didn't just dispense medicines at the apothecary; in cases of ordinary winter ailments, he would also diagnose and prescribe. Every day, many people would come to the shop to be examined and receive medication from him. He would inspect the patient, ask questions, take something from this drawer, something from that, pound them up, mix them together, and who is to say that the brews he concocted didn't cure a good number of his patients? He even had folk remedies for some of the more obscure and intractable conditions, and his abilities gained him the local soubriquet of 'The Immortal of the Many

Medicines'. He had known Song Ci's father, Song Gong, as an honest and upright official, and through his dealings with Song Ci, held the son in similar respect. In the current circumstances, he thought, it could certainly do no harm to have Song Ci's assistance, so why not tell him about what was going on? He pursed his lips for a moment and then explained that the lad was Gong, the son of the local basket-maker, Tong Da. Tong Gong used to go up the mountain to gather bamboo, and had once come to the aid of a hunter in distress. Because that hunter could supply the apothecary with monkey fat, tiger bones and suchlike, a degree of friendship had developed. While he was away, a few days ago, the *yamen* officials had come pursuing this year's advance taxes and had taken everything of value from the Tong household. After the soldiers had gone, Chai Wanlong had also come over to demand his rent.

"Chai Wanlong?" Song Ci jumped as though stung by a wasp.

The pharmacist explained: "Chai Wanlong owns all these shops. The Tong household was already two terms in arrears, so they had no chance of paying the rent. Tong Gong was away from home, hunting in the mountains. The only people in the house were his father Tong Da and his elder brother Tong Ning and his wife. Chai Wanlong told them: 'Don't worry if you can't pay the rent, just send your wife over to my house to do some chores.'"

It happened that Tong Ning's wife was the prettiest woman in Wulijiang, and as she grew up, there had been any number of local ne'er-do-wells vying for her affections. One of these louts once thought he could take advantage of her, and she bit him on the nose. The story got around, and when Chai Wanlong heard about it, he decided he had to see her for himself. Not long after, she married Tong Ning.

And now, Tong Ning most certainly was not going to allow his wife to go to Chai Wanlong's house, so he pleaded: "Master, let me go instead." At first Chai refused, but eventually he gave in and agreed. How was anyone to know that this visit to the Chai household was to prove fatal for Tong Ning? The story put about was that he had climbed up to Chai's daughter's bedroom to assault her, but had been caught by one of the guards and fallen to his death from a wall while escaping. Now was that at all a likely story?

But the affair was not yet over. Chai Wanlong summoned a mob to his house to raise a rumpus, and ordered Tong Da to come and collect the body. Tong Ning's wife was consumed by grief, but wanted to go, too. Fearing Chai Wanlong's evil intentions, Tong Da persuaded her to stay at home while he went at night with a group of neighbours to fetch his son's body. To their amazement, when they got back, Tong Ning's wife had disappeared, and though they searched everywhere, no trace of her could be found.

Tong Da was furious, and after their searching had found nothing, told his companions that the only explanation was that Chai Wanlong had kidnapped his daughter-in-law. As we know, Tong Ning's wife had always been a spirited individual, so there was no way this situation was going to end well. So, there they were – Tong Gong had still not returned and no one knew where he was. Tong Da was powerless to snatch his daughter-in-law back from the Chai residence and, think as he might, he could see no way forward. All he could do was get someone to write out a formal accusation to be laid before the *yamen*, requesting the officials to step up to the mark and search Chai Wanlong's house.

"What happened next?" asked Song Ci, eager to hear how the officials had handled the matter.

"It all happened very quickly. They sent a man over to the Chai mansion, but he didn't spend very long there. As soon as he came out, he went in front of the court and laid a charge of giving false witness against Tong Da, who was then flogged and thrown into jail."

"What about the charge against Chai Wanlong of abducting Tong Ning's wife?" Song Ci asked.

"Ha!" Pharmacist He laughed, wryly. "What can I say?"

In the past, the pharmacist had furnished Chai Wanlong with aphrodisiacs and so knew more about him than most. But he wasn't going to mention this.

"Surely, sir, you must have heard Master Chai's reputation. Even among the rich and powerful he is a byword for depravity. Early this year, all the tenant farmers were in dire straits and facing lawsuits if they couldn't pay their rent. Master Chai took advantage of the situation to spy out the prettiest of the farmers' wives, and suggest a way out of their difficulties if they came to work as a servant girl in his household. A few months later, when their bellies began to swell, he sent them packing. There were a number of families, at the end of their tethers, who endured the ignominy of this course of action, and afterwards were obliged to pay lip service to the charity of the great Chai Wanlong. So, you see, Chai fixed his intentions on Tong Ning's wife, Tong Ning objected and this is the result."

"How does Chai think he can get away with this?"

"Haven't you heard?" said the pharmacist. "He keeps a private army of hired thugs and has influence in the right places."

Someone else in the crowd piped up: "And anyone who tries to take him to court gets a night-time visit and is beaten up or has an ear cut off. And that's just for starters."

"I know some who've had their eyes gouged out, or even been killed," said another.

Song Ci was shaken by what he was hearing. Then everyone started joining in with their version of events, until they reached the point where

Tong Gong arrived. He had heard what was going on and had come hurrying down from the mountains where he was hiding, determined to get his father out of jail even if it cost him his life.

Song Ci frowned and took stock of the young man. He was an ordinary looking youth, of seventeen or eighteen, Song Ci guessed. His short, buttoned tunic revealed a broad-chested and muscular physique. His brow was furrowed with anger, with a murderous look in his eyes, but there was a touch of childish petulance about his tight lips.

"So, what makes you so intent on dying?" Song Ci asked him.

Pharmacist He took it on himself to respond. "Master, you have a lot of experience of this kind – why don't you take up his case?"

At this, all the others joined in.

"His father is all that he has left now."

"You've got to find some way to help his father."

"The two of them are in fear of their lives."

Song Ci listened to what they had to say, then looked down at the razor-edged stave-shaving knife the youth had dropped. He picked it up and went over to stand in front of Tong Gong. "Very well, I will help you. But you had better remember that the way the law is handled locally is very different from imperial law. Under no circumstances must you do anything hasty."

# 3

## A LEGAL REPRESENTATIVE

The events of that night were far outside Song Ci's previous experience. He was a fundamentally self-confident man. His failure in his first examinations all those years ago had not really affected this, as in the end, no one could gainsay his third place in the highest level imperial examinations. But these past few days had given him pause for thought: his twenty-odd years of dedication to his studies had left him with a fine reputation as a classical scholar and as a skilled rhetorician, but had ill-prepared him for these real events involving real people. When he helped Tong Gong to his feet, it seemed to him he wasn't just helping this man, he was also helping himself. With the opportunity to do something that actually mattered right in front of him, he questioned the point of taking up his official post.

He ordered someone to fetch him a brush and paper. In general, scholars are not much use in drawing up indictments, unless they themselves have been in a situation requiring one. Although Song Ci did not have such personal experience, he was determined to use the skills he had learned from writing so many essays and from passing the official examinations. He felt this must be of some use to him in composing his very first indictment, against Chai Wanlong. He decided that, next morning, he would go in person to visit the chief provincial magistrate.

That same autumn night, as Song Ci was writing his indictment, Chai himself was gathering up some silver, and also going to visit the chief magistrate. He took the Tian brothers with him as bodyguards. The purpose of his visit had nothing to do with any potential court case, however; he wanted to ask the magistrate to help him collect his rents.

Before the Song dynasty, there was no precedent for an official helping a private individual collect rents, nor was it a common occurrence in the Northern Song. By the Southern Song, however, as the imperial tax burden on the people grew almost daily, they increasingly had trouble meeting their taxes, let alone their landlord's rent. The rich began to bribe officials to collect the rent on their behalf. As the practice grew more common, some kind of demarcation became essential to avoid conflict between the landlords' rent and the official taxes. An imperial edict was issued, stating that the period when magistrates would hear cases brought by landlords over their tenants' rents should run from the beginning of the tenth month until the end of the third month of the following year. But this year had been a particularly difficult one for the farmers, and despite the edict, officials had been out all year collecting rent. As a case in point, although it was only the ninth month, here was Chai Wanlong already going to the magistrate for help.

Chai was forty years old, in the prime of his life and with a roving eye. When he reached the gates of the *yamen*, the bailiff let him in and the magistrate came out to greet him. Chai handed over the silver he had brought, with a murmured: "Just a small token of respect."

The magistrate's name was Shu Gengshi. He was thirty years old, and his eyes were always narrowed as if in amusement. He invited Chai to sit down, and before the landlord even opened his mouth to explain the reason for his visit, said: "The people are having trouble meeting their taxes. I already have quite a number of private rent cases."

"I realise that," replied Chai.

As they spoke, the magistrate put a pile of official documents on the table and casually pushed one over towards Chai Wanlong: "This one, for example, is from Master Dong in Jianning Prefecture, and it alone is pursuing a hundred or more households for monies owing. I also have cases from the Ministry of Appointments, the Provincial Chamberlain and the Privy Council."

A servant brought tea, and Magistrate Shu invited Chai to take a cup. Accepting, Chai replied that he was, himself, all too well acquainted with the current problems around the collection of rents, and that was why he had come to seek His Honour's help.

"I need to make it clear at the outset," Shu said, "that you cannot take the law into your own hands. In the current circumstances, it has become a commonplace for tenants to be unable to pay their rent once they have handed over their taxes. And I have heard that your minions have been over-zealous in their methods. You need to be careful lest you stir things up to such an extent that your tenants bring a group action against you. If that happens, you and I will both be in trouble."

Chai replied that this was an accurate assessment of the situation, and for that reason the affair should be dealt with only by local officials. The two men continued their negotiations for half a stick of incense, and then Chai Wanlong swore out his affidavit. It was the morning of the next day when Song Ci arrived at the *yamen*.

When he was announced at the gates, Magistrate Shu himself came out to welcome the guest and escort him to the inner hall of the *yamen*. Once they were seated, Shu started by praising Song Ci's great scholarship. Song politely half rose from his chair and murmured: "Not at all, not at all. I am a mere student."

"You are too modest," Shu replied, and then went on to ask Song what brought him there today. Song told him that he had stumbled across a difficult situation, but... well, he wasn't sure quite how best to explain it.

"Tell me all," said the magistrate. "And the resources of the province will be at your disposal."

"Well, there is a family that lives in my village..." Song Ci hesitated. "Perhaps it would be best for Your Honour to read this indictment."

Shu took the document and unrolled it. Without a word, he sat down as though deep in thought. Song Ci remained silent and then, after a while, Shu turned to him with a smile and said: "Honoured Father's reputation for scholarship is clearly well deserved."

"Your Honour is too polite. I'm afraid it is poorly worded."

"You assert that Tong Ning was deliberately and maliciously killed by Chai Wanlong, and further that his wife's disappearance is the result of kidnap on the orders of the same Chai Wanlong?"

"That is correct."

"What proof do you have?"

"It is common knowledge that Chai Wanlong does as he pleases in the area and forces himself on local women."

"Such accusations most certainly require substantiation."

"But it is not the place of the aggrieved parties to provide that evidence. This is a troublesome and vexatious case, and it is the responsibility of the family's local officials to investigate it and collect evidence."

"And how do you know this office has not already done so?"

"What have you done, then?"

"We have viewed the corpse, and it is clear that Tong Ning fell to his death. There were no marks indicative of any kind of beating. He had climbed up to the chamber of the young lady of the household, with felonious intent. He was pursued by one of the family retainers with the intention of bringing him before this court for punishment but, in the course of the pursuit, he fell to his death from the top of the compound wall."

"On whose evidence?"

"That of the Chai family retainer."

"How can Your Honour rely solely on the word of a family servant?"

"Honoured Father, however you look at it, this case originates in the Chai family compound, so where else should we look for evidence?"

"Master Shu, it is self-evidently nonsense to claim that Tong Ning went there to assault Mistress Chai."

"And how can you be so sure of that?" the magistrate asked, looking hard at Song Ci.

Song was momentarily lost for words.

"In fact," the magistrate went on, "I can tell you that indeed he did not go there to assault the young lady."

"What do you mean?"

"He went there specifically to rape her."

"Rape her? On what evidence?"

"On the evidence of the young lady herself."

"And that is reliable?"

"You are well acquainted with court procedure. In cases of rape and attempted rape, the primary source of evidence is the victim."

"Even so, how can you be sure the evidence is reliable?"

"Chai Wanlong was accused of having his way with the local women and of planning to assault Tong Ning's wife. In forcibly entering Mistress Chai's chamber, Tong Ning reckoned he was simply taking revenge on behalf of those other wronged women. It is quite common in revenge crimes such as murder and arson for the action taken in revenge to escalate beyond the original offence. Can you prove that is not the case here?"

Song Ci was stumped. He didn't believe the magistrate's scenario, but how could he disprove it?

"Honoured Father," Magistrate Shu said. "It would be best if you did not pursue this case. Your intentions are good, but you don't have the stamina for it. Look what is going on around us. With invasion from outside the borders and the government in turmoil within, the country is awash with court cases that will never be resolved. And what's more, the Chai family have connections in the capital, and no matter where you seek a judgment, no one will give one."

"So, what will the court do?"

"Do? It will do what it ought to, of course. In this case, have I not viewed the body, collected evidence, taken every measure as I should? It is not as though this is the only business I have to attend to. I tell you, if you ever decide to become a magistrate, you would see for yourself that even though I am one of the busiest government officials and am beset with matters both high and low, every one of them must go through the same painstaking process."

Having delivered this short homily, Magistrate Shu asked Song Ci if he had any other business with him, and he assured him that the court would spare no effort if the Song household needed its assistance with anything. After a moment's thought, he added: "The Chai family has a lot of influence in this area, and you need to be very careful while you stay at home to observe the mourning period for your father. If anything happens, this court will not be able to protect you."

With these words, Magistrate Shu escorted Song Ci from the *yamen* with all due courtesy, leaving him bewildered, with red face and burning ears, trying to fully understand what exactly had just happened.

Tong Gong had been waiting in a little shop just outside the gates, and when he saw the magistrate escorting Song Ci so politely, his hopes were raised. He hurried out, asking: "Master, what did the magistrate say?"

"Let's go home and talk about it there," Song Ci replied.

# CHAPTER III

## THE WASHING AWAY OF WRONGS (1218)

Throughout the nation, both town and countryside are in turmoil. Song Ci is considering his alternatives: to enter the court to put his intellect at the service of the emperor; or to go to the battlefront to help devise strategies to recapture territories lost to the invaders; or to stay on home ground and try to curb corruption and control the local tyrants, bringing succour to the local people. All of these are worthy ambitions. What he didn't expect was to see lives being snatched away, one after another, before his very eyes; or that his own efforts to seek legal redress on behalf of these ordinary folk would be thwarted. All ambitions in more lofty spheres have fallen away in the face of this local bloodbath...

# 1

# LAW IN THE SONG DYNASTY

Song Ci decided to re-submit his case in the prefectural court at Jianning.

Tongyou was the local name of the river that flowed through Song Ci's home town, but it is actually a tributary of the Min River and its proper name is the Jianxi Stream. Jianning Prefecture is now called Jian'ou City, in Fujian Province, to the south of Jianyang.

Song determined to take the river route to Jianning. This was a busy commercial thoroughfare in Song times, and every day several hundred local boats moored at the south-eastern pier outside the east gate of Jianyang. Accompanied by Tong Gong, he boarded a skiff.

The East Gate city wall and gate towers receded into the distance, and the only sound was the swishing of the water against the sides of the boat. This departure felt different to Song Ci from any other. He stood at the prow of the skiff with the river breeze gently ruffling his gown, his heart as agitated as the waters flowing past the sides of the boat.

He heard his mother's parting words: "My son, your father always used to say that officialdom has a habit of engulfing people in its processes and drowning them in a sea of empty words. You have been quite correct in not taking up your post to mourn your father, but because of this, I am afraid that the high officials at the prefecture may not listen to you."

And he remembered her whispered advice as she escorted him to the gate: "If you don't succeed, come straight back and think of another way."

Watching the gentle flow of the water, Song Ci thought again of his old colleague Liu Kezhuang. In his days at home, he often reflected on the importance of friendship. Last year in the capital, the day after he had passed the examinations, Liu invited him to go out into the countryside to enjoy the spring weather. They left the city by the Qiantang Gate and came to the Six Harmonies pagoda, which is situated beside the Qiantang River on Yuelun Hill. Song Ci had been studying in the capital for quite a few years, but now he realised, as if seeing it for the first time, what a peaceful and secluded position the pagoda enjoyed.

Black-tiled and red-walled, the Six Harmonies pagoda towered above the hillside, surrounded by shady green trees alive with noisy birdlife. It was only infrequently visited by travellers, so the whole area was quite densely overgrown. But there was a narrow path leading up to the pagoda that had mostly been worn by the feet of pilgrims going to burn incense. There, indeed, were some bundles of incense sticks, lit by who knows whom, still burning in front of the pagoda, their smoke gently dispersing in the breeze. The two men went into the building, through the central chamber, and began climbing the spiral staircase. When they reached the topmost storey, and were leaning on a windowsill gazing into the distance, they began to argue.

"You first entered imperial service in the second year of Jiading, eight years ago, and I'm wondering how it is that you have come to despise your official career." Song Ci spoke freely, as to an old friend.

"I don't know what you mean!" said Liu Kezhuang. "It is, however, true that I don't necessarily believe a life in the civil service is the best way to make a real contribution. In the olden days, many men of great ability would spend years in hard study, struggling for advancement, only gradually to get bogged down in the petty squabbles of bureaucracy. None of their studies proved adequate to render proper service to the state, and they ended up fawning on their bosses, and wasting time on the private affairs of the rich and powerful. One cannot be proud of that sort of a life."

"So what do you think constitutes a productive life?" Song asked.

"Well, something like our forebears erecting this pagoda, or like Li Bai and Du Fu leaving thousands of fine poems for posterity, or like Master Zhu Xi, who, after fifty years of imperial service, re-took the nine examinations and only forty days into his new appointment founded the White Deer Grotto Academy to nurture the young shoots of tens of thousands of new scholars."

Looking out from the top of the pagoda, they could see the winding belt of the Qiantang River connecting them to the ocean. It was the rainy season south of the Yangtze, and the river was clamorous and swollen. On its banks nearby, wearing clothes as full of holes as fishing nets, a crowd of watermen were strenuously hauling at the ropes of a flotilla of grain barges. Government soldiers were standing in the prows of the barges that were flying banners reading 'Army supplies'.

"That may be so," Song Ci said to his friend, "but what I need to consider, since town and countryside across the nation are in turmoil, is what it is best to do. Should I enter the court to put my abilities at the service of the emperor, go to the battlefront to help devise strategies to recapture territories lost to the invaders or stay on home ground and try to curb corruption and control the local tyrants, bringing succour to the local people? They are all worthy ambitions, in my opinion."

"Your high ideals do you credit. But when the Qingli Reforms failed, and Fan Zhongyan's efforts proved to be for nothing, all the redundant officials became a blight on the court. Wang Anshi's changes to the legal system were designed to dispose of Fan Zhongyan and all that he had hoped to achieve. And what was the result? All the reforms were abolished. Now the court is full of unemployed officials, and appointments rest in the hands of a talentless and dishonest claque. Here you are, having come third in the palace examinations, and all they offer you is a minor post in the Department of Military Affairs in Yin County in Zhejiang. Don't you feel like an eagle with clipped wings?"

This was the same conversation they had had a year before in the capital. But since then, Song Ci had met a man like Magistrate Shu and had seen sinister forces running rampant in his home town; and his experience of the peculiar injustice meted out to the Tong family had led him to question the rule of law under the Song dynasty.

The river route from Jianyang to Jianning was about 150 *li* (around forty-five miles), so it was the middle of the night before Song Ci and Tong Gong arrived. As the city gates were already shut, the two men took their leave of the boatman and found a small inn outside the walls to bed down. They rose the next morning and ate a makeshift breakfast before hurrying into the city towards the gates of the provincial *yamen*.

As they reached the road in front of the *yamen*, they heard the sound of horses and carts, and saw a dozen or so empty wagons approaching. There had been a downpour at dusk the day before, and the road was still full of puddles. As they passed, the wagon wheels threw spray over Song Ci and Tong Gong that they had no chance of dodging. Looking at the wagons as they went on their way, Tong Gong suddenly exclaimed: "That's Liang E!"

"Liang E?" Song Ci turned to look, but the wagons were already too far away.

Liang E was the chief of police in Jianyang, and the sudden sight of him emerging from the *yamen* in Jianning gave the two men a sinking feeling.

This Liang E was the younger son of a rich family from Mafu village on the west road out of Jianyang. He was monstrously large – the body of a lion and the arms of an ape, was how he was described – and had long wavy hair and moustaches like a young dragon. From childhood, he had trained himself in the arts of the sword and staff, and as an adult he exercised himself in the violent collection of grain taxes, so that, almost by default, he became a true expert in martial arts. In his twenties, he began to teach martial arts, but then he got into a fight. He knocked down his opponent, then picked him up again and attacked him with redoubled fury so that he ruptured the man's abdomen. He ended up facing a murder charge.

It so happened that the case came before the recently appointed prefectural magistrate to Jianyang, Shu Gengshi. Liang E's family members came clustering round from all sides, distributed a substantial sum in bribes, and ensured that this major case became a minor one and that the minor one then disappeared completely. Magistrate Shu took note of Liang E's fighting prowess and arranged a contest between him and Chai Wanlong's hired thugs, the Tian brothers, Tian Huai and Tian Ju. The brothers were recognised champions of the four provinces, but in the end could only fight a draw, two against one, with Liang E. Shu Gengshi was delighted, as he realised the *yamen* had need of just such a man, who could intimidate local despots and bullies. So he appointed Liang E chief of the prefectural military police. Liang E was very grateful for this appointment, which allowed him to further hone his skills with sword and cudgel. He found the job most congenial, and threw himself into it. For Liang E suddenly to appear like this could only mean that he was there on the orders of the Jianyang magistrate Shu Gengshi to help the Jianning local worthy Master Dong in the collection of his private rents.

Master Dong's family came from Mafu in Jianyang, the same village as Liang E. When he realised that this year Magistrate Shu was going to help with the collection of his rents, which took the form not just of grain, silver and cash, but all kinds of other household valuables, he understood that Shu was going out of his way to assist him and so was highly appreciative. Of course, Song Ci as yet had no experience of these commonplace semi-official arrangements. But even if he had, what could he have done? It would, however, have reinforced his belief that, under the current state of Song imperial law, the common people had no recourse against injustice. So now, watching the wagons disappearing into the distance, he just said: "Pay no attention. Let's go."

The two men reached the *yamen* and Song Ci knocked on the main gate. He explained who he was and presented his petition along with a letter he had written to the chief magistrate. When the porter realised it was the newly graduated imperial official from Jianyang who had come calling, he cupped his hands in front of him and bowed low, saying: "Please wait a moment, Master Song." He then turned and went in to report to his superior.

Master Dong was playing chess with one of his concubines in the rear hall. The chamberlain of the inner court came in and presented him with the letter and petition, saying: "Master, this is a letter from the new imperial official from Jianyang, Song Ci, and there is also a petition he has prepared on behalf of others."

Master Dong kept surveying the chess board and finally asked: "Whom is the petition against?"

"A local gentleman from Jianyang called Chai Wanlong."

After another pause, Dong moved a piece on the board and then asked: "Why doesn't he present it to Magistrate Shu in Jianyang?"

The chamberlain replied: "Magistrate Shu is included in the indictment."

"What!" This time Dong looked up and took the letter and tore it open. After reading it, he smiled faintly and put it down on the table. Then he took the petition, read it cursorily, and exclaimed: "Bring me a brush."

The chamberlain hurriedly brought a writing set, and Master Dong took the brush and wrote a few columns of characters on the petition. He returned it to the chamberlain and turned his full attention back to the chess game.

While this was going on, Song Ci and Tong Gong sat under a camphor tree outside the gates of the *yamen* to wait for a response. It was late autumn, and the seasonal wind was making the branches of the camphor tree sway gently and rustling the few remaining dreary, dead leaves. The two men had rushed to the court that morning and so were a little sweaty; several hours of waiting under the tree left them chilled to the bone.

"Hello, there!" The gates opened and the porter stuck his head out. The two men hastily looked up.

"Go home, you two," the porter said, smiling insolently.

"What?" exclaimed Song Ci.

"The master has approved your petition for hearing before the magistrate in Jianyang."

"What?" repeated Song Ci, in disbelief.

"The master has approved your petition for hearing before the magistrate in Jianyang, and is sending it back with the properly authorised officials. You had better go home."

The gates closed with a clunk, and Song Ci's heart dropped like a stone. He looked at the gates, but they were already shut, leaving two ring handles in the shape of monster masks staring fixedly at him. Song Ci turned to Tong Gong to find Tong's eyes staring back at him, both pleading and despairing. Song had never seen such a look in his life. The last thing he had expected was to make the journey to Jianning only to be turned away at the gates of the *yamen* without even being admitted, and to be sent home peremptorily.

2

# ANOTHER HUMAN LIFE

A cold moon hangs high in the sky. Under the clear, cold moonlight the courtyard seemed particularly desolate to Song Ci. The dim light fell on him as he stood by the window, a motionless silhouette. There was no sound in the room, and only the chirruping of invisible insects outside. He was thinking about all the 'what ifs': if he hadn't needed to come home to collect more travel money, he could have taken the case straight to the court in Fuzhou; if Pharmacist He hadn't found them in time, then they would have had no way of knowing of the death of Tong Gong's father, Tong Da, on the evening of the day they left for Jianning; the jailer said it was a sudden illness that took him, and because there was no one left in the Tong family to arrange it, he had been buried without ceremony.

So as he contemplated another human life snuffed out pointlessly, Song Ci was completely at a loss.

He couldn't sleep that night, and he didn't know what he was thinking, if indeed he was thinking anything at all. In the end, he remembered his father who had often acted as prefectural judge for the provincial governor, and investigated prison punishments. When Song was a child, his father was at home after being dismissed from office, and during that time he had often heard his father telling stories about cases regarding prison matters. From this, Song had developed a great interest in the different aspects of incarceration. When he was at the academy, he had been particularly diligent in his legal studies of the *Xing Tong* and the *Bian Chi*. Since the *Xing Tong* was the first compendium of law compiled since the start of the Song dynasty, and the *Bian Chi* was the encyclopaedia of punishments ordained by imperial edict, he could hardly avoid paying particular attention to them.

And now he remembered how self-satisfied he had been when he said to Tong Gong: "Very well, I will help you. But you had better remember that the way the law is handled locally is very different from imperial law. You absolutely must not do anything hasty." Now he hung his head in shame and with a cry of disgust threw all the books and scrolls on the table onto the floor.

His wife came into the room carrying a bowl of lotus seed porridge. Lian Yulan had known her husband from childhood, and for twenty years now had been Song Ci's kindred spirit and faithful soul-mate. Seeing the books scattered on the floor, she put the bowl of porridge down on the table without any fuss, and said gently: "Eat it while it's hot."

Song Ci seemed not to hear her and just stood there, quite still. She bent down and gathered up the pile of books, before saying: "You mustn't get agitated. It was just the same in the early days of the Great Song dynasty before it was fully established – the countryside was left defenceless, corruption was rife, and law and order non-existent. Many people in the empire suffered great injustices."

She continued: "In fact, what's going on now is barely comparable. In the Shaoxing period,[1] were not even heroes like General Yue Fei executed on trumped-up charges?"

Song Ci turned to her as though about to say something, but he remained silent, his eyes fixed on the candle. He seemed to be staring into an imaginary world where there were two rows of flaming torches, two slow ranks of ceremonial procession with long lances and halberds, great broadswords glinting with a cold, bright radiance. The torches illuminated an inscribed tablet over the door of a tall pavilion – the Wind on the Waves Pavilion (Fengbo Ting in the hills above the West Lake). He had once gone with Liu Kezhuang to offer sacrifices there. It had been in the first year of the Kaixi period of Emperor Ningzong (1205-1207) when he had just gone up to the academy. The academy was established in the former residence of General Yue Fei. After Yue Fei's murder, his family property was seized and his residence became the Imperial Academy. Not far to the west of the academy stood the Wind on the Waves Pavilion. Song Ci entered the academy the year after Chancellor Han Tuozhou had petitioned Emperor Ningzong to bestow on Yue Fei the posthumous title of Prince of E. At the Qingming festival that year, a great host of the common people, the able bodied supporting the old and carrying the young, had flocked from all corners of the empire to the Wind on the Waves Pavilion to mourn the death of their father figure, Yue Fei. All students from the academy went along, too. What a solemn and moving spectacle it was. A great wave of people flowing ceaselessly from early morning until dusk; a seemingly limitless conflagration of paper money burning from dawn far into the night…

"Tell me what you're thinking." His wife seemed to know what was on his mind even before the thoughts were fully formed.

"I've had a premonition," Song Ci replied.

"What premonition?"

"He's going to meet with some misfortune."

"Who is?"

"Tong Gong."

3

## A TUNNEL INTO THE ABYSS

A black-clothed man stole up to the perimeter wall of Chai Wanlong's compound – it was Tong Gong. His father was dead, but he was still alive and had important business to carry out. His sister-in-law had disappeared, dead for sure but with no body to be found, so it was up to him to find her. Although he had no proper plan in coming here, and had no real appetite for murder, he decided to throw caution to the winds. It was less than a year since his sister-in-law had married into the household, and she was carrying his small niece or nephew in her womb. Even before the marriage, she had often come over to help with household tasks. For Tong Gong, who had recently lost his mother, she reinforced the soles of his cloth shoes in winter, and mended his short tunics in summer as scrupulously as his real mother had. He had come to the perimeter wall now with death in his heart, and if he could not find his sister-in-law, then he would find Chai Wanlong, and blood would be shed.

The Chai mansion was set in a sprawling compound slightly apart from the village of Tongyou. It was surrounded on all four sides by a high wall that was topped with brickwork tiles that stuck out about six inches. He scouted round the compound for a while and settled on a thickly branched, leafy maple tree that abutted the wall. Using the skills he had acquired as a child in climbing bamboo, and with his hands clasped firmly on either side and his feet planted in the centre of the trunk, he swooshed his way up the tree.

A rustling sound came from the end of a branch, where several startled night birds and some nearby jackdaws took wing from their nests. Tong Gong hooked his feet round a branch and sank into hiding among the foliage. Peace was restored after a short while, and he took a look around from the safety of his branch, then dropped down inside the courtyard.

The compound was so big, he could scarcely see all four walls, and the flickering shadows of the trees confused him, so he didn't know where to start searching. A waning moon was just bright enough to light the way. It would be a good idea, thought Tong Gong to himself, to search where there are lamps burning. But I can't see lamps anywhere, only the moonlight.

Then he thought he could see a light and made his way towards it. It turned out to be the kitchen, where people were busy at work. "Take it now," a voice said, and two maids emerged from the door. One was carrying a lantern and the other a wooden basket containing an earthenware cooking pot and a wine jug.

I wonder who those are for, thought Tong, and he quietly followed the maids.

They passed along a covered corridor, carried on a fair distance along a narrow alley past a black brick storehouse, passing through a moon-gate into another courtyard, on a little bit, then round an ornamental hillock, before finally reaching their destination. Here there was a grapevine pergola made of dark-coloured stone. The leaves of the vine had begun to wither but still provided thick cover so that a tunnel was formed beneath them; there was a pond either side of the tunnel. Following the maids' lantern, Tong Gong went in and immediately caught the smell of rotting leaves and green moss, and the scent of flowers he could not name. He went a little further in, and a shiver of cold ran down his back, as though he had just stepped into a demon's cave.

Still shadowing the maids, he heard a knock on a door somewhere ahead of him. A sliver of light appeared and the maids went in, shutting the door behind them and plunging the tunnel back into darkness. Holding his breath, Tong Gong crept up to the door and, before he had even come to a halt, he could hear someone walking about inside the room...

"Open the door!" Tong Gong attempted to hide by pressing himself against the side wall and, luckily for him, at the end of the tunnel on both sides there were earth banks about three feet high, on top of which, right by the room, had been planted a profusion of trees and flowering plants. Tong Gong climbed up onto one of the banks and hid among the foliage. The door opened and out came the two maids, carrying their lantern. They closed the door and disappeared back down the tunnel.

Tong Gong cautiously followed the earth bank towards the room until he reached a window, where he stopped and climbed down. The window was narrow and tucked away, and in addition someone had planted Japanese creeper on the earth bank. The leaves and branches almost covered the window lattice, blocking out most of the light that was coming from the room. Tong Gong parted the foliage carefully and slowly pressed himself close to the window frame so that at last he could see the layout of the room.

It was a big room and very deep, and while dimly lit he could see it was covered in elaborate decoration. A net curtain divided the room. In the front half against the walls were a number of tables and two divans; in the middle stood a large oval wooden flower pot and, through the dividing curtain, Tong Gong could dimly make out a bed decorated with carved dragons and painted flowers. Tied to the bed by her arms and legs, lay a young woman.

His heart leapt. Could that be his sister-in-law?

There was a man in the room too, and it was none other than Chai Wanlong. Fire sprang into Tong Gong's eyes, he ground his teeth and the short-handled, broad-bladed knife he carried began to shake uncontrollably in his hand. The fiend was actually in the room, and he was saying something that Tong couldn't quite make out. He began to make his way to the door; he could see it was flimsy and would give at a single push. Then he would suddenly reveal himself in front of the devil Chai, plunge the knife into his heart and tell him who the avenger was so that he would fully understand his fate. He reached the door and gave it a careful push. There was a slight creaking noise as the door opened slightly, and light spilled out. He stopped to listen, but no sound came from inside. Holding his breath, he worked his hand into the crack of the door and, lifting it on its hinges, pushed it noiselessly open.

He stole in through the door. He could see the light flooding out of the main part of the room, but it was still not enough for him to make out clearly what was going on in the inner section. He began to think things through – if he went into the body of the room, and Chai Wanlong saw him, then they would have to fight it out. If he didn't kill him instantly, then he would have real trouble escaping from him and getting out of the room. If Chai's cries roused the household, people would come to his aid. The only entrance was that door, and, unquestionably, that door could be the death of him. He silently picked up a wooden door bar that was leaning against the wall. It was about the thickness of the width of a rice bowl, and once in position, it would delay anyone trying to get into the room.

After barring the door in this manner, Tong Gong made his way into the main part of the room. He could see Chai Wanlong had started to untie the young woman and already had one hand loose. He looked again at the woman, and this time he could see that it wasn't, in fact, his sister-in-law. It was a woman he didn't recognise, wan and sallow, her hair in disarray. It was only his eagerness to rescue his sister-in-law that had deceived him into thinking this was her.

Even though the woman wasn't his sister-in-law, the man was certainly Chai Wanlong.

The sight of Tong Gong, knife in hand, froze the woman into silence. Chai Wanlong sensed the movement behind him and turned to look at Tong Gong. Startled, he dropped the rope he had just untied and called out: "Who are you?"

"I am Tong Ning's younger brother, Tong Gong," he replied slowly and clearly. "And I've come to avenge my brother and his wife."

A double-edged sword was hanging on the wall to the left of the bed, and Chai Wanlong glanced across at it, while saying: "Hold on there, my good fellow. How much money do you want?"

"The only thing I want is to smash your brains out!" Tong Gong replied, flourishing the knife at his enemy.

Chai Wanlong knew a trick or two himself, and he started grappling with Tong Gong, dodging the knife and yelling: "Help! Help!... Assassin! Assassin!"

By chance, there was a side-annexe behind the pillars of that half of the main room, where two maids were busy heating water. They were in the act of ladling the hot water into the water-butt when they heard Chai's cry for help. In alarm they dropped the butt, and scalding water splashed out. Tong Gong hadn't expected anyone else to be in the room, and he froze in surprise. Without hesitation, Chai snatched the broadsword off the wall.

A vicious hand-to-hand fight broke out between the men, and as the two maids cowered in the side chamber, Chai shouted at them: "Get out of here and fetch help. Don't let this Tong fellow get away!" The maids ran out into the main room and, seeing the door was secured, together lifted the bar and fled from the chamber.

"Help! Help!" Tong Gong was distracted by the maids' cries for assistance coming from outside the room, and Chai slashed him on the right hand, making him drop his knife. Chai had already assessed the extent of his opponent's combat skills, and the sword blade danced in his hands as he coolly thrust left and then right, step by step advancing on Tong Gong, who found himself backed into a corner. Chai laughed coldly and slashed down with the sword. Tong Gong tried to dodge the flashing blow, but the blade caught his left arm, opening up a gash from which blood flowed freely through the sleeve of his tunic.

Chai Wanlong pressed home his advantage, and Tong Gong, eyes fixed on the flashing blade, tried to dodge the blows that came at him left and right. He retreated into the side annexe where the maids had overturned the water butt. In a panic, he snatched up the barrel to use as a shield, and the fight raged on.

Blinded by blood-lust, Chai slipped on the wet floor, and the two men fell in a tangle of limbs and weapons. Tong Gong was already wounded in the right hand and left arm, and his strength was ebbing, especially with Chai's weight on top of him. Seizing the advantage of his position, Chai rained blows on Tong Gong's head. Then, suddenly, a round object hammered down on Chai's own head, and blood spurted out and flowed down his forehead. He fell to the ground. Standing behind him was the woman who had been tied to the bed, in her hands a pewter wine jug, now dented out of shape. Tong Gong was astounded. He scrambled to his feet and looked down at Chai Wanlong, who was lying face-down, twitching. The woman threw down the wine jug and picked up the broadsword that Chai had dropped. Standing four-square in front of Chai's head, she hammered the blade down, and more blood came gushing out, splashing over the four-character inscription cast into the sword blade, which read 'May all your affairs prosper'.

Abruptly, the room fell silent. Tong Gong's eyes met those of the woman. Then, from outside the room, they heard the sound of distant footsteps...

"Who are you?" Tong Gong asked.

"Run away," the woman said.

"We must run together." Tong Gong saw that the woman's clothes were liberally spattered with blood.

"Then neither of us will get away." As she spoke, the woman grabbed the red-gauze octagonal temple lantern from beside the bed, tore off the cloth covering and dropped it burning to the floor. She also set fire to the set of hanging couplets in the middle of the room and the red gauze canopy of the bed. Finally, she put the flame to a painted lacquer clothes rack that had been knocked over in the fight. Not only was the room itself of wooden construction and highly flammable, but also the decorative fretwork carvings had been recently oiled, so the contents of the room were soon crackling and popping away fiercely.

The woman pointed at Tong Gong and said: "Quick. Go now. If you hesitate, you'll never make it."

"No! You go first," Tong replied.

The footsteps outside the room were getting louder. The woman put the bar back across the door, shutting it tight. She picked up Tong Gong's knife and grasped it firmly in her hand, before shoving Tong Gong away, saying: "Go out of the broken window. I have a plan, but if you stay, you'll be the death of me."

Tong Gong did not understand how his failure to leave would harm the woman, but he didn't stop to think about it. He looked at her again, but she was clearly not going to accept any argument, so he clambered through the broken lattice of the window and made good his escape.

The footsteps were already clattering down the tunnel, and there was a battering on the door. By this time the fire was licking across the floorboards, and the gusting flames crackled loudly…

## 4

# A KNOCK ON THE DOOR AT THE DEAD OF NIGHT

Along the cobbled street outside the Song courtyard came the sound of dogs barking, getting closer and closer. Startled, the birds roosting in the pear trees beside the walls took flight, and from the cover of shadow on top of the wall, a figure dropped down into the court.

Song Ci and his wife had not yet gone to sleep, and when they heard the excited barking of the dogs, they turned to look at each other. Song Ci felt he had to go out and see what was causing the noise, but just as he was about to open the door of their chamber, there came the sound of gentle knocking. He crossed the room and opened the door. In came Tong Gong. In the candlelight, Song could see that he was covered in bloodstains, and on his left arm there was an open knife wound, still bleeding.

"You!" he exclaimed.

"Chai Wanlong is dead," said Tong Gong.

"What!"

"Chai Wanlong is dead."

"Did you kill him?"

Tong Gong hesitated slightly and then said with a grin: "Yes, it was me."

Song Ci turned back into the room and sat down on a chair.

Tong Gong followed him in, knelt down and said: "Master, I know murder is against the law. But there is no justice to be had for ordinary people in the imperial courts. The officials just do as they like, and we have to go along with it."

Song Ci felt as though he had been stabbed in the heart. He tried to think of something to say, but no words came. Seeing Tong Gong's open wound,

Song's wife fetched a lacquer dish of salve and said: "Stand up, and I'll dress your wound."

Tong Gong stayed on his knees, and Mistress Song again ordered him to get up. He did so, and she made him sit on a porcelain stool. The little three-year-old, who was affectionately called Qi'er, now woke up too, and she crawled out from under the bed canopy, rubbing her eyes.

Out on the street, the barking of the dogs grew louder, supplemented from across the wall by the sound of hoofbeats from many horses. Tong Gong's heart skipped a beat; he realised it must be the mounted police patrol hot on his trail, and he snatched back the hand that Mistress Song was in the act of bandaging and sank to his knees again. "I came to say goodbye," he said. "I can't stay. Farewell." With these words, he kowtowed three times, stood up and left.

Seeing Tong Gong going out of the door, Song Ci called out: "Stop!"

Tong Gong stopped.

"Where will you go?"

Tong Gong shook his head forlornly.

In his mind, Song Ci was frantically running through legal precedents under Song law, and he realised that, according to the *Xing Tong*, Tong Gong's case would be treated as murder punishable by beheading. But if you followed the *Bian Chi*, a capital sentence could be avoided. In Song history, there were precedents for clemency in the case of revenge killings. In the Yuanfeng period of Emperor Shenzong (1078-1085) in Qingzhou, a commoner called Wang Bin killed an enemy of his father, laid the man's head, arms and legs on his father's grave as an offering and then surrendered to the authorities. The Qingzhou magistrate considered this a highly complex case that he could not resolve easily, and he handed it on to the provincial court. The chief justice there, in turn, laid the case before the emperor. Emperor Shenzong consulted the legal records and passed judgment thus: "Although this is a capital case, the accused killed his father's enemy as an offering to his parent and accepted responsibility himself. We have sympathy with him. He is to be spared the death penalty and exiled to the neighbouring province."

But even so, if Tong Gong came before Magistrate Shu, then there was no hope for him. In the circumstances, Tong Gong had to flee. But where? If he left that night, it would be hard to evade capture the next day. Even as these thoughts were going through his mind, Song Ci was writing a letter. It was a short letter, addressed to Song Xie. The best thing was for Tong Gong to seek refuge with Song Xie, his father's old retainer, who could provide him with a safe hiding place. Song Ci instructed Tong Gong: "Go to the Rushi Temple on Mount Lianyuan and take shelter with a monk called Song Xie. He will be able to help you."

Tong Gong took the letter and once again knelt tearfully in front of Song Ci and kowtowed. Song Ci raised him up, saying: "Go, quickly." The hoofbeats outside were getting closer and then halted in front of the Song mansion's gates. A loud knocking followed.

Little Song Qi burst into tears and clutched her mother's skirts. Mistress Song held onto her daughter with one hand and with the other thrust a cloth bundle at Tong Gong, asking: "Can you swim?"

"Yes."

"Slip into the river from the back gate."

"Good idea," Song Ci said to his wife. "You go to the back gate and I'll go to the front."

Under the light of the waning moon, Mistress Song led Tong Gong to the rear courtyard. Following her directions, he clambered up onto the high wall. From the top, in the distance he could see Chai Wanlong's compound lighting up the sky with its blaze. The fire was getting fiercer. He wondered what had happened to the woman who had saved his life. He thought perhaps he should tell Mistress Song about her, but no words came to him. From the top of the wall, he made a deep obeisance, and then he dropped from the wall into the deep water of the Jianxi River…

Song Ci took Kang Liang with him to the front gate, but he didn't open it. He stood listening to the frantic knocking, then ordered Kang Liang to lift the bar. When the gate opened, there, sure enough, in the lamplight, at the head of the crowd, was the chief of the prefectural military police, Liang E.

Liang stepped over the threshold and bowed to Song Ci. "Master Song, I am under orders to hunt down a murderer. We heard the dogs barking here, and I wonder if he might have hidden in Your Honour's courtyard."

Song Ci stood squarely in the gateway and asked Liang: "What exactly do you mean by that?"

"Please don't misunderstand me, Master Song," Captain Liang said hurriedly. "It's just that the dogs were so excited, they were almost climbing the wall. I'm afraid lest, unknown to Your Honour, the vicious felon may have gone to ground inside."

Song Ci stared at Liang E in silence for a moment, then snapped: "Come in."

Liang led his archers into the mansion. Mistress Song had already gone back into the bedroom where she noticed, with a start, a bloody handprint on the door – it must have been left there by Tong Gong when he knocked. What to do? The soldiers' torches were already lighting up the reception room and their footsteps were getting closer. There was no time to clean up. Eventually, she simply opened the door and tried to use her body to hide the bloodstain. Unfortunately, it was around the height of her neck, and she couldn't cover it completely. Hastily, she picked up little Song Qi and stood by the door, holding her daughter so her back concealed the incriminating stain.

The archers rushed into the inner courtyard and one of them took up position by the door to Song Ci's living quarters so that Mistress Song couldn't get out. The soldiers mounted a search. By this time, the lamps in all the rooms had been lit. Song Ci's mother had also been roused from her bed, and she asked the archers what they were searching for. They told her they were hunting a murderer. "What murderer?" she asked.

The search spread over every part of the house and courtyards, except for Song Ci's own room, which the soldiers didn't dare enter without permission. When Liang E came over and saw Mistress Song standing in the doorway holding her daughter, he couldn't help thinking there was something odd about it.

Song Ci didn't know why his wife was standing there cradling his daughter like that, and said to her: "Wife, why are you standing in the doorway? Step aside and let Captain Liang in to have a look around." Song Ci's tone was a little sarcastic, but his wife didn't dare move.

"If the captain wants to look, then by all means let him come in," she said.

Liang E peered into the room. The lamps were burning brightly, and there didn't seem to be anyone hiding there. But they had already searched every other part of the Song residence, and there was only this room left. Suppose the man was actually hiding inside! In any case, he was under orders, and turning back now would be hard to explain later. So Liang E entered the bedroom, looked in every corner, satisfied himself that there was no one there, then turned and left.

When Liang reached the door, he clasped his hands to take a respectful farewell of Song Ci, but then he stopped and dropped his hands to his sides. He turned his attention to little Song Qi who was still cradled in her mother's arms. "Did you see a stranger come into the house just now?" he barked at her.

Song Qi looked at this monstrous, hairy man with the bulging eyes, and snuggled deeper into her mother's embrace. As she did so, she shifted her body so that a corner of the bloodstain was revealed. Song Ci saw what had happened, and his eyes warned his wife. She shifted her hold on Song Qi, turning slightly as she did, so that the stain was covered again.

"You saw him, didn't you," Liang demanded, staring at the child. Fortunately, he had not shifted his eyes from her face. Song Qi burst into tears. She gazed imploringly at her mother, who remained speechless. Finally, she shook her head.

"Well, did you see him or not?" Liang E repeated his inquisition.

"I didn't see anyone," Song Qi replied in a little girl's whisper.

Liang E snorted, then turned to Song Ci and clasped his hands in a respectful farewell: "I am sorry for disturbing you. I will take my leave."

The archers withdrew from the residence as swiftly as they had arrived. When she heard the sound of Kang Liang dropping the bar back across the main gates, Mistress Song was still standing in the doorway of the bedroom. Song Ci said: "Yulan! You…" His wife finally came into the room and turned to look back at the door. The bloodstain had almost disappeared from where Song Qi had pressed against it.

So this was how Song Ci helped Tong Gong escape. It was a turning point in his life. With his own hand, he had helped a murderer escape justice!

Song Ci stood thinking about this inexplicable turn of events for quite some time. Reading his mind, his wife said to him: "Try not to think about it. All Tong Gong did was do for himself what the courts should have done, but didn't."

The dogs were still barking excitedly in the distance, and the Chai mansion continued to burn fiercely, the red glow in the sky visible from Song's residence. Mistress Song brought some water, and with her own hands scrubbed the bloodstain off the bedroom door. Meanwhile, Song Ci found himself thinking about the series of visions that had crept into his dreams over recent days: Qiu Juan, Tong Da, Tong Ning and his wife all walking towards him, neither laughing nor weeping, just looking at him with wide-open eyes. Behind them was the Wind on the Waves Pavilion wreathed in the smoke of incense sticks. Feeling something stirring inside him as he entered the library, he unrolled a scroll of fine writing-paper on the desk. He took up his brush and wrote two elegant characters: '*xi yuan*' – 'washing away wrongs'.

"Good! Now we can go to bed," said his wife, coming into the library.

Song Ci put down the brush and made to follow his wife back out of the room, when suddenly she stopped and said: "Listen!"

"Listen to what?"

"In the vegetable garden… at the back gate. Someone's knocking."

Song listened carefully but heard nothing. "You're imagining it."

"I tell you, I heard something."

"Who can it be?"

"Tong Gong?"

"Let's go and see."

The two of them went out into the vegetable garden, which was next to the library. This time they both heard it: someone was knocking on the gate, very softly. They made their way over to the small sturdy gate in the encircling wall of the garden and stopped.

"Who is it?" Mistress Song called out softly.

"Mistress... it's me." It was a woman's voice, weak and indistinct.

Song Ci and his wife both opened their eyes wide in astonishment and gave a great start.

"Who are you?" Song Ci asked.

"It's me, Qiu Juan." The voice was as faint as a wisp of smoke.

Song and his wife were astounded. The candle in her hand trembled uncontrollably, and its light flickered across the vegetable garden, as though about to go out. Could it be a ghost?

"Who are you?" Song Ci asked again.

There was no sound from outside. Then, strangely, there was another noise, as though someone had fallen to the ground on the other side of the gate. Song looked at his wife and then exclaimed: "I'm going to open the gate." Which is just what he did.

There, outside, was the limp figure of a woman who had been half sitting, half leaning against the gate, which she fell through as it opened. Her hair was in disarray and her body was covered in blood. Mistress Song lowered the candle to light the woman's face and said in amazement: "It's Qiu Juan... it really is Qiu Juan!"

# CHAPTER IV

## A CITY OF BOOKS IN THE EAST (1218-1219)

As I wrote this chapter, my mind turned to the library in the ancient city of Alexandria, more than two thousand years ago, which also served as the national publishing house. The method of book production was simple: the scribes sat in a large room, facing a man who read the text out in a loud voice as they made multiple copies. What people in later times have found hard to understand is that in Alexandria, all that time ago, the studies of philosophy, mathematics and astronomy were all well advanced, so why did Europe not discover printing until the fifteenth century? European scholars believe this was because paper suitable for printing had not yet travelled from China to allow the development of this mysterious art. In the thirteenth century, my home town of Jianyang was already one of the three great printing centres of the Song dynasty, and this gave Song Ci access to the knowledge of those who came before him.

1

## SILENT WEEPING

That night, the people all came out to watch the fire. The late autumn winds were fanning the flames so they burned with some ferocity. The Chai compound was situated a little way apart from the other houses of the village, and the villagers stood at a respectful distance enjoying the entertainment, as the conflagration gradually reduced most of the compound to ashes.

Once it was light, Magistrate Shu came to survey the scene. Among the ruins, he could see the firewalls still standing proudly against the skyline, and he thought this very odd. The Chai mansion had contained many of these firewalls, all carefully positioned, so how had this fire been able to spread so widely? It seemed that it must have been started by several different people in several different places.

The rumour spread around the village that Chai Wanlong had been murdered by Tong Gong, son of their very own basket-maker, Tong Da. There were varying degrees of belief in the truth of this rumour, until around midday when 'wanted' posters for Tong Gong began to appear on the walls beside the city gates and at every major intersection. At this point, everyone accepted it as the truth and excitedly began propounding their own theories about the affair.

Kang Liang had been out and about shadowing the police patrols, and he came back to report on what he had seen. When Song Ci heard about the posters, he breathed a sigh of relief, as this told him that Tong Gong had escaped capture. But had he managed to find Song Xie? His wife reassured him: "Try not to worry. In this case, the absence of news is a good thing."

By the evening of the next day, Qiu Juan had at least partially regained her senses. When Song's wife went into the bedroom to light the lamp, she suddenly sprang fully awake. Mistress Song hurried to the bedside and urged her to rest some more: "Lie down and don't be afraid. You're safe at home."

Qiu Juan realised her clothes had been changed and her old ones were laid out clean and dry next to the bed. She clasped Mistress Song tightly by the hand. Mistress Song repeated: "Don't be afraid. You're safe at home and can sleep in your own bed." Qiu Juan wept silently but heartrendingly.

This silent weeping was scary in its intensity. Mistress Song let her cry for a while, then urged her: "Don't cry. It's all over. Everyone said you were dead! What happened?"

Qiu Juan kept on weeping, her lips trembling uncontrollably. Her cheeks and forehead were wet with tears and perspiration. Her face was much thinner and bonier than before, and she looked like a different person from the one who had left home all that time ago.

Little Song Qi came rushing in: "Qiu Juan! You're awake!"

When she saw Song Qi, Qiu Juan tried to stem her tears, but to no avail.

"You had better go, for the moment," her mother told Song Qi.

In a while, Song Qi came back with her father and grandmother in tow.

"Little Juan, you've decided to wake up!" Madame Song said, taking Qiu Juan's hand. Song Ci stood behind his mother, not speaking. Presently, Madame Song said: "I'm so happy you're still alive!"

Gradually, Qiu Juan stopped crying. Madame Song asked her: "Whose was the body your brother and the other men carried out of Chai Wanlong's mansion?"

Qiu Juan burst into tears again and didn't look up. Song Ci and his wife, and Madame Song, exchanged a look. They realised it must be something so terrible that Qiu Juan couldn't bear to talk about it. Mistress Song said: "Mother, go and have something to eat. I'll stay here."

2

# NO ORDINARY MAID

The day after Qiu Juan woke up, Song Ci himself suddenly fell quite seriously ill. He lay in his bed with a high fever, his lips and tongue dry, and racked by coughing. When he coughed, the muscles and tendons in his face stood out, his chest burned as though it was being branded, and his phlegm was a dull rust colour; sometimes he even coughed up fresh blood. Trying to suppress the coughing just made him faint and dizzy. Song Ci told the others not to worry – he had just caught a chill, and he would recover after taking some medicine.

Kang Liang went to the Jianning apothecary in town, and when Pharmacist He heard what was going on, without needing to be asked, he went to see Song Ci. After examining him, he told the distraught Madame and Mistress Song: "There is no cause for concern. He has indeed caught a chill from the wind and rain on his trip to the court in Jianning. The chill has gone to his lungs, and his fire element has over-compensated and is out of balance. His lungs are over-heated, which is why there is blood in his phlegm. There is pathogenic heat in his heart that is causing the dizzy spells. All we need to do is rebalance the hot and cold, clear the phlegm in his lungs and, with careful nursing, he will make a complete recovery."

Pharmacist He hurried back to town and returned with several packets of medicine, including some heart-thread lotus leaf, common dayflower herb and Japanese ardisia, which he boiled up into an infusion for Song Ci to drink. The next day, Song began to feel much better.

Not long after he had drunk the medicine, his fever broke. He had just got up and changed into some fresh clothes when Pharmacist He returned. He brought news. "Have you heard, Master? As the story of what happened has done the rounds, Tong Gong has become something of a hero. Your own reputation hasn't suffered either, Master", he added.

"What do you mean?" asked Song.

"The gossip in the city is that you and Tong Gong were working together, and local respect for you has increased as a consequence," he replied.

"That is not the kind of reputation you want!" Mistress Song chipped in.

"What other news is there?" Song Ci asked.

Pharmacist He began to talk about the fire. He said that, according to two maids from the Chai household, the murderer was called Tong. He hadn't been caught because, when the fire began to spread, everyone went to help the Chai family save their valuables. The household had a troupe of armed guards – a mob of hired thugs in reality – who had started out by helping save the property, but had soon run off. Even their weapons instructors and drill masters, the Tian brothers, had disappeared no one knew where.

"Is that so?" said Song Ci.

"It is indeed," replied Pharmacist He. "Old Chai had committed so many outrages, on a daily basis, that many of the servant girls really hated him. In the confusion when the fire broke out, it was hard to tell whether some of them were trying to put it out or actually helping it to spread. What is more, the few areas that escaped the fire, and indeed some of the ones that were still burning, were all looted and stripped bare of valuables. That's why the fire was able to spread the way it did."

Song Ci had never imagined that a single fire could have so many ramifications. The case had indeed become much more complicated.

"Well, the first thing will be to send someone to investigate," he said.

"That's not going to happen," Pharmacist He replied. "Magistrate Shu is far too canny to cause trouble for himself by investigating."

"How would that cause him trouble?" Song asked.

"Well, if the report finds that there are many culprits, but none of them can be brought to book, wouldn't you call that trouble?"

"But doesn't the Chai family have people in the capital?"

"They used to have a lot of influence because they were rich and could bribe people, but the fire has changed all that," Pharmacist He explained.

Song felt ashamed when he heard this reply, but he didn't show it.

"In fact," the pharmacist continued, "the person who should be investigating is the chief provincial magistrate. But over the years the people have suffered many injustices that he has covered up and failed to rule on. Sooner or later, the case of the fire is going to go the same way, isn't it?"

Song Ci had to agree that this was indeed the case.

Pharmacist He addressed Song Ci again: "I have some other news, Master.

The girl's body they brought out of Chai Wanlong's house all that time ago wasn't your maid Qiu Juan, it was Tong Ning's wife."

Song was startled: "Surely Qiu Juan's mother and younger brother saw the body."

"Hah! It was so bloated and decomposed that no one could have identified it. They say that Tong Ning's wife counted for so little that Chai Wanlong gave her to the Tian brothers to defile."

"What about Qiu Juan?" Mistress Song asked.

"Apparently, Chai took her straight away and locked her up somewhere in the house."

"What happened then?"

"Nobody knows."

In fact, as we know, Qiu Juan was alive and in Song Ci's house. Song and his wife had begun to feel there was something very strange about the way Qiu Juan had escaped from the Chai mansion during the fire, not least because of the amount of blood on her clothes. They had discussed it with Song's mother, and had also told Kang Liang and Song Qi not to tell anyone what they had seen. So they did not tell Pharmacist He anything either. On the third day, Qiu Juan wanted to get up, but she was still too weak. Song's wife told her to stay in bed until her strength returned. After quite a while, she said to Mistress Song: "I wanted to come and see you and ask after my little brother."

Mistress Song had already told her all about how her brother had run off, they knew not where, after their mother's death, so she realised that Qiu Juan was explaining why she had come knocking on their door that night. "Whatever your reason, you and I are family, so of course you should have come here." She didn't, however, tell her about how all the serving girls had run away from the Chai mansion after the fire, or about the 'wanted' posters for Tong Gong that had been put up everywhere.

Suddenly, Qiu Juan burst out: "That man wasn't killed by Tong Gong."

Mistress Song didn't reply immediately, but after a pause she asked: "So who did kill him?"

"I did!" said Qiu Juan.

Mistress Song stepped back in amazement: "You killed... who did you kill?"

"I killed Old Man Chai. And I started the fire."

"Are you telling the truth?" asked Mistress Song both disbelievingly and perplexed, since she couldn't help feeling there was some truth to the girl's words. When she repeated the question, Qiu Juan started weeping uncontrollably. Later that day, Mistress Song told her husband what had been said, and, thinking about it, Song Ci also felt there must be some connection between Qiu Juan and Chai Wanlong's murder. Following on his train of thought, he realised that this was no ordinary maid, and if she had stayed alive only in order to seek revenge, now that she had had that revenge, would she not be rather more careless of her life? What was going to be the best way of protecting her? Hide her in the house? No, that certainly wouldn't be safe. But if she wasn't in the house, would any of them rest easy?

He turned different options over in his mind, and in the end decided the best one would be to send her to his wife's maternal uncle, Mr Wu Zhi. Wu Zhi was a leading disciple of Zhu Xi, who had taught building construction in Tongyouzhen. In his old age, he had retired to a thatched cottage on Mount Yungu in Jianyang Municipality. Mount Yungu is a place where the mists curl endlessly round the crags, and is covered in the lush green of ancient trees. Zhu Xi himself had once lived in a cottage there, and he wrote this poem about it:

*The mountain peak waves a curt greeting;*
*No sign of human activity here,*
*Just the faint sound of threshing grain drifting up from below.*

Perilous as it was, it seemed to Song Ci that this was the best place to send Qiu Juan.

But how to get her there? Whenever Kang Liang went out on errands, it was always in company. Song himself couldn't do it, nor was there anyone else in the household who could. Could Qiu Juan slip out of the back gate at night and make her own way to Mount Yungu? She was no Tong Gong, and it wouldn't be right to expose her to that kind of danger. Then Song Ci thought of Pharmacist He – he could ask him to find an excuse to go to the Rushi Temple on Mount Lianyuan and ask Song Xie to come back with him. Together with Song Xie, surely they could come up with a plan. And what was more, he would have news of Tong Gong. But there could be a problem: Pharmacist He had been in and out of the Song house many times recently and suppose he attracted the attention of the police, wouldn't this trip to Mount Lianshan be putting Tong Gong in danger?

A few days later, Song Ci was completely recovered, and Qiu Juan was also out of bed and looking to get on with her life. Song Ci and Mistress Song went to have a quiet word with her.

"You can't do anything just yet," she said. "You can't even leave the house. If you were suddenly to reappear, and word got to the *yamen*, who knows what Magistrate Shu would do."

"So I've just got to stay hidden away all day?"

"To be on the safe side, yes. We'll think of something."

That night, Mistress Song talked to her husband. "I don't leave the house often, and if I go out people won't notice me. It would be best if I were to take Qiu Juan."

Song thought this was a very risky strategy, but his wife reassured him: "All we have to do is to find a way for us to leave the house safely, then I know the way. First, we head north, then when we're out of town, we go to the west road where we can hire a horse and carriage. That's the main road to the Masha publishing house, so there will be lots of business travellers and merchants. Qiu Juan and I can put on men's clothing – the weather is cold, so since everyone will be wearing lots of layers, no one will notice. After a little while we can change carriages. If anyone asks why we're going to Mount Yungu, I'll say I'm going home to visit my parents. It won't be a problem."

Song Ci disagreed: "We need to think again."

But his wife thought to herself: If Qiu Juan is comfortable with the plan, the two of us are not stupid, and we are sure to make it if we go together.

The next day she went to sound out Qiu Juan, but much to her surprise, couldn't find her. All she saw was her mattress neatly tidied up and stowed away in her bedroom. Amazed, Mistress Song hurried to tell her husband. The whole household started searching for Qiu Juan, but there was no sign of her anywhere. The only clue was that the gate in the rear vegetable garden was closed but unlocked.

"She must have gone last night." Mistress Song burst into tears.

3

# A WIFE HAS HER SAY

Qiu Juan had disappeared just as suddenly as she had appeared. She had no family left, so where could she turn?

Song Ci was deeply troubled – for all his extensive study and education, was he actually any more use than anyone else? He thought to himself: In intelligence, worldliness, broad-mindedness, courage, in none of these can I compare to my wife. How, then, do I stack up against Qiu Juan? She had been willing to pay a heavy price for the opportunity for vengeance. And now, fearing lest she involve us, she didn't hesitate, but just upped sticks and went. Can I compare myself even to this little maidservant?

In the past, he had been guided mainly by his book-learning, but now he didn't know what to make of himself. Later that day, he stood in front of the scroll on which he had written the characters 'washing away wrongs', and wept.

He recalled the argument he had had with Liu Kezhuang on top of the Six Harmonies Pagoda that spring day; and then he felt ashamed of himself. Qianfu, as Liu was affectionately known, was certainly not devoid of emotion, but how did he manage to remain so detached? "Qianfu! Yes indeed, what about Qianfu!" he thought. He wished he could be as detached as Qianfu. Moved by these thoughts, he recited a verse of poetry:

*Oh, to be a mountain hermit*
*With only the clouds for friends;*
*And take three leisurely cups of wine*
*Amid the flurrying raindrops.*

This was not his own creation but had been written by Zhu Xi when he was living as a hermit on Mount Yungu.

In the Song household there was a Confucian-style, narrow-shouldered zither known as the 'Ice in the Jade Ewer'.[1] Mr Wu Zhi had let Mistress Song bring it with her when she left home to get married. It was a treasure among zithers, and in its soundbox was written in regular script characters: 'Made by Gong Lu Jin Yuan in the second year of the Shaoxing period of the Song dynasty'.

Jin Yuan's zithers were famous for their delicate construction and pure sound, but when Song Ci went to play this instrument to dispel his gloomy mood, the only sound he could produce was a harsh tone like tearing cloth. He switched from music to wine and drank until his face was flushed and his ears burning, with a pounding in his head, but he couldn't drown the knowledge that this was the first time he and his wife had argued about anything.

The room was oppressive, so he went out into the courtyard and started pacing up and down. The ground was carpeted in petals scattered by the autumn wind, which was sighing through the withered leaves of the pear trees. He found himself touched with sorrow by the transience of the flowers and the leaves on the trees: a man has a whole lifetime, but they only saw one autumn. He felt like one man standing against the whole world, and for several nights this thought kept him awake, as he tossed and turned.

Finally, there came a night, a night with a glorious moon drifting through a cloudy sky, when the exhausted Song fell into an uneasy slumber. He dreamed he was on the misty, cloud-covered slopes of Mount Lianyuan. There was Song Xie, from whom he had parted so long ago now. He asked him about Tong Gong, but Song Xie knew nothing about him, and Song Ci was greatly alarmed. Then he heard the sound of hoofbeats and iron chains clanking on the ground, and with that was suddenly transported to the entrance of the village. He could see a group of armed military police to-ing and fro-ing. At their head was Liang E mounted on a horse behind which he was dragging in chains a bedraggled, blood stained figure... it was Tong Gong! The vision startled him awake, his body drenched in sweat, and he sat up unsteadily in bed.

The bright moonlight was flooding in through the window so the room was lit just as things had been in his dream. Then his eye fell on the scroll hanging on the wall opposite on which he had written the characters 'washing away wrongs'. An indescribable feeling swept over him, propelling him out of bed and across the room so that he stood in front of the scroll. He remained there for some time and then, with a great shout, tore down the scroll from the wall.

Startled awake, his wife got out of bed, too. Without a word spoken, the two of them stood looking at each other. Yulan had no conscious intention of reproaching her husband, but the words just came tumbling out: "You are a principled man, and you are determined to avenge injustice. But after Tong Ning's death, your brains have become a little scrambled and your body has been muddled. People said he slipped and fell from the Chai mansion wall, and you had no way of proving he didn't. People said Qiu Juan fell into the pond and drowned... the body that was carried out wasn't hers, but it was so bloated and decomposed, there was no way of telling. Didn't your father use to say that, without honesty, a man has no foundation, yet honesty is no qualification to hold office? The dishonest people of the empire don't know you, but if you stick to your principles, they will come to know you for what you are. Throughout history there have been bizarre and baffling court cases. If you are called to be a judge, how many of those do you think you will actually be able to untangle?"

Song Ci didn't know how to answer. He knew he was well versed in the law and had a firm grip on the principles of conducting a case and passing judgment, which he had studied at the academy, but this was all book learning. Rather to his surprise, however, in the face of his wife's interrogation, he began to find some indefinable stirrings of a resolution to his doubts.

"Let's go to sleep and not think about it."

Seeing his distracted look, his wife picked up the scroll from off the floor, put it carefully on the desk and began to push him gently back towards their bed.

"You really mustn't distress yourself," she said again gently. "When the Marquis of Wu lived in seclusion and withdrew from worldly affairs to immerse himself in his studies, didn't people call him a sleeping dragon?"

Of all the wise men in history, the one Song Ci most admired was Zhuge Liang, Marquis of Wu.[2] Despite the man's motto of 'Strive your hardest, and only stop when you are dead', and despite his perspicacity and almost divine wisdom, had he not, indeed, withdrawn from the world? Later generations extolled his talents and achievements after he came out of seclusion, but how many spoke of his great efforts before that? Before emerging from his thatched cottage, had he not overseen the division into Three Kingdoms, an extraordinary feat by any measure?

His wife's words that night had kindled a spark in Song Ci like a flint on steel, and illumination came to him – he had thought of a way out of his difficulties. What about the famous publishing houses of Jianyang? Even before the Song dynasty moved south, Jianyang district was already established as one of the country's publishing centres. It was known as the

Prefecture of Maps and Books, and its publications were admired across the empire. In those publishing houses there must be many works on legal precedents that he could systematically research.

"Yulan," he said, "tomorrow I'm going to the publishing house."

"The publishing house? Which one, Masha or Chonghua?"

"Chonghua."

"But that's a hundred *li* away."

"It wouldn't matter if it was a thousand!"

4

# THE HALL OF TEN THOUSAND SCROLLS

Masha and Chonghua are both on the western road out of Jianyang, Masha about seventy *li* from the city and Chonghua another twenty or more. The books from both places were primarily distributed from Jianyang, so they were known everywhere as the Jianyang publishing houses. As Chonghua was further away, Song Ci decided to visit it first and then take in Masha on his way back.

The next day dawned bright and pleasant. Accompanied by Kang Liang, Song rode into Jianyang by the north gate, made his way through the city and left by the western Jingshu Gate. The road led them through a countryside of desolate trees, their yellowing leaves clinging to the branches and carpeting the ground, but Song's heart was much lighter than it had been the day before. In his eyes, the leaves glowed in the sunlight, as if the landscape were sheathed in a suit of golden armour.

China was already using woodblock printing by the Sui dynasty (581-618 CE), and paper had been discovered well before that. Now, in the Song dynasty, the publishing houses of Jianyang towards which the two men were riding were not only printing whole books but had also developed special paper for the purpose. On the road, Song Ci and Kang Liang watched the carts carrying paper to Masha and Chonghua, and they delighted in the sound of the small bells on the horses' harnesses. The road was busy; because the immediate environs could not produce enough paper to supply the two houses, all the villages and hamlets on the north road were also involved in its manufacture.

Many different trees grew in the country between Masha and Chonghua, primarily red-date and pear. There were several varieties of pear, including snow pear, winter pear, iron pear, wood pear and date-flower pear, all of them good for making woodblocks for printing. Jianyang is also bamboo country, and the types that grew there, *huangzhu*, *mianzhu* and *chijianzhu*, were also ideal for paper-making. It is perhaps surprising then, that despite this abundance of raw material, Jianyang was not, in fact, the birthplace of both paper manufacture and printing.

The surroundings reminded Song Ci of a similar autumn day when he was a boy. He had accompanied his father on a trip to Chonghua, and on the road his father had explained to him how the rise of Chonghua's woodblock-carving industry had begun at the end of the Tang dynasty (618-907 CE). Because Fujian Province was at the south-eastern extreme of Chinese territory, it hadn't been affected by the wars and chaos at the end of the Tang and the beginning of the Five Dynasties period,[1] and its economy had remained prosperous. Scholarship was on the rise, and as the number of people involved increased, the woodblock industry started up in Chonghua to meet the demand for books. The mountains around Chonghua were full of the materials needed for printing: pear trees, Chinese elm and wax gourds. There was even the famous Heiqiu or 'Black Hillock', a black spring that flowed out of the coal- and ore-bearing strata, its waters coloured by the coal, oily black and glossy, in a seemingly endless supply of printing ink. It could be said that heaven had created a natural treasure house for printing.

Some childhood memories really take root, especially when they are about something as extraordinary as this home of printing. As they went along, Song Ci recalled how all the countryfolk were involved in the industry, how all the street markets were crammed with bookstalls. He remembered the names of the scenic spots in the forests of trees used by the printers: Warm Jade Immortal Pavilion, Southern Bamboo Mountain, Daizhang Cold Spring, Dragon Lake Spring Water; there was even a Book Hall Temple. Little wonder it was known across the civilised world as the Peerless City of Books of the Orient. He had asked his father: "Why are there so many people buying books in the markets?"

Since Tang and Song times, there have only been two main commercial roads through Fujian Province. One is the postal relay road through the interior along the Red River, the other is the trunk road through Shangrao to Hangzhou and Suzhou. Jianyang is situated at the intersection of the two roads, so what better place for booksellers of the empire to gather and sell their wares to graduates of the academies and other scholars?

The road was teeming with travellers, almost all of whom were heading for the publishing house. Around midday, the roadside inns and foodstalls opened up for weary travellers to eat, sleep or just rest their feet, but it was sunset before Song Ci and Kang Liang arrived at their destination.

The publishing house! Ah yes, the publishing house, on which the eyes of the world were fixed. It was even more prosperous-looking than Song remembered it from twenty years before. The sun was dipping below the horizon, its last reddish-purple rays illuminating the western part of the sky. Varicoloured lanterns were being lit in the township. Spanning the main road was a ceremonial entrance arch on top of which were carved the four characters 'Tang Yang Shu Lin' (Tanyang Forest of Books). The setting sun and the light of the lanterns reflected off the gilt lettering. Along both sides of the road there were countless bookshops and wood-carving workshops facing each other, and everywhere were tall flagpoles with banners advertising the various establishments:

> 'Best selection of books in the country'
> 'The six classics and their commentaries'
> 'Diamond-quality printing blocks'
> 'Fine calligraphy printing'
> 'Radiant ink sticks'

On the street, books of all kinds spilled over from one stall into the next, and the customers wove in and out, intoxicated by the atmosphere. Song Ci was exhausted from the long journey, but he threw himself into the sea of books and people like a fish diving under the waves. As Song Ci went rummaging through the books in shop after shop, he frowned and asked himself: How is it that, in this veritable city of books, I can't find a single volume on precedents for incarceration?

In the end, he asked a shopkeeper: "Do you have any books on legal precedents in court cases?"

"No, we don't," the shopkeeper replied.

He went into another shop and, after another fruitless search, asked the same question. This time, the shopkeeper pulled a volume out from a pile of books and gave it to him. Song Ci looked at it. It was *A Legal Commentary*, a book he had already read when at the academy.

"Don't you have anything else?"

"No."

There was nothing for it but to keep looking. Song went from shop to shop, searching pile after pile of books, and apart from one copy of *A Few Words on the Study of Law*, he couldn't find a single volume of the kind he wanted.

The Hall of Ten Thousand Scrolls![2] Why don't I go to the Hall of Ten Thousand Scrolls? It had slipped his mind until then.

The hall already had a history of more than two hundred years. It was the earliest established block-carving house, as well as the largest and most distinguished. The name of its owner, Yu Renzhong, was known throughout the civilised world, and it had the resources to carve blocks for any kind of book. Song Ci decided to abandon his fruitless search of the bookstalls, and go and find the Hall of Ten Thousand Scrolls.

The hall stood in the busiest part of the street market with a large, shiny, eye-catching *zitan* wood tablet carved with gold characters: 'Hall of Ten Thousand Scrolls'. The words stood out with an air of supreme self-confidence. They had been written by the great Northern Song calligrapher, Mi Fu. Mi Fu was the father-in-law of the prefectural governor of Jianning, Wu Ji, who was a palace graduate and had previously been minister of imperial tributes. He was a fine poet and an accomplished painter and calligrapher. In the first year of the Daguan period of Emperor Song Huizong (1107 CE), Yu Renzhong's grandfather had made the journey to the Northern Song capital of Bianjing to ask Wu Ji to write the calligraphy for the tablet. Wu Ji wrote the three characters but then his father-in-law Mi Fu, who happened to be staying with him at the time, inspected the work. In his opinion, although the calligraphy was extremely elegant and refined, it would be difficult to reproduce on a tablet that would be worthy of the great woodblock-carving house of the Hall of Ten Thousand Scrolls. Thereupon, he took up his own brush and rewrote the three characters. Mi Fu died that same year, so this tablet was the very last one that he wrote, and it became of inestimable value. With this tablet above its gate, the Hall of Ten Thousand Scrolls inspired great respect in visiting scholars before they even crossed the threshold.

The hall was unusually busy when Song Ci entered, full of the sounds of people rummaging through books, requesting particular volumes, striking bargains, calling out prices, laughing... all rolled together into a great clamour. There was a group of Koreans, dressed in their national costume, buying books. The shop staff gave them three lacquered wood balls the size of hens' eggs to roll into a large basin that was as big as the table it sat on. Inside the basin were seven small holes arranged in the pattern of the seven stars of the Great Dipper. The shop staff rotated the basin to imitate the movement of the stars, and if the ball the customer rolled fell into one of the holes, he was given a copy of a book of illustrated folk tales. It was the kind of book that was enjoyed by scholars and casual readers alike, and it had been specially produced as a free gift for the pleasure of customers of the Hall of Ten Thousand Scrolls. Rather to his surprise, the sight of this bustling scene reassured Song Ci and strengthened his resolve. Even so, search as he might in the Hall of Ten Thousand Scrolls, he still couldn't find what he wanted. Sighing deeply, he sat down on the bench provided for customers to rest their book-weary feet.

"We have been on the road all day, Master," said Kang Liang. "And we've already visited many bookshops. Let's find an inn where we can sleep, and perhaps tomorrow you will find what you are looking for."

Song Ci did not reply but just sat silently for a while. Then he stood up and made his way over to the shop counter. This time, almost in a single breath, he ordered a pile of books: dynastic histories, general histories, histories of specific periods, unofficial histories, private political diaries. He then went on to financial records, local chronicles, obituaries and memorials, collections of folk stories and fairy stories… books of all kinds, as many and varied as possible. Helping Song Ci bundle up his purchases, the astonished shop assistant said to him: "Honoured Sir, may I ask who you are buying these books for?"

"I'm not buying them for anyone," Song replied.

"They are for yourself?"

"Yes."

"That can't be so! You must be setting up a business."

"What kind of business?" Song put down the volume he was leafing through and looked at the shop assistant.

"A block-carving business!"

"Block-carving?" Song was amazed. "No, not at all."

"Hah! Come now, you can't fool me! Why else would you be buying so many books?" As he spoke, the assistant took a book down from the shelves. It was Su Shi's *Biography and Collected Works of Dongpo*. He flicked through it, looking for a particular page, which he showed to Song Ci.

Song Ci read: "The riches to be found in books are like the riches of the ocean, everything is there. You can never fully fathom their depths, but you will always find what you are looking for. Thus, a man seeking knowledge should always have a purpose in his search."

The assistant addressed Song again: "It has been written that 'True scholarship does not try to encompass everything'. You have a great pile of books here, one of almost every kind imaginable. If Your Honour is not buying them to set up a block-carving business, what other possible reason can there be? I have had several customers like Your Honour before. The only thing is, they usually come from distant parts to buy the books for their businesses back home, and that I can understand. But I have heard Your Honour's accent, and you seem to be from this province. Where can you be thinking of setting up your business?"

Song Ci burst out laughing. Now he understood! Because the Hall of Ten Thousand Scrolls only carried the finest calligraphy, carving and printing, there was no shortage of block-carvers from other provinces who came here to buy sample books; the assistant had taken him for one of these. From their conversation, he realised the assistant must be an educated and intelligent man. In fact, he wondered whether the man might not be the owner Yu Renzhong himself. But he didn't ask and simply said: "You just quoted the saying 'True scholarship does not try to encompass everything'. I believe that comes from the academician Cheng Yi. He had another saying – 'Knowledge accrued should be put to use'."

This was, in truth, what Song Ci believed himself. Although he had not found any specialist books on legal precedents, there would certainly be examples of court judgments and sentences from the past in a hundred different books. If he found a volume with one or two examples of records of the kind he was looking for, then he bought it. He also bought *Childhood Illnesses*, *Married Women's Health*, *The Illustrated Circulatory System* and *Essentials of Surgery*. He bought these titles because they dealt with subjects that had great relevance to the conducting of autopsies. By now he had spent nearly all the money his wife had sent him off with, leaving only just enough for a night's board and lodging – which he now set off to find.

The next day, Song Ci embarked on the return journey. Although his purse was empty, as they passed the Masha publishing house, he couldn't resist the temptation to go in to have a look around. He found that the book market there was about the same size as the one at Chonghua. But here, too, he was unable to find the specialised books he sought, so he headed home. Over the next few days, he began a careful analysis of the case studies on intractable diseases that Dr Haiting had bequeathed him, and although he couldn't for the moment tell just how helpful these were going to be in the future, he did begin to understand their inestimable value.

In no time, it seemed, it was the spring of the following year. Yulan decided she wanted to pay a visit to her parents, and Song Ci went with her to pay his respects to his father-in-law, Master Wu Zhi. As they were chatting one day, the old man told Song Ci: "I was talking to your father once, and he told me that old Mr Cai Qi at the Yijing Hall in Masha had a book called the *Anthology of Difficult Cases*, which laid out the collected precedents of difficult historical court cases."

"Really?" said Song Ci, his eyes widening.

"Yes indeed, but when your father went to try to buy the book, Old Man Cai made an excuse, claiming the story wasn't true. He certainly wasn't willing to admit that he had the book. Not long after that, he died. Then one day, your father bumped into the old man's son in town, and he asked him about this matter. The son told him the book had been bought by Yu Renzhong of the Hall of Ten Thousand Scrolls for a very considerable sum. 'So, that's it,' your father said to me. 'If he paid a lot of money for it, he is not going to want to part with it.' This was all a good few years ago, and I have no idea where the book is now."

Song Ci was both pleased and doubtful at the same time. He was pleased because he now knew such a book existed, and there was some chance he could get to read it. He was doubtful because he couldn't understand why, if it was such a rare book, Yu Renzhong had not turned it into a money-making bestseller? Still, the first thing to do was to raise some substantial funds. But how?

His father's long illness leading up to his death had severely depleted the family coffers, leaving them only with just enough to live off. After Song's initial spending spree at Chonghua, and following several return visits to Masha, in the course of which he had bought large quantities of every imaginable type of book, he had had to sell the family jewellery to raise the money and was now reduced to asking friends for help.

The news of the existence of this book immediately made Song Ci want to return home that very day. His wife understood the urgency he felt and went with him. That night, she took out a green jade belt ornament carved in the form of two cranes, which she had worn since she was a child. Each of the cranes had one eye showing, and where the pupils should have been, there were two holes. If you looked closely through these holes, you could see that inside each one was a tiny carving of a Buddhist image: on one side was Guan Yin of the Southern Seas, and on the other was Tathagata, the Buddha of Medicine. Mistress Song handed her husband this priceless jade to give to the book shop.

"No! No, that won't do." Song Ci saw the jade and immediately understood his wife's intention. He snatched his hand away, as though the jade was red hot, and repeated: "No! Absolutely not. This is the only heirloom left to you by your mother."

"We'll find a way to get it back later," his wife said.

"No. I have a plan," Song replied.

"What plan?"

"Look," Song turned and pointed at all the books in the room. The carved bookcases were full to overflowing, and the surplus lay in piles on the floor. "I can take them to the book shop and sell them."

"You? Sell a book?" his wife laughed.

Song joined in the laughter, then after a moment, said: "I'll take them to the Hall of Ten Thousand Scrolls. I'll exchange a hundred of them for just that one volume."

"I'm afraid you could take this whole library and the owner wouldn't think it worth the exchange for that book of his. If you…"

Before Song's wife could finish her sentence, the library door was pushed open, and little Song Qi appeared outside.

"Mummy, what's this purse doing here?" she asked.

Song and his wife looked across the room, and there, sure enough, in the middle of the doorway, at Song Qi's feet, was a purse. They were astonished – what on earth was a purse doing there?

Song Qi didn't wait for her parents to reply, but reached down and picked up the purse. It was quite heavy and made a noise when it knocked against the door frame. Song Ci hurriedly took the purse, put it down on the desk, in the lamplight, and opened it.

"Silver!" Song Qi cried out in delight.

Song and his wife looked again, and they were even more astonished.

Mistress Song had certainly not seen any purse in the doorway when she came into the library. In the course of their subsequent short conversation, someone must have put it there. Who could it have been? Song went out of the room to have a look around, and his wife followed. But outside, all that could be seen were the hazy moonlight, the pear trees in the garden and the black silhouette of the melon shed. The only sound was the dull drone of insects, like rain pattering on the ground. All was just as it should be.

"What are you looking at?" Song Qi had also come outside.

What, indeed, were they looking at? There was nothing to see. The three of them went back into the library. Suddenly, as her eyes fell on the purse, Song's wife exclaimed: "Tong Gong! It's Tong Gong!"

"Tong Gong?"

"Yes. It's him. Look – this is the purse I gave him when he ran away that night." She removed the silver from the purse, revealing a silk tea flower. "I embroidered that flower myself… What's the matter?" Her anxiety had turned to excitement until she looked at her husband and saw him frowning.

"Where did Tong Gong get this much silver?"

"You're afraid he stole it?"

"Tomorrow, I'm going to the Rushi Temple."

"Do you have to go?"

"I have to."

## 5

# THE LIANYUAN RUSHI TEMPLE

This unexpected turn of events caused Song Ci to postpone his plan to go to the Hall of Ten Thousand Scrolls; instead he would go to the Rushi Temple. That starless autumn night when he had so recklessly helped Tong Gong escape, he had done so out of sympathy for the youth's situation. Yes, he had killed a man, but it was to avenge his father. Moreover, the man deserved to be killed. He didn't expect anything from Tong Gong in return for letting him go, but if he had now committed some crime in order to do so, then Song Ci would feel deeply hurt. He had to find out for himself how Tong had come by the money.

The Rushi Temple was first built in the Tang dynasty and was situated within Jianyang Municipality on Mount Lianyuan. When Song Ci set off there at the break of dawn, he did not ride, but went on foot, dressed as a Buddhist pilgrim. He followed the Jianxi Stream north for thirty or so *li*, then branched off eastwards along the Futun Stream for another thirty. The road was cold and desolate with few other travellers, and it was hard going. When he reached the prosperous village of Luotianli, it was already past noon. He ordered a cup of tea at a small wayside teashop and gulped it down gratefully. Then he set off up the mountain. As he plodded on, he could already see the eaves of the temple in the distance. The sun was setting early, and it was already half hidden by the distant peaks when he passed through a black stone ceremonial gateway and started up the long flight of stone steps that led to the temple. In front of the ancient building stood a row of immensely tall dawn redwood trees, densely covered in luxuriant foliage, which cast deep shadows over the top end of the flight of steps. The last of the evening light filtered through the redwoods onto a tablet bearing the three-character inscription 'Rushi Temple'. On either side of the main gate were two converging red-washed walls on which was inscribed detailed information about the name of the mountain, the name of the place where the temple stood and when it was built:

*On Tianzhu Peak the evening sun*
*Falls on the sacred lotus throne,*
*Illuminating the passing of five hundred years.*
*Clear waters grace the slopes of Lianyuanshan*
*And through shady bamboo groves,*
*Far off sounds the bell of the Rushi Temple.*

Song went in through the temple gate and found himself in a wide, square courtyard, in the middle of which was a covered walkway made of stone. This led him to the inner gate, and as he stood in front of it, he suddenly heard the sound of martial arts combat. Beyond the inner gate was an even larger courtyard, in the middle of which he could see Tong Gong spinning a 'fire and water staff'[1] like a miniature tornado. He was advancing, in step-and-thrust form, the staff under tight control, on an unarmed Song Xie. Song Xie dodged the thrusts, left and right, retreating step by step as though timidly resigned to defeat. Then, suddenly, in a movement as swift as a tiger pouncing on its prey, he shifted his stance and struck out with a thunderous blow that sent Tong Gong tumbling to the ground.

Song Xie stopped and said angrily: "You see! I keep telling you. If you are short and not particularly well-built, you have to perfect your evasive techniques."

With Song Xie so firmly in control, I really doubt that Tong Gong could have got up to any mischief, Song thought to himself.

Tong Gong rolled over on the ground. The blow had not been a light one, and his nose was bloodied, but he made no attempt to wipe it clean. Staring at Song Xie, he half-picked himself up, and kneeling in front of the other man, said: "Master, I want to learn to fight, not to dodge."

Song Xie turned to walk away, leaving Tong Gong kneeling in the middle of the courtyard. Then he saw Song Ci.

"Lord Song!" He fell naturally into the same form of address as he had always used in the past, and he went over to greet Song Ci.

As Song Xie greeted him, Song Ci thought to himself: Here's a man who accompanied my late father all over the country and has considerable experience in catching wanted fugitives. Is it really any surprise he saw straight through my disguise?

Hearing the voices, Tong Gong took a close look at the new arrival and he, too, immediately recognised Song Ci. All thoughts of what had just happened were forgotten. Song Xie formally welcomed his old master and invited him to wash off the dust of his journey.

A little later, as night was drawing in and the Rushi Temple was clothed in a drizzly mist, Song Ci saw Tong Gong sweeping the entrance to the Hall of the Four Heavenly Kings, and he decided to go over and ask him about the silver.

"Did you come down from the mountain last night?"

"Come down from the mountain? No." Tong Gong stopped sweeping.

"Don't try and hide the truth from me. Where did you get that silver?" Song Ci said severely.

Tong Gong was startled. "Silver? What silver?"

"Don't play dumb. I saw the purse we gave you that night."

At the mention of the purse, Tong Gong said: "Master, I don't understand what I have done wrong."

"Go and get the purse!"

Tong Gong didn't move.

"Go and get it!"

Tong Gong still didn't move.

"You…" Song felt all his previous suspicions flooding back, bringing anger with them. He reined these feelings in and asked again: "Just tell me, where did you get that silver?"

"What silver?" Tong Gong's eyes widened in even greater puzzlement. "Truly, I don't know anything about any silver."

Song Ci himself began to wonder what was going on. Certainly, Tong Gong had not wanted to fetch the purse, but he had repeatedly denied any knowledge of the silver and he did seem genuinely puzzled.

"Quick now! Get the purse and show it to me."

Tong grunted, put down the broom and hurried to his sleeping quarters.

Song Ci followed him into a small hall, and when Tong Gong produced the purse for him, he could see it was, indeed, the one his wife had given the man the night he escaped, complete with embroidered tea-flower. As soon as he saw the purse, Song felt himself blushing right to his ears. He was no longer concerned about where the silver had come from, and he had already worked out who had left that identical purse outside the door. He felt deeply ashamed. He had recently read up on a number of old court cases, and he felt he had really made considerable progress in his studies. But if he were to look on this affair of the purse as though it were a case that had been brought before him as a judge, he now realised that all the deductions that he had made about it were completely wrong.

He didn't say anything more but just turned and left. He found himself in the Manjushri Hall. In the middle of the hall there was a statue of the Bodhisattva, a five-pointed crown on his head, a jewelled sword in his hand, seated on a lion. In two rows on either side were the twenty-four other celestial beings, each with their particular attributes. At the front of the hall, Song Xie was seated alone on a prayer mat, his eyes almost closed, deep in meditation. As Song Ci was wondering whether or not to disturb him, he heard Song Xie say softly: "Lord Song, please come in."

Song Ci did as he was bid, and Song Xie stood up.

"I thought you might come," he said.

"How did you know I needed money?"

"You have been borrowing from friends for some time now."

"When you came home, why didn't you stay for a few days?"

"If I had done that, would you still have come here?"

"What do you mean? Is there a problem here?"

"No problem, other than that you entrusted Tong Gong to me."

"Has he... has he broken the temple rules?"

"That's not it," Song Xie said. "As soon as he arrived here, he asked me to teach him martial arts. Knowing his compulsion to see things through to the end, I guessed he had some purpose in mind. When I asked him, he denied it at first, but when I pressed him, he finally admitted that there were two people he wanted to kill."

"The Tian brothers?"

"That's right."

Song Ci knew that the local gossip was that Tong Gong's sister-in-law had been raped and then killed by the Tian brothers. The story had started to do the rounds after the fire at the Chai mansion, and came from the servant girls who had fled from there, so Tong Gong must have heard it too.

"I'm worried that he may just disappear at any moment," Song Xie said.

"After Chai Wanlong died, the Tian brothers made off, no one knows where, with a great quantity of silver they had looted from the household. But you probably know that."

"Yes, indeed. And I told Tong Gong. People set on revenge will go to extreme lengths, and I rather think Tong Gong is the same. But I'm afraid that with his level of martial arts, if he comes up against the Tian brothers, it won't be an even contest."

Song Ci was sure this was true. He remembered the saying that failure to seek vengeance is the mark of an ignoble man, and he knew that it would be difficult to persuade Tong Gong to relinquish his chance at revenge.

"Lord Song, there is another matter I have been thinking about for a long time and would like to discuss with you."

In the light of the lamps in the Manjushri Hall, Song Ci could see the serious look on Song Xie's face as he said this.

"What is it?"

"I have been thinking that, in these chaotic times, the job of a government official is going to be a dangerous one. When Your Lordship comes out of self-imposed seclusion, if you don't have a devoted companion at your side, however wise you are, you are going to find yourself in danger. I have grown too old to serve you myself, so I now only have one aim – to find someone trustworthy whom I can instruct in some of the martial arts so that he can become Your Lordship's defender in your quest for honour and justice. I have considered the matter from every point of view, and I am convinced that Tong Gong is a man of exceptional loyalty and courage. The only problem is that his fighting skills are just not good enough, and he is too pig-headed to learn properly. Moreover, he is determined to go back and have his revenge, and I'm afraid that, with his skills still so rough and ready, he will meet with disaster. That is why I asked him to stay up here with me."

So that's how it was. Now Song Ci understood why Song Xie was taking such pains. The man had been his father's constant and devoted companion for more than twenty years, and now he was deeply concerned about the trials and tribulations he knew Song Ci himself was going to face in future.

"I have already seen that Tong Gong is devoted to you and listens to what you say. But you are afraid I haven't thought about all this, and rather than discuss it with me, you think you can sort it out by yourself."

So saying, Song Xie sat back down on the prayer mat, closed his eyes and began to meditate.

The lamplight illuminated Song Xie's tranquil face, and it was as though this was the first time Song Ci had really seen him properly. There he was: Song Xie, never married and a lifetime on the move, he had certainly grown old now, and yet as he sat there so dignified in his stillness, he seemed to radiate the mystical strength of a jade boulder and the stability of a temple bell. On his heavily-lined but open and generous face, the veins were like the rivers and streams, and his forehead was as wide as the oceans. The ineffable Song Xie! Song Ci watched him for a moment, and then left the Manjushri Hall without a word.

Tong Gong was waiting some distance away, in front of a large bronze incense burner in the middle of the courtyard. He had gone up to the threshold of the Manjushri Hall, and heard what Song Ci and Song Xie had said. But he was afraid it wouldn't be proper for him to be found listening outside the door, so he had retreated back to the incense burner. His head was still full of the affair of the purse and what Song Ci had asked him about the silver. When he saw Song Ci emerging from the hall, he went over to greet him.

"Master, do you have any more orders?" he asked.

"Ah, no... no, I don't," Song Ci replied. "Don't worry, go to bed."

6

## THE TIMID FIST

The night breeze brought the clear cool air of the mountain temple in through the bedroom window, and it caressed Song Ci's face. The new developments since his arrival at the Rushi Temple were keeping him awake. He kept going over and over his deductions about the silver, trying to work out what had been the first step that had led him down that false trail. In the end, he decided it was his wife's mistaken identification of the purse that had fixed his opinions at the start and overridden later evidence. He wondered how many of the cases he had been reading about were similar, with the judge deciding his verdict on first appearances, thereby establishing a false precedent? And how had he fallen so easily into this trap of pre-judging the affair? He was not in the mood to make excuses for himself. The reality of this 'case' should have been obvious from the start: in essence, had he really thought that Tong Gong had the necessary skill to have deposited the purse outside the door without a sound, without a shadow, without leaving a trace or footprint, without even waking the dogs? Even if he did have some skill, he would still have disturbed the dogs. And then there was the purse – he knew his wife had given Song Xie an identical purse. How many more false turns was he capable of making?

He saw now, too, that matter of Tong Gong's reluctance to get the purse had also given rise to false assumptions: on Tong Gong's part, he thought Song Ci wanted to take the money back; and at the same time, he himself had presumed it was because Tong couldn't produce it.

Ha! How could I have been so poor at understanding someone else's thought processes? Song Ci scolded himself inwardly. He knew that Tong

Gong was at heart an honest fellow, so how was he going to fare as a judge if he came up against someone who was truly wicked and devious? Some words of his wife came flooding back to him: "Throughout history, there have been bizarre and baffling court cases. If you are called to be a judge, how many of those do you think you will actually be able to untangle?" And he reflected on the fact that this trip of his to the Rushi Temple had, in fact, all been subtly engineered by Song Xie, who had lured him obediently up the mountain. That of course was a product Song Xie's twenty years of hard-earned experience attending the old judge, Song Ci's father, and sitting in on his court cases and judgments. How slow-witted he must seem in comparison.

With these thoughts tumbling around in his head, it was only at dawn that he finally managed to snatch a few moments sleep. And then the temple bell began ringing, regularly and incessantly. When it finally stopped, it was replaced by the sounds of the monks going about their morning routines. All vestiges of sleep left Song Ci, and he rose wearily from his bed, with just one thought left in his mind: I have to get back to the Hall of Ten Thousand Scrolls.

Straight after breakfast, Song Ci was ready to leave. Song Xie did not try to detain him, nor did he accompany him very far to see him off. This made Song Ci wonder whether his old companion had not already spoken to Tong Gong. And it was indeed Tong Gong who escorted him down to the outer gate. As he reached the bottom of the long, stone staircase down from the temple, Song Ci turned to look at Tong Gong. He noticed that he had lost a lot of weight, and there was some bruising on his dark-complexioned face around his nose, which must be from the blow he took from Song Xie the day before. Song Xie had said he was persistent, not to say stubborn, and had thrown himself whole-heartedly into his study of martial arts. The problem was, however, that he wasn't happy with making slow but steady progress, and he could do something rash at any moment. With this in mind, Song Ci asked him: "Why don't you study the evasive forms?"

"I don't want to."

"Why not?"

Tong Gong pursed his lips and paused for a moment, and then the words poured out of him as suddenly as a bean exploding in a pan: "My father, my brother and my sister-in-law worked hard all their lives. They were prudent and kept themselves to themselves, but they both ended up being beaten and killed. When I came here and had the chance to perfect my fighting skills, why should I have wanted to waste time studying how to dodge?"

Song Ci thought he knew the real reason, and wondering how best to explain things to Tong Gong, he came to a halt at the bottom of the staircase.

"Do you know what the evasive forms entail?"

Tong Gong didn't reply.

"The essence is that you evade your opponent's blow and slip away from them in order to put yourself in a position to make your own strike. This is how you blunt his attack and turn the tables on him. If you can side-step in your advance, then you can make him waste his energy striking at empty space, and use suppleness to overcome solidity. Then, at the right moment, you can switch from soft to hard, and use the element of surprise to achieve victory. That is how Song Xie knocked you over yesterday."

"That was because... that was my lack of technique."

Song Ci thought for a minute and then asked again: "Do you know what Master Song's most mysterious skill is?"

Tong Gong shook his head.

"It is his Timid Fist form."

"Timid Fist?"

"That's right. There is the Drunken Fist form that has two aspects – one is to draw strength from the wine, and the other is to harness the wine to confuse your opponent. In a similar way, the Timid Fist uses timidity to confuse the opponent, but that in itself is not enough. Master Song's Timid Fist form goes very deep, right to the secret heart of his evasive technique. This form was not developed lightly. Once, when Master Song was young, he was ordered by the local governor to take a tiger-hunting party up into the mountains. When they killed a pair of adult tigers, they took a cub out of the lair and raised it in a tiger enclosure they built on one of the other mountains. Every day, Master Song practised fighting that cub, and no matter how the beast attacked him – pouncing, slashing, kicking, biting – it never managed even to scratch him. That was how he developed his Timid Fist, and when other men matched themselves against him, they saw what seemed to be his weak and timid attitude, and thought they could knock him down in no time. None of them anticipated being unable to lay a finger on him, just like the tiger cub, no matter how they strike – left, right, up, down. Then, at last, when they were exhausted and dispirited, Master Song would unleash a blow like a thunderbolt and knock them down. The ancients used to say that the greatest wisdom is like stupidity, and the greatest courage like timidity. That is why Master Song used the word 'timidity' to call his form 'Timid Fist'. If you study this form, you will never be troubled by any opponent, even the strongest and most powerful."

This story had quite an effect on Tong Gong. Although he was stubborn by nature, with a little push, he could be made to change his mind very quickly. In a moment, his face became wreathed in smiles, and Song Ci knew he had achieved what Song Xie had desired of him.

"You stop here. There's no need to escort me any further." Song Ci patted Tong Gong on the shoulder, looked at him and said with great seriousness: "Listen to me. You stay here and study hard at your martial arts, and later we will come up with a plan for your revenge." He kept his eyes fixed on the young man, waiting for a reply.

Tong stopped smiling, and looked wide-eyed at Song Ci. Song noticed that his pupils had become a little indistinct, and then the tears welled up and began to fall. In the end, tight-lipped, Tong Gong bowed to Song Ci.

"I'll be on my way."

Song Ci turned and strode briskly down the mountain. After a while he turned back to look and saw Tong Gong still standing there on the tall rock under the towering crags.

7

# A SURPRISE ACQUISITION IN A CELLAR

Song Ci returned to the Chonghua publishing house.
 He was determined at least to lay eyes on the famous *Anthology of Difficult Cases*. Little did he know that at the same time as he was making his way to see Yu Renzhong, Yu had himself sent someone to find him. Sometime after Song had bought all those books, one of the bookshop staff casually mentioned to his boss that they had recently had a most unusual customer. The news made Yu Renzhong uneasy. He didn't for a moment think that this unusual customer was buying the books for a rival block-carving business; he had his own opinion and wanted to find out the truth of the customer's motives. Since that first visit, Song Ci had only been back to Masha, not to Chonghua, and when he returned on this trip, the shop attendant's eyes lit up. He sent a colleague to report the arrival, and himself came out from behind the counter, smiling broadly.

"Ah! Your Honour has returned. Please come in." He turned and called out in a loud voice: "Bring some tea."

Song Ci considered all this carefully and came to the conclusion that something dubious was going on. The shop was very busy, so why was the attendant being so solicitous just of him? And the young lad hurrying off to the back of the shop, surely must have something to do with his arrival. Song Ci made sure his face didn't betray any of these thoughts, and he decided to keep watching and waiting to see what unexpected turn of events might occur. He walked through the throng of customers to the main hall of the establishment and had just sat down when the tea arrived.

"What books might our honoured customer be after this time?" the attendant asked with a smile.

"I'll have a look around and let you know," Song replied promptly, wondering who might come out or what might be said as a result of the young lad's disappearance into the back of the shop. Quite soon there was indeed the sound of footsteps, firm and regular, and quite unlike the hasty pattering of the young lad on his errand.

The man who emerged was somewhere between fifty and sixty, of medium build, strong and capable-looking, his upper body slightly out of proportion to his lower. A pair of piercing brown eyes looked out from under heavy eyebrows. Judging by his clothes, Song Ci decided this must be the owner, Yu Renzhong.

It was indeed he, and as soon as he spoke, Song knew there was something special about him.

"Ah! There you are, Honoured Sir. You have come a long way, I think. Come now and take your ease in the inner hall." He made a deep obeisance with clasped hands.

Song Ci stood up hastily to return the courtesy. "I thank you for such a generous reception."

"Not at all, not at all. Our honoured customers are our livelihood, so it our duty to look after them well. If you are not in any hurry, please come and rest in the inner hall."

Song Ci thought to himself: I've come here to see Yu Renzhong, and the front of the shop is certainly no place to discuss my business. So he promptly replied: "Thank you, that would be most acceptable."

Song Ci followed Yu Renzhong into the inner part of the building and could see that it was divided into different workshops. There were discrete areas for drafting, patterning, block-planing, carving, proof-reading, printing, paper-cutting, binding... people of both sexes and all ages were hard at work at their particular tasks, and the place was a hive of industry. Yu led Song Ci to a bamboo-partitioned office. The office was decorated in the most refined taste. At the entrance was a row of bright blue-and-white porcelain planters, in each of which grew a flourishing spring orchid that perfumed the room with its delicate fragrance.

On entering the room, the first thing the eye rested on was a fine painted screen. Its subject was 'Xun Shu and Chen Shi of the Later Han Go for an Outing' and it was the work of two famous artists of the Northern Song who were natives of Jianyang, Zhang Yanyue and Huang Sheng. Beyond the screen, hanging over the office, was a tablet in the calligraphy of Zhu Xi that read: '*Wu suo bu zhi* – Leave no stone unturned.' On either side hung two imposing landscape paintings: one was Huang Qi's 'Solitary Appreciation in a Mountain Village' and the other was Hui Chong's 'Dawn on the Spring River'. Both these artists were also from Jianyang, and they were famous painters of the early Song; their works were highly sought after by collectors. Hui Chong was of particular appeal, because he was an artist monk, and people said he had the real spirit of Daoism and captured the true likeness of the rivers and mountains of distant lands in his paintings. Because of this, his works inspired poetry in many scholars and men of letters. As a case in point, on the painting in the office there was inscribed a poem specially written by Su Shi:

*A few branches of peach blossom beyond the bamboo.*
*The ducks are the first to feel the warmth of the spring river waters.*
*Mugwort covers the ground and the rushes are just sprouting.*
*It's time for the river dolphins to start their upstream journey.*

As well as these paintings, there were also many pieces of calligraphy, and even at a glance, Song Ci recognised that most of them were by famous artists from the north of Fujian Province: Cai Yuanding from Jianyang, Zhen Dexiu from Pucheng, Liu Yong from Chong'an, Li Gang from Shaowu. There were even works by Li Gang's maternal grandfather, Huang Lü, and Zhu Xi's teacher, Li Dong.

Among all these fine pieces of calligraphy, the one that really stood out was in Yuan Shu's small character regular script, where he had written 'A complete examination of all the events of the age' in honour of the book collection of the Hall of Ten Thousand Scrolls.

As soon as he entered the office, Song Ci felt himself immersed in its solemn and dignified atmosphere, and he forgot his original intention of trying to figure out just what Yu Renzhong was up to. This new environment made him think that all these great men of the area had somehow been brought together by fate in the Hall of Ten Thousand Scrolls. So perhaps if he, insignificant as he was, were to explain himself openly to Yu Renzhong, and gain his support, then maybe he might…

When Yu Renzhong saw Song standing in admiring wonder in front of the calligraphy, he didn't disturb him. He had brought him there precisely so that he could see all this, as though he knew beforehand how much it would interest the young man. Now he knew his instinct had been right, he waited until Song Ci finally tore his eyes away from the walls of the office, and only then invited him to sit down.

"Ah, yes," Song Ci replied and sat down on an x-frame chair that was covered in a fine satin cloth. A young lad brought in a basin of hot water, and Song immediately stood up again.

"Sit down," Yu Renzhong said, indicating with a gesture that there was no need for Song Ci to stand.

The lad produced a face towel and handed it to Song Ci. A young girl made the tea. The teacups she used were black-glaze 'hare's fur' cups from the Luhuaping kiln in Chongzhi Village near Jianyang. Although these were local ware, the Jian kiln had recently become an imperial kiln, and its products were no ordinary pottery, so Yu Renzhong really was treating Song Ci as a highly honoured guest.

"A little while ago, one of my assistants told my lowly self that Your Honour was setting up a block-carving business. May I humbly say that I do not believe this is the case," said Yu.

"Hmm?" Song Ci remembered that on his previous visit, the shop assistant had indeed made this conjecture.

"Your Honour is clearly an extraordinary man and a seeker of knowledge. May I humbly enquire what kind of book it is that you are looking for this time?" Yu Renzhong had clearly decided it was time to get down to business.

Seeing the smiling Yu Renzhong asking this question that went straight to the heart of his intentions, Song Ci decided there was no point in prevaricating, so he stood up and bowed deeply to him. "This humble student has come here today with the sole intention of asking if he may purchase the *Anthology of Difficult Cases* that your honourable self has in his collection."

Yu Renzhong sat in silence for a while, giving nothing away, and then returned the bow. When he spoke, he changed the way he addressed Song Ci: "Your Lordship is mistaken. Your humble servant has not purchased this book and is unable to satisfy Your Lordship's aspiration."

Song Ci replied: "This humble student had heard that, some years ago, Your Honour bought a copy of the *Anthology of Difficult Cases* from the son of a certain Mr Cai Qi. I foolishly thought Your Honour would have desired this book to add to the prestige of your collection. But do not the ancients say that a true gentleman does not ride on the coat-tails of another man's credit? I know that I myself am now going against that adage, but for my own professional ambitions, I find I must ask for Your Honour's help. I entreat your honour to take pity on my obsession, and if it is not possible for you to sell the book, might your honour at least allow this poor student the opportunity to have a look at this rare treasure? My gratitude would be boundless."

Yu Renzhong looked at Song Ci a while, deep in thought, and then he, too, decided there was nothing to be gained by not getting to the heart of the matter. "There is no point in denying it. Your humble servant did, indeed, acquire the book. Even if Your Honour was willing to hand over all his family's wealth just for one read of the book, I would still not be able to accommodate Your Honour."

"Why not?"

"Your humble servant has some advice he would like to offer Your Honour."

Song Ci realised Yu Renzhong had already gone to some pains to find out about him, but he did not yet know why. He half-rose from his chair in a respectful gesture and said: "This poor student will be honoured to hear it."

"Your Honour has been specifically searching all manner of books for examples of unusual court cases, ancient and modern. I believe this is not because you wish to set up a block-carving business but because you are writing a book of your own. Is this not so?"

"Writing a book? No, this poor student has no intention of writing a book."

Yu Renzhong clearly did not believe him, but his tone remained cordial as he went on: "Your humble servant believes that, of all the affairs of this great world, writing a book advancing one's own opinions is without rival. Given the urgency of your searching, like a man seeking water in the desert, surely you have no options left, so why hide the fact that you are writing a book?"

Song Ci thought Yu Renzhong's words did not display his intelligence in the best light.

"Your humble servant assures Your Honour that he really is not writing a book."

"No?"

"No."

"Then what is it?"

Song Ci suspected that, in the past, there had been many illustrious visitors to the Hall of Ten Thousand Scrolls, most of whom were researching their own books, and that was why Yu Renzhong did not believe him. However, even on this short acquaintance, he had come to see that Yu was a true gentleman of great vision, and he thought to himself the time had come to take this admirable man into his confidence. So, without holding anything back, he began to tell him all about himself, his family circumstances and everything that had happened to him over the last twenty years. But when he came to most recent events, his voice unexpectedly choked.

"Our government is in disarray and public morals are slipping. This poor student knows it is a dangerous path he is following. I have no experience of the real world, so where can I find a solid foundation, where can I find the determination I need to carry this through? I entreat your honour to take pity on this poor student…"

Song Ci fell silent, and just looked expectantly at Yu Renzhong, waiting to hear if he had succeeded or failed.

The silence in the office was broken only by the sound of Yu Renzhong's footsteps as he paced up and down, deep in thought with his hands clasped behind his back. How long was it since he had last heard such a speech? It had contained all the clarity of a mountain stream, and all the force of a mighty river. At last, Yu Renzhong stopped pacing and said: "Follow me."

The two men left the office, went along a long corridor, through a gallery and turned into a winding alleyway. At the end of the alley was a book storeroom in the form of a large cellar excavated from the hillside. Yu Renzhong opened a large bronze lock and led Song Ci into the interior. Before he had taken more than a couple of steps, Song was aware of a cold draught that chilled the bones. In the thread of light that came in through the open door he could see a wall made up of row after row of books, and cabinets overflowing with scrolls, most of which he had not even seen at the academy.

"Why did you dig this cellar out of the hillside? Aren't you worried about the damp?" Song asked, before, to his surprise, he saw a dehumidifying apparatus in the middle of the cellar.

"The damp is certainly to be feared, but the greater danger is from arsonists and thieving employees!"

They both made their way over to a row of bookcases, and Yu Renzhong gestured abruptly at one of them: "Come on. Do you think you can shift it?"

Song Ci looked at the large bookcase, which was crammed full of volumes, and then he looked at Yu Renzhong, whose age was showing in the greying hair at his temples. He was rolling up his sleeves! Did he really expect to be able to move that heavy bookcase?

"Let's give it a try," he said.

Yu Renzhong's strength surprised Song Ci, and he himself had not neglected to keep up the training he had received from Song Xie. Otherwise, it would have been a hopeless task.

The two men pushed aside the bookcase to reveal a small cave. Yu Renzhong lit a red candle and went down a few steps into a small room. In the middle of the room was a stone ledge on which some smaller bookcases were arranged. Yu put the candle down on one box and picked up another and blew the dust off it. He opened it and handed it to Song Ci, saying: "Take a look."

Song looked inside and gasped. The box was full of books: all four volumes of the work *A Collection of Difficult Cases*, compiled by He Ning and his son in the Five Dynasties period – the first two volumes were collated by the father and the last two by the son; a copy of Wang Hao's *A Reading of Difficult Cases*; Yuan Jiang's *Judicial Sentencing*; Zheng Ke's *Collected Studies in*

*Legal Interpretation*; Gui Wanrong's *Comparative Case Studies from Tangyin*; as well as several anonymous works and anthologies. All these records of difficult cases throughout history gathered together in one place! This was the kind of rare treasure that would never been seen on the open market.

Song Ci stared at them in silence, and he could feel himself breaking into a cold sweat. After a while, he asked: "These books... how much do you want for them?"

"Not a single coin. I am giving them all to you."

Song Ci stared blanking, not understanding what had been said.

Yu Renzhong then started opening box after box, and every one of them was full of books on difficult cases and complex judgments – so many that Song Ci lost count.

He was astounded: "There are so many! Is Your Honour sure he doesn't want to sell them?"

"I am quite sure. Over the decades I have been in business, I have bought up just about every book of this kind that has come on the market."

"Why so?"

"Ha!" Yu exclaimed emphatically, and then went on: "Books can help the nation prosper, or they can throw it into disorder. When such books appear on the market, most of them are bought by precisely the wrong kind of person. They seldom fall into the right hands. If men with evil intentions study them and apply the knowledge in false judgments, the country will be thrown into chaos."

Song Ci wondered what it was that had brought Yu Renzhong to this philosophy. "Master, what is it that happened?" he asked cautiously.

Yu Renzhong replied: "In its early years, the Hall of Ten Thousand Scrolls suffered a great loss when my father was murdered. The authorities captured the culprit, who surprised everyone by conducting his own defence. He had found his argument in a copy of *An Anthology of Difficult Cases* that he had bought from our own shop."

Song Ci remained silent and listened as Yu continued to explain that, although the two publishing houses of Chonghua and Masha were privately owned, just as the wrestlers and performers of Lin'an had independently formed their own guild, the Wrestlers' Society, so had the publishers formed the Clear Print Society. And Yu Renzhong was the president of the society. Over the years, he had persuaded the bosses of the block-carving houses in Chonghua and Masha to forbid the production of this kind of book, and had himself bought up all copies that were already in existence wherever he could find them. Because of the fame of the two houses, it was inevitable that all kinds of books found their way there, so gradually this particular type of book vanished from sight. Song Ci had had no inkling that Yu Renzhong, the head of the Hall of Ten Thousand Scrolls, could possibly have had exactly the same idea as he himself about how to preserve the peace of the empire. Moreover, sparing no expense, he had put it into practice unknown to anyone except the bosses of the block-carving houses in Chonghua and Masha.

As the two men went to leave the room, Song Ci realised that he felt rather uneasy about receiving such a generous gift, and he wondered what he might do in return to show his gratitude. All he had was some silver and the jade belt ornament. Then he reconsidered – why not give Yu Renzhong the jade as a memento. Yes, that was the thing to do. With that thought in mind, he took out the precious jade ornament carved in the form of two cranes, which had remained in his purse until now.

To his surprise, Yu Renzhong pushed his hand away and said in a voice trembling with emotion: "My Lord, please don't. I may just be a humble local man, but I do know what is going on around us. Since the end of the Jingkang period,[1] the empire has been in danger on a daily basis. Not only are the borders under threat, disorder is spreading everywhere. In my humble way, I would like to make a small contribution to help the people of the great Song dynasty. Beyond any expectation, Your Honour has the determination to avenge injustice and protect the people from violence and insult. I had thought to keep these books hidden away from view, but then I met Your Honour. You must simply accept them, and say nothing to anyone. I.... I beg you!"

So saying, Yu Renzhong fell silent and bowed deeply to Song Ci, holding the bow for a very long time.

Song Ci was deeply moved by this speech, and tears of emotion came to his eyes. In a choking voice, he replied: "Your Honour... Master! I, Song Ci, will never forget the instruction you have given me today. If, in days to come, I have the chance to do some good, I will not fail you." He knelt down in front of Yu Renzhong and bowed his head to the ground.

"That is too much, My Lord, too much. Let us say no more about it." Yu Renzhong also fell to his knees. The tears of the two men, one old, one young, mingled on the ground.

There are few things more precious than this kind of immediate and complete mutual understanding; it is a treasure beyond price. Song Ci felt himself the most fortunate of men. Not only had he been given this collection of rare and valuable books, but he also felt, most deeply, that he had been entrusted with the safety of the empire.

# CHAPTER V

## A SHOCK FOR QIANFU (1224-1226)

A new magistrate was posted to Jianyang – none other than Liu Kezhuang. When the two old academy friends met, Liu discovered that Song Ci's historical researches already encompassed innumerable cases of precedent from as far back as the Spring and Autumn period[1] right up to the start of the Song dynasty. These included cases such as the assassination attempt on Su Qin, the corpse in the dried-up well and the upright corpse in the temple gateway. He had made a particular study of the psychology of murder cases and the rationale of judgments passed on them. Feeling his way forward, often stumbling, he had tried to draw inferences from unsolved historical cases. But by this time he had already been living at home for seven years, without being found employment by the imperial authorities, so what, exactly, was the use of all this? Quite soon, however, a most unusual case came before Liu Kezhuang, which was to be turned on its head by Song Ci's newly acquired legal knowledge...

# 1

# THE ASTONISHMENT OF LIU KEZHUANG

Time flowed swiftly, and seven years passed with Song Ci still at home.
In the third month of the seventeenth year of the Jiading period (1208-1224), the Song and Jin had already been at war for six years. In the face of stubborn resistance from the Song and the increasing threat of the fearsome Mongol horsemen, the Jin advance southwards was halted. Thus, six years of war between the Song and the Jin ended in stalemate.

Some time before this, the magistrate of Jianyang, Shu Gengshi, had been transferred, and the same had happened to his successor in the winter of the year in question. To Song Ci's surprise and delight, the new replacement was none other than Liu Kezhuang.

Liu's family came from Putian Prefecture in Jianyang municipality, and although he was a year younger than Song Ci, the two of them had entered the academy in the same year. They were quite different in temperament, but the similarity in their interests engendered mutual respect, and the two became bosom companions. In their fourth year, Liu passed the imperial examinations, and the pair were finally separated. However, when Liu took up his official duties, he was not in the top flight, but rather was assigned as a supplementary officer.

Previous members of Liu's family had not made any great mark at court through their achievements, and his own appointment was something of a reflection of this. From the start of the Song dynasty, provincial officials of the sixth rank and above, and prefectural officials of the fifth rank and above, were entitled to bestow rank by right of their service. The privilege to do so extended to sons and grandsons only, for the lower ranks, but for higher levels it was not restricted to immediate family. Even family physicians and such-like could bestow this patronage on anyone they pleased. In the Qingli period of Emperor Renzong (1041-1048), when Fan Zhongyan was in political office and initiated his reforms, he proposed a change to this system. The emperor officially adopted the new policy and issued an imperial decree to take effect across the whole empire; but it was rescinded a little over a year later. In the second year of the Jiading period (1209), Liu Kezhuang received his post through the patronage of a family member of a cabinet minister for whom he had composed some poetry. And now, when he arrived in Jianyang and heard that Song Ci was still living in the family home, that very afternoon he left the city for Tongyou, to visit his old friend.

Once at the house, he did not wait to be announced but went straight in and found Song Ci in his library. On seeing the collection of priceless books and scrolls arranged on three ranks of expensive bookcases, and the racks full of bamboo slips, Liu Kezhuang couldn't imagine what his friend could possibly be doing with so much literary material. He called out: "I can see you haven't changed over the years. You're still a book-hoarder."

Song looked up in amazement at the sudden arrival of his old friend. He assessed him up and down, taking in his smooth forehead, the same old expression of knowing cynicism in his eyes and the neatly trimmed beard on his chin – they all added up to the impression of lofty severity that he remembered so well. The two men looked steadily at each other for a moment and then sat down. Kang Liang brought in some tea, which Liu drank without waiting for any invitation from Song Ci. Then, finally, he said: "So, how have the years treated you?"

Song Ci told him everything that had happened, and as Liu listened he felt that some change he couldn't quite define had come over his old friend. When he heard what kind of books actually filled the bookcases, he said: "So, have you now read every court case that has ever been recorded?"

"You're teasing me," Song replied.

As they talked, Liu discovered that Song's researches had, indeed, taken him from the Spring and Autumn period right up to the present day. He learned what had been written about the investigation of wounds and injuries, written and oral evidence, cross-examination and sentencing, with references going right back to the *Book of Rites*. He heard that Wang Mang of the Later Han dynasty was one of the most contentious people in history but might also be considered the father of the science of autopsy, for he had ordered his doctor to open up the skull and weigh the five vital organs of any corpse that came before him. Of course, Song Ci had also seen the account of an autopsy in the *Classic on Medical Problems*, but that might be a later gloss; if not, then the origins of autopsy were actually to be found with the famous physician of the Warring States period, Bian Que.

Liu had no idea how many historical cases Song Ci had actually read, but he did know that his friend had meticulously committed a very large number to memory, including examples such as: the case of the corpse burned by Zhang Ju of Wu in the Three Kingdoms period, recorded in the *Zhe Yu Gui Jian*; the assassination of Su Qin in the *Chun Qiu Hou Yu*; the case of the corpse in the dried-up well in *Su Shui Ji Wen*; and the case of a corpse found standing upright in a temple doorway, recorded in *Hou Han Shu*. Song had read them all carefully and studied the defences offered by the accused, as well as the judges' verdicts. In fact, he was almost punch-drunk from his labours working out the implications and inferences to be drawn from so many cases.

"And do you still think taking up a government post is the only way for you to make an effective contribution to society?" Liu asked.

Song Ci smiled ruefully.

"It's just that I am wondering why, after so long, you have not yet done so and fulfilled your duty to the emperor."

"After I'd been in mourning for three years, I did send a request to the Ministry of Appointments, but they never replied."

Liu leapt to his feet: "The country is already overflowing with officials and I have heard that the Ministry of Appointments is bursting at the seams with scholars looking for official posts. I will have to think of a better way for you."

"What better way?"

"I have some contacts in the capital. They are not in the Ministry of Appointments, but they might still be able to wield some influence."

The two long-parted friends continued to talk, earnestly and with complete candour. Liu Kezhuang told Song Ci all about his experiences over the years. As before, he wasn't wholly committed to his official career. In the thirteenth year of Jiading, Mr Zhen Dexiu returned home to observe mourning for his recently deceased mother, and he took up a job lecturing at the West Mountain House in Jianxi, Fujian Province, where he invited Liu Kezhuang to join him as a teacher. So, Liu retired from his official post and made his way to Pucheng. Before Liu joined them, already at the school were Mr Zhen's old friend and colleague, Wei Liaoweng, and his disciples Wang Yening, Lü Liangcai, Liu Hanbi and Ma Guangzu. After he arrived, Liu and Mr Zhen Dexiu discussed one of Mr Zhen's pet projects – to create a shrine to his teacher, Zhu Xi. So, foremost in Liu Kezhuang's mind was his desire to turn Mr Zhen Dexiu's dreams into reality, by building the memorial in Kaoting College outside Jianyang.[1]

Song was delighted at the news. The two men talked until dusk began to fall. It was only when Song's daughter Song Qi came to summon them to the evening meal, that they finally stopped.

2

# THE STRANGE CASE OF THE HARE'S FUR CUP

Another year flew by. It was then the winter of the first year of the Baoqing period (1225). The servant whom Liu Kezhuang had sent to the capital with a letter had returned at the beginning of the new year. Liu's friends had all cheerfully agreed to help try to find Song Ci a post, but so far without success. The memorial to Zhu Xi had already been built in Kaoting College. The many sons and grandsons of Zhu Xi's eldest son, Zhu Shu, from Jianning, and those of his third son, Zhu Zai, from Wuyuan in Jiangxi Province's Huizhou Prefecture, had all come to Jianyang. Zhu Xi's second son, Zhu Ye, already lived there. Now they were only waiting for Mr Zhen Dexiu to arrive so they could hold the grand opening ceremony. Liu Kezhuang was very busy with all the arrangements, when, quite by chance, he stumbled on a most unusual case.

The man who was to report the case was Zhu Minghu, the owner of the Kaiyuan Teahouse on Jianyang's West Road. He was among the wealthiest men in the prefecture, and one of the many benefactors of the Zhu Xi memorial. The officials at the gate of the *yamen* recognised him when he arrived and had immediately taken his report. Liu Kezhuang was talking to Zhu Xi's three sons in the rear hall when he heard the report. He immediately came out to see Zhu Minghu.

Zhu was a man of about thirty, sturdily built and with a long face and wide forehead. Normally he was of stately and dignified bearing, but on this occasion, because he had been running, he was dripping with sweat and out of breath. As soon as he saw Liu Kezhuang, he kowtowed to him and said: "Master Liu, I'm afraid my younger brother has been murdered."

"Afraid?" asked Liu. "Why 'afraid'?"

"I believe it to be the case, sir."

"Where is your brother's body now?"

"I don't know."

"You don't know?"

"It's..." Zhu Minghus's face went bright red.

Seeing the man's agitation, Liu asked: "Is it the case that you saw your brother's body, but it is now lost? Or have you not seen it at all? Stand up now, and speak slowly."

Zhu got up from his kowtow and then sat in a chair that one of the bailiffs had brought. He ordered his thoughts and began to speak, while a clerk, ready with ink and paper, took down what he said.

"Shi Houji is an official at the imperial kilns at Luhuaping, and yesterday, when my younger brother returned from the capital, Shi came to invite him over to his house that evening for some wine. My brother went, but never came back. Early this morning, I was in my courtyard doing my exercises when I heard someone knocking at the gate. I went to open the gate and saw it was Shi Houji. When he saw it was me, he asked: 'Is Mingtan in?'

"I said: 'Wasn't he drinking at your house last night?'

"He said: 'He went home quite early.'

"I said: 'Well, go and look for him at his house.'

"He went off, and when he came back he said: 'He's not there.'

"'That's strange,' I retorted. 'Where has my brother got to, then?'

"'I'll go and have another look,' he said, before turning and leaving. This time he didn't come back, and I thought to myself: He said he was going to have another look, but have a look where? It all seemed a bit odd, so I summoned some of my own men to go and look for my brother. We searched everywhere in the area but couldn't find a trace. I'm afraid my brother has come to no good at the hands of Shi Houji..."

"Slow down a bit," Liu Kezhuang said. "How can you say that if you haven't seen a body? Is there some kind of dispute between your two families?"

"No, no dispute. But there is one thing that might have stirred up some resentment."

"What's that?"

"Shopkeeper Wan at the Fuchengchun provisions store in town has a daughter, just sixteen and very beautiful. People call her White Teaflower. Shi Houji and my brother have both been showering her with gifts, but Shopkeeper Wan only allowed my brother's to be accepted. I just wonder whether this might have put murderous thoughts into Shi Houji's head. I respectfully ask Your Honour to investigate on my behalf." At this, Zhu Minghu began to weep.

"Don't get overwrought," Liu Kezhuang said. "Your brother might just have gone to seek some entertainment elsewhere. You go and wait in the gatehouse. I will send people to bring in Shi Houji, and perhaps we can clear up this matter. Go now!"

After Zhu Minghu had gone, Liu immediately dispatched an express messenger along the east road to Luhuaping. It was the middle of the night before the messenger returned, reporting that the whereabouts of Shi Houji were unknown.

This Shi Houji was a bachelor, with no family to question his comings and goings, and Liu Kezhuang began to feel there might be some urgency to this affair. Having sent someone to fetch the captain of the military police, he also summoned Zhu Minghu to ask him more about Shi Houji – where was he from, if he had any family in the prefecture and so on. Zhu told him Shi originally came from Chong'an and had an elder sister who still lived there. As far as he knew, he didn't have any family in the Jianyang area.

As they were talking, the captain of police arrived. This was no longer the Liang E spoken of before – he had left on Shu Gengshi's coat-tails when the magistrate was transferred. This new captain was Wei Cipei. Liu informed him of the situation and issued him with an arrest warrant, saying: "Take some of your men to Chong'an, leaving tonight, and see if you can find Shi Houji there. If you do, arrest him and bring him back."

That night, Wei Cipei led twenty mounted patrolmen out of the city, and the next day, quite late in the morning, they reached Chong'an. When they found the house of Shi Houji's elder sister, they surrounded it and knocked on the gate. Shi's sister was greatly alarmed.

"Has your younger brother returned here?" Wei Cipei asked her.

"No."

"Search the house!"

Wei Cipei motioned with his hand, and the patrolmen entered the house. They made a thorough search but found no trace of the man. They then asked all round the neighbourhood, but everyone said they had not seen him either. Wei had no option but to lead his patrol out of the city. After they had gone about thirty *li* and reached the Chongyou Daoist Temple at Mount Wuyi, one of the patrolmen, who knew Shi Houji, suddenly shouted: "Look, isn't that him?"

There, in a wine-shop on the corner of a side-road, they saw a man in a felt hat sitting drinking wine and warming himself by the fire. It was indeed Shi Houji.

"Seize him!" Wei Cipei clapped his heels into his horse's flanks, spurring it forward, and the other patrolmen followed. They took hold of Shi Houji roughly and searched him. In his purse they found a large number of gold ingots. They bound him with rope and took him back to Jianyang. Liu Kezhuang came to the courthouse to interrogate him.

"Shi Houji, you are being questioned on the authority of this prefecture. Be sure to reply truthfully!"

Shi Houji knelt before the court, trembling even before he replied. Nonetheless his bright eyes under dark eyebrows were darting shrewdly this way and that – as an official at an imperial kiln, he was clearly no fool. He kowtowed to Liu Kezhuang and replied: "Your Worship, I shall speak not even half a word of falsehood!"

"Tell me then – the evening of the day before yesterday, you invited Zhu Mingtan for a drink. Is that so?"

"It is, your worship."

"Where did you take him after that."

"Nowhere, Your Worship. He had a drink and went home."

"What time did he leave your house?"

"Around the third watch."

"Was he drunk?"

"He was tipsy. I asked him to stay the night, but he thanked me and said he had to go."

"The next morning, you went to look for Zhu Mingtan?"

"Yes."

"Why?"

"I... I was afraid that the wine might have got the better of him, and he had met with some accident on the way home."

"Did you find him at the Zhu residence?"

"No."

"Did his brother ask you where his little brother was?"

"He did."

"What did you reply"

"I said I didn't know."

"Nonsense! You said: 'I'll go and look for him again', didn't you?"

"Yes..., ah, no... I didn't say that."

"Bring in Zhu Minghu!" Liu Kezhuang called out in a stern voice. There was an answering shout from the *yamen* bailiffs and when Zhu Minghu was brought in to confront him, Shi Houji was struck dumb.

Liu asked him once more: "Where did you go then?"

Shi Houji had no reply.

Liu asked him again, sternly: "Why did you run away from the imperial kilns yesterday? Where did you get all those gold ingots? Even if they are just what you have been able to save up, why did you have them hidden about your person?"

Shi Houji stuttered incoherently. It was only when he was asked directly if he had killed Zhu Mingtan, that he said, firmly: "No, I didn't."

Liu Kezhuang lost his temper, and banged down the judge's wooden sound block: "Torture him!"

As soon as the torture instruments were laid out, Shi cried out: "I confess!"

Liu ordered the implements to be put away and instructed Zhu Minghu to leave the court. Then he turned to Shi Houji and ordered: "Speak."

Shi composed himself and began his confession: "Your Honour, I have no way out, I will own up to everything, but absolutely not to killing anyone…"

We have already mentioned that Shi Houji was an official at the imperial kilns, and it is at the kilns that an account of this case must begin.

In the Song dynasty, the huge popularity of tea-tasting competitions spread from high-ranking officials, the aristocracy, scholars and students into the wider population. Particularly prized in these competitions by the cognoscenti, were the 'rock teas' of Wuyishan (Mount Wuyi), such as Iron Bodhisattva, Mid-day Demon, White Cockscomb and Golden Water Turtle. The popularity of these competitions also had a great influence on the production of tea-ware. The kilns at Luhuaping on Jianyang's east road produced a particular type of porcelain tea bowl, the deep purple-black glaze of which had a clear lustre like lacquer. By candlelight, when one of these bowls was full of tea, the body of the vessel revealed a pattern like hare's fur, with a shimmering blue halo effect when viewed from any angle, which entranced the drinker. Cai Xiang, author of the essay *A Note on Tea*, written around this time, made a special study of tea-ware. He said of these hare's fur bowls that they were "good at retaining heat and slow to cool, and especially recommended". Huang Tingjian also praised them in verse:

*A precious bowl the colour of hare's fur shot with gold thread;*
*The wind sighs through the pines*
*As the water boils with bubbles as small as crabs' eyes.*

This sort of bowl also has the great advantage of keeping the tea fresh-tasting. It was Emperor Huizong of the Song dynasty who first called them hare's fur bowls and who proclaimed the Jian kilns imperial kilns. He also decreed that their porcelain was only to be used by the imperial household, and was forbidden to commoners. As soon as anything was declared 'imperial use only', its price increased a hundredfold, and people were more inclined to sharp practice and risky ventures involving it, so inevitably the number of court cases around it also increased. The case in question here had a hare's fur bowl at its root.

At this time, some Japanese merchants came by sea from the south to Fujian, hoping to obtain the secret of making hare's fur bowls; but as it was produced at an imperial kiln, they had no chance. Then they found out about the tea merchant Zhu Mingtan, who was selling a particular tea called White Tree Peony in the capital. White Tree Peony was a special tea grown by Zhu Kaiyuan, the owner of the Kaiyuan tea plantation. The hills around Luhuaping provide the perfect conditions for its cultivation – the hillsides are networked with streams, and the weather is warm with plentiful rainfall. After tea-drinking became popular in the Han and Tang dynasties, the Luhuaping area became famous far and wide for the quality of its tea. Following the invention of hare's fur porcelain, Zhu Kaiyuan developed a special white tea, the leaves of which were covered in a fine white down and turned ash-grey when brewed. It had a pure, sweet flavour and was particularly aromatic. Because its leaves resembled the white peony, the tea was named after that flower. If you infuse White Peony Tea in a hare's fur bowl, the liquor froths up like snowflakes,[1] and the contrasting colours of the white tea and black bowl are particularly attractive. The two are a perfect match, each accentuating the qualities of the other, and this is what made Zhu Kaiyuan a millionaire and his tea plantation famous the world over.

When Zhu Kaiyuan died, he left two sons. The younger one died childless, of a seasonal illness, soon after marrying. The elder left three sons and two daughters. The second son died of cholera, leaving four sons of his own. By this time, the method of production of White Peony had been obtained by other tea-growers, and the Kaiyuan plantation lost its monopoly. There were no longer such great profits to be made from it, so the two remaining grandsons of Zhu Kaiyuan began to develop their tea business in the capital. The eldest remained at home managing the plantation, while third grandson sold white tea in the capital. Together, they maintained the family's position as the wealthiest in the area.

According to Shi Houji's confession, the whole affair started in the summer: "Zhu Mingtan suddenly came to see me, saying that he had some Japanese customers for White Peony at his shop in the capital, who were offering a lot of money for hare's fur bowls, and could I supply him with any? Well, I thought there's no real money to be made without taking a few risks, so, despite the dangers, I was tempted, and agreed a fifty-fifty deal. Come winter, I found an opportunity to get hold of some bowls. I knew that Zhu Mingtan had returned from the capital two days before, so I went to find him. As we were sharing a drink, he told me that the plan had changed and the bowls shouldn't be sent to the capital, but to the Yulin Temple at Wuyi, where the deal could be settled.

"I asked why. Shi Houji said there were two Japanese disciples of Daoyuan (Dogen)[2] at the Yulin Temple, called Katasiro and Saemonkagemasa, and they were secretly studying porcelain manufacture there. On his return journey, he had met with them in the Chongyou Hall and agreed a substantial price for the hare's fur bowls. As I listened, I thought about this. In the sixteenth year of Jiading, here were these two men wanting to go to an imperial kiln to study porcelain manufacture, but because the secret of the process used there was kept secret by order of the emperor even from other kilns in China, what hope did they have, as foreigners? So, since there was no point in coming here, they had taken the initiative to go to the Yulin kiln.

"Then Zhu Mingtan told me about the whole business and said it had to be done quickly. He wanted me to go with him the next day, because it would be safer with two people rather than just him alone. It occurred to me that I was well known at both the Yulin Temple and the Yulin kiln, so although I agreed, I insisted that I would be waiting for him at home before daybreak. My house is at the top of the village, so it was easy to get on the road unnoticed. To my dismay, I found it was already getting light, and Zhu Mingtan had not yet appeared. I was afraid he had overslept, so I went to rouse him. When I got to his house, there was no one there. When I asked his brother, I was thinking he must have already set out to meet me. I was somewhat out of breath, so said without thinking: "I'll go back and look." When I returned, there was still no sign of him. By this time it was full daylight, and I reckoned that, getting to my house and finding I wasn't there, he must have thought I had gone on ahead by myself. In that case, he would have followed me, so I set off after him.

"To my surprise, I saw no trace of Zhu Mingtan, although I kept looking as I went along. Then I wondered whether he might not be ahead of me, but even when I got to the Yulin Temple, I still couldn't find him. So I sought out the two Japanese gentlemen, and concluded the business with them myself. I left the temple and looked for somewhere to stay the night. This morning I had intended to go to my elder sister's house, but I was arrested on the way there. Every word of this confession is the truth. I do not know where Zhu Mingtan is. Your Honour is known as an upright and incorruptible judge, and I beg you to believe me."

As Shi Houji finished his confession, the courtroom fell silent, and Liu Kezhuang remained deep in thought for a while. Then he banged the judge's sound block hard on the desk and shouted: "You are a brazen scoundrel!

From what you have said, it is obvious you arranged the whole deal on your own and then plotted to kill him."

"Your Honour!" Shi Houji spoke again, but where fear had made him loud and urgent before, this time he bowed his head, because he could see the judge was angry. "I plead guilty to stealing and selling imperial property, but I did not kill anyone. The gold ingots are Zhu Mingtan's half share of the deal, which I was going to give him."

"Half share? If you were going to give him a half share, why were you taking the gold north when you should have been heading south?"

"Your Honour, I have said, I was going to look..."

"Be quiet! Are you confessing or not?"

"I have confessed everything. Truly, I have not killed anyone! Your honour must believe me."

"You scoundrel, I'm afraid only torture will screw the truth from you. Bring the torture instruments!"

The court attendants sprang into action, shouting, and Shi Houji cried out: "Stop." He looked up at Liu Kezhuang: "Your Honour, I have something else to say. Please allow me to speak, and then you may execute me if you wish."

"Speak," said Liu Kezhuang.

"I could not take being tortured, so I will continue my confession. Your Honour undoubtedly would like me to produce the body and the murder weapon. The murder weapon is not a problem, any old knife from my home would do as evidence, but the body? I didn't kill anyone, so where could I find a body? At that point, Your Honour would say I have made a full confession and would order me to be tortured. Then I would die in this very courtroom and that would be that.

"As for my fate, well, I am guilty of stealing and selling imperial property, so my death would be justified in those terms. But supposing, some days later, Zhu Mingtan reappears? Then I'm afraid Your Honour's reputation would be sullied. As I see it, Your Honour should delay my execution – I'm not going to be able escape in any case. And if Your Honour sends men to look for Zhu Mingtan, after four or five days you should know his whereabouts, and all will be plain sailing for Your Honour. Your Honour's magnanimity is as wide as the ocean, so please consider all this very carefully before passing judgment."

Shi Houji stopped speaking and kowtowed. Liu Kezhuang thought to himself: "There's some logic to what he says. At the very least, Zhu Mingtan is an accomplice in the theft of imperial property, and there's no harm in sending a patrol to look for him. And if there's still no sign of him, the prosecution of this fellow can go ahead anyway."

So, Liu ordered Shi Houji to continue his confession detailing how he had managed to steal the hare's fur bowls, how many there were and so on. Then he ordered him to sign the document. He further ordered the prisoner to be put into a twenty *jin*[3] cangue[4] and placed in the condemned cell. He summoned Zhu Minghu back into the court and instructed him to go home and send some of his men out in search of his brother. If there was any news, he was to come back and report immediately. Finally, he ordered Pei Ci, the chief of police, to take a patrol post-haste to the Yulin Temple to confront the purchasers of the stolen bowls, and bring them back to face the court.

Liu retired to the inner hall to consider the case so far. If Zhu Mingtan is found, he thought, then that's that, but what if he is not? His head hurt – this was a lot more taxing than composing poetry! Then he remembered his old friend Song Ci and slapped a hand to his forehead: "How stupid can I get? He is the one who has the brains for this."

3

# HANDLING A BUTCHER'S CLEAVER WITH EASE

When Song Ci arrived at the courthouse, he listened to Liu Kezhuang's summary of the case and then read the statements of the plaintiff and the accused. Satisfied, he put down the scroll and said to Liu: "There is no point in looking for Zhu Mingtan."

"Why not?"

"He's already dead."

"Dead? How do you know?"

"Well, unless I am very much mistaken, the murderer is his elder brother."

"You mean Zhu Minghu?" asked Liu.

"He is certainly the prime suspect." Song unrolled the scroll again and put it in front of his friend. "Look, here is his witness statement. He says that someone came knocking at his gate early in the morning. He went to open the gate and found it was Shi Houji. Shi asked him if Mingtan was there, to which Zhu Minghu replied: 'Wasn't he drinking with you last night?' If you think about it, isn't there something suspicious about that?"

"Go on."

"In normal circumstances, if you have a drink at someone else's house, you go home afterwards. So, now we have the person who invited his brother over the night before, knocking on the door the next morning asking for him. Surely, the normal answer would be: 'I'm afraid Mingtan is still asleep.' Or perhaps: 'It's very early to be coming knocking, what's the matter?' But when he immediately replies something to the effect of 'Wasn't he with you last night?', that clearly implies he already knows his brother isn't at home."

"Slow down a minute," said Liu Kezhuang, trying to think it through.

"Supposing he had already gone to his brother's room and seen that he hadn't returned. Wouldn't it be quite natural for him to reply as he did on seeing Shi Houji?"

"But he has, in fact, shown quite clearly that he hadn't gone to his brother's room. Look, if the other party tells him that his brother went home the night before, then his reply would be: 'Go and have a look in his room.' Of course, he might indeed already know his brother isn't there but think the other party won't believe him, so again tell him to go and look. So the point is that, if the other party went and looked and said there was no one there, Zhu Minghu would be surprised by that. And when we read what the statement says, it shows he said: 'That's strange. Where has my brother got to then?' Doesn't that tell us he hadn't gone to look in his brother's room?"

Liu Kezhuang didn't reply. He realised that his own previous thinking on the case had been turned upside down, and he had to accept his friend's meticulous reasoning. But he still had some concerns. Eventually, he said: "But we still haven't seen a body, so how can you be sure Zhu Mingtan is actually dead?"

"From Zhu Mingtan's point of view, his most pressing business was to get rid of the hare's fur bowls. If that was already accomplished, then why wouldn't he come home? Where else would he go? Of course, strange and unexpected things do happen, but the point is that all the indications are that his elder brother, Zhu Minghu, had definite murderous intent towards him."

"How do you make that out?"

"Look, here is the court transcript again. It says you asked the suspect Shi how drunk Zhu Mingtan was when he left. Zhu Minghu is the elder brother, and if he really wanted to find his little brother, once he heard he was missing, why didn't he ask the same vitally important question? Unless of course he is an imbecile – which he certainly isn't. Even supposing Shi Houji left so quickly, he didn't have a chance to ask him. Surely he would have gone after him to ask – but he didn't."

"So what you are getting at is that Shi Houji had already left the village before Zhu Minghu came to make his complaint, but he didn't mention the fact that Shi had absconded."

"That's right. Supposing he had gone looking for him, he would have discovered that Shi's house was all locked up, and he wouldn't have left something as important as that out of his statement. The fact that he made only cursory enquiries before coming to lay his case against Shi Houji on suspicion of murdering his brother, must mean that he already knew his brother was dead. And in that case who else could possibly be the murderer?"

"So Shi Houji is telling the truth, and he didn't kill anyone?"

"Well, if I was a murderer, how would I act? Assuming I wanted to stay in control of the business of the tea bowls, I certainly wouldn't choose this most dangerous of days to try to close the deal. I would act as though nothing had happened, watch how the situation developed and then choose the right moment. Judging by his confession, Shi Houji's thinking was quite lucid – he's certainly not stupid, and in fact he showed considerable guts. He is surely not the type to commit a murder and then straight away off-load the tea bowls. That's why you can be certain that the essential parts of his confession are true."

As Liu Kezhuang listened to Song Ci's train of thinking, he found the reasoning sound, so he nodded his head and asked: "So what was Zhu Minghu's motive in killing his brother?"

"That is also clear from his complaint."

"How so?"

"He didn't mention the matter of the hare's fur bowls and it's unlikely that was because he was trying to cover for his brother. Much more likely, his brother never told him about it. We know, after all, that each brother had his own area of responsibility in their tea business. Moreover, when he accused Shi Houji of killing his brother, he raised the possibility that it could have been because the two of them, Shi and his brother, were vying for the affections of White Teaflower, the daughter of Shopkeeper Wan, the owner of the Fuchengchun provisions store. From that we know Zhu Mingtan was unmarried, and on his wedding day, the two brothers would have had the problem of dividing up the family wealth. So, Zhu Minghu got rid of his brother before that could happen. If you look back through history, this is not an uncommon occurrence."

As Liu Kezhuang listened to his old friend leading him step by step through his thinking, exposing the different layers of deductions like peeling an onion, he once again had the feeling of his own thoughts on the affair being scattered to the four winds. He considered Song Ci's analysis and what had been said by both the plaintiff and the accused, and he understood how his friend had been able to use both their truths and falsehoods to get to the nub of the case. First, he had separated what was clearly true from what was clearly false, and then, like a master builder, he had used this raw material to construct his case. Taking a truth here, a lie there, he pieced them together, each in their proper place, so that the reality of the case was clear to see in the final assembly. It was the first time Liu Kezhuang had realised the full extent of Song Ci's knowledge and perspicacity, and he looked at him closely.

"What I still don't understand is where you started from in your unravelling process."

"Oh, there's nothing extraordinary about that," Song replied. "As you know, I have read up on a lot of cases, and there are often similarities to be found within them. There is no shortage of precedents for this kind of case. If you had read all the cases I have, I rather think you would be better than me at all this."

For Liu, this comparison of his abilities to those of his old friend was as delightful as a draft of fine wine. For him to attain the same perfection in being able swiftly to sum up a case from every angle, and to unravel its every twist and turn, this was something he scarcely dare imagine. If, on first arriving in Jianyang, he had been rather taken aback by the way his old friend had spent the last few years, that surprise had certainly now turned to the deepest respect and admiration.

The two friends stayed there talking until evening, and then parted.

After he had seen Song Ci to the door, Liu Kezhuang returned to the inner court with a curious sense of loss and frustration. He suddenly felt very tired and sat down in a chair, thinking about the problem of finding Song Ci an official post: "Someone of his talents simply can't be left languishing in obscurity."

At that moment, one of the gatekeepers came in to report that someone had just arrived from the capital and was asking to see him. Liu perked up, thinking it must be news from one of his friends there: "Bring him in immediately," he said.

As the gatekeeper turned to leave, Liu called him back: "Wait a minute. After you've sent him in, find Master Song Ci and ask him to come back here."

The gatekeeper acknowledged his instructions and left. Almost immediately, the visitor appeared, and it was indeed someone from the entourage of one of his friends, bearing a letter. Liu was delighted and tore open the envelope he was handed. As he read the letter, the smile left his face.

Song Ci hadn't got very far after leaving his old friend, and he soon returned. As he entered the rear chamber, he saw Liu sitting there, frowning at a letter on the small table in front of him. He had already formed a shrewd idea of what was in it before Liu handed him the letter without speaking. He read it, and then, also without speaking, put it back on the table.

The letter said that Song Ci's name had been removed from the register at the Ministry of Appointments. The reason given was that an official in the magistrates' office had lodged a complaint of misconduct against Song Ci with a senior minister. The allegation was that, while at home and observing the mourning period for his mother, Song had consorted with a person or persons wanted for murder. This complaint rendered it impossible for Song to hold any office, and since he was not yet employed, the Ministry of

Appointments, without further enquiry, suspended his eligibility for any post. The constantly changing personnel in all government departments, combined with the permanent problems caused by the huge number of unemployed officials since the capital moved south, meant that, however hard one tried, a situation like this was very seldom resolved.

As night approached and a chill wind began to blow, the two friends sat in silence. Neither said it, but they both knew the identity of the magistrate who had made the complaint. Without even taking up office, Song Ci was already experiencing for himself the ruthless and treacherous face of public service.

## 4

# THE ZHU XI MEMORIAL

The next day, before dawn, Wei Cipei returned. He had obtained all the proof needed in the case of Shi Houji's illegal sale of the hare's fur bowls. Liu Kezhuang ordered him to go back to Luhuaping the following day, and arrest Zhu Minghu and bring him back for trial.

On the day that Wei Cipei left on this mission, Mr Zhen Dexiu arrived in Jianyang. Liu had made up his mind that, come what may, he would personally lobby Mr Zhen to exert his influence to find Song Ci a posting. As far as Liu knew, Mr Zhen had observed three years of mourning for his father and had then been ordered by imperial command to Hunan Province to take up the post of regional administrator in Tanzhou. So, when he sent someone to invite him to the opening of the Zhu Xi memorial, the 'express' messenger found himself going first to Tanzhou, then to Lin'an, until he finally discovered that in the eighth month of that year, Mr Zhen had received an appointment back in the capital as an imperial personal secretary, and then been promoted to a senior post in the Ministry of Rites and the Hanlin Academy.

Even if I had known this sooner, and asked for his help, there's no guarantee that anything would be achieved any quicker, Liu comforted himself.

Mr Zhen Dexiu's arrival had been very unremarkable. He came in civilian clothes with only two mounted escorts, and there were no gongs and drums or banners – in fact no fuss or ceremony of any kind. Liu hurried out to greet him and seeing him arrive thus, although he knew all about Mr Zhen's practice of simplicity in all things, he couldn't help feeling that the effect went beyond simplicity and was verging on impoverishment.

The day was almost over, but Mr Zhen declined the offer of rest and refreshment and wanted to go straight to see the memorial. Liu accompanied him, explaining the story of the building of the shrine as they went. Kaoting College stood on a river promontory known as Cangzhou about five *li* southwest of Jianyang. To the north were mountains, but the other three sides were surrounded by the river. With deep and mysterious terrain for several *li* all around, it was a beautiful and secluded spot. On approaching the college, visitors would look up to see a stone memorial arch of unusual design on which were carved phoenix, cranes, qilin,[1] lions and other symbolic birds and beasts.

Beyond the arch, via the ceremonial gateway, was the newly-built shrine to Zhu Xi, modelled on the Confucius Temple in Qufu, Shandong Province. The outer wall was plain and unadorned, and above the main hall hung a large tablet bearing the calligraphic inscription 'Jicheng Dian' or 'Hall of Unification'. On entering, through the clouds of incense smoke, the hall was bathed in a mysterious light. At the front, in solitary splendour, stood a lifelike painted stone statue of Master Zhu Xi, carved on the propitious first day of spring in the fifth year of the Shaoxi period (1194). Its base carried the inscription: 'Memorial Portrait of the Great Master Wen Gong'. The statue showed Zhu Xi wearing the gown of a Confucian scholar with a silk head-cloth. It captured all the dignity of the great man in his later years.

Standing in front of the statue, Zhen Dexiu was deeply moved. He knelt before it and wept. He thought of the seventy years of Master Zhu Xi's life, the greater part of which had been devoted to the promotion of learning. He had started out on his official career at the age of twenty-four, when he had taken up an appointment as official registrar of the Tong'an district of Quanzhou, in Fujian Province. While there, he had established the Tong'an District Academy, and after that also founded the prefectural academy at Zhangzhou. On Mount Lu in Jiangxi Province, he set up Bailudong College, while in Tanzhou in Hunan Province, he renovated and extended Yuelu College, and in Wuyi in Fujian he established Ziyang College. At the age of sixty-three, in the third year of the Shaoxi period (1192), he built the Cangzhou monastic retreat at Kaoting College in Jianyang. It is hard to believe that only five years later, Han Tuozhou, the statesmen with supreme control over all national military and administrative affairs, would label Zhu Xi's philosophies as 'bogus teachings', ban them and purge as many as fifty-nine of his followers from government office.[2] Zhu Xi himself was labelled 'chief architect of bogus learning'. Terminally ill, he persevered in lecturing to his students at the Cangzhou retreat. On his deathbed, he suddenly lost his sight and his arms became swollen and intensely painful, but he worked on, compiling and editing his lectures until, his life's work complete, he passed away.

When Zhen Dexiu was fourteen, in the year that Zhu Xi established the Cangzhou retreat, he came to study at Kaoting. At twenty-one, he moved straight into a high-level government post. He had returned to Kaoting for the funeral rites when Zhu Xi passed away. In front of the grave were placed two stone candle-standards to represent the light that the master had brought into people's lives. The government attempted to play down and limit access to the funeral rites, but thousands of scholars from all over the country came to attend. From that time on, Zhen Dexiu nurtured the dream of building a memorial to Zhu Xi at Jianyang – a place for scholars to come to pay their respects, to lament the chaos of current times, to contemplate the serenity of the past and to dedicate themselves to the education of the people.

The years passed and Han Tuozhou, the man who had banned the teachings of Zhu Xi, was executed. Zhen Dexiu's acolyte, Liu Kezhuang, was conducting the offerings at the shrine, and the old man was not only delighted at the realisation of his long-cherished dream, but also felt that at last he could see clearly the path his own life should take henceforward.

Inside the Hall of Unification, Liu led Zhen Dexiu into the memorial shrine itself. They sat down, and, fretting slightly, Liu took the opportunity to broach the topic of Song Ci. Zhen Dexiu had an excellent memory, and immediately recalled the student at the academy who had written a poem entitled *Ode to Time*. He heard Liu Kezhuang out, and then, with a bitter smile, said softly: "Qianfu, you can't have heard. I have already retired."

Liu couldn't believe what he was hearing, but there was no doubt about it; he could see there was no point in pursuing the matter further. Zhen Dexiu was not the kind of person to joke about matters like this, and it suddenly dawned on Liu the significance of the simplicity of Zhen's arrival in Jianyang. He was struck dumb.

However, when Zhen heard that Song Ci was still at home in mourning for his father, he was extremely interested and said to Liu: "Why are you looking so astonished? I need men of his exceptional talents. You must take me to see him later. I am going to return to my home town of Pucheng to expand the West Mountain College, and I want to employ him to come and lecture there."

Liu Kezhuang knew that promoting education came before everything else for Mr Zhen Dexiu, but he had to tell him: "I'm afraid that won't work. All he wants is to be a government official."

"A government official? There are so many other uses for his knowledge and experience! Why does he want to be an official?"

"Well, that's how it is. Perhaps you find it hard to understand."

Zhen looked at Liu and thought to himself: I may not fully understand Song Ci, but being an official is something I do know about!

Formerly, because of his vehement opposition to Shi Miyuan's proposed reconciliation with the Jin, Zhen Dexiu had been unable to establish himself at court, and he had taken up a post in Jiangdong as an auxiliary officer supervising merchant shipping. Just before he left, he had admonished Emperor Ningzong: "Our national humiliation cannot be overlooked, and our rapacious neighbours should not be taken lightly. Trusting to luck is not a viable strategy. Flattery is not to be trusted. The opinions of the just and virtuous must not be neglected."

On arriving in Jiangdong, he found the area devastated by drought and locusts, with countless people dying of thirst and starvation. He focused his initial efforts on the two worst-affected districts of Guangde and Taiping. There, he lowered the price of grain and purged corrupt officials, bringing relief to those in the direst straits with such efficiency that even those at court who had previously mocked him as being hopelessly naive and impractical, had to applaud him. In the thirteenth year of Jiading, before Zhen had observed the full three years of mourning for his father, he was given another appointment as a mediator in Tanzhou in Hunan Province. Following the maxim for those in office of 'Enact four benefits, remove ten harms', among the latter he concentrated on unjust court judgments, poorly investigated litigation, prolonged detention on remand, excessive use of torture, vindictive interrogation, double taxation, profiteering from court fines and other such corrupt practices. In this way, he gradually established himself as a firm foundation of honest administration for the people. After the death of Emperor Ningzong, his successor, Lizong, ordered Zhen Dexiu back to the capital as a confidential advisor with responsibility for military and civil appointments. It could be said that with this, Zhen Dexiu had achieved his lifetime ambition, of using his scholarship in the service of his sovereign. Unfortunately, Emperor Lizong's ascension to the throne had been the result of a coup d'état, which is something that stuck in Zhen's throat. Although it is covered up in the official histories, Zhen was denounced by another senior official to whom he had expressed his reservations. Further accusations piled up until he had no option but to relinquish his position and return to the south.

On his journey home, Zhen Dexiu thought deeply about what had happened to him. It was clear to him that, although there were huge numbers of court officials, very few were of real talent and virtue with the vision to govern justly. Thus, his only ambition now was to educate a new generation of virtuous and talented young men who would selflessly exert themselves to the proper service of the nation.

"Qianfu, you must still try to persuade Song Ci to come with me. Nothing could be better than for him to join me in this great enterprise of training a new generation of talent."

"Master, I'm afraid there is absolutely no way he will do this," said Liu Kezhuang.

"Why not?"

Liu gave a detailed account of what had happened to Song Ci over the last few years, explaining all about the most recent case and how easily Song had deduced the true state of affairs. Zhen Dexiu listened very carefully and couldn't suppress a small gasp of astonishment at what Liu told him. Thinking of his own circumstances, he said: "I wish I could help him, but my hands are tied."

"Not at all. There is something you can do," Liu said. "There are many instances where official intervention may not get anywhere but a quiet, private word can achieve results. Although you may have retired from office, there must be several acquaintances at court you are still in touch with. If you were to make earnest entreaties to one of two of them, surely we would get some result."

Zhen Dexiu knew there was some reason to this. He had also begun to feel that Song Ci was a man he had yet to fathom, and that his intellect was very different from his own. Song was also very different from most of the court officials he knew, and he was coming to recognise that this was a quite extraordinary man. He was about to say that perhaps there was no harm in trying, when they were interrupted by the sound of heavy footsteps entering the memorial hall – Wei Cipei had returned.

"My report, Lord! The murderer is locked up, but it is not Zhu Minghu, it is a sixty-year-old man."

"What?" exclaimed Liu Kezhuang.

"When I got to Luhuaping, I met this old man who was on his way to turn himself in to the authorities."

"What about Zhu Minghu?"

"I didn't dare act without further orders, so I brought the two of them in and locked them both up."

Liu Kezhuang rolled his eyes at Zhen Dexiu who was sitting beside him, and he found that Zhen was looking straight back at him. They were both amazed – could it be that all Song Ci's careful reasoning had in fact led him to an entirely erroneous conclusion?

5

# WHITE TIGER JOINT DISEASE

The next day was the day of Zhu Xi's memorial rites, and that night, Liu Kezhuang opened the hearing of the case against the old man. Song Ci was invited to attend, and Zhen Dexiu had developed a lively interest in the case, so he was there as well.

"Why did you want to kill Zhu Mingtan?" Liu asked the old man.

"Last year..." said the accused, whose surname was also Zhu, with the given name Baiyou. He was a worker on the Kaiyuan tea plantation. He had a thin, almost gaunt appearance, and spoke in a gruff voice as though there was something lodged in his throat.

"Louder!" Liu ordered

"Last year, Zhu Mingtan raped and murdered my daughter." The accused spoke more loudly, his voice becoming so hoarse it sounded as though it was coming not from his mouth but from deep in his throat.

"If your daughter was raped and murdered last year, why didn't you report it?"

"What would have been the point?"

"What do you mean?"

"After she was raped by Zhu Mingtan, she drowned herself."

"Well, why didn't you report the rape?"

"I didn't see him do it, so what difference would reporting it make?"

"How did you find out about it?"

"She came to her mother in tears and told her..."

Liu Kezhuang continued his careful questioning, asking the man when he had killed Zhu Mingtan, where the murder had taken place, were there any bloodstains and so on. The old man answered everything. Liu then asked him why he had turned himself in.

The old man replied: "I was afraid someone else might be blamed falsely. Besides, my daughter had come to us about her ordeal and no one had been told the true reason for her suicide."

Finally, Liu asked if the old man had been acting on behalf of someone else, to which he replied with some vehemence: "No, no one. I acted alone, without orders from anyone."

As Liu Kezhuang questioned the man, he was racking his brains trying to find some hole in his story, but try as he might he could see no flaws or contradictions. He looked at Zhen Dexiu, but that serious and conscientious man was giving nothing away. Then he looked at Song Ci, who silently waved his hands in dismay. Liu ordered the prisoner to sign his confession, then had him locked into a broad, iron-bound cangue and taken down to the condemned cell.

Suddenly having to stand up after kneeling for so long, the old man's legs began to shake uncontrollably so that the court staff had to hold him up and lead him away. And with the case having reached this point, there was no justification for keeping Zhu Minghu locked up, so Liu ordered him to be released into temporary house arrest. When everybody else had left the court, Liu said to Song Ci: "Well, my brother…"

Song interrupted him: "Quick! Send someone to Luhuaping to bring back the corpse and the murder weapon. We need to examine them again."

The next day, Captain Wei Cipei went, as ordered, to Luhuaping to exhume the corpse and collect the murder weapon, blood-stained clothing and other items of evidence, which he found where the accused had said they would be. He hurried back with them. Song Ci examined the body with the county coroner, and completed both the body charts and the examination record.[1]

Liu Kezhuang was still busy with the final stages of the memorial rites for Zhu Xi and had no time to return to the case. But he was content in the knowledge that the accused was under lock and key. The case was set aside for three days.

In the morning, three days later, a group of staff formed a perimeter at some distance from the main examination hall of the *yamen*, allowing no one to approach any closer. As well as the corpse itself, the murder weapon, clothing and other evidence were all assembled on a table in the examination hall. This had all been done according to Song Ci's recommendations. There were only three people in the hall: Zhen Dexiu, Liu Kezhuang and Song Ci.

"Zhu Baiyou is not the culprit," Song Ci said quietly.

Liu Kezhuang had suspected his old friend might say this. But the old man had confessed, and the murdered corpse, murder weapon and everything else were all laid out in front of them as proof. Zhen Dexiu looked at the autopsy records that Liu handed him, and listened carefully as Song Ci continued: "According to Zhu Baiyou's confession, he struck Zhu Mingtan in the neck from behind with a broad-bladed axe. Zhu Mingtan staggered forward a few paces and then fell to the ground. He then rolled so that he was lying supine and Zhu Baiyou struck him again with the axe in the face. Zhu Mingtan then stopped moving. The autopsy results support this version of events. The blood-flow pattern from the wound in the neck shows it running from the neck down the back, while from the single wound on the face, the blood has spattered equally in all directions. However, this is deceptive – the two wound sites both exhibit very neat, slender entry points from the weapon used, especially on the neck where the rear end of the entry point is particularly thin. In addition, the bottom of the wound is flat all the way across, and not indented. We can be quite certain it was not made by an axe, but by a knife with a honed edge, with the attacker drawing the blade across the neck from behind. When the victim turned over, he slashed the face with the same knife. This is the first reason for doubting the confession.

"The second reason is that the wound in the neck slants down from the left, meaning the blow was struck obliquely downwards, left to right, so we can be sure it was struck by someone who uses a knife in their left hand. But when Zhu Baiyou signed his confession, he used his right hand. So we know he is right-handed.

"Third, in the matter of the blood-stained clothing, although it is what Zhu Baiyou habitually wears, it is, in fact, not the killer's."

"How can you tell that?" Liu Kezhuang let out a sigh of relief as the hope dawned on him that Song Ci's original conclusion might, indeed, not have been mistaken.

"In his confession, Zhu Baiyou states that most of these bloodstains came from when he was carrying the body on his back up the hill to bury it. But if these clothes are the murderer's, and he was actually wearing them on his body, how can you explain the remarkable pattern of the staining?"

As he spoke, Song Ci spread out the bloody clothes. Zhen Dexiu and Liu Kezhuang could see that both front and back were heavily stained, and that the stains were exactly the same shape and size on both sides.

"These stains have been faked. Since there was actually no body in the clothes, front and back exactly replicate each other as closely as if they had been printed. So where did the blood come from? A chicken perhaps, or maybe a dog. Human blood is comparatively thick, but animal blood is thin. The blood on these clothes is thin and can only have come from an animal."

"In that case, the murderer…"

"Is still Zhu Minghu."

"Explain," said Zhen Dexiu.

"From my examination of the body, we can eliminate revenge as motive. It has always been the case that most revenge killings involve a face-on attack so that the victim knows it is their enemy who is killing them, and that they are taking pleasure in the act. But with this body, the wound on the face starts above the left eye and ends just below the right eye. This clearly indicates that the initial attack came suddenly from behind, and when the victim fell face down, he turned over to see who was attacking him. But the assailant didn't want him to see that he was being attacked by his own elder brother, so he slashed him across the eyes with his knife – it was a deep-seated impulse that he couldn't resist."

Zhen Dexiu listened to what Song said, and he nodded his head.

"And apart from all that, as I have already ascertained from brother Qianfu, Zhu Minghu wrote out his deposition in his own hand, and the characters clearly shows that it was written by someone who is left-handed."

"But why should this Zhu Baiyou fellow be willing to take the blame for a murder on someone else's behalf?" Liu asked.

"That's not so strange," Song Ci exclaimed. "From the tenth year of Jiading, the Jin have been pushing south, and the war has been going on for six years. The soldiers and officers in the border regions have been giving up their lives in defence of the country. In the interior, the people have been taxed as never before and their livelihoods pared to the bone. Although there is now a truce, the people have not been able to regain any of their losses. Zhu Baiyou is a tea farmer, his family is poor and you can see how thin he is from lack of food. If he was to get into serious debt, or some family emergency arose that needed money to sort out, suppose someone came along offering cash for him to accept the blame for something. Well then, even if it meant his death, as long as his family was saved, don't you think he would consider that a reasonable proposition?"

"In that case, do you think Zhu Baiyou was coached in his confession by Zhu Minghu?"

"That's right. Furthermore, we can say that Zhu Minghu wouldn't have given him the knife that he used as the murder weapon, because someone might have recognised it if it was used as evidence. But Zhu Baiyou wouldn't have had such a knife of his own, and if he had pretended that he had used a tea-pruning knife, the size and weight would have been wrong. So he chose a broad-headed axe, instead, as the purported murder weapon. As for the blood-stained clothing, naturally Zhu Minghu couldn't hand over his own, so the best they could do was fake some of Zhu Baiyou's."

"In that case," Zhen Dexiu said, "when Zhu Minghu laid information against that official from the imperial kilns accusing him of murder, the official was already under arrest, and when he returned here, he was under no kind of suspicion. So why did he still want to find someone to take the blame for him?"

"That's why I have asked Qianfu to take some extraordinary measures today. I was pretty sure that there had to be some minor official in the *yamen* who was working for Zhu Minghu. He must have overheard Qianfu and me discussing the case that afternoon, and during the night gone to inform Zhu of what we said. That's why he thought up this complicated deception. But that's enough discussion for the moment – we must bring up Zhu Baiyou for some further questioning, and all will become clear."

Liu Kezhuang and Zhen Dexiu thought about all this for a while, and deciding that Song Ci's deductions more than held water, agreed to question Zhu Baiyou again. Soon they heard the clatter of footsteps outside, and the sound of someone groaning hoarsely. The *yamen* guards arrived carrying Zhu Baiyou on a door panel. He was in a bad way: his eyes were staring blankly and his body was rigid as he lay on the panel, twitching occasionally. During three days of imprisonment, his thin body had become bloated, and after he had been carried in to the court he lay there without a word, grinding his teeth and breathing stertorously. His chest was shiny with sweat, and the smell of foul urine seeped from his body.

Liu Kezhuang dismissed the rest of the guards and turned to the jailer, asking: "What is the matter with him?"

"My Lord," the jailer replied. "The morning after he was put in the condemned cell, he began to behave oddly, shouting and rolling about on the floor. And there was something odd about the way he rolled, stiff and rigid like a log of wood, not bending or twisting at all. When I asked what was wrong, he didn't reply. On the third day, he stopped eating. We gave him some water and he drank it all up, which quietened him down for a bit. But after a while he began shouting again and rolling around even more violently. Today we didn't give him any water, and he knocked over the piss bucket…"

"Has anyone been to see him in his cell over the last three days?" Liu asked severely. He was worried that the unknown minion who was helping Zhu Minghu might have been able to get in and poison the old man.

"No one, my lord. I took his food in myself."

"Qianfu," Song Ci interrupted. "There's no point in asking further. I'm sure you remember that, after he had been kneeling in court, he had couldn't stand up and had to be carried down to the condemned cell."

"In that case…" Liu began, remembering also the man's hoarse voice.

"No." Song Ci pre-empted Liu's train of thought. "It isn't that someone gave him something before he came to court."

"Then…"

"It's an illness."

"An illness?"

"I have read about something just like this in the old casebook of a doctor I knew." Song Ci could almost see Dr Haiting standing in front of him, as he reflected that the book left him by the old doctor, *Personal Record of the Diagnosis of Intractable Disease*, was now proving its worth.

"What kind of disease is it?" Liu Kezhuang asked quickly, when Song Ci stopped talking.

"People who suffer from this kind of disease usually have a history of chronic joint and muscle pain. Its onset is fast and fierce, and it reaches a critical point after only a few days. The muscles swell and the patient is unable either to flex or extend his joints. He cannot stand up or move, and he develops a raging thirst. But if he drinks, within half a day his throat becomes intolerably sore, as though it is being gouged by tiger claws, and for this reason, it is called White Tiger joint disease.[2]

"White Tiger joint disease," Liu repeated emphatically, looking at Zhen Dexiu, who returned his gaze. It was clear neither of them had heard of it before.

"I believe that when he was kneeling in the courtroom, and he appeared to be inappropriately and rather insolently shrugging his shoulders, it was in fact because his shoulders were aching severely. Then, when he was put into the condemned cell, which is the one deepest below ground and consequently very damp, and also extremely cold at this time of year, his clothes being so thin and flimsy, he had no protection and that is when he contracted this disease."

"Is there any cure for it?" Zhen Dexiu asked with concern.

"If it is not treated immediately, he will deteriorate very quickly and die."

"So there is a cure?"

"There is."

"And can you treat him?" Liu asked.

"There is a prescription for the treatment in my book, and a description of how to administer it."

"Do you remember the prescription?"

"I do."

"Quickly then, write it out."

Liu Kezhuang stood up to give Song Ci a brush and ink, but Song Ci shook his head: "There's no point."

"Why not?"

"Most of the ingredients will need to be dug up or picked, up in the mountains. Things like leaves from the mulberry, willow, maple, poplar and pagoda tree; and kadsura vine, 'dragon across the mountain creeper' and chicken blood vine. If you go to the pharmacist to try to buy the ingredients, the only one you will find will be sulphur. You had better order some men up into the mountains where they can split up and gather what is needed."

"No, no," Liu Kezhuang said. "I'll call them here first so you can explain what they are looking for."

Liu hurried out of the room, and ordered all the *yamen* staff who were standing around outside to come in and listen.

"Now listen carefully, you men. Master Song Ci is going to give you some orders in a very important matter. You are to split up and do as he says. There's no room for any mistakes."

The staff all chorused their assent. Song Ci proceeded to give them their orders in groups of two or three, and sent them on their way immediately. He then ordered the jailers to dig a trench seven feet long and just over seven inches deep in the prison yard, and to level off its bottom so it was flat and even as a sleeping mat.

Around noon, one by one, the *yamen* staff returned, each bearing the leaves or vines they had been instructed to collect. Song Ci carefully arranged each piece of vegetation in the trench he had dug, poured over some grain spirit, scattered some sulphur, and then set light to it all. The flames took instantly, and the leaves and vine were burnt down to ash. Song ordered the ash to be removed, and then poured yellow wine into the pit, from the bottom of which smoke erupted with a hissing noise. After a while, Song Ci squatted down and felt around in the bottom of the pit. Then he stood up and ordered: "Strip Zhu Baiyou of all his clothes, and put him in the trench so he can feel its warmth."

The jailers hurried to obey, and laid Zhu Baiyou out in the bottom of the pit. Zhu had been crying out in pain incessantly, but as soon as he was in the pit, the noise stopped, and he closed his eyes and mouth and lay there in silence, quite still.

"The book says that once the patient is put in the pit, his body begins to feel numb, and the pain recedes. It looks as though that's what is happening," Song Ci said.

"Let us hope so," said Liu Kezhuang.

Song Ci waited until the trench had cooled down completely, then ordered Zhu Baiyou to be removed. That afternoon, dressed in padded-cotton jacket and trousers, Zhu was put into a wooden shed with a medical attendant to watch over him. Song Ci took some pig and ox bones, roasted them and ground them to a powder. Then, following Dr Haiting's prescription, he mixed the powder with wine and gave it to Zhu Baiyou to drink, sip by sip. That night, Zhu neither cried out nor thrashed about, but slept contentedly. As the sun came through the shed window the next morning, he suddenly woke up, smacked his lips and looked expectantly around him.

"He's hungry," said Song Ci, looking in through the window.

Food and wine were sent in. Zhu Baiyou looked at it wide-eyed in alarm, thinking it was the condemned man's last meal. If I'm going to die, I might as well be a full ghost, he thought to himself, but when he tried to get up to eat, he found he couldn't.

"You must feed him," Liu Kezhuang told the jailer.

The jailer went to follow these orders, and after a moment's hesitation, Zhu Baiyou opened his mouth and consumed all the food and drink that had been brought in.

At midday, Zhu Baiyou was put in the trench again. This time, when he was taken out, he found he could roll his neck, move his body and even flex his wrists. He was carried back into the wooden shed.

Song Ci told Liu Kezhuang and Zhen Dexiu: "Now you can go and question him."

The three of them went to where Zhu Baiyou was sleeping. Mindful of the ordeal the man had been through, this time Liu questioned him much more gently, gradually drawing the truth out of him. It turned out to be precisely as Song Ci had deduced.

After he had heard the real story from the old man, Liu immediately ordered that Zhu Minghu be brought for interrogation. However, Zhu Baiyou's new confession wasn't the only extraordinary thing that happened that day. The court officer who had been sent to bring in Zhu Minghu, returned in a great hurry to report: "Your honour, Zhu Minghu is dead!"

6

# PLUM BLOSSOM FALLING IN THE WIND AND SNOW

In the blink of an eye it was early spring in the second year of the Baoqing period (1226). In Jianyang, a heavy snow had fallen such as was seldom seen south of the Yangtze. The morning dawned crisp and clear, and outside everything was dazzling white. All over the city, the roof-tiles were covered in a blanket of fresh, fluffy snowflakes. The branches of the fruit trees were thick with snow and glistened like silver bars. On the ground, the thick carpet of snow was unmarked by any shoes.

Song Qi, who was now twelve and had never seen heavy snow like this, was thrilled. After breakfast, she and her maid hurried out into the courtyard to build a snowman, and they played in the snow, romping and rolling around until it was suddenly already afternoon.

This was a day that no one was to forget. At noon, a man tramped through the snow to Song Ci's front gate and knocked loudly. He was bringing some unusual news. The maid went to the gate and saw an officer from the *yamen*.

"Magistrate Liu requests the attendance of Master Song Ci," he said.

"What's the matter?" asked Song Ci, who had just come out into the courtyard to admire his daughter's snowman.

"Master Song," said the officer, making an obeisance to Song Ci. "Magistrate Liu requests you to officiate at the court."

"What are you saying?"

"Magistrate Liu requests you to officiate at the court."

This was a most extraordinary request, and the one that Song Ci had been waiting for ever since he had returned home after entering the upper-middle ranks of officialdom ten years before. Needless to say, this was the result of

Zhen Dexiu's efforts. Song Ci remembered that last winter, when Zhen was about to return to Pucheng, he had had a long conversation with his old intimate, during which Zhen had finally accepted there was no chance of Song fulfilling his wish and coming to lecture in Pucheng. No two men's abilities are the same, and each has a responsibility to make the best use of the talents and tools available to them.

"I most certainly do want to help you get an appointment," Zhen said.

The case of the death of Zhu Mingtan had clearly demonstrated to Zhen the extent of Song Ci's abilities. But, Song reminded himself, I did make some mistakes in that case. Otherwise, that final outcome could have been avoided.

Zhu Minghu had been poisoned in a house near the *yamen*, and there could be no doubt that the poisoner was Zhu's unknown informer on the *yamen* staff. It hadn't been a difficult affair to ferret out, and Song had worked it out within a day. The resultant confession went along these lines: the fellow had had no previous connection with Zhu Minghu, nor had Zhu Minghu bribed him. But, after he had overheard Song Ci and Liu Kezhuang talking together, on his own initiative he had paid a night-time visit to Zhu Minghu and blackmailed him with the information. This was what had put the twist into the case. Song Ci hadn't thought of blackmail.

Whenever Song Ci thought of the death of Zhu Minghu, he castigated himself over not having anticipated this. He had, after all, saved Zhu Baiyou. He had worked out that Zhu Minghu must have a co-conspirator among the *yamen* staff, so how was it he had neglected to put an extra guard over him? It left him with an uncomfortable feeling whenever he thought about it.

"Tell Magistrate Liu that I am coming at once," Song told the messenger, and he went inside to let his wife and his mother know what was going on. He had a hasty lunch, pulled on his boots and got ready to go.

"Father, can I come too?" Song Qi came rushing out of the kitchen and hugged her father, her mouth still half full of food.

"No, Qi'er, don't go. The snow is too heavy," her grandmother said, following her out of the kitchen.

"No, Grandma, I want to go," Song Qi pouted.

Song Yulan came out into the courtyard, hugging herself with both arms, but not saying anything. When she heard about Song Ci being summoned to take up office, she was completely taken aback and didn't know what to do.

"All right, I'll take you," Song Ci said, taking his daughter by the hand, even though he didn't know how long he would be gone.

The snow had stopped before dawn, but there was no sun, and the sky was one vast expanse of white. The air was cold, but crisp and clear. The snow on the high-road wasn't as thick as in the courtyard, and as Song Qi walked along she kicked at it, scattering a frosty spray in all directions. Song Ci led his daughter into the *yamen*, where Liu Kezhuang was in the courtyard admiring his plum blossom.

On seeing Song, he told him: "The news has just come in from the capital. I'm only sorry that the post they are offering you is quite beneath you."

"What is the post?"

"Official registrar for Xinfeng County in Jiangxi."

"That's all right," Song Ci said. "So far this year, the only other job they have handed out has been a military posting in Yinzhou in Zhejiang."

"I see little Song Qi has come too. Let's go and look at the plum trees in the snow. It's a sight you don't often see in Jianyang." Liu Kezhuang was particularly keen on horticulture. "Plum blossom, pure and noble, orchids with their serene perfume, the elegant rustling of the tea bush, the chrysanthemum that defies the frost..."

Of all the hundreds of flowers, Liu loved plum blossom the best. His passion for that particular flower had originally been considerably influenced by the poet Lu You.[1] He had become acquainted with the great man the year before his death, and he had read all the hundred or more poems Lu You had written in praise of plum blossom. He particularly liked the poet's description of plum blossom as "the truest and most virtuous of flowers". In his own garden, he had cultivated at least eight different types of plum tree: the jade butterfly plum, the fragrant mouth plum, the red-speckled plum, the green-stemmed plum and so on; and he had several more varieties in *penzai* (bonsai) form. He tended all these trees himself, without any help from a gardener. He planned the plantings with meticulous care and did all the work on his own. It brought him enormous pleasure.

In his youth, Liu Kezhuang had not seen any point in wasting time poring over the classics or religious texts, nor had he been willing to grind away mastering scansion, rhyme and meter in versifying. Few people, however, understood his overriding passion for horticulture. But Song Ci considered that his friend's fascination with developing new types of *penzai*, and his unwillingness to be bound by convention, were two sides of the same coin. And the satisfaction he got from growing a *penzai* was no less than that to be had from composing a finely-turned ode or poetic essay. Nor was the time he spent with these plants every morning just a way of whiling away the time; he devoted all his skill and knowledge, tirelessly and gladly, into tending all of the little trees, one after the other. In this activity he could work through each of his worries and annoyances and resolve them. And he drew new resolve and inspiration from his beloved *penzai*. In poetry too, his love of plants allowed him to free himself of the constraints of verse forms and rhyme patterns. It gave him a direct and powerful access to his inner feelings. It gave him a reservoir of inspiration like an ocean of ink. It gave voice to an energy, freed from reason, that could topple walls. Along with Lu You and Xin Qiji, he was considered the third member of the triumvirate of Song poetry.

On this day, when Liu Kezhuang just told him to come and admire the plum blossom, Song Ci couldn't help suspecting his old friend had an ulterior motive.

"Well, my honoured friend," Liu continued. "Perhaps you remember what kind of plum tree that is to the left of the trellis on the veranda?"

"It's a Hunan plum tree."

"And is there anything particular about it?"

"I seem to remember you telling me that it has many flowers, and each flower can have more than twenty petals. It's sometimes called the thousand-leaf yellow fragrant plum."

"Many flowers? Don't you mean the fewest flowers of any plum tree?" Song Qi piped up. She was looking at the pot containing the *penzai* that Liu and her father were talking about, whose branches, pointing up to sky, were covered in icicles. Of blossom, however, there was not a single petal to be seen.

"Little Qi," Liu Kezhuang said, smiling. "Yesterday evening, it was covered in blossom, but it was ambushed overnight by the wind and snow, and the flowers were all taken prisoner. If you don't believe me, have a look in the snow on the ground beneath it."

"Is that really true?" Song Qi asked, wide-eyed.

"It's really true."

Song Qi scrabbled around in the fresh snow and dug out handfuls of bright petals.

"Do you see the tree to the right?" Liu asked.

"That's an ancient tree."

"Do you see how its branches are old and twisted, and covered in moss? It can only put out buds in the gaps in the moss, so it doesn't have many flowers."

"But although it doesn't have many flowers, they all proudly resisted the onslaught of the wind and snow. Is that what you mean?" Song Ci asked.

"That's right."

In Liu Kezhuang's company, this was always the way. Even if the mood of other people might be completely different to his, they gradually found themselves being redirected, and their urgent concerns being put aside for considerations of his own. But this time, Song Ci realised it wasn't going to be too much of a diversion, and whatever it was, was somehow connected with his new appointment. He saw that Liu was about to say what was on his mind, and he anticipated him, saying bluntly: "Is there something you have to say to me?"

"I was going to say that, it is of course a good thing for a man to have talents. In our civil service at the moment there is much talent, but also much vexation. Look there at the plum tree, standing defiantly against the frost and snow, but look also at how many flowers it lost."

When Liu Kezhuang stopped speaking, he gestured at the sky, as though about to declaim one of his poems to the heavens, but then he stilled his hands and dropped them back to his sides. He turned to Song Ci and said: "This morning, when I looked out of the widow and saw the snow and the fallen blossom, and then heard the news about your appointment, I wrote a poem. Shall we go and look at it?"

"Yes, let's go." Song Ci was looking forward to sitting down in the library and talking things over. Song Qi followed the two men in, clutching some of the petals she had dug out of the snow.

The library was simply furnished. There was a Mume plum *penzai* on the book case and a Chinese plum on the *zitan* wood frame of the east window. Leaning disorderly against the west wall were piles of the essays and poetry that Liu dashed off every day. A white copper brazier on the floor, full of fresh charcoal, was burning away merrily. Liu had already inscribed the poem he mentioned on a narrow hanging-screen that was lying on the desk, weighted down with an uncut gemstone.

The ink was still glistening on the freshly written characters. They were written in 'wild cursive' script that looked like a tornado about to launch itself from the paper. Liu Kezhuang took the screen and hung it on the wall. Song Ci read the poem:

> *Each fallen petal carries a world of sorrow*
> *As they pile up on the steps like a snowdrift*
> *Drifting in the wind like an exiled official,*
> *Lost like a scholar without a patron.*
> *So many blossoms once proud and lofty*
> *Now reduced to the mud and the moss,*
> *But if their petals brush against your sleeve*
> *The fragrance lingers long.*
> *Surely it is wrong for the east wind to wield*
> *Such power of life and death.*
> *It is jealous of the blossom's lofty grace*
> *And ravages it wantonly with no shred of respect.*

He realised that Liu Kezhuang had been using the impermanence of the plum blossom as a metaphor for the paucity of opportunity for talented officials entering government service, the heroes who lose their way, the bleakness of serving one's country with no prospects for advancement. And, in his own case, the resentments of those jealous of the virtuous and envious of his talents. There, too, was the envy of those who resented Mr Zhen Dexiu and caused his demotion.

"Honoured friend," Liu Kezhuang said. "We have to part and I wanted to give you a poem. But this verse *Fallen Plum Blossom* would not be an auspicious gift."

Song Ci felt the emotion bubbling up inside him. Over the years, his attitude had toughened, becoming more and more cool-headed, so that he was not easily stirred. But today was different. He didn't know what to say. It was Song Qi who suddenly spoke, breaking the silence and exciting great interest in Liu Kezhuang.

"Uncle Liu, your wild cursive script really has the feeling of the brushwork of Zhang Bogao."

"Zhang Bogao!" Liu exclaimed. "How do you know about Zhang Bogao?"

"Of course I know about him," Song Qi said. "He was a master of cursive script in the Tang dynasty. His surname was Zhang, his given name was Xu, and his courtesy name was Bogao. Even Yan Zhenqing asked him to teach him calligraphy!"

"What else do you know?" Liu asked even more animatedly.

"Zhang Bogao is most famous for his wild cursive script," Song Qi said, looking at her father. "His contemporaries all said 'His brush moves like lightning, with ten thousand changes at the turn of a wrist'. His wild cursive script, Li Bai's poems and Pei Min's swordsmanship were the three incomparable achievements of the age."

"So, what made you say that your Uncle Liu's script had the feeling of Zhang Bogao's brushwork?" Liu asked.

"Zhang Bogao's characters don't follow in the tracks of previous generations. He used to get drunk and run around madly, yelling and shouting, and that's when he would pick up his brush and write. So his characters are drunk and crazy. People at the time called him Madman Zhang. I thought Uncle Liu's characters…"

"What?"

"Looked a little crazy."

"Excellent!" Liu Kezhuang said, laughing. "Calligraphy must be your hobby."

Song Ci looked at his daughter and said: "She hasn't really got on to poetry calligraphy yet, but her writing is very good. She's already finished copying all the old characters in those books I bought."

"Very good. Very good. When your father has gone, you can come over here and your Uncle Liu will teach you calligraphy."

"I don't want to learn your crazy characters though!"

"Hah! How charming," Liu said. He knew that most of Song Ci's collection were character scrolls, and there weren't many Buddhist stone-rubbings, so he took out a volume of *Rubbings from the Chunhua Pavilion* printed in Quanzhou during the Chunxi period. He picked it up and said: "Take a look. Here we've got rubbings of inscriptions by Master Xixian and his son, Emperor Taizong of the Tang dynasty, Emperor Xuanzong, Yan Zhenqing, Ouyang Xun, Liu Gongquan and many others."

"Give it to me! Give it to me!" A delighted Song Qi went over to take the book and started looking through it.

A little later, Liu Kezhuang told Song Ci that the current magistrate in Xinfeng was a man called Shan Zilin. Shan Zilin came from Changzhou in Jiangsu Province, had had dealings with Liu Kezhuang in the past, and he considered him a friend. Liu was going to write a letter for Song Ci to take, which would have the dual purpose of maintaining contact with an old friend and of benefitting Song Ci.

The charcoal in the copper brazier was gradually going out, leaving only some grey ash in the bottom. Song Qi had stopped reading the volume of rubbings and was sitting, leaning her cheeks on her hands, quietly listening to the conversation of Liu Kezhuang and her father. The sky grew dark, and almost imperceptibly, night closed in.

7

# HEAVEN IS HIGH AND THE ROAD IS LONG

Song Ci's wife, Yulan, felt the days and nights had become very short. That night, she was quietly sorting out her husband's travelling clothes. She fiddled around with them, picking them up and putting them down. Normally neat and capable, Yulan had become clumsy and disorganised, and she kept thinking she had forgotten something important. Previously, when she had seen Song Ci fretting around the house with no job to do, she had really hoped that he would soon be given an appointment. Then, when she learned that someone had accused him of misconduct, and he might be struck from the government rolls, she burned with anger. Now he was going to take up a new appointment, her emotions were all tangled. Although she had never experienced the challenges of an official career, she had often heard it said that, quite apart from all the petty squabbling within the court, all manner of other dangers lurked. She remembered Song Ci's father saying that there had been many occasions when he had almost been killed by a criminal he was trying to track down, and if it hadn't been for Song Xie, he would have met his death alone and far from home. That was when Yulan remembered Tong Gong.

"Why don't you take Tong Gong with you? He's become quite an expert in martial arts over the years."

"I can't do that. Provincial registrars aren't permitted to have attendants."

This upset Yulan, and her eyes reddened.

"You just have to wait a bit. Once I get to be a magistrate, then you, and mother and Song Qi can all join me. We'll get Tong Gong to escort you then."

The day of departure dawned. Yulan and Madame Song bought the wine for Song Ci's farewell dinner. The whole household, including the maids and man-servants, all sat round the table.

Madame Song had aged quickly over the last ten years. Although she was not much over 60, her ash-grey hair hung loose down her cheeks, already thinning, and her forehead was speckled with liver spots. She had lost many teeth, and the buxom charms of her youth had all disappeared. After the death of her husband, Song Gong, she often felt lonely and abandoned, and this tended to make her touchy and perverse. Her particular resentment centred on her daughter-in-law's failure to provide a son, and she would often fly off the handle for no apparent reason. Now Song Ci was about to leave his aged mother, he was deeply worried but couldn't quite put his finger on why.

Song Ci had spent all his youth and early childhood in the company of his mother. While his father had been posted to distant parts, it was his mother who had raised him. He had forgotten much of what had happened during his childhood, but there was one thing he always remembered quite clearly, and that was how much both he and his mother missed his father. It was a deep and indefinable feeling, an almost mystical longing. He didn't know in which part of the country his father might be, only that he was serving the emperor with the army far away. The pear trees in the courtyard had blossomed and fruited, and he and his mother made sure they kept most of the pears for his father's return. Countless evenings and nights had passed with him sitting at his mother's knee, listening entranced to her telling oft-repeated stories about his father's exploits and then gradually falling asleep. And countless beautiful mornings too, when he and his mother had walked slowly down to the little stone bridge in front of their gate, and sadly watched the wild geese and other birds flying across the empty sky, vainly hoping to see his father appear on the distant horizon. But his father never did appear. Once, when he was four, his mother taught him Du Fu's poem *Waiting for Spring*. Then, when they went on to *A Letter Home is Worth Ten Thousand Pieces of Gold*, he suddenly asked: "Has father sent any letters home?"

"He has," his mother replied. "It's a shame you can only recite poetry and can't read and write yet."

From then on, he began to learn his characters with his mother. Now, forty years on, all he did was read, as though there was nothing else he should be doing for the household. Even though the family was in straitened circumstances, short of money for daily necessities, he really couldn't say he was doing anything constructive for it. Over those same forty years, his mother had dedicated herself heart and soul to him, consecrating her life's blood to him. But what of him? Had he ever been as considerate of his mother's difficulties and sorrows as she had been of his? Had he ever done anything to try to assuage his mother's loneliness? And now he was about to go away himself, leaving his mother just as his father had done. How much was his mother going to miss her only son?

For years, Song Ci had been longing for an official appointment, but now the dreadful day of parting had come, he did not know what to say to his mother, how to console her... but then, his mother stood up, smiling, raised the wine cup her daughter-in-law had filled and, trembling slightly, offered it to her son.

"Ci, my son, a man's duty is a mother's good fortune. You must fulfil that duty with all your heart. Your father has passed on to the Nine Springs of the Underworld, but even so he rejoices. Come, my son, drink this cup of wine from your mother. Put aside your worries, this is no time for heavy hearts."

Song Ci took the wine cup and put it to his lips. As his tears fell into the dark red wine, he drank it to the last drop.

Yulan, who never drank herself, took the wine jug and refilled her husband's cup to the brim. As she offered it to him, she looked at him with eyes filling with tears. What could she say to her husband who was so soon to be parted from her?

Her heart was full of a thousand things she wanted to say, but as she looked in a daze at her husband, she didn't know where to start. Perhaps it would be better to say nothing, she thought, staring blankly. Then she said, very softly: "Drink up."

Song Ci took the cup and drained it again. His wife took the cup from him, refilled it, and, without saying a word, put it to her lips and drank.

Liu Kezhuang had also bought some wine to toast Song Ci on his way, and he escorted him ten *li* out of the west gate of the city to the pavilion specially built for receiving officials. Song was going to take the post-road through Shaowu County to Jiangxi, and just as the two old friends were about to part, they suddenly heard the sound of approaching hoofbeats. A horse came galloping along the road and astride it was Tong Gong. He rolled out of the saddle, knelt in front of Song Ci and said: "Master, take me with you."

"How is it that you are here?" Song Ci asked.

"Master Song Xie told me to come."

"How did he know?"

Tong Gong hesitated and said nothing.

"It's... it's Tong Gong, isn't it?" Liu Kezhuang asked.

"It is!" Song Ci replied.

"Bring the wine," Liu ordered his attendant in a loud voice.

Liu poured three cups of wine, offered two of them to the others and, keeping one himself, said: "Come, come, come. How can you refuse such a loyal and valiant man who truly deserves to be asked to join us?"

Song Ci took the cup of wine that Liu was offering to Tong Gong and gave it to him himself, saying: "All right then. Get up!"

The three silver wine cups touched together in a toast with a crisp, clear ringing sound.

In fact, Song Ci had anticipated Tong Gong's arrival. He knew quite well that his wife would have sent someone to take the news of his appointment to Mount Lianyuan and that Song Xie would then dispatch Tong Gong. Since this was the case, he said nothing and just waited for Tong Gong to arrive. This is how it came about that Song Ci took Tong Gong with him as he set out to take up his official duties. By then it was 1226, the second year of the Baoqing period of the reign of Emperor Lizong. At the age of forty, Song Ci finally began his career proper as a government official.

Several weeks after he left home, a totally unexpected event occurred – Qiu Juan came home. In the middle of the night seven years before, Qiu Juan had returned to the Song house, covered in bloodstains, confessing to the murder of Chai Wanlong, and to setting fire to his house. Greatly alarmed, Song and his wife took her in and hid her. Qiu Juan was afraid of implicating the Song family in her crimes and left after only a few days, without saying goodbye, and the Songs lost track of her thereafter. Seven years later, she had now reappeared, and Madame and Mistress Song were even more alarmed than before. The young woman's strength of character in enduring disgrace and shouldering heavy responsibilities was clearly exceptional. She had heard about Song Ci's departure to take up office and had thought that some of the other members of the Song household might be in need of care and attention. So there she was...

# CHAPTER VI

## PERSONAL INVESTIGATION (1226)

Forensic medical examination in China has its roots in the Spring and Autumn period (771-476 BCE), earlier than anywhere else in the world. Through the Han and Tang dynasties and into the Song, the system advanced significantly; specifically, the responsibilities of the investigating official and the scope of the initial examination were established by law, as were the circumstances for secondary examination and those when examination was not required. Also established were the framework for autopsy along with the complete set of body charts and other documentation. None of this, however, was proof against corruption, and if the investigating official was bribed by the accused, a miscarriage of justice always ensued. In 1226, Song Ci is in post as the registrar for Xinfeng County in Jiangxi. Although he is full of scholarly knowledge about judicial matters, this knowledge has yet to be tested in earnest...

# 1

## SMOKE FROM AN INCENSE BURNER

Xinfeng is situated in the south of Jiangxi Province, on the banks of the Taoshui River. Its climate is warmer than in Jianyang, but just as rainy. Song Ci and Tong Gong didn't encounter a single dry day on the road there. But on their arrival the sky cleared, and the hillsides were ablaze with the deep red of Indian azaleas.

Magistrate Shan Zilin read Liu Kezhuang's letter with great pleasure, and he called all the administration staff in to meet Song Ci. Magistrate Shan was in his early forties. His square face was lively and alert, his expression genial; his eyebrows were short and thick, and slanted upwards like the character for 'eight', 八. The overall effect was one of great vitality. Song Ci couldn't help remembering that Liu Kezhuang had told him Shan Zilin was a hereditary official – "not a brilliant administrator, but an honest and genuine man".

The place was soon crowded with all the court staff, and Magistrate Shan began by introducing Song Ci to everyone. One by one, the county deputy Zhou Anping, the sheriff Huang Jintai, the clerk of the court Lü Gui'er, the head bailiff Cao Ruteng and several others were all made known to him. A little later, after the hubbub had died down, Magistrate Shan called in one of the officials who was standing in the doorway: "This is our county coroner. His name is Yuan Gong. Instant autopsies are always nasty, messy things, and he has cleared up quite a few difficult cases for us."

Yuan Gong was about thirty years old, powerfully built and dark-complexioned. It was the coroner's responsibility to arrange the transport of bodies and to record the injuries. Normally this is a low-ranking function in the *yamen*, but Magistrate Shan showed considerable respect to the man. This made Song Ci think of something else Liu Kezhuang had said about him: "As an administrator he may not be the best organiser, but he knows how to listen to other people."

That evening, Shan Zilin held a banquet in honour of Song's arrival, and after the wine had been round three times, the magistrate was quite red in the face and had become very talkative. Perhaps because he remembered something complimentary Liu Kezhuang had written about Song Ci in his letter, he said: "Qianfu says you are a man of great talent and ambition. I can see..."

"To my great shame," Song Ci interrupted, "I have frittered away many years achieving nothing. Now I am here, I shall always look to Your Honour for guidance."

"Not at all, not at all!" Magistrate Shan pointed at some of those who were sitting at the table, the county deputy, the prison sheriff, the court recorder and others. "But there are a number of other very capable colleagues here in the *yamen*, and they keep the region in excellent order."

The county deputy Zhou Anping picked up the story: "The Xinfeng region has had full coffers over the last few years, and the army is well provisioned. That is all down to Magistrate Shan's good management."

"You are too kind," Shan said, blushing. "In fact, the people of Xinfeng are straightforward, frugal and hard-working, and that's why they are self-sufficient."

Huang Jintai, the prison sheriff chipped in: "When Magistrate Shan first arrived, there were a lot of bad elements, but he soon put a stop to them. He handed out severe punishments and showed no-one any favours, so now the number of disputes has fallen dramatically."

As the banquet continued, Song Ci noticed that the clerk of the court, Lü Gui'er, smiled a lot but said very little. The dinner continued in this convivial atmosphere, with the wine flowing freely, for another couple of hours. Song soon had a clear idea of the state of things both in Xinfeng and in the *yamen* itself. He could see Shan Zilin's genuine concern for the people under him, and he found himself agreeing completely with Liu Kezhuang's assessment of the man as both honest and genuine.

After the Qingming festival, the weather in southern Jiangxi was getting warmer by the day. A few leisurely white clouds drifted across the sky, and the silky willow fronds hung silently over the riverbanks, all with irresistibly soporific effect. Everywhere was quiet and peaceful. A month had passed since his arrival almost without Song Ci noticing, and apart from a few run-of-the-mill, undemanding cases, no serious or complicated litigation appeared before the court. He began to find his duties rather boring. Then, out of the blue, someone came and struck the court drum to demand attention. The supplicant was an old man, and when he was brought in front of Magistrate Shan, he knelt, huffing and puffing, and said: "I have found two dead bodies outside the city at Kuzhuping in the southern mountains."

"Did you recognise them?" Shan Zilin asked.

"Yes, yes, I did recognise them. They are fellow villagers of mine who went up the mountain to clear some land for planting yesterday, and they met their deaths there."

"Did you find them yesterday?"

"No, I found them this morning."

"Didn't anyone go looking for them last night?"

"There was no call to."

"Why not?"

"The place they were going is a long way from the village, and they were planning to spend several days there."

"How did you come to discover them?"

"I have some land there, too, and I went up there this morning. I didn't expect to find two corpses!"

"What connection with the dead men led you come to court today?"

"No special connection. They were just neighbours of mine."

"Did the dead men have any relatives?"

"They did."

"Why didn't they come to report the matter themselves?"

"In one family there is only a newly married young wife, and in the other, only the man's old father, who is not well. That's why they asked me to come and make the report."

It was mid-morning by this time, and once Magistrate Shan had got the facts of the situation clear, he sent one of the *yamen* staff out of the city to investigate. Song Ci asked the old man some further questions: "Where are the dead men's relatives now?"

"They've gone off to the mountain," the old man replied.

Song Ci turned to Magistrate Shan: "In that case, please send an express messenger to the mountain to preserve the scene."

"Very well," Shan agreed.

The deaths had taken place on an, as yet, uncultivated mountain about twenty *li* from the city along the south road, and it was past midday before Magistrate Shan reached there. The scene of the incident was a newly reclaimed patch of land, on which, some distance from each other, were lying two hoes and a tea jar, its mouth covered with a tea bowl. Not far away was a small thatched shack used for sleeping and storing ash from the land clearance. Of the two corpses, one was lying in front of the hut, and the other was inside. When Shan arrived, the relatives of the two dead men, who had been kept some distance away from the scene, stopped their tears. He immediately ordered an examination of the bodies, and a thorough investigation of the *locus in quo*. Yuan Gong took out a small incense burner, put it down a few feet away from the corpses on the ground and lit some sandalwood in it.

"If you want to get rid of the corpse stench, you should use *atractylodes rhizome* and honey locust. Why are you burning sandalwood?" Song Ci asked.

"I know that is what the ancient texts say, but sandalwood smells much better," Magistrate Shan replied, with a smile.

The *yamen* attendants brought two wooden stools and put them down close to the incense burner. Magistrate Shan was the first to sit down, and then he turned to Song Ci, who was carrying the body charts, front and back, on which to record their findings: "Don't get too close. Come over and sit down here to write."

Grateful for Shan's concern, Song Ci did as he was bid. The incense burner was well alight by then, and a rich, strong smell of sandalwood was being carried towards them on the breeze. Yuan Gong stood up from beside the burner, took out a lump of fresh ginger root and put it in the side of his mouth without chewing it. Then he produced a small narrow-necked bottle, removed the stopper, poured out a small amount of scented oil and anointed the tip of his nose with it. He gave the bottle to the two other *yamen* officers appointed to inspect the bodies and then himself went over to the corpses. The two officers took the bottle, twisted some straw paper into wicks, soaked them in the oil, plugged them into their nostrils and followed Yuan over to the bodies. As they made their way over to the front of the shack, the efficient Yuan Gong had already brought out the body that was inside the hut, and, in the bright sunlight, the three of them began to examine the corpses. They began with the short, rather slight body of the man who had died outside the shack.

"Hair in a loose topknot... no injury to the crown of the head... four-inch knife wound to the left side of the forehead, laying open skin and flesh..." Yuan Gong called out his findings in a loud voice and Song Ci recorded them verbatim.

After the examination of the body, the whole scene was carefully searched, but nothing could be found to indicate the presence of a third party. The next stage was to determine the cause of death according to the findings of the examination. Magistrate Shan scrutinised the completed body charts, pondered for a while and addressed the assembled company: "Well everyone, how do you think he died?"

After a moment's silence, the county deputy, Zhou Anping, said: "There are a number of knife wounds on the body. I believe he was stabbed to death by persons unknown."

"I agree," Sheriff Huang piped up.

"And what do you think?" Magistrate Shan asked Song Ci.

It was the first time Song had assisted in an affair like this, and he didn't hurry to reply. He remembered Magistrate Shan saying that Yuan Gong had solved many problematic cases, so he turned to him where he was standing a little apart from the others and asked: "What do you think?"

Yuan Gong wiped his nose on his forearm, thought for a moment and seemed about to speak. But then he looked at the county deputy, who had just voiced his opinion, and at the court recorder and the sheriff, and said nothing.

"Speak up!" Magistrate Shan said impatiently.

Yuan Gong still hesitated and then said softly: "I think these two men died after fighting each other."

Song Ci stared hard at Yuan Gong.

The county deputy and the sheriff both exclaimed at the same time: "What makes you say that?"

Yuan Gong replied: "Three reasons. Number one, although there are many knife wounds on both bodies, on the body of the taller man who died inside the hut, there is a three-inch knife wound to the left side of the neck. It is deep at the entry point and shallow at the other end – this is a suicide wound. Moreover, in his right hand, which was his knife hand, there is a blood trail flowing from the *he gu*[1] to the *qu chi*[2] acupuncture points. This is evidently the result of the fresh blood flow from the wound in the neck. Number two, the wounds on the bodies were made by wood-cutter's knives, and there are just such blood-stained knives beside both bodies. The edges of the blades have nicks in them which are the result of knife-to-knife fighting. Number three, the two deceased were here clearing land on the mountain side and weren't carrying any money, so it is highly unlikely they were murdered in the course of a robbery. Besides, the few catties of rice they brought with them to eat are still in the shack. Thus, I can't help but conclude that these two men quarrelled, over business most likely, and came to blows. One killed the other and then committed suicide out of fear of the consequences."

Sheriff Huang Jintai said: "I think we need to give this some more consideration." The lesser officials all murmured in agreement.

Magistrate Shan thought for a while before seeking Song Ci's opinion: "And what do you think happened?"

Song Ci thought it would be inappropriate to stay quiet, but what to say? Yuan Gong's conclusions were quite reasonable; a point of view he had not reached after listening to Yuan's exposition, but when he was filling in the body charts. But apart from that, what still needed to be considered, he felt, was that even if the two men had quarrelled, would it necessarily have led to such a vicious fight. And if it had, what was the cause? In that case, they needed to make a close examination of the two men's daily lives, which would take some time. Having reached this conclusion, he said: "Given the results of the examination, this seems to be the correct interpretation."

Magistrate Shan raised his eyebrows at this, as though he had some suspicion of Song Ci's bland agreement with the others. But, he thought to himself, perhaps these were indeed the facts of the case, so why make further enquiries? He then asked the county deputy, the sheriff and all the others whether anyone had any other interpretation that contradicted Yuan Gong's findings. They all looked at one another but no one spoke, so Magistrate Shan declared the case closed on that basis.

Once again, Song Ci remembered Liu Kezhuang's words: "As an official, Shan Zilin never equivocates and is firm in his decisions." But, he thought, there is something a little too 'firm' about this decision. He wanted to say he thought it had all happened too quickly, and that the verdict might be a little premature, but he said nothing.

The relatives of the two deceased, along with a small crowd of fellow villagers, who were being held at a distance by the *yamen* guards, were all looking on eagerly waiting for the magistrate's decision. When it was relayed to the relatives, everyone was shocked. There was a moment's silence, then one young woman burst into wails of anguish and, shrugging off two elderly female villagers who were supporting her, rushed over to Magistrate Shan and fell to her knees in front of him. Through her tears, she cried out: "No! No! It's not possible! Great Father, my husband had no quarrel with that man. They couldn't have fought each other like that. They couldn't." She wailed mournfully.

The woman's name was Qiu, and she was the wife of the man deemed in the verdict to have committed suicide. An old man with a wan and sallow complexion and greying hair also staggered forward and knelt in front of the magistrate, wailing: "My son... it's not possible... not possible. Please reconsider. Catch the murderer... for my son's sake... for Mistress Qiu's husband's sake... avenge them!"

Magistrate Shan was greatly embarrassed by this display of grief. But since the verdict had been reached, what could he do? Normally so forthright, he became tongue-tied and didn't know how to explain the matter clearly to these grief-stricken villagers. Even though they had not initially fully agreed with the verdict, County Deputy Zhou Anping, Sheriff Huang Jintai and the others all hurried forward to explain, and they were joined by area and village functionaries, and neighbours, all offering consolations and commiserations. This saved Magistrate Shan from having to find the right words himself.

When Tong Gong arrived in Xinfeng with his master, he had been given a supplementary post in the *yamen*, and he was among the party that had come to examine the bodies. He now went over to a nearby bamboo grove and cut down several mid-size canes, all of the same length. Then, using his former skills as a maker of basket staves, he swiftly fashioned two lattice frames, on which the villagers placed both corpses and carried them down the mountain.

2

## ONE NIGHT

The late spring evenings in southern Jiangxi had lost the chill of early spring, but were not yet properly warm. The southerly wind blowing in off the Taoshui River kept the whole area fresh and clear, but cool. It was the best season of the year for restful sleep. But that evening neither Song Ci nor Tong Gong were asleep, kept awake, as they lay in the same room, by thoughts of what had passed that day. Tong Gong's ears were still full of the keening and weeping of the young wife and the elderly father, and in the end, he had to ask Song Ci: "Master, did those two men really fight to the death?"

"Unless there is something we don't know, that must be what happened."

"In that case, might there be something we don't know?"

"It's hard to imagine. If the verdict from the examination differed from the original report or from a verbal confession, then that would be immediately obvious. Or if there was an eyewitness who could say 'This is what I saw for myself', that too would be something we could rely on. But I just think…"

"What do you think?" Tong Gong interrupted excitedly.

"If they did fight to the death, then it must have been for some quite extraordinary reason. And that reason could well involve a third party, whether or not he was present at the time of the fight. In addition, the taller of the two men, whether or not he killed the other one, would he really kill himself out of fear of the consequences? Might there not have been someone else who forced his hand?"

"Why didn't you say so at the time?" Tong Gong suddenly sat up in bed and fixed Song Ci with his gaze in the faint starlight that was filtering in through the window.

In the dark, Song Ci felt Tong Gong's censorious gaze fixed upon him and knew that this perspicacious, forthright and courageous young man understood he was holding something back. But in handling a criminal case, just trusting in this excellent young man was not enough. Then he thought about how Tong Gong had followed him so faithfully, and he suddenly realised that if he was going to continue to rely on the young man, he needed to educate him. So he turned to Tong Gong and said: "I'm going to tell you about an ancient case that will help you understand." Tong Gong waited expectantly in the gloom.

Song continued: "This case is recorded in the account of Liu Zhenghui in the *New History of the Tang Dynasty*. The judge in the case was an official of the Tang dynasty called Liu Chonggui. He held many posts including domestic secretary, director of the Bureau of Military Affairs, vice-minister in the Bureau of Finance, chief secretary for financial review in the same ministry and governor of Guangzhou. At the time of this particular case, he was in charge of the Garrison of the Southern Seas..."

"Where are the Southern Seas?" Tong Gong interrupted.

"It's another name for Guangzhou. Liu Chonggui was a senior official in charge of the navy in Guangzhou, a very important post in the defence of the empire. One day a case came his way involving a young woman from Jiang'an who was killed in her own home. Her family members found the scene covered in blood, and they followed the blood trail to the banks of the river, where it disappeared. They then went and reported the matter to the local officials. Liu Chonggui sent someone to question the residents of Jiang'an, who reported that recently there had been a visiting vessel moored on the riverbank, which had suddenly departed the night before. Liu sent an officer in pursuit of the boat and he detained its captain, who turned out to be the son of a rich merchant. The young man was handsome and dressed in very expensive clothes. The story he told the court when he was taken there was that, on the day in question, he had been on the riverbank where his boat was moored, and he saw a young woman of quite bewitching beauty in the doorway of a fine house nearby. Encouraged by the fact that she didn't turn away when he stared at her, he called out to her: 'I am going to come to your house tonight.' On hearing this, the young woman didn't blush at all, but just smiled faintly.

"That night, the young man did just as he had promised, and when he got to the house found the door was unlocked, and it opened with a single push. He went in, but as soon as he was through the door, he trod in something liquid and slipped. At first he thought it was water, but when he felt it with his hand, he caught the smell of blood. That was when he discovered there was a body lying on the ground, and he could hear the sound of dripping blood. He panicked and ran away immediately, and once back at his boat, cast off and sailed away.

"Now the thing is, beside the girl's body there was a butcher's knife, the kind used for slaughtering livestock, and what would the son of a rich merchant be doing with a knife like that? So Liu Chonggui kept the young man in jail, while at the same time he started searching for the real murderer. He devised a clever plan that involved taking a condemned man from the cells and having him beheaded, pretending he was the merchant's son. This gave the impression that the case was all settled. The real killer, who had gone into hiding, relaxed, and with a bit of effort, Liu Chonggui soon found him and had him arrested."

Song Ci stopped at this point and hadn't intended to go on, but Tong Gong was fascinated by the case, and he asked: "So who was the real murderer?"

"It was a burglar," Song Ci replied. "He had gone to rob the young beauty's house that night. He saw that there was no light on, and the door opened at a push – that was because the girl had unlocked it in anticipation of the young man's arrival. So, when the girl saw there was someone coming in through the door in the dark, she thought it was the young man and ran over to greet him. The robber thought someone was coming to grab him and struck out with his knife, catching the approaching figure in the neck. In the confusion, he dropped his knife, made to look for it, but heard footsteps outside the door. Afraid of being captured, he fled.

"Well then, I haven't gone into all details of the case, just the parts that are relevant. Do you understand now?"

Tong Gong thought about it quietly for a while and then said: "What you are saying is that, by allowing the verdict of death as the result of a fight, you are also lulling the real murderer into a false sense of security?"

"Maybe, maybe not. But the verdict will certainly help us towards uncovering the reason behind the case."

Tong Gong suddenly understood exactly why Song had kept quiet during the investigation. After another pause, he asked: "In that case, I can't quite see what your next move is."

"I think tomorrow I will have a detailed conversation with Magistrate Shan and ask him to let me leave the city incognito and ask around a bit, to see if I can find any new information."

"Then you had better take me with you," Tong Gong said.

"Of course. But that's enough talking, let's go to bed."

The two men fell silent. Quite soon, Song Ci heard the sound of deep, even breathing coming from the bed on the other side of the room. But Song himself could not get to sleep, and he lay there thinking over all aspects of the case, deep into the night. Sad to say, in the middle of that quiet night there was another development in the case that he could not possibly have foreseen: Qiu Shi, the widow of the man who it had been decided had committed suicide, herself died during the night.


The next morning, the captain of police, Cao Ruteng, came hurrying into the rear hall of the *yamen*, leading the old man who had first made the report the day before. He told Magistrate Shan about the death of Qiu Shi. Shan was greatly surprised: "What? She is dead as well? What happened?"

The old man kowtowed and said: "Today is the day of her husband's funeral, and some of us neighbours went over to help. No one opened the door when we shouted, so someone climbed over the wall and discovered her."

"How did she die?"

"We don't know. Some people think she took arsenic."

"Quickly!" ordered Captain Cao. "Assemble the *yamen* guard, and go to the scene."

The deceased woman lived in a village called Huangnicun, about ten *li* south of the city, with a population of thirty or so households. It was surrounded by arid, rocky countryside, and the yellow-coloured soil was very poor quality. The outer walls of the homesteads were all made of the same yellow mud and were topped with rush mats to protect them from the rain. When Magistrate Shan reached the village, he saw that a crowd of villagers was already clustered round the doorway, and the gate was unlocked and open. The villagers shouted at each other to make way as they saw the magistrate approaching.

Yuan Gong approached the front, pushed open the gate, and everyone followed him in. The courtyard was empty except for some birds, which were shut up in a coop and were clucking and pecking at the bars trying to get out. Going into the house itself, in the middle of the first room there was a coffin laid out ready for the funeral. On the east side was the living room, and Yuan Gong pushed aside a blue-and-white pottery screen that was in front of the door. Inside he saw Qiu Shi's body lying face up on a couch. Because, in this instance, the deceased was a woman, they had brought along a chaperone for the examination. Magistrate Shan sent Yuan Gong and the chaperone in to turn the body over and begin the examination. Qiu Shi's fine, thick hair was loose, her clothes were disordered and were very unusual in the circumstances. On her upper half she wore a red sleeveless jacket over a red damask bodice; on her lower half, a green skirt beneath which were red under-trousers and patterned, knee-length bloomers. On her feet were embroidered red shoes, and the whole effect was as eye-catching as that of a young bride, except for the lack of make-up on her face.

The chaperone removed the clothes and underclothes piece by piece and examined her breasts, genitals and anus for any sign of injury, but found nothing unusual. Then she re-covered the body and, with Yuan Gong, turned to the crown of the head, the face, the torso and every part of the arms and legs. Yuan Gong called out his findings item by item, and Song Ci recorded them. Song was already very surprised and intrigued by the nature of the young woman's death.

Even the normally rather carefree and feckless Tong Gong felt the same frisson. Although Song Ci was always Gong's prime concern, when the occasion arose he paid particular attention to what his trusted master was doing, in the hope of picking up some useful ideas. The nature of this examination had caught his interest, and when Song Ci was recording the findings on the body charts, he noticed him frown quickly. What did that mean? Yuan Gong and the chaperone soon finished the visual examination of the body. Yuan then took a silver hairpin and put it in Qiu Shi's mouth, before covering the body with the quilt that was on the couch. He picked up off the ground a broken bowl in which there were still some dregs of wine, and he came out of the room.

"Your Honour, I'm afraid this woman did indeed poison herself with arsenic. You can see traces of white arsenic in this bowl. I will test it again." So saying, he went into the kitchen.

At this point, Tong Gong saw Song Ci suddenly look at Yuan Gong, and it was no ordinary glance. In a moment, the efficient Yuan Gong returned from the kitchen. In one hand he held the bowl, in the other, a handful of rice. He made his way out into the courtyard, stirring the rice with his hand, followed by Magistrate Shan, the county deputy and all the others.

Song Ci didn't go with them, but instead went into the room where Qiu Shi was lying. Standing in front of the couch, he took the quilt off the young woman's body, and, as he looked at her, his brow suddenly furrowed deeply. After a moment's thought, he took the pillow from under the neck of the corpse, turned it over and inspected it closely. He put it back in its original position, and then went out towards the courtyard. As he passed through the outer room, he stopped to look at the coffin. Tong Gong, who had been paying close attention to his master, seemed to anticipate Song Ci's thoughts and joined him in front of the coffin. Song saw that the lid was already nailed down, and he said to Tong Gong in a low voice: "Open it!"

Tong Gong gripped one of the nails tightly in his fingers; there was a slight creaking noise, and then it came out. One by one, he prised out the remaining nails and opened the lid of the coffin. Song Ci leaned his head in and took a careful look at the corpse. Then he gestured to Tong Gong, who put the lid back on, re-inserted the nails and followed Song Ci into the courtyard.

"Shoo! Shoo!" They heard Yuan Gong's shouts in the yard. He had released the two pheasants that had been shut up in the coop, and the birds, hungry after a night without food, were pecking at the rice in Yuan Gong's bowl. But the two birds stayed put, fluttering their wings and scuttling round in circles.

"We must inspect the silver hairpin," Yuan Gong said.

"Go and get it," Magistrate Shan ordered with a wave of his sleeve.

The crowd trooped back into the house, where Yuan Gong removed the hairpin from the girl's mouth. He brewed an infusion of honey locust fruit and stirred the hairpin around in it for a while. Then he took it out, wiped it dry and gave it to Magistrate Shan, saying: "Look, Your Honour!"

They could see that part of the pin was still bright shiny silver, but the other part was now a greenish-black. Magistrate Shan let out a long breath as if to say: So, she did die of poison.

Instead, he pursed his lips and then called Zhou Anping, Song Ci and the others, and asked: "What do each of you think?"

The county deputy said nothing, but the normally reticent court recorder Lü Gui'er suddenly spoke out: "I always thought there was something fishy about her death."

"What do you mean 'fishy'?" the magistrate asked, looking at him.

"This young woman's husband died yesterday," Lü Gui'er said. "So how is it that she is not wearing plain mourning clothes but is all dressed up like a bride-to-be? I think she must have been having an affair."

"How do you come to that conclusion?" Magistrate Shan asked. "Explain!"

"If she was having an affair, then that man yesterday..."

Magistrate Shan frowned, as though he knew what Lü Gui'er was going to say next.

"Your Honour, may I say something?" interrupted Yuan Gong.

"Speak!" Shan replied.

"This young woman knew that, if she died, there would be no one left in the household. Other people would come to lay out her body, certainly, but would they feel able to change her clothes? This is not something easy to talk about, or an auspicious thing to organise in advance. So, the young lady dressed herself in her wedding clothes so that she could accompany her husband to the other side in fitting style."

"So, we are still saying she poisoned herself?" Magistrate Shan looked first at Yuan Gong, then left and right at the assembled company.

At that moment, Magistrate Shan's eyes met Song Ci's and he saw that they were burning with an inner light. He heard Song give voice to a totally contrary opinion: "This young woman did not die from poison."

Yuan Gong was shaken to the core, and he whipped his head round to look at Song Ci in a daze.

"And what is your brilliant idea then?" Magistrate Shan asked.

Song replied: "The woman's hair is loose and disordered, and her clothes are fine, but in disarray. Although this does, indeed, look like the result of death throes after taking poison, she is supposed to have died specifically from taking arsenic. Arsenic causes spasms of the stomach and intestines that results in the vomiting of foul matter. There is no sign of this beside the woman's couch. This is the first cause for doubt. In addition, as you were all coming out into the courtyard, I inspected the body for myself. There are traces of blood in the mouth and nose, and the neck and chest show a greenish-black discolouration. These are, indeed, symptoms of arsenic poisoning. But below the waist, her skin is snowy white and unblemished, and her nails are not discoloured at all. This is not consistent with death by poison."

"So how do you explain the symptoms on her upper half? Magistrate Shan asked.

"Come and see for yourself, Your Honour."

Song Ci and the magistrate went back into the house together, took the quilt from the body and also removed the red damask bodice that was covering Qiu Shi's breasts. Magistrate Shan saw the green-black discolouration on the woman's neck and chest, and how it spread downwards from the top of her breasts, but faded as it spread outwards, so that the inner surface of her breasts was lightly tinged and the outer surface was still completely white.

Song Ci said: "Immediately after death, the blood is not completely static and coagulated, so if white arsenic is introduced at this point, the poisoned air can pass through the throat into the respiratory tract and upper thorax."

"So what you are saying… the arsenic was administered after the woman had died, to simulate death by poisoning."

"That's right," Song Ci agreed.

"And according to your version, how did the young woman die?"

"Not only is there purple discolouration to her face, there are also traces of blood in her mouth and nose, and her front teeth are broken. This is consistent with her mouth and nose being smothered with something and her suffocating to death."

As he spoke, Song Ci lifted up the woman's neck, removed the pillow, and handed it to Magistrate Shan. "This is the murder weapon."

Magistrate Shan took the pillow and looked at it carefully. He saw that there were indeed tooth marks and bloodstains. "So, that's how it was," he said. "She was murdered."

"Not only her, but the two men on the mountain too," Song Ci said.

Magistrate Shan was stunned. Only now did he begin fully to understand the real weight of what Liu Kezhuang had said in his letter. He thought for a moment, then looked at Song Ci and said: "Very well. Take your time and tell me exactly how you reached this conclusion."

"Your Honour, come and take another look." Song Ci led Magistrate Shan towards the coffin, and without waiting to be ordered, Tong Gong again took out the coffin nails that he had previously loosened, and lifted the lid off the coffin. Heedless of the decay of the body, Magistrate Shan followed where Song Ci was pointing and took a long, careful look.

"I examined this body myself just now. Your Honour can see the wounds he received while he was still alive. The skin around the cuts is puckered up, there is a criss-cross pattern and bloodstains on every side – these are the indications of wounds made in living flesh. But look at the difference with the knife wound in the neck."

Magistrate Shan looked intently, as though having difficulty making out any difference. He pursed his lips and said: "I'm looking – go on!"

"Take this knife wound. It's very neat and even, the skin has not contracted, there is negligible blood flow and no blood tracks from its end. These are the marks of a knife wound faked after death."

"Ah!" Magistrate Shan exclaimed as he came to understand Song Ci's explanation.

"And if the man who faked the knife wound wasn't the murderer, then who else could it possibly be?"

Magistrate Shan was too taken aback to say anything.

"Now have another look at the head. On the crown, hidden by the hair, there is a deep wound penetrating the skull. This was the fatal blow, struck with a knife, without warning, from behind by the murderer. That is what killed him."

"So, the murderer..." Magistrate Shan seemed to be waking abruptly from a dream.

Song Ci turned and pointed to Yuan Gong: "You can ask him!"

"Me?" Yuan Gong cried out in surprise.

"Yes, you! When you called out your findings as you examined the body, you should have been reporting what you actually found. So why did you lie?"

"Lie?" Yuan Gong shook his head. "I... I didn't know..."

"But this is all common knowledge. You spent the last two days making a careful and meticulous examination. How could you not have known?" Song

Ci's eyes bored into Yuan Gong as he continued: "Not only did you know – it was you who made that post-mortem knife wound!"

Yuan Gong was thrown into confusion and said shakily: "My Lord Registrar, sir, how can you say that? I… how could I dare?"

Song Ci replied quite gently: "If the murderer had wanted to make this wound, he would have struck before the last breath had left the body and before it had gone cold. In that way, it would have looked the same as the blows struck when the victim was still alive. But this wound was clearly made post-mortem, when the body was already cold and in rigor.

"Let us also consider, how could the murderer come back here, far from the scene of the original crime, to strike another blow? It takes no great thought to see that such an act was unnecessary. Without this wound, it would still have looked as though the men had fought and that he had bled to death. You made the new wound because you thought it would cover up the presence of a third party, and support the verdict that there had been a fight to the death between the two of them. In fact, in adding the wound, you were 'painting legs on the snake'."[1]

"My Lord, I… I was in company all that day. Even when I was examining the body, there were three others with me. How could I have made the wound?"

Song Ci saw he still needed to spell things out, so he continued: "As everyone will recall, you went into the grass shack alone, and in there was a wood-cutter's knife lying on the ground beside the body. Thus it was all too easy for you to use that knife to make the cut on his neck, before you brought the body out of the hut."

Yuan Gong hung his head and said nothing. He couldn't look Song Ci in the eye.

This was a totally unexpected development from Magistrate's Shan's point of view. In the past, the *yamen* staff had been rather condescending towards Yuan Gong, but previous magistrates had begun to take notice of his talents. No one, however, had suspected just what a base creature he actually was. All of a sudden, Magistrate Shan found himself incapable of knowing what to do next.

"Your Honour," Song Ci said. "The decision now is straightforward. These three people were all killed by the same person, or the same gang, and they all had some connection with Yuan Gong. If you arrest him, it will lead you to the murderer."

Magistrate Shan nodded his head as his mind cleared. He looked up and stared furiously at Yuan Gong. In a fearsome voice, he ordered: "Arrest him and take him back to the *yamen*."

3

# SILVER THROUGH THE WINDOW

The case was heard in the public hall of the provincial *yamen*. By now, not just Magistrate Shan, but County Deputy Zhou Anping, Sheriff Huang Jintai, Court Recorder Lü Gui'er and the others had all come to the conclusion that Song Ci was an extraordinary individual. They were in awe of his ability to see things that were hidden to others and amazed by his solution of this case in particular. The case was watertight, solid as a brick wall. All the accused could do, in the face of such a wall, was hang his head and plead guilty.

As a consequence, Song Ci was very much the centre of attention in the courtroom, and from the time Magistrate Shan uttered his first words to open the case, everyone kept looking from the accused to Song Ci, wondering what rabbit he would pull out of the hat next. Song Ci himself gave nothing away. The onlookers could have had no idea what was really going through his mind, but since he had first uncovered Yuan Gong's deception, he had, in fact, been berating himself for his own shortcomings. He deeply regretted his failure to examine the corpse for himself the previous day, as he had in the case of Zhu Mingtan back in Jianyang. Had he done so, he might have caught Yuan Gong straight away, and in that case, the young woman might still be alive. However he looked at it, he couldn't help holding himself responsible for her death.

But regrets were of no use now – the important thing was to catch the real killer currently hiding in the shadows. Song had little doubt that the trial of Yuan Gong would flush him out. He focused his whole attention on the current trial and, as he always did in such circumstances, deployed both his spirit and acuity to their utmost. The complex web of knowledge and experience he had gleaned from his study of both historical and contemporary cases now spread very wide, and in it he could find solutions to even the smallest problems. But, as he was soon to discover, his plan to catch the real murderer through Yuan Gong's trial was going to run into difficulties. Nor did these difficulties stem from an unwillingness to confess on Yuan Gong's part.

"Your Honour, the truth is I... I accepted a bribe..." These were his very first words as he knelt in front of the court.

"Who is the murderer?" Magistrate Shan asked.

"I don't know."

"Nonsense! How can you have taken a bribe without knowing the culprit?"

"Your Honour, I truly don't know."

Magistrate Shan slapped his sound block down on the desk with a bang. "So, you have the audacity to withhold information! Summon the torturers!"

Magistrate Shan showed his determination to bring the full severity of the law to bear on the case. The sound of shouting emanated from inside the *yamen*, and two of the guards appeared and laid hold of Yuan Gong.

"Just a moment," Song Ci interjected. "Your Honour, let us hear what he has to say first. It is possible that he took the bribe without knowing the culprit."

"Very well, you interrogate him!"

The two guards released Yuan Gong, who kowtowed and said: "Your Honour, the night before I examined the bodies, someone threw five taels of silver over the wall of my house..."

Bang! Magistrate Shan slammed down the block again and said angrily: "More nonsense! You risked all this for five taels of silver?"

"Your Honour, I... I haven't made myself clear..."

"Go on!"

Yuan Gong shot a glance at the court and then felt the magistrate's stern gaze upon him.

Yuan Gong thought deeply, steadied his nerve and stammered out the story of something that had happened two years before. At the time, he was living in a house in an alley in the east of the city. The house had three rooms and a small courtyard, and was occupied only by him and his family. There were three generations living together, and because his wife, whose family name was You, was a large and domineering woman, he was more than somewhat hen-pecked. One night, he and his wife were sleeping drunkenly in their room, when his wife suddenly cried out and clutched hold of him. He woke up and realised that his wife was speechless with terror and pointing at the room's pivot window. He was surprised to see it swinging backwards and forwards. As he stood up, he heard the sound of something falling off the bed onto the floor. He looked down and could just make out that it was a money bag of some kind. He jumped from the bed and looked for a flint to light the lamp. In the lamplight he could see that it was, in fact, a fine silk scarf tied up into a kind of purse. When he opened it and looked inside, he saw a bag of silver and a dagger that gleamed in the lamplight. His wife started trembling uncontrollably with fear, and she clutched him even tighter than before. Yuan Gong, too, was stunned. He freed himself from his wife's embrace and went outside to look around.

It was just before dawn, and the moon was sinking in the west. There was no one to be seen in the quiet moonlight, just an old tree that cast a deep shadow, and behind the tree, a high wall. Yuan and his wife were too worried about what might happen next to go back to sleep. Quite soon, after the sun had fully risen, one of the *yamen* guards came to summon Yuan to examine a body. The death had been reported by a servant from the household of the local millionaire, Old Man Feng – it was Feng's wife, Mistress Yang.

"Old Man Feng?" When he heard the name, Magistrate Shan couldn't help interrupting.

"That's right. Your Honour will remember that, as soon as I arrived at the *yamen*, I accompanied you to go and examine the body. Mistress Yang lived in the apartments on the east side of the mansion. When we went in, Your Honour couldn't help remarking on the fact that the furnishings of Mistress Yang's rooms were not at all in keeping with Old Man Feng's wealth and status. The bamboo curtains in front of the windows were covered in dust and looked as though they hadn't been raised in a long time. The bed canopy was old and faded, and the make-up table was empty, except for a bronze mirror that had fallen over. When we saw Mistress Yang's body, she was lying on the bed, her hair loose and disordered, her clothes in disarray, shoes on her feet…"

"Just the same circumstances as the body of the young woman we examined yesterday?" Song Ci interjected.

"Very much the same. The difference was, Mistress Yang was wearing her everyday clothes, whereas the young woman was all dressed up."

"Go on."

"I couldn't determine the cause of death from my examination, but I could see that someone had put white arsenic in her mouth to make it look as though she had taken poison. I thought about the purse of silver that had appeared the night before and knew it wasn't likely that someone was just giving me money for no reason. It had to be the culprit in this case trying to bribe me."

"Hold on a minute," Song Ci again interrupted. "How could you be so sure someone was trying to bribe you? Weren't you afraid it might be someone trying to set you up and frame you?"

"No, that wasn't possible," Yuan Gong replied. "In general, I was a very lowly official, dealing with rotting corpses and not respected by the rest of the staff – but in court, it was a different matter. When rich families came to court, they would try to curry favour and certainly wouldn't scruple to offer substantial bribes."

"Go on."

Yuan Gong looked at Song Ci, then at Magistrate Shan. By now, his confession had become solely directed at those two men.

"At that point, I went outside to look around, and I saw Your Honour over by the gate, talking to Old Man Feng. I could see that he didn't seem particularly upset, and that standing beside him was a very beautiful young concubine, with a complexion like white jade. And I thought to myself that, although Mistress Yang was the principal wife, she was already past forty, and her charms had faded. Moreover, she hadn't borne any children, not even a daughter. Old Man Feng had three concubines, and if perhaps there had been some discord between them and Mistress Yang, didn't that explain the latter's death?

"I also remembered that Old Man Feng was one of the town's richest men, and that he had a son by one of his concubines who was already in an official post. I knew that he was a close acquaintance of Your Honour, and I was wary of the consequences if I began to make waves. What is more…"

"Spit it out!"

"What is more, there was also a dagger in that money bag, and I knew what that meant – if I didn't take the bribe, sometime, somewhere, somehow, that dagger would… that dagger would be used on me. So what else could I do but go along with what they wanted and fake my finding of death by self-administered poison?"

Bang! On hearing this, Magistrate Shan slammed the sound block again, and he roared at Yuan Gong: "So you took the money and deceived this court. You knew the penalty – weren't you afraid of being executed?"

"I… it's just that… it's just that…" Yuan Gong mumbled.

"It's just that what?"

"It's… it's…"

"Speak!"

"It's just that Your Honour was present at the autopsy, and you know that it is said the smell of smoke clings to anyone near it. You were in charge of the proceedings and allowed me to make my report. So if I faked my findings, it wouldn't be difficult…"

Magistrate Shan was completely taken aback. Fortunately, he had considerable self-control, and he did not lose his temper easily. He just remained speechless for some time.

"So you are saying that the murderer came from the Feng household?" Song Ci followed up.

"No!" Yuan Gong shook his head and went on with his statement. "There were a number of further cases like this, so that each time someone threw some silver into my house, I knew that the next day I would be called on to examine a body. The thing is, though, that in these later cases, the deaths all took place outside the town. And the money that came through the window was never more than ten taels – sometimes just a handful of copper coins. I realised that the same person must be behind all these cases. If he was bribing me, he must be afraid of being tracked down – and once tracked down, he would surely be arrested. The strange thing is that I couldn't see any connection between all these other cases and the Feng household, so I am not at all certain that Mistress Yang was killed by someone from her own family."

Magistrate Shan had broken out into a sweat as he listened to all this. He had had no idea that, over the last two years, all the suicide cases he had heard that were pronounced self-immolation, or 'threw self down well' or 'jumped off cliff', were, in fact, just the same as this one! And when he thought that the murderer was still at large and unlikely to be brought to justice, he found himself sitting most uncomfortably.

He stood up and asked in a loud voice: "And you never once saw who it was who threw the money in through your window?"

"No, Your Honour. And I really didn't want to be an accomplice in shielding the culprit. I was even keen to arrest him. But the problem was that, if he was captured, he was bound to implicate me. So I thought, maybe I would catch him myself and kill him. I even had a knife ready, hidden under my pillow every night – but I never got him. Then I thought I could get away from him, and my wife and I moved in with her parents who lived right at the back of a large courtyard. I even nailed up the window shutters. Even so, that villain still managed to slip the money into my room. So the next day when I examined the body, I still had to take the lead, put up with the stench of the corpse and perjure myself for him. And now, as the gods are my witness, I have told you everything I did over the last two days, leaving nothing out, and I entreat both Your Honours to take it all into consideration."

This was a case that Song Ci would remember for the rest of his life. It was all quite beyond his previous imaginings. Clearly, Yuan Gong had made a full confession, but they still had no idea of the identity of the killer. The hearing was temporarily suspended, and after Yuan Gong had signed the confession that Song Ci had taken down, he was led back to jail. Magistrate Shan looked earnestly at Song Ci and asked: "Brother Huifu, what do you think can be done about this case?"

Song Ci thought for a moment and said: "All we can do is keep our eyes and ears open, and explore every avenue."

"Very well," Shan said. "All the *yamen* staff are at your disposal."

"No, no! I may be able to give Your Honour some ideas, but Your Honour must give the orders."

"And do you have any ideas now?"

"I am going to take Tong Gong with me to Huangnicun to make some enquiries."

4

# ENQUIRIES AT HUANGNICUN

No one knows when the isolated village of Huangnicun was established, but what *is* known is that the whole population, gentry and peasants, men and women, young and old alike, were all addicted to gambling. In particular, during the season between the end of the harvest and the beginning of winter, people came from far and wide to try their luck at all types of gaming in the village. The whole place was a hive of activity, with every household either touting themselves as gambling dens or advertising food and lodging. The gaming on offer was plentiful and diverse – individual bets, side bets, dice, lotteries – either seated at tables or squatting on the ground. The losers pawned their clothes and the winners drank, ate and womanised. During the years of war, many women from poor peasant families in the countryside were forced by poverty and hunger to turn to servicing the winners, though the villagers were very disapproving of this practice. And so, with winners and losers coming from all over, there was a constant flow of silver into the pockets of the villagers, and gambling had become a way of life for them.

At some point, no one knows when, the men of the village had established the convention that, much as they loved gambling, they would not bet with each other, but only provide the opportunities for visitors to do so. The women had a similar agreement. Unlike rich families, the women and children of the common folk in the village did not live secluded in upper floor apartments at the back of residences, nor again in the desolate isolation of peasant women. Whenever it was time to eat, if they didn't see their menfolk returning, they would put the food to stew in a pot, wash their hands, burn some incense for good luck and go to the gaming tables to take their husbands' place, saying: "Go home and eat – I'm here." Thereupon, the menfolk would get up and go home, and the women would take over at the table. Or perhaps the men might be on a losing streak, in which case they would get the women with their 'lucky hands' to swap places, and as often as not their luck changed.

Often, the gamblers, eyes red from lack of sleep, were not even willing to leave their game to eat, so there were women who made steamed buns, fried dumplings, green onion pancakes and suchlike to sell at the tables. If a gambler was hungry, he would slap money down on the table, and one of the women would appear and put some tasty snack in his hand. However, all the out-of-towners who came to gamble in Huangnicun knew there was a strict rule: although the women of the place were quite willing to earn some money providing night-time companionship, during the day they were even less open to any approach than women elsewhere. If anyone did try to get fresh, the alarm would sound, and all the men of the village would seize whatever weapon came to hand, and go mob-handed to the woman's defence. The lecher could be sure to receive a sound beating.

When Song Ci arrived in Huangnicun, this was all explained to him, with no attempt to hide anything. "When Mistress Qiu got married, both her parents were already dead, and she had no career of her own. She had previously worked as one of the night-time 'companions', but she stopped after the wedding." This was what the old man who had made the original report told Song Ci.

"After she married, did her family run a gambling den?" Song asked.

"They did – there isn't a single family in the village that doesn't."

"Has anything unusual happened to her family over the last few days?"

The old man's house was not in good repair – the windows were broken, the door rickety and there were missing roof tiles through which you could see the sky. Light filtered in through these gaps and dappled the floor in patches the size of hen's eggs. Looking around the room, all the furniture and fabrics were old and tatty, except for a shiny new lacquered gaming table at the top of the room. Song Ci sat at this table and explained the situation to the old farmer.

"As for any suspects among the visiting gamblers, it's hard to say. I don't think anything unusual has happened recently," the old man said.

His daughter-in-law, who was in the room with them, shook her head and said: "Well, last winter, wasn't a gambler beaten up in her house?"

"That was nothing unusual – it happens all the time." It was the woman's husband who spoke.

"What happened?" asked Song Ci.

"A gambler known as Old Gourd took a beating," the old man replied.

"Why?"

"He broke the rules."

"You need to explain."

"He was a regular at Qiu Shi's table. Sometimes he won, sometimes he lost, but that day he hit a winning streak and wouldn't leave the table. Qiu Shi tried to sell him some green onion pancakes, but he yelled out that he wanted better food and wine. So Qiu Shi went back to the kitchen to make him something. Having put together several dishes, she called to Old Gourd to come and eat. Not too long after that, Qiu Shi started yelling, and everyone rushed in to see what was the matter. There was Old Gourd, red in the face from drink, trying to force his attentions on Qiu Shi and shouting: 'I've got money... I've got money.' Money or not, it was against the rules, and the rules can't be broken, so he was given a beating. That's all there was to it."

"Was it a severe beating?"

"It wasn't light! Old Gourd couldn't walk afterwards. The villagers used his winnings to pay some people to carry him away. I don't know where he went, and no one has seen him since."

"Is it likely he would come back after a beating like that?"

"I don't see why not. He took his beating and that's that. If he wanted to come back, the villagers would be happy to see him – that's the rule, too."

"Who took part in the beating?"

"Lots of people. Anyone who was there joined in." It was the old man's son who spoke.

"Qiu Shi's husband hit him the hardest," a woman added.

"Where was Old Gourd from?"

"Somewhere along the north road, I heard."

"He was the younger son of a rich family called Hu," the old man said. "His father was a keen gambler – a long time ago, he also used to come here to play."

"What about his father now?"

"He's dead."

"How did he die?"

"He was murdered."

"Who was the killer?"

"Don't know."

"Was he ever caught?"

"Don't know."

This was all the information Song Ci gleaned from his visit to the old man's house, and it was enough to make him think Old Gourd was a lead he needed to follow up. A spot of sunlight, the size of a copper coin, filtered through the broken roof tiles onto the surface of the tea in Song Ci's bowl. He drank the tea and took his leave.

The next day, he returned to the *yamen* and reported everything he had found out to Magistrate Shan. Old Gourd was indeed the younger son of a rich family called Hu who lived out on Xinfeng's north road. They lived in a small township, bigger than Huangnicun, which also hosted gambling, but not on the same scale as its smaller counterpart. By the time Old Gourd was eight or nine, he was often to be found at the gambling dens buying food for his father, bringing drinks and, if his father was losing, running back and forth between the gaming house and home, fetching more money. And so it was that, win or lose, the family fortunes gradually diminished. Then there came an occasion when Old Gourd's father had a big win, after which he was murdered in his bed during the night and his winnings disappeared. No one was ever arrested for the crime. When Old Gourd grew up, he had inherited his father's love of gambling but not his astuteness in the fundamentals of estate management. The family got poorer by the day, until even the few remaining properties had gone. And once they were gone, it was only natural for Old Gourd to turn to gambling.

He spent his days loafing around, and by the time he had lost everything and had no work of his own to perform, he was happy to take on odd jobs such as collecting corpses, keeping watch over coffins, washing and dressing the dead, and even sounding the death knell and digging graves. Unpleasant as this work was, it did afford him the opportunity to strip any unwanted clothes from the bodies and find a patch of ground to spread them out and sell them. Some people suspected him of robbing the graves as well.

"But the crux of all this is that he was a gambler," Magistrate Shan observed.

"Indeed – a dyed-in-the-wool gambler. For the last few years he hasn't been doing any of the other work, collecting bodies and so on. But when he was on a losing streak, he always seemed to get more money from somewhere – it kept happening. As to where the money came from, people just said he had a knack of finding his way out of difficulties."

"What do you mean?"

"Well, there was one occasion when a local butcher threw a handful of copper coins at Old Gourd and told him to climb a tree to fetch down a bird's nest. Old Gourd took a deep breath, swung himself up into the tree and climbed it as easily as anything. In the blink of an eye, he had thrown down the nest and slid back down the trunk of the tree."

"So do you think Old Gourd might be a suspect in this case?"

"You decide."

"No, you tell me!" Magistrate Shan said good-humouredly.

"I think you should bring him in for questioning."

"Very well."

The problem was, Old Gourd spent his time wandering from place to place and had no fixed abode, so first they had to find him. The word was put out and searches started, until news came that Old Gourd was keeping the gaming books at a small tavern outside the east gate of the city. It was dusk when the report of his whereabouts came in, and Song Ci hurried off to the tavern with Tong Gong and some other attendants. Night had fallen when they got there, and lamplight was spilling out of the tavern, along with the laughter and curses of the gamblers. The doors were shut, but through chinks in the panels, they could see the drunken gamblers, and, standing in the banker's position, a bald-headed, middle-aged man holding a pair of wooden dice boxes, which he was in the act of shaking.

"That's Old Gourd," said the man who had brought in the report.

Old Gourd had a broad forehead and a tapering jaw with a short beard, which did indeed make him look rather like his nickname. Veins stood out on his forehead, his eyes were glinting like an eagle's and he was biting his lips. He was red in the face and shaking the dice boxes faster and faster, as though they were caught up in a whirlwind. Finally, head trembling with excitement, he stopped shaking the boxes, put them down on the table and leaned forward, glaring at the people standing around the table. He took the lids off the boxes and stared wide-eyed at the dice inside. On the instant, his body jerked and his head dropped like a chicken with its neck wrung; he started twitching uncontrollably. The other gamblers were shouting and cheering loudly enough to shake the rafters...

"In with you!" Song Ci ordered his men, and in no time Old Gourd was in Tong Gong's grasp.

5

## TAKING RESPONSIBILITY

"So as it turned out, when he ran into Old Man Feng's house that night, two years ago, he had no intention of killing anyone."

"The most unexpected things can happen!"

The trial was over. Old Gourd, bald head gleaming in the lamplight, was brought up into the courtroom, and all the *yamen* staff stared at him, studying the perpetrator of this most unusual crime. But, in fact, the case hadn't proved as difficult as some expected. The pillow, the woodcutter's knife, the dagger that had been thrown in through Yuan Gong's window, and all the other evidence, had been put in front of Old Gourd and he had had no defence; bit by bit, he confessed. His account of how he had bribed Yuan Gong tallied with what Yuan Gong himself had admitted. His account of killing the two men on the lonely mountainside, and of smothering Qiu Shi, also matched Song Ci's deductions. The audience gasped, both in admiration at Song Ci's prescience and in horrified wonder at Old Gourd's evil machinations.

After the case was over, everyone was talking it over, but Song Ci himself took his leave of Magistrate Shan, and went straight back to his lodgings. He thought about the matter and reflected that, while Old Gourd had seemed a very commonplace sort of defendant, he had committed so many hair-raising crimes and turned out to be a cold-blooded killer. What did it mean? He felt that this was a case that a good lawyer should study very carefully…

That night two years ago, sometime after the third watch, Old Gourd had crept into the Feng mansion. As he went into the inner residence, he heard the sound of women weeping and wailing, followed by a man's voice. He ignored the commotion, except for thinking what good cover it was for his burglary. He saw that the door of the eastern chamber was open, and the room itself was lit but empty of people – he slipped in. He rifled the place for a while, putting his loot into a large satchel. He swung the bag onto his back and was about to leave when he heard the sound of a woman weeping, approaching the room. It was too late to make his escape, so he hurriedly stowed the satchel under the bed, and followed it himself. While he was tucking his head in under cover, he took a last look round, and his eyes fell on a large wicker chest with its lid still open. He scrambled up to close it, but just as he reached the basket, the footsteps also reached the doorway. He had no time to get back under the bed, so, thinking quickly, he climbed into the chest and pulled the lid back down. As the lid settled into place, Old Gourd heard the 'click' of the room door being locked. He couldn't be sure whether or not the woman had caught a glimpse of him, and he huddled inside the chest, trembling. But when he heard the sound of continued weeping, he realised he hadn't been seen, and he let out a sigh of relief. Then, to his consternation, as well as the tears, he also heard the sound of footsteps coming over and stopping in front of the chest.

Damn, he thought to himself, not daring to breathe. Then he heard the woman's hand on the bronze latch of the chest, and he froze in terror. Before he could think what to do next, the lid began to open. Acting on instinct, Old Gourd shot up out of the chest, and as he did so, he heard a faint gasp from the woman and saw her fall to the ground. When he recovered from the surprise, he bent down to look at the woman who was lying there on the floor, and what he saw shocked him rigid. He had laid out many people who had died from various causes, but he had never seen eyes bulging with fear in such an unearthly expression. Dead? he thought to himself. Then he stretched out his hand over the woman's mouth and nose to feel for breathing. She's gone, not a trace of a breath, he concluded. Old Gourd was still rigid with fear, and the room felt as though it was closing in on him. He had just killed someone – he had taken a living woman and scared her to death! Through his terror, he heard the sound of someone else approaching and stopping outside the door.

Then a voice said: "Mistress! Mistress!" It was the voice of a maid, calling out very softly, as though she was afraid of being discovered. Old Gourd wanted to go and blow out the lamp, but it was as though his feet were nailed to the floor in fright, and he couldn't move. It was several moments before he was able to make his way over and put out the light with a muffled 'huff'.

"Mistress! You must take care of yourself. Open the door. The Master ordered me to bring you some ginseng tea."

Old Gourd hid himself again and held his breath. The maid called out once more, then waited; then waited and called out again. He couldn't tell how long it was before she finally heaved a sigh and went away. Old Gourd cautiously emerged from under the bed, soaked with sweat. It was a bright, moonlit night, and light was filtering in through the slats of the bamboo shutters, casting a silvery radiance over the room. Looking round, he noticed that there was a box of fine white powder on the dressing-table. He quietly made his way over and lifted up the box to smell the powder. Then he took it over to the window to examine it more carefully. He was right – it was white arsenic!

"She must have been planning to kill herself," he thought. Then he noticed that, on the dressing table, there was also a wine jug and a small cup that was half full of wine.

That must be it! Old Gourd had laid out the corpses of suicides before, and he knew that, as the time approached, many of them changed into their best, most auspicious clothes in which to greet death. That must have been why the woman was opening the chest. She really was going to kill herself.

This thought made him feel much better. Then, as he had done so often before with other bodies, he gently lifted the woman off the floor and laid her out on the bed. After a moment's thought, he mixed some of the arsenic into the wine, then he pressed gently on the *qi chi* acupuncture point to open her tightly closed lips, and, pressing more firmly on the *tian tu* point,[1] he poured some of the wine down her throat. He accomplished the task with ease, as it was one of the tricks of the trade of all undertakers. Very often, after the deceased had been washed and laid out, the family wanted to have some wine poured down their throat and a triple hard-boiled egg placed in their mouth.

When he had finished, Old Gourd realised he couldn't bring himself to keep the clothes he had stuffed into his satchel, and he pulled the chest back out from under the bed where he had stowed it, and put them back. However, he was unable to resist the gold and silver jewellery, and he put that into a smaller bag and made off. Fear set back in when he reached home. He had seen people who had died from arsenic poison, and he knew what they looked like. While his faking might deceive ordinary folk, he didn't think it would fool the specialist official who conducted autopsies for the *yamen*.

What to do? He thought hard and finally remembered a story he had heard about someone fixing a coroner's verdict with a bribe. He considered the advantage of this idea – if he could succeed in silencing the coroner, then his little artifice would never come to light. So he took half of the silver he had stolen, added the dagger, and quietly made his way to Yuan Gong's lodgings.

After this he committed many more robberies, and, more often than not, since he wasn't a very skilful burglar, he ended up being surprised by the householders and having to kill them. Gradually he became inured to this and began to think of murder as just another occupational hazard. He stopped providing any of his undertaker services, laying out bodies, digging graves and so on, and all he could think of was gambling, gambling and more gambling.

The reason he had killed the two men on the mountain was that they had been part of the group of villagers that beat him up. He had stayed away from the village for quite a while as he recovered from the beating. The villagers bore him no ill will once the punishment had been administered and would have welcomed him back, but he did not return, for one, because it had been no light beating, and for another, because, for quite a while afterwards, he intended to report the matter to the authorities. Finally, however, when his injuries had healed, he did return. He went, by night, to the house where he had been beaten up, and it brought back all the pain of the assault. He gritted his teeth and settled down to wait for the owners to go to sleep before showing his hand.

Then he heard the woman of the house, Qiu Shi, say to her husband: "When you go up the mountain tomorrow, don't stay more than three days. I get very lonely all alone in the house."

Qiu Shi didn't say what her husband was going to be doing, but the news was enough to make him decide not to act that night: I'll wait until tomorrow and kill him somewhere up on the mountain. Then I'll come back down and deal with his wife – that's even better!

The next morning, he saw that Qiu Shi's husband wasn't going alone, but he still decided to follow at a distance. The two men were out on the open road, and he was skulking in the shadows, but an opportunity didn't present itself to kill his target. Besides, just killing one of the pair and making his escape would leave the other one to tell the tale – he had better take the chance when it offered itself and kill them both. When they reached the mountain, Old Gourd realised they had come to clear some land for farming, and he thought to himself: If I'm going to do this properly, I'd better wait until they've done a day's work and are tired out.

So he waited until evening. Before the sun set behind the mountain, he picked up a wood-cutter's knife that was lying on the ground and crept into the thatched hut to hide. Quite soon, Qiu Shi's husband came down from the slopes by himself and made his way over to the hut. Holding his breath, with one hand clutching his chest and the other grasping the knife, Old Gourd almost lost his nerve: If he turns around now, he thought, I'll slip away and not kill him.

But the footsteps made their way straight into the hut, and then the dreadful deed was done. The victim didn't make a sound as the deadly knife struck.

Old Gourd wanted to escape but knew that the other man would see him if he tried. I should get away, he reasoned. But no, if I do, the other one will inform on me, and I'll be executed if I'm caught. But if I don't, and I don't manage to kill him, then I'm a dead man too. But if I do succeed, then my way is clear! His murderous resolve wavered – the bloodstains on his body would warn the other man, and it might not be so easy to kill him.

A bloody knife fight ensued in the crimson light of the setting sun. They were far from any village or homestead, and there was no one to hear the fracas and come to the rescue; life and death were in their own hands. The poor farmer was exhausted from a long day's labour, and, in the end, he took a knife cut to the left-side of his neck, dropped his own knife... and it was all over. The idea came to Old Gourd of staging a fight to the death between his two victims, so he went back into the hut and added some more knife slashes to the body as it lay there in a pool of its own blood. He didn't, however, think to make a cut on its neck.

The sun had set properly by then, and he hurried down the mountain and made his way to the county town as though nothing had happened. When he got there, the drawbridge was up for the night, so he scrambled up its ropes and over into the town. He made his way to Yuan Gong's lodgings and threw in the five taels of silver. The next morning the rumours began of a fight to the death on the mountain between two farmers. That night he went back to Huangnicun and slipped into Qiu Shi's house, intent on settling the debt from the night of the beating. The helpless Qiu Shi tried to resist and cry out, so he took a pillow from the bed and smothered her face with it and she lay still. Although the wretched Qiu Shi lay there, suffocated to death, Old Gourd was still not satisfied and he pulled down her trousers and raped her. When he was finished, he callously recalled what he knew about suicides putting on fresh clothes before killing themselves, so he stripped the body and changed it into the finery in which it was found.

So now, apparently, all the facts of the case were laid bare. But Song Ci still felt there was a piece missing. When he got back to his lodgings, he started pacing across his room. There were many leads he hadn't followed up completely, he thought. Watching him, Tong Gong wanted to ask what was going through his mind, but he held his tongue. What Song Ci actually was thinking was: Could such a dullard of a failed gambler really be responsible for so many deaths? Could a coroner so easily pull the wool over the eyes of an experienced judge? The woman was supposed to have died from white arsenic, but the test for arsenic poisoning was an easy one to interpret. She had been raped, but no proper examination had been made. How was this cover-up allowed to pass unremarked? If the judge had based his verdict on a proper examination of the body charts and the autopsy report, and if he had fully considered the behaviour of the accused and of the coroner, he would immediately have uncovered the coroner's deception. If he had wilfully misinterpreted the clear evidence of the autopsy, then surely there was something crooked going on.

Song Ci felt it was up to him alone to set the record straight. In these times of political and official corruption, when law and order was largely disregarded, how important had his own involvement in the autopsy become! But this was no straightforward matter – it was one of those things that can change the whole course of a person's life. Quietly, but confidently, Song Ci made his decision.

"What would people say if, from now on, I were to conduct my own autopsies?"

"They would say it was bad form," replied Tong Gong.

"So I shouldn't examine any more bodies?"

"Yes, you should. From now on, whenever I am called on to deal with a body, you stand beside me and observe – simple as that."

Song Ci smiled.

"Don't you think that will work?"

"It will work."

Now he could relax and go to sleep. But as he went to lie down, he suddenly thought of something. He could visualise the green-black discolouration spreading down the chest of Qiu Shi's corpse, and across her breasts, and how closely it resembled the bodies of other people he had seen who had died from arsenic poisoning. That was down to the way Old Gourd had known how to open her mouth and pour the wine laced with arsenic down her gullet. At this point, he threw off the quilt and said to Tong Gong: "Get down to the condemned cell! Go!"

"Am I looking for Old Gourd?" Tong Gong guessed.

"That's right."

"Is there something you need to clear up?"

"Ask him how to find the *qi chi* and the *tian tu* acupuncture points."

"Can't I go tomorrow?"

"I won't get any sleep if you don't go now!"

# CHAPTER VII

## DRUMS OF THE YAMEN (1226-1227)

Following the resolution of the case of the two men murdered at Kuzhuping, and that of the rape and murder of Qiu Shi, the truth emerged about a number of other supposed suicides in the Xinfeng area. The *yamen* was now a hive of activity, with all manner of complicated cases and lawsuits. Some were genuine, some bogus, but Song Ci treated each on its merits, and Magistrate Shan's eyes were opened to a whole new world…

# 1

## THE STRANGE AND THE GROTESQUE

Following the resolution of the case of the two corpses, and that of the rape and murder of Qiu Shi, the truth emerged about a number of other supposed suicides in the Xinfeng area over the previous two years or so, causing a county-wide sensation. Previously, the county had been known as the least litigious in the country, but now the *yamen* was a hive of activity, with locals raising lawsuits left, right and centre. The latest case to come before the court was brought by the father of one of the *yamen* messengers, whose surname was Feng. He was from one of the wealthy families of the county, and the case involved one of his elder kinsmen, Old Man Feng, and how he had cheated them over their estates. Magistrate Shan had already given his verdict on the case. It had seemed straightforward: the tenancy agreement would prove, indisputably, who had rights over the estates. But the plaintiffs said they couldn't produce their copy of the agreement, as it had been destroyed in a fire. There certainly had been a fire, but there was no way of knowing whether the papers had actually been destroyed. When Old Man Feng was asked for his copy, he had no trouble producing it. "It's a forgery!" the plaintiff cried, pointing at the paper.

But the document Old Man Feng produced had been passed down through the generations, over a very long period of time, and it bore all the hallmarks of age; so how could it be a forgery? The black ink characters on the white paper were still quite clear, and they showed that the agreement had been made with Old Man Feng's grandfather, and that it had been handed down father to son, so that now, naturally, it rested with Old Man Feng himself. In the light of this, Magistrate Shan had given judgment in favour of Feng. Now the case had been resubmitted, and the magistrate's eyes were glinting with suppressed irritation. Nonetheless, he had Old Man Feng brought in and ordered him to produce the document, which he asked Song Ci to examine.

Song Ci took the paper, and before he had even begun to assess its authenticity, he had a thought that rather disturbed him. Would this case have been treated in the same way, he asked himself, if it had been brought before any other judge?

"Your Honour," Song Ci said with an earnest look. "If I were to overturn this case that you have already settled..."

"If it is overturned, then it is overturned, and that's all there is to it," Magistrate Shan said. "If I don't act when the people are in need, how can I be at peace with myself? Brother Huifu, if you can bring some clarity to this case, then I will consider it my good fortune."

Song remembered Liu Kezhuang's description of the magistrate as "an honest and genuine man". He took the document and examined it carefully all over, but could find nothing wrong. Then he tore off a corner, and after inspecting the tear, said to magistrate Shan: "The document is a forgery."

"How can you tell?" asked the startled magistrate.

"The agreement may be old, but although this document has the appearance of age, that's only superficial – underneath is a different story. Look here," Song Ci said, showing him the tear. "The colour is uniform all the way through. That shows it is a forgery."

"But the document..."

"Has been stained with tea, that's why it is uniform."

"How do you know?" Magistrate Shan was still doubtful.

"There are several different types of forensic examination," Song Ci explained. "There is autopsy, evidentiary examination and so on. Evidentiary examination is just what it says: examination of the physical evidence. Just as there can be real and faked injuries on a body, so the marks on items of evidence can also be real or faked. There are ancient precedents for this kind of forged agreement, and while I was living at home I conducted my own experiments in staining paper so I could be able to tell the difference. That's why I can state quite categorically that this document is a forgery."

Magistrate Shan understood immediately, and without hesitation he reopened the case to question Old Man Feng. Feng made no response to the accusation, so Magistrate Shan ordered that a corner be torn from a different old document. When it was examined, the surface of the document showed all the signs of age, but the tear showed white. Then he ordered that a fresh sheet of the kind of paper used for such legal documents be stained with tea, and when that was torn too, the result was identical to Old Man Feng's document. He was summarily convicted.

The story spread rapidly around town, enhancing Song Ci's reputation considerably. And on the back of it, several more bizarre cases came to light.

The next day, while Magistrate Shan and Song Ci were busy with other cases, the gatekeeper came rushing in to make a report.

"Your Honour, there is a local man outside who has been beaten black and blue, and his family have carried him here to lodge an accusation."

Postponing the case he was currently hearing, Magistrate Shan said: "Tell them to bring him in."

After a short delay, two men appeared, carrying the wounded man, and set him down in front of the court.

The weather in southern Jiangxi was particularly hot at the time, and the wounded man's jacket was unbuttoned, revealing his body to be a mass of bruises from a severe beating. He was moaning incessantly.

"Present your case!" Shan ordered.

The two men knelt before the court, and the older one kowtowed and said: "Your Worship, we don't have a case."

"Then who are you accusing?"

"I don't know"

"What do you mean, you don't know?"

"Your Worship, this is the situation. Last night, someone came to rob our house. Our father heard the noise and got up to try to catch the burglar. He was beaten with a cudgel of some kind, and you can see the result."

"What did the thief get away with?"

"He had filled a bag with things, but he left it behind. My two brothers heard the commotion but the thief had already run away."

The man then produced a strip of cloth and presented it to the court. "My father managed to tear off part of the burglar's sleeve."

Magistrate Shan went over to have a look at the piece of dark green material, and then he gave it to Song Ci. Song inspected the cloth, then raised his eyes and exchanged a look with Magistrate Shan, but said nothing. He went to stand beside the wounded man and bent down to inspect his injuries. The man started groaning piteously, but Song said to him: "You have nothing to groan about."

"But it hurts," the man said.

"No it doesn't." Song Ci stared into the man's eyes. "So, you surprised a burglar last night?"

"That's right."

"And the burglar had enough time to give you a beating like this?"

"Yes. These bruises..."

"Are fake!" Song Ci had already straightened up as he spoke to unmask the deception to the court.

He went on to explain: "You used Japanese elm to fake the injuries. You smeared the leaves and branches over your skin, and they left these marks that look like bruises. If you crush the foliage and brush it over your body, then apply a hot iron, you get these fake bruises with black centres spreading to a greenish colour at the edges. Leaving an indelible impression, they look just like the marks of a beating. The only difference is that with real bruises the blood coagulates under the skin and goes hard. With these fake ones, although the colour is convincing, you don't get the hardening."

Song Ci was so clear and certain in his explanation that Magistrate Shan believed him without question. He smacked down his sound block and said to the man who was still lying on his door panel: "Tch! Stand up and confess, man!"

The man rolled over onto his knees and said: "Your Worship, I was telling the truth."

"The truth? How can you dare to say that!"

"No, no! I meant to say I will tell you the truth."

"Speak!"

The facts were that the man's house had, indeed, been burgled, but not the previous night. It had actually taken place a fortnight or so previously. The man had received a beating too, but not with a cudgel. After he had been disturbed by the noise and got up to investigate, he met the burglar face to face. The latter was a sturdy fellow, wearing a mask, who landed two savage punches on the left side of the man's face. His cheek swelled up and his left eye began to bleed, so that he couldn't see anything. He had thought of reporting the incident at the time, but then he reconsidered: the burglar hadn't got away with anything, and he was afraid that if he did make a report, the magistrate wouldn't take it seriously. So he let it drop for the time being, while still harbouring thoughts of doing something at some stage. The reason he was acting now, so long after the fact, was that he had heard of the arrival of the new county registrar, Song Ci, with his serious reputation. He not only hoped that the registrar would be able to apprehend the burglar, but also calculated that if he exaggerated his injuries somewhat, the magistrate would impose a heavier punishment... and that is how this laughable case came to court. The men involved had little thought that they themselves would end up in prison, while the burglar remained at large.

This case with its mixture of fact and fiction, truth and fakery, was born out of a particular set of circumstances that aroused Magistrate Shan's interest. After the men who had made the complaint had been taken down from the court to be held on remand, Shan turned to Song Ci and asked: "Brother Huifu, do you think you can catch this burglar?"

"I think I can."

"Will it be difficult?"

"Probably not."

"So, will you…"

"I will try."

Song Ci left the *yamen* with Tong Gong and a few others.

Just before noon, they returned with a man in custody. It was, indeed, the burglar, and there was no need for a trial as he had already confessed everything. From then on, the whole *yamen* viewed Song Ci with increased respect.

After lunch, Magistrate Shan went to Song Ci's lodgings to ask about the arrest.

Song invited his guest to sit down. "It all started with my original examination of the evidence," he said

"You mean that piece of material?"

"That's right. You know that it came from the sleeve of a jacket? Well, it was very grease-stained, and when I washed it, a rainbow-coloured slick of fat came off. That told me the man was a butcher. This morning I went out and asked around. I discovered that there are three butchers in the neighbourhood where the complainant lives. Two of them are right-handed, and one left-handed. I could eliminate the latter from my enquiries."

"Is that because the complainant was struck on the left side of his face."

"Just so!"

"But you still had two right-handed suspects?"

"One of them was a bachelor, so I eliminated him too."

"How so?"

"The piece of sleeve that was torn off has been mended, and I could see from the neat stitching that there must be an expert seamstress in the household of the jacket's owner. When I searched the butcher's house, I found this green jacket. Although it had been mended again by his wife, when I unpicked the new repair, the old damage exactly matched this fragment. Quite clear enough proof to convict him."

When Magistrate Shan heard the solution to the puzzle, he thought back over the cases he had tried in recent days. He saw now that the reason all the defendants had made full confessions was that Song Ci's careful unpicking of all the evidence had left them with no alternative.

"Brother Huifu, I can see now that, in conducting a trial, it is much better to spend time re-examining the evidence rather than have to call for a retrial."

"That's right," Song Ci replied, laughing.

Magistrate Shan let out a sigh. He had been in office for so many years, but only now, it seemed, did he fully understand the meaning of 'adjudication'.

Over the next few weeks, Song Ci was busy collaborating with Magistrate Shan over a host of similar cases that turned up, one after the other. None of them proved too baffling for him. On Magistrate Shan's part, he found his new colleague to be not just very useful, but also worthy of respect, and a closeness developed between the two men.

2

# THE UNUSUAL SOUND OF THE YAMEN DRUMS

After a period of hectic activity, Song Ci was finally able to rest. A month passed, then another and another… and before he knew it, summer had turned to autumn, and Song was still idle. The court drums announcing a case were seldom heard in Xinfeng during that time, and Song was beginning to feel rather homesick. On top of that, the county deputy, the sheriff and the other *yamen* staff seemed to be less respectful of Magistrate Shan than before, and this also applied to Song Ci himself.

"Brother Huifu, one day you'll be a real bigwig."

"Master Song, don't forget me on your way up."

"Master Song…"

Whether on purpose or not, County Deputy Zhou Anping seemed to be implicitly criticising Magistrate Shan when he addressed Song Ci. This put Song Ci on his guard; he thought to himself that if word of any of the faulty judgments Magistrate Shan had presided over in the past got to the imperial court, then he would certainly be censured, and perhaps even demoted. He realised that, within the *yamen*, there was a conspiracy against Shan and that they wanted to implicate him, too. Thinking about the matter dispassionately, he decided that his concern for the magistrate was not just because he was a friend of Liu Kezhuang. Over the last days and weeks, he had come to recognise him as an honest and genuine man who acted, in his official capacity, in the best interests of the people. During autopsies, although he sat at a distance, sheltering behind the incense smoke, he did at least go to the crime scene, in contrast to the many other officials who stayed away.

However, his most honourable trait was the absence of regard for his own reputation in his desire to right injustices – something that could not always be said of many of the 'wise and sagacious' officials of the past.

Song Ci thought about the minor officials who were all so keen to pick over Magistrate Shan's perceived failings. They all clearly had their own opinion of the man, but they were not brave enough to voice it, and flattered and fawned instead. But if anything went wrong, they would pick apart his mistakes or omissions one by one. These were the kind of officials to be wary of, so Song decided to try to protect Magistrate Shan. As Song quietly but determinedly launched his campaign, Tong Gong could see something was going on, but he was not sure exactly what. So he asked: "Master, what is the use of interviewing these people?"

"It's going to be very useful," Song Ci smiled broadly. "Just wait and see – then you'll understand."

Over the next few days, Song worked his way through the ranks of minor officials, quietly and tactfully explaining to them where everyone stood. Magistrate Shan, however, remained unaware of any of this. Shan's wife, who lived with her husband in Xinfeng, was an excellent cook, and Shan often invited Song Ci over to share a meal. Song never refused, not just because he appreciated the sincerity of Shan's invitation, but also because he thought it would do no harm for the other officials to see how intimate the two of them had become. His tactics seemed to be effective: peace reigned in the *yamen*, and the lesser officials' respect for Magistrate Shan increased again.

Nonetheless, the days were dragging for Song Ci. Every time he ate Mistress Shan's Jiangxi-style fermented rice, he couldn't help thinking of the Jianyang-style sweet lotus soup made by his own wife, Yulan. His heart flew over the wide rivers and high mountains that separated him from home, and he found himself missing, more and more, his mother, wife and daughter. Sometimes he felt he had spent a whole lifetime waiting for things to happen; at first it had been waiting with his mother for his father to come home, then he had been waiting to get married, waiting for his first child, waiting to take the examinations, waiting to enter imperial service, waiting for his first posting... what was he waiting for now? He was waiting to be reunited with his family. How long had he been away now?

He remembered a day, when he was five years old, when, unexpectedly, a letter home arrived from his father: it told them that his father had been posted to the capital, Lin'an, and that he would soon be coming home to take his wife and son back there with him. His mother was so happy and excited she couldn't sleep that night. Every day after that, he went with his old grandmother down to the little stone bridge beyond the gate to watch for his father. The whole household began preparations for the move to the capital in expectation of his arrival. Not long after, his father did indeed come home, accompanied by a hulking stranger, who turned out to be Song Xie. However, things didn't work out as expected: his father had been dismissed from office. But this meant nothing to the young Song Ci. As long as his father was home, he was happy.

It was only many years later that he learned of the circumstances of his father's dismissal. Song Xie had given shelter under their roof to a woman, her name now forgotten, who had been assaulted by some soldiers. A fight had ensued that resulted in a murder case being brought, and his father had become implicated because of his defence of Song Xie. He still remembered the words his father said to him at the time: "A man of true character may be born without righteousness, but he should die a righteous man. Anything acquired through iniquity should be justly surrendered."

It was these years spent together that had truly cemented his deep respect for his father. His father told him many stories, ancient and modern, of court and country, of the high-born and lowly, of his exploits following the army on its campaigns to his adventures apprehending murderers... a seemingly endless fund of anecdotes. He had an extraordinary memory and was often able to repeat, almost word for word, some of these stories for the entertainment of his father's important visitors; a feat that made his mother very proud. But what Song Ci found himself thinking of most was his time with his wife Yulan. He remembered the day, aged ten, when he had been out exercising his horse. Just as he got home, Song Xie took the reins from him and said: "Quickly, get down. Your father is sending you off to school."

"To school?" He was astonished. "Aren't I studying well enough at home?"

"Your father wants to send you to study under Mr Wu Zhi."

Helped down from his horse by Song Xie, Song Ci hurried inside. There he learned that his father had been called back into imperial service, and although it was only a minor post as a prefectural judge, his father treasured it and immediately accepted. In Song Ci's childhood, Jianyang was already well established as a seat of learning thanks to Master Zhu Xi's educational foundations. Close neighbours in the area included the Kaoting Academy, the Yungu Academy, the Lufeng Academy, the Yingshan Academy, the Aofeng Academy, the Yunzhuang Academy and the Ruizhang Academy, all with national reputations for scholarship. But his father had, somewhat contrarily, chosen Mr Wu Zhi's Tanxi Academy. Mr Wu Zhi, whose courtesy name was Hezhong, was a celebrated scholar from Jianyang, and a disciple of Zhu Xi, and it was to his academy that the young Song Ci was sent that very day. On the road, his father again exhorted him: "Mr Wu Zhi is a man of great scholarship, and you must pay close attention to your lessons, not mess around as you do at home…"

"Yes, sir," he replied, half-heartedly, his eye distracted by a lotus pond up ahead. It was the season when the lotus was in bloom. The pink morning light was flooding over a sea of lotus blossom, and the morning breeze rippled across the surface of the water, making it flicker with a wonderful radiance. Across a stone bridge over the pond stood Mr Wu Zhi's thatched cottage. In front of the cottage was a small bamboo-fenced courtyard, the gate to which was half open and just inside the fence could be seen a pile of jade-green vegetables; there were also several pear trees and a modest melon frame.

It looks much like the courtyard at home, he thought.

A little later, as he was in the cottage, kneeling to pay his deep respects to Mr Wu Zhi, he heard the sound of tinkling laughter coming from somewhere outside. He sneaked a look under his arm and saw, crowding outside the door, the heads of several children of about his own age. The laughter, directed at his current situation, came from the only girl among them, who looked to be a few years younger than him.

"Look! Look! A hunchback! He's a hunchback!" The young girl was calling out merrily to her companions.

He was confused for a moment, then remembered, and reached round and took the book bag off his back. The laughter redoubled. Then it stopped abruptly, and he sneaked another look. For some reason, the children who had been clustering noisily around the doorway had all scattered – perhaps the master had given them a look. But the little girl was still there.

"And this is…" he heard his father asking.

"That is my niece," Mr Wu Zhi replied.

That was when he first met Yulan. As the days of his childhood went by, he remembered how she would often come and grind the ink for him, and bring cakes and pastries from home to share with him. Once, she said to him: "Brother Ci, my uncle says you are the cleverest student in the whole class, and he has high hopes for your future."

"Is that so?" He looked at her, as if for the first time, and took in her beauty. The days slipped by for the two young innocents, until a time came, and neither was quite certain when it started, when they no longer dared to be alone together. When he was twenty, with the same respectful ceremony as when he arrived, he once again knelt in front of his master beside the lotus pond in front of the cottage, to take his leave. He was going up to the Imperial Academy in Lin'an. It was very peaceful beside the pond, the scent of the lotus wafting on the breeze. Yulan was standing silently behind her uncle, and when he looked up into her tear-stained face, for the first time in his adult life he felt the true pain and sorrow of parting.

And so Song Ci spent his time in Xinfeng thinking over past events, until, one autumn day, another murder case arrived. It was a case that would make him miss his family even more.

3

## ANOTHER MURDER

One clear morning, two young men arrived in a rush to lodge a report. Their neighbour, Madam Bian, had been murdered in her bed by her daughter-in-law, they did not know how or why, and her body was lying there covered in blood. On the way to the scene, Song Ci urgently questioned the two men about the circumstances. He learned that: Madam Bian was about forty; she had lost her husband while still young and had lived as a widow ever since; she had single-handedly and with great difficulty raised a young son to adulthood. When the boy was twenty, he had married a village girl from Huangnicun called Yao Shi; the three had lived together peacefully for more than a year. After that however, relations between mother-in-law and daughter-in-law had gradually deteriorated, and they often argued. Then a time came when, to everyone's surprise, things improved between them. The daughter-in-law fell ill with a seasonal flux, and her mother-in-law was constantly at her bedside. She cooked for her, washed her and brewed her medicines, making sure they were at the right temperature, tasting them herself and feeding them spoonful by spoonful to her daughter-in-law. Then, when the young woman was feeling better, the old lady sprained her back, and it was the daughter-in-law's turn to bring food and drink to the bedside, and wash and feed her mother-in-law. This display of familial affection and support warmed the hearts of their neighbours, but when they discussed it among themselves, they couldn't help worrying that no good would come of such a sudden change in affections.

In the middle of one night, about a month later, there was a sudden strange occurrence. No one was clear who first heard the 'shink, shink' of a knife being sharpened coming from Madam Bian's house, but there it was, carrying, stroke after steady stroke, through the still night. One of the neighbours scrambled up to look over the wall, and he saw Madam Bian's son sitting alone in the main room, sharpening a knife. A moment later, the lamps were lit in the rooms of both Madam Bian and her daughter-in-law, their doors opened and the two women followed each other out into the main room. The three of them all seemed struck dumb with surprise for a moment. Then the old lady summoned her son into her room; he put the knife on a shelf and followed her. When he emerged, he went back to his own room with his wife. The lights went out in both rooms, and nothing further happened that night. After this, the months passed and friendly relations continued between the two women, so everyone forget their previous concern that something untoward might happen. This lasted for about a year until, once again, the relationship between the two women soured. Madam Bian began to berate Yao Shi for not getting pregnant, and the young woman would shout back in response.

Things went from bad to worse, until the previous day, when a furious row broke out between the two women, and the sound of smashing crockery echoed round the neighbourhood. Then came the sound of Madam Bian cursing her son for not showing her proper respect, and her son storming out, cursing her back. He didn't return for the whole night. So, that evening Madam Bian and her daughter-in-law were alone in the house, and the lamps remained lit until daybreak. At dawn, Madam Bian's son had still not returned, but Yao Shi packed a bag and left the house. A villager bumped into her on the street and asked where she was going. She laughed and replied that she was going home. Not long after she had left, the Bian family's big black dog scrabbled open the door, and it was running to and fro, barking incessantly. Someone noticed blood on the dog's muzzle, and that's when people began to suspect something was not right. They rushed into the house and found Madam Bian lying in a pool of blood...

The Bian house was on the city's west street, and a crowd had gathered outside. Song Ci pushed the door open and went in. As soon as he saw the body stretched out by the bed, he cried out: "She's not dead! We can still save her."

This news greatly cheered the crowd of onlookers. Song Ci took a hairpin from Madam Bian's head and used it to stimulate the *guanyuan* acupuncture point.[1] At the same time he instructed: "Take the wick out of a lamp, dip it in cooking oil and light it."

When it was burning well, he took the wick and applied it to the *yinbai* and *dadun* points on her big toe. "Quick, give me a moxa stick," he said.

Someone produced a moxa stick, and Song Ci applied it to the *baihui* point on the crown of her head. Madam Bian revived quite quickly after this treatment.

"Come over here," said Song Ci, pointing at some of the women in the crowd of neighbours. "Bring some hot water and help her to wash and change clothes. Then put her into a clean bed."

The women obeyed his instructions. Song then ordered Tong Gong to go to the pharmacy to get palm charcoal, ginseng and matured monksfoot. Tong Gong went off on his errand.

"Are you writing a prescription?" Magistrate Shan finally asked when he saw Song Ci writing down a list of ingredients.

"Mmm," Song grunted as he went on writing. Magistrate Shan looked at the prescription: mock dragon bones – eight *qian*;[2] mock oyster – eight *qian*; mountain cherry pulp – eight *qian*; Indian madder root – three *qian*; lyceum bark – six *qian*; stir-fried haws – four *qian*; schizandra – one *qian*; motherwort – eight *qian*…

Magistrate Shan saw the concentration on Song Ci's face, and thought he looked much more like an eminent doctor than a county registrar. When Song had finished writing the prescription he again dispatched someone to the pharmacy. Not long after, when Tong Gong returned with the palm charcoal, ginseng and monksfoot, the women of the village already had Madam Bian washed and changed into fresh clothes. Song Ci took the five *qian* of palm charcoal, which had been ground into a fine powder, mixed it with freshly boiled water, and gave a dose to Madam Bian. He then gave instructions for the ginseng and monksfoot to be boiled in some water over a fierce flame, and he dosed Madam Bian with this as well. When this was all done with great speed, Song Ci appeared to be exhausted, and he sat down on a long wooden bench. He looked up at a distant patch of empty sky and let out a long sigh.

"Huifu, look…" said Magistrate Shan, oblivious to the fact that Song Ci was not in the mood for explanations that day.

"Aah!" Song Ci sighed softly. "This isn't attempted murder."

"If it's not attempted murder, then what is it?"

"It's an illness."

"What illness?"

"Let's go home and I'll explain."

"But for the moment…"

"You should send people to look for her son and daughter-in-law, to tell them to come home and look after her. Once she is better, we can discuss the matter."

"So what should we do now?"

"We should go back to the *yamen*."

Magistrate Shan couldn't help feeling this was all a bit hasty, but by now he was used to going along with Song Ci. He knew that there always reason behind what he did, and this faith had frequently been justified. So he made preparations to leave, as Song Ci suggested. He requested the local officials and neighbours to make sure Madam Bian was looked after, and they set off back to the *yamen*.

"Now you can tell me what kind of illness it was."

The two of them had barely sat down in the rear hall of the *yamen*, before Magistrate Shan began questioning Song Ci impatiently.

"Blood avalanche."

"That's a woman's illness, isn't it?"

"That's right."

"How did it happen precisely at that moment, and how were you so sure it wasn't an assault by her daughter-in-law?"

Song Ci thought for a moment and then said slowly: "There is an old saying that there are three great calamities in life. One is to lose your mother when you are young, another is to lose your spouse in middle age and the third is to lose a child when you are old. We don't know if this lady lost her mother when she was young, but we do know she buried her husband in middle age. After that, she endured great hardship to bring up her son single-handed. All her hopes and aspirations rested on that son. How could she have expected that he would marry a woman who wouldn't bear him any children? Is that not, in the end, much the same as actually losing a child? What is more, although she is only just over forty, her hair is already grey, her face wrinkled and her body wasted. It is obvious that both her blood and her *qi* have been depleted by years of drudgery. Blood avalanche occurs during a woman's menses, when her vessels of conception are too weak to withstand the flow. In the case of this woman, both her spirit and her physical body were compromised and by bad chance it was also a sickly time of year. On top of that, the day before she had been in a violent argument, so it was inevitable that her internal organs would contract, the fire element in her liver would overheat and this heat would be transmitted to her whole reproductive system. The reproductive system is intimately connected with the kidney meridian – if the kidney meridian is constricted, it can be damaged and close down. This causes loss of control of the reproductive system, the over-heated blood then overflows and this is what causes 'blood avalanche'. This corresponds exactly with what happened to Madam Bian, and now the crisis has passed and she is on the mend. So there is absolutely no reason to suspect her daughter-in-law of assault."

The explanation gave Magistrate Shan much to ponder. Suppose, for instance, the woman had died and he had had to conduct the case by himself: he would have investigated the woman's son and daughter-in-law; he would have asked about the sudden, strange changes in relationship between mother and daughter-in-law; he would have followed up the sound of knife sharpening that disturbed the neighbours in the middle of the night.

As it was now, he still could not see any connection between these events, so he asked Song Ci: "Huifu, do you know what happened a year ago to improve the relationship between the two women?"

Song Ci didn't reply immediately, as if he considered the question superfluous.

"It is said that even an honest and upright official will have difficulty resolving a family dispute. The good thing is, no laws were broken, so there is no need to investigate."

However, Magistrate Shan wasn't willing to let the matter drop: "But it is something of a mystery, isn't it? Don't you have a theory?"

"A theory is just a theory. We'll never know for certain."

"Even so, why don't you tell me?" Magistrate Shan looked earnestly at Song Ci.

Song Ci paused for a moment in thought, and then he began to explain: "I think perhaps, one day, the son said to his mother something along the lines of: 'Mother, if you could bear to be nice to my wife for a month, then I will kill her!' 'Kill your wife?' 'That's right!' His mother couldn't believe what she was hearing. The son might have gone on to say that brothers are like your hands and feet, but wives are like clothes – when clothes are worn out you can throw them away and buy new ones, but if you cut off your hands and feet, you cannot replace them. If this was so for brothers, how much truer was it for a mother with an only son.

"Alternatively, he may have said: 'Mother, if you are nice to her for a month and let all the neighbours see how well you are treating her, if she were suddenly to die, no one would suspect the two of us of plotting anything. And perhaps, as they discussed it, they might be moved by our tears of grief.' So the mother may have been half convinced. At the same time, the son may have been saying the same things to his wife: 'If you can bear to be nice to my mother for a month, then I will kill her'. Of course, his wife wouldn't believe him. But a husband can pledge undying love and pluck at his wife's heartstrings with honeyed lies, and so he did until his wife too half-believed him."

"What then?"

"Then, the mother and her daughter-in-law were probably both mulling it over, trying to decide whether to believe it or not. But in the meantime, for a month they were nice to each other and let all the neighbours see this miraculous change for themselves."

"So what you are saying is that, over this period, everything the two of them said and did was for the benefit of the neighbours?"

"I think that must be so. A month passed, and that night of the knife grinding must have marked the culmination of that period, when one of them was going to be killed. The neighbours found the sound of the knife sharpening most disturbing. He was doing it very slowly and deliberately because he was waiting for his mother and his wife to come and stop him."

"You think they were sure to come out and stop him?"

"Of course! They must have been worried out of their wits – what would happen if he really did kill someone? So they came hurrying out of their chambers at the same time, and there they were, all three of them in the same room. The son presumably made up some story to explain why he was sharpening the knife, but his mother was still worried, so she took him into her chamber to talk to him. And to calm his wife's fears as he went into his mother's room, he left the knife behind and went empty-handed. I am guessing his mother said to him: 'For heaven's sake, don't kill her!' Then, when he came out and went with his wife into their own room to sleep, I am guessing his wife said exactly the same thing."

"So you are saying what this was all about was that the mother and her daughter-in-law did not in fact have such irreconcilable differences, and that after a month of being nice to each other, they found that they did actually have some genuine mutual affection."

"That seems only natural to me."

"So after that night passed without incident, they continued to get along with each other for the next year. And when they fell out again after that, it must have been over something different."

"I think that must be so."

Magistrate Shan let out a long sigh, as though a great weight had been lifted from his shoulders. He really hadn't expected the affair to turn out like this. He was silent for a while, then said: "So the son handled things very shrewdly, considering he was caught in the middle of those two."

"Who would have thought it of him?" Song Ci said, laughing. "It was all a pretence."

"So it was. But there is one more thing. Did the girl leave before or after her mother-in-law suffered her 'blood avalanche'? If it was afterwards, and she left her to die, then that needs to be properly investigated."

"No, it wasn't like that," Song Ci said firmly. "She left before the 'blood avalanche' happened."

"Are you sure?"

"The onset of this condition is very sudden and dramatic. If it had already started before the girl left, no matter how quickly I hurried, I would not have go there in time to save the woman."

Magistrate Shan nodded contentedly, thinking to himself that the way Song Ci had handled the affair was just what he had come to expect from him. A cup of jasmine tea had been placed on the table in front of him. Magistrate Shan reached forward to drink some, before realising that it had gone cold. He put his own cup down and stood up to pour Song Ci a fresh cup. Song Ci realised Shan's intention as soon as he stood up and, to save both their face, hurried to pour some hot tea for himself. Shan sat back down. His respect for Song Ci had increased enormously. Previously, he had thought of him only as an expert in matters of forensic investigation and judicial sentencing, without realising his expertise extended so remarkably into the field of medicine.

"Huifu, if I had had to handle this case by myself, without your contribution, that woman would not be alive now. And if she had died, I would certainly have convicted her son and daughter-in-law, and it would not have been just one life that would have been lost. As it is, you opened up a whole new field of understanding."

"I discovered for myself, unexpectedly, some years ago," Song Ci replied, "that this ancient medical knowledge can have a direct bearing on the cases that come before us today."

4

# THE LONELY MILES OF SEPARATION

Days passed, and the *yamen* was quiet again. Song Ci was made restless by the inactivity, but at the same time, he didn't wish to see the good order of the district disturbed by more cases. It was something of a paradoxical situation. Perhaps, he thought to himself, I should be travelling across the empire, finding cases to solve and wrongs to right. But then again, how would this be possible when my official standing is so modest – I'm not even a magistrate. Gradually, he began to feel more and more uncomfortable with his current status. His rank was too low, and he longed for advancement. This longing grew steadily stronger.

Two years later, in the spring, there was a lot of rain. Both the Qingming festival and the Dragon Boat festival had passed before the weather began to improve and get hotter, and then summer gave way to the bleaker weather of autumn. It was deep into autumn, when, far away, back in his home town, Song's mother fell seriously ill and took to her bed.

Come winter, Magistrate Shan had been in his current post for three full years, and he was looking for a change. On the day in question, he came in search of Song Ci to talk over some of their old cases. He had himself made great strides in understanding the complexities of these cases, but if he were to reach Song Ci's level of ability to draw on historical analogy, he needed a much firmer, broader-based foundation of knowledge on which to build. He was too young, still, to have built up such a knowledge base, and so it seemed there was little difference in how he treated the different cases that came before him, and this gave him limited scope for development. Even so, his enthusiasm remained undiminished from day to day. But now, when he came hurrying into Song Ci's lodgings, he was brought up short... Song Ci was sitting on a chair with tears flowing down his cheeks. Beside him stood Tong Gong and another man he didn't recognise. On the desk lay two envelopes and beside them their letters.

"What's the matter?" Magistrate Shan asked.

Song Ci stammered out: "It's my mother..."

"How is she?"

"She's dead."

There are no words sufficient to console even the most steadfast soul in these circumstances.

The letters from home had been brought by the stranger who stood next to Tong Gong. From them, Song Ci finally learned what grief had befallen his family during the autumn just past. The autumn weather in Jianyang had been much colder than in Xinfeng; the leaves and grass withered away with only the weakest of sunlight, and the leaves had all fallen from the pear trees in the Song family courtyard. The autumn wind got up, blowing the leaves all over the yard, and the rain fell incessantly. It was left to Yulan alone to summon the doctor and to look after the invalid with tender care. Pharmacist He came assiduously every day and showed the utmost concern, but Madam Song's health steadily worsened, and there seemed no prospect of recovery.

Yulan was desperate to send someone to Xinfeng to inform Song Ci of what was going on, but Madam Song exerted her authority and forbade it. Yulan did not dare disobey. Many times, she stood beside her mother-in-law's bed, pleading with her tearfully: "Mother, please let me send a messenger to Jiangxi."

"No!" the old woman always replied, her own eyes filled with unshed tears.

"But mother..." Yulan pleaded with her.

"No!" Madam Song remained determined.

Day after day, Yulan kept asking, until one day, Madam Song, almost without realising what she was doing, grasped Yulan's hand and clasped it tightly to her bosom: "Lan'er, you once sent for Tong Gong behind your husband's back. This time, you must not trick me and secretly send for my son."

Yulan nodded in understanding. She had, indeed, considered this course of action, but because she so well understood the old woman's feelings, she always thrust the thought aside.

"Lan'er!" The old lady spoke again. "These last few days I have seen your father-in-law in my dreams. He called out my name, and I am sure this means my time is nearly up and I will soon be dead. Calling Ci'er home would be of no use. Besides, after your father-in-law died, Ci'er stayed at home for many years, which brought him only misery and hardship. If the same thing happened again, it would cause his father's spirit too much anguish."

"Grandma!" the thirteen-year-old Song Qi interrupted tearfully.

"Lan'er, listen to me while I still have life. After I die, you must tell Ci'er that it is my express wish that he must not come home and stay here in mourning for me. That would only serve to stall his career even further."

Yulan's tears fell on the old woman's thin and withered hand, and she didn't know how to respond: "Mother... are you... are you cold?"

The old woman's hands were trembling continuously. Yulan tried to put them back under the quilt, but with one of them she clutched Yulan's own hand more tightly, and she stretched out the other, shakily, to stroke her daughter-in-law's glistening cheeks. She seemed about to say something important. Indeed, when she did speak it was to give voice to the one thing that had truly worried her all her life.

"Lan'er," she said, finally letting flow the tears she had been holding back so long. "Over many generations, the Song family has descended through a single line, and now here you are, with only a daughter and no son. After I die, please hurry to Ci'er's side while there is still a chance for you to have a son. If you do fall pregnant but have another girl, then you must find your husband a concubine. You and I are both of the Song family, and the most important thing is to have a son. I beg you to do this for me."

Yulan's tears fell like strings of pearls, and she slowly nodded her assent. Madam Song died that night, and she passed away peacefully. She had been such a mother as occurs only once in a generation, and in a time of turmoil and destruction, she had raised for the world an extraordinary son. Even in her dying moments she put her son's interests first, and so she died content.

After Madam Song's death, Yulan had her buried next to her husband, and after thinking long and hard, finally sent a messenger to Xinfeng with news of the old lady's death. She also relayed Madam Song's last will and testament, and her final instructions to her son. She urged her husband not to ignore his mother's wishes and not to come home to observe the mourning period. She well knew what a dutiful son her husband was, and realised how difficult he would find it not to do so. She further told him, therefore, that she would not come straight to join him, and exhorted him to let her stay at home to observe the mourning herself. Every year they would go to clear the overgrowth of wild grasses from the tomb, bringing company and companionship for the departed and some measure of consolation for the living.

Song Ci understood all this; but things had happened so quickly, he had had no chance to repay his mother's loving kindness. He had been able to observe the mourning period for his father, but now, after taking up office at the age of forty, he was not to have the chance to do the same for his mother.

Yulan's letter also brought news of Qiu Juan's return to the household. "We have always worried," she wrote, "about the way she left all those years ago, without saying goodbye. Well, after she left, she made her own way to Anshan and stayed all that time at the Lingquan convent. As soon as she heard you had gone away to take up office, she thought the family might need some help, so she came back."

Apparently, when Qiu Juan left, she was already thinking that one day she might return. She had remained unmarried. Now she was back, Yulan had told her about Madam Song's wish for Song Ci to take a concubine. She said that as she herself could not be with her husband, she was of no help to him; and if they waited until they finally could be together, then she would be too old. That was why she was asking Song Ci to think about all this very carefully, and to accept Qiu Juan as his concubine. She was, after all, a very nice girl.

Song Ci was deeply moved when he read this, and he reflected on how stoically Qiu Juan had endured everything that had happened to her. He had always been worried for her, but now, as she had shown herself too strong-willed to contemplate taking her own life, she had come back – and that was all to the good.

Nor was all this the only news in the letters the messenger had brought. Song Ci carefully picked up the second letter from the desk and handed it to Magistrate Shan: "This is from Qianfu."

"From Qianfu?"

"Yes, take a look."

The letter was on notepaper printed with a plum blossom watermark letterhead, and it was written in cursive script that looked like rain being whirled in the wind. It gave the clear impression that the author was in a state of some agitation. Who would have thought that Liu Kezhuang, the man who had so forcefully warned Song Ci how careful he would have to be when he took up office, had himself been dismissed!

Shan Zilin opened the letter and read it: "To my brother Huifu. You will remember how, last spring, I was moved to write the poem *Fallen Plum Blossom*? Well, the imperial censor has taken exception to the lines: 'The east wind is jealous of the blossom's lofty grace / And ravages it wantonly with no shred of respect.' He says they are disrespectful and defamatory to the emperor, and I have been removed from office. But things could be worse – I am going to the retreat on the West Mountain at Pucheng to teach, and there, among the rivers and mountains, will be a place where I don't have to concern myself with disgrace or favour, and I can declaim my poems and write my odes in peace.

"Huifu, you are worried for the safety of the country, and the desire to right wrongs is indeed worthy of respect. But corruption within the empire increases daily, and it is very hard to be an upright official, just as Li Bai describes in his poem *The Road to Shu is a Hard One*. Although you are a man of exceptional talent, strong as the plum tree we admired that year, yet even the plum tree sheds its blossom under the onslaught of the cold and snow. I beg you to take very good care of yourself. I have not written separately to Zilin, so please pass on my deepest respects"

After he had finished reading, Magistrate Shan let out a deep sigh and put the letter back on the desk. Gesturing helplessly, he said: "I would never have thought it. I would never have thought it."

Conceivable or not, there it was. Song Ci's mind was in such turmoil, he could not speak. He was grieving for his mother, debating with himself over taking a concubine and outraged at the injustice inflicted on Liu Kezhuang. He looked through the window at the overcast sky outside, and it seemed to him as though he was witnessing a swirling snowstorm, and he was wading across an endless, borderless snow-bound wilderness.

# CHAPTER VIII

## A FAMILY OF CORONERS (1232-1233)

One day, an old man took Song Ci to a lonely mountainous spot away from the city, and he pointed out a patch of Chinese wormwood, saying: "Look! What do you think that is?" The wormwood had taken on a particular oily black colour, and the most luxuriant growth was in the shape of a human body, with the head and four limbs clearly distinguishable. The old man said: "When a body is cremated, the fat enters the soil. After two years, any plant that grows on the spot looks like this. A body must have been cremated here." When Song Ci inspected the vegetation more closely, he could tell that the body had been that of a woman. He searched the surrounding area but found no other evidence. How did Song Ci solve this case?

# 1

# THEFT OF A CATTY OF SALT

In the fifth year of the Shaoding period of Emperor Lizong (1232), the forty-year old Song Ci received orders to take up a magistrate's post in Tingzhou. Tingzhou is a poor mountainous district, situated in the border area between Fujian, Guangdong and Jiangxi. A single river runs through it, flowing southwards. Both the river and the county are named in accordance with the *Yi Jing* (*Book of Changes*).[1]

Song Ci and Tong Gong took the road to Tingzhou via Huichang and Ruijin during the rainy season. By the time they arrived, spring had ended, and once the Dragon Boat festival had passed, the summer sun came out in the skies above Tingzhou. As soon as they arrived, the very first thing Song Ci did was to send Tong Gong with all speed back to Jianyang to see Yulan and Song Qi. Tong Gong understood completely his master's emotions, and he needed no second bidding. He changed horses at the *yamen* and set off northwards out of the city. Hardly was he out of the north gate, when he was startled by a commotion at the side of the road and he reined in his horse.

Outside the gate, a group of men had formed a circle, and in the middle of the circle two young men were fighting; both were already badly battered with torn clothes and bloody faces. With some difficulty, a sturdily built middle-aged man managed to separate the pair.

"What's going on here?" he asked loudly, standing between the two youths.

"He stole this fortune-teller's salt." The taller of the two pointed at the other one and also indicated a fortune-teller who was standing next to them.

"It's not true," the shorter youth said.

"It is," shot back the tall one.

"Tell us what happened," said the man who had intervened, looking first at the youths and then at the fortune-teller.

The fortune-teller had wide open but sightless eyes, and in one hand he held a bamboo cane, and in the other a small bag. He clicked his tongue and stalled for a while, before finally telling his version of events.

It turned out that the fortune-teller had been in the city to buy a catty of salt, which he had put into a small alms bowl. He then wrapped the bowl in a cloth bag and stowed it in his backpack. He had gone far outside the city gates when he was attacked and robbed. A passer-by heard his cries of "Thief! Thief!" and set off in pursuit. Soon he heard someone shouting "Sir! Sir! Come here!"

Leaning on his bamboo cane, he tottered towards the voice. When he reached the place where the shout had come from, he heard the increasingly violent sound of two men fighting. He called out to them to stop fighting, and just as he repeated his plea, he heard someone say: "Here, sir! Take it and get away."

Almost simultaneously there came the dull thud of something hitting the ground at his feet. He felt around and found it was his stolen bag of salt. The two men kept fighting, and he could hear the sound of them pummelling each other. The fact that he couldn't see what was going on made him all the more agitated, and he cried out again: "Stop fighting! Stop fighting!" At which point a crowd of passers-by gathered round.

Tong Gong was not at all surprised that such a fuss was being made over a catty of salt. That very morning, he and his master Song Ci had discovered that it was as expensive to buy table salt in Tingzhou as it was to buy land. As chance would have it, Tong Gong recognised the taller of the two combatants as the person he had met that very morning. Could he be the salt thief?

That morning, Song Ci had been disguised as an itinerant doctor when the two of them made their way into Tingzhou. Over the last few years, from time to time and for no particular reason, Song Ci had often done this. He would wind an old black cotton turban round his head, put on a black sackcloth outfit and order Tong Gong to dress himself as a servant and carry a medicine bag on his back on which was written: 'Bring the dead back to life – Hua Tuo[2] reincarnated'. Dressed in this manner, they would walk through the streets of the towns and villages. Now a magistrate, arriving in Tingzhou for the first time, Song Ci had again donned this disguise, a ruse he found highly entertaining and enlightening. Not long after they had entered the city that morning, they were accosted by someone asking for medical advice, and that man was indeed the taller of the two men who were fighting. He had been in a state of considerable agitation and had flung himself headlong at Song Ci and Tong Gong saying: "Doctor! Doctor! My mother…"

"Lead the way," Song Ci replied immediately.

The man lived in a large house nearby, and the three of them hurried there, to find that his mother had fainted. Her face was very white and her body thin and pallid, but apart from the fact that she looked very weak, there seemed to be no emergency. Song Ci first applied an acupuncture needle obliquely to the patient's *ren zhong* point on the nasal philtrum, then loosened her topknot and applied another needle slantwise into the *bai hui* point on the crown of her head. In response to this emergency treatment, she gradually began to come round.

The family's name was Qin. The patient, who was in her early forties and the mistress of the household, had three sons and two daughters. The one who had gone in search of a doctor was the middle son, and now all five of them were clustered round the bedside. The husband, who was in his fifties, was also there, standing woodenly, and when he saw his wife regain consciousness, he didn't speak, but gestured to his children to kneel and kowtow to Song Ci.

From Song Ci's point of view, reviving the woman hadn't presented much difficulty and he didn't think of it as anything special. His interest had, however, been piqued by the woman's illness and he wanted to find out more about it.

"What is that?"

Song Ci had seen the eldest daughter stirring some water in a bowl and putting it down in front of her mother. Clearly something had just been mixed into the water, but it hadn't been heated, so what could it have been? Song Ci had to ask.

"It's salt water," the daughter replied.

"Doesn't your mother have enough salt in her food?"

"That's just it," said the husband, speaking for the first time. "She gives all her salt to the rest of us."

"Why? Can't you buy enough salt?" Song Ci asked.

"Ha!" the husband gave a hollow laugh, but he didn't say anything.

The eldest daughter, who was helping her mother to drink some of the salt water, said: "Doctor, you are not from around here, so you won't know that in Tingzhou salt is worth its weight in silver."

"Why is it so expensive?"

"Well," the daughter said, "our salt comes from Fuzhou, along the upper reaches of the Min River, and that is a long and difficult route. A return journey can take more than a year, and the price of the salt reflects that."

"Why can't you get any from down the Han River in Chaozhou, or the Ting River?"

"There are some merchants who do that, but there is a band of pirates on the Ting River, not many of them – I have heard only ten or so – but their captain is a very clever man. After their salt boats were robbed a few times, none of the salt merchants dare use that route any more."

"Doesn't the government know about this?"

"Of course. But even though the pirates are active on both sides of the county border, neither county's officials have been able to do anything about it."

As Song listened to her explanation, he noticed how well-spoken she was, and how fair and plump. She was also wearing much finer clothes than either her parents or her siblings. She had an embroidered white silk flower in her hair, which showed that she had been married but was now widowed; and, as the silk flower looked new, the bereavement must have been very recent. By rights, she should have been in mourning clothes, but she was in fact wearing a green skirt and a spring jacket patterned with purple flowers... Song Ci had noticed over recent years how much more willing people were to flout convention, and this young widow's attire was a case in point.

All this had occurred when Tong Gong was out with Song Ci that morning, and after they left the family, Song told his companion about the peculiarities he had noted. And now, Tong Gong had bumped into the middle son in these rather unusual circumstances. Since the Qin household was short of salt, and had urgent need of it, surely it was very likely... but Tong Gong stopped himself, and reconsidered, knowing there was no way he could be sure of this.

"If you rely on first impressions, it only serves to impede your reasoning, and can lead you seriously astray." Song Ci had reminded himself of this warning on many occasions. Over the last few years, he had passed on much of what he had learned through experience – the world is endlessly full of surprises, and unexpected events can arise from the most ordinary of circumstances. Tong Gong's thoughts were interrupted by the sturdily built man who had begun interrogating the two combatants again, in very judicial fashion, and Tong Gong stationed himself at the edge of the circle of onlookers to listen.

"So according to what you have said," observed the man addressing the fortune-teller, "the one who shouted 'Sir! Sir! Come here!' and 'Here, sir! Take it and get away!' was the one who tried to help you."

"Er... that's right," said the fortune-teller.

"In that case, I'll get the two of them to repeat those words and you can tell which one it was."

"Very well – I'll try."

"Right you two, speak up! And if one of you doesn't dare, then we'll know he's the thief," the man said sternly and with no little authority.

"Sir! Sir! Come here!"... "Here, sir! Take it and get away!" The taller of the two was the first to speak.

"Sir! Sir! Come here!"... "Here, sir! Take it and get away!" the other one repeated.

The onlookers all turned to the fortune-teller who opened his sightless eyes wide and craned his neck forward. It was clear he was making a huge effort, but he remained silent.

The self-appointed adjudicator ordered the two youths to repeat the phrases.

"Sir! Sir! Come here!"... "Here, sir! Take it and get away!"

"Sir! Sir! Come here!"... "Here, sir! Take it and get away!"

The youths kept repeating the two phrases while the fortune-teller listened with an intent expression on his face, his lips pursed. Finally, he said: "I... truly, I can't tell which it is."

"Ha!" exclaimed the man. "So much for blind people having better hearing! I know you can't see, but I can't believe you're deaf as well."

The fortune-teller's face was beaded with sweat. "It's just... one of them is a nasty, violent thief and the other is an honest fellow who came to my aid. If I pick the wrong one, everyone will think I'm just a stupid old blind man..."

The crowd of onlookers were all scratching their heads and offering differing opinions on what to do next. So there they were: the blind man had been through the whole experience but hadn't seen it; the sighted people hadn't witnessed it; and the thief was manipulating the situation, so even the innocent party would have trouble proving his case. No one could shed any light on the situation.

"Good townspeople," said Tong Gong, walking into the circle of onlookers. "A new magistrate has just arrived. I think the best thing to do would be to take these two to the *yamen* and explain the case to the magistrate. I expect he will quickly get to the bottom of it."

The onlookers turned to Tong Gong in his working man's disguise and agreed that he had a point. The middle-aged man said: "In that case, we'll hand the two of them over to you."

"No." Tong Gong made an obeisance to the crowd. "I have to tell you, I'm on urgent business. I would ask you all to help this poor old blind fortune-teller to take the suspects to the *yamen*."

As he spoke, he noticed that the taller of the two young men seemed to be looking rather flustered, but he couldn't be sure whether this was just his imagination.

"Very well," the middle-aged man replied, before turning to the two men. "Let's go then, and if one of you chickens out, we'll know he's the thief."

Of course, the two men immediately both said they were willing to go, but their injuries made walking difficult. So the townsfolk supported them back into the city, willing to help because they knew that one of them had had the honesty and courage to help the old fortune-teller.

Tong Gong stood in the middle of the road, watching them all go back in through the north gate. Then he turned, remounted his horse and set off northwards with all speed towards Jianyang.

2

## THE DISC OF THE MOON

Midsummer came to Tingzhou in all its beauty. The sky was clear and blue, and the countryside was at its very best. Trees, plants, animals and people all basked in the sunshine, and harmony ruled.

Along came the sound of galloping hoofbeats and the sweet tinkling of small bells. Carriage wheels threw up the comforting smell of the earth of the southern post road. The sweet wind-borne scent of rice seedlings was particularly rich and fragrant in the countryside of the south. When Tong Gong returned home and saw Qiu Juan, he couldn't help being surprised; surely this wasn't the same young woman who had once saved his life. Qiu Juan, on the other hand, had no such difficulty in recognising the young man who had tried to kill Chai Wanlong that year, and who currently attended on Master Song. Now Mistress Song, her daughter Song Qi and Qiu Juan were all accompanying Tong Gong to Tingzhou, which at that moment was just appearing ahead of them.

"You're here! You're here!"

As the entourage arrived outside the *yamen*, Song Ci had already come out to greet them. The first person to alight from the covered wagon was an exceptionally elegant young woman, and at first Song Ci couldn't believe his eyes. He knew that Qi'er was no longer a little girl, and he had imagined her often and seen her in his dreams. But, in those dreams, she was still the tender child he had left behind. Song Ci stared in wonder at his daughter... his eighteen-year-old daughter!

She was covered in the dust of travel, but even that could not hide her fresh, spring-like appearance. Her skin was white and glowing, her body slender and elegant but well formed; her features were regular, with pleasantly dimpled cheeks. All in all she was an even more beautiful and vivacious version of her mother in her own youth, except that her hair was a little less glossy – but that was probably only because it was covered in dust from the road. A lock of hair clung to the perspiration on her forehead and only seemed to emphasise the impression of elegance. She got down from the carriage and stood, looking at her father.

Mistress Song followed her daughter down from the carriage, and after her came Qiu Juan, who by now was thirty years old, but still looked a decade younger. Song Ci came down from the threshold of the house and said first to Qiu Juan: "Juan'er, you had us worried for a while, but we always knew we would see you again."

"Thank you, Master," Qiu Juan replied.

Yulan hadn't changed much since the last time her husband had seen her; except perhaps she was a little thinner, which, when she stood alongside her daughter and Qiu Juan, only served to make her look more like their elder sister than their mother and mistress.

Song Ci stood in front of his daughter and looked her over carefully before saying: "Qi'er, you've grown up."

Song Qi looked back at him and exclaimed: "Father!"

"Qi'er, let me show you your chamber."

Song Ci had prepared a very elegant chamber for his daughter: outside the window a banana palm leaned its fronds against the eaves, and a thicket of tall bamboo swayed gently in the breeze. Inside the room there was a bowl of evergreen asparagus grass on a *zitan* wood stand. Its stems drooped elegantly like jasmine, and the small green leaves were dappled with the morning sun that came in through the window. The chamber was furnished with a make-up table, a bookcase and a reading desk. On the desk were some of the texts by eminent legal scholars that Song Ci had collected over the years, a stack of fine Anhui writing paper, two Duan-stone inkstones from Zhaoqing and several sticks of *qianqiuguang* Anhui ink. A brush pot contained ten or more brushes of different sizes, all with the finest quality Huzhou hare's fur from Zhejiang. These brushes are famous for the firmness of their tips, their capacity to absorb ink, and the way their rigidity and suppleness combine when used for calligraphy. Song Ci had bought all this equipment specially for his daughter. Song Qi had loved calligraphy from an early age, and even though, as a girl, she could never have an official career, both to have excelled at her other studies and, at the same time, to have perfected a fine calligraphic hand, was no small achievement.

When Song Qi went into her chamber, the first thing her eyes rested on was the writing equipment on the desk, and she began to jump up and down with excitement. Over the last few years while she had been at home, most of her studies had been devoted to her love of calligraphy. One by one, she had taken down and copied every one of the texts her father had collected over the years: Wang Xizhi's *Commentary on Yue Yi*; Yan Zhenqing's *Stele from the Duobao Pagoda*; Liu Gongquan's *Stele from the Xuanmi Pagoda* and *Shencejun Stele*; Ouyang Xun's *Inscription from the Jiucheng Palace*; Su Shi's *Record of the Fengle Pavilion* and later copies of his *Thousand Character Text*. They were all grist to her mill. 'First copy, then imitate: copy the structure and imitate the spirit; first seek the form, then follow the expression'. Following these principles, she had gradually developed an exceptionally elegant hand. So when she saw all the precious materials, the fine paper, the Duan inkstone, the Anhui ink and the Huzhou brushes, she couldn't help rubbing her pretty hands in delight. Song Ci picked up one of the sticks of *qianqiuguang* ink, and he began to grind it for his daughter.

"Come, Qi'er. Write some characters for me."

"Ha!" His daughter was delighted at the prospect of showing off her calligraphy to her father. She smiled sweetly and asked: "Isn't this *sichidan* paper?"

"It is indeed," her father replied. "Now, Qi'er, write something."

*Sichidan* is a type of fine writing paper, named after a man called Kong Dan from the Eastern Jin dynasty (317-420 CE) who invented it in his youth, and its production had continued ever since. Song Qi carefully selected a medium-sized hare's fur brush and then looked at her mother, who smiled back and nodded her head. She loaded her brush from the ink-stone, made sure she was holding the brush correctly with 'empty palm and firm fingers', then, her wrist poised, she began to write without haste. And what she wrote, in large characters, with brush strokes, now swift, now slow and controlled, were the following lines:

> *I want to be an example to others in life*
> *And remain a hero in death.*
> *I will always remember Xiang Yu*
> *And never admit defeat.*

It was *Quatrain of a Summer Day* by Li Qingzhao that her father had taught her when she was little. Song Qi was finished writing in a moment. Her father raised his eyes to look at his daughter with surprised pleasure. Although he expected Qi'er's calligraphy to have improved, he had never imagined it would be as remarkable as what he now saw. His eyes moved from his daughter's satisfied face to the characters she had written. Song Ci was no great calligrapher himself, but he was an avid collector and something of a connoisseur. He could see that, in their form, his daughter's characters were perfectly proportioned: in those that divided top and bottom, the upper and lower portions were clear and distinct, their weight evenly distributed; in those characters that divided left and right, the two sides were evenly balanced, close but not crowded, distinct but not separate. In the single form characters, their few strokes were carefully defined, their relationship clear and the transition between them smooth and even. He could see that the writing on the paper in front of him had all the qualities of fine calligraphy: it was perfectly proportioned; had an inner strength; held a balance between vigour and passivity; moved easily between restraint and release; was tight but not cramped; relaxed but not loose; changing but harmonious. The strokes were satisfyingly powerful, round and voluptuous, full of meaning and glowing with vitality. It was hard to find any fault with them.

"Not bad, really not bad at all," Song Ci said, looking in delight, first at the calligraphy and then at his daughter.

"Father," said Song Qi, suddenly changing the subject. "Did you know you have been swindled over one of the scrolls of rubbings you bought?" She then began searching in the trunk of scrolls she had brought with her.

"Do you mean that copy of Wang Xizhi's *Preface to the Collected Works of the Orchid Pavilion*?" Song Ci understood that his daughter was already sufficiently expert to be able to identify inferior work.

"It's certainly not by Mi Fu."

"I know."

"Why did you buy it then?"

"How do you mean?"

"Tell me!"

Song Ci looked at his daughter's eager expression and couldn't resist explaining.

"I bought that in the capital outside the door of the Hanlin Painting Academy's painting and calligraphy store. At the time, your Uncle Liu was still around, and he and I were coming out of the shop when we were stopped by a hawker selling calligraphy scrolls."

"A hawker selling calligraphy?"

"That's right. In a place as large as the capital, you come across all kinds. The hawker was very mysterious about it. He said he had been watching the two of us for a while, and he could tell that we were serious collectors. He said he had a rubbing of Wang Xizhi's *Preface*, one of the most sought-after works in the empire. Then he took the scroll out of his sack."

Song Qi raised her eyebrows in amusement. "The *Preface* was buried with the Tang emperor, Taizong, in his mausoleum."

"That's right. So your Uncle Liu and I just ignored him. But then the man hurried after us and said that what he had was a copy made by the great calligrapher Mi Fu, and that Mi Fu's work was so good it could pass for the original. It was not something that keen collectors like the two of us should pass up."

"He was certainly persistent," Song Qi said, laughing. "But how could a real copy by Mi Fu possibly come onto the market like this?"

"That's right. So we kept ignoring him and continued on our way. But the man ran ahead of us, and with a great flourish, unrolled the scroll, so we had to stop and look. The calligraphy certainly had the style of Wang Xizhi's work, three hundred and twenty-four characters in twenty-eight columns, repeated characters were highlighted in a different script, and in the bottom left-hand corner was Mi Fu's seal reading 'The Eccentric Scholar of Xiangyang'."

"Ha!" Song Qi gasped. "So it did indeed need a close inspection. If its condition was too good, if the balance between moist and dry brushwork, and the shading of the ink were not right, and if the layering of the brush strokes was too neat, then it couldn't be the work of Mi Fu."

Song Ci looked at his daughter's rather disappointed expression, and said, in an amused tone: "So, you think your father only realised all this after he'd been duped?"

"Mmm," Song Qi nodded.

"Not at all. We spotted it straight away, and when the hawker saw that we really did know our stuff, he rolled up the scroll and made to leave. It was we who told him to stay."

"Why?"

"For years I had been looking for a copy of Wang Xizhi's *Preface* but had never found one. Although this scroll was a fake, it still had some merit. When the hawker saw that we did want to buy it, but weren't going to offer the kind of price he wanted, he tried to slip away. But your Uncle Liu stopped him, and after some discussion he agreed to sell it for just enough for him to buy ink and paper. And that's how we acquired it."

Evening was approaching and the whole afternoon seemed to have passed in a flash. Song Ci told his daughter about all the wonders inside the capital's Hanlin Painting Academy bookshop and Song Qi listened in rapt attention.

"Father, next time you have an opportunity to go to the capital, you must take me with you," she said.

"Very well."

· · ·

The night sky looked vast in summer south of the Yangtze. On this particular night, the moon was full, and the warm breeze was laden with the scents of the plants and flowers in the courtyards at the front and rear of the houses. There were two lofty ancient pine trees inside the district *yamen*, which, according to tradition, had been planted at the beginning of the Tang dynasty. Their trunks were enormous, with a girth three men could only just encircle. Their branches were closely entwined with each other, winding in and out like tow ropes on the river, forming a shimmering canopy that enchanted all who saw it. It was pleasantly cool there on this summer night in the dense shade of the trees, and the light breeze made it the most delightful of spots. Song Ci, along with his wife and daughter, and Qiu Juan too, had been sitting there talking for ages, until, before they knew it, night had drawn in and they finally made their way home to sleep.

At last Yulan was back with her husband. As she gazed at the man she had been parted from for six long years, she saw that the wrinkles around his eyes had deepened, his skin had darkened and he had lost weight.

"I'm forty-three already. You need to give careful thought to your mother's dying wish. Qiu Juan is a very suitable young woman. And at this time in her life, if you don't take her as your concubine, she will probably never get married."

"Have you discussed it with her?" Song Ci asked.

"No."

"Then for goodness sake don't!"

"Why not?"

"She saved Tong Gong's life. I think the two of them were brought together by fate, and they are well suited."

"What about you?"

"Aren't you here with me now?"

"I can't have any more children."

"Yes, you can."

"Besides, you are no longer young yourself. Much better you take Qiu Juan as your concubine. I think she wants it too."

"Talk to her about it. She might want to marry Tong Gong."

"You really should settle for her – you won't find anyone better."

"Tong Gong isn't young any more either. Think about it... Song Xie never got married – do you want to consign Tong Gong to the same fate?"

"You could find him another woman to marry."

"Let's not talk about it any more," Song Ci said, folding his wife in his arms.

3

# GRANDFATHER AND GRANDSON OF THE HUO FAMILY

The next morning, Tong Gong took advantage of a quiet moment to raise the case of the salt thief.

"That's still on your mind? Very well, I will explain. When those two men were bundled into the *yamen* by the townsfolk, I made sure I found out all the surrounding circumstances, and I was reminded of a larceny case recorded in the Tang dynasty by Fang Xuanling in the account of the life of Fu Rong[1] in his *History of the Jin Dynasty*. There were many similarities."

Tong Gong asked what these similarities were.

"The main difference was that the victim was an old woman, and the reason she could not identify the culprit was because it happened at the dead of night. The way Fu Rong dealt with it was to order the two suspects to run a race. He reasoned that the slower of the two must be the thief, because the slower man had been caught by the faster one. But our two men were both quite badly injured and not able to run a race. In fact, there was no need for a race – since they were both injured, why not start by examining their injuries?"

"Have the two men stripped of their clothes," Song Ci ordered, once the basic facts of the case had been established.

The court officer repeated the order, and four of the *yamen* staff came forward and stripped the two men. Song Ci stood up and went over and walked round the two men, inspecting them. Then, addressing the shorter but more able of the two youths, he asked, quite amiably: "What is your name?"

"My family name is Huo, and my given name is Xiong," the youth replied.

"Very good. Now stand up." Song Ci turned to the *yamen* staff and ordered: "Bring a chair."

A chair appeared immediately, and the young man called Huo Xiong sat down. Song Ci turned to the other man, who was still kneeling at the front of the court, and gazed at him sternly. This one was the second son of the Qin family. Song Ci said: "As for you, hadn't you better confess now?"

When the young man had entered the *yamen* and recognised Song Ci, he experienced quite a shock. But now that Song Ci had addressed him thus, he replied in his own defence: "Your Honour, my family is indeed short of salt, but I beseech you not to believe that I am a thief. I beg Your Honour to clear up this matter."

"There are many people in Tingzhou who are short of salt, but they don't all go and steal some. If this court convicts you of theft, you cannot use that to excuse your crime."

The youth was stunned. He couldn't believe what he was hearing.

Song Ci pointed at the injuries on his body and said: "Both of you have marks on your bodies, but yours are clearly those of someone who has been grabbed by another. It's clear that when the two of you were fighting, your opponent was afraid you would get away, and he reached out and grabbed you, leaving these marks behind. If you look at his body, all you can see are the marks of a fist fight. All you were concerned with was making him let go so you could run away, and you had no reason to grab hold of him. What do you have to say to that?"

This speech made everything clear to the crowd of townsfolk who had gathered in the court. When they looked at the two young men's bodies, they could see quite obviously the marks left by blows from a fist and those left by being grabbed. The thief had no option but to confess immediately. With the case settled, Song Ci ordered the *yamen* staff to take Huo Xiong into the back room to have his wounds dressed. Although he insisted there was no need, the youth was escorted into the back room. But when Song Ci himself went there with some ointment, he found the *yamen* staff searching for the young man.

"Where is he?" Song asked.

"We don't know where he went."

"How strange. I wanted to give him a reward."

Song Ci had always recognised the benefits of a system of rewards and punishments, and in this, his first case as district magistrate, he had very much wanted to reward the young man for his honesty and courage. So it was a great shame that he had made off without waiting.

This, then, was the whole story of the case. Tong Gong had listened very carefully and had certainly taken it to heart. Mistress Song and Song Qi had also been there while Song Ci was telling the story, and they were greatly intrigued by it. The only thing they thought odd was the way the young man had left without a word. Mistress Song thought to herself that, if only he had waited for Song Ci to apply the ointment, then his wounds would have healed much more quickly.

Song Qi asked: "So, Father, have you not seen him since then?"

"No, I haven't," Song Ci replied.

"Father, could all of this really happen here in Tingzhou just over the theft of a catty of salt?"

"What do you mean? You heard the whole story. Don't you believe me?"

Song Ci could see from the expression in his daughter's eyes that she was still wavering between doubt and belief, so he told her about some of the cases he had dealt with in the period after Tong Gong left Tingzhou to return to Jianyang. And the fact was that the majority of these cases involved salt in some way. As she listened, Song Qi's doubts were resolved, and her dubious expression was replaced by one that was almost melancholy. Never in her eighteen years had she thought there was any reason to be worried about something as basic as salt, nor could she have believed that there were people who were willing to rob, steal, assault or murder just for the sake of acquiring a small quantity. Of course, what she also didn't know was why edible salt had been a state monopoly for hundreds of years over many dynasties; or why so many beacons of war had been lit because of it. In fact, in the second year of the Shaoding period (1229), in Tingzhou itself, a major uprising had erupted over the black market trade in salt. It was led by Yan Mengbiao, and the rebels quickly seized and occupied the county town. Fearful of being killed in his own *yamen*, the magistrate at the time had left office and fled. The ranks of the rebels swelled rapidly, and the movement spread across the counties of Ninghua, Qingliu, Jiangle, Liancheng and Shanghang, then north into Jianning, Taining and Shaowujun and into the coastal regions of Quanzhou and Xinghua. It was so serious that the government was forced to send an elite detachment from the armies fighting on the front line against the Jin forces west of the Huai River. They had only succeeded in putting down the rebellion in the spring of the previous year.

While Song Ci was explaining all this to his daughter, his wife was listening with a frown on her face. When Song had finished, she said: "So it would be a great thing if someone could solve the salt problem in Tingzhou?"

"Of course. The people need to eat, so there should never be a shortage of salt."

"Can it be solved?" asked Song Qi, taking an interest herself.

"It's a matter of time, really. With good planning, I'm sure it could be done."

But at the same time, Song Ci was thinking to himself that it would be no easy matter; certainly much harder than any of the tangled and complicated cases he had previously resolved. It reminded him of the importance of Mr Zhen Dexiu's maxim "Enact four benefits, eradicate ten wrongs". So, when he took the matter in hand, he first presented a petition to the emperor asking for a remission of fifty per cent of land tax, and displayed announcements of a bonus for private cultivation. The aims of these measures were to increase local production and support the farmers of the region. At the same time, he recruited a squadron of able-bodied, expert boatmen and waited for Tong Gong to come back from Jianyang so he could put him in charge of an expedition to Chaozhou in Guangdong Province to bring back salt.

Three days later, the boatmen set off.

This was the first time Tong Gong had taken on such a responsibility on his own, as he stood at the prow of the lead boat, making his parting respects to Song Ci. Song Qi, who had accompanied her father to the wharf on the Ting River, suddenly felt worried as she watched the boats casting off from the shore. Quietly, she said: "Isn't this journey rather dangerous?"

"Not at all," Song Ci replied.

Three months later, Tong Gong returned. The boats were fully laden with salt, and Tong Gong had also managed to apprehend several salt smugglers.

During these three months, Song Ci had also heard a number of cases involving salt, had halted several violations and arrested some corrupt officials who were profiteering from the salt trade. Now he started a series of hearings for all the related cases, and he had all the convicted either tattooed on the face or sent to the district penitentiary, or severely beaten and sent back to the fields. As a result of all these measures, the price of salt fell sharply, and life for the people began to improve considerably. The district of Tingzhou gradually began to settle down, and Song Ci once again found himself with little to do.

From time to time, Song and his wife returned to the matter of Qiu Juan and whether to take her as a concubine. Song still thought they should make an arrangement between Tong Gong and Qiu Juan, and the two of them could not agree on the matter. They still had not talked about it to Qiu Juan herself.

The year passed quickly, and very soon it was the start of summer of the following year. Song was called on to investigate a most unusual case that involved the upstanding young man who had disappeared without taking his leave the year before.

One bright, early summer morning, the city was covered in a light mist, and the moist air blowing in off the Ting River felt pleasantly cool. A pair of couplets hanging on the Zhengchen Pavilion in the rear courtyard of the *yamen* read:

*Birds are singing in the jade-green willows,*
*Dew drops cluster on the green bamboo.*

It summed up perfectly the feeling of place and time.

As was his custom, Song Ci was up early practising his 'internal' form Xingyiquan.[2] Tong Gong had risen even earlier to practise his own 'Timid Fist' form. On this particular day, Song Qi had also got up early and, as always, was standing some distance away from Qiu Juan. As she watched Tong Gong's evasive moves, soaring like a dragon and leaping like a tiger, her hand would occasionally trace calligraphy characters in the air, just as admiringly as the poet Du Fu when he saw the Tang dynasty dancer Lady Gongsun perform her dagger routine. And Song Qi, who preferred regular script and running script, and detested wild cursive, as though inspired by Tong Gong's Timid Fist, found herself taking pleasure in that very script.

At this point, the gatekeeper came into the courtyard to report to Song Ci: "Your Honour, there is a man called Huo Xiong waiting on the street outside. He says he wishes to consult you on an important matter."

"Huo Xiong?" Song Ci stopped his exercise for a moment to think and then remembered that this was the same upstanding and courageous youth from before. "Tell him to come in."

Huo Xiong hurried in, and Tong Gong came across to join them. Song Qi had made to retire, but she couldn't resist eavesdropping. She naturally wanted to get a good look at this mysterious youth who had disappeared last year without so much as a by-your-leave, and who had now suddenly reappeared. Huo Xiong was of average size, dark-complexioned, with a fuzz on his upper lip. He looked to be in his early twenties, quick-witted and well able to handle himself.

"Master Song!" Huo Xiong greeted Song Ci respectfully when he saw him. "My grandfather requests you to come and investigate an extraordinary occurrence. Are you, by chance, willing to do so?"

"Your grandfather?"

"Yes."

"Who is your grandfather?"

"He is a medicine-seller, but he is an old man now."

"Ah, so that's why you didn't need my ointment and just slipped away."

"I..." Huo Xiong hesitated. "My grandfather has some skill in treating bruises and sprains from fighting."

"Is that so? And what does your grandfather want to consult me about?"

"Your Honour will have to come and see for himself."

"Is that so?" Song Ci repeated, beginning to think there really must be something extraordinary about the affair. "Very well, I'll come."

"In that case, you will have to change into some ordinary clothes. It is a long way from the city and there are some hills to climb," Huo Xiong said matter-of-factly.

"Change my clothes? Is that also an instruction from your grandfather?"

"Yes, sir."

"Clearly," Song Ci thought to himself, "this grandfather is something of a character." He ordered Tong Gong to go and change too.

"So where is your grandfather now?"

"In the Tingjiang Inn."

The Tingjiang Inn was situated in a street not far from the east gate of the city. In front of its doors hung a couplet in clerical script that read:

*Brewed with sweet autumn water from the Jade spring*
*On a beautiful spring day by the Ting River.*

A pole stuck out from the eaves displaying a blue-and-white banner, on which was written: 'The beautiful scenery of the Ting River'. The brilliant rays of the morning sun were striking full on the banner, making the characters of the inscription stand out in a golden glow.

The three men had reached the inn and were just about to go in, when out of the door came an old man carrying a deep bamboo basket and with an exceptionally large wine gourd hanging from his belt.

"Grandfather!" Huo Xiong cried out happily and took the basket from the old man.

The old man clasped his hands in greeting to Song Ci: "Thank you, Your Honour, for not ignoring such an ignorant old man."

"Not at all, not at all," Song replied, returning the salute.

The old man had twinkling eyes and a silver-grey beard, and he was dressed in a long, pale-green gown that had faded almost to white from constant washing. Although it was clearly old, it was still very neat and in good condition. His voice was clear and full of vigour, and his demeanour was that of a dignified, seventy-year-old man. Song Ci noticed that, hidden among the wrinkles on his forehead, almost imperceptible, was an unusual scar. The nature and positioning of the scar led Song Ci to the conclusion that the old man had probably once been tattooed as a punishment and that the character had been removed with considerable skill. The scar gave the man a rather mysterious air, but Song Ci put this issue out of his mind and asked him: "Venerable Father, may I ask your name?"

"I am ashamed that you should ask. My name is Huo Jing. I have lived all my life in Tingzhou, and for many years I have collected medicines in the mountains to sell in the market. Yesterday, up in the mountains, I happened on an extraordinary sight, and I had heard that Your Honour has a penchant for such things. I thought it might interest you, so I sent my grandson to ask Your Honour to come. I little thought you would come so quickly."

"Venerable Father, I could not have dared to refuse you."

"I do not deserve such attention. I am just a simple mountain man, and I beg forgiveness for my impudence in inviting Your Honour." When the old man finished speaking, he looked up at the sky. "We have quite a long way to go, so let us slowly make our way."

4

# THE CASE OF THE WORMWOOD IMAGE

Although he had said "slowly", the old man set off with great strides, so that Song Ci, following behind, had to hurry to keep up. The four men left the city by the east gate, crossed the Guanyin Bridge out of the eastern suburbs and began to climb Tongjiyan. Tongjiyan is a towering mountain full of strange rock formations. It is divided into the upper and lower slopes, and at the top stands Tongji Temple. Despite the many strange rock formations, the mountain is not made up completely of barren crags. In early summer, the slopes were lush with vegetation, with a profusion of mountain flowers, white as pure jade, and blazing red. The branches twined overhead and you could reach up and pluck the fruit and leaves.

As the four of them passed over the mountain's ridges, they forded a crystal-clear stream, where the water eddied round the broken rocks and arrived at a spot known as Black Rock Ridge. Above them were rocky cliffs and below they could see the river winding through the valley. A hundred weird and wonderful rock formations rose as though pulled up from the earth, towering mightily above them, steep and awkward and full of potential hiding places. The old man came to a halt.

"Look, Your Honour. What's that?"

Looking where the old man was pointing, Song Ci could see a field of wormwood, in the middle of which was an area that had grown especially tall and lush and had taken on a particular oily black colour. This luxuriant growth was in the shape of a human body, with the head and four limbs clearly distinguishable. The old man said: "A human body has been cremated here, and if that is the case, then it was surely a murder, and someone brought the body here and burned it."

Song Ci immediately realised its significance, and he raised his hands in a respectful gesture towards Huo Jing: "How do you know this?"

Old Man Huo returned the salute: "When a body is cremated, the fat enters the soil. In the following years, the grass grows oily black and lush, in the shape of the body, and it keeps on doing so over time."

He led Song Ci down from the ridge to the meadow where they carefully inspected the body-shaped patch of wormwood. They could see for certain that the victim had been a woman.

Despite searching, they could find no other evidence. So who was the murderer, and how could the case be solved? Song Ci was quite taken aback, not least because he had never before seen anything like this human outline in the grass. He again asked the old man: "How do you come to know all this?"

Huo Jing hesitated for a moment, as though he was having trouble forming the words. Then, looking up at the expectant Song Ci, he said: "My grandfather had seen a case like this before."

"Your grandfather?"

The old man nodded: "My grandfather was a coroner. He served Deputy Chief Justice Li Ruopu for many years and gained a lot of specialist knowledge. During the Shaoxing period, after General Yue was framed on trumped-up charges and his body was spirited out of the city one night by the jailer Kui Shun, officers of Qin Hui's faction dug a new grave outside the city walls and sent for a coroner to formally identify the body. My grandfather didn't want any part of it, and he slipped away home. Not long after, he heard that, by imperial order, the chief investigator in the case of Yue Fei, He Zhu, deputy chief justice of the Court of Revisions, Xue Renfu, deputy chief justices Li Ruopu and He Yanyou were all dismissed from office."

On hearing this, Song Ci's respect for the old man grew considerably.

That affair had happened after the posthumous rehabilitation of Yue Fei, and the imperial court had kept it very quiet, so for Huo Jing to talk about it in such detail showed that his grandfather had indeed been very close to Li Ruopu. Song Ci himself did not know much detail about this case, which by now was almost a hundred years old, so he asked: "Perhaps you can tell me – He Zhu was originally one of Qin Hui's henchmen, so why was he dismissed for presiding over the Yue Fei case?"

"I did hear my grandfather talk about it a little."

"Please tell me." Song Ci, of course, was very familiar with the monstrous miscarriage of justice against Yue Fei.

"He Zhu was indeed part of Qin Hui's faction and participated in the impeachment of Yue Fei. In fact, the imperial court appointed him chief investigator in the case. But he was not really in accord with Qin Hui. When, during the proceedings, he saw with his own eyes the words 'Total loyalty in the service of the country' carved with a knife on Yue Fei's back, he was deeply ashamed. After that, he argued powerfully for a 'not guilty' verdict and actually confronted Qin Hui in court. So a little more than a month into the trial of Yue Fei, Qin Hui got Emperor Gaozong to decree that He Zhu... well, the rest you know."

"Wasn't he secretary of the Duanming court, with responsibility over the Bureau of Military Affairs, and comptroller of tributes to the Jin?" Song Ci did indeed know all about the imperial decree over He Zhu, and filled in the information.

"That's right," Huo Jing said. "It was all designed to get their chosen man in place and they wanted He Zhu dismissed as governor of the imperial prison. After he had gone, the reactionary minister Moqi Xie was appointed by the emperor as deputy censor. He was totally on the side of Qin Hui and was able to see this unprecedented miscarriage of justice through to the end."

"And why were those other senior officials – Xue Renfu, Li Ruopu and He Yanyou – also removed from office?"

"Xue Renfu was a sympathiser of Yue Fei and had offered a veiled defence of him. Li Ruopu and He Yanyou were not afraid to risk their official positions and stand up for what they thought was right. But on their own, rowing against the tide as they were, how could they hope to achieve anything? Of course, Qin Hui couldn't possibly tolerate it, and that was that."

"I remember," Song Ci said, "that the other investigator in that case was Chief Justice Zhou Sanwei…"

"Zhou Sanwei was the deputy chief investigator and also a sympathiser of Yue Fei, but during the case he was too scared to speak out and kept his mouth shut. So when the case was over, at the same time that Moqi Xie was promoted to a senior post in the government, Zhou Sanwei was appointed assistant minister in the Ministry of Justice, and later became chief minister. Ha! But that's enough. Let's say no more about such things."

So saying, Huo Jing took the wine gourd from his belt and took some deep, gurgling draughts. He put the gourd down and wiped his snowy white beard. Then he pointed to one of the towering cliffs and asked Song Ci: "Does Your Honour want to climb to the top?"

"Let's go."

The sun was high in the sky and scorching hot. There was not a breath of wind, and the atmosphere was stifling and sultry, as though the weather was about to break and rain was on the way. The four men had just reached the top of one section of cliff, and they were dripping with sweat, their mouths parched. Fortunately, as they passed beyond this first cliff, a spring appeared beside them as they climbed. It widened and then narrowed, sometimes dispersed into many rivulets, sometimes a single stream, and they could drink at will to slake their thirst. Only Huo Jing didn't drink a single drop of water, applying himself, instead, to his wine gourd.

"Master, have you ever seen the plant known as 'barbarian iceplant'?" Huo Jing asked as he walked along, his voice still strong and clear.

"I have heard of it. It is also known as wild chrysanthemum, yellow rattan, torchflower and heartbreak grass. But I've never actually seen it. I do know that it is a deadly poison, and just three leaves are enough to kill you."

"I know it. There is a waterfall that comes down from the crag up ahead, and there is a place near it where that plant has always grown."

Not much further on, they did indeed hear the sound of a waterfall echoing round the valley. Then it came into sight, a torrent of water flowing down the cliff face, like a water god descending from the clouds. The four of them approached until they were standing by the crag, and the noise was thunderous. Looking up towards the top of the waterfall and down into its depths, they felt as though they were suspended in mid-air, surrounded by a bewildering whirl of white and green. Looking up, they couldn't see the top of the waterfall and they calculated they must be standing right at its mid-point. Above them the water was pouring down, and below them the spray was billowing upward – a whirl of pearls and snowflakes, clouds of vapour like waves reflecting the sun. It was an experience so intense, only by being there could you fully appreciate it. Song Ci gazed in awe for a while, and then he urged the old man to go down to find the iceplant. As they stood in front of the patch of creeper, they saw it suddenly begin to tremble slightly.

"Look, Your Honour! This is the barbarian iceplant. It always trembles when someone approaches. See how the leaves are long and narrow, and taper to a point. The stems are variegated blue-green and yellow, the flowers when they open are red as torches and shed their petals like wild chrysanthemums. If you dry the stems and leaves in the sun and then grind them to powder, they are a very potent poison."

"Is there an antidote?" Song Ci asked, as he inspected the plant. "The ancient texts say that the liquid from human faeces can counteract it, if taken soon after the poison has been swallowed, but I don't know if it is true or not."

"In that case the liquid acts as an emetic. In fact, if you take an unhatched chicken embryo, grind it and take it with sesame oil, not only does that too act as an emetic, it also counteracts the poison. But in either case it has to be done quickly. If there is any delay, then there is no hope."

"Have you ever seen anyone cured in this way?"

"No, I haven't, but..."

"But what?"

"My father cured someone who had been poisoned by this plant."

"Your father?"

"My father was also a coroner."

"Is that so?" Song Ci was amazed and pleasantly surprised.

"One year my father chanced on a most extraordinary affair. There was a local man who had started a feud with someone. Because he knew he wasn't going to win in a fight, he determined to use his own death to get the better of his rival. He gave himself a dose of barbarian iceplant and then went to pick a quarrel with his enemy. They set to fighting, and then the poison took effect and the man fell to the ground. By chance, my father saw what had happened, and when he turned the man over, he discovered he still had two leaves of iceplant in his pocket. When my father realised the man had poisoned himself with the plant, he rapidly sought out a chicken embryo from the neighbours and mixed it with sesame oil. He dosed the man with this and he did, indeed, recover. Otherwise, if the man had died, and the case had come before an official who took no account of the suspicious circumstances, then the other family in the feud would have been lucky not to pay with their lives."

Song Ci listened to all this very attentively, thinking that he had indeed learned something very useful. Without being ordered, Tong Gong began gathering some of the stems and leaves of the iceplant, since he knew Song Ci would want to keep some to study.

The summer sun was very changeable, and although it was still very hot with no breath of wind, the distant clouds were beginning to close in. The blue sky grew dark, the wind got up in an instant and the clouds came rushing over like a stampede of wild horses. The peaks became shrouded and clouds filled the valleys, as the trees and plants swayed and bent. Thunderclaps burst overhead, and a torrential rainstorm was about to be unleashed.

"Your Honour!" said the old man. "The Tongji Temple is up on the mountain top, and behind it, below the cliff, there is a place where a kind of Indian madder grows. Have you ever seen that plant?"

"Indian madder?" Song Ci shook his head. He had never even heard of it, let alone seen it.

"South of the river, countryfolk steep the plant in vinegar and sell it as a treatment for wounds – it makes the scars disappear. But if you then put liquorice root juice on them, the scars come back again. Does Your Honour want to go and have a look?"

"Let's go."

Song Ci was always interested in anything new and unusual, and he would go to almost any lengths for something that might turn out to be useful in a case. Of course he wanted to go.

All around them, the peaks were towering into the sky, piercing the clouds. The thunder was still pealing mightily, making the cliffs shake. Following a long stone path and looking up at the uniform grey of the sky, the four men climbed to the top of the mountain. The rain was pouring down by then, and Huo Jing led Song Ci into a cave at the base of a crag. An icy wind blew through the cave, and water dripped steadily down from the rocky ceiling with a tinkling, splashing sound. Huo Jing led the way deep inside, through the drips, until they reached a drier spot where they each chose a flat-topped rock to sit down.

"Have a drink," Huo Jing said after he had sat down. He took the wine gourd from his waist, unstoppered it and offered it to Song Ci. "I brewed this myself. It will warm you up and dry you out, get your *qi* flowing and relax your bones, get your blood pumping and put some starch back in you."

Song Ci didn't refuse the offer, and he drank heartily from the gourd. With a few mouthfuls of the wine in his belly, he came to see that this was no ordinary drink. It was highly fragrant, sweet, mellow and powerful, making its effect felt all through his body and straight to his *dantian*.[1] When Song had finished drinking, the old man took the gourd and gave it to Tong Gong who also knocked back several good draughts. Finally, the old man took back the gourd to sit by himself on a rock and slake his own thirst.

The rain was still falling outside the cave, and Song Ci took a seat on a rock, facing Huo Jing. He studied him for a while and then asked: "Venerable Huo, may I presume to ask – you are an old man now, I dare say you saw many things when you worked in the *yamen*."

The old man looked up abruptly and stared hard at Song Ci. Song returned the gaze, and he could see how much was hidden behind his eyes. He continued his questioning: "Coroners run in your family. You clearly have so much deep knowledge gleaned from experience, you must have been a coroner yourself. I am just wondering… why did you stop?"

"…"

"Did you suffer some injustice?"

Huo Jing opened and closed his mouth, mumbling indistinctly. Then he gulped down some more wine, and the strange scar on his forehead began to turn red.

Song's gaze still rested on the old man, who finally began to speak: "I was indeed once a coroner." And as he started, the words came tumbling out. He continued: "Your Honour, in the cases you handle you put great weight on the physical evidence, and less on verbal confessions, and I think you also like to sort truth and fiction from people's everyday conversations. I'm afraid I won't be able to persuade you of the truth of what I tell you today, but… but you can trust me that it is true."

"Speak up then." Song Ci looked eagerly at the old man.

Huo Jing took the stopper out of his gourd and drank several mouthfuls. Then he began to speak, taking more pulls at the gourd as he did so. The first thing he talked about was his family history, which could almost have been something out of a fairytale…

It was in the Five Dynasties period (906-960 CE) in the time of Wang Shenzhi[2] of Min (Fujian). A mother was living with her son in Tingzhou. The son was an expert snake-catcher, which was how he made his living. At the age of twenty he married a girl called Xie Shi. Mother, son and wife lived together, and although their circumstances weren't easy, it was a very harmonious household.

But bad luck was to strike. Before the couple had been married six months, while out hunting, the husband was bitten by an Indian cobra and died. This left the nineteen-year old Xie Shi a widow. The poor girl had already fallen pregnant, and not only did she have to bear the misery of losing her husband, and endure the hard grind of her daily life, on top of that her mother-in-law was constantly berating her for having been a scold and a bad wife. Despite all this she remained tenacious and determined. The child in her belly was always restless and agitated, and, in fact, was born unexpectedly early. Xie Shi endured a long and difficult labour, but the baby was stillborn. After this, her mother-in-law cursed her even more for being star-crossed and cursed.

Five years passed with the two of them scratching out a living. The old woman grew weaker and feebler, and a day came when she went blind. For those five years, Xie Shi had been deep in grief, toiling away at what woman's work she could perform, and looking after her mother-in-law as a dutiful daughter should. Two more years passed, and the old lady took to her bed and never rose from it again. Xie Shi saw to the sightless old woman's every need. The illness lasted another two years, with Xie Shi even sleeping in the same bed, the better to look after her. The effect of Xie Shi's faithful heart, truer than gold, began to rub off on the old woman. One day, as she was gently stroking her daughter-in-law, widowed for nine years already at the age of twenty-eight, she began to weep and said in a trembling voice: "You are still young. You should marry again as soon as you can."

The two of them wept bitterly together for a while, and then Xie Shi stopped her tears and said firmly: "No, I will not."

Later that same day, the old woman waited until her daughter-in-law had gone out for a while, then fumblingly tied a rope around one of the bedposts and hanged herself. When she died, she was still kneeling on the ground beside the bed. Her relatives were deeply suspicious of the death, and they took Xie Shi to court, accusing her of murder.

The local magistrate interrogated Xie Shi, asking: "How is it possible for someone to hang herself while her feet are still on the ground? Come on, speak up!"

"I... I don't know." Xie Shi shook her head, by now thoroughly terrified.

"You are a shameless and contrary woman to have the impudence not to confess. Officers, she is to suffer the highest level of torture!"

How could such a weak and defenceless woman endure that kind of torture? She made a false confession and pleaded guilty. The case was then referred up to the prefectural magistrate for sentencing. Xie Shi's younger brother was perplexed; he remembered how good his elder sister had always been to him in the past, and he hurried through the night to plead with the prefectural magistrate that a grave injustice was taking place. The magistrate re-examined the defendant, but Xie Shi seemed set on dying, refusing to retract her confession.

Then an aged coroner from the *yamen* took it on himself to speak to the magistrate: "There have been cases in the past of people hanging themselves while kneeling on the ground. If you judge this case to be one of murder by strangulation on the basis of what we have heard, then I am afraid it will indeed be a miscarriage of justice. There would be no harm in sending someone to re-examine the old woman's body, so we can know for certain."

The prefectural magistrate accepted the old coroner's suggestion, sending an officer to escort him to conduct a second autopsy. On examining the body, the old coroner found enough evidence to prove that the old woman had indeed hanged herself, and Xie Shi was exonerated.

Once Xie Shi was freed from prison, she really wanted to thank the unknown coroner, but she never saw him again and could not see any way of doing so. Two years later, when Xie Shi was thirty-one, she was just as beautiful as she had been when a young woman, and she married a man from the mountains who was ten years older than her and had never been married before. The man's name was Huo, and he gathered medicines for a living. As time went by, Xie Shi bore three sons, and even after they had grown up, Xie Shi never forgot the old coroner who had saved her life all that time ago. So she arranged for her third son to become a coroner too. Of her three sons, the youngest was by far the most able.

Xie Shi lived on until she was over seventy, by which time her husband had already died. As she herself approached her end, she summoned the son who had become a coroner to her bedside and told him of all the regrets and frustrated hopes of her life. She finished by pleading tearfully with him: "My son, it is the gift and blessing of a coroner to be able to right the wrongs perpetrated on the common people. It is a noble thing. Promise me that you will choose one of your own sons to become a coroner, and he will do the same with his sons, and his son's sons and so on down the generations."

When she had finished, she stared at her son, waiting for his reply. Tearfully he assented, and with this last consolation after a lifetime of toil, Xie Shi died. From then on, the profession of coroner became a tradition in her family, and has indeed been passed on from father to son over the generations. Time rolled on, and rulers came and went. The Kingdom of Min was overthrown by the Later Tang, and the Later Tang was superseded by the Song. As the dynasties changed, each generation of the Huo family continued to produce a son who would later become a coroner. When Chancellor Xiang Minzhong of the Northern Song solved the notorious case of the body in the dried-up well, it was Huo Jing's forebear Huo Gang who acted as coroner in the affair. That case was recounted by the Northern Song historian, Sima Guang, also known as 'The doctor of the Su River', in his *Records of the Su River*. Song Ci had read it himself, but the name Huo Gang was not mentioned. That was not, in itself, surprising. The role played by a very minor coroner in the case, although pivotal, would not have been of sufficient importance.

The story reached the time of Huo Jing's grandfather. Even after he had left office and returned home, he still passed on his knowledge to his own son. Now, in Huo Jing's lifetime, not only had he inherited the ideal of his ancestors to use his skills to right the injustices perpetrated on the people, but he had also distilled the essence of the skill and knowledge of all the previous generations. Even though, down through those generations, the post of coroner was somewhat held in contempt by the officers of the *yamen*, their consummate skill and knowledge, handed down father to son, always caught the attention of those officials genuinely concerned with the well-being of the nation, right up to the chancellor himself. Sadly, however, such officials were few and far between. And in the cases handled by such officials, their devotion to duty, their honesty and candour, and their unwillingness to compromise their conscience, tended to jeopardise their position in the *yamen*...

"Telling the truth often got one into trouble, while telling lies and covering up brought great rewards. It... Ach!" Having said this much, the old man sighed deeply and stopped.

Silence fell in the cave. The only sound was the faint drip, drip of the water falling from the ceiling and the glug, glug of Huo Jing drinking from his gourd. Song Ci understood, for the old man had just told the story of Song's own experience.

Huo Jing took a few more swallows from the gourd, then put it down at his feet and let out another sigh. By now, beads of sweat were standing out on his face, the crown of his head seemed almost to be steaming and the strange scar in the centre of his forehead had turned such a deep red, it was almost purple. After a while, he started up again and told the story of a case he had encountered several decades before. He told it as it had happened to him, his manner calm and open and his voice clearer than it had been before. It was a tale to make the hearts of listeners quake. Song Ci was familiar with countless strange cases from the past, but this one even shocked him.

5

# THE CASE OF THE SWIM ACROSS THE LAKE

A biting wind was blowing into the cave, and outside it was still raining. Rolls of thunder were punctuated with lightning that lit up the interior and pierced the downpour that was falling like a curtain in front of the cave entrance. Still grasping his wine gourd, the old man began to tell his tale.

"Forty years ago, I came across a most extraordinary case. I won't go into too much detail about who was involved, and what caused it and so on. But I will describe the nature of the case, as I know that is what most interests Your Honour. The guilty party was ruthless in the extreme. Just consider, Your Honour – he made a wooden barrel, as tall as a man, filled it with water and mixed in several catties of lime. He then put a man in there, upside down, and fixed the lid in place. Of course, the man died. Have you ever seen or heard of such a thing?"

"No, indeed. This is the first time," Song Ci said.

"There was another case in the ancient past. I heard it passed down from my great grandfather. It is known as 'The case of the swim across the lake'."

"The case of the swim across the lake?" Song Ci thought that he had read up on every unusual ancient case that had been recorded, but he had never heard of this one before. But then there must be hundreds of strange cases over the years that went undocumented. He realised he was being presented with a field of human activity he had never encountered before.

"The lime prevented any blood flow from the body that was stuffed in the barrel, and although the blood did congeal in the face, it was dissolved by the action of the lime. When I washed the body, there was no sign of any injury, and the flesh tone of the face was a pale yellowish white. It appeared as though the man had died from some ordinary illness."

"So, how did you conduct your examination?"

"The case took place in the compound of a very eminent family, with a population of fifty or sixty people. The body had already been examined by another coroner, who had certified death through unspecified illness. I was away examining a body in a different case, but when I returned and heard about all this, I immediately had my suspicions. These suspicions were aroused in the first instance because I knew that the deceased had been the best *cuju*[1] player in the district and was in excellent health. So how did he die so suddenly of some illness?

"I was very young at the time and always keen to find an explanation for things that puzzled me. Besides, there might well be some very important people involved in the case, so I decided to take the opportunity to examine the body for myself. That night, I crept into the compound and did just that.

"I won't go into the twists and turns and alarms of that night. Suffice it to say that I went, and as I examined the body, when I opened its mouth and took a sniff, I caught the smell of lime. That's when I remembered the story my great grandfather had told me. I realised that the current victim must have inhaled a large quantity of lime through his mouth and nose, and although it might have been rinsed out, the smell was still discernible, even over the stench of decay. Moreover, I was able to use a bundle of thin bamboo slivers to dig out some of the actual lime from the corpse's ears. At the time, I did not know that when a body dies, lime can enter the cranium through the nostrils, and because it is so dense, it stays there and doesn't come out. If you want to be sure this is so, you can open up the skull, and you will see that the inside is completely white. After I had finished, I slipped back out of the compound and returned to the *yamen* to report the matter to the magistrate.

"To my surprise, the magistrate was very angry, and he reprimanded me, saying: 'What kind of strange drug have you taken that you come here spouting this wild nonsense?'

"I replied that it wasn't wild nonsense at all, and that just made him angrier: 'Surely you are aware that entering someone else's property without permission is a criminal offence. If you weren't ordinarily such a loyal servant, I would have you locked up!'

"I was young and fearless then. I thought this was a particularly cruel and violent murder, and I was genuinely concerned for the magistrate. So I continued to plead with him: 'Your Honour, if you have made a wrong judgment in this case, then surely that will cause trouble for you.'

"The magistrate just got angrier still, but I continued to argue my case as vehemently as I could. It was no use, and eventually he sentenced me to a night in the holding cell and ninety strokes of the cane. Then I was thrown out of the *yamen* in disgrace.

"But I was hot-headed too and couldn't let the matter rest. I reported the case to the prefectural magistrate, who listened with great interest and sent an officer to reinvestigate.

"I was very excited, the day they exhumed the body. The prefectural magistrate was there, and the head of that important family had also been ordered to attend. I watched them behaving as though they hadn't a care in the world, and thought to myself that it would all come out once the body was dug up…"

The old man stopped.

Song Ci looked at his face, which had lost its red colour and taken on a grey-green tinge. He took up where the old man had left off: "But when the grave was opened, the head was nowhere to be seen!"

"That's right." Huo Jing hesitated, then went on: "There was a great clamour from all the onlookers, but I kept calm. I said: 'The fact that only the head was taken shows that the killer is trying to hide his tracks. The case can be properly registered now.' I little thought…"

"The case had been registered, and the person put on trial was you."

"That's right!" Huo Jing smiled wanly. "Things happened rather quickly. The magistrate's assertion was that I had stolen the head from the grave, then misled the officials with false evidence and acted with malice aforethought. I still wasn't worried, however, because I had seen that neither inner nor outer coffin had any trace that might have been left by being exhumed. So there could be no doubt that the head had been taken before the body was buried. That being the case, the guilty party must have been someone from inside the eminent family's household. I explained all this, but…"

Seeing that the old man had stopped again, Song Ci thought to himself that, although he had never previously heard of this case, he was familiar enough with the way court cases went to have a pretty good idea of where this one was going. So, to prompt the old man, he asked: "And was the body still unburied on the day you were thrown out of the *yamen*?"

"It was."

"So they could, quite reasonably, claim that the night after you were dismissed, you crept back into the compound and stole the head."

"Exactly so. I was taken into the courtroom and tortured to the limit of what is permitted. The family had made a careful inspection of the contents of the coffin, and they falsely accused me of stealing money and other valuables that had been put in there… Ha! How foolish I was then."

"But you… you stayed conscious through the torture?"

"Absolutely! And at that point I realised why they were so unconcerned when they went with the magistrate to exhume the body. And I also wondered how the guilty party had known the head had been taken before the body was buried. I said all this to the magistrate. I was beginning to see my way through the complexities of the situation. But I did wonder why the official who had just arrived to conduct the second autopsy was quite so closely in agreement with the magistrate. The only explanation was that the wealthy family involved had been distributing bribes. It was quite clear that they were all of the same mind, and they wanted me dead and out of the way."

"What happened next?" Song Ci had been listening with clenched fists and gritted teeth, but couldn't stop himself interrupting.

"Next?... I confessed," the old man said calmly.

"What? You confessed?"

"That's right, I confessed. But I only confessed to using the opportunity of my examination of the body to steal the valuables. I didn't confess to going back and stealing the head."

"Why?"

"It's quite obvious really. If I didn't confess at all, they would certainly torture me to death. And all I could think of was that, if I died, then the tradition passed down from my ancestors of each generation producing a coroner, would end with me, Huo Jing. I would be shamed in front of those very ancestors. So I decided I must not die at any cost. I was no fool, knowing that if I confessed to the theft of the valuables, according to the Law on Larceny established by Emperor Shenzong, the heaviest penalty that could be imposed was to be tattooed and sent to some remote military penitentiary. And they knew that if they tried to make me confess where I had put the head, and I did actually confess, they certainly wouldn't find it wherever I said it was. So, as I had already confessed to the theft, why not just sentence me for that? And if they still wanted me dead, rather than have me die in the courtroom of the *yamen*, why not arrange to have me quietly disposed of en route to the penitentiary? So I confessed to the theft, and they sentenced me for that. They gave me forty strokes of the cane, arranged for my forehead to be to tattooed, fixed a forty-catty iron cangue round my neck, signed the orders and sent me off into the deep south to serve my sentence."

"And then you escaped!" Song Ci said, smiling faintly, as he saw the colour returning to Huo Jing's face.

Huo Jing scratched the reddening scar on his forehead, smiled and then continued: "You are right, Your Honour, and we will soon get to the nub of my case. It was high summer at the time, and the sun was scorching down on the trunk road to the south – every step burned our feet. I said to my two escorts: 'If we don't take some medicine to counteract this heat, we will all die of sunstroke on the way.' They knew about such medicines, and together we set about collecting the plants we needed. I had made the suggestion, because quite recently I had learned from my father of a medicinal plant called *menghangu*. It is very rare. Your Honour may never have seen it, and, another day, I will collect some for you to study. The thing was, I had seen it growing by the roadside, and I collected some, along with the other herbs. That evening, we brewed up our medicine in a little local tavern, and I, of course, found some excuse not to drink it. But the two guards did, and very soon they were sleeping like the dead. I took the keys off them, unlocked the cangue and escaped."

Reaching this point, Huo Jing unstoppered the gourd again and drank some more. Still scratching the scar on his forehead, he said, smiling faintly: "I know that Your Honour will have made certain assumptions about me because of this scar. Indeed, if I don't do something about it, it will continue to haunt me all my life. It was a good thing that that miscarriage of justice took place in Tingzhou – otherwise I might never have returned to my old home, and I would never have met a man of such wisdom and sagacity as Your Honour!"

"You are too kind to me," Song Ci replied with humility. "I have learned a great deal from what you have spoken about, and it has been my good fortune to meet you."

"Your Honour!" The old man's eyes were alight, and his words were clear and sonorous as he spoke from his heart. "To tell the truth, when you arrived in Tingzhou that day and solved that case about the catty of salt, Xiong'er came home and told me about it. It was as though I had encountered one of the great sages from the past. And then when you announced the remission of half the land tax, and so judiciously resolved the salt shortage for the people of Tingzhou, I was filled with respect and it set up a longing in me to realise a long-cherished hope. After we had inspected the human form in the wormwood up on the mountain yesterday, I took the liberty of bringing you to this ancient cave. Please forgive me."

After Huo Jing had finally finished his secret history, he drank again from the gourd, draining it to the last drop before putting it down.

The old man's words had had the same effect on Song Ci as if he himself had just drunk a whole jar of fine wine, so much did they warm his heart. The old man was so full of righteous energy and the desire to settle old grievances, and his family had such a venerable tradition of service as coroners, started by that simple peasant woman so long ago – how could that not command the greatest respect! In the face of such a life full of dashed hopes and extraordinary experiences, Song Ci was at a loss how to respond.

"Old friend, that must be quite some wine," he said in the end.

"Ha! If you can't drink, you can't be a good coroner." Having finished the wine, the old man had perked up considerably, and his white-bearded face was glowing. "Have a drink before you examine a body to concentrate your *qi*. Have a drink while you examine it to hide the smell. Have a drink after you have finished and spit it out onto the charcoal to keep away the evil spirits of the departed."

The four men all laughed heartily.

Almost imperceptibly, outside the cave the rain stopped and the sky began to clear. They left the cave and felt the cool, moist mountain breeze blowing gently over them, incomparably refreshing. The sky had cleared after the rain and was beautiful to behold. A dazzling rainbow arched across the heavens.

The four of them set off back through the remoteness of the cloud-covered mountains, skirting round the Tongji Temple until they came to the vine-covered cliff with its curtain of waterfall, where they had gathered the Indian madder. Song Ci came to a stop, dazzled by the wondrous beauty of nature. He sighed inwardly to himself. How magnificent his country was, truly a crouching tiger and a hidden dragon, that it could shelter unnoticed among its people so many priceless treasures.

# CHAPTER IX

## FLYING DETECTIVES (1233-1234)

Nowadays, the use of dogs in criminal investigations is commonplace across the world. Seven hundred years ago, China was already using houseflies in such investigations – the first instance of a living creature being used in this way. At that time in medieval Europe, the Church took the place of courts of law, and ordinary people's criminal cases could be abandoned or quashed at will. They were still a long way from using animals in investigations. In contrast, Chinese legal officials at the time already had several different categories of crime scene examination: examination of injuries, autopsy, examination of tools or weapons, and so on. This example of using flies in a case can be considered one of the first instances in history of forensic medical investigation.

# 1

# THE DISMEMBERED BODY IN THE FIRE

High summer had passed, but the weather had not yet cooled down. From the moment the sun rose, a heat haze began to ripple across the landscape. Even the occasional breeze that came from the direction of two ancient pine trees in the courtyard of the *yamen* was baking hot, and the pair of tilework unicorns on the roof ridge of the main building seemed to be gasping for breath.

Song Ci had gone to pay a visit to Huo Jing and his grandson. Since Tang times, there were villages in Tingzhou where Han Chinese and the local She people cohabited. Huo Jing and his grandson were Han but lived in a small She mountain village some way outside the city. Bamboo was plentiful in the mountains, and like all the other families in the village, the Huo home was made of bamboo and almost all their furniture and household fittings were of the same material. For Tong Gong, who came from a family that made bamboo staves for baskets, it felt rather like coming home.

The family circumstances were somewhat straitened, and the house contained little, except for medicinal plants of all kinds hanging on the four walls. In his lengthy chats with Huo Jing, Song Ci always gleaned much knowledge that could not be found in books.

He was still brooding over the case of the human outline in the wormwood up on Black Rock ridge, but since no other clues could be found at the scene, even his frequent discussions with the old man failed to result in any further enlightenment.

Until one day, in the course of their roamings in the mountains, Huo Jing and Huo Xiong found a freshly cremated body near the site of the first one on

Black Rock Ridge. The two of them had left early, before the heat set in, and they reached the ridge just as the sun was coming up. In the early dawn light, Huo Xiong noticed a column of grey-green smoke rising from beside the path that cut across the ridge.

"Look, Grandfather! What's that?"

"Fire! It's a fire! Quick!"

Huo Jing set off in the direction of the smoke, taking great strides and parting the branches with his hands as he went. When he breasted the ridge, he saw the fire burning on a stretch of grass not far from the first cremation. It had been stacked with enough grass and branches to burn for many hours.

"Surely someone can't be burning another body!"

Grandfather and grandson looked at each other and simultaneously came to this same conclusion. They scanned all around, but there was no sign of anyone. The fire had been lit so recently that whoever was responsible must still be in the vicinity. What to do?

"Quick! Put the fire out."

The two of them rushed down the ridge to extinguish the blaze. The fire was getting bigger, fanned by the wind, and was crackling loudly. They had got there just in time, and, after a fierce struggle that left them with blackened clothes, they managed to bring the blaze under control.

"Spread it open and see what's there."

"Ah!" Huo Xiong pulled apart the pile of charred grass and firewood, and almost immediately found a cloth sack covered in blackish-purple stains.

"It's blood!" he called out.

"Open it."

The neck of the sack was tightly fastened, and Huo Jing used a serrated pruning knife to cut the string. Inside was a body, a recently dismembered body, completely naked. A glance was enough to show that the corpse was male.

The two men looked around; above them was a towering rock formation and, some way below, a stretch of wormwood that had clearly never been mown, as it had grown at least to the height of a man. Apart from the babble of a nearby stream and the smoke still rising leisurely from the fire on the meadow, the mountains and valleys were quiet and undisturbed by any human activity. There was no one to be seen.

"Don't worry about him," Huo Jing said and the two of them began to examine the body. As they worked, Huo Xiong noticed there were unmistakable knife wounds on the body, and he said: "That's strange. Grandfather, have a look. It seems he was attacked with a sickle."

"You're right. And it must have been a new one – the cuts are very clean and neat." The old man spoke in a matter-of-fact way, and it was clear he already appreciated the significance of the wound for himself.

"The cuts were made while he was still alive."

"Yes. Look at the one here on the back of the neck. It has severed the blood vessels right down to the vertebrae – a fatal wound."

"The cuts indicate that he was lying down when he was attacked."

"One, two, three…"

The two men counted the wounds as they continued their examination; there were sixteen in total, of varying depth and quite widely spaced. The blows had all been inflicted at the same time, and there were no cloth fibres in any of them. It was evident that the man had been naked when he was attacked. After they had learned all they could, Huo Jing said: "Xiong'er, hurry and report this to Master Song Ci."

Huo Xiong looked round the dark and lonely valley. He was afraid that his aged grandfather might meet with some mishap if he was left there all alone.

"You go, Grandfather. I'll stay here."

Huo Jing was not happy with the suggestion, but Huo Xiong was determined, and, in the end, the old man decided he had better go himself.

Mid-morning that day, Song Ci was watching his daughter practising her calligraphy. Huo Jing rushed into the *yamen*, and as the gatekeepers recognised him and heard that he had urgent business, rather than take his report in themselves, they let him go straight into the rear courtyard.

The old man was sweating profusely and steaming from the heat. His clothes were travel-stained and covered in dust from the road. When he saw Song Ci, before saying anything, he took the familiar wine gourd from his belt, unstoppered it and drank several good mouthfuls. Only then did the tale of what they had seen come rushing out in a single breath.

As Song Ci listened, he realised that this was indeed an unusual case: the corpse had been dismembered with a knife, but rather than use that, the murderer had chosen to kill his victim with a sickle. This indicated a ferocious hatred. What is more, with such a ruthless killer at large, Huo Xiong was alone on the mountain. Song leapt up from his seat and said to his daughter: "Qi'er, go and look for Tong Gong, and tell him to take two men up to Black Rock Ridge immediately and find Huo Xiong."

"Yes, Father," Song Qi replied, hurrying from the room.

Song Ci left his daughter's chamber and ordered his men to assemble the *yamen* messengers to prepare for immediate departure.

Looking back, he asked Huo Jing: "You say there are more than ten wounds from the sickle. How are they distributed?"

"They are concentrated on the face and the lower body."

"Did you recognise the victim?"

"He is the shaman from the Dong She Village at the bottom of the mountain."

"What state is the body in?"

Huo Jing understood that Song Ci was asking if the murder had been committed recently. In the heat of summer, after only two days, there would be obvious changes to the colour of the face, abdomen and the flesh over the ribs and upper chest.

There had been no such changes visible, so Huo Jing replied: "The murder must have taken place yesterday."

"Do you think the same person is responsible for this case and the one last year?"

"Well, the two scenes are quite close to each other, and both bodies were set alight, so there does seem to be an association. But…"

"You mean the bodies are different – one was intact while this one has been dismembered?"

"Yes, but it could be that the murderer had noticed the body-shaped markings in the wormwood from the first one, and then cut up the body so as not to leave similar traces this time. Then again, he could have destroyed those markings. But…"

"Are the marks still there?"

"They are. As I said, the two scenes are quite close, but he might not have had time."

"You said that the cuts that dismembered the body were very clean and neat. That shows that they were done soon after he was killed and not after the body had been taken up into the mountains."

"I think that must be so."

"In that case, if the murderer cut up the body because he had found out about the shape in the wormwood, surely he would have destroyed that too. Since the shape is still there, it may well not be the same man."

"That's what I think too."

"Hmm," Song Ci said, beckoning to Huo Jing. "Let's go."

"Go where, Master?" Huo Jing asked, as he followed Song Ci out of the room.

"Dong She Village," Song Ci replied immediately.

"You think the murderer must be from there then, Master?"

"I can only think so."

"But," Huo Jing said, "when I came down from the mountain, I made a special detour to Dong She. I saw that the shaman's house was looking just as normal and I could hear the sound of someone spinning. I knocked on the door and went in, pretending I wanted the shaman's services to exorcise a spirit. The shaman's wife was sitting at her spinning wheel, and her first words to me were: 'He left yesterday.' I thought to myself: The shaman usually carries out his work away from the village, so the culprit must be from outside the village too."

Song Ci replied: "If his wife was having an affair with another man, then of course she would try to pretend nothing had happened. Then again, when you examined the body, you said the knife wounds were all on the face and lower body, and that the body was naked. That certainly indicates that he was having an affair himself. So it is possible the wife is not the murderer, and she does indeed know nothing about it."

Huo Jing understood that, even though Song Ci had not actually made any enquiries about the circumstances in the shaman's household, he had already worked out that, whether or not the shaman's wife had anything to do with the murderer, she would, in any case, continue to act as normal.

"So, Master, you think we will find the key to the case in Dong She?".

"I think so. Dong She is very close to Tongji Crag. The area all around Tingzhou is very mountainous and there are any number of places to bury a body. Why would the murderer kill his victim at home there and then carry it all the way to Tongji Crag?"

"So, Master, where are you going to start?"

"First, let's find the sickle."

"How do we do that?"

"Put the word around that all the locals need to produce their sickles."

"But suppose the murderer doesn't produce his?"

"It's a small village, with only thirty or forty inhabitants, and there is a blacksmith's shop there. Each household will have several sickles and the blacksmith will be able to recognise every one of them. If he's uncertain, the other villagers will tell us. Moreover, you determined that it was a new blade, and the farmers hereabouts mostly buy their sickles, hoes, knives and suchlike, on credit. The blacksmith is bound to know if any family has recently bought a new sickle. If we make sure everyone understands this, then the culprit would not dare fail to produce his sickle. But let's take a step back and suppose the culprit has already discarded the sickle – he may think better of it and produce it after carefully scrubbing it clean. If he doesn't hand it over, then we can be sure that it is the murder weapon. If he does produce it, then we can use that method you told me about to identify it. So I am confident that, as long as the culprit does come from the village, he can't escape identification, whether he hands over the sickle or not."

As Song Ci finished talking, he heard the sound of men assembling outside the room, and he beckoned to Huo Jing, saying: "Let's go."

Seeing Song Ci work out this well-developed strategy in such a short time hugely increased Huo Jing's respect for him. He marvelled at the way Song Ci had taken all the various pieces of information he had seen and heard, and woven them into a net so comprehensive that the culprit didn't stand a chance of escape. His own life had been one of toil and hardship, and he was deeply moved. Whereas before he had only heard other people talk about Song Ci's miraculous ability to solve cases, and had been content to marvel at and envy the agility of mind the master had displayed in their various conversations, now here he was, experiencing it for himself.

However, it often seems to happen that some apparently tangled and mysterious affair resolves itself abruptly in front of one's eyes, and one suddenly becomes sceptical of it.

Can that really be how it is? Will it really happen the way the master has predicted? Huo Jing was having this inward debate as he made his way out of the room, taking his usual great strides.

2

## DEPLOYING HOUSEFLIES

The sun was at its highest point, and the heat was intense. Under the blistering golden autumn sky of the south, the countryside was silent and peaceful. The rows of crops glinted in the sun, and from all over the ripe paddy fields came the flash of sickles. A horse came galloping down the road, startling twittering flocks of sparrows into the air from the fields of harvested and unharvested grain.

The country folk were taking their midday rest when the express messenger arrived in the little village under the mountain. He was under instructions to beat his gong to gather the villagers and announce the magistrate's orders. The intention was, of course, to give the culprit time to make up his mind what to do; and if he chose to produce his sickle, it would make the case a great deal easier.

When Song Ci arrived, the sun had already passed its zenith and was descending into the west. The noise of the gong was still reverberating around the village, two strokes at a time, and between each burst, the *yamen* messenger was shouting: "All sickles from every household,"... Clang! Clang! "Everyone must produce them immediately,"... Clang! Clang!... "Anyone withholding a sickle will be considered guilty,"... Clang! Clang!

Song Ci made his way to the threshing floor in front of the village, and soon the villagers began arriving in twos and threes, each carrying a sickle. A clerk labelled each implement's short handle with the name of the head of the household, and one of the *yamen* orderlies stacked them, one by one, in a small pavilion next to the threshing floor. In order to calm suspicion, the blacksmith added all his unsold stock of sickles too. Those blades were not yet affixed to handles, and not suspected of being the murder weapon, so the orderly made a separate pile of them off to one side. After they had handed over their sickles, the villagers all waited in a patch of shade next to the threshing floor. The shaman's wife came too. No one had yet said who the victim was, and she chose an inconspicuous spot to wait with the others. By then, the villagers were all assembled, and there were no more sickles to be handed over. Huo Jing produced an eel – it was not at all clear where from – and went into the pavilion to kill it. He used a double-edged pruning knife to gut the eel, and then chop it up. The eel was soon motionless, the floor around it liberally spattered with blood. Huo Jing then stood up and went to wait, a little distance apart.

The villagers were all puzzled by the eel, which lay on a plank of wood, still dripping blood. They couldn't work out why it had been killed, and they kept stealing glances at the magistrate, who sat motionless under the shade of another tree. What was he waiting for? They looked at each other in concern and exchanged whispered conversations.

Song Ci was indeed waiting. Quite soon, he saw houseflies beginning to land on the eel – first one, then two, then three… more and more of them, until they were swarming all over the bloody plank. All of a sudden, Huo Jing looked at Song Ci and spread open a piece of cloth that he flapped at the swarm of flies and then used it to wrap up the dripping plank. Deprived of their delicious meal, the flies buzzed around the interior of the pavilion…

Only Song Ci and Huo Jing understood the reason for the flies. There were a dozen or more sickle cuts on the body of the victim, so the blade used must have traces of blood on it. Although human blood can be washed off, it leaves behind a taint that is hard to get rid of; moreover, these sickles had toothed edges. The reasoning was that even if a human nose couldn't detect any odour after the blood was washed off, flies, which are attracted to blood, are much more sensitive. Of course, the culprit could have burned the blood off, but that would have left visible scorch marks. So now, in their quest for blood, the little creatures would reveal if the murder weapon was in the pile of sickles.

The flies buzzed around the room for a while, until, finally, some of them began to settle on the pile of sickles. But it was all very random – they settled, then took off again, settled, then took off again as though they had no real purpose.

Then something extraordinary happened.

"There! There!" shouted Huo Jing.

A swarm of the flies was settling on the jumble of handle-less blades from the blacksmith's shop.

Song Ci jumped up from his chair: "Lay them out, lay out that pile of blades."

Huo Jing hurried forward and methodically laid out the blades in neat rows, and very soon, all the flies began to settle on a single blade.

"That's it! That must be it!" Huo Jing cried.

The villagers were all staring at the blade in amazement. The most startled of all was the blacksmith, and before he had time to react, he heard the clang of an iron collar being padlocked round his neck.

The main room of one of the larger houses in the village was commandeered as a makeshift 'public court'. Song Ci sat in the middle, flanked by the *yamen* staff and the villagers assembled outside the door, as they had been ordered, waiting in turn to be questioned.

Finally the blacksmith reacted to his situation and began to cry out: "Great Lord, I am wrongly accused. I am innocent."

Song Ci looked at the strong-armed, well-built blacksmith for a moment and then began to question him: "How are you wrongly accused?"

"I didn't kill anyone."

"If you didn't kill anyone, then why were the flies attracted to one of your blades?"

"I... I don't know."

"Tell me where you went this morning."

"I was working in my forge."

"Can anyone confirm that?" Song Ci asked. The blacksmith's forge was on the main road at the top of the village, and there were bound to be witnesses if the smith had been hammering away there that morning.

"Yes, yes," the blacksmith cried. "My apprentice can confirm it."

"He was with you all the time?"

"He was. He was."

"And if he can't back you up, is there anyone else?"

"Yes... yes, there is."

The blacksmith then came out with a whole string of names of people who could vouch for him. When Song Ci questioned them, there was no single person who had been with him all the time from morning till noon. However, one way or another they had all been in the forge, and taken together were enough to prove that, right from early morning, the blacksmith had had no opportunity to get to Black Rock Ridge. Could it be that one man committed the murder and another transported the body? Or perhaps the blacksmith wasn't the culprit at all.

A swarm of flies had settled on the sickle blade, and Song Ci brushed them away before picking up the blade and examining it minutely. Suddenly his eyebrows shot up in surprise as he discovered traces of sawdust in the fixing hole of the blade, and the marks of a blunt instrument of some kind around its edges. Clearly the blade had had a handle at some stage, but who had removed it? There could be no question but that someone had gone into the forge and swapped the blade for an unused one. But who was it?

Song Ci turned the possibilities over in his head, and then he asked the blacksmith: "Where were you when the gong started?"

"I was working in my forge."

"Did anyone come into the forge?"

"No one."

Song Ci ordered the *yamen* staff to go into the pavilion and search for an unused blade among the villagers' sickles.

Clearly, Song Ci was convinced, the murderer must have switched blades after the gong had started sounding, otherwise what would be the purpose? Now that the blacksmith had said no one had entered his forge, the only thing to do was to search the blades of the sickles handed in by the villagers. Understanding Song Ci's intentions, Huo Jing followed the attendants into the pavilion. The sickle blades were all still laid out as before. The old man and the two attendants split the task between them and soon found what they were looking for. But there was a problem: they found not one, but three fresh blades. Song Ci inspected them closely and saw that all of their handles were newly attached, but there was nothing else to distinguish them. So he gave orders for the heads of the households to which the sickles belonged to be brought before him.

Three people were promptly led in: a man, a woman and a child. The man was tall and powerfully built, the woman was thin and ill-looking and the child was just eleven or twelve years old. The child was too young to understand what was going on, but the man and the woman both looked very nervous.

Smiling reassuringly, Song Ci first asked the child: "Now, tell me – how is it that you are the head of the household?"

The boy knelt, wide-eyed, at the front of the court and replied: "My father is ill."

"What about your mother?"

"She got up early and went to town with someone to buy medicine."

"Your father has been ill a long time?"

"Yes, sir."

Next, Song Ci questioned the woman.

"And what is your story?"

"My husband died last year."

"Why hasn't your sickle been used?"

The woman burst into tears and couldn't speak.

"Your Honour!" The other man, who was also kneeling at the front of the court, suddenly spoke up. "I beg you not to ask her again."

"Why not?" Song Ci fixed the sturdily built man with his gaze.

"Someone else... I killed him."

The whole courtroom gasped. They were amazed not just that the killer had revealed himself, but that he had done so of his own accord and not under interrogation.

Song Ci nodded dispassionately and said to the woman and the boy: "You two may leave now."

The woman kowtowed, stood up and left. The boy stayed on his knees, showing no inclination to stand up, until one of the attendants went over to help him and ordered him to go.

Only then did the boy scramble to his feet and make his way over to the door, where he stopped and looked reluctantly back into the court. Then, at last, he disappeared through the door.

3

# MURDER FOR REVENGE AND MURDER FOR ADULTERY

The moon was not yet up, but countless distant stars were twinkling in the sky.
Autumn nights are different from summer nights, and a cool breeze blowing off the Ting River quickly dispelled the blazing heat of the day. Song Ci was sitting with his wife, daughter, Qiu Juan and several others under the two lofty ancient pine trees in the inner courtyard of the *yamen*. Song Ci had just finished recounting the details of the day's case, and everyone had sunk into silent thought. Another extraordinary case! Song Ci had originally assumed that if the victim had been killed in Dong She Village, there was no way anyone would have carried off the corpse to some distant spot. But he had been wrong.

The victim had been killed in the house of a widow in the village called Qin, and that is where he was dismembered as well. Widow Qin turned out to be the woman with the embroidered white flower in her hair, whom he had met on his first day in Tingzhou. She had been wearing a green skirt and a spring jacket patterned with purple flowers, he remembered, and had been the eldest sister in the case of the stolen salt. This new case had similarly aroused Song Ci's interest. But of course, he had not yet unravelled all of its complexities.

The guilty party in the case was called Lei Sanquan – a very ordinary-looking man. He was born into a mixed Han-She farming family, which was nothing unusual in the area. Just when he had reached the age to be of some use around the farm, his parents both died from the same illness. At the time, they had as a neighbour a solitary old Han Chinese man called Zhao, who willingly agreed to shoulder some of the burden left by the death of the parents. Between them, the old man and the boy managed to scratch a living.

One year, out of nowhere, the old man bought a five-year old girl from another village. By the time Lei Sanquan was twenty-six, the girl was sixteen, and the old man gave her to him to marry. Not long after, the old man died of old age, and a year later, the girl gave birth to a boy. Within a year, the little boy was already toddling, and his mother had transformed from a thin and sickly little girl into a strikingly beautiful young woman. Lei Sanquan himself was a very well-built young man, of exceptional strength, and the best field worker in all the mountain villages. Although they could not be called well off, they lived together very harmoniously.

But one day in the autumn of the previous year, Lei Sanquan's wife left their son with a neighbour, who was called Lan Shi, set out to take her husband some food and never came back. Lei frantically searched everywhere for her, but he could find no trace. Meanwhile the little boy stayed with Lan Shi, who was the sickly woman Song Ci had questioned in court.

Some of the villagers speculated that the young woman might have come across her real parents and run away home. But old man Zhao had never revealed the identity of her biological parents, or where they lived, so no one had any idea. Lei Sanquan completely rejected that theory; her home was there in the village with her husband. He believed that she was devoted to him and their young son, and would never have run away, deserting them. He kept searching everywhere, no matter whether it was a tiny hamlet of two or three houses deep in the mountains, or the Tongji Temple, perched on the very top of Black Rock Ridge. And he had kept up his fruitless quest right up to the time of the spring sowing of the current year. He came home just long enough to plant his rice and then set off again.

One day at the start of summer, he found a clue. He was in Tingzhou when he saw a pedlar trying to sell a pearl-inlaid copper padlock. It closely resembled his wife's favourite piece of jewellery. He examined it carefully and, sure enough, it was the piece he remembered. He looked all around, his heart beating fit to burst. He wanted to detain the pedlar to ask him where he had got it, but the man had seen Lei's expression on recognising the padlock, and he immediately slipped away into the crowds, disappearing without trace.

He spent the whole of the rest of the summer searching day and night for both the pedlar, and of course, his wife. Before long it was harvest time and, remembering his little son still lodged with his neighbour Lan Shi, he went back to the village to bring in his crops. The day before the harvest, as he was getting everything ready, he suddenly saw the pedlar on the main road outside the village. Pandemonium ensued: Lei Sanquan swooped on the man like an eagle on its prey and dragged him into the woods at the side of the road. The pedlar took one look at his bulging eyes and started to quake with fear. He knew that the knuckles Lei was cracking could easily break his skull. But Lei didn't lay hold of him – instead, he took out a shiny new sickle, held it across the man's neck and took from his pocket the pearl-inlaid padlock that he carried with him night and day. Then he barked: "Right! Where did you get it?"

"I... I... I... stole it."

"Stole it?" Lei Sanquan was a straightforward young man, and he took the pedlar at his word. "Where did you steal it?"

"The... the next village. Qin Erniang's house."

"Qin Erniang?" Lei remembered the widow – in fact, she had something of a reputation in the surrounding area. But remember her or not, he wasn't going to let the pedlar go until he found out what had happened to his wife. Glaring at the man, he ordered: "Let's go. Take me there."

The pedlar didn't dare dawdle, and he scrambled up, rubbing his throat, where a few drops of blood were appearing from the mark left by the sickle. Cowed by Lei's stern, ashen-faced countenance, he didn't say a word, just set off, obediently leading the way. The two villages were only about ten *li* apart, and by hurrying, they got there before half the morning was past. Widow Qin's house was in the middle of the village; the men were all out in the fields, and the place was quiet except for the voices of the women and children coming through the half-open doorways. The widow's house was shut tight, and the pedlar led Lei up to the door. "That's the place," he said, pointing.

"Go in," Lei ordered.

The man hesitated, and Lei grabbed his arm so tightly it made him grimace. Without a sound, he stepped towards the door. Lei gave him a shove, and the door flew open as he crashed into it with a thud. The pedlar tumbled in and sprawled into the courtyard.

"Who is it?"

A woman's voice called softly from the house in the yard. The pedlar didn't dare speak as he lay there, and Lei stayed silent too. He turned and shut the door, then propelled the other man towards the house. As they reached the door, it opened with a creak, and there on the threshold stood Widow Qin. She was wearing a round-collared, pale-red autumn jacket and jade-green trousers. She had the round, plump, white face of a classical beauty, which emphasised the limpid black gleam in her deep-set eyes. As soon as she saw the two men, all the softness left her.

"You two gentlemen..."

Lei Sanquan didn't say anything but kept pushing the self-confessed thief in through the door, forcing Widow Qin to give way. Once in the house, Lei turned and closed the door. The widow didn't have time to recover from the initial shock and had no idea what the two men wanted. Lei took out the padlock and thrust it in front of her face, saying: "Tell me! Where did you get it?"

The widow shivered involuntarily, considered the padlock for a moment, then shook her head and said: "I've never seen it before."

"Never seen it before?"

"No, never."

Lei snorted, and with his right hand took the sickle from his belt, and grabbed the pedlar by the neck, as though he were catching a chicken. The man was left dangling with his feet in the air, and he cried out in a strangled voice: "Slow down… slow down and listen to me."

Lei Sanquan put him down and he tumbled to the floor. He scrambled to his knees in front of the widow and began kowtowing furiously: "Qin Erniang, my life is in your hands. Please tell him where you got the lock from. If you don't, he will kill me."

By now, the widow was trembling with fear, and the pedlar's knees were knocking together as he addressed Lei Sanquan: "My good fellow, I truly did steal that padlock from here. And if you want to know how she got it, you'll have to ask her. Even if you were to kill me, I wouldn't say anything different."

Beads of sweat stood out on Lei's forehead as he tried to decide who was telling the truth. How could he tell? With clenched teeth, he kicked out at the pedlar and heard him yelp as he flew across the room and came to rest in a heap in the corner. He stayed there, curled up in a ball, not daring to move. Lei Sanquan turned to stare at the widow, then walked towards her, sickle raised. Terrified, she fell to her knees and stammered out: "Don't kill me… I'll talk… I'll tell you everything."

Slowly, and with long pauses, she began to tell her story. She had been having an affair with the shaman from Dong She Village, and he had given her the padlock as a love token. That was all she knew about it.

It is no trivial matter for a woman to confess to having an affair with another man. If Lei Sanquan were to report her to the authorities, it would be considered a very serious crime and she would be punished severely. This made Lei think she must be telling the truth. Then he remembered something that had happened the previous year. His wife had fallen ill with a raging fever, babbling deliriously, so he had consulted the shaman. The shaman said she had been possessed by a demon and had to be taken to visit the immortals. Once she had been blessed by them, she would recover. The shaman took her, alone with him, into a darkened room, where he danced to raise the spirits. There was a great commotion, and then the room fell silent. Several hours later, the sound of an indecipherable recitation came from the room, and a heavenly fragrance wafted out. Finally, the shaman emerged and told Lei Sanquan that his wife had returned from the immortals; she was sleeping peacefully and shouldn't be disturbed. A few days later, Lei thought that his wife was still rather dazed and confused, but that her illness was improving, albeit slowly, and he forgot all about the matter. But now he thought about it again, he felt very uneasy. The news that the supposedly sage-like shaman had been carrying on with this woman gave him pause for thought, and he felt certain that the shaman had also killed his wife.

Lei Sanquan pushed the man and woman away from him and, without saying a word, turned and left. He had a score to settle with the shaman.

To his great surprise, not far out of the village he saw the shaman himself directly ahead in the distance, coming his way. But he wasn't alone; there was someone with him. Lei slipped off the road into the woods where he waited for them to go past, then he started to follow. The shaman had been summoned to perform another exorcism and his companion led him back to the village and into a large family compound. The exorcism took the rest of the day, and until sundown, all manner of wild noises came from the house. When it was done, the family gave him food and drink, until finally he got up to go.

The moon was not yet up, and the road out of the village was quiet and deserted. The shaman reached the elm tree that marked the end of the village, where the highway began. Lei Sanquan intended to follow until they were far enough away for him to grab the shaman and get to the bottom of the affair. But instead of leaving the village, on reaching the elm, the shaman turned off onto another smaller road that led back into the village. He stealthily made his way to the widow's house and knocked quietly on the door. In an instant, he had slipped inside.

Lei made his way over to the house and tried to pry the door open with his sickle, but the door was shut tight by a wooden bar, and he couldn't shift it. He was a tall and strong young man, however, and not to be thwarted, he measured up the surrounding wall of the compound, then climbed up and over it, to land in the small courtyard.

"And how are you today?"

The shaman had embraced the widow, but she just stood there silent and unresponsive. She had wanted to tell her lover about everything that had happened that day, so that he could help her think of a way out. But when she thought about it, she was suddenly afraid that if she told the man in front of her now, he might decide to kill her in order to keep her quiet. As she hesitated, the shaman swept her in his arms onto the bed, took off his own clothes and began to unfasten hers. From nowhere, a shiny new sickle blade was laid across his neck...

There is no need to go into too much detail about what happened next. The shaman's knees buckled at the sudden appearance of Lei Sanquan, and the deed was done almost immediately. Lei was strong as an ox, and besides, he had the sickle across the man's neck, and it had already drawn blood. The shaman heard Lei say, through gritted teeth: "If you don't tell me where my wife is, I, Lei Sanquan, will not just kill you, I will kill your whole family too."

The shaman didn't doubt that Lei was a man of his word, so he shut his eyes tight and told Lei what he wanted to know. A red mist descended on Lei Sanquan, and he slit the man's throat with a single thrust of the sickle. Not content with that, he rained a dozen or more blows onto the man's body and face.

Widow Qin fainted dead away but Lei paid no attention. He sat down, panting and sobbing, to rest a moment, then went into the kitchen in search of a knife, with which he dismembered the shaman's corpse. He then found a sack, which he filled with the body parts. Satisfied, he slung the sack over his shoulder and left the village.

Under the faint light of a waning moon, he carried the sack towards Dong She Village. But instead of entering the village, he hurried on to Tongji Crag. When he reached Black Rock Ridge, he used his sickle to harvest armfuls of wormwood and collected a plentiful supply of firewood. His wife's body had been cremated here by the shaman, and, to avenge her memory, he wanted to do the same to the shaman in the very same spot. The sky was gradually getting lighter, and just as he had built his fire and got it blazing, he heard the sound of footsteps running towards him. Instinct took over and he just had time to hide. When he saw a man putting out the fire, he hesitated for a moment over what to do, but then remembered he had a child at home and he cautiously made his way back to the village. Later on, when he heard the *yamen* runner beating his gong, ordering all villagers to produce their sickles, he thought about the formidable reputation of the district magistrate. He hadn't made any arrangements for the care of his son, and he didn't want to be arrested just yet, so he took advantage of the blacksmith's absence and slipped into the forge to exchange his sickle for one of the new, unused ones. He little suspected that the blacksmith would add those to the collection too...

The trial was concluded that afternoon. The sun had already set, and a purplish, silver-grey light was just beginning, faintly, to illuminate the sky. Lei Sanquan had only intended to confess to the murder, and to make no mention of the pedlar and the widow. But under Song Ci's piercing interrogation, he told all.

Song Ci sat in silence for a while. He was thinking to himself that he had made a few erroneous deductions about both the murderer and the weapon. For example, although the assassin had indeed been filled with hate, he had used a sickle because it was the only weapon to hand; and he had dismembered the body so he could make a sacrifice to his wife, and had carried it a long way from the murder scene. Court cases are often tortuous and complicated, and even the seemingly most obvious of things may turn out quite differently from expected. He also knew from experience that, although inference and deduction were important skills, only absolute proof could be used to decide a case.

Finally, he asked: "Lei Sanquan, do you have any other relatives, apart from your son?"

Lei looked at Song Ci through bloodshot eyes, then shook his head.

"What arrangements do you intend to make for your son?"

Lei Sanquan cleared his throat, as though about to speak.

"What is it you want to say?"

Lei prostrated himself and said, finally: "I thought my neighbour Mistress Lan might be willing to take him in."

"The district authorities will arrange this for you."

On hearing this, Lei Sanquan's eyes lit up, and he kowtowed continuously: "Thank you, Your Honour. Now I can die without regret."

All this time, Tong Gong had been waiting for help to take the dismembered corpse down the mountain, so that the murder scene would no longer need guarding. Meanwhile, Song Ci took the court to the neighbouring village to inspect the other murder scene there, and to check that Widow Qin's account tallied exactly with Lei Sanquan's. Thus, he was able to confirm the direct connection between the 'case of the human form in the wormwood', which he had been brooding over all this time, and the current 'case of the sickle murder'.

On the road back to the city, Song Ci reflected on the fact that even the most unusual cases, which might seem quite baffling at first, would become childishly simple once all the facts were known.

As Mistress Song, Song Qi and Qiu Juan finished listening to Song Ci recounting the case, their amazement at all its twists and turns was gradually replaced by feelings of sympathy and pity for the plight of the defendant Lei Sanquan.

"Father," Song Qi could not help exclaiming, "wouldn't it have been so much better if Lei Sanquan had just come and lodged a complaint yesterday?"

Song Ci looked at his daughter and said nothing.

"Little Mistress," Tong Gong said. "What you cannot yet know is that, when a man is consumed by some great grievance or hatred, often the only way he can rid himself of this feeling is to kill the cause of it with his own hands."

Song Ci looked sharply at Tong Gong. Although he understood quite well the reason for Tong Gong's words, he had expressly forbidden Tong Gong from taking matters into his own hands if he ever, by chance, came across the Tian Huai brothers.

"Father, Lei Sanquan is blameless, just like elder brother Gong when..."

"Qi'er!" Song Ci cut her short.

"I still remember, Father, how you told me that the emperors of our dynasty all established precedents for pardoning revenge killings. When Lei Sanquan killed to avenge the death of his wife, it is easy to understand both the emotion and logic of his act. You must pardon him too."

"Those revenge killers who have been pardoned in the past have all first surrendered themselves to justice."

"But Lei Sanquan didn't wait to be found out – he gave himself up, didn't he. Please help him, father. He has a child."

"Capital cases are not things you can play around with. Now this case has been settled in the first court, it will be referred upwards. Once the prefectural magistrate has looked at it, he will want to refer it on himself to the provincial administration for final appraisal and sentencing. It's not that I don't want to help, it's just that I have already done everything I can within my remit."

Qi's compassionate expression was tinged with bewilderment as she said: "Father, you are the most important person in the county. Surely, if you are determined enough, you can do something to save one of your people who is in such dire circumstances."

"Come then, get your brush, and I will dictate a plea in mitigation for Lei Sanquan. If it's accepted, then he can escape execution. He will still be sent to prison for quite a few years, but at least when he gets out he will be reunited with his son."

Because Qi'er's calligraphy was so excellent, since arriving in Tingzhou she had often helped her father by transcribing official documents. Song Ci was endlessly amazed at her accomplishments. And on her part, she was delighted every time her father called on her to help. This evening, however, she took no such pleasure and said to her father: "I don't want to do it."

"Why not?"

"I... I'm too tired."

So saying, she threw her father a look and turned and left. How difficult a nineteen-year old girl is for her parents to understand. From childhood, Song Qi had been educated at home by her mother and father, and was well versed in the classics. She also had no little understanding of the deep-rooted corruption of government bureaucracy. In Jianyang, she had greatly admired Liu Kezhuang for the way he would stop at nothing to do what he thought was right, even to the point of being dismissed from office. By contrast, at this point she felt her father was too bound by convention.

Back in their room that night, Mistress Song asked her husband whether there might not be some way to save Lei Sanquan.

Song Ci heaved a deep sigh: "What else can I do?"

Song and his wife did not sleep well that night. As the last light of the waning moon merged into the first light of morning, Mistress Song had only just fallen asleep when her husband shook her awake.

"Yulan, I'm going to set Lei Sanquan free this morning."

"What did you say?" Yulan thought she must still be dreaming.

"I'm going to set him free."

Startled awake, Yulan rolled onto her side and propped herself against the lattice of the window, through which the faint light of dawn was just beginning to filter. From the determined look in her husband's eyes, she could tell this was a position reached after long and serious thought, but even so, she could not help being taken aback. Had it been the result of what their daughter had said? No, it couldn't be. Her husband was not a man to allow his principles to be swayed by the words of a young woman.

"How have you come to this decision?"

"In these troubled times, law and order no longer prevail. The common people either have no way to bring a lawsuit, or no chance of succeeding if they do. And it's not just in isolated places, it's everywhere. That's why revenge killings like this are becoming more common."

"You can't mean that these killings are only happening because the people involved don't trust the authorities?"

"I think it must be so. I also believe that the law of the land should work for the benefit and happiness of the people. At heart, Lei Sanquan is a law-abiding fellow, and he deserves legal protection. But now he has committed this murder to avenge his wife, even if I submit an official plea in mitigation, he is unlikely to escape execution. So all my best efforts will result in this upright man, albeit a convicted murderer, being snatched away from the happiness of his home and sent to the headsman. What else should I do, but set him free to be reunited with his son?"

Still somewhat concerned, his wife asked: "But how are you going to account for this?"

"I've been very stupid. I should have remembered that, according to the statutes, if an adulterer is killed where the adultery actually took place, the killer cannot bear criminal responsibility. The shaman was killed during the act of adultery with Widow Qin, so if I change the charge from 'revenge killing' to 'killing of an adulterer', then Lei Sanquan is in the clear."

"Ha!" exclaimed his wife. "Won't this make Qi'er's day."

"Perhaps she was right, and this really is a 'washing away of wrongs'."

4

## THE LIFE OF QIU JUAN

In the first year of the Duanping period (1234), Song Ci was in his third year as magistrate in Tingzhou. In the first month of the year, just after the spring festival, there were extraordinary goings-on in the great Song empire. Early the year before, the Mongol army had penetrated the territory of the Jin right up to the gates of their capital city of Nanjing (modern day Kaifeng, in Henan Province). Wanyan Shouxu, the Jin emperor Aizong, was helpless against the mighty Mongol horsemen, and he fled the capital first to Guide (modern day Shangqiu in Henan Province) and then immediately on to Caizhou (modern day Runan, also in Henan). Genghis Khan's third son, Ogedei Khan, sent an embassy to the Song emperor, proposing an alliance between them to eradicate the Jin. Believing that such an alliance would help to redress the national humiliation of defeat by the Jin, Emperor Lizong agreed.

In the seventh month of the previous year, the Song general Meng Gong led his troops north out of Xiangyang (modern day Xiangfan in Hubei Province). Spurred on by a deadly hatred of the enemy, the Song troops carried all before them and inflicted a resounding defeat on the Jin army at Madengshan. By the eighth month they had reached the gates of Caizhou, where they united with the Mongol army. In the first month of the current year, the last Jin emperor Wanyan Shouxu finally ran out of food and weapons. With his troops helpless and in dire circumstances, he committed suicide in Caizhou. The Jin army was destroyed, and 150 years of Jin rule over north China came to an end. Express messengers were sent out from the capital, Lin'an, by imperial order, along every road in the country, to spread the news as swiftly as possible. The whole country celebrated, revelling in this great victory. In little Tingzhou, the people thronged the streets, rich and poor, men and women, old and young alike. Even the little peasant girls with unbound feet crowded into the city, dressed gaily in red. There were dragon dances and lanterns and fireworks, and the celebrations lasted three whole days.

All three days, Song Qi dragged her mother and Qiu Juan out onto the streets to join in. The emperor announced a general pardon across the empire. Widow Qin, who was languishing in jail until her death warrant was signed, was set free. By chance, Qi bumped into her on the street. She was wearing a pale-green padded jacket and plain trousers, and she had lost a lot of weight. Much to everyone's surprise, when Qi saw the widow, she went over to greet her with every evidence of pleasure.

One day in mid-autumn, Song Ci received an unexpected letter from Liu Kezhuang, which the latter had entrusted to a merchant to deliver. Although Song was both surprised and delighted by the letter, it also worried him.

The letter had been sent from Fuzhou. It started by telling him the current situation of Liu Kezhuang and Mr Zhen Dexiu. The year before, after the death of Shi Miyuan, the emperor had appointed Mr Zhen as chief magistrate of Fuzhou, with responsibility for maintaining order across the province of Fujian. Liu had accompanied his friend to Fuzhou and taken up a senior post in the legislature. This news delighted everyone in the Song household, but especially Qi. She was still young enough to be completely open in her emotions, and she was as happy as if it was the spring festival.

Liu went on to raise his worries over the state of the nation, and this was the part that troubled Song Ci.

He talked about the previous alliance between the Northern Song and the Jin against the Liao, and the bitter lesson of the havoc subsequently wrought by the Jin. He suggested that the current alliance with the Mongols against the Jin might not be such a cause for celebration. Although he said little, his words resounded thunderously with Song Ci. They took him back in history to the time when Zhuge Liang and Liu Bei[1] met and discussed plans to move west into the territory of Shu to establish a firm foundation, and then to form an alliance with Sun Quan to the east and hold back Cao Cao in the north. Thus would be formed the legs of a tripod that was to be the power base of the Three Kingdoms; there they could find safety and plan their future expansion. Under the planning and strategies of Zhuge Liang, this power base was indeed established. Of the Three Kingdoms, the Cao Wei in the north remained the most powerful, but found it no easy task to defeat the Shu and the Wu. The Shu had great generals and leaders such as Zhuge Liang, Guan Yu and Zhang Fei, while the Wu had the natural defences of the Huai and Yangtze rivers. But after the deaths of Zhuge, Zhang and Guan, the kingdom of Shu fell to the Cao Wei, causing the balance of power to shift, and the Eastern Wu also fell soon after.

And wasn't the state of affairs in the empire very similar now? Genghis Khan had swept to power north of the Great Wall and raised his troops against the Jin, forming a pincer movement around their southern advance. In the tenth year of Jiading, Emperor Xuanzong of Jin attempted to enlarge his territory in the south in order to hold back the Mongols. The resulting rout of his forces was due not only to the stubborn resistance put up by the Southern Song, but also because of the Mongol army massing to the rear of the Jin advance. So it turned out, these new circumstances for the much-harassed and plundered Song were similar to the situation in the Three Kingdoms period: they could repair the damage done by the depredations of the Jin; re-establish control of their land; repair and restore their city walls and reservoirs; economise on state expenditure to refill their coffers; restore the rule of law in the prefectures and provinces; and recruit soldiers from the border regions to shore up the nation's defences. The current capital, Lin'an, was located in what was the ancient Kingdom of Yue in the Spring and Autumn period (771-476 BCE), and if the Song were able to emulate that kingdom in developing its resources of money and grain, strengthening its army and consolidating its base, then it would be able to deploy its forces in timely fashion. But now that the Jin were destroyed, having previously threatened both front and rear, the Song found themselves surrounded on all sides by an even more powerful adversary – a situation that was no cause for celebration.

"The state of the nation is as fragile as an egg", "The north wind is strong in our faces" – these words of Liu Kezhuang were no mere scaremongering. As a keen student of history, Song Ci was well aware of the country's parlous state, but he had been so preoccupied with local legal affairs over the last few years that he had given little thought to the matter. But now, reading his old friend's letter, this realisation hit him hard. But what could he do to help the nation? 'Restoring the rule of law' was at least in his power, but only to a limited degree.

In his letter, Liu also told Song Ci that Mr Zhen Dexiu was working hard on his behalf and that he intended to send him to Fuzhou as judicial commissioner for the province of Fujian. This was precisely what Song Ci had hoped for. If things worked out as he planned, he could exercise his talents over a jurisdiction of considerable size, and fulfil his duty as an official of the great Song state.

. . .

The days lengthened so that a single month seemed to last sixty days. Mistress Song was now forty-five years old and past childbearing. She felt that she had not yet fulfilled Madame Song's dying instructions. But as she thought about it, she found herself not completely comfortable with the idea of interfering in her husband's domestic arrangements, so she continued to hesitate. She knew that, if she discussed the subject with her husband, he would take her side and refuse to take a concubine. But there was no point in further delay, nor in consulting Song Ci. So, one day, she called Qiu Juan to her room and presented her with the situation.

To her surprise, Qiu Juan immediately fell to her knees and said beseechingly: "Mistress, you and the Master have treated me like a daughter, please don't talk like this."

Mistress Song replied: "Please get up. These words come from my heart. You have always wanted to help the Song family and I have thought about this for a long time. You are by far the most suitable candidate, and Qi'er already thinks of you as a member of the family."

Qiu Juan did not get up: "Qi'er is like my little sister, but Mistress, forgive me, I cannot obey."

"Stand up before you speak again. Stand up."

Qiu Juan stood up and Mistress Song, taking her hands to lead her to sit down, discovered that Qiu Juan's hands were like ice.

"Now, tell me why you can't obey."

"I want to serve Mistress and the whole family."

"We are already like a family, and you are so considerate of Song Ci. With luck, you might bear the Song family a son. What could be wrong with that?"

"Truly, truly, I can't."

"I don't understand. It would be a fine and noble thing, so why can't you?"

Qiu Juan burst into tears and fell silent.

"Juan'er, what's wrong? Just tell me."

Qiu Juan sobbed quietly and still didn't speak.

Mistress Song clasped her hands tightly and said: "Child, what is the trouble? Tell me, your mistress will understand."

So Qiu Juan told the story of how, when she was sixteen, she had been defiled by the brutish Chai Wanlong. If she survived the experience, she was not willing to take her own life and resolved to live with the shame until she found the opportunity to kill Chai Wanlong. So, that night when she encountered Tong Gong coming to take his revenge on Chai, Tong Gong was himself almost killed by Chai. This gave her the opportunity she was looking for while Chai's attention was focused on defending himself against Tong Gong. She seized this chance and took her mortal revenge. Then she would happily have gone to her death, but Chai's maidservants had seen Tong Gong and were telling everyone that he had killed their master. The authorities were hunting him, and if he was caught, only she, Qiu Juan, could prove that he wasn't the killer. She couldn't allow Tong to be implicated, so she had to stay alive. Thus, unable yet to seek death, she went to the nunnery on Mount An. Then later, when Song Ci took up his official posting, leaving only Mistress Song and Qi'er at home, she came down to find them.

"Of course," Qiu Juan continued, "you knew of my disgrace, but you didn't abandon me, and my life had a purpose again. While we were in Jianyang, Mistress, you urged me to get married, and I was worried you didn't want me any more. I wept in secret at this thought. But when I realised you weren't trying to drive me away, I couldn't bear the thought of leaving Mistress and Qi'er… since I was sixteen, I never wanted to marry but was happy just living day to day. I still don't know where my younger brother is, so I have no family of my own. All these years, since I first came to this house, you have treated me like family, and I will never be able to repay that kindness. Whatever you ask me to do, I will do… except this, Mistress. This I cannot do."

Qiu Juan wept as she told her tale. Mistress Song embraced her, her own eyes filling with tears and her heart full of emotion. Finally, she said: "Juan'er, you are the best person in the world. That is all in the past, and you have had your revenge and erased the shame. Now you can hold your head high. Song Ci and I never asked before about what had happened to you during this period, because we didn't dare. But Song Ci said to me at the time that he held you in the greatest admiration and respect. It is important that you know that. If you were to marry Song Ci, it would be a great blessing to the house of Song. There is not another woman like you."

Mistress Song had not expected the conversation to turn out like this, and it left her feeling helpless and full of regret. That evening she couldn't hold back from telling Song Ci what had transpired, which only served to reduce her to tears again. Song Ci was deeply moved, since, as he said, Qiu Juan had always seemed so apparently happy in her work and gave no clue she was in such deep distress. He had had no idea that her violation by Chai Wanlong had left such an indelible mark.

"Go and talk to her," his wife said.

"What could I say?"

"Ask her to marry you."

Song Ci thought for a moment, then said: "I will talk to her."

• • •

Some days later Song Ci was strolling along the little path in the garden, when he saw Qiu Juan and called her over to him: "Qiu Juan, come over here and walk with me. There's something I want to discuss."

Qiu Juan came over to him.

"Don't be alarmed." Song Ci's words were tempered by his smiling and relaxed demeanour.

"I'm listening," Qiu Juan said.

The two of them walked side-by-side, talking.

"There is something I need to say to you. It is not something anyone else has told me, these are my own thoughts."

"What is it?"

"There is someone who is beholden to you for saving his life. You know I mean Tong Gong. But, I can assure you, this is not something he has told me, because you know he would never speak of it. What I think is that, Tong Gong is a year older than you and needs to get married soon. If I were to act as go-between for you two, is that something you would happily consider?"

At first, Qiu Juan didn't know how to answer. She felt it would be disrespectful to Song Ci to simply decline, and probably disrespectful to Tong Gong too. So what should she say? She looked at Song Ci's open and benevolent face, and thought to herself that he hadn't ordered her to do this thing, but simply asked if she would be happy with the arrangement. Plucking up courage, she smiled and replied: "Thank you for your concern, Master, but I will never get married. I get along very well, and Master does not need to worry about me."

Song Ci stopped walking: "You are quite sure about this?"

"I am quite sure."

Song Ci didn't ask any more questions, just said: "Very well, we'll say no more about it."

But as he left the garden, he turned back to Qiu Juan and said: "Nonetheless, you might have another think about it."

5

# THE DEATH OF HUO JING

Everyone in the Song household was eagerly awaiting news of Liu Kezhuang and Mr Zhen Dexiu, and most excited of all was Qi, who had not yet mastered the art of hiding her emotions. She wasn't interested in her calligraphy, and she neglected her martial arts, even though for the past few days she had been learning several different styles with Tong Gong, so as to improve her self-defence. One day, she dragged Qiu Juan with her to ask her father if the two of them could pay a visit to the Golden Sand Temple on Crouching Dragon Mountain.

"I'm afraid that if we leave Tingzhou, we won't ever come back and I will have lost my chance," she remarked.

Song Ci agreed but stipulated that his wife should go too, with Tong Gong as escort.

Crouching Dragon Mountain is to the north of Tingzhou, rising in solitary splendour among the fields with no other mountains in the vicinity. It is a tall and imposing ridge, formed into tortuous zigzags so it does indeed look like a crouching dragon. Its peaks are covered in towering ancient pine trees, and when the sky clears after rain, it is shrouded in a blue-green haze with lingering white clouds, so it is sometimes also known as the White Cloud Dragon Mountain. Every day there is a constant stream of pilgrims, climbing the mountain to the Golden Sand Temple to offer prayers. On the road there, Qiu Juan stayed close to Mistress Song, and she was constantly at her side every step of the climb up the mountain.

Song Qi walked by herself at the front of the party. Halfway up the mountain, they chanced upon a young peasant girl who had collapsed on her way to burn incense at the temple and was sitting down on one of the stone steps. She didn't even have the strength to make it to the pavilion a little way up ahead, and the young married girl she was travelling with wasn't strong enough to support her. As soon as she saw the situation, Qi hurried ahead to help the girl up to the pavilion. As she did so, she realised the girl was running a fever, and she said to the other girl: "She's sick. You mustn't try to go any further, you won't make it. Take her to see a doctor."

When Song Qi and her three companions reached the summit, they saw the Golden Sand Temple, its many ramshackle storeys clinging to the peak like a half-built city wall, huge and imposing, but possessed of an exquisite delicacy too, and affording a magnificent view. Looking down from the topmost storey, the whole Ting River was spread out below in a stunning panorama. It was one of the happiest days of Song Qi's life, but on the way down, she too began to develop a fever: she started to shiver uncontrollably, had pains in her chest, began to vomit and her whole body ached. Worst of all, her head felt like it was splitting open and she had a raging sore throat. Dark fever-spots began to appear on her usually clear forehead, and they spread gradually across her chest, down her back, on her abdomen and all along her arms and legs. Within the day, they covered her whole body, some small and almost insignificant, but others as large raised discs. In the creases of her arms and upper legs, the spots merged into red weals. She was barely recognisable as the beautiful young woman of a few short hours before.

Song Qi had caught a serious form of seasonal scarlet fever, well known to locals.

She was hurried back to see the doctors in Tingzhou, who diagnosed the illness and began treating her. Over the next three days, although the rash began to disappear, she remained delirious from the fever; her throat was inflamed and ulcerated, and it felt as though she was swallowing sharp knives if she tried to drink anything. Her skin was peeling off in patches, so it was still hard to recognise her.

Because the disease was so contagious, from the very first day Song Ci didn't allow his wife anywhere near Qi'er, as he was afraid her constitution was too weak to take the risk. But Qiu Juan ignored all his admonitions to be careful and careless of the risk to herself, stayed at Qi'er's side, day and night. The two of them had developed an exceptionally close and loving relationship since Qi'er was a little girl, and now Qiu Juan's concern and distress were every bit as great as Mistress Song's.

When the doctors came to examine her again, they looked at each other in dismay and didn't dare say anything. Song Ci understood – the poison was trapped in Qi'er's internal organs, and the disease had mutated. This was the worst development that could happen with such a condition. Once the poison enters the system, the body attacks its own nutrient blood and then infects the heart, lungs, liver, kidneys and other internal organs. By this stage, it is a life-threatening illness.

"Quick, go and find Huo Jing," ordered the normally calm Song Ci, waving his hands in great distress. He turned to give the instruction to Tong Gong, and in doing so knocked a medicine cup off the bedside table.

Tong Gong left immediately.

Towards dusk, they heard the sound of approaching hoofbeats, and finally Tong Gong returned drenched with sweat and covered head-to-foot in scratches from tree branches.

"Did you find Huo Jing?" Song Ci asked anxiously.

"I found him." Tong Gong had indeed found the old man deep in the mountains accompanied by his grandson. Huo Jing had put down the medicinal plants he had been collecting and told Huo Xiong to go off and gather the ones needed to treat Song Qi.

"Which plants?"

"He didn't say. He just told me to come straight back here and tell you not to worry. He'll be here himself before daybreak tomorrow."

All they could do was wait.

That night, Song Ci, his wife and Qiu Juan all waited in Qi'er's bedroom, with Tong Gong just outside the door. Qi'er moaned restlessly from time to time. Her normally sparkling eyes were closed and sunk deep in their sockets. Her once rosy lips were pale and mottled, and drawn back in a grimace. Huo Jing had told Song and his wife not to worry, but how could parents not do so in such circumstances?

Mistress Song could not hold back her tears, and she was almost at breaking point. Qi'er was only just twenty, and raising her from a baby to adulthood had not been an easy road. From the time the old, blind Dr Haiting had saved her at birth, Qi'er had clung on valiantly to life. For the first month, when she weighed less than five catties, she had nestled in her mother's embrace, crying very little but not having learned how to feed. At a little over a month, she had started to look for her mother's breast, but by this stage Yulan's milk had dried up. Twenty years of careful nurture, twenty years of tears and tantrums, twenty years of togetherness for father, mother and daughter; shared worries and shared laughter, and now… Song and his wife could not bear to think any further. They were eternally grateful to Dr Haiting, but, if only, in that book of remedies for unusual diseases he had left behind, there had been one for Qi'er's illness. But there wasn't.

Dawn began to break, and there was no sign of Huo Jing and his grandson.

The sun was up, and Song Qi, who had been restless all night, drenched in sweat, finally drifted off to sleep. Her father took the opportunity to take Qi'er's pulse: it was as rapid as if she had been running, just as, indeed, were those of her parents.

"Tong Gong, go and look for Huo Jing again," Mistress Song said.

"Quick as you can," Song Ci added.

Tong Gong was gone for the rest of the morning, and when he returned he was carrying a deep basket full of medicinal plants that Huo Jing had collected. But he was also the bearer of unexpected bad news.

"Master, I found Huo Jing up on the mountain road. He was being carried on a litter and was covered in blood."

"What did you say?" Song and his wife chorused in alarm.

"He was on his way home in the middle of the night last night, when he lost his footing and fell down a cliff. Huo Xiong got the help of some mountain men, who were up there distilling camphor oil, and during their search this morning they found him at the bottom of a gully. He doesn't have long to live."

"Where is he now?" asked Song Ci.

"He's been taken home." Tong Gong pointed at the plants in the basket he was carrying, a mixture of leaves, branches and stalks. "Huo Jing told me which ones to boil and which ones to apply externally. The last thing he said…"

"What did he say?"

"He wants to see you, Master!"

This was all too sudden and unexpected. Song Ci asked Tong Gong: "Do you remember exactly what Huo Jing told you about how to use these medicines?"

"I wouldn't dare get it wrong."

Song Ci grasped his wife's hand: "I am handing Qi'er over to you."

"Go," his wife said, choking back her tears. "And come back soon."

Song Ci mounted his fastest horse, and sped off.

There was the same old bamboo-framed hut, poorly furnished but neat and tidy, with medicinal plants and herbs hanging on the walls. Huo Xiong greeted Song Ci and led him into the hut. Huo Jing valiantly tried to sit up in bed, but he quite clearly didn't have the strength.

"Wine… bring me some wine."

Huo Jing was trying to shout, but he had lost so much blood, his face was pale and his voice too weak.

Song Ci rested his hand on the old man's shoulder: "Lie back, lie back."

"Wine! … Wine!"

The old man's lips were moving, but the voice was very faint. Huo Xiong had fetched the wine gourd and held it to his grandfather's mouth. Song Ci saw that the gourd's neck was cracked from the fall down the cliff. Huo Jing took it in trembling hands and drank deeply. Some of the dark red wine spilled through the cracks in the gourd, flowing down the old man's snowy white beard and onto his chest. Suddenly, Huo Jing thrust the gourd aside and pushed himself up with both hands.

"Master," he stammered out, clasping Song Ci's hand. "My son died young and never became a coroner. The sons of the Huo family have always been coroners. The tradition must not end with me." His breathing had become harsh, and he grasped Song Ci's hand more tightly. "Master, please do as I ask. Tomorrow, take him…"

Song Ci kept hold of the old man's trembling, icy hand and nodded: "I promise."

"Master," the old man spoke again. "With your talents, it is easy for you to handle the cases of common folk. The difficulty lies with cases involving the rich and powerful… you must look out for yourself."

Song Ci could not hold back his tears.

With trembling hands, the old man took from beside his pillow a fine old porcelain jar, and he gave it to Song Ci. Beads of sweat the size of beans stood out on his forehead.

"There is a little musk… no more than two *liang*… one *liang* of spring water… one *liang* of chuanxiong rhizome… grind it fine and roll it into pills… you can use them at your autopsies to overcome the smell…"

When Song Ci took the jar, the old man heaved a deep sigh and quietly passed away. Song Ci cradled the jar in both hands, and his eyes misted over with tears. It was some time before he noticed the label on the jar, which read: 'Stench-dispelling pills'.

# CHAPTER X

## THE EXTRAORDINARY CASE OF THE BURNT BODY (1238)

In this year, Song Ci travelled to take up a new post as local magistrate in Nanjianzhou, Fujian Province, when there was an unexpected and unusual crop failure. Under orders from Emperor Lizong, the prime minister was making a tour of inspection of taxes and grain reserves in the interior of the southern part of the empire. On the road he encountered peasants stealing food, and he handed the culprits over to Song Ci for punishment. Song Ci's judgments astonished the prime minister. He told him that, in the current dire circumstances, the roads were almost deserted, even in daylight, and human flesh was being sold in the marketplaces. This was giving rise to all manner of strange cases. One night, a burnt body was discovered, and Song Ci ordered an autopsy. All the skin had been burnt away, so it was a challenge to examine. The method used is one recorded in the ancient classics and remains, to this day, an important way of determining ante- and post-mortem injuries.

# 1

# FAMINE IN A DROUGHT-STRICKEN LAND

In the second year of the Jiaxi period (1238), when Song Ci was fifty-two, he was moved from being prefectural magistrate in Shaowujun to the same position in Nanjianzhou (modern day Nanpingshi in Fujian Province). Four years previously, while he had been in office in Tingzhou waiting to take up the post of judicial commissioner for Fujian Province in Fuzhou, he had received a letter from his old friend Liu Kezhuang, informing him of a change in Liu's circumstances.

Mr Zhen Dexiu had been summoned to the capital to become revenue minister, and he had taken Liu Kezhuang with him. Mr Zhen made every effort to get Song Ci promoted to a post in the Supreme Court in the capital. But the autumn had passed, then winter, and now in the summer, three years on, the tragic news of Mr Zhen Dexiu's death through illness reached the Song household. In the letter, Liu Kezhuang only mentioned that Mr Zhen's patronage had secured him the post of secretary to the Privy Council, and it did not say anything about his efforts on behalf of Song Ci. Song Ci understood – clearly Mr Zhen had tried his hardest, but without success.

Mr Zhen was fifty-seven when he died, and his wise instruction would no longer be heard, and no one would gaze on his compassionate countenance again. The entire Song household mourned his loss, while the whole country was deprived of a wise and virtuous statesman.

Then, in the winter, Song Ci received news of his unexpected move to the post of local magistrate in Shaowujun. This was the result of the efforts of Mr Zhen's old friend, Wei Liaoweng. At the time, Wei was military commissioner in charge of cavalry mounts in the Jinghu region. In the Song era, military commissioner was one of the top-ranking posts, with rank equivalent to the secretariat and carrying the title 'prime minister', with joint responsibility for military and civil affairs. Wei was eager to recruit men of talent and virtue, and he willingly endorsed Song Ci's appointment to oversee his staff. He himself was a man of great learning, with a deep knowledge of the classics. He was an individualist, deeply respected by contemporary scholars, and Song Ci had sought his help in the past. But Song's heart was not really in military affairs, and Wei Liaoweng, who was very wise, recognised that Song's unique talents for solving difficult cases would be wasted in the army. So, after long consideration, he resigned himself to losing the benefits of Song Ci's abilities, and changed tack by appointing him prefectural magistrate, despite his previous lack of experience and in the face of his own preferences. He sent Song Ci to take up the post in Shaowujun.

The duties of a prefectural magistrate were not confined to trials and sentencing. The office was, in fact, second in rank only to the provincial registrar. He had authority over the public affairs of the prefectural government and oversaw all its bureaucrats. Indeed, the post was often referred to as prefectural supervisor. All in all, the powers were much greater than those of a county magistrate.

Song Ci had been in post in Shaowujun for more than a year. Just as Huo Jing had said with his dying words, Song found no difficulty in handling the cases of the common folk; he had settled a considerable number of them. Although one or two of these cases had been somewhat unusual, Song had resolved them all with no great effort. Now, in the second year of the Jiaxi period, he was once again uprooting his household, to move to the prefectural magistracy in Nanjianzhou.

The horses and carriages hurried along the empty post road. Song sat in one of the carriages, silently pondering, preoccupied by the uneasy feeling that this was going to be a difficult year.

The climate in Nanjianzhou is hot and humid, with copious rain. There are three tributaries of the Min River, the Jian, Sha and Futun, which join the trunkline there as it flows east towards the sea. The surrounding area had always been fine farming land, but highly susceptible to natural disasters including flooding. The river levels could rise by several *zhang*,[1] even over the height of the city walls, flooding houses and fields and destroying property and livestock. The devastation could be total, with many fatalities. Flooding was a constant concern, but there was seldom any danger of drought. But the previous year, Nanjianzhou did, indeed, endure its worst drought in a hundred years. There was no rain at all between the fourth month and the tenth, resulting in an unprecedented crop failure across the whole territory.

It was the time of the spring sowing, but the fields were empty of farmers and there was not a seedling to be seen; the land was covered only in withered weeds and wild plants. The hillsides were dotted with the burial mounds of those who had starved to death, their bodies washed down on the flood of the Min. As he saw these tombs, Song Ci's professional sensibilities inevitably led him to think that they could not all be the victims of famine. Nor were his eyes the only ones to survey this scene of desolation.

Close behind Song Ci's carriage was a covered wagon carrying his wife Lian Yulan, his daughter Song Qi, and Qiu Juan. Tong Gong and Huo Xiong were riding escort either side. Life changes and moulds people, and such changes were especially apparent in Song Qi, now grown to adulthood. Four years before, she had been restored to health by the medicinal herbs picked for her by Huo Jing, but the illness had left its mark, and she was a much more prudent and cautious young woman than before. Although she did not dwell on the past, there were times when she went quiet, frowning slightly, as though deep in thought. That frown was there now as she watched the ravaged countryside passing on either side, and her eyes were full of melancholy.

Crowds of displaced people, carrying their possessions on shoulder poles and begging for alms, looked up at the carriages as they passed. Song Ci halted his convoy, considering trying to turn the flood of people back, but what could he actually do to fill their starving bellies? All the faces he saw were jaundiced and shrunken, the bodies emaciated, clear evidence of their battle against starvation. Tried beyond endurance, they were being forced to leave their homeland.

Song Ci ordered his party to the side of the road, and watched the steady flow of refugees for quite some time, before resuming his journey. As they neared the city, he saw two farmers using a plank of wood to carry a body wrapped in reed matting, and following behind them, a short, middle-aged man. As they got nearer, he saw that the man's eyes were red and swollen, and lifeless, and as they passed, he also noticed that his clothes were old and tattered, with three large square patches on the back…

"The deceased must be his wife," Song thought to himself.

He sighed deeply and closed his eyes. Before they had gone much further, he opened them again to see two children, a boy and a girl, their clothes worn and ragged, standing beside the road. The girl must have been about ten, and she carried on her back a tatty old bed roll strapped tightly to her shoulders. The boy was about eight. The two of them were hugging each other in fright and staring at the horses and carriages. There were tear tracks on their faces, indicating they had only just stopped crying.

After the convoy had passed, behind him Song Ci heard the sound of the boy wailing, and he threw up his hand. "Stop the carriages," he ordered.

Song got down from his carriage and went over to where the two children were standing. The boy stopped wailing, and clasped the girl even more tightly, looking up at Song in fright, with eyes full of tears. Song crouched down and surveyed the children with a kindly expression. Their faces had the abnormally large appearance brought on by starvation, and their hair was yellowed and brittle. Song asked the girl: "Are you his sister?"

She looked at him and nodded.

"Are you escaping the famine?"

She nodded again.

"What about your mother and father?"

The girl was silent for a long time and then finally said: "They starved to death."

Song Qi and Qiu Juan had also got down from their wagon and came over.

"Father, we must take them with us," Song Qi exclaimed.

"Bring them along," Song Ci ordered, standing up.

Song Qi and Qiu Juan each picked up one of the children and carried them over to the covered wagon. Tong Gong also dismounted and helped them lift the children into the wagon.

Now, as the convoy continued on its way to the city up ahead, Song Ci's thoughts were no longer preoccupied with legal matters: to treat the illness, find the cause. He realised that, if he wanted to return stability to the region, one thing was staring him in the face. He had to see the provincial governor to discuss an emergency distribution of grain to relieve the immediate dire situation. But some tasks are more easily said than accomplished.

There is a very strict hierarchy surrounding ministers and their advisers at national government level. It may be compared to the writing of a medical prescription: the principal active ingredient is the minister of state, the secondary one is the junior ministers and the third one is their advisers. Each has their own unique status, and each office has its particular responsibilities and acts strictly according to convention. This is not a chain of command that can be by-passed. If someone higher up the chain hasn't considered something, chooses not to do it or doesn't dare do it, it is next to impossible for his subordinate to change that situation.

Song Ci's current position was very different from what he was accustomed to. When he held office in Xinfeng, although he had only been in an advisory post, Magistrate Shan Zilin had proved to be an honest and upright man, open to Song's advice. In Tingzhou, he himself had been the chief local authority. But now, as prefectural magistrate, although it was a higher office than local magistrate, he was subordinate to the provincial registrar; and the current registrar happened to be Shu Gengshi, formerly the local magistrate at Jianyang.

"It's not straightforward. There is no imperial decree regarding grain reserves, so who would take charge?" They were sitting in the business chamber of the prefectural seat, and Shu Gengshi had just listened to Song Ci's proposal.

"My suggestion is that the distribution of grain for the starving people should come from the wealthy families of the area," Song Ci replied.

"You are joking, of course!" Shu Gengshi said, smiling, but looking shrewdly at Song Ci. "If country gentry have put aside grain, it is their own private store. How could we just appropriate it?"

There was a babble of agreement, as the other prefectural bureaucrats showed support for their boss. At a stroke, Song Ci had become something of a laughing stock, but he pressed on: "My Lord, it is time for spring sowing, but all the farmers have gone. If we don't find some way to get them to come back, next year…"

"I know that!" said Shu Gengshi, who had stopped smiling. "But what you are suggesting is impossible. Do you know who is the richest man in the prefecture?"

Song Ci saw Shu Gengshi's inscrutable expression and realised it must be someone from a very important family.

"Who is he?" he asked.

"He is the brother-in-law of the imperial prime minister, Li Zongmian. Moreover, Prime Minister Li is on an imperial tour of inspection of the south. He has already passed through Guangdong into Fuzhou Prefecture, and will pass through here any day on his way back to court. Are you really suggesting we should impound his relative's private grain stock?"

There was another murmur of agreement from the assembled officials, and Song Ci was left feeling isolated.

He felt as though he had stepped into quicksand, with no means of escape. This was a far more difficult situation than any case he had previously been involved in. Of course, he could not back down – all his life he had done what he thought needed to be done. But, equally, he could not see his way ahead. Even though he was second in rank only to the prefectural registrar, he could do nothing without the support of the officials from the Ministry of Supervision. He looked at the sea of unfamiliar faces in the business chamber and realised that he would have to talk to each and every one of them, in the hope of finding a dissenting voice whom he could persuade over to his side. Only then would he have a chance of enacting his proposed famine relief.

When Li Zongmian passed through Nanjianzhou, it had not been his intention to trouble the local officials, but simply to spend the night with his brother-in-law, Du Guancheng. However, as he was about to leave, his mistress had asked him to "come home and have a look at something", so before he arrived, he sent word ahead to Du Guancheng.

Du was delighted at the news of the impending visit, and he set about preparing the very best food and wine. He then led a welcome party, which included his eldest son and third son, along with his drill instructor and others, ten *li* out of the city to meet Li Zongmian. However, before they had gone half that distance, the sedan chair-bearers had had to stop to rest, and that was when, out of nowhere, they heard a tremendous commotion. A great crowd of country folk, armed with knives, sticks and rocks, came hurtling down the hillside, yelling and shouting.

"The people are starving... The people are starving..."

Du Guancheng lifted the curtain of his sedan chair and tumbled out. The great famine that year had resulted in mobs of starving country folk who were afraid of nothing and dared anything in their search for food.

"Run away... run away!"

But despite his cries, Du Guancheng found himself rooted to the spot, unable to move. Two of his sons came rushing to his aid and bundled him back down the road towards the city and safety. In an instant, the whole entourage were scrambling after them, leaving only Du's drill instructor standing there, staring at the on-rushing mob.

And who was that drill instructor? It was none other than the man who had once worked for Chai Wanlong in Jianyang, and who had murdered Tong Gong's sister-in-law: Tian Huai. Du Guancheng had recruited him to his household to instruct three of his sons in sword and stick fighting, along with other martial arts. Now he stood there without fear, shouting at the fleeing attendants: "Stay where you are. Don't run. Don't run."

But to no avail, as they were already disappearing into the distance.

The mob was formed of country folk who had been scraping a living up in the mountains eating roots, leaves and tree bark. There were fifty or sixty of them, all carrying makeshift weapons. They surrounded Tian Huai, who was armed with his 'fire-and-water' staff, while some of them gathered up the food left behind by the fleeing attendants.

"Put it down," Tian Huai barked, and, whirling his staff above his head, he aimed a blow at the leader of the mob. In an instant, there was the sound of clashing staffs as a hand-to-hand fight broke out beside the road. Although the peasants had the advantage of numbers, they could not match Tian Huai's skill. It wasn't long before they were being knocked over like skittles, dropping their makeshift weapons. They soon fled, yelling as they went.

Tian Huai wasn't finished, and he charged up the mountain, still flourishing his staff. The peasants, who had picked up laden baggage poles, realised that they couldn't get away if they kept on carrying them, so they dropped them as they ran. The poles clattered down the steep slope and came to rest at the roadside, where the packages split open, scattering food and wine across the highway.

At that moment, the clatter of horses' hooves and the tinkle of sedan chair bells was heard, and a party of mounted men appeared. When they saw the extraordinary state of affairs, their rearguard escort of infantrymen smartly formed up on either side of the road in most impressive style.

"The prime minister! It's the prime minister! The prime minister is here."

When Du Guancheng, who had already gone quite some distance in his flight, saw what was going on, he came rushing back and staggered to a halt in front of the minister. He ordered his sons to pay their respects, and then he explained what had just happened. When Li Zongmian saw all the fine food and wine strewn over the road, he was furious.

"Seize them!" he ordered.

In response, his bodyguard drew their swords and swept up the mountainside to round up the looters. By the end of the morning, they had caught twenty or more of them, and they were dragged in front of Li Zongmian as he sat in his carriage. Through gritted teeth, Du Guancheng asked the prime minister to punish the offenders himself, but Li said: "That won't do."

"Why not?"

"Because I have family connections to the affair, I cannot get involved."

Li gave orders for the men to be arrested and tried in the local court.

It was noon, and the spring sun was high in the sky. The twenty or so prisoners, with torn clothes and bloody wounds, were led, bound and roped together, into the great courtyard in front of the main hall of the prefectural court. Many of them, weakened either by hunger or their injuries, were shivering violently in the cold. Song Ci ascertained the background to the case and then had them lined up in the courtroom. This wasn't a particularly unusual case, but it was clearly going to be a difficult one to handle.

Mass looting! No matter how you looked at it, they had all quite clearly broken the law. But what lay behind it? As a tribune of the people, surely he should show sympathy for their plight. If he were to take the most serious view, what was the appropriate sentence? If he were to treat them leniently, how would he justify it to the prime minister? There was no shortage of historical precedents for virtuous ministers who were willing to risk their lives rather than compromise their principles and try to curry favour. If he were to show clemency, he would offend the prime minister. The worst he could expect would be to be dismissed from office, and it was unlikely to go as far as execution. Did he dare? No, no, he couldn't countenance dismissal. In clinging to this idea of 'not fearing to lose one's job' he would be deluding himself. If he was actually dismissed, then these people would be far worse off, and he would have sacrificed his own career in vain. Yes, that was right – he could not be dismissed, he had far too much still to do. He was fifty-two already and life was too short. He needed to be prudent.

Song Ci looked up at the sun, which was already past its noonday height, and its rays were falling slantwise onto the eaves of the court. There was a swallow's nest under the eaves, from which came the cheeping of fledglings that oddly disturbed him. Suddenly, after thinking the matter over, he screwed his eyes tight shut as though reaching a final decision, turned to the men in court and barked an order to the court attendants: "Release them."

The attendants, thinking that they must have misheard, didn't move. Even Tong Gong and Huo Xiong failed to react.

"Release them. Release them all," Song Ci repeated.

This time the attendants hurried forward to untie the prisoners. And that, thought Song to himself, settles the case the prime minister handed over to me.

The freed men all bowed and kowtowed innumerable times, then linked arms and left. But for Song Ci, despite the careful consideration he had given the whole affair, his troubles were just about to begin.

That afternoon, the chamberlain of the ministerial court arrived at the prefectural court with four soldiers from the ministerial guard. Once in Song Ci's presence, he announced with great pomp and ceremony: "The prime minister requests your attendance."

"Where is the prime minister now?"

"At the Du family residence."

"Then let us go."

Song Ci had been expecting this and, taking Tong Gong and Huo Xiong with him, he followed the chamberlain out of the court compound.

Mistress Song had been worried ever since she had heard at noon that her husband had freed the prisoners handed over to him by the prime minister, and her concern only intensified. Now, as she and Qi'er saw Song Ci off at the gate, she was almost beside herself.

"Don't worry about me," Song Ci said to his wife, smiling as he stood on the threshold.

Watching him disappear in the direction of the ministerial court, she clutched her daughter's hands tightly and discovered that Qi'er's hands, too, were as cold as ice.

2

## THE DU FAMILY COMPOUND

The Du family compound, which was situated in the north of the city, was a great deal more luxurious and ostentatious than the ministerial court. Inside the walls, there were three sets of lodgings, one for each of the sons. Du Guancheng himself lived in the principal residence at the rear of the compound. He had numerous wives and concubines who lived in seclusion and seldom ventured out, but had servants to see to their every need. In front of the compound was a broad open space, little used by passers-by and usually deserted. That was the case today, as security was particularly tight.

From a distance, as they approached the compound, they saw the gates opening. Although there was no one about outside, inside, Li Zongmian's squadron of armed bodyguards was on parade, helmets, breastplates and weapons glinting coldly in the sun.

Song Ci followed the chamberlain in through the gates, and just after he had crossed the threshold, he heard a clanging sound as two long-handled halberds flashed down in the hands of the guards, shutting out Tong Gong and Huo Xiong, who were following close behind. Song glanced back briefly, saying nothing, and continued following the chamberlain across the courtyard.

As Song Ci walked along, he looked at the three sets of buildings, each one different, but all lofty and imposing, and arranged with artful eccentricity. When they reached the entrance of the hall in the main courtyard, the chamberlain went ahead to announce their arrival: "Worshipful Prime Minister, Prefectural Magistrate Song Ci is here."

Song Ci heard a deep voice from within give the curt response: "Enter."

Song Ci obeyed and bowed to Prime Minister Li Zongmian, who was seated at the top of the hall.

"Your servant, Song Ci, respectfully greets the Worshipful Prime Minister!"

"Sit," Li Zongmian instructed him as abruptly as before.

The chamberlain brought a silk-upholstered X-frame chair. Song Ci sat down unhurriedly and waited for the prime minister to question him.

There was a silence. Song Ci noticed that, while there was no trace of good humour on the prime minister's face, Du Guancheng, who was seated beside the minister, had a secret half-smile playing across his lips. He also saw the huge painting of a tiger hanging over the middle of the hall, so vivid and realistic, it looked as though the beast was about to spring out of the scroll. Framing the painting was a couplet in running script. Song Ci did not recognise the calligrapher, but his hand was free-flowing, bold and individual. It read:

*When fortune smiles, the sacred trees flower every day*
*And golden blossoms burst forth all over.*

The silence was broken by Li Zongmian's opening question: "Song Ci, by what law did you release all the looters?"

"In reply to Your Honour," Song Ci said, half rising from his chair, "I would remark that these people were starving to the point where they were living off grass and roots."

Li Zongmian raised his eyebrows in apparent disbelief.

"So according to you, they were justified in looting my convoy!" Du Guancheng interjected.

"No. But it is important to investigate the reasons behind their actions."

"Go on," Li Zongmian resumed.

"Worshipful Prime Minister, Nanjianzhou is currently in dire straits. People are starving to death and outside the city walls they are reduced to eating tree bark, grass and roots. Within the city, there is no shortage of grain, but people are still starving for a different reason. All the rich and powerful families are using this natural disaster as an excuse to speculate and profiteer. They are asking ten thousand copper cash for a single *dou*[1] of rice. The common people are starving and at the end of their tether, so they are willing to take any risk to get food."

"And you say that is a reason not to investigate this outrage?" Du Guancheng asked.

Li Zongmian appeared to frown slightly, as though irritated by Du's interruption.

"Of course it must be investigated," Song Ci replied. "But it needs to be carefully thought through."

"Go on," Li Zongmian said.

Song Ci did not respond immediately, but thought for a while before saying: "I cannot lie. I thought long and hard, considering all the options, before I released the prisoners. And it is true that doing so was contrary to what the law dictates. I am new to this area, and I have no connection of any kind with the prisoners, nor have they tried to influence me with gifts. The only reason I was willing to turn my back on the law and release them, was out of concern for their plight. But I do not know if this concern is misplaced."

"Go on."

"Your Honour, when I talk about Nanjianzhou being in dire straits, it is not just for effect. Things really have reached the utter limit. Please consider, Your Honour, in Nanjianzhou today, the roads are practically deserted, human flesh is being sold in the marketplaces..."

"Human flesh is being sold?" Li Zongmian interrupted in amazement.

"It is," Song Ci confirmed. "I had the culprit up before me in court yesterday, and I can give Your Honour a full account at another time. In the light of all this, the hijacking of food on the highway is hardly a surprising occurrence. It is my personal opinion that, in years of famine such a this when local despots start hoarding grain, if the government doesn't take exceptional measures to relieve the situation, but instead adheres to the letter of the law and suppresses the common people, they will take matters violently into their own hands and see it as a reason to justify looting. This is something that history has already shown us. Moreover, our country suffered more than a hundred years of aggression and invasion from the Jin, and now, only a year after the defeat of that enemy, we are suffering similar incursions from the Mongols. The country has not had a chance to recover from its old injuries before being wounded anew. The whole nation, from emperor to peasant, is in deep distress."

As he spoke, Song Ci could not restrain his own emotions, and his normally slow and considered speech gradually became more animated and urgent. He continued: "Your Honour, our borders may be hard pressed, but famine is already with us in Nanjianzhou. Just consider the trouble it will cause if the people are forced, by want and resentment, to band together in the countryside and raise the ragged standard of revolt."

Song Ci stopped at this point, and a silence fell on the chamber.

Li Zongmian narrowed his eyes slightly, but the rising anger previously apparent in his face seemed to have subsided and his expression was impassive. "Only a year after the defeat of the Jin..." It was true, and for a high-ranking official such as Li, who had himself seen much suffering and hardship, Song Ci's words stirred a genuine concern...

In the second year after the defeat of the Jin, the beginning of the second year of the Duanping period, the Mongol leader Ogedei Khan had massed his crack cavalry, defeated both the Jin and Chinese armies, and mounted a major two-pronged invasion of the south. Only a year later, Ogedei's second son, Kadan, led a division through the breach in Sichuan's defences already opened by the main Mongol army, and invaded the province. In response to the emergency, thousands of local people joined the army to fight the invaders. Government troops and irregular soldiers together manned the defence of the passes, but they were wiped out to a man, spilling a veritable ocean of blood. At the same time, Ogedei's third son, Khochu, led the Mongol army, which had occupied Xianghan, in taking Yingzhou and Xiangyang... Xiangyang, which had previously been freed from under the iron boots of the Jin army by General Yue Fei; which had been restored to its role as a strategic military stronghold for more than a hundred years. Xiangyang was now razed to the ground: 300,000 taels of valuables and grain, and twenty-four armouries in the city were plundered by the Mongol army, inflicting a grievous loss on the Song.

'Worries in springtime may not return until the autumn, but this morning's worries will be back in the evening.' Not long before, Li Zongmian had said something very similar in audience with Emperor Lizong. With great depth of feeling he had said: "Previously, we were concerned about advancing prematurely from our defensive position. Now, our problem is that we wish to defend ourselves, but cannot. Where can we establish a stronghold? Which troops should we dispatch? Which general should command our defences? Where do we find provisions for the troops? These are all things we need to plan for." It was the conviction in Li Zongmian's voice that persuaded the emperor to send him to the interior of the south to levy a grain tax.

On reaching Nanjianzhou, and encountering this case of mass highway robbery, he had thought to himself that, with the border areas under so much pressure, the heartland needed to be kept stable and well-fed. A band of robbers like that were quite close to being in open revolt, but it could be quashed before it really took flight. So how could they possibly be let off so lightly? But quite unexpectedly, despite his apprehension over the possibility of rebellion, along came this prefectural magistrate who gave voice to his own innermost thoughts.

This was the first time Song Ci had met Li Zongmian, and he knew very little about him either as a man or as an official. All he knew was that his courtesy name was Jiangfu, and that he had passed the imperial examinations in the first year of the Kaixi period, the same year as Mr Zhen Dexiu. He had held office as director of the Imperial College and as national state academician, but that was all after Song Ci had left the Imperial Academy. Now that he was face to face with the prime minister, Song Ci had several considerations over his release of the looters. In these extraordinary times, Li Zongmian had received imperial orders to levy a grain tax in the south and was already travel-stained and weary from visiting many different districts. But now, when he saw the looters with his own eyes, and had them arrested, when he could have taken personal charge of the case... Instead of doing so, he handed the affair over to the prefectural magistrate. Clearly, at this crucial harvest time, not only was the prime minister a man of decision, it would seem he was also an old-fashioned guardian of the law. That being so, it would be possible to reason with him. And now, as he watched the prime minister's brow gradually unfurrowing, he began to believe it might be possible to really speak his mind.

So he continued, unhurriedly: "Your Honour, for the last ten years, the majority of my work has been done in the interiors of Fujian and Jiangxi provinces. Ten years ago, a farmer from Ganzhou, named Chen Sanqiang, raised a rebellion at Songzishan. Nine years ago in Tingzhou, the salt merchant Meng Biao did the same in Tanfeizhai. It was entirely due to government oppression and the slaughter of the innocent, that the people retreated into the natural fastness of the land and raised the banners of rebellion.

"Now, here I am in Nanjianzhou, which guards the bottleneck in the middle reaches of the Min River. From ancient times it has been prized by military strategists. In attack, troops can move across it unhindered to provide support, and in retreat it becomes a redoubtable defensive base. When Wang Shenzhi was establishing the Kingdom of Min, he took this area as his base of operations.

"I also remembered that, in those days, the first move in putting down a rebellion was to execute a number of officials. Although there were protests among the courtiers, in fact it was a logical thing to do. Once the hearts of the people are lost, the country is endangered, and what use is an official who cannot keep order in his own district? Moreover, the common folk are very changeable in their ways – sometimes it is best to ignore them, but at others, one neglects them in peril. I had to take all this into consideration. My personal opinion was this: Nanjianzhou is currently in an extremely parlous state because of the famine, and if the starving people can only get sufficient food, they will return to the fields and Nanjianzhou can regain its rightful role as a national bastion, contributing its fair share of taxes and helping to restore the nation's stability. Otherwise..."

Song Ci stopped at this point, as though the rest of the sentence went without saying. While speaking, his voice had remained soft and relaxed, but each phrase had the weight of a drum beat echoing in Li Zongmian's heart.

Li sat in silent thought for a while and then said: "In your opinion, what is the best way to proceed?"

"I believe we should implement a distribution programme of part relief aid, part commercial sale."

"Are you suggesting that, with our army in its current difficulties, we should start dispensing grain to the people from the state granaries?"

"There is no need to empty the state granaries. We can use Nanjianzhou's five-tier household system to supply the necessary grain for the relief programme."

In Song times, households were categorised in five ranks. The first rank consisted of major landowners, the second and third of medium-sized landowners, and the fourth and fifth were individual farmers. Li Zongmian understood that Song Ci meant the categorisations as recorded in the local population census, but was not clear about how he intended to apportion responsibilities.

"So what about the first rank?" he asked.

"The first rank are all wealthy households. They should be instructed to hand over half their grain stocks for relief aid, and to sell the other half to those in need at the official price."

All trace of a smile had left the face of Du Guancheng, as he sat to one side listening to this. He fixed Song Ci with a stare and seemed about to speak. But in the end he said nothing and just spat on the floor of the chamber.

"What about the second rank?" Li Zongmian continued his questioning.

"The second rank should be instructed to sell their stocks at the official price."

"The third rank?"

"They should be exempt."

"The fourth?"

"They should receive half their grain in aid and buy half at the official price."

"The fifth?"

"They should receive all their grain as free relief aid."

Li Zongmian listened carefully and gradually began to look less stern. When Song Ci had finished, he impulsively rose from his chair and went over to Song Ci. He slapped Song on the back, saying: "Excellent! Excellent! The Tang emperor Taizong often used to quote Xunzi, saying: 'The ruler is like a boat and the people are the water – water can support a boat, but it can also capsize it.' We should always bear this in mind. Since you have come up with this plan to use the grain hoarded by the rich families of the area to provide for those in distress, without having to empty the government granaries, I must ask you to put it into effect without delay."

Thus, in taking on the original case and exploiting Li Zongmian's imperially ordained mission to levy a grain tax in the south, Song Ci was able to save the lives of the starving looters and also gain Li's approval for the enactment of a sale and distribution system.

The same day, Li Zongmian followed up on Song Ci's mention of the case of the sale of human flesh, and Song gave him a detailed account. While Song Ci was busy with this, Tian Huai emerged from the residence and bumped into Tong Gong on the street outside. Tian Huai stopped and swept his gaze over Tong Gong and Huo Xiong, but he failed to recognise Tong. When he had gone to Tong Gong's house with Chai Wanlong to collect the rent, Tong Gong had been away in the mountains, hunting. And then, when Tong Gong had slipped into the Chai mansion with the intention of killing Chai Wanlong, it had been the household maidservants who had identified him as the assassin. So Tian Huai had never actually seen Tong Gong, and he had no idea that the man in front of him now had long ago vowed to kill him to exact revenge and to expunge his family's humiliation.

The Tian Huai brothers had been notorious in Jianyang, and were well known to Tong Gong, so when he saw the object of his vengeance standing in front of him, staring at Huo Xiong and him so rudely, his face flushed with anger, but he managed to hold himself in check. Did he do so because his master was currently inside the Du mansion, with his fate in the balance, or because of the training and experience he had received during his long years in Song Ci's service? Whichever it was, he clenched his fists but didn't use them and, once Tian Huai had dropped his insolent gaze, contented himself with staring after the man's disappearing form as he came out of the gate and walked off down the road.

Inside the residence, Li Zongmian was listening to Song Ci's explanation of the case, asking occasional questions, which Song answered one by one. Li could not help but be impressed by the agile mind of this prefectural magistrate. The two of them kept up this dialogue until, before they knew it, dusk was upon them. As Song Ci rose to take his leave, Li Zongmian rose too and accompanied him to the door, as though he did not want the conversation to end.

Li Zongmian stayed in Nanjianzhou for just one night. Early the next day he summoned Shu Gengshi and Song Ci, and, in their presence, ordered the enactment of the famine relief scheme. He then departed.

The government of the time had a strict hierarchy, dictating who directed whom, and who reported to whom. The implementation of the relief programme would have proved immensely difficult had the responsibility lain solely with Provincial Magistrate Shu Gengshi. But the day after Prime Minister Li Zongmian had given his brief instructions, it became straightforward.

Straightforward to an extent, at least, but there were still many twists and turns in its enactment. After the prime minister had left, Song Ci and Shu Gengshi and his fellow bureaucrats wrangled over the details for three full days before everything was finally agreed in accordance with Song Ci's original proposal. Thereupon, a memorandum was written for Prime Minister Li, and an official announcement was drafted.

At last, the announcement was to be posted in the marketplaces, and Song Ci could only imagine the joy with which the people would greet the news of the arrangements for the distribution of grain. His own pleasure was almost too great for words. He little thought that, the very night before the announcement was to be made, he would encounter the most gruesome case of his long career.

## 3

# FIRE ALARM AT THE DEAD OF NIGHT

It was just an ordinary night.

At the second watch, the waning moon had not yet risen, and the starlight was pale and uncertain. Under the vast, empty night sky, the ancient city walls of Nanjianzhou loomed dark and still. On the battlements appeared the stealthy silhouette of a black-clad figure. It slid hand-over-hand down a rope and landed at the base of the walls.

An early spring breeze was blowing gently. On the distant mountains, luminous points of light danced like will-o'-the-wisps, while insects provided a mournful accompaniment. Occasionally, the wind blowing off the Min River stirred the banner hanging over the doorway of a countryside inn. Who was it slipping out of the city on this dark spring night?

The same light wind was rustling through the willow fronds in the rear courtyard of the prefectural headquarters. A light shone through one of the shuttered windows, where someone was still awake.

It was Song Qi's chamber, illuminated by a number of candles in silver candlesticks. They also lit the young girl's slender figure, already dressed for bed with elegant simplicity. She wore a snowy white, light silk sleeveless jacket that perfectly complemented the lines of her body. A pair of pale jade-green, embroidered knee-length trousers showed off the shape of her calves. Her supple hair was piled in a loose bun, not held by any hairpins. In the heart of a young girl such as Song Qi, the cool of a spring night can actually generate a kind of languorous warmth. She was holding a Huzhou brush in her hand, her lips were pursed in concentration and she was frowning slightly as she looked, lost in thought, at a large calligraphy scroll that hung on the wall.

The characters on the scroll were Su Dongpo's *Remembering Your Charms – Memories of the Past at the Red Cliffs*, and, as she had done countless times before, Song Qi began to recite the poem as she read it from the top of the scroll:

*The mighty Yangtze River crashes eastwards,*
*Carrying the souls of long-dead heroes.*
*On the west bank, the ancient fort lays claim to be*
*The Red Cliffs of Three Kingdoms fame.*
*Great waves crash on the shore, hurling rocks high in the air*
*And scattering a blizzard of foam.*
*The river and mountains are like a painted backdrop*
*To the countless heroes of the past and their daring deeds*
*Remember the time when Zhou Yu,*
*Newly married to his bride, the maiden Qiao,*
*With silk cap and feather fan,*
*Laughed and joked while far below,*
*The enemy ships disappeared in clouds of smoke and ash.*
*I travel with the spirits of the past*
*While, in the present, people mock*
*My hair, gone grey before its time...*

It was a remarkable piece of calligraphy, the characters spilling down the scroll with the force of a thousand *li* river in spate, and with an inner energy that was both profound and uplifting. Whether moved by the poem itself, or inspired by the calligraphy, Song Qi felt almost as though she actually was on the banks of the river, hearing the crashing of the waters and seeing the light of the signal beacons filling the sky. She read the characters one by one, savouring them. The calligraphy ended with the words 'My hair, gone grey before its time' and below that there was a blank space. Song Qi stood staring at the blank paper, turning the brush handle round and round in her hand. Could it be that the young lady had forgotten what came next?

"What are you thinking about?" Qiu Juan's voice interrupted the silence.

As she had been in the habit of doing for many years, Song Qi had asked Qiu Juan to come and watch her at her calligraphy. She liked it when Qiu Juan was there, as though her presence allowed Song Qi to express herself particularly freely. She now said to her companion: "Sister, I can't write it."

"Why not?"

"I don't understand what Mr Dongpo means. Look, this character '情' in the last line – which reading of it does he intend here? Later, he goes on to say that 'human life is like a dream', so I'm sure that he is making some sophisticated reference, but I don't understand it and don't know how I should write it."

"You need to think it through, and then write. But now, it's getting late. You should go to sleep."

"Very well," Song Qi said. "Don't go tonight. Stay here and sleep with me."

There was someone else in the prefectural headquarters who couldn't sleep that night. In another part of the complex, that person got out of bed and went over to open the window with a soft creak, letting the faint starlight into the room.

"What are you doing, Husband?" Yulan asked from the bed.

"Go back to sleep," Song Ci replied as he stood by the window.

"The arrangements for the food relief have gone just as you wanted, so what else is worrying you?"

In point of fact, Song Ci didn't know himself what was bothering him. All he really wanted was to forget about everything and get a good night's sleep. He had even gone to bed far earlier than usual, but sleep had eluded him and, as he felt more and more awake, he decided to get up and open the window to look at the stars and breathe in a little cool air. Then he returned to bed.

A quiet night, an ordinary night, but the stillness was suddenly broken by the whinnying of a horse... it was Song Ci's saddlehorse craning its neck out of its stall, and neighing and stamping its hooves. The commotion was enough to rouse several of the other horses in the stable, and it set them off whinnying too.

The noise startled Song Ci. He leapt up and hurried barefoot out of the room to investigate. At the same moment, Tong Gong came hurtling out his room. As they rounded a corner of the building, the two men could see the red glow of fire lighting up the northern horizon.

Tong Gong was the first to speak: "Master, the north of the city is on fire."

"Damnation!" Song Ci exclaimed, looking up at the heavens. Then he turned to Tong Gong and said: "Quick, go and wake the staff. We must go the scene immediately."

Tong Gong acknowledged the order and made off, when Song Ci shouted after him: "Change of plan. You go and have a look first."

Tong Gong waved a hand in acknowledgement. Song Ci went back inside to change, and as he re-emerged, Huo Xiong was leading his saddlehorse out of the stable. Mistress Song, Song Qi and Qiu Juan were also all up and about, and the three of them made their way to the front courtyard. Soon, all the *yamen* staff were also up, dressed and assembled in the middle of the yard.

Seeing that Song Ci was intending to ride, one of the prefectural officers suggested: "Your Honour, we have a sedan chair inside."

"No need, a horse is quicker."

Even as he spoke, Song Ci was taking the reins from Huo Xiong's hand, and he led the horse out of the *yamen*, followed by the crowd of attendants. Once outside, Song Ci flung himself on the horse and headed off in the direction of the fire. The only people left in the front courtyard were Mistress Song, Song Qi and Qiu Juan, along with an aged gatekeeper, whom Qiu Juan helped to close the gates. Song Qi suddenly felt a strange emptiness inside her, and she turned to ask her mother: "What's going on?"

"Your father is afraid someone has set fire to some grain," her mother replied.

"What for?"

"When the people are starving to death, some of the wealthy families try to take advantage of the situation by selling grain from their warehouses that has been spoiled by rodents and insects. In revenge, a disgruntled buyer might try to set fire to their personal grain stocks. It happened quite often before the famine-relief programme was announced."

Song Qi nodded in understanding, then turned and took Qiu Juan by the arm. Qiu Juan realised that Qi'er must have remembered the time when she, Qiu Juan, had set fire to Chai Wanlong's mansion.

The glow on the northern horizon was turning a deeper red, and the people gathering on the street were causing dogs to bark, near and far. The three women stayed in the front hall for a while, and then they made their way back to the rear courtyard. On arriving there, they discovered that the young girl and her little brother had also got up. These were the two children Song Ci had met on the post road some days ago, and brought home with him. The girl didn't have a proper name. At home, her mother had called her 'Little Kitten' and her brother 'Little Puppy'. Song Qi didn't much like the sound of those names, so she had given the little girl the name 'Qingqing' and the little boy 'Jianjian'.

The two of them were dressed in very decent clothes and were standing at the door of their bedroom, holding hands, and looking as though they were used to responding to all kinds of emergencies. Greatly moved by the sight, Song Qi thought to herself: What a hard life those two must have had, and how strong and self-reliant they must be.

# 4

## ON-THE-SPOT INVESTIGATION

At the scene of the fire, dense smoke was roiling around, and the sky was lit up by the flames.

Surveying the scene from the top of the north city gate, by the light of the fire, farmers could be seen scurrying around everywhere, bringing water to put out the flames and carrying long ladders, poles, gunny sacks soaked in water, pitchforks, thick ropes, iron lances… suddenly there was a tremendous crashing sound, and the building that was on fire collapsed, filling the sky with a great cloud of smoke and flames.

Then came the dull thudding of a horse's hooves, regular as heavy rain. It was Tong Gong, already galloping back along the road from the northern sector of the city. In a moment, he was reining in his horse and making his report to Song Ci.

"Master, I can report that it is a farmer's house outside the city walls that is on fire." Tong Gong spoke from astride his horse.

Song Ci seemed to sigh in relief as he heard this, but even so, fire was something that had always deeply concerned him. His horse whinnied and stamped its feet, and Song Ci hauled on the reins as he said: "Let's go and see."

"The city gates are still closed."

"Open them!"

Tong Gong, turned his horse, gave it its head and galloped off.

The drawbridge was slowly lowered, and the gates opened wide. Song Ci hurried to the site of the fire, which was almost out by then. As he arrived, he heard the sound of wailing. Seeing an official arriving, the country folk made way for him. Song Ci dismounted and passed through the crowd. As he reached the main scene of the fire, he saw a group of locals carrying a badly burnt body out of the fire. He stood in front of them and raised a hand to halt the procession, asking: "Who is the dead person?"

"He's a bricklayer," one of the men replied.

"His name was Zhang. Everyone called him Shorty Zhang," another added.

"Was there no one else in his family?" asked Song Ci, noticing the absence of anyone standing next to the body, weeping.

"His wife and child both died two weeks ago."

"Is this his house?" Song Ci asked, pointing at the place from which the body had just been carried.

"It is," the men replied.

Looking around the scene, Song Ci could see that the house in question was evidently the seat of the fire. The houses on either side were both badly damaged, so the house in the middle was clearly where the fire had started. A simple question confirmed this. Song Ci then asked if anyone knew what had caused the fire. The locals all looked at each other, murmuring apprehensively, until, after a pause, one of the older men said: "I'm afraid he must have done it himself."

"Why do you say that?" Song asked, looking at the man.

"Shorty Zhang had no quarrel with anybody, and he was as poor as could be. No one would have wanted to kill him, and he didn't have anything worth stealing."

"Before you brought the body out," Song asked the men, "where in the house was it?"

"It was by the door," a middle-aged man replied.

"Which way was the head pointing?"

"The head… inside the house, the feet were pointing out."

When he heard this, Song looked very serious. He was quite clear in his mind: most people trying to escape from a fire would make for the nearest door. If they were overcome by the flames and fell, then surely their head would be pointing towards the outside, and their feet towards the interior. This body had been found by the door, but facing the other way. If he hadn't been murdered, then what other reason could there be? He must consider other possibilities. Supposing the man had already escaped from the house and suddenly remembered something he wanted to save from the fire? Song Ci turned to Huo Xiong and ordered him to examine the body.

The *yamen* staff chivvied the crowd out of the immediate vicinity, and Huo Xiong took his shiny utility knife with a saw-edged blade from his belt. He and Tong Gong knelt down beside the body. The locals were astonished when they saw that the officials were going to examine it.

"He burned to death. What is there to examine?"

"That's right. There's no skin left, it's just like a block of cinder."

Nonetheless, Huo Xiong used his knife to prise open the oral cavity, and Song Ci bent over to take a look. What he saw, made up his mind. When a person is burned alive, they struggle for breath and their nose and mouth become clogged with ash and cinders; this does not happen to someone whose body has been burned after death. There was no sign at all of any ash in this body's mouth, so he must have been killed first and then the body was burned to conceal any evidence.

So, if the man had been murdered, who was the killer?

The most urgent thing now was to make a painstaking examination of the crime scene.

The area was lit by many torches, and although the locals didn't really understand what was going on, they were all eager to help. Working with the *yamen* staff, they cleared away the burnt and broken bits of timber, carefully turning over and inspecting each piece, and did the same with all the broken pots and pans. Amid the rubble, one of the searchers found an iron tool that turned out to be a bricklayer's knife. They also found iron hooks, plaster brushes and other tools, but these they put to one side, as they seemed unlikely to be the murder weapon. The first thing Song Ci did was to examine the place by the door where the body had been lying. In a spot no more than a body's length from the door, he found a scorched oil lamp. The sight of it started off a chain of images that unfurled in his agile brain like the horses on a moving lantern:[1]

In the middle of the night, when no one is about, someone knocks on the bricklayer's door... the bricklayer picks up a lamp and goes to open the door... as the door opens a crack, the person outside gives it a shove and goes in... the lamp is extinguished, and in the darkness there is the sound of someone falling to the ground or perhaps a muffled scream... a little later there is the flickering of flames inside the house... the killer hurries out of the house and slips away into the darkness... the fire burns more and more fiercely, thanks to the oil lamp dropped by the victim...

The investigation proceeded. Following Song Ci's instructions, all the least suspicious objects, including the random pieces of broken timber, were examined and excluded by a process of elimination, then put to one side. Bit by bit, the ruins of the dead man's house were emptied, until, finally, the accumulated ashes were swept away, leaving just an empty space.

No more suspicious objects had been discovered. Once they had tidied everything, the men got up to go, certain that the killer had left nothing behind him.

"What next, Master?" Tong Gong asked.

"Examine the ground. That's all we can do," Song Ci replied.

Examine the ground, indeed – not the same thing as examining the scene.

This was Song Ci's own particular kind of examination. Over the years he had cast his net wide to absorb new knowledge and ideas with a single-minded dedication. Not only had he acquired many new investigative techniques, he had also taken the science into areas never reached by any of his predecessors throughout the ages. And because he had all kinds of almost miraculous techniques at his disposal, he was never defeated even by the most baffling of cases. At the very least he knew just where to start, what to do next and the sequence of steps that would quickly lead to a resolution. So now, once it was clear that the culprit had not left any objects behind, he had decided to examine the ground, from which he would be able to tell how the victim had died, and what traces had been left behind, and where. He whispered instructions to Tong Gong for him to make some swift preparations. As Tong Gong left, Song inspected the general area where the body had been burnt, in the space he had had cleared, and marked out the area for closer scrutiny. Suddenly, his eyes fixed on a certain spot, and, taking one of the large muslin lanterns marked 'Prefectural Court' from a nearby attendant, crouched down to have a closer look. He was convinced he had found a vital clue and decided to follow it up immediately.

"Go and bring Tong Gong back," he said, turning to one of the *yamen* staff.

"Master!" said Huo Xiong, who had just come hurrying back from examining the pile of ruined items that had been set off to one side. He held a wine jug that had been squashed out of shape and handed it to Song Ci: "Look, Master!"

Song Ci examined the jug and up-ended it so that a few dregs tipped out into his hand. He put them to his nose. They smelled like a normal strong wine. Even so, it roused the shadow of a suspicion in Song Ci's mind. He turned to Huo Xiong, who was looking at him, waiting to hear what he had to say. He murmured softly: "You're right. The bricklayer had long since run out of grain, so where did he get the money to buy wine?"

As he spoke, Song Ci thought of the banner outside the wine shop, only a hundred paces away, and he decided to find out where the wine had come from.

"Let's go to the wine shop," Song Ci said.

The barman from the wine shop by the north gate was called Zhao, and he happened to be in the crowd of onlookers. When he heard that he and his shop were being implicated, he became agitated and broke out into a sweat.

He pushed his way through the crowd and fell to his knees in front of Song Ci, saying: "Your Worshipful Honour, I kowtow in front of you, Your Worship!"

"Stand up!" Song Ci said.

Barman Zhao stayed on his knees and didn't move.

"His Honour told you to stand up," Huo Xiong said, standing beside him.

"You mustn't be alarmed," Song Ci said. "The fire is over and your wine shop has not been destroyed, so you are not under any kind of suspicion."

"Ah, thank you, Your Worship." Barman Zhao kowtowed again, and only then stood up.

"When I speak to you, you must reply."

"Ah! Ah!"

The man stared blankly and hesitated.

"Speak up, now," Song Ci urged, quite gently. "Did the bricklayer come to your wine shop today?"

"Ah, yes... yes, he did."

"What time?"

"Around dusk."

"Did he have money to buy wine, or did he exchange some goods?"

"He didn't actually come to buy wine, to begin with, he..."

"Don't be nervous. Tell me."

"He came to change money, because he already owed us some." Barman Zhao's speech speeded up as he began to remember, and he gestured as he spoke, sounding more and more business-like. "When he came into the shop, he produced a ten *liang* silver ingot. I was really surprised and asked him where he got it. He gave a shifty smile and didn't say anything. Then he finally said: 'I didn't steal it'. So I said: 'Well, in any case, now you've got some money, just think how many cups of wine you can have!' But he shook his head and said: 'No, no!' So I gave him broken silver in exchange for the ingot, and he took it and left. But then he came back not long after with a wine jug, which I filled for him and he left again. It didn't occur to me that he might get drunk and run into trouble."

Barman Zhao finished talking, exhaled a long breath and stood there looking dejected. Then he suddenly added: "Ahhh, I'm afraid someone must have killed him for the money."

"You mentioned some silver?" Song Ci could see he had more to tell.

"Yes. Silver!" Barman Zhao said loudly. "How come there was no sign of the broken silver I gave him? Even if it had got melted in the fire, there would surely have been a lump of it left."

"How much did you change for him?"

"After I'd settled his account, I gave him seven *liang*."

"Is there anything else you want to tell me?"

"No." Barman Zhao thought for a moment, then repeated: "No."

Song Ci then asked him if, over the last few days, he had seen the bricklayer in company with someone called Tian. Barman Zhao shook his head and said that, as far as he knew, there was no one called Tian from the area.

Song Ci said: "Isn't the drill instructor in the Du household called Tian?"

It wasn't just Tong Gong who had seen and recognised Tian Huai. Barman Zhao replied that Sergeant Tian wasn't from the area. And in any case, why should he have had anything to do with Shorty Zhang? Song Ci didn't reply and didn't ask any further questions. He just waved his hand at Barman Zhao, saying he could go. The barman knelt and kowtowed twice to Song Ci, and said: "If it please Your Worshipful Honour." Then he stood up and retreated into the crowd.

Song Ci instructed Huo Xiong to ask around the locals whether any of them had seen a man called Tian in company with the bricklayer over the last few days. They were in luck, because very soon a young slave girl of about eleven or twelve came forward and said: "Sergeant Tian came to this house three days ago."

"Are you quite sure it was Sergeant Tian?"

"Quite sure. I was letting out the cattle at Master Du's house. They all called him Sergeant Tian."

"What time was it when you saw him here three days ago?"

"The sun was just going behind the mountains."

"What were you doing then?"

"I was bringing the cattle back in."

At this point in the investigation, Song Ci felt he had made his first breakthrough. In trying to find a man called Tian, where there had previously been no connection with Tian Huai and the Du household, he had now firmly established just such a connection. Looking back, before he had discovered the dregs of wine in the wine jug Huo Xiong had found, Song Ci had uncovered an important clue in the spot where the dead man had been attacked – as soon as he had approached the place where the lamp had fallen, as he cleared away the ash, he had seen a straggly, badly-written character 'Tian' scrawled in the mud. Then he had learned from Barman Zhao that, at dusk on the day in question, the bricklayer had produced a ten *liang* silver ingot. So it was clear that the case was most likely connected with one of the rich families of the area. On top of that, there was no local man called Tian, so Song Ci immediately thought of Tian Huai. Of course, it was only a suspicion for the moment. But then there was the young girl who had seen the bricklayer in company with Tian Huai, so if you put together the wine, the silver and Sergeant Tian Huai, a clear picture began to form. By now, Tong Gong had returned, and Song Ci took him and Huo Xiong to one side, and said quietly: "It's quite possible the culprit is Tian Huai."

When he heard this, Tong Gong's blood boiled.

"You will have to restrain yourself for a while," Song Ci told Tong Gong. "Tian Huai is currently Du Guancheng's drill instructor, and Du is no ordinary country gentleman. Are you clear about that?"

"So, what do we do now?" asked Huo Xiong.

"We will go straight to the Du compound and see if Tian Huai is there. The incident happened during the night, when the city gates were closed. Given his skills, he could quite easily have got back in, but equally possibly, he may not yet have returned. If he has already returned, we need to find some evidence against him. This case will hinge on the evidence. And as yet, we don't have any."

Tong Gong grimaced and spat. When he considered the importance of Du Guancheng, his blood ran cold. It wasn't that he was afraid of Du Guancheng, but rather that he was thinking of everything he had seen and heard while in the service of Song Ci. He had come to know a lot about the complicated ways of the world, and where previously he had not been worried for his master, now he was. When he heard that Song Ci was going to search the Du compound, he felt very uneasy. He thought to himself that the reason they were going to search the Du household was to find incriminating evidence. But the master of the household was Du Guancheng, not Tian Huai, and Du was the brother-in-law of the imperial prime minister. Not only that, but he would also have the protection of the provincial magistrate Shu Gengshi, and probably all the other provincial officials too. So, if this search didn't produce any concrete results, they were surely in for real trouble later. In Tong Gong's opinion, it would be better not to go and search at all.

"Master," Tong Gong said. "I think we should just go and see if Tian Huai is there or not. If he isn't, then we can wait until morning and arrest him then. If he is there, then we can interrogate him and still have time to consider what best to do next."

"It will be too late," Song Ci said.

"Why?" Tong Gong and Huo Xiong asked together.

"I'm afraid Tian Huai may not be the only person we need to arrest. Just consider, why did Tian Huai kill the bricklayer? I rather think he was acting under orders, and there is some other plot afoot. So his master Du Guancheng must be a prime suspect, and if we just concentrate on Tian Huai, it will alert him to what's going on."

"You mean to arrest Du Guancheng too?" Tong Gong blurted out.

"You said yourself, it's only a suspicion at the moment," said Huo Xiong, equally alarmed.

"It's a suspicion we can confirm," Song Ci said.

"Confirm?"

"Absolutely. If Tian Huai hasn't returned to the Du residence, then of course we can arrest him tomorrow. If he has returned after committing the crime, there's bound to be something that gives him away, and we can catch him unawares…"

Song Ci kept exhorting the two men, until they finally understood, fell in with Song Ci's wishes and left.

They went off together. Song Ci left two of the *yamen* staff behind to guard the crime scene, and himself led the rest of the attendants back to the city on horseback. After he had departed, the area outside the north gate remained busy. A house fire meant a lot of trouble and bother for the neighbouring households. Those locals who had been affected by the fire began to sort out the possessions they had managed to rescue from the flames, and women were weeping and wailing. Then there were the households that hadn't been affected by the fire, who began to wonder why the new magistrate had stopped his enquiries, gathered up the troops and gone away, once he had started asking questions about Tian Huai from the household of Du Guancheng. And why had he left two of the *yamen* staff behind to guard the crime scene?

# CHAPTER XI

## EXAMINING GROUND AND REVEALING FORM
### (1238)

In China, the study of forensic medicine did not concern itself just with establishing the causes of ante- and post-mortem injury. It was also used to track down offenders. The examination of wounds and the autopsy of dead bodies, including those that had been burned by fire, shared many of the same techniques. But in the case of immolated bodies, since in ancient times there was no knowledge of DNA, how was it possible to identify the individual, or tell whether in life they had been tall, short, thin or fat? Song Ci's concept of 'examining the ground' was not just concerned with examining the actual ground of the crime scene, but formed part of the autopsy in trying to establish the site of the fatal wound. It was unique to ancient Chinese forensic medicine and is, even today, still considered extraordinary.

1

# A NIGHT-TIME ARREST

It was past the third watch, and the waning moon was high. Its pale light spread across the boundless night sky, creating a magical landscape.

Inside the prefectural headquarters, Mistress Song and Song Qi were still up. Qiu Juan had taken the two young children off to bed, leaving mother and daughter alone together.

"Don't worry. Nothing bad will happen," said Song Qi, having seen her mother's troubled expression.

"I'm not worried," her mother said, smiling wanly.

But despite her words, she was clearly in considerable distress. She did not know whether it was just because she was getting older, but Mistress Song found herself increasingly worried for her husband. Song Qi, however, felt that most of her mother's fears were groundless. Even so, tonight, Song Qi could not sleep either. To start with, she hadn't been able to finish her calligraphy. Then there had been the fire, of which she knew neither the location nor the cause, and the fact that all the men seemed to have disappeared from the compound. Looking at her mother's stricken face, although she would not have admitted to being worried herself, it was all enough to keep her awake.

The moonlight was seeping into the room like a thin, luminous mist, making Song Qi even more wakeful, and she went over to the side of the room where the Ice in the Jade Ewer zither lay. She had hoped that its music would dispel the melancholy mood, but hardly had she plucked the first chord when her mother stopped her, saying: "Qi'er, what are you thinking. Look at the time!"

Her mother was adamant, so Song Qi pouted, and stopped playing.

"There's no point in waiting up for them. Let's go to bed." This time it was the mother reassuring her daughter.

They put out the lamps and went to bed, but they still couldn't sleep. Mistress Song lay in bed with her eyes shut, but Song Qi's eyes were wide open. Finally, just as her father had done in the second watch, she went over to the window to look at the sliver of moon that was now visible.

*The waning moon hangs above the spreading parasol trees.*
*The water clock is empty and all is quiet and still.*
*There is no one to see my lonely pacing,*
*Only the fleeting shadow of a solitary goose.*

Song Qi found that the words of Su Dongpo's poem, *Song of Divination*, had sprung unbidden into her head. She knew that he had written it while living in Huangzhou. The image of the wild goose represented his lofty isolation and disengagement from mundane concerns, along with the loneliness created by the disappointments in his official career and his despondent mood. Song Qi wasn't sure why she had thought of this poem; perhaps the references to the waning moon in the quiet of night had triggered it, but she didn't pursue the thought any further.

"But what are Father and the others up to at the moment?" This was the one thought she could not dismiss.

At that moment, under the pale moonlight, Tong Gong and Huo Xiong were arriving in front of the Du residence. There was a broad, open area in front of the compound, silent except for the chirruping of insects and the chirping of birds. The sky was lit with silver-grey moonlight, as though covered by a boundless net, which bathed everything below in an eerie light. Flying eaves projected over the main gate, under which were displayed, swaying gently in the night breeze, two large red lanterns bearing the character '杜' (Du). The two men made their way round to the outer wall of the rear courtyard. They scouted the area and stopped at a place where there were some tall trees inside the compound, next to the wall. Tong Gong took the large knife from his belt and gave it to Huo Xiong. Then he climbed on his companion's shoulders and clambered up astride the top of the wall, before dropping quietly into the shadows of the trees.

Lamplight was spilling out of one of the buildings in the courtyard. Vaulting over the surrounding balustrade, Tong Gong crept up to the window and looked in. On a large round table, there were the remains of a drinking party, except that there was only one wine cup and one set of chopsticks, which a maid was in the process of tidying up. Clearly someone had just been refreshing himself with food and drink. Grasping a smaller knife he had concealed in his clothing, he crept into the room and said quietly to the startled maid: "Don't worry, I'm not going to hurt you."

The maid started and was about to cry out, when the tray of dishes she was carrying slipped from her hands... but there was no sound of plates crashing to the ground, because Tong Gong caught the tray before it fell.

"Who has just been drinking here?" Tong Gong asked, carefully setting the tray back on the table.

The maid had clutched her hands to her chest in surprise, and it took a while before she spat out the name: "Sergeant Tian Huai."

"Has he been out tonight and just got back?"

The maid nodded.

"Do you know where he went and what he was doing?"

The maid shook her head.

"Where is he now?"

"He's gone to his room to sleep."

"Thank you." Tong Gong put away his knife and took out a piece of silver that he put on the table in front of the maid.

"Now, Sister, please don't tell anyone you saw me." So saying, he slipped out of the door and disappeared into the night.

Huo Xiong stood in the shadows of the trees, looking up at the top of the wall... eventually, he saw a small rock being thrown over the wall and heard it land with a soft thud; a second rock followed almost immediately. Huo Xiong picked them both up, and hurried off to report.

Having thrown the rocks, Tong Gong himself hurried off to check on the maid. When he saw her washing up the plates and dishes in the kitchen, and acting as if nothing had happened, he relaxed. As he turned to leave, he heard someone knocking on the gate of the main courtyard, setting the dogs barking. He realised that his master had arrived with his men in front of the Du compound.

The flickering light from a lantern approached, carried by an old retainer who acted as gatekeeper. Tong Gong hid behind an ornamental rock and let him go by. Then he quietly fell in behind him. The gatekeeper made his way along the covered corridor and climbed some stone steps to a multi-storeyed tower that had been hidden behind some lush bamboo. There was a small ornamental pond in front of the building with two floating lanterns on it. It was impossible to tell the original source of the water, but a small stream ran into the pond with a gentle babbling sound. The pond was surrounded by luxuriant foliage and flowers, and although their colours were indistinct in the gloom, they gave off an intoxicating fragrance. Faint candlelight was showing from the several smaller buildings either side of the tower, and the old gatekeeper hesitated for a moment before knocking on the elegantly carved door of one of them to the east of the tower, and calling softly: "Master. Master."

After a moment, a woman's voice answered from within: "The Master isn't here".

The old man turned and made his way to another similarly carved door to the west: "Master. Master."

Another pause, and then a rather refined woman's voice softly repeated the call: "Master. Master."

"What is it?" Du Guancheng had been roused by the cries.

"Someone is asking for you," the woman's voice replied.

"Master," the old gatekeeper spoke up. "The prefectural magistrate has come to visit, and he's waiting outside the main gate."

"What?" It sounded as though this information had made Du Guancheng sit up in bed.

"The prefectural magistrate wants to see you, Master. He's waiting outside the main gate," the old man repeated.

Tong Gong had slipped to one side and was pressed close to the widow lattice. He could see the room was half-lit by a large, eight-sided temple lantern that was imparting a reddish tinge to the beaded curtains and embroidered screens. The curtains were shot with all kinds of gold and silver thread that glittered and twinkled when they were moved. The naked figure of Du Guancheng emerged from behind the bed curtains.

"What do you want to do, Master?" It was the woman's voice again.

Du Guancheng stood in a daze beside the bed for a moment. Then he began to get dressed and shouted to the gatekeeper outside his room: "Liuhe!"

"Here, Master."

"Go and tell Sergeant Tian not to worry about what is going on. He should stay in bed and go to sleep."

"Sir," the gatekeeper called Liuhe replied. "I am going now. Are there any other orders?"

"Tell Sergeant Tian I am going to meet the prefectural magistrate myself, and invite him in. Now go!"

Tong Gong silently followed the gatekeeper as he left to carry out his orders. He was going to Tian Huai's bedroom; the bedroom of the man who had killed his sister-in-law; the bedroom of the man who had almost certainly killed the bricklayer too. Tong Gong could hear his heart pounding, sweat breaking out on his forehead, the hairs on his forearms standing up on end and his whole body filled with a burning anger. As he followed the old man, he kept shutting his eyes tight as he tried to keep himself under control. His master's words echoed in his ears: "...the most important thing is to get proof."

2

# THE FIVE-BLADED STEEL CLAW

Tian Huai's lodgings were in a small building apart from the others in the front courtyard. In front of them was an old banyan tree, so thick three people couldn't encircle it. Its luxuriant foliage spread out like a white canopy, half-obscuring the small chamber. In the shade of the tree were a number of tall ornamental rocks arranged haphazardly, looking, in the dark, like crouching monsters.

The gatekeeper went into the chamber, startling a flock of roosting birds that flapped off noisily from their perches in the tree. They were followed by a cloud of bats that made grotesquely shaped shadows in the moonlight under the foliage.

"Who's there?" said a startled voice from inside the building.

The gatekeeper started, then composed himself and stepped up to the threshold where he said through the lattice: "It's me, Liuhe."

"What's up?" Tian Huai asked.

"The Master asked me to tell you, Sir, that Prefectural Magistrate Song has come calling in the middle of the night. The Master has gone to meet him at the front gate, and you are not to get up, but just go back to sleep."

"Understood."

"May I go now, Sir?"

"Go."

Liuhe picked up his lantern and hurried off, plunging the area around the window back into stillness and darkness, disturbed only by the gentle rustling of the night breeze in the leaves of the banyan tree. The moonlight filtered down through the trembling foliage and bathed Tong Gong in its flickering light. This only served to increase his sense of uneasiness and further test his self-restraint. Suddenly, a lamp was lit inside the window. Tong Gong stepped up onto the stone ledge that encircled the building and crouched under the window. When he peered through the lattice, he saw that Tian Huai was out of bed and seemed to be searching for something: he patted himself all over and finally pulled out a silver ingot from under his clothing.

Hah, thought Tong Gong, so it really was him.

Tian Huai put the ingot on a small tea stand beside the bed and then took another object from under his pillow, which he also put on the tea stand – a five-bladed steel claw.

Still peering through the lattice, Tong Gong saw Tian Huai lift up his sleeping mat to reveal a wooden coffer. He opened its lid and dropped the steel claw into it with a muted thud. Then he took out of the coffer a gold-inlaid wooden box that he placed on the tea stand. From a hidden drawer in the stand he retrieved a key that opened the bronze padlock on the box. The lock removed, he opened the box that proved to be full of gold, pearls and other precious objects. He took the silver ingot from the tea stand and put it in the box too. At this point, Tong Gong gave a great yell, and burst in through the window. Taking advantage of Tian Huai's surprise, Tong Gong seized the hand that was holding the silver ingot. But with one quick, skilful move, Tian Huai clasped both hands together, and with a deft twist, broke Tong Gong's grip and escaped from his grasp. Tong Gong seized the moment to put the lid back on the wooden box, and, in an instant, had locked it with the padlock.

A sneer of a laugh came from Tian Huai. Almost casually, he put the ingot back under his clothes, then, drawing back for an instant, he leapt forward aiming a double-handed scything blow at his shorter opponent. Tong Gong dodged like lightning, and, with a crash, Tian Huai's hands smashed into the tea-stand, shattering it into pieces. At the same time, Tian Huai let out a great shout, not because he had hurt his hands on the tea stand, but because Tong Gong, having dodged his assailant's blow, had landed a thunderous one of his own.

A life-or-death battle ensued in the confines of the room. It was a mighty contest. Soon, wood panelling and assorted pieces of furniture were smashed, the lamps had been extinguished and the room was in turmoil. Twenty years had passed from the eleventh year of Jiading, and Tong Gong had finally got his hands on the object of his hatred. But as far as he was now concerned, the man wasn't just his ancient enemy, he was also a murderer wanted by the state, so he must be taken alive. As for Tian Huai, he knew he had all the influence of the Du family behind him, he was confident in his own combat skills and his opponent was half a head shorter than him. He was confident it would be an easy victory as he mounted his ferocious attack. The two men fought their way out of the building and into the courtyard...

By now, the main gate of the Du compound was open, and Du Guancheng had gone out to greet Song Ci with hands clasped respectfully in front of him: "It is late for Your Honour to come visiting. Please come in."

"No need," Song Ci replied.

"What?" Du Guancheng stared at him blankly.

"I just want to ask you a question."

"What is it?"

"Has your drill instructor, Sergeant Tian Huai, left the compound at all tonight?"

"Ah, so that's what you want to know. No, not at all, not at all. He is asleep in his bed at this very moment."

As he spoke, the sound of fighting came drifting over from the rooftops. Everyone looked up, and saw, silhouetted in the moonlight, the figures of Tong Gong and Tian Huai locked in combat on the roof tiles. Tong Gong kept evading his opponent's attacks with the nimbleness of a monkey, fighting then retreating, gradually drawing Tian Huai closer to the roof of the main gate. Suddenly, Tian Huai noticed the red lanterns inscribed with the characters 'Prefectural Magistracy', along with the crowd of *yamen* attendants, and his attention was distracted. Tong Gong saw his opportunity, and, taking advantage of the lapse, halted suddenly, feinted to retreat and sprang to the attack. He landed a melon-splitting blow flush on Tian Huai's forehead that caused his opponent to see stars. While Tian was still off balance, he saw Tong Gong aiming a double-handed strike to his face; he raised his own hands in defence, but the blow was just a feint, and, swift as a rabbit disappearing down its burrow, Tong Gong delivered a kick flush over Tian Huai's heart. It was an extraordinary blow, and Tong Gong let out a shout of "Down you go!" as he delivered it. Tian Huai lost his footing and fell backwards. His body hit the tiles, and, unable to stop himself, he slid with a clatter to the guttering and then down onto a mounting block in the form of a reindeer, next to which Du Guancheng was standing. Finally, he collapsed to the ground. Tong Gong pulled back his foot from the kick, steadied himself and jumped down to the roof edge. From there, he leapt down nimbly and landed on the same reindeer mounting block, before removing the silver ingot from under Tian Huai's clothes. Tian Huai had been badly injured by his fall, and he couldn't move. All he could do was watch, as Tong Gong extracted the ingot.

Song Ci took the broken ingot that Tong Gong handed him, turned it over in his hand, and estimated that it was about the weight Barman Zhao had described. He listened to Tong Gong's account of what had happened in the courtyard, then turned to Du Guancheng, saying: "Squire Du, I am sorry to disturb you like this, but I must send some of my people in to search Sergeant Tian's quarters."

"This…" Du Guancheng didn't seem to be able to grasp what was going on. He spread his arms out as though to prevent anyone passing.

Song Ci ignored this attempted obstruction, and with a nod of his head, said to Tong Gong: "In you go, and be quick about it."

Tong Gong raised his hand in summons, and Huo Xiong and several of the *yamen* guards followed him swiftly in through the gates. Du Guancheng tried again to obstruct them, but just as he raised his hands, he himself was stopped by the attendants.

Tong Gong and the others hurried through the front hall, straight to Tian Huai's lodgings. Then Tong Gong stopped and raised his hand to halt Huo Xiong and his companions. As he strained his eyes and ears, he heard the sound of footsteps running away from other side of a moon gate; although they were very soft, they carried clearly through the still night air. He said to Huo Xiong: "Quickly, take some men and follow whoever it is."

Huo Xiong and his colleagues took up the chase into the rear garden, and, in the moonlight, saw someone in a panic throwing a bundle into the ornamental pond. Huo Xiong rushed in and seized the unknown person. Then he carefully fished the bundle out of the pond. It was a set of scorched, mud-stained clothes.

By now, Tong Gong had retrieved the five-bladed steel claw from Tian Huai's room, and discovered that it was a left-handed set. Carefully inspecting it under the lamplight, he saw what seemed to be some traces of blood. He sniffed it, and it was indeed blood. He searched the rest of the room but found nothing else of interest, so he took the claw and hurried out of the room over to the rear garden. As he reached the gate, Huo Xiong was dragging his captive out, and Tong Gong immediately recognised the man as the gatekeeper he had heard being called Liuhe.

It had only been about half a stick of time[1] from the moment Tong Gong had first entered the Du compound, to the broken ingot, the steel claw, the mud-stained clothes, along with Du Guancheng, Tian Huai and Liuhe all being assembled in front of Song Ci.

In the streets either side of the open ground in front of the Du compound, a good number of householders had heard the commotion and came out of their homes to see what was happening. When they saw the normally high-and-mighty bully Lord Du surrounded by soldiers, although they didn't fully understand what was going on, they were all secretly delighted. Even though it was the middle of the night, word spread quickly. Soon, some of the more courageous locals had made their way onto the normally forbidden parade ground, and were standing there, gawping and chattering among themselves.

Song Ci looked at the gatekeeper, who was trembling all over, and decided to interrogate him first.

"What is your name? Tell me everything from the beginning."

The crowd went quiet. The gatekeeper was kneeling in front of Song Ci, not daring to look up. He stammered out: "My name is Hu... Hu Liu... Hu Liuhe."

"Where did you get these clothes from?"

"Sergeant Tian gave them to me earlier this evening, and he said to me: 'Liuhe, take these and wash them, then give them to the household cobbler to mend shoes with.' But when I looked at them, I could see that, when washed, they would still be quite good enough to keep the cold out... so I kept them."

"So why did you then throw them away?"

"When I saw Sergeant Tian being arrested, I realised that it wouldn't do me any good to be found in possession of these clothes, and I just wanted to get rid of them. I didn't think that I'd be... that I'd be arrested too."

"They are evidence in a murder case."

"No, no, they're not... they're just a set of... a set of dirty old clothes."

Verbal evidence is not something that can be taken simply at face value. It remained to be proved whether or not that mud-stained set of clothing was evidence of murder; and to do that, all the mud had to be washed off.

"Bring some water," Song Ci ordered.

One of the locals heard him and hurried off to his house, returning with water in a bamboo bucket. When the mud was cleaned from the clothes with the water, the process did not reveal the slightest trace of bloodstains, but it did uncover a number of patched repairs. Closer inspection revealed three large square patches on the back of the clothes, which caused Song Ci to frown slightly. They instantly reminded him of the day of his arrival in Nanjianzhou, and the short middle-aged man whom he had encountered leading a funeral procession. His clothes had been patched on the back in just the same way. Could it be that he and Shorty Zhang the bricklayer were one and the same person?

"Hang up the clothes so that everyone can see them," Song Ci ordered.

The clothes were spread out and lifted up on a pole.

"Take a good look, all of you. Does anyone recognise whose clothes these belong to?" Huo Xiong shouted, holding the pole up high.

There was a moment's silence, and then the locals all began competing for attention to be the first to identify the clothes as being the ones bricklayer Shorty Zhang from the north gate wore every day.

The details of the case were, by now, largely laid bare, but Tian Huai would admit nothing under questioning. Tong Gong ground his teeth in fury. Du Guancheng protested vociferously for a while, but then became very matter-of-fact and offered his own explanation of events in an unconcerned manner.

"There's nothing unusual going on here," he said. "Three days ago, I sent Tian Huai to find a bricklayer to make some repairs to my buildings, and these are the clothes that he left behind. What use were such rags to me? Naturally I had them thrown out. As for the silver, it doesn't have any owner's mark, so how do you know it isn't Tian Huai's? There are traces of blood on the steel claw because he used it to kill a dog today – what's odd about that?"

Song Ci listened without interrupting. Once he had finished his explanation, Du Guancheng was quiet for a moment, before speaking up again and asking Song Ci: "May I ask Your Honour, how did the bricklayer die?"

Song Ci looked hard at him, knowing that there was more to this question than just a simple enquiry. But after a moment's thought, he decided to answer straightforwardly: "He was murdered."

"And were there any marks from a steel claw on the body?" Du Guancheng pursued.

"It was burned in the fire."

"How badly burned?"

"Completely."

"Completely?" Du Guancheng asked in amazement, and his voice became ominously gentle. "Judge Song, I am sure you are aware that even the ancients had no way of identifying a burned body. So how do you know it is the bricklayer? For all we know, he might have killed one of his customers and burned the body before running away himself. I have the greatest respect for Your Honour, and your wisdom is well established, but it seems to me that you should be very careful with such a difficult case as this."

Song Ci knew full well that this was the real reason behind Du's question about the body. This wasn't any ordinary suspect in a case – he was a person of standing at court and would not easily be led into making a confession. Further proof was needed to make a cast-iron case at trial. Song Ci considered for a while, then called Huo Xiong over and whispered in his ear. Huo Xiong left to carry out his instructions. Then Song Ci turned to Du Guancheng and said: "Master Du, I wish to take Tian Huai to the scene of the murder. May I trouble you to come too?"

"Will you be taking your men with you?"

"Yes."

"I won't go."

Still choking with fury, Tong Gong stood in front of Du Guancheng, who looked sidelong at the powerful figure before him, then turned and made to leave. Song Ci could see that the sidelong look was not one of disdain, but of fear, so he pressed home the advantage: "You really had better come with us."

Du Guancheng closed his eyes in exasperation, as he realised he had to follow. As he would lose less face if he went of his own accord rather than having to be escorted, he snapped: "Very well, let's go."

Tong Gong stepped forward to lay hold of Tian Huai, and two *yamen* guards bound him with a stout rope and shoved him on his way. At that moment, the half-closed door of the Du mansion was flung wide open and a voice called from inside: "Let the man go."

A mob of men armed with knives and cudgels rushed out, with Du Guancheng's three sons in the lead. Du's wife and children had their bedrooms in the east wing of the main building, and, at first, had taken no interest in the goings-on outside, wanting only to sleep. His concubines, although well aware that the prefectural magistrate had come calling in the middle of the night, had not wanted to meddle in their lord's affairs either, and had also addressed themselves to sleep. Each of Du's three sons had his own set of apartments, and his own wives and concubines, and they were all deep in slumber. In the end, however, Du's wife could tell there was something amiss in the front courtyard, and she got out of bed to look out of the window. When she saw that the government men were already inside the residence, she knew that things were going badly wrong, and she summoned the gatekeeper. She hurriedly roused Du's four concubines, who were asleep inside the building, and ordered them to go and wake their master's three sons and all the family servants. Under their mother's instruction, the three sons hid themselves just inside the main gate to gauge the situation. Now, on seeing Song Ci leading the men away, they came rushing out on the offensive.

When Tong Gong heard their shouts, he drew his knife in a flash. Before his master could say anything, he threw himself forward with a clashing noise from the steel knife in his hand, and engaged with the mob who were hurtling out of the gate. Song Ci had still had no chance to speak, when Huo Xiong and the *yamen* guards also drew their blades and made to join the attack. But Song Ci stopped them with a commanding gesture. As Tong Gong used his knife to drive Du's sons and their mob of men back at bay inside the gate, Song Ci impassively ordered his own men to be on their way.

The guards shoved Du Guancheng in the back, and he set off – but after only a couple of steps, he turned to shout back at his sons: "You dogs! That's no way to go about it. Get back inside."

His sons, who had trained every day in sword and staff play with Tian Huai and were now being held at bay by one knife in the hands of Tong Gong, were very aware that going on the attack was certainly no way to go about it. So, all they could do was stand and watch as Song Ci led the group away.

By now there was a crowd of more than a hundred locals gathered outside the Du mansion, carrying all manner of torches and lanterns, and they began to follow the official party towards the north gate. None of them could ever have thought they would see such an extraordinary official as this; or, indeed, witness the newly arrived prefectural magistrate dealing with the great Tian Huai of the Du household, let alone the brother-in-law of the prime minister himself!

Tong Gong, who had been standing in the doorway all this time, knife in hand, sheathed his weapon, casually stepped down from the threshold and followed the others.

3

# MIRACULOUS COLLECTION OF EVIDENCE

The waning moon was high in the star-filled sky, and the faintest early glimmerings of dawn were just showing on the distant horizon. In the shadows of the tall trees in the prefectural *yamen*, the birds were beginning their dawn chorus. A faint morning mist was creeping in through the window of the bedroom where Mistress Song had spent a sleepless night. No longer able to lie still, she sat up in bed, moving very softly for fear of waking her daughter. But to no avail – Song Qi dragged herself upright too.

"Go back to sleep," her mother said.

"If you're awake, then I'm awake!" Qi'er replied.

For a long time now, Song Qi had made a habit of getting up before her mother to watch Tong Gong at his boxing practice, and to study swordplay with him.

"Grandfather allowed father to learn martial arts as well as his literary studies," she used to say to her mother.

"But your father is a man," her mother would always reply.

"Well, what about women, then? Wasn't this dynasty's Lady Peacemaker, Liang Hongyu, wife of Han Shizhong,[1] a woman?"

But that morning, when she got up, Song Qi was all alone. Her father, Tong Gong, Huo Xiong and the others had not yet returned, so what was she going to do with herself?

"Mother, I'm going to the north gate to see what is going on."

"You're not to go," her mother replied severely. "But don't worry. If anything was amiss, Tong Gong and the others would have come back to tell us."

"I'm not worried," Song Qi pouted. "I just want to see what's happening."

"Don't go. It's not even light yet, and a young girl like you can't be out alone."

"If I wait until it's light, can Qiu Juan and I go together?"

"Let's wait until it's light and then see."

Song Qi didn't pursue the matter. She just looked towards those faint glimmerings of dawn in the east, willing them to hurry up and turn into proper daylight.

A new scenario was unfolding outside the north gate.

Countless torches and lanterns were forming a sea of flickering flame, making the area where the fire had been as bright as day. It illuminated a pile of dry firewood that had been heaped up around the spot on the scorched ground where the burnt body had been. The mountain breeze fanned the flames of the torches so they crackled into greater life, setting the scene ablaze with light. Tian Huai was standing, tied up, next to the bonfire, and beside him was Du Guancheng, all trace of his former pomp and authority now extinguished. In the flickering torchlight, they were seen to be shivering in the chill north wind, and cold sweat was beading their foreheads. Song Ci sat silently to one side.

A bazaar-like atmosphere was developing as more and more of the locals gathered from near and far, standing around six-deep and chattering away nineteen to the dozen: "They're saying that Lord Du is involved as well," people at the edge of the circle were saying.

Others said: "I've heard they are both going to be thrown onto the fire!" Others still were clasping their hands in prayer to the heavens, asking the gods to witness what was going on. Some were even beating their fists on the ground in delight, crying that justice was being served on the villains.

But the most popular cry of all was simply: "Burn him!" The Du family had always been arrogant and overbearing, acting like local despots and generally the cause of many grievances among the locals, which were clearly manifesting themselves now.

"Make way. Make way." Some people were pushing their way through the crowd from the back. It was Huo Xiong, who was carrying a sack and a short broom, and one of the *yamen* guards who was shouldering a copper-gilded door panel. They made their way into the middle of the circle.

Song Ci watched the flickering circle of scarlet flames, then stood up and ordered: "Put out the torches."

The *yamen* guards started grabbing and pulling, pushing and shoving, until, quite soon, all the torches were out, sending plumes of black smoke into the gradually lightening morning sky. The locals started muttering to each other, wondering why the magistrate had ordered the torches, which had just started burning nicely, to be put out.

Song Ci raised a hand to Huo Xiong and ordered: "Scatter it."

Huo Xiong immediately opened the sack he had brought, inside which were the sesame seeds Song Ci had instructed him to obtain from the local pharmacist. Sesame seeds have a clean, sweet flavour, and act on the kidney meridian. As a medicine, they increase the vital essence to relieve constipation by nurturing 'yang' blood. Because they contain a lot of oil, they are also sometimes called 'oil seeds', and there are two types, black and white. It is the black that are most commonly used in medicine. Huo Xiong lifted the bag and scattered the seeds evenly across the ground so they looked like a black-coloured reed sleeping mat.

"Now take the broom and sweep them gently," Song Ci ordered.

As Huo Xiong duly swept away, a patch was revealed where the sesame seeds were left behind, and it gradually assumed the shape of a human torso with two outstretched arms. Picked out in black on the ground, it was a blood-curdling sight.

What really caught the eyes of the on-lookers was the strange black heap of seeds left stuck where the head would have been, impervious to Huo Xiong's broom. What was more, as the broom swept over the area of the shape's right hand, beside where the hand would have been, clearly visible was the character '田', 'Tian'…

The onlookers being held back by the *yamen* guards were roused to a peak of excitement. They stared in amazement at the human form on the ground, the ones at the back standing on tiptoe and craning their necks to get a better view. As Song Ci himself contemplated the shape that had been revealed, he was quite clear that he understood how the murdered man had met his death. But knowing for himself was not enough – he needed proof that would convince any other judge it might be presented to. So he gave Huo Xiong some more instructions: "Now burn off the seeds."

One of the torches was relit, and passed over the heads of the crowd, temporarily blinding the people at the back, but they could soon hear the crackling sound of the burning sesame seeds.

"Now get the door panel and put it very carefully over the top," Song Ci said.

Adopting a wide-legged stance either end of the blackened human form, Huo Xiong and one of the *yamen* guards carefully lowered the panel, like a printing block, so it covered the shape completely. After a moment, Song Ci ordered: "Lift it."

The panel made a slight noise as it was raised. An amazing sight greeted the onlookers – the sesame seed human shape had been transferred exactly to the under surface of the panel. There it was, the shape of a man, short of stature and thin in body, just like Shorty Zhang, the bricklayer from the north gate. On the crown of the head was a broad bloodstain, and however you looked at it, no one could gainsay that it was the result of a violent assault, and certainly the site of the fatal blow. But again, the most remarkable and chilling thing was that the bricklayer's right hand was pointing at the character '田', 'Tian'!

Because the door panel was being held upright, like a standing figure, those at the back of the crowd who had previously been unable to see the shape on the ground, were now able to clearly see the human form. Not only had the locals never witnessed anything like this, they had not heard of such a thing before even in the traditional fairy stories that were handed down in the region. They were quite dumbfounded.

The next thing was to examine the body. Since it was already known that death was caused by a blow to the head, that was the starting point. Huo Xiong took his saw-toothed double-edged knife, and, with practised strokes, scraped away the upper layer of burnt flesh, exposing the skull. There on the cranium, clear as could be, were five shallow pits exactly resembling claw marks. Song Ci took the left-handed steel claw, and fitted it to the pits in the cranium – they matched precisely.

More and more of the locals were arriving, and the circle was getting bigger and bigger, and increasingly crowded. Inevitably, there was a lot of jostling and toes being trodden on, but no one seemed to mind. They were all trying, without success, to work out how the miraculous human form had appeared, and they had no idea what manner of phenomenon it was. Varying emotions bounced around the crowd: amazement, respect, resentment, excitement, all growing more intense as time went on. The area outside the north gate was like a seething cauldron of heat, noise and passion, and a hubbub of voices, all mingling incomprehensibly.

Song Ci had not expected so many people to converge on the spot, and he was unable to move either forward or back. But once he raised his hand to the crowd, a part of it, at least, quickly fell silent. The people at the front stopped talking first, and then those behind, hearing that their fellows in front had gone quiet, realised the judge was about to speak and immediately followed suit. This, in itself, was something rather extraordinary, and very far from an everyday occurrence. Song Ci was secretly very moved by this display of unity by the locals.

Dawn was already colouring half the sky, and the east was gradually turning from milky white to pale blue as full daylight spread. It was at this point that Song Qi and Qiu Juan arrived. As they came out of the city gate and looked towards the open space outside, they suddenly became aware of the dense crowd of people up ahead, all standing in total silence, as if in shock. Song Qi had a very vivid, not to say lurid, imagination, and to her, this mass of people all gathered together looked like an army on the eve of battle, waiting to fall on the city in tumultuous attack.

In the silence at the centre of the circle, the on-the-spot investigation was proceeding with great expedience. As the damning evidence was laid before Tian Huai, Song Ci said softly to him: "Sergeant Tian, when Squire Du sent you to find the bricklayer, it wasn't to get him to do any repairs, was it? So, tell me now, why did he send you?"

Tian Huai was nobody's fool, and a very capable man, and up to now had made a great show of indifference to his situation. But since the time of the third watch, all manner of things he had never seen or heard of or experienced before had come piling in on him. He had no idea how this human figure had been made to appear where there had been no trace of it before, but he knew that his black deeds of the night-time had been laid bare and there was no hiding them now. He shot a glance at Du Guancheng and saw that his boss's face had lost its colour and his beard was trembling with fright. It was almost as though Magistrate Song's last question had not been directed at Tian Huai, but at Du Guancheng himself.

"So, Sergeant Tian, are you still not willing to confess?" Song Ci asked again, noting Tian Huai's reactions.

After a moment's silence, Tian Huai looked up and then kowtowed once, saying: "Master, I have spent half a lifetime out in the world fending for myself, and I have never encountered a magician of an official like you before. I give in."

Song Qi and Qiu Juan hurried towards the open space in front of the city gate. Like many of the crowd, they could not see the interrogation going on in the middle of the circle, and could only listen from the back. Song Qi really wanted to hear her father's questioning, but she could not; all she could make out was an unfamiliar voice pouring out a confession. Although the voice wasn't loud, every word was clear and unambiguous. It turned out that everything was as Song Ci had anticipated: Tian Huai had killed the bricklayer, clearly under orders, and there was some other affair at the heart of it. It seemed to be intimately connected with the famine-relief programme and the sale of grain.

What had happened was that, as a result of Li Zongmian's interview with Song Ci, the former's support for the proposed famine relief had come as a considerable surprise to Du Guancheng. Du knew the prime minister both personally and in his official capacity, and was sure that the prefectural government would waste no time in enacting the scheme. This caused him to sit very uncomfortably. So, while the prime minister and Song Ci were discussing the case of human flesh being for sale in the marketplace, Du had slipped out of the room and went looking for his most capable henchman, Tian Huai. He ordered him to visit the bricklayer, Shorty Zhang, and tell him to visit the Du compound at noon the next day to conduct some business. Du Guancheng knew that the prime minister was intending to leave in the morning. It was that same day that Tong Gong, who was waiting outside the gates of the Du residence, happened to catch sight of Tian Huai.

The next day, Li Zongmian had summoned Shu Gengshi and Song Ci to give his personal instructions for the famine relief, and then had indeed departed from Nanjianzhou. After he had gone, Shorty Zhang arrived at the Du mansion at midday and was told to wait in the rear courtyard. There, he had been able to observe some unusual activity in the Du household.

Nanjianzhou is a mountain city, and many of its houses perch in disorderly fashion on the hillsides. Du Guancheng had long ago arranged for a cellar to be dug into the slopes underneath his main residence, and while Shorty Zhang was waiting in the rear of the compound, he had seen the household servants busily carrying sacks of grain into that storehouse.

Du had ordered the bricklayer to his house to instruct him to build a mound of stones in front of the cellar to look like an ornamental mountain. He had chosen Shorty Zhang because he was not just a builder, but also an expert landscaper.

It was towards dusk on the third day that Shorty Zhang was looking to complete the job. Du Guancheng's original intention was to kill Shorty Zhang in the rear courtyard. But after consideration, he decided that this would be inauspicious and might bring back luck on the house in future. So instead he gave the man a large ingot of silver, swore him to secrecy about the work and told him to go home when night had fallen.

Because of the famine, no one in the area was much concerned with building new houses, or even repairing old ones, and Du was worried that Shorty Zhang's muddy clothes would arouse suspicion. So before Zhang left, Du ordered him to take off his soiled clothing. After he had gone, Du instructed Tian Huai to go and take care of things during the night. He was sure the spirits would not concern themselves with a murder outside the city walls. Climbing over the walls at night was not a worry for Tian Huai, who was skilled in the use of the steel claw.

That night, before the moon was up, Tian Huai had already slipped out of the city and made his way to Shorty Zhang's house. Through gaps between the panels of the broken old door, he could see an altar table with ancestral tablets, on which some wax candles were burning, and bundles of incense were sending spirals of smoke into the air. Shorty Zhang was kneeling in front of the altar, sprinkling wine as an offering to his wife, who had died two weeks before. Tian Huai stood outside the door for a while, and just for a moment, felt some pity for the man. Nonetheless, he raised his hand and knocked on the door... and everything that happened after that was just as Song Ci had deduced from finding that lamp.

The clerk of the court recorded Tian Huai's confession, which Song Ci ordered Tian to sign. In the same proceedings, he also obtained Du Guancheng's signed confession.

It was full day by then, and the rays of the morning sun were scattering light like fire flowers, bringing life to the desolate and neglected patch of land outside the city walls. Song Qi had listened to the whole affair and now caught hold of Qiu Juan, and stuck her lips out at her. Qiu Juan understood: the young mistress wanted to go home. Her father had been away all night, and her mother was stuck at home, anxiously waiting for news. Song Qi and Qiu Juan linked arms, looked around at the crowd, then turned and left. They had not gone far, though, when they heard the clanging of a gong being struck inside the walls. After a moment, two placards reading 'Make way' and 'Respectful silence' were carried out of the gates, followed by an official sedan chair, complete with attendants, front and rear. There was no need to ask – it was clearly the provincial magistrate Shu Gengshi arriving on the scene.

There was a rider in front of the sedan chair, tall and well built, with an imposing presence. As he got closer, Song Qi thought he looked familiar. After a moment's further consideration, she realised that, when she was a child, she had often seen that spreading beard like a young dragon's horns and those piercing blue eyes on the streets of Jianyang.

Although she had been very young, she still was able to remember the year when Qiu Juan's father had been arrested by this man and locked up in prison to die of starvation; and when her mother had been kicked in the stomach by him until she vomited blood and died of her injuries. All Qiu Juan's bad luck had stemmed from that time... it was indeed Jianyang's ex-captain of police, Liang E.

Song Qi felt a nameless hatred rise up in her heart. She fixed the man with a glare, then turned and left without looking back. She saw the same hatred in Qiu Juan's eyes, too, and the pair of them, by tacit agreement, made their way back to the scene of Shorty Zhang's murder. Who could have anticipated what Shu Gengshi's arrival was to presage...

## 4

## AN EVENTFUL DAY

The crowd shifted restlessly, and a passageway quickly opened up through it. Song Ci understood that this new arrival was the result of Du Guancheng's angry words to his three sons, and it was they who had summoned the provincial magistrate.

But what could Shu Gengshi do now he was here? The magistrate got out from the sedan chair, and he and Song Ci exchanged formal greetings. Song handed him all the evidence and the signed confessions to inspect. After he had looked at it all, Shu Gengshi seemed just as amazed as the locals had been. All within a single night – no, half a night in fact – Song Ci had investigated the case so clearly and comprehensively, and had furnished such strong evidence, that the result was indisputable. What was there for Shu Gengshi to say?

The magistrate was at a loss. He could not get his head round the human form on the copper-gilded door panel. As Shu looked at the panel, in a daze, Song Ci's brain was also in a whirl. He knew that Shu Gengshi was under Du Guancheng's patronage and had had no option but to come; but also that, now he was here, there was actually nothing he could do. Song Ci thought about the fact that the announcement enacting the famine-relief programme had not yet been posted; and the fact that, after today, he would still have to work with Shu Gengshi. He decided that he couldn't let all these local people see any sign of disharmony between himself and the provincial magistrate. With this in mind, his only course of action was to explain the riddle of this case as clearly and frankly as possible.

"My Lord Shu, there is nothing extraordinary about these minor skills of mine," Song Ci said quietly to the magistrate. "When a body burns, the fats and oils drain into the soil. If you apply fire to them again, they, naturally, are drawn out once more. When you scatter sesame seeds over them, the seeds bind the fats together. As for the '田' character, the seeds just filled in the indentations of the finger-strokes. In this case too, the heat drew the oils out of the sesame seeds so that, when the copper-gilded panel was placed over them, they adhered to it, revealing the human form you can see now."

Of course, once a miracle is explained, it no longer seems so miraculous. But sorting the miraculous from the commonplace was not what was currently at the forefront of Shu Gengshi's mind. Although he was not a man of great scholarship, he was quite accomplished. He knew that in the 'dog-eat-dog' world of a government career, it was all too easy for an official, no matter how learned, to suddenly find himself ensnared in unexpected toils and travails. So far, his own progress, with the benefit of patronage, had been smooth and uneventful. And he was quietly confident of climbing higher still up the ladder, because he had an exceptional ability to size up the potential risks and advantages of any given situation.

"My Lord Shu, please take another look at this," said Song Ci, indicating a large sheet of fine writing paper that Tong Gong and Huo Xiong had unfolded. On it was the imprint of the human form taken from the gilded door panel.

Song Ci went on: "In this manner, it can be stored in the records and produced as needed for the Ministry of Punishments or even if the case is petitioned before the emperor."

Shu Gengshi realised that Song Ci was implying it was a certainty that a case involving so high an official would be referred up to the emperor.

So far, Shu had not said a word – there was nothing he could say – and he had simply listened as Song Ci recounted the circumstances of the arrest of the two malefactors, Du and Tian, and waited for the matter to be dealt with. In the end, as the two officials discussed the case, it seemed only fair that the huge audience of locals should be informed about the announcement of the famine-relief programme. Everyone then could hurry into the city to look at the official proclamation, and then proceed on to the *yamen* to register for the scheme so that they could take advantage of it.

Shu Gengshi agreed with this plan, but he still was not willing fully to commit himself, so all he said to Song Ci was: "Very well. You go and make the announcement."

Song Ci excused himself from this task, instructing Huo Xiong to make the announcement in his place. As soon as Huo Xiong did so, in his strong, clear voice, the huge crowd outside the north gate began shouting with joy, and the noise, like a spring thunderclap, shook the city walls and echoed for miles around the district.

It was the most eventful day in the history of Nanjianzhou. People rushed into the city to spread the news, and the whole place erupted. When the official proclamation was brought out to be posted, crowds surged up to it so that the *yamen* staff who had been sent to carry out the task were trapped by the throng of people wanting to see it with their own eyes. Express messengers were sent to carry the proclamation round the whole district of Nanjianzhou, and the same happened wherever they went.

But what was going on in the Du residence all this time?

It was in a similar state of upheaval. Du Guancheng's wife was forty years old, and of a scheming disposition. Over the years, she had, by one means or another, ensured that none of the children of her husband's concubines had grown to adulthood. While the rest of the household, including Du Guancheng's sons, had been at their wits' end, she had calmly written a family letter to Li Zongmian's wife, Du's younger sister. She had personally given the letter to her second son, who was an expert horseman, with the instruction: "Take this post haste to Lin'an, and don't delay."

"Lord Shu, please think of some way to help our father." This was Du's eldest son, also following his mother's orders and pleading with Shu Gengshi in the rear hall of the provincial magistrate's headquarters.

Shu was not long back from outside the north gate, and was at a loss what to say. He listened to the lengthy pleas from Du's son, before heaving a deep sigh and saying: "Song Ci is just too clever for us."

"Lord Shu, you are the most important man in the district. How can you let him control you?"

Shu Gengshi was not a man who was easily roused, and he just closed his eyes in response.

"Lord Shu!"

"There's no need to shout," Shu Gengshi said in measured tones. "It's not up to me any more. The prime minister is involved and there may be nothing I can do."

"What do you mean?"

Shu did not reply immediately but sat murmuring to himself for a while, before opening his eyes. He seemed to be still mulling something over and his gaze was turned inwards. His lips moved as though about to say something, but then his mouth closed again. There was another silence before he pursed his lips, as though reaching a final decision, and said: "Generally, in a court case, if you want to find a way round the law, you have to act before conclusive proof has been produced. In the situation we are in now, there is nothing that can be done to refute it."

"So, what is the best thing to do?"

"You..." Shu Gengshi hesitated for a moment. "You had better go home and discuss things with your mother." Then he rested his head on the back of his chair and shut his eyes again. No matter what Du Guancheng's son said, he didn't utter another word.

So all Du's son could do was go home and report to his mother. Experienced conspirator that she was, Du's wife seemed to understand the hidden meaning behind Shu Gengshi's words, and an evil scheme began to form in her head...

All this happened in the course of the same day.

During that same day, Song Ci, who was in charge of making arrangements for the famine relief, was busier than he had ever been in his life. As for Song Qi, when she and Qiu Juan had returned to the rear hall of the prefectural *yamen*, and had reported everything they had seen and heard to Mistress Song, she went back to her own chamber. Once again, she stood in front of the unfinished calligraphy scroll and looked at the characters as they hung on the wall. Now her eyes glittered like black jewels. She took one of the fine Huzhou brushes from the brush pot. Qiu Juan could see that she was ready to write, so she took the cover off the inkstone and began to grind the ink. First forming the characters in her head, Song Qi loaded her brush and began to write. With brushstrokes now slow and controlled, now swift and wild, unhurriedly she wrote the final ten characters:

人生如梦，一樽还酹江月
*Life is like a dream; let us offer wine to the moon's reflection in the river*

The characters were controlled but full and mellow. Song Qi stepped back to look at her work and smiled to herself. Then she took a smaller brush, stepped forward again, and in the empty space on the left of the scroll, wrote two columns of characters that read: "Written by Song Qi in the Wuxu year of the Jiaxi period in honour of the poetry of the great scholar Dongpo."

5

# A YOUNG LIFE IN FULL BLOOM

The waning moon had not yet risen and the stars were casting a flickering, uncertain light. Nanjianzhou, which had been in uproar all day, was now quiet and still, but the people were finding sleep elusive. Rich and poor alike were gathered in courtyards, or in their bedrooms discussing the day's events and making plans for the forthcoming days.

There is a proverb that says: 'Good news doesn't travel, but bad news has wings', but such was not the case here. No one knew which insider started the word off, but by the end of the day, everyone in Nanjianzhou knew that the famine relief was the result of extraordinary efforts on the part of the new prefectural magistrate. There were some who hated him for it and others who praised him.

Inside the prefectural *yamen*, the flowers and plants were lightly bedewed, and everywhere was blanketed in a soft and comfortable feeling of peace. Song Ci had been busy all day with the relief programme. Now, after dinner, as they sat quietly for a moment and the drum in the drum tower sounded the second watch, Mistress Song urged him: "Husband, you haven't slept for a day and a night. Go and get some rest."

But Song Ci's mind was still abuzz.

The human spirit can support quite extraordinary efforts. An extremely important task can keep one busy night and day, and it is only when the work is done that, suddenly, exhaustion takes over. Song Ci was at the height of his powers and he felt that there were still some vital public works to be carried out, so how could he think of sleeping? He made his way over to his daughter's chamber. Song Qi had not slept much the night before, and her thoughts were turning to bed. She had changed into her night attire, which, as always, was simple but elegant: a light silk, snow-white sleeveless top and a pair of pale jade-green knee-length trousers. Her hair was put up comfortably in a loose bun, not held by any hairpins on top. She was delighted to hear the sound of her father calling her. She pushed a jade hairpin into place, fastened an emerald green pleated skirt around her waist and went over to open the door.

"Father," Song Qi said. "Come and have a look. I've just finished that piece of calligraphy."

Her father, as always, was charmed by his daughter's elegance and her high good humour. He knew the scroll she was referring to and went into the room with a feeling of pleasant anticipation. Wet ink still glistening, the lofty and imposing waterfall of characters greeted him as he entered, and were reflected in his eyes.

"Qi'er," he remarked, "I thought you said you didn't know what style to use to finish it."

His daughter raised her eyebrows and then smiled sweetly. She seemed as though she had been about to make some sharp retort to her father, but had thought better of it and kept her mouth closed.

In the end, Song Qi had written those last ten characters so they crowded up against the preceding four. Her thinking was that this poem of Mr Dongpo captured so movingly the atmosphere of the rivers and mountains, that it was close to perfection; until right at the end when the mood changed to what seemed to her melancholy verging on despair with the words "life is like a dream". She thought long and hard about those characters, turning over all sorts of possibilities, and in the end concluded that, however she wrote them, they could not be the same as the rest of the poem. Anyone else might have found this explanation rather quaint and amusing, but Song Ci completely understood his daughter's fine-tuned sensibilities. He listened attentively to her heartfelt explanation with an appreciative smile.

"Yesterday," Song Qi went on, "I thought that Mr Dongpo was getting old and had written these lines for another poem, but in the end he just dropped them in here, where they have no particular merit."

"And what do you think now?" her father asked.

"I no longer think they have no merit."

"Tell me your thinking." Song Ci was in a particularly buoyant mood that evening.

"Mr Dongpo wrote this poem when he was in exile in Huangzhou and made a trip to Chibi. I don't think he was necessarily despondent though."

"Why do you think that?"

"When he says 'life is like a dream', it's like a sigh," Song Qi said thoughtfully. "He still has ambitions and things he wants to accomplish, but he is already an old man. You can see it as him lamenting the brevity of life. But, using the phrase here not only reveals his wide-ranging ambitions, it also vividly shows that, even with his awareness of the approach of his end, his determination to serve his country is undiminished."

"So, to reflect both those aspects, you wrote the characters alternately wet and dry, part complaint, part lament." Song Ci continued his daughter's train of thought.

Song Qi smiled. It was the sweet, happy smile of a daughter delighting in a father who understood her so well.

Song Ci did indeed understand his daughter, often down to the finest nuance of mood. But did the daughter understand her father so well? In fact, she could sometimes be a little thoughtless. So perhaps she did not think how her little speech about the poem might have resonated in Song Ci's heart. She had spoken of Mr Dongpo's regrets over not having achieved his ambitions, and getting old. Her father reflected that he had already passed fifty, and what had he actually achieved to benefit the nation? This sombre introspection somewhat dampened his cheerful mood. It also reminded him why he had come to his daughter's room in the first place.

"Come with me," he said. "I need your help with an official document."

"Is it the official account of the murder case of the burnt corpse for the provincial court?"

"Precisely so," Song Ci said. "It is a most unusual case. There are two main considerations right now. First, I want to get it done as soon as possible, so I don't lose any sleep over it. And second, the wording of such a report has to be just right, and I want to give it my most careful attention."

"Very well, let's start."

Still wearing her white silk sleeveless jacket and long embroidered skirt, Song Qi followed her father out of her room. The night was so quiet and still, all she could hear was the faint chirruping of crickets, and the sighing of the night breeze. A few fireflies dotted the darkness with their lights. It was a most enchanting scene.

Once out of the room, Song Qi had skipped ahead of Song Ci, and called back to him as she walked: "Father, you known the line by Xin Qiji: 'The calling of startled magpies in the moonlight; the chirruping of cicadas on the midnight breeze'? I think that's all about the magical stillness of the night."

"Is that so?" Song Ci replied absently.

"Of course. Think about it – the moon itself has no sound, but when it rises suddenly, it disturbs the birds roosting in the trees. You can see from that just how still and quiet it must be."

"What made you think of that now?"

"I don't know." Song Qi turned to look at her father, then walked back, thinking, before she continued: "I just thought that tonight has not been at all quiet and peaceful. I wanted to say something of my own along the same lines as Xin Qiji's but… but the words wouldn't come to me."

Then she turned round again and continued on her way, staring up into the boundless night sky.

Song Qi had changed over the years. She had matured a great deal and seldom displayed the naivety of former times. Even so, the innocent passion of her youth sometimes still erupted in a body now burgeoning into maturity, and when it did, it was even more ardent than before. So perhaps, in the heart of this meticulous but passionate young woman, a quiet night like this really did represent something rather different. Even though the half-moon had not yet risen, still there were countless small, twinkling stars, each striving in its own way to assert itself through the screen of the night breeze and shed its own light, however limited, across the landscape. Even though they were hidden from sight, the flowers and plants were singing their own soft songs, and spreading their soft and comforting fragrance…

Who could have guessed that the course of Song Qi's short life would come to an end that very night?

She reached the library and went in, her heart filled with pleasure at the thought of being able to help her father. How attentively she listened, how conscientiously she wrote. Her wrist moved like flowing water, and not a single hair of her brush landed out of place – all in the cause of righting injustices, punishing evil and upholding righteousness in the world.

The night was dark, and the world outside the window was harbouring grim and unexpected deeds. The shadow of a masked man clad in dark clothes appeared on top of the roof to one side of the library. He concentrated on the flickering light from lamps and candles on the widow lattice, and the lit room within, as his objective.

The masked man stretched, stood up and clambered nimbly across the tiles as easily as though he was still on the ground.

The masked man eased himself down from the roof and landed without a sound.

The masked man fixed his eyes on the slats of the window lattice.

A flash of light cut through the dark of the night – the masked man had a weapon.

History is full of examples of violent and treacherous acts bringing disaster on the good and the righteous, and this was to be another instance.

There was the sound of footsteps walking along the colonnade outside the library… the masked man started, then slipped into the shadows. The newcomer was Tong Gong.

As he approached the library, he heard Song Ci's serious voice, mid-dictation. He stopped in front of the door then pushed it open and went in. Song Qi, who was sitting at a desk at the far end of the room, writing studiously, looked up briefly and smiled. Tong Gong nodded to her and then said to Song Ci: "Master, Mistress would like you to come back soon to get some rest."

Song Ci nodded in acknowledgement and continued pacing the room dictating his text. It was Song Qi who replied with a slight smile: "We'll be finished soon."

Tong Gong knew that once his master had started on a task, he couldn't stop until it was finished. He stood there for a moment, then decided he had better report back to Mistress Song, so he turned and left the room, shutting the door behind him. For the rest of his life, he was bitterly to regret not staying.

Song Qi finished writing and, smiling happily, handed the document over to her father, saying: "It's finished, Father. Sit down and look it over."

She helped Song Ci, who was exhausted from his constant pacing, to a chair and pushed him down into it.

As Song was concentrating on the beautifully written, unblemished document, the door of the library was flung open, there was a glint of light, and a throwing knife sped like an arrow from a bowstring, whistling straight towards Song Ci's heart. Song Qi, who was standing beside her father, waiting for any corrections, gave a startled glance, and, with a strangled cry, threw herself across her father, taking the knife in her own body. When Song Ci realised what had happened, he gave a great cry of: "Assassin!"

Two more short-bladed knives flashed in from outside the door, but Song Ci dodged them and snuffed out the candle next to him. Tong Gong, who had not gone far along the colonnade, heard the cry, whirled round and flew back towards the library. By this time, the assassin had already clambered back onto the roof and was making good his escape. Ignoring for the moment whatever was going on in the library, Tong Gong set off in hot pursuit.

In the darkness, Song Ci clutched his wounded daughter to his breast, and felt the handle of a knife sticking out of her back. Cold terror clutched his heart, as, with a shudder, he groped again for the handle of the knife. He felt the warm blood flowing out of his daughter's back and onto his own body. A fiery heat flooded through him.

"A lamp! A lamp! Bring a lamp!" he shouted in a frenzy.

The household was in uproar. Mistress Song came rushing out, as did Qiu Juan and all the *yamen* staff... up on the rooftops, the assassin was flinging roof-tiles at the pursuing Tong Gong, who was dodging them all. Finally, the assassin sprang down from the roof and left the compound, with Tong Gong still in chase. Inside the compound, Huo Xiong and the *yamen* guards sized up the situation, opened the main gates and made to join the chase. But they could see no sign of Tong Gong or the assassin.

The library was now flooded with light, and Song Qi lay in her father's arms, already close to death.

"Father… you… must not worry…" She struggled to form the words.

"Qi'er!…."

"Qi'er!…."

Song Ci and his wife both choked out her name, their insides wrenched by fear and grief. They looked at their daughter's clothes: the snow-white jacket was scarlet with her blood, and the jade-green trousers now a deep purple.

"Qi'er… you… you must stay alive…" Her mother stroked the girl's breast with a trembling hand and wept soundlessly.

Qi'er's downcast eyes fell on the document that lay between her and her father, and she gestured at it, trying to pick it up. Song Ci picked it up, spread it out and placed it in front of his daughter. It was, of course, the formal statement of evidence that Qi'er had just finished writing, the beautifully formed characters now stained red with blood. Qi'er looked at her father and said: "Father… I really wanted… to go to Lin'an… to see the Hanlin Academy gallery… and all the paintings and calligraphy…"

As she spoke, a great shudder ran through her body, a frown creased her forehead and she closed her eyes.

"Qi'er!"

"Qi'er!"

Song Ci and his wife thought that she had passed away, and Qiu Juan, standing beside them, burst into tears. The sound of the weeping from both Qiu Juan and Mistress Song seemed to revive Qi'er, who sighed deeply and slowly opened her eyes.

"Qiu… Juan… sister!" she said, haltingly.

"I'm here!" Qiu Juan knelt in front of Qi'er.

"Sister… promise me…"

"What is it?" Qiu Juan replied, still weeping.

"There's… one… thing…"

"Tell me, little sister."

"You… must… promise me…"

"I promise."

"You must…"

"I'll do it."

"Marry… Tong Gong…"

Qiu Juan nodded her head.

"Tong Gong… has never forgotten that… you saved… his life… if… you…

don't marry him… he will… never marry… anyone else… you must… promise… me"

"I… I promise."

Song Qi smiled, looked at her mother and smiled again. Then her gaze became fixed and motionless. After a long time, she blinked once and turned her eyes to the distance, as though looking for someone. "Older Brother Gong… " she mumbled.

"He's on his way, Qi'er," her father reassured her.

Her eyes rested on her father's face, and her lips, which were growing paler and paler, began to move as she just managed to whisper: "Father… Mr Dongpo said… life… is like a dream… you must… look after yourself…"

Song Ci grasped his daughter's hand more tightly; it was clammy with sweat. And then she was gone. Two crystal teardrops rolled down from her long, delicate eyelashes. Were they from pain, or sadness or perhaps from a simple reluctance to leave this world? She was only twenty-four, and she was gone.

"Aaah! Qi'er! Qi'er…" Song Ci's voice choked on his grief, and tears he had held back for so long, flooded out. For a long time, he lay on the ground and could not rise. Mistress Song was speechless with grief too, weeping as she cradled her daughter.

Tong Gong returned, drenched in sweat and empty-handed. Before he had even reached the compound, one of the *yamen* staff was pulling open the gates for him. Through the crack between the gates as they began to open, Tong Gong caught the sound of weeping and wailing coming from the rear courtyard. A terrible presentiment froze his heart, and he grabbed the doorman by his jacket, shouting: "What's that noise?"

"It's… it's…" the doorman stammered fearfully. "It's the young mistress…"

With the force of a thunderbolt, Tong Gong thrust past the doorman, who fell to the ground and did not dare to rise. Tong Gong flew towards the rear courtyard, and hurtled into the library. When he took in the scene that lay before him, he gave a soundless cry and fell to his knees beside Song Qi's body. All the *yamen* officials and servant girls followed suit.

That night, no one in the prefectural *yamen* slept, as they were engulfed by grief.

Song Ci never imagined that such a calamity could befall his daughter in the prime of her life, wrenching her from the springtime of her youth.

Song Ci and his wife both aged ten years in the course of that one night. Their precious only daughter was no longer with them.

The sky was gradually lightening, and broken white clouds were drifting across the eastern horizon, meandering like silken threads. A new day was beginning to dawn and the world was waking up. But Song Qi would never wake again.

In the depths of his grief, Song Ci could find no way to comprehend his daughter's death. The murderer had escaped and not been caught, and Song Ci was incapable yet of raising the hue and cry. But, in the clear light of that morning, angry beyond enduring, Tong Gong quietly slipped out of the prefectural *yamen*...

# CHAPTER XII

## 10,000 PEOPLE WORKING TOGETHER (1238-1239)

In this period, Europe lagged behind China not just in legal matters. The Mongol horde had swept across Europe without meeting effective resistance, and withdrawal from the continent was certainly not the result of defeat in battle. In 1241 a dispute over succession arose in the Mongol empire, and the armies far away in Europe were recalled. Their horsemen passed like a whirlwind through central Europe on their way back east, as easily as if they were on manoeuvres on their native steppes. After that, the Mongol's principal battlefront was with the Southern Song. Although the Southern Song has been described in later times as weak and degenerate, it still put up a stiffer resistance than any country in Europe managed. In Europe, the Mongols advanced as they pleased, but they were not able to make the same headway into the territory of the Southern Song. Why not? Because, with the country in such a parlous state, people like Song Ci concentrated on cleaning up the penal system, righting miscarriages of justice, resolving apparently intractable disputes, consolidating the power of the people, and in general addressing their talents to the most important issues.

1

# THE MANGDANG WINERY

With murderous vengeance in his heart and without a backward glance, Tong Gong set off in pursuit of Tian Ju. For the assassin was, indeed, none other than Tian Huai's younger brother, Tian Ju. Perhaps because he had carried a mental image of the Tian brothers in his head for so many years, he had had a feeling that night, while dodging the roof tiles his adversary was throwing at him, that the man had the look of Tian Ju. His pursuit led him out of the *yamen* and into the deserted streets and lanes, until he finally ran his quarry down in a blind alley. A fierce hand-to-hand fight ensued under the pale, uncertain light of the newly-risen moon.

On any ordinary day, Tong Gong would have had no trouble evading his opponent's attacks, exploiting his weaknesses and wearing him down into defeat and capture. But that night he was too anxious to get the culprit back to the *yamen* as quickly as possible, and also desperately worried about what might have happened in the library. In addition, he realised as soon as he engaged with the man that he was no ordinary opponent, and the fight developed into a fierce and evenly matched contest. Tong Gong's greatest accomplishment in the course of it was to strike the mask from his opponent's face, revealing him, indeed, to be Tian Ju. At the same moment, Tian Ju caught him with a side-kick right over his heart, which sent him tumbling into a block of limestone in the alleyway and knocked him to the ground. By the time he scrambled to his feet, Tian Ju had climbed over a wall and disappeared from sight.

Tong Gong made to go after him, but felt himself held back, as if by some invisible force. On reflection, he knew who the assassin was, and there was no danger of him not being apprehended, so he stopped, turned and hurried back to the prefectural *yamen*. As soon as he reached the gates, the sound of wailing coming from within, froze his marrow...

During the rest of that grief-stricken night, he never left Song Ci's side. Since the assassination attempt had failed, there was a real danger the culprit might return. But come daylight, he could restrain himself no longer; he went to the kitchen to get something to eat and drink, and, soon after, set out from the *yamen* alone.

Nanjianzhou was only a small mountain town, and everybody knew Tian Ju. Tong Gong quickly discovered that he had opened a wine shop known as the Mangdang Winery, about ten *li* outside town at the top of the Mangdangshan Road. Mangdangshan is situated to the north-west of Nanjianzhou, and is a fine, picturesque spot. The mountain has abundant clear springs and flying waterfalls, exotic plants and flowers, and fantastical rock formations, more beautiful than any landscape painting. Back in the fifteenth year of the Jiading period, the prefectural magistrate Chen Mi had had an inscription carved into the cliff face extolling the mountain as being as beautiful as the famous mountains of Lushan, Tiantai, Yandang and Wuyi. If you travel west from the top of the Mangdangshan Road, you will find, perched on the mountainside, the Xiyuan Temple, which by this time had already been established for more than a hundred years, and was famous far and wide across the region, attracting countless pilgrims. If you travel north-east, you will find yourself on the steep and arduous road cut through the mountains from Fujian to Jiangxi by the generals of the Yang family, known as the 'Thirty-Eight Hundred Pits'; it remained the principal thoroughfare between the two provinces. Clearly, this was a very profitable spot to open a wine shop.

Of course, on such a busy road across the mountains, Tian Ju's was not the only wine shop. At first, Tong Gong could not find the establishment he was looking for, as he made his way along the road. After asking in two other wine shops, he finally discovered that Tian's was the largest place on that stretch, located at the top of the road just where it was about to enter the mountains themselves. Outside its door, it had a sign that read 'Mangdang Liquid Jade'.

Tong Gong hurried on his way and soon saw the inn, just where he had been told, at the place where the road began to climb into the mountains proper. It was located on a wide, flat area, with its door facing the road and its back to the cliffs. It stood by itself, shop in front, courtyard behind, of a good size and, all-in-all, the image of a prosperous winery. Having reached his destination, Tong Gong stopped to catch his breath, and then he strode briskly towards the main entrance.

In front of the door grew a red bean yew tree, so called because, although it resembles an ordinary yew, every autumn it produces little red fruits that look like red beans. The inn sign that read 'Mangdang Liquid Jade' was hanging from this yew tree, and as Tong Gong made his way to the door, he silently pulled it down and broke it in two. He flung the pieces through the door and hurtled into the inn after them, trampling them under foot as he went. He looked around, searching for his quarry. Two waiters tried to get in his way, but he lashed out with a couple of punches and sent them flying.

"Stop fooling around and get Tian Ju," he shouted.

One of the waiters ran to tell Tian Ju what was going on. The man himself had hurried back through the night from Nanjianzhou, and was asleep in his concubine's room in the inner courtyard. When he heard the waiter's report, he rolled hastily out of bed, thinking that it was government officers who had come to arrest him. He knew full well that he had committed a capital offence that night. The *Book of 36 Stratagems* says, if all else fails, flee, and that is what Tian Ju intended: he was going to slip out of the back door and onto a little track that wound up the mountain, until he could join the Thirty-Eight Hundred Pits Road that would take him into Jiangxi. From there, he could disappear anywhere he liked.

"Tell your boss to come out."

The shout was so loud it overturned tables and shattered dishes and wine jars.

This was decidedly odd, Tian Ju thought. Perhaps it wasn't government officers after all, but one of his rival innkeepers come to turn over his establishment.

"How many of them are there?" he asked.

"Just one – a big fellow wearing white."

Tian Ju began to relax. He hadn't recognised the man he had fought the previous night and so reckoned that, even though his mask had been knocked off, his opponent wouldn't have recognised him either. So why be worried? Tian Ju strode out confidently.

When the two men met inside the shop, Tian Ju was considerably surprised. The man in front of him was, indeed, his pursuer from the night before. But why had he come alone? It still hadn't dawned on him what was going on: just like his brother, Tian Huai, he didn't recognise Tong Gong.

"I'm going to kill you. Do you hear me?" Tong Gong bellowed through clenched teeth.

Tian Ju stared at him. He had expected his opponent to say he wanted to capture him, not to kill him. But before he could dwell on the matter, the man rushed at him. At the same moment, a dozen or so of the inn's waiters saw what was happening to their boss. They plucked up their courage and intercepted the attack.

A battle royal ensued, and although the waiters were armed, they were no match for Tong Gong's skills and were soon being battered. Tian Ju was incensed and yelled at them: "Get out of my way!"

He leapt into the fray and engaged with Tong Gong. But this was not the same Tong Gong as on the previous night; he had got himself under control and was determined to take Tian Ju alive. He advanced circumspectly and attacked with restraint. Tian Ju, on the other hand, seeing that there was only this white-clad man standing against him, thought he could swiftly prevail and soon be able to make his escape. So he hurled himself at his opponent with great force and fury. But even when he exerted his fighting skills to the utmost, he could not lay a finger on Tong Gong. Instead, he found himself on the receiving end of a continuous torrent of blows that left him dazed and disoriented. Eventually, he stopped in his tracks, turned and fled to the back of the inn.

Tong Gong was in no mind to let him get away, so he set off in pursuit. The fight turned into a running battle between the two men, as they chased all over the inn, overturning furniture and smashing crockery as they went. Tian Ju's womenfolk and the waiters from the inn all stood watching, but none of them dared intervene. Seeing his escape route cut off, Tian Ju ducked into a storeroom and slammed the door shut. When he saw what was happening, Tong Gong made to stop him and, pausing briefly to gather his strength, launched himself with a great shout at the door. With a crash, Tong Gong burst through the door, carrying it bodily with him into the storeroom.

But Tian Ju was nowhere to be seen.

It was a very large room, full of wine jars and vats, and Tong Gong scanned it carefully. Suddenly he felt a gust of air behind him, and he turned, with both arms raised to protect himself. An empty wine jar came flying in his direction and struck him on the elbow, shattering as it did so. Scarcely had the pieces hit the ground, when another jar came whirling through the air. This time he dodged it, and the jar struck a wine vat, smashing both vessels and flooding the floor with the dregs and lees inside them.

The storeroom turned into a new battleground, and after several exchanges, once again Tian Ju found himself on the losing end and had no option but to flee. Tong Gong sprang after him in remorseless pursuit. But all of a sudden, the floor under his feet gave way with a great cracking sound and he disappeared from sight.

Gasping for breath, Tian Ju stopped and turned back to look down into the hole where Tong Gong had fallen. Gritting his teeth, he picked up a large vat, full of wine, and threw it down the hole. Then he lifted the trap-door that had been concealing the opening, put it back in place over the hole and strode out of the storeroom.

Tian Ju's wife and concubines, and the waiters, were all standing outside the storeroom door, and when they saw Tian Ju come out, they all clamoured to know what had gone on inside. Now, this inn of Tian Ju's had originally been several smaller wine shops. When he arrived on the scene, he started by setting up a number of small establishments of his own, and then he began intimidating all the other shops. He relied on the fact that his brother was the drill instructor to the Du household, a household with close ties to the local officials, so the other establishments had no hope of legal redress, while he had no compunction in bringing lawsuits of his own against them. Thus, he had been able to build this substantial winery with its saloon at the front and courtyard at the rear.

But once he had established his own little fiefdom, Tian Ju did not have it all his own way. A man is nothing without his good reputation, and several of the wine shop owners refused to be intimidated, despite having no recourse to the law. They brought in some itinerant mercenaries from the river margins to take their revenge. A number of skirmishes followed, and although none of the mercenaries had been able to defeat Tian Ju, they had certainly caused him no little bother. So, when Tian Ju had heard the crashing of furniture and smashing of crockery, at first he had thought it must be one of his competitors causing all the trouble. Moreover, he had long ago constructed an escape tunnel leading from the winery, partly so that he could indeed avoid anyone who came along whose martial arts were superior to his, and partly because, in choosing that spot to build his inn, he had planned to develop a sideline in assassination and highway robbery. So far, however, any travellers carrying significant amounts of money with them had tended to be accompanied by expert bodyguards.

Now, the escape tunnel had demonstrated its usefulness and saved him from the threat of this mysterious white-clad fellow. But he knew he was still in danger, since he reckoned that the man must be an agent of the prefectural court and that, at any moment, soldiers might surround the winery. In the face of such an imminent threat, he had to make hasty preparations to flee.

No point in standing around, he thought. I'd better get to my room and collect my valuables.

He started yelling orders at his wife and concubines. For their part, the womenfolk were mystified: hadn't their master not just got the better of his opponent, so why was he so agitated and in such a rush? They still thought that the white-clad man was an agent of one of their competitors, but they didn't dare question Tian Ju's orders and each of them hurried off to their own quarters. Tian Ju himself picked up a long steel knife from the ground where it had fallen, and he ordered one of the waiters to go out onto the main road to keep watch.

Tong Gong had not been too seriously injured by his fall from the storeroom. When he looked up from the ground on which he had landed, he could make out an opening about the size of a large temple lantern and a hinged trapdoor; he realised he had accidentally discovered some kind of secret tunnel. His body ached all over, and he had still not got to his feet when he saw Tian Ju lift up a wine vat and hurl it down at him. He twisted out of the way and wildly fended the vat off with both hands as it headed straight down at him. There was a great crash as the vat hurtled into the wall and broke into pieces almost at his feet, splashing him with dregs. At the same time, the impact of the vat sent him hurtling backwards; he yelled out in agony and surprise as a shooting pain spread across his back, as though he had been struck by ten thousand arrows. Before he could gather his senses, everything went dark, as Tian Ju closed the opening to the tunnel above his head.

Tong Gong gritted his teeth and stretched out his body, panting heavily. He could feel there was something on his back, and not just the wine he had been splashed with. He put a hand behind him and felt about, then brought the hand up to his nose and sniffed – blood, definitely blood. He wasn't in any doubt.

Everything was still pitch black in front of him. He sat on the wine-soaked ground and closed his eyes. On opening them again, he could just make out some dim shapes in the darkness, thanks to the faint shafts of light filtering through chinks in the panelled trapdoor above him. He felt around and, as he moved, the pain in his back shot through him again. Now he could make out some kind of shadings in the blackness that looked like an iron grating. He stretched out his hand and felt metal spikes. He realised that he must have fallen onto those spikes, and that was what had caused the injury to his back. But he could not work out what kind of spikes they were, nor what they were doing there. He had never seen or felt anything like them before: they were like saw-teeth, but then again not exactly the same. He felt them carefully and inspected them as closely as possible, and when he added the evidence of touch and sight together, he was certain that what was in front of him was a door with an iron grille. The areas of deepest black were the door, and the slightly lighter areas were the bars of the grille, and the lightest bits of all were the openings in the grille. It wasn't a circular grille, but triangular, and all three sides were edged with tooth-like metal spikes. He groped his way to his feet, and discovered that this peculiarly designed iron door was less than the height of a man, and above it was a lumpy, uneven rock face.

He turned and felt around behind him. He worked out that space that was neither round nor square, enclosed on all sides by the same uneven rock surface, and about the size of a cattle pen. He turned again, so he was facing the iron door and grille.

I can't see beyond the door, he thought, but there has to be an underground passage up to the surface. And if it is a door, it must open.

He felt around some more until he located a cold, black iron chain. He followed the chain with his hand, reaching carefully through the metal teeth, until he found what appeared to be a bronze, ox-head padlock. This gave him a slender thread of hope. He set his feet and exerted all his strength and skill against the heavy lock and chain, but other than drawing blood on both arms from rubbing against the iron teeth, he produced not the slightest result. Thereupon he took a short-bladed knife from his boot. He carried this knife everywhere with him, and he had hoped to use it that day on Tian Ju. He had certainly not expected to find himself in this particular situation, and now he had to find some way of using the blade to get himself out of it. But how to use it? Cut? Saw? Chop? Stab? All equally ineffectual.

"Ah! A lever!"

Inspiration had struck: he could try using it as a lever. He inserted the knife into one of the chain links. He was afraid that the knife might snap, but there was no help for it. He applied sudden, fierce pressure. There was a sharp crack, and the blade snapped off at the handle.

The blade fell to the floor and Tong Gong's spirits fell with it. Nonetheless, he quickly squatted down to find the broken blade. Locating it, he probed round the frame of the iron door, looking for a place where he might prise it away from the rock face. But he soon found that it was not possible. The frame was flush to the solid rock, all round. He began to realise just what a serious position he was in. If he couldn't get out through the door, he was trapped in this small cave, no bigger than a cattle stall, as surely as if it was indeed a cage.

His thoughts turned to dying; in effect, to being murdered. Perhaps, if he could only get through that dimly visible door, he could quickly find a lamp or candle. Then equally quickly, he would hear the sounds of footsteps and find himself face to face with his enemy. Then, just as he had planned, he would fight him, hand to hand, and kill him. That was it – if he could only get through the door, he would have no trouble in swiftly dispatching his foe.

Tong Gong was not afraid of dying. The lady Song Qi was already dead; she was only twenty-four, but she had met death without hesitation, braver than any man. Tong Gong himself had no regrets. He had already decided that his life had no meaning without Song Qi and he would gladly follow his father, brother and sister-in-law into eternity. He was happy with his life over the last twenty years. Although he had met with great calamity, he had never given up. Happy as a man, and happy in his deeds, he had always been honest and straightforward. It was only when he realised that he might not be able to kill his enemy with his own hands, that he had some regrets. Nevertheless, he was quite confident that Tian Ju would not escape the net of justice. His disappearance would soon be noticed by his master, Song Ci, whose almost superhuman intellect would quickly discover his whereabouts. And then Song Ci would, in a different way, avenge him, his brother, his sister-in-law and Mistress Song Qi. As long as this vengeance was certain, he, Tong Gong, would die content.

His back was on fire and still bleeding, but he paid it no attention. The ground underfoot was cold and damp, and the place was quiet as the grave. Except that water was dripping from the rocks somewhere: drip, then a pause, then another drip... the faint tinkling noise suddenly gave Tong Gong hope. As he thought about finding that dripping water, he realised how thirsty he was, and how parched his lips and mouth were. He felt around until he located the drip, opened his mouth and craned his neck to drink... that first drop of water was cool, sweet and refreshing, blissfully moistening his lips and throat. The sensation roused his spirits once more and fanned his will to live. No, he was not going to die! He had seen countless dawns in the company of his master, but today Song Ci had lost his only daughter, and he, Tong Gong was not there to support him in his grief... No, he could not die! His place was at his master's side.

But, how to get out alive? He yearned for Song Ci to arrive at the winery, but could he wait for that?

By this time, Tian Ju had returned from the main road without having sighted any government soldiers. He decided he should go straight back to the underground cave to find out whether that white-clad fellow who had threatened so vociferously to kill him, was actually dead or not.

2

## ANOTHER WOMAN STABBED

"Where can he have got to?"

When Huo Xiong discovered, at breakfast, that Tong Gong was nowhere to be seen, he immediately reported the matter to Song Ci. Song's wife was also there to hear the news, and, even in the midst of her grief for her daughter, she was deeply worried. She looked at her husband.

Song Ci had been almost knocked out by the terrible loss of Song Qi, but this news roused him. Tong Gong might have met with some misfortune. After a short pause for thought, he said: "He's gone to the Du mansion."

There were probably many reasons why the normally decisive and sagacious Song Ci made this false assumption, but most important was that Tong Gong had concealed a crucial piece of information, a vital clue, from his master.

"My Lord, did he not go off in pursuit of the assassin?"

"He did not."

"Did he have any idea of his identity?"

"None at all."

Earlier, when Huo Xiong had pressed Tong Gong on the matter in front of Mistress Song, Tong Gong had said the same thing. In all the years Tong Gong had followed Song Ci, he had never concealed any pertinent information, so why should his master suspect otherwise now? In the circumstances of Tong Gong's current disappearance, Song Ci could only deduce that he must have gone to the Du mansion to settle accounts with Du Guancheng's wife.

The question seemed quite straightforward: if the assassin hadn't come from the Du household itself, he must have been hired by Du's wife. And if that was where Tong Gong had gone, then it could only be to seek revenge for the murder of Song Qi. And he would stop at nothing to take that revenge. But if the assassin had escaped from Tong Gong's pursuit, then he must be a man of considerable ability. Moreover, he would know that the attempt on Song Ci's life had been unsuccessful, so he would be very much on his guard. By rushing out so rashly and hastily, Tong Gong might have put himself in serious danger.

"Gather the men and horses, we must make haste to the Du mansion."

The clatter of galloping horses threaded through the city streets and across the open ground in front of the Du compound. Song Ci led the troupe through the gates into the main courtyard.

The previous day, the Du household had opened its granaries to start selling grain. Now, all over the compound, the flowers and plants had been trampled by the feet of the crowds of locals and no one had tried to restore them to order; nor had anyone swept up the grain that still lay scattered all over the ground. The whole place was silent and sombre. A search of the place revealed that Du Guancheng's middle son was missing, but his wife and concubines and his two other sons were all present. Of Tong Gong, there was no sign, nor any indication that he had ever been there. Indeed, it seemed, that morning, as though nothing out of the ordinary had taken place.

Song Ci's concern deepened. He summoned the servants and maids to be questioned individually, since he knew from experience that the household staff were always the best place to start with matters like this. But they all said the same thing: they hadn't seen anyone breaking their way into the compound.

Suppose Tong Gong had fallen foul of some evil scheme conceived by Du's wife? Would the maids and servants know anything about that? Perhaps not. He decided to question Du's wife and sons again.

Song Ci was conscious that, in a case like this that involved his immediate family, he should recuse himself, just as Li Zongmian had done. But he was not a man who always felt himself bound by the strict letter of the law. Extraordinary events call for extraordinary action – he was quite clear about that. What he was thinking now was that, no matter what, Du's wife knew the identity of the assassin. But for any potential court case to succeed, first he had to find Tong Gong.

Beset by grief over his daughter's death, and concern for Tong Gong's life and safety, Song Ci ordered that Du's wife and sons be detained and paraded in front of him.

They all knew full well who the assassin was, but, what with Song Ci's sudden appearance in their midst that morning, they did not know what had happened to him. When Tian Ju had not returned by daybreak, they had begun to feel a little uneasy. Then, when the sound of hoofbeats heralded Song Ci's precipitous arrival, they were frightened in earnest, the cold sweat running down their backs. Now, as the *yamen* guards made them kneel in front of Song Ci in the front hall, their expressions were even more alarmed, the colour drained from their faces and their teeth began to chatter.

"Speak up now. Where is your second son?" Song Ci rasped.

Even the normally quick-witted Mistress Du was at a loss, and she just knelt there in silence.

"Speak up. Quickly now."

Mistress Du's eyes were darting this way and that in her alarm, but she had greater resolve than Du's concubines, let alone his son's wives. But even so, she was afraid there was no escape from her current situation. As she saw it, the magistrate had come in pursuit of the assassin, her second son was not there and she herself was under suspicion, so keeping silent was not an option.

Grasping courage in both hands, she said, tremulously: "My son left the city yesterday morning."

Song Ci knew that the martial arts skill of the assassin far surpassed anything Du's second son could master, so he chose his words deliberately, attacking directly to try to force them to reveal the identity of the assassin. He followed up immediately by asking where the second son had gone, and then continued by pointing at the eldest son, saying: "In that case, the assassin must be the eldest son. Guards, take him away!"

The *yamen* guards gave a shout of acknowledgement, and Huo Xiong swiftly put a chain around the son's neck and pulled him away.

"I'm not... not... me..." Totally unused to such rough treatment, the son stuttered and stammered in a daze. His knees trembled and began to give way, and he scrabbled vainly at the chain with both hands, unable to move a step.

"Take him away," Song Ci repeated, in steely tones.

Two of the *yamen* guards stepped forward and began to drag Du's eldest son away.

"Mother, Mother..." he cried out, looking back over his shoulder.

"My Lord," Mistress Du suddenly kowtowed to Song Ci, "please wait."

Song Ci gestured to the guards to stop and turned to ask Mistress Du: "Do you have something to say?"

"Your Honour spoke of an assassin... but who was the target?"

Song Ci realised she was planning some way of extricating her son, so he answered directly: "I was the target."

But having asked her question, Mistress Du fell silent. Song Ci knew she was playing for time, so he tried to lead her on: "Do you know who the assassin was?"

"No… no, I don't."

"Then who do you think it might be?"

"Well, I was thinking of saying to Your Honour…"

"Go on."

"I know Your Honour must think my son is the assassin because of what happened last night, but he doesn't have either the skill or the courage…"

"So it must be some master assassin who tried to kill me?" Song Ci understood that Mistress Du was by far the most cunning member of the household.

"I was just thinking that my husband wasn't the only person arrested last night. There was Sergeant Tian as well…"

"Say what you have to say."

"Sergeant Tian has a younger brother called Tian Ju who is an even better fighter than him. Everyone in Nanjianzhou knows that Tian Ju heard about what happened last night, so perhaps…"

The woman left her words hanging and looked expectantly at Song Ci. Realisation came to Song like a bolt of lightning. It was obvious to him now that Tong Gong had not come to the Du compound, and he hadn't done so because he had gone off in pursuit of the assassin: the man he had fought with the night before, and whom he had recognised as Tian Ju…

"So tell me, where is Tian Ju now?" Song Ci shouted.

"He runs an inn at the top of the Mangdangshan Road."

"Let's go."

Leaving Mistress Du and her sons behind, Song Ci led Huo Xiong and the others out of the compound, and headed for the north gate. On the road, Song inwardly berated himself. Once Tong Gong had learned of Song Qi's death, he had kept his recognition of Tian Ju to himself and left without saying a word. His intentions were obvious. He already had one ancient wrong to be avenged, to which a fresh one had been added, so of course he had determined to kill the culprit himself.

Song Ci knew all about Tong Gong's courage and persistence, but he had never let him undertake any particularly dangerous assignments. Now he had gone off alone and without a word, anger burning in his breast… and when two tigers meet, one will come off worse. If Tong Gong could keep his cool, then all would be well. But if…

The sun was high in the sky and Tong Gong had already been gone half a day. Song Ci knew intuitively that his fears for his man were not imaginary.

• • •

Tian Ju's winery hove into view at the top of the Mangdangshan Road.

Even from a distance, they could see the shattered door and the broken fixtures and fittings, and when they got up to the inn itself and looked inside, the place was in disarray. Song Ci knew for certain that Tong Gong had been there.

There was not a sound to be heard from inside, and no one to be seen. In the rear courtyard, the signs of battle were quite evident, but there was still no sign of anyone. Song Ci's unease mounted.

"Search the place! Quick! Search everywhere," he ordered.

The *yamen* guards spread out to search, and almost immediately one of them found a blood-stained sword in a corner of the surrounding wall. Huo Xiong noticed a side room with a broken lattice-windowed door and made his way over. As he cautiously approached the room, his nose was assailed by a strong smell of blood coming from inside. Looking through the broken lattice, he saw the blood. And not just blood – on the floor was an embroidered door curtain covering a human form, and the blood was flowing from under the curtain. Greatly alarmed, he pushed open the door and went in. All was quiet. He hurried over and lifted the door curtain – it was a woman, ashen-faced and hair in disarray. When he reached out a hand to touch her, the flesh was still soft, and when he covered her nostrils, he felt the faintest of breaths. All the furniture in the room was overturned, and the decorations smashed beyond recognition. Clearly Brother Gong had fought a pitched battle with Tian Ju here. But who was the woman? He couldn't figure it out, so hurried out to report to Song Ci.

Song Ci was mightily worried. He didn't know the whereabouts of Tian Ju, and there was no sign of Tong Gong. Instead, they had found a half-dead woman who was totally unknown to them. His anxiety increased a level. He ordered someone to fetch the landlord and staff from one of the neighbouring establishments, and then he went into the side room to see if anything could be done to save the life of the injured woman.

She was about twenty years old, and when Huo Xiong lifted the curtain that was covering her, they saw she had been stabbed in the stomach. Some unknown person had already loosened and pulled aside her clothing, so the wound was exposed. Song Ci took one look and said: "She can be saved."

He could see that, although the blade had entered the abdomen, it hadn't damaged any of the internal organs, and the woman had passed out from the combined effects of pain, shock and loss of blood. He took out a universal salve he always carried with him, and applied it to the wound. Then he prepared a decoction of ginseng and ashitaba that he tipped down her throat, before carefully lifting her onto a couch.

Soon, the landlord and waiters from the neighbouring inn came hurrying over in response to his summons, and Song Ci asked them if they could identify the woman. Several of them cried out simultaneously: "That's Tian Ju's new concubine."

Song Ci was shaken – could this be Tong Gong's doing?

"It must be the work of one of Tian Ju's rivals," the landlord said.

"Rivals? What rivals?" Song Ci asked.

The landlord explained about Tian Ju's campaign of destruction and intimidation of the other inns; and how the innkeepers had not been willing to take that treatment lying down and had sought outside help. This news raised hope in Song Ci that it might not have been Tong Gong who had fought with Tian Ju that day. But he was soon to realise that was just wishful thinking, and Tian's mortal adversary really had to have been Tong Gong.

Song Ci asked about the set-up in the Mangdang winery, and was told that there were ten or more staff who were there every day, and as well as the injured concubine, there was a wife and two small children. For the moment, there was no sign of any of the staff, or of Tian Ju's wife and children.

Can the whole household just have upped sticks and fled? thought Song Ci, his concern increasing enormously.

This was the bleak reality of the situation that confronted him. If Tian Ju had been able to uproot his whole household and make off, that meant that Tong Gong... no... no... Song Ci cudgelled his brains. This was just his anxiety speaking, he needed to inspect the surrounding area and think it through.

"Master, we need to find Tong Gong." Huo Xiong saw Song's furrowed brow, and he tried to urge him into action.

That was right. Setting aside everything else, they had found no trace of Tong Gong. Song Ci forced himself to calm down and follow a different chain of thought...

## 3

## XIYUAN GORGE

A drear, soughing wind began to make itself heard, carrying on it the smell of moss and mud. Something soft and warm was caressing his forehead, and he felt warm breath on his face. Ahead of him there was a thin ribbon of light... he rolled over, fully awake now, and saw, standing stock still in front of him, a mountain muntjac.

His back was as cold as ice, and his limbs were on fire. He rolled over again and tried to sit up, but couldn't manage it. The muntjac hesitated for a moment, then ran off.

Where am I? How did I come to be lying here?

He could see a dim strip of light that was the sky, and rock faces on either side of him. Pallid light from a waning crescent moon suffused the dark, boundless sky; it was just before daybreak. The shattered moon seemed just to be hanging there, waiting for the sun to rise and take over from its own feeble light.

He heard the babble of running water and realised there must be a stream nearby; his throat felt even more parched. He licked his lips and tried to go in search of the water, but still he couldn't even crawl.

Nevertheless, his mind was beginning to clear. He was in the ravine of a mountain stream – that was it! It was the Shiliqing Stream in a ravine in the Forest of Ten Thousand Trees. He wasn't dead. He was still alive. Or was he dreaming? No...

But everything that had happened since he had fallen down the hole in the storeroom yesterday morning had a dream-like quality to it. He had been trapped like a beast in a cage, in an apparently hopeless situation. But his desire to return to the side of his master, Song Ci, and the determination to exact revenge, spurred him on. He had seen a glimmer of hope in the broken wine jar that lay at his feet. He had turned over and groped around in the darkness picking up one shard of pottery and then another. Then he sat up and took off his jacket, and tore it into strips. He took the pieces of broken pot and strapped them tightly all the way round and up his right arm. He had decided to use his arm to batter down the door with the saw-toothed triangular grille. Once his arm was wrapped securely, he steadied his stance and gathered his strength for this all-or-nothing, do-or-die attempt. He hurled himself without hesitation at the iron door: once, twice, three times… he lost count. The shards of pottery were smashed into smaller pieces. As the cloth wrapped around his arm became more and more tattered, each successive blow turned the pottery into dust, which gradually trickled out of the bindings onto the ground. Then a movement; at last, a movement. He could feel it: the frame of the iron door was coming loose. The iron teeth had bitten into his arm, gouging his flesh. But he didn't hesitate. Hope had lit up his spirits like a ray of sunshine. He was going to get through this death trap of a door. He gathered all his strength, and, with a great shout, charged the door one more time like a maddened lion. In an explosion of irresistible force, he heard a cracking sound as the door gave way, and he carried it with him out of the cattle pen of a space he had been trapped in, into another underground passage.

His arm was a solid mass of pain, but his heart sang with the knowledge he had cheated death. With that last charge of the door, the cloth wrapped around his arm had given way completely; most of the remaining pottery dust spilled down onto the floor, but some of it stuck to the bloody wounds on his arm. He didn't care.

Ahead of him was still darkness, but panting heavily and steadying his nerve, he groped his way forward. He could tell that the passage was on an upward incline, and finally he heard the footsteps of someone moving around above him and someone rummaging through chests and cupboards. Then a voice said: "Have you found it yet?"

"No."

"Have another look in the cupboard."

The voices belonged to two women. Tong Gong realised he must be in a cellar under one of the side rooms of the inn. He found some steps leading up to the cellar entrance where he felt something blocking the opening. It was a floor board; no, it was the base board of a cupboard. With only a plank of wood separating him, he could clearly hear someone searching in the cupboard.

"It's not there." The woman's voice came from inside the cupboard, directly above his head. He heard another set of heavy footsteps hurrying into the room and knew there was no time to lose. He steadied himself, put both hands on the base of the cupboard, held his breath and heaved. He heard a cry of alarm, as the base board went flying upwards. The woman, who had thrust her whole body into the cupboard searching for whatever it was, was sent tumbling to the ground. Tong Gong hurled himself up and out of the cellar and landed on his feet in the middle of the room.

Coming out of the darkness, the light in the room dazzled Tong Gong, and he couldn't see a thing.

"Ah!... Ah!..."

The other woman cried out in alarm – the sight of Tong Gong was certainly enough to alarm anyone. His naked torso was streaked with blood, and his right arm was a mass of gouged, bleeding flesh. As he burst up from under the ground and planted himself foursquare in the room like a cast-bronze statue, he might as well have been Yama, the King of Hell, rising from the Underworld. The women cried out again and rushed from the room.

The heavy footsteps that Tong Gong had heard entering the room belonged to Tian Ju. When he had turned back into the shop from the road outside, his first act was to grab a sword and hurry to the side room, intending to haul the white-clad fellow out of the cellar beneath the cupboard and settle with him once and for all. But when he reached the room and heard the cry of alarm from inside, he was pulled up short, wondering what on earth could be going on. When he heard the further frightened yells, he knew there must be something serious amiss, and he hurled himself into the room. It was at that point that the tragic accident occurred – simultaneously with her blood-curdling shriek of terror, the woman came running through the curtain over the doorway, straight onto the point of Tian Ju's sword. She fell to the ground...

Supporting the woman with one hand and parting the door curtain with the other, Tian Ju caught sight of Tong Gong. A shiver of fear ran through him. When Tong Gong saw Tian Ju, he rolled his eyes in hatred but stayed stock still, not moving. He drew in great gulps of fresh air now he was free from his underground prison, but he did not speak, letting Tian Ju just stand there, staring at him in amazement.

Tian Ju shook his head, as though to clear it. He didn't really understand what was going on, but, nonetheless, he quickly dropped the woman, took firm hold of his sword again and swept through the curtain into the room. With a great shout, he hacked down murderously at the unarmed Tong Gong.

An earth-shattering, life-or-death battle broke out. Freshly released from the jaws of death, Tong Gong faced his mortal enemy. Although his eyes were aflame with hatred, he was still intent on staying alive. In the face of the flashing blade of the sword, his footwork remained precise and his martial arts skills at their peak. The two men fought their way out of the room and then out of the building. All Tong Gong's attention was concentrated on their close-quarter exchanges. After some time, he felt Tian Ju begin to falter and start to look for some way to escape. Tong Gong pressed him even closer to stop him from escaping. Out of the inn, they fought a running battle, heading towards the great mountain to the east. They lost track of time as they fought and ran, ran and fought. They also lost track of where they were... or did they? Suddenly Tong Gong realised what the crafty Tian Ju was up to. He wasn't heading for the Thirty-Eight Hundred Pits track, but had turned towards the Xiyuan Gorge.

Fear lent Tian Ju wings as he fled through the mountain forest, but fortunately for Tong Gong, he himself had grown up among the bamboo groves, and he matched his opponent stride for stride, blow for blow. The chase continued up and down mountain ridges, in and out of forests, from morning until afternoon and from afternoon until dusk. They lost track of the hills they climbed, the tracks they followed, the tumbles they took and the blows they exchanged. They fought until their noses were bleeding, their faces swollen and their bodies streaked with blood. They stopped neither to eat nor drink, one fleeing for his life, the other chasing with mortal vengeance in his heart. They fought and ran, ran and fought. Finally, they reached the limit of their endurance and the two men came to a halt, facing each other and gasping for breath.

The sun went down and all was quiet in the gorge, disturbed only by the calling of birds returning to their nests, and the babble of water running through the forest grove. A wind blew off the mountain, which cooled their burning bodies. They stood there, panting, for a while. Tian Ju would have fled, but he was too exhausted, and Tong Gong, in turn, was too tired to even lift a foot in pursuit. They stood, facing each other. But they both knew they were still engaged in a battle of strength, a battle of skill, a battle for life or death. Then, at last, Tian Ju suddenly took a step backwards, looked up to the sky, and, with a great cry, fell to the ground. Tong Gong let out a deep breath, then felt the darkness close in around him, and he knew nothing more...

Now, as the sky was lightening into dawn, Tong Gong woke up. Perhaps it was the gentle licking of the muntjac, or perhaps it was his burning desire for revenge, but something had roused him. As he recognised his surroundings, and remembered what had happened, his waking thought was: First for Tian Ju... he's still alive...

This thought revitalised him, and he struggled into a sitting position, looking around in the sombre light for some sign of his enemy. But he could see nothing.

He still didn't have the strength to stand, and he felt as though his legs belonged to someone else. He gritted his teeth and began to crawl. He remembered his opponent falling to the ground last night, and he was sure he must still be lying there.

He was at the bottom of the gorge, on a narrow meandering track, flanked by luxuriant wild grasses and shrubs, and a dense tangle of Indian azaleas. Falling petals and drips of water landed all over his face and body, arms and legs. The growing daylight still was not enough for him to see very far, but it gave him renewed strength. Finally, beside the path in front of him, he could make out a leg with its foot sticking up in the air: it was Tian Ju, lying there with his body submerged in the undergrowth.

This discovery restored Tong Gong to himself, and he struggled to his feet and staggered over to Tian Ju. Tong Gong took a good look at his enemy: he was lying motionless, as if dead.

With a grim smile, laden with hatred, contempt and the knowledge of victory, Tong Gong forced himself over to stand beside the fallen body. He tried to crouch down, but his knees trembled and wouldn't bend. He forced himself to drop down with both knees onto one of Tian Ju's shoulders. Tian Ju didn't move an inch. He reached out to touch Tian Ju's body. It was cold as ice.

"No! He can't be dead!"

The icy chill spread into Tong Gong's heart, and he shook Tian Ju repeatedly, shouting at him:

"Tian Ju! Tian Ju!"

Still, Tian Ju did not move.

"Tian Ju! You can't die! You can't die like this!" Tong Gong grabbed Tian Ju by both shoulders and shook him.

Tian Ju had to know how he was going to die, why he was going to die and who was going to kill him. Tong Gong kept shaking him and shouting his name. Finally, Tian Ju let out a deep sigh. Tong Gong stopped shaking him and looked closely. He put his hand over Tian Ju's nostrils, and yes, there it was: he could feel his breathing. Tian Ju was alive!

The time of reckoning had come for this evil monster of a man, and Tong Gong could feel his heart thudding against his chest. Very deliberately, he reached for the short-bladed knife that he always kept strapped to his leg, but it wasn't there; it was lying on the floor of the cave back at the inn. Then he noticed a sharp-edged rock on the ground next to him, so he picked it up. Pressing his knees hard into Tian Ju's chest, he waited for Tian to open his eyes. When he did, there was no great surprise in them, as if he had long been expecting just this turn of events. He furrowed his brow, as though about to struggle, but his strength had deserted him.

"Tian Ju, do you recognise me now?" Tong Gong asked expectantly.

Tian Ju looked at Tong Gong before shutting his eyes again.

"Take a good look. I am Tong Ning's brother, Tong Gong."

Tian Ju opened his eyes again. This time there was a strange look in them, part fear and part a slow, dawning understanding of why this fellow had pursued him so remorselessly.

"Quickly now. Tell me how my sister-in-law died."

Tian Ju stared at Tong Gong, but he didn't say anything.

"Speak up!"

Tian Ju gave a great sigh and said: "For days on end, she didn't eat, and she starved to death."

"Why? Why?" Tong Gong seized the collar of Tian Ju's jacket.

Tian Ju kept staring at Tong Gong, wanting to move but frozen to the spot. He knew he was surely going to die. His expression gradually took on a look of savage defiance in the face of death.

"It is something you should know, so I will tell you. Your sister-in-law wouldn't do what Chai Wanlong wanted, so the master handed her over to me and my brother. We took turns to…"

Slap! Slap! Two stinging blows to the face shut Tian Ju up, and Tong Gong roared at him: "Her body! Where is her body?"

Tian Ju had closed his eyes when Tong Gong slapped him, but now he opened them again in response to the question and said: "If you were to go and look under the vine trellis in Chai Wanlong's garden… but I'm afraid she'll already be rotted away. Otherwise you would be able to see how your sister-in-law's tits were…"

Smack! Tong Gong hit him in the face with the rock he still had in his hand, stopping him from saying any more. Tian's head snapped to one side, and blood began to seep from his mouth.

A bell sounded somewhere up the mountain, and the ringing seemed to be travelling along the meandering path from its invisible point of origin. It was the morning bell of the Xiyuan Shrine. Tong Gong noticed how the sky was already brightening to the east, the sunlight supplanting the slanting moonbeams and announcing the start of a new day.

Tong Gong put his hand to Tian Ju's nose again, to check that he was still breathing and had not died yet. Now was the time to settle the score once and for all. Tong Gong was not going to let him live to see another day.

He discarded the stone he was holding and picked up another larger, jagged rock in both hands. Solemnly, he raised it above his head…

## 4

## INTO THE HEADWIND

With Huo Xiong behind him, Song Ci followed a Buddhist monk along the winding, maze-like path until they came to the Xiyuan Shrine, which stood amid towering trees and lush bamboo.

The shrine was divided into two sections, the upper hall and lower hall. The upper hall stood to the west of the mountain peak and, pressed close to it and right in front, was a strange and wonderful rock formation rising out of the bottom of the gorge. It rose to the same height as the hall, piercing the sky, almost as though it had deliberately chosen the spot. Leading up from the lower hall to the upper was a flight of two hundred or more stone steps. It had a zig-zag bannister with vermilion balustrades, half of which was visible from below, and the muffled ringing of a bell could be heard winding down the staircase. The lower hall stood beside the stream to the north, and the sound of the water flowing across its stony bed was sweet to the ear. Surrounded as it was on four sides by mountain ridges, the lower hall had a dark, secluded air, and when the clouds wreathed it like fine muslin, it had the mysterious and imposing appearance of a place where the immortals might dwell.

Hurrying in the footsteps of the monk, Song Ci arrived at the lower hall.

Crossing a bridge, he caught sight of Tong Gong in a small room in the eastern corner of the hall. When Tong Gong heard the familiar footsteps, he jumped up from the bamboo couch on which he was sitting.

They met again. Song Ci and Tong Gong. Tong Gong and Song Ci. Although the two had only be apart for a day and a night, to them it seemed as though it had been years, twenty years, even.

They stared at each other for a long time. Tong Gong seemed about to speak, but although his lips moved, no sound came out. There was no need for words. Song Ci already knew everything that had happened.

The previous night, with careful searching, they had quickly discovered the cave. Knife in one hand, torch in the other, Huo Xiong opened the cupboard and climbed down into the cave. He followed the underground passage until he came to the area past where the broken iron-toothed lattice door lay. There he found a man and a woman, leaning against the rock face, not daring to move.

"Who are you?" Huo Xiong shouted, grasping his knife.

"Ah... Spare us! Spare us, Sir! I am one of the waiters at the inn. Please spare us, Sir!"

On hearing Huo Xiong's voice, he came away from the wall and knelt, pleading continuously for mercy. The woman followed suit.

"Come out," Huo Xiong ordered.

The man looked at the knife in Huo Xiong's hand, hesitated, and then kept kowtowing, pleading for mercy.

Huo Xiong held up his torch to make sure there was no one else there, and then he began to retreat, repeating his order for the two of them to emerge. When they did so, the landlord of the neighbouring inn identified them as the bookkeeper from Tian Ju's establishment and the maid of Tian Ju's concubine.

The man's hands were bloody and there were bloodstains on his body too. Song Ci didn't bother to ask what the two of them had been doing, but fixed them with his stare and barked: "Who stabbed this woman?"

"It wasn't me," the man said, falling to his knees. "It wasn't me. It wasn't me."

"Who was it then?"

"It... it was a man dressed in white."

Song Ci started, then asked: "Did you see him with your own eyes?"

"No... no." The man shook his head

"Do *you* know anything?" Song Ci turned to the maid.

"No, Sir, I don't know anything," the maid replied, also kneeling.

She was, in fact, the same maid who had been knocked to the ground by Tong Gong when he erupted out of the cupboard. Because she had been hiding in there, scared out of her wits, she really hadn't seen anything. Once Song Ci heard her say she knew nothing, he didn't interrogate her further, except to ask: "Where did the man in white go?"

"He was fighting with the boss, and they wrestled their way out of the door," the man said.

Song Ci looked at all the clothes, scattered under the overturned furniture, and realised that they must have been piled up for packing, preparatory to flight. He asked the maid: "Where was your master going to escape to?"

"I heard his wife say they were going to take the ancient Thirty-Eight Hundred Pits Road into Jiangxi."

This information coincided with what Song Ci had deduced. He ordered Huo Xiong to dispatch some of the fleetest of the *yamen* guards in pursuit.

Once Huo Xiong had seen the men off, Song Ci turned back to the bookkeeper and ordered him to start from the beginning and describe everything that had happened. But as to the overall picture of how Tong Gong had arrived, his fight with Tian Ju, how he had fallen into the cave and, indeed, how Tong Gong had managed to escape from there, neither the man nor the maid could shed any light. On the matters of Tong Gong and Tian Ju fighting their way out of the inn, and the general consternation among Tian Ju's womenfolk and the inn's staff, the man was more useful since it was he who had discovered Tian Ju's concubine lying in a pool of her own blood.

Song Ci went on to question Tian Ju's wife and the rest of the waiters, and they were all certain that it was the man in white who had stabbed her. It was unclear who had then raised the cry, but a shout of "Run away" came from inside the building, and the whole crowd of them scattered in an instant. But, as they ran, the bookkeeper turned to look back from the middle of the courtyard. He had been having an affair with the young concubine and was wondering whether there was any chance of saving her. He had just turned back into the inn, when he heard a woman cry out, and, mustering courage, he went to have a look. Sure enough, he saw the cupboard move and the maid trying to crawl out from it as it lay overturned on the floor. He hurried in, lifted the cupboard and helped her up, because this particular maid knew all about his affair with the concubine and had often acted as go-between. He urged her to help him do something for his lover. He loosened the injured girl's clothing and exposed the wound. When he saw the blood still flowing from the great gash, and saw her intestines exposed, he didn't know what to do for the best. Then he heard the sound of galloping horses on the main road outside and, an instant later, running feet entering the inn. At this point he realised it was too late for him and the maid to escape. Hastily, he snatched up the door curtain that was lying on the floor, laid it over the body of the unconscious concubine and then grabbed the maid by the hand and pulled back into the room. They dropped down into the cave and pulled the cupboard over the opening...

By this time, the *yamen* guards searching the surrounding area had discovered Tian Ju's wife and the other staff members, and brought them back into the winery. In fact, they had only just fled and so had not got far. When Song Ci learned from them that Tong Gong and Tian Ju's running battle had taken them off in the direction of the great mountain to the east, and that this mountain was the location of the Thirty-Eight Hundred Pits Road, he left them all in the inn and ordered the guards to set off in pursuit.

But once again, Song Ci was at fault in his deductions. He did not give enough thought to the psychology of such a desperate criminal as Tian Ju when on the run, and dismissed the possibility of him taking some other direction. This meant that, when he sent Huo Xiong and the guards ahead of him to press forward the pursuit, they came up empty-handed. By the time Song Ci, following on behind, determined that Tong Gong and Tian Ju had actually not taken that route, the sky had already begun to darken. They hurried back through the night, heading west to search the Xiyuan Gorge. As dawn broke, they met a Buddhist monk who had come looking for them with new information.

In another hut nearby lay Tian Ju… still alive. As it turned out, Tong Gong had not killed him.

Just as Tong Gong had been about to bring that jagged rock smashing down on Tian Ju's head, as he lay there with his eyes shut, a thought came to him. What could it have been that stayed the hand of this hot-blooded man and made him land his blow elsewhere?

When he saw Song Ci, Tong Gong's lips moved as though he were about to speak, but then he closed them tight and looked away.

There was no need for words. As soon as he saw the mixture of distress and gratification on Tong Gong's face, Song Ci knew all that needed to be known.

Had Tian Ju committed the murder in retaliation for the arrest of his brother? If there was another reason, then he must have been acting under orders. If that was the case, then killing Tian Ju would simply have been protecting the even greater villain behind his actions. Also, had the young woman who had been stabbed by Tian Ju's sword, died or not? If she had, and Tian Ju also died, there would be no witnesses left to the deed, and Tong Gong himself would have fallen under suspicion of murder. Following the same reasoning, killing Tian Ju before a confession could be extracted from him would make the whole case infinitely more troublesome. The old Tong Gong might not have been troubled by such issues, but this was no longer the carefree Tong Gong of former times. He was Song Ci's personal attendant, and the principal player in this case was Du Guancheng, who happened to be the prime minister's brother-in-law. If he, Tong Gong, were allowed to escape punishment for his actions through preferential treatment or a legal loophole, then that would rebound on Song Ci and cause him untold trouble. Were that to happen, Tong Gong would never have been able to look Song Ci and his wife in the eye again, and after death he would be too ashamed to meet his ancestors... so perhaps all these thoughts went through his head as he picked up that rock and was about to bring it crashing down. Perhaps determination faltered, and he changed his aim so the stone struck the ground instead. He knelt down and wept bitterly as he looked towards his old hometown hundreds of miles away. After a while he chanced upon a group of monks from the Xiyuan Shrine and, with their help, carried Tian Ju back to the temple.

Song Ci watched Tong Gong as he looked away. He put his hand on Tong's shoulder and said gently: "Let's go home."

And so, Tong Gong emerged from this most perilous adventure and went home.

Huo Xiong rode ahead on a fast horse to alert Mistress Song, who had not slept for two nights and a day. As soon as she heard the news, she came out of the compound to greet the party, her eyes filled with tears.

With Tian Ju still alive, the plot to kill Song Ci was swiftly unravelled. Du Guancheng's wife and eldest son were arrested, and Song Ci showed them no clemency. Inevitably, the case of his attempted assassination was passed on up to the provincial court for trial.

"If we get rid of Song Ci, we can certainly find our way out of all this." These were Du Guancheng's wife's words. She could see that Shu Gengshi, who was very protective of his own power and authority, was scared of Song Ci, and knew that her brother-in-law, the prime minister Li Zongmian, was too far away to be of help in the current situation. So she devised her own plan and sent her eldest son to fetch Tian Ju. Some years before, there had been an estrangement between the Tian brothers and they had gone their separate ways. Tian Ju might not want to get involved in this shady and murderous enterprise, but Du's wife did not let little things like that discourage her, and she offered him a lot of money.

Tian Ju was a clever man, and he knew that Du's wife had come looking for him, both because of his martial arts skills and because he was Tian Huai's brother. Unlike in other murder cases, if the crime was committed to help the assassin's brother, no one would look for anyone else who might have commissioned the deed. Thus, Tian Ju was the obvious choice.

Tian Ju was under no illusions about this, but he did not expect to be caught, so he went along with the plan. Now, however, although he was still alive, he did not expect to remain so for long. Nor did he have any intention of covering up for Du's wife, who had landed him in this situation, so he made a full confession of the whole affair.

Meanwhile, the famine relief programme was still in full swing.

On the same day that Tong Gong returned safely, one of the local constables brought a middle-aged man into the *yamen*, who turned out to be the uncle of the two little children, Qingqing and her brother, whom Song Ci had taken in. Some time ago, Song had sent men out to find him and bring him in.

"Your Honour," the man said, kneeling and kowtowing to Song Ci. "It has been a time of great calamity, and the whole area has been devastated. But as soon as everyone heard about Your Honour's merciful implementation of the famine relief, we all came hurrying back."

Song Ci was gratified to hear this. He nodded gravely, thought for a moment and then said: "You should go and get your grain today, and take your nephew and niece with you. It's up to you to look after them now."

"Thank you, Your Honour. Thank you, Your Honour," the man replied, kowtowing continuously.

When the children saw their uncle, they flung themselves into his arms. As they were about to leave together, the girl took her brother by the arm and led him over to Song Qi's coffin, where they both knelt and wept piteously. This moved Song Ci and his wife to tears too.

The grieving parents arranged memorial sacrifices for their daughter. They raised a banner in the courtyard and erected a catafalque inside the main hall. A large group of monks from the Xiyuan shrine came down from the mountain to conduct the ceremonies for Song Qi and to chant sutras for her peaceful passage into the next life. Huo Xiong took responsibility for making all these complex arrangements and supervising the whole process.

Shu Gengshi brought all the local government officials to join in the mourning and pay their respects to the grieving parents.

When the day of the funeral came, Song Qi's coffin was taken to the chosen burial spot on Nine Peak Mountain, some way outside the town of Nanjianzhou.

Nine Peak Mountain is on the south side of the Min River, facing the city across the water. As its name indicates, it is made up of a succession of nine peaks that form a crown on the mountain range to the south of the city. The reason Song Ci chose this place to lay his daughter to rest was because it was the location of the Yanping Academy. The Yanping Academy was where Master Zhu Xi's own teacher, Mr Li Dong, had lectured. After Li Dong's death, a memorial shrine to Duke Li Wenjing was erected there. In the second year of the Jiading period, after the arrival of Chen Mi as provincial magistrate, flanking the shrine, along the model of the White Deer Cave Academy on Mount Lu, they built an academy for the study of sacrificial rites. Song Ci thought that, although she had never officially enrolled at the academy, his daughter had always been in love with writing and had a deep appreciation of literature. In laying her to rest on the mountain behind the academy, she could continue in the afterlife as she had done in life: by day she could go down to the academy to admire the paintings and calligraphy, and in the evening she could listen to readings from literature. This was the only way her father could still demonstrate his love for his daughter.

It was a typical bright spring morning, the sky blue like sapphire, and, as the sun climbed higher, it bathed the landscape in dazzling golden light. The wings of the waterfowl flashed white as they flew over the Min River, now skimming the surface, now soaring back into the heavens. The water lapped gently against the banks, like naughty children teasing their mother. The distant mountains were aflame with the red of azaleas. But that morning everything seemed as hazy and indistinct as a dream to Song Ci and his wife.

Under the kingfisher blue arc of the sky, fanned by a gentle morning breeze, the solemn funeral procession filed down to the banks of the river. Because of the recommencement of the famine-relief programme, many local farmers were away tilling the land, great numbers of whom spontaneously joined the procession behind the party of government officials. Among them were two children with hempen belts around their waists: Qingqing and her brother, weeping with every step and bereft with sorrow.

The procession reached Nine Peak Mountain. The road up to the Yanping Academy was lined with numerous ancient plum trees, branches like twisted iron and the flower buds tipped with red. As Song Ci walked along between these living walls of vivid green, he could not fail to remember his old friend Liu Kezhuang's poem *Fallen Plum Blossom*, and his heart filled with countless, nameless emotions...

5

# THE SUN BREAKS THROUGH THE WIND AND SNOW

Night descended on the day of Song Qi's funeral.
Now they were bereft of the sight of Song Qi's slender and elegant figure, and the sound of her eloquent entreaties. Only in the shadows of their dreams could they seek their witty, intelligent daughter and talk with her.

Mistress Song suddenly fell ill. Song Ci sat by her side as the night breeze blew around them. In the middle of the third watch, Mistress Song caught the sound of sobbing carried faintly from afar on the wind. She half sat up in bed and listened carefully. No, she wasn't dreaming, and now the sound didn't seem so far away.

"Husband, listen…"

"What is it?" asked Song Ci, although he, too, had already heard the sound.

"Weeping. Who is weeping?"

"Lie back down and don't worry about it."

But Mistress Song insisted on getting out of bed to find out. Song Ci couldn't dissuade her, so he gave her his arm and the two of them went out of the bedroom.

There was no moon, just the shimmering light of a sky full of stars. As the two of them entered the courtyard, the sound of weeping became more distinct. It was the crying of a man, and it was coming in through the moon gate. Still supporting his wife, Song Ci led the way to the side of the gate, and they peered through it. In front of the Greet the Moon Pavilion close by they saw a candle and some incense sticks burning, and a man kneeling, facing Nine Peak Mountain, sobbing bitterly.

"It's Tong Gong."

Song and his wife looked at each other. They stopped beside the moon gate and stood there for a long time, not wanting to disturb him. The sound of his grief moved the two of them so deeply, that they, too, fell to weeping.

In local families, a woman of twenty-four would already be married, but Song Qi had remained a maiden. It was not that her parents preferred her to stay single, but they wanted to choose someone who was her match and worthy of her. But as the years passed, no such person presented himself.

Such affairs are properly the preserve of the mother. There had been an occasion, actually in front of the very same pavilion, when Song and his wife had been watching Qi'er practising swordplay with Tong Gong. Mistress Song had turned to her husband and whispered: "Husband, have you had the same thought?"

"What thought is that?"

"Qi'er and Tong Gong are very well matched."

"Hmm," Song Ci did not agree. "Tong Gong is almost part of the family, and Qi'er is very offhand with him."

Despite this exchange, there was another occasion, when Song Ci was by himself, again watching Tong Gong and Song Qi practising with their swords. He observed the delight on his daughter's face and how, when they took a break, she spontaneously brought Tong Gong a cup of tea, calling him 'Brother Gong'. When Tong Gong looked embarrassed, she laughed and said: "What are you waiting for? Drink up!"

Tong Gong took the cup and drank the tea. At the time, Song Ci found himself thinking: "Tong Gong, eh? Well, what about Tong Gong?"

But Song Ci had always thought of Tong Gong and Qiu Juan as a couple, and how much more suitable it would be, if *they* were to get married. Moreover, it was indeed he who had responsibility for arranging any marriage for those two, and if they were to come together, then it would be a great thing for them.

Now, as he thought of Qi'er, he was brought back down to earth. Twenty-four tranquil years, but perhaps it was a rather lonely life; and apart from her passion for books, brush and ink, a life of easy pleasure. And before she had any dealings with young men from outside, there, always, was Tong Gong, practising Taijiquan and swordplay with her. Perhaps she had indeed developed feelings for him…

But that was all in the past. Now Qi'er was parted from her father, was parted from Tong Gong, for all eternity. Song and his wife also remembered how, as she died, Qi'er had urged Qiu Juan to marry Tong Gong. Now they could see that it was not just a demonstration of her concern for Qiu Juan, it was also her last expression of love for Tong Gong.

The sound of Tong Gong's weeping gradually died away, but Song Ci and his wife still did not disturb him. Silently, they went back to their bedroom, thinking that Qiu Juan's promise to their daughter must now be fulfilled. They discussed when best to arrange the marriage between Tong Gong and Qiu Juan. But time slipped by, and winter came still with nothing settled.

Over the previous six months, Song Ci seemed to have spent much of the time as if in a trance. Fortunately, nothing problematic had arisen. All the defendants had been transported under armed guard to the provincial court, and those sentenced to summary execution had been promptly dispatched. Those banished to penal colonies had been sent there, and everything had been done according to the letter of the law. And, contrary to the expectations of all the Du family, Li Zongmian had not put in an appearance.

The pain of the loss of their daughter seemed without end. Despite Li Zongmian's absence, Mistress Song couldn't rid herself of an abiding unease, as though one day some great thunderbolt of a calamity would descend from above and strike her husband down.

The year ended.

The day came when Song Ci and his wife asked Qiu Juan if she would become their adopted daughter. Qiu Juan knelt before them and said: "For more than twenty years, you have treated me as one of your own. After my little sister died, I have always thought of myself as your daughter."

Soon after, the wedding between Qiu Juan and Tong Gong was held. In the bridal room that night, Qiu Juan suddenly burst into tears. Tong Gong asked her what the matter was and whether, in fact, she had not really wanted to marry him. Through her tears, Qiu Juan assured him how much she treasured her little sister's kindness and how much she wished to fulfil her last wish.

On New Year's Eve, a great snow blew into Nanjianzhou, such as was seldom seen in the south. As New Year's Day dawned, the people who had risen early to set off firecrackers to welcome in the new year were confronted by a strange and wonderful sight. A night of wind-driven snow had wrapped the mountain city in a boundless white cocoon. The roadways and rooftops were blanketed by the drifting snowflakes, presenting a desolate scene of blinding white everywhere you looked.

This was the most important festival of the year, and in every household, young and old, women and children alike all gathered in their halls to celebrate noisily. At the prefectural *yamen*, all the minor officials and other staff who had families in the area had gone home to spend the holiday with them, and the place was cold and silent.

It was a time for the younger generation to pay their respects to their elders, and for the elders to hand out tangerines, as symbols of good fortune, and red envelopes full of new year money. Song Ci and his wife rose early with a feeling of indescribable loneliness. Although Tong Gong and Qiu Juan, Huo Xiong and some others all came to offer their new year good wishes, this did not bring them much consolation. On this day, when everyone exchanges messages of good will and good fortune, the two of them put on a show of good cheer, and their mood lifted only a little.

For breakfast, they ate the food left over from the New Year's Eve banquet the night before. This was in keeping with the transitional new year saying 'Every year, may you have more than you need', and Song Ci wondered what more there was that he could need. He could think of nothing. After breakfast, he went to his study. As the sun rose towards its midday mark, it burst through the gloomy sky with a limpid brilliance that made the snow lying on the ground sparkle with a myriad of colours. All the remaining staff and soldiers in the *yamen* hurried out to admire the scene.

"Husband, the snow is very beautiful. You should come and look." Mistress Song had gone into the study and seen that the fire in the brazier at her husband's feet was covered in a layer of white ash, and she spoke as she bent down to stir the coals. The fire crackled back into life. Song Ci stretched out his hands to the warmth and finally unfolded his body from his chair and went outside with his wife.

In the courtyard, a maid called Ting'er and one of the kitchen girls were building a snowman, and tinkling laughter echoed round the snow-covered scene. Song Ci could not help remembering the year he had first taken up office, when the countryside around Jianyang had also seen just such a snowfall. Song Qi had been twelve at the time, and she had built her own snowman, even putting firecrackers in its hands and setting them off. How carefree she had been.

The snow was still lying when Song Ci received the news of his appointment, and he had taken his daughter along with him through the snowy streets to the district *yamen* to see his friend Liu Kezhuang. Liu had taken him and his daughter to look at the snow-covered plum trees…

He would never forget the miniature tree called 'The thousand-leaf yellow fragrant plum', which the day before had been covered in countless blossoms. Which had been stripped from it by a night of wind and snow, leaving only its snow- and ice-covered branches stretching into the air. He would also never forget another gnarled, old tree, covered in moss, which still retained a few fine blossoms as if in defiance of the snow.

"Brother Huifu, it is, of course, a good thing for a man to have talents. In our civil service at the moment there is much talent, but also much vexation.

Look there at the plum tree standing defiantly against the frost and snow, but look also at how many flowers it has lost."

His old friend's words echoed in his ears. He thought of his twelve-year-old daughter scrabbling around in the snow for some of the deep red petals of the fallen blossoms, and then he also saw, in his mind's eye, the deep red bloodstain spreading across his twenty-four-year-old daughter's sleeveless white jacket...

"Father... Mr Dongpo said... life... is like a dream... you must... look after yourself..."

These were his daughter's last words.

As the new year midday sun burst through the snow and wind, bathing the world in glorious light, Song Ci went out into the courtyard to join the maids in building their snowman, his breath steaming in the crisp, clear air. It was at that very moment that a great shout came from outside the *yamen* gates, sounding as though it came from heaven itself: "By imperial edict. Song Ci to receive the orders of the emperor!"

Song Ci heard this and froze to the spot...

6

## PURE OF HEART

Mistress Song could not understand what was happening.
Some months before, Du Guancheng's second son had ridden non-stop to Lin'an and gone to the prime minister's office to see his aunt, Du Shi. When she read the letter he had brought from home, Du Shi was greatly alarmed. She burst into tears, and, still sobbing piteously, went to her aunt's chambers to beg for help for her brother. The aunt was a woman who was easily swayed, and the tears moved her to promise that she would make every effort to help the family.

Li Zongmian had just arrived back in the capital and was making his report to the emperor, so he had not yet returned home. The two women discussed how best to proceed and then waited for his return. When an old retainer hurried in to tell them the master was back, they stood up and made their way to the front courtyard. They knelt down together on the main path across the yard and tearfully greeted Li Zongmian.

The prime minister had been away a long time, and, having just made his report to the emperor, coming home was like lifting a heavy weight from his shoulders. He little expected to be greeted immediately, but this scene of woe startled him.

"What has happened in the household?" he asked. "Stand up. Stand up, the two of you."

The aunt stood up, but Du Shi remained kneeling, howling piteously. When Li Zongmian asked again, she produced her sister-in-law's letter and presented it to him. On reading it, he found the contents to be quite straightforward: there had been a fire in a house outside the city walls of

Nanjianzhou, in which a bricklayer, totally unconnected to the Du family, had burned to death. The prefectural magistrate, Song Ci, was insisting that the bricklayer had been murdered by an agent of Guancheng. Guancheng was currently in prison under arrest. She begged the prime minister to take charge as soon as possible and see that true justice was done, and so on and so on.

When Li Zongmian had finished reading, he could not immediately think what was going on. On questioning Du Guancheng's second son, he learned that the provincial magistrate was siding with Song Ci. Li couldn't help thinking that the affair was, in fact, far from straightforward. He had met Song Ci and recognised him as a man of talent and virtue. He knew that such a man would not level such accusations lightly, and there must be good reason behind his actions. Li really did not want to involve himself in the affair; but he could not ignore his wife and his honoured relative in their tearful entreaties, so he told them he would dispatch someone immediately to look into it.

Li Zongmian was a cautious and prudent man. He knew that, in sending someone to investigate, he was setting off a chain of actions that, like the wind taking the helm of a ship, could completely alter the course of the case. He chose one of his most reliable agents and instructed him to make his own private investigations, while being careful not to alert or alarm any of the local officials.

It wasn't long before his agent returned. He had made discreet enquiries in Nanjianzhou and had also gone to Fuzhou where he had slipped into the Office of Punishments and sneaked a look at Song Ci's case report, and even seen the autopsy chart drawn up from the results of Song's 'investigation of the ground'. He had also succeeded in not drawing any attention from the local officials.

Li Zongmian listened attentively to the man's report, and then summoned the two women to tell them what he had learnt. He told them, very solemnly: "I cannot get involved in this case, nor is there any way of getting round the law. You are not to mention it again."

Thus, the affair seemed to be settled. Li Zongmian did not wish to have his loyalties divided by it. On his recent southern tour of inspection, he had seen with his own eyes the state of the interior of the country, the suffering of the people and the dishonesty of local officials; it had moved him deeply. When he went on to consider the state of the whole nation, he could see that two of the four routes into Sichuan were already lost; Chengdu was isolated and might be lost; fields were left fallow even in the fertile river basin between the Huai and Yangtze rivers. The country was truly in great danger. Li Zongmian needed to make a comprehensive plan of action to present to the emperor. On his tour, he had inspected everywhere from the centre of power to the nation's furthest reaches, and every level of society from the emperor down to the common people, and he recognised that there were far too many incompetent officials in positions of responsibility.

Among the clamour of voices that always surrounded the emperor, Li Zongmian strove to make his own voice heard in admonition and entreaty: "Please listen to these humble and urgent words of advice. I realise this will be painful for you to announce, but as the model for the nation, I urge you to cut back on excess in your court, end the lavish feasting, release the captured concubines in your harem, reduce any frivolous government spending to a minimum, stop the practice of giving gifts to your favoured subjects and put an end to the commissioning of great works."

With so many urgent matters of state occupying his mind, Li Zongmian quickly forgot Du Guancheng and his problems.

But he did not forget about Song Ci and, indeed, often thought about him – the deep lines around his eyes and his impassive expression that impelled people to tell the unvarnished truth.

So many letters and petitions arrived in the capital from the interior that it was impossible for the emperor to read them all. The imperial secretaries used a system of yellow fiches when presenting them for the emperor's consideration. One type of sticker was affixed to the front of a letter with a general, simplified summary of its contents; another type, however, gave a detailed exposition of the salient points of the petition and was stuck to the back of the document. While Li Zongmian was going about his daily business one day, he saw a memorandum to the emperor that had arrived from Guangdong, giving a detailed account of the principal long-standing cases of prisoners held in the Guangdong jail, and a good number of other intractable cases that had been passed down through the years. The people were vociferous in their complaints and the emperor was beseeched to send a representative, with the full power of the court, to re-establish the rule of law and dispense justice.

Li Zongmian pondered deeply over this petition. He recalled that, when he himself had been in Guangdong, many officials had raised this matter with him, but at the time, his primary concern had been with his tour of inspection of grain levies and taxes, and the provision of supplies for the army, so he had little thought to spare for the disarray in the prison system. Now, however, as he read, he remembered Nanjianzhou and the case of the starving highway robbers, and how Song Ci had suggested the hard-working people of An Jun could contribute to the guarding of the border and the implementation of imperial decrees. It was as if he realised for the first time the importance, in the current circumstances, of reforming the prison system and redressing miscarriages of justice. An idea formed in his head that must have been lurking there for some time.

Once the shrewd and experienced statesman Li Zongmian had formed this idea, he first consulted many of the topmost officials in the Golden Hall, the highest legislative authority in the empire. Not meeting with any dissenting voices, he was determined not to waste another day and went straight to the palace to seek an audience with the emperor.

Winter was well advanced, and Lin'an was under snow. That afternoon, however, the snow had stopped and there was glorious sunshine. The young Lizong emperor was playing polo with his imperial concubines and other palace ladies at the Deshou Palace.

Polo had begun as a form of training for the army's cavalry and a popular way of honing their mounted fighting skills, but now it was also a fashionable pastime in palace circles. The Deshou Palace had grown out of the former residence of Qin Hui, the official said to have betrayed General Yue Fei. It was a magnificent sight, glittering with gold and precious stones. It contained the Wan Sui Bridge,[1] built entirely from bricks of white jade from Baiyü County, with railings intricately carved in the form of eagles and other birds of prey – a dazzling sight. The bridge spanned a clear-water pond with an area of more than ten *mu*, in which grew thousands of lotus plants.

Although still comparatively young, the Lizong emperor was affected by poor health, suffering from crippling pains in his legs, poor hearing and dizzy spells. His doctors had recommended exercise to counteract these ailments, so he had ordered that the pond be filled in and turned into a polo field. A dragon gate was built on either side of the field, each formed of two columns and a cross-beam with a pair of carved dragons on top – these served as the goals. After the light snow of the morning, the sky had cleared, and the emperor and his ladies were delighting in their game of polo on the snow-dusted field. The young emperor had stationed himself under one of the dragon gates, to defend the goal; one of his concubines by the name of Shu was guarding the other goal. At the sound of a drum, two teams of palace ladies galloped onto the field. The ball was dropped in the middle of the field, and the game began. Off the field, the drums kept playing to urge both teams on.

As the two sides became lost in their contest, an old eunuch in informal attire led Li Zongmian into the Deshou Palace, across the Wan Sui Bridge to the side of the polo field. At the top of the field, sitting under a phoenix fan, was the empress Xie Shi. The empress did not know how to ride and had no desire to learn, so she was not taking part in the match. Nonetheless, she enjoyed watching and was wrapped up in the game, her eyes gleaming and her lips parted, so she did not notice Li Zongmian's arrival until he greeted her. She turned to look at him.

Zhao Yun, who had taken the imperial name Lizong, was thirty-three and fond of his amusements. However, since coming to the throne at the age of nineteen, he had succeeded in maintaining his authority despite the almost continuous social and political unrest in the country. He took very seriously all reports submitted to him by his senior ministers. In fact, he had a standing order for all his ministers to come to the palace immediately with anything they considered important. So, when the normally taciturn Empress Xie Shi saw the prime minister, she thought it must be something urgent. When Li saw her wave a gong stick at the referee on the field, he realised she was ordering him to sound his gong to stop play.

"It's not urgent, it's not urgent," he told her hurriedly.

But the gong had already sounded, and the two teams dismounted to take a rest.

The emperor stood up to look around and saw Li Zongmian. He came over to find out what was going on. Li immediately kowtowed in greeting. The emperor gave permission for him to rise and asked: "What pressing matter does Our Beloved Minister bring before us?"

Li Zongmian had hoped to wait until the emperor had finished his game of polo before presenting his memorandum, but now the emperor was already in front of him, so all he could do was offer with both hands the petition that had arrived from Guangdong.

"Your Majesty," he said, "when I first saw this I did not think it so urgent, but after careful consideration I have changed my opinion and did not dare to delay."

The emperor took the petition and looked first at the golden fiche on the front and then at the one on the back. He raised his eyebrows slightly, as though he thought his minister was playing some kind of joke on him. But he thought about what Li Zongmian had just said and did not reply that he could see nothing urgent enough to bring the prime minister hurrying to the Deshou Palace. Instead, he just said: "We would like to hear the details."

Li Zongmian then proceeded to tell the story of how Song Ci had handled the case of the starving highway robbers and its greater relevance to the safety of the nation. He explained in detail the most important aspects of the matter and, as the emperor listened, he gradually lowered his raised eyebrows. Then he began to frown, as he came to see that, if this was how things stood in the case of Guangdong, and the people were becoming vociferous in their discontent, then the situation was indeed as threatening as an arrow on a taut bowstring, and most certainly should be considered urgent. In the end, he asked: "Does My Beloved Minister think I should send someone from the court to handle this matter?"

"I do not believe the task should be given to someone from the capital."

"Why not?"

"I believe there is only one man I can recommend to undertake this task."

"Who is that?"

"The prefectural magistrate at Nanjianzhou, Song Ci."

"Song Ci..." The emperor thought there was something familiar about the name.

Li Zongmian continued forcefully: "Although this man is not particularly exalted in office, he has extraordinary talents and achieves results. He has faced down petty local tyrants and shown great compassion to the worthy. Over recent years in Jiangxi, Fujian and other places he has been very shrewd in his use of rewards and punishments to encourage or reprimand. He has used the strict letter of the law to bring peace to the district. Many of the cases he has resolved have been of the most unusual kind, and he is truly of a calibre that occurs only once in countless generations."

When Lizong heard his old prime minister praising such a lowly official in such an exalted way, he had to ask: "How can you prove this to me?"

Li Zongmian thought for a moment and then recounted how Song Ci had solved the case of the burned body in a single night. The emperor thought that, by the sound of it, this man's ability to solve cases exceeded even that of Bao Zheng[2] of the Northern Song, and to his own surprise found himself listening with rapt attention. His original plan had been to make a quick decision and then return to his polo, but now, all thoughts of polo were forgotten. Empress Xie Shi and the palace ladies could also be heard clicking their tongues continuously, in amazement.

Seeing the effect he had had on the emperor, Li Zongmian continued: "Your Majesty, although Song Ci is not a palace official, the difficult cases he has solved up to now are beyond counting. Time and time again, he has conducted his own autopsies, increasing his knowledge on each occasion. His abilities at trial and in sentencing surpass those of anyone we have at court. We must be sure we use such a man to the best effect in the service of Your Majesty. Not to do so would be like having a bow but not firing it, or a horse but not riding it. May Your Majesty bring down blessings from on high."

On hearing this speech, the emperor remembered where he had heard the name Song Ci before. This was the man that Zhen Dexiu had once recommended so passionately in the Golden Palace, but another senior official had presented a memorandum accusing Zhen Dexiu of acting out of personal interest. He recalled that there had been bad blood between these two senior officials, and that both of them had been among his closest companions and most trusted aides. At the time, Lizong had felt that if he were to promote such a lowly official, it would just serve to deepen the feud; and to have the two men constantly at loggerheads would be of service neither to the country nor to himself. So he hadn't followed Zhen Dexiu's recommendation. But now, Li Zongmian was urging him to promote the same man – moreover, Li Zongmian was on good terms with everyone at court, and they all seemed to regard him as an unbiased, upright and honest minister. So, using this fellow recommended by Li was not going to light any fires of dissent at court.

The emperor went on to ask Li Zongmian how he came to know Song Ci. Li could not avoid replying, and did not dare hide anything, so he gave his personal account of what had happened at Nanjianzhou, including his own brother-in-law's involvement in the case of the burnt body that Song Ci had investigated. The emperor listened carefully and was greatly moved by his prime minister's honesty. He stretched out his hand and said: "We permit it."

Li Zongmian thanked the emperor. He thought of the man who had originally recommended Song Ci for his current post. Leaving the palace, he made his way to Liu Kezhuang's official residence and told Liu what had passed that day. Liu was almost lost for words. He thanked the prime minister reverently and thanked him again on behalf of his old friend. Without waiting to see in the new year, he rode non-stop to Nanjianzhou to deliver the news... but of all these twists and turns, Song Ci and his wife knew nothing.

When Liu Kezhuang's yellow-covered wagon carrying the imperial decree halted outside the prefectural *yamen*, and as the official summons for Song Ci to receive the decree penetrated the front gate, Liu himself carried the decree into the front hall – how little Song Ci and Mistress Song could have expected to see him! And how little could Song Ci have anticipated that the decree would be promoting him to Inspector of Prisons for Guangdong. And, to cap it all, how could he have possibly thought that the man who had recommended this promotion was none other than Li Zongmian!

When Song Ci finally grasped what was going on, his heart overflowed with a mixture of emotions: surprise, pleasure, sadness – he couldn't distinguish between them. To have control of every prefecture and to have total charge of the judicial system, this had been his crowning ambition for many years. He felt that, contained within this great responsibility, were all his childhood dreams; his youthful ideals; the toil of many years; the goodwill of the venerable prime minister; the youthful hot blood of his beloved daughter; and the expectations of countless elders of the empire.

It was the third year of the Jiaxi period. The snow of the old year had not yet melted when Song Ci and his wife, accompanied by Liu Kezhuang, took Tong Gong, Qiu Juan, Huo Xiong and the others to Nine Peak Mountain to offer sacrifices to Song Qi's departed spirit and to say farewell to her. When they arrived at her grave, they saw that some unknown person had surrounded it with twenty or more ancient plum trees, their branches like iron bones, just coming into their season of blossom. The flowers were white as snow in front of the tomb, a focus of purity and serenity.

On his return from Nine Peak Mountain, Song Ci set out to take up his new post. On the day of his departure, all the people of Nanjianzhou, supporting their elders and carrying their children, poured out into the city and thronged the streets to see him off. Astride his horse, Song Ci fought back his tears and saluted the people with raised hands, sending them his warmest good wishes.

As he went out of the city gates, he spotted, among the crowds of well-wishers, little Qingqing and her brother. They were standing with their uncle and had come to see him off. He dismounted in front of the two children and patted the girl on the head, as if about to speak. But no words came out, and he got back on his horse and proceeded on his way. When he reached the post road, the whole multitude of people knelt on the snow-covered ground and wept as they sent him on his way. Song Ci could hold back no longer, and his own tears came flooding out…

# CHAPTER XIII

## THE JUDICIAL COMMISSIONER DISPENSES JUSTICE (1239)

Song Ci was fifty-three and, for the first time in his career, he had reached a position of judicial commissioner, the highest authority in the control and administration of the penal system. Guangdong already had the largest number of remand cases awaiting trial of anywhere in the country. Since the majority were difficult cases where there was no body to autopsy, or where too much time had passed for a proper examination of the scene of the crime, Song Ci's practice and study now had to extend to exhumation and the examination of skeletal remains. He built up the most exhaustive knowledge of this subject of anyone in the world at the time and applied it to cases that had been mired in injustice and controversy for many years.

1

# THE PENAL COLONY AT PANSHAN

Song Ci's father had held office in Guangzhou. As a child, Song had often heard his father describe the scenery and customs of the place and tell anecdotes from its history. He had been particularly interested by the sea routes established since the Tang dynasty between China and southeast Asia and east Africa, of which his father spoke. He longed to go and see the thousands of ships that arrived every year in Guangzhou from Persia, Borneo, Ceylon and countless other countries whose names he could not now remember. He wanted also to see those strange barbarians with red hair and blue eyes. He could still remember his father saying that such barbarians from all parts of the globe gathered in Guangzhou to trade in pearls, tortoiseshell, spices, precious stones and every other imaginable kind of treasure. But it was the stories of the bizarre legal cases thrown up in the courts of Guangzhou by the glamour and glitter of these precious objects that really fascinated the young Song Ci.

Now, at the age of fifty-three, he was heading east on the Guangnan Road to take up his new post as judicial commissioner with supreme authority over the control and administration of the penal system for the whole of Guangdong. But what adventures was he going to confront as he dealt with all those long-delayed cases – more of them than anywhere else in the country?

Travelling fast and light, Song Ci soon passed through the south-western part of Fujian and entered Guangdong. This part of the country did not really have a winter, but passed directly from late autumn into early spring. As he travelled further southwest, the colours of spring became more and more abundant.

There were skylarks above, singing bright and clear, and by the roadside, banana trees and sunflowers swayed gently in the breeze. Palm trees and betel palms stood tall and elegant, and the delicate leaves of the Chinese redbud trees glowed with myriad points of scarlet. With the spring wind at his back, on a fast road, Song Ci soon reached Guangzhou.

The judicial commissioner's office was situated on Panshan Hill, inside the south gate of the city. The buildings dated from the time when the Later Tang (923-937 CE) was established and Panshan Hill was flattened off. Inside, and dating from the same period, was Guangdong's largest jail, occupying a spot that formed a naturally strategic and inaccessible stronghold. After Song Ci had arrived there and formally accepted his post, he rested overnight and, the next day, began to work his way through the court records.

Office guards brought over the prison lists, volume by volume, and the case records bundle by bundle. Even though each volume and each bundle was given a good beating, plenty of dust and mould still clung to them; and when they were opened or unrolled, worms and insects came crawling out. Tong Gong and the others made sure to give them an extra whack before handing them over to Song Ci. All this made Song Ci think to himself: Just from the state of the prisons in Guangdong, I'm getting an inkling of what the bigger picture must be like.

Song Ci began his examination of the cases in earnest, and the more he looked, the more his brow furrowed. In so many instances he found that either the grounds for the case were not clear, or were self-contradictory, or that countless other areas of doubt were thrown up. He tried to remain collected as he conscientiously read through them all, but from time to time he couldn't help exclaiming to the heavens in exasperation. At such a point he would take a break, put down the documents, close his eyes and wait until he had regained sufficient composure to continue.

"Hah!" he sighed deeply, putting down the current scroll and leaning back in his folding chair.

"Have some tea, Master," said Huo Xiong, handing him a cup.

"Come and have a look at this so-called statement of evidence!"

Huo Xiong knew that his master didn't really want him to look at it, and that he was just letting off steam, so he didn't move, and asked: "What's wrong with it?"

"This is a serious capital case, and the autopsy finding just reads 'loss of blood from a wound'. What kind of use is that? Of course blood is going to come out of a wound! It doesn't give the dimensions of the wound, its shape, its depth, its length… nothing. What use is that as evidence on which to base a judgment?"

"Take a break, Master," Huo Xiong suggested.

After a few mouthfuls of tea, Song Ci continued reading, adding, as he went, a few annotations of his own. This went on all day, until he could read no more, even by candlelight, at which point he was obliged to put the documents down. He sank deep into contemplation.

For years he had been waiting for the opportunity to undertake his great plan, for him to have sufficient authority to see it through, and for there to be enough problematic cases for the purpose. Now here was the opportunity, here was the authority and here were the cases, all right in front of him. So, was he up to the task?

Although he had only been looking through the records for one day, that was enough to show what was confronting him: a whole day of reading had only dealt with a small section of the huge pile of records in the storehouse, and, of those, there had not been a single one in which the evidence was clear enough to make a decision. And if they were re-opened, so much time had passed that it would be almost impossible to search out the evidence or to re-examine witnesses. There were so many of them, not at all like the comparatively limited number of cases he had solved in Tingzhou and Nanjianzhou – 'The Wormwood Image', 'The Burnt Body' and the others. How should he begin and where should he begin were questions that needed considerable thought.

"You should have your supper now, Master," said Huo Xiong, coming back in.

Song Ci stood up and went off to eat. But after supper, he was still mulling over how to set about things the next day. Should he keep reading the records, or should he summon all the bureau staff and listen to what they had to say?

Actually, best of all, go and see the prisoners, he thought.

This thought became a decision, and Song Ci was too eager to wait until the next day. He pushed himself up from his chair and said to Tong Gong and Huo Xiong: "Come along. We're going to the prison."

One of the departmental aides led the way, with Huo Xiong carrying a large lantern inscribed with the words 'Judical Commissioner'. Tong Gong followed behind his master, with four officers from the military academy, all of them silently climbing the cold stone steps that led from behind the ministry up to the prison.

A string of dim yellow lanterns hung over the closed prison gates, which were of middling size and undefended, but the guards on top of the walls were just visible. The aide stepped forward and knocked on the gates with one of their monster-mask ring handles.

After a pause, there was a noise from the upper section of the gate, and a small, square hole appeared in the panel. A pair of eyes looked through the opening, and a voice said: "What business?"

"Don't your eyes work? The judicial commissioner has come to inspect the prison."

"Sir!"

The gates, which were studded with nails and reinforced with iron bands, gave a groan and then were flung open. The jailer informed them very nervously that the prison governor was not there, but had gone back down the mountain before sundown and was not going to return until much later. Song Ci was in no mood to wait for anyone. He had come to see the prisoners, so he ordered the jailer to take them into the body of the jail to do just that.

The jailer led them across a large courtyard, round a high wall and stopped in front of large, wooden double doors, where their nostrils were assaulted by a dreadful stench. After a lot of trouble, the jailer finally managed to open the door's large ox-head padlock.

As Song Ci descended the steps, the smell intensified. The jailer was holding his nose as he led Song along a long corridor that was flanked by wood-partitioned cells.

Song Ci inspected the cells and saw that they were no more than five paces wide and four *chi* long, and each held twenty or more prisoners. They were lying in tightly packed rows on the floor, and those who couldn't find space to lie were sitting squashed into the corners. All of them were long-haired and emaciated, sallow and haggard in the extreme.

Song asked his aide, who had followed him in: "Are all these prisoners locked up according to their crimes, or are they mixed together?"

The aide did not know.

"Your Honour," the jailer answered, "they are mixed together, and among them there are quite a few being held on remand pending investigation."

"Remand prisoners?" Song Ci stopped and asked the aide again: "Why are remand prisoners being held here?"

"It's always been like that."

"How long are they held on remand?"

"The longest, four or five years, and even the shortest, three or four months."

A barely perceptible ripple of anger passed across Song Ci's brow. Were the officials here really so careless and dismissive of the law? With the judicial process taking so long, even the most straightforward case could become mired in complexity.

As Song Ci was speaking, some of the prisoners in the cells began to scramble to their feet, and as he proceeded inside, they began shouting: "Great Lord! I'm innocent, I've been falsely accused!"

As the first voices died down, others took up the cry until the place rang with pleadings of innocence and unjust treatment. The jailer and the aide scurried forward and started shouting in return: "Silence! No talking!"

The four military officials drew their swords with a clatter and waited for orders. Song Ci stayed standing where he was, and Tong Gong and Huo Xiong stood still too, not speaking. The aide and the jailer kept up their shouting for a while, until gradually they quieted the hubbub, and silence returned to the cells. But all eyes were still fixed on Song Ci.

Song Ci singled out the man who had first called out, went forward so they were just separated by the wooden partition and asked him: "Whatever your grievance is, tell me now."

On hearing this, everyone began clamouring again, which made Song Ci frown in annoyance. When Tong Gong saw this, he stepped forward and bellowed: "Shut your noise!"

At the sound of this thunderous shout, many of the voices were scared into silence, and Tong Gong pointed to the original complainant again and said: "You begin."

He was a man of slim build, with long straggly hair, very dishevelled, and his face looked particularly thin because of its pallor. At first sight he could be taken for forty or more, but in fact, he was no more than twenty-five years old.

"I didn't kill my sister-in-law."

That was all he said.

"Why were you sent here?" Song Ci asked.

"My sister-in-law disappeared."

"What had that to do with you?"

"A… a young woman was killed."

"What had that to do with you?"

"She died where I was sleeping."

"Who was she?"

"I don't know. But I think she was my sister-in-law."

"You didn't know your own sister-in-law?"

"Her head was missing."

"A dead woman in your bed was missing her head?"

"That's right. Ah, but… but she didn't die in my bed."

If it weren't for Song Ci's patient questioning, the prisoner would have had no hope of explaining the circumstances of his case by himself. After a few more twists and turns in the evidence, Song Ci established the story behind the man's arrest and incarceration.

The story went like this: the prisoner had a sister-in-law whose younger brother was going to marry a country girl. His elder brother was away from home and could not attend, so the man accompanied his sister-in-law to the celebrations. On the day of their return, it started to rain heavily, and the two of them took shelter in an old temple. Rumour had it that several people, both men and women, had hanged themselves there. It was old and neglected, fallen into disrepair, with wild grasses growing on its threshold. After he and his sister-in-law had run in out of the rain, he was overcome by the wine he had drunk at the wedding and lay down to sleep it off. When he woke, to his consternation, he saw that his sister-in-law had been murdered, and her head was missing. Scared out of his wits, he ran back to the village to call for help and was promptly hauled before the local magistrate. The court decided that he had raped the woman and then killed her. Because he knew that he could not withstand the extremes of torture and would certainly confess, he made a false statement that he had thrown the head and the knife he had used into the river, and he was, thereupon, sentenced to death.

But three days later, after his elder brother had returned home to prepare the body for burial, and when he was changing his wife's clothes, he discovered that, although the body was clad in his wife's clothes, and was the right size and build, it was not, in fact, his wife. It wasn't difficult to spot, since his wife had two, small supernumerary nipples. He immediately brought the body to the *yamen*, kowtowing continuously in front of the judge, and petitioning for his brother's release and for a search to be instituted for his missing wife.

These distinguishing features had been on his wife's body since childhood, and his mother-in-law could testify to it. The judge conducted further questioning and examinations, but he was not willing to release the younger brother. The fact still remained that a dead woman had been found next to the prisoner, and in order to dispel any murder charge, they needed to find the missing wife to give the true account of events. Only then could the case be decided.

As word of the affair spread, someone else came forward to identify the body. The daughter from a wealthy household in a neighbouring village had been missing for several days. The representative of that household came looking, inspected the body closely and confirmed that it was the missing woman – she had a birthmark about the size of a copper coin on her back, which she, too, had had from childhood. But how had she come to be found dead in the dilapidated old temple outside her home village? This was another puzzle that could only be solved by finding the missing sister-in-law.

The magistrate ordered searches to be made throughout the area, and the prisoner's elder brother made his own enquiries. However, despite three years of hunting, she could not be found, so the case was left hanging.

As a result of his patient questioning, Song Ci was able to recognise some similarities between this case and 'The Case of the Headless Woman' in the *Anthology of Unusual Cases*. But he was not happy to proceed just on the basis of this first impression, so he took the details of the prisoner, who was called Jiang Qing and was a farmer from the village of Boluo in Huizhou. When he had finished his questioning, the other prisoners could not hold back any longer, and they began vying with each other to speak. But Song Ci chose a rather scholarly looking individual, who had not yet opened his mouth. "You haven't said anything. Does that mean you have no grievance to air?"

"No, My Lord, my grievance is as vast as the oceans."

The man answered promptly and clearly, with the bearing and diction of an educated man. He made a move as though to kneel and kowtow, but he was jostled out of the way by someone and ended up just nodding his head through a crack in the panels of the partition. Song Ci ordered him to explain the nature of his grievance, and, speaking swiftly and precisely, he summarised his case in a few sentences.

He was twenty years old and lived in the countryside. Two years previously he had come up to the city to sit the civil service exams and was staying in a tavern on Guangta Street, next to which was a lodging house that catered for foreign merchants and travellers. That night a foreign woman was raped and murdered in her bed. The blood trail led to the man's room, and a bloody knife was discovered under his pillow. In his trunk of books they also found some foreign coins, so he was arrested, and that was how matters now stood.

Song Ci listened to the scholar's brief account and was struck by the similarities with the other prisoner's story. But for the moment he couldn't think what more to ask, so he turned and said: "Let's go."

At this, all the other prisoners began shouting again, and the jailer barked back at them to stop. But this time, Song Ci really did leave, and as he passed through the big wooden door, he could still hear the racket from inside the jail…

"My Lord, the man died in my doorway, it had nothing to do with me…"

"My Lord, I had a row with my wife, but I didn't kill her…"

"My Lord…"

"My Lord…"

Having left the men's jail, Song Ci decided he should also visit the women's prison.

The women's prison was on the same level as the men's and had originally been the death row for prisoners awaiting execution. It had only recently been put to its current use, because of overcrowding.

The jailer's wife led Song Ci over to the prison, and they were about to go in, when Song Ci stopped. He had heard a young child weeping and wailing.

"Is that a child crying?" he asked.

"Yes, My Lord," the jailer's wife replied.

"The jail is a restricted area. How can there be a child crying?"

"It's the young son of one of the woman prisoners. He has prison sores and he never stops wailing."

"Are the women prisoners allowed to bring their children into the jail?"

"He wasn't brought in, he was born here."

"How old is he?"

"He's three."

Song Ci frowned: "Why hasn't he been taken out?"

"He doesn't have any relatives on the outside."

"Go and bring the woman to the interrogation room."

Acknowledging the order, the woman went along the snaking corridor to the women's prison. It wasn't as crowded as the men's prison, and all the women were able to lie down. When they saw the jailer's wife, they clambered to their feet.

"Listen to me, all of you. Put on your clothes. It's likely My Lord is going to come in to inspect the prison," the woman shouted.

There was a rustling of clothes as the women stood up, and the lamplight showed that many of them had been lying down, stripped to the waist. The jailer's wife went over to a wooden door and unlocked it, at the same time calling to the young mother: "Ah Xiang, come here."

Two women were inside the cell, one old, one young, along with a small child. The young woman was comforting the child, who had now stopped crying, and did not get up immediately.

"Come on, now. The Master wants to ask about your case," the jailer's wife said.

The young woman handed the child to her cellmate and stood up.

The interrogation room was a fairly spacious stone chamber. It contained a floor lamp with three candle lamp stands, each covered in cobwebs and lacking oil, so the jailer refilled them. There was an array of torture instruments, which gave the room a sinister air, along with a writing table and several low benches. Everything was covered in a thick layer of dust. The aide produced a folding chair that the jailer usually sat on to keep his records.

It, too, was covered in dust, and the aide used his sleeve to wipe it down before placing it behind Song Ci, who sat down. Soon they heard the sound of footsteps outside as the jailer's wife and the young woman approached.

Perhaps it was the sinister, icy atmosphere of the interrogation room, or perhaps because she didn't understand why she had suddenly been brought, all alone, to be questioned, but whatever the reason, a great shiver ran through the woman as she entered the room. As Song Ci looked closely at her, he suddenly felt he could see something of his daughter Song Qi in the prisoner. Could it be that it was the memory of Song Qi that had brought him here? He looked at the woman again and thought that there were indeed many similarities: the prisoner was about twenty-three or twenty-four, and although her frame was thin and haggard, her face was very well formed, and her expression gentle and refined. Her hair was loose but not dishevelled, and although her clothes were old and tattered, they were neatly mended.

"Why are you not kneeling in front of His Lordship?" the jailer's wife asked loudly, but not unkindly.

Not daring to look up, the young woman fell to her knees.

There was a ripping sound as she knelt. Her knees had got caught up in the dress, and the pressure as they made contact with the ground had torn a new hole in the shoulder, exposing her snow-white skin. She was greatly perturbed by this, and hurriedly put her hand over the tear.

"Stand up and talk to me," Song Ci said.

The woman's eyelashes fluttered a little, but she still didn't either look up or stand up, as if she hadn't heard.

"His Lordship told you to stand up and speak," Tong Gong told her. He, too, had noticed the slight resemblance to Song Qi.

The woman finally raised her eyes to look at Song Ci, then dropped them again and stood up shyly. Song Ci began to question her gently: "What is your name, and where do you come from?"

She hesitated, before replying: "My family name is Song, and I only have the pet name Ah Xiang. I'm from Dongguan."

"Why are you in prison?"

She didn't reply but suddenly burst out wailing.

"His Lordship asked you a question. Why are you crying?" the jailer's wife asked.

Song Ci motioned at her to be quiet and then listened carefully to her weeping. To his ears, the way a prisoner wept and wailed was a very useful piece of evidence. He was expert at distinguishing many different kinds: there was the crying of someone deeply wounded by injustice; there were the tears of remorse of someone who had committed a crime; there were the fake tears of someone trying to hoodwink the court... but the woman only let out two sobs before she clapped her hand over her mouth, quashing the noise, and forced herself to calm down.

"This is the new judicial commissioner," Tong Gong said. "If you have a grievance, just tell him."

The woman lifted her head slowly and timidly. But when she looked into Song Ci's eyes, she suddenly thought she recognised in them something that she had never seen in an official's eyes before. Was it dignity? Was it compassion? She couldn't decide, but whatever it was, she felt hope of salvation stirring in her heart. She tried to look at him properly, but suddenly her eyes filled with tears, and she could see nothing clearly…

## 2

## THE GIRL AH XIANG

The majestic Pearl River flowed swiftly, day and night, watering the year-round luxuriance of the land and bringing innumerable blessings to its inhabitants. But it also brought catastrophe. In the first year of the Duanping period, five years before Song Ci arrived in Guangzhou, the Pearl flooded as seldom seen before. The flood started in the upper reaches of all three tributaries of the Pearl – the North, East and West rivers – and came bearing mightily down on Guangzhou, overflowing both banks, overturning houses and drowning countless people. Guangzhou is situated at the apex of the Pearl River delta, at the confluence of the three rivers, and the combined effects of the floodwaters, sudden typhoons and tidal surges pounding the city, turn the place into an almost permanent wetland.

Dongguan County is in the southeast of Guangdong Province, and the heavy rains that year had caused flash flooding in the East River, which had swept away Ah Xiang, her family and fellow villagers in its muddy torrent. When Ah Xiang came to, she was lying in the crook of the branches of a massive old banyan tree, her body covered by a boy's jacket. In front of her was a young man, stripped to the waist. She recognised him as a local lad who had recently failed the county-level imperial examinations. She remembered he had the double-character surname Sima and the given name Ding. She made her living mounting paintings and calligraphy on scrolls, and had done several pieces of work for him. When he saw that she was awake, Sima Ding smiled at her and then turned away. Ah Xiang made to take off the boy's jacket that was covering her, but what she saw when she lifted it made her clutch it more tightly about her.

When the weather begins to get warm in Guangdong, between spring and summer, the young girls of the province used to wear a very lightweight top that became translucent when wet and did nothing to conceal their modesty. Ah Xiang forgot all about her current situation and blushed furiously, her ears burning. But, in the circumstances, there was no point in being ashamed and no point in being afraid. Everywhere around them was water, as far as the eye could see. The wind was blowing keenly, and every so often a corpse floated past. Ah Xiang had to accept that the young man's actions had kept her alive. But she had lost her mother and father, and her brothers, and she was hungry, cold, frightened and sad. All this began to overwhelm her, and Ah Xiang began to wail.

Without a word, Sima Ding clambered further up the tree and began collecting twigs and branches, like a bird collecting material for its nest. And, having found the most suitable spot, he did indeed build a kind of large nest.

"Come over here, Miss," he called to Ah Xiang.

He made his way to another nest he had built. Perhaps because of his calm manner and his exceptional ability to adapt to such an unusual and perilous situation, Ah Xiang stopped wailing, clutched Sima Ding's jacket around her and clambered up to the nest he had made for her. It was big enough for her to lie down in, and much safer and more comfortable than the crook in the branches she had been in before.

It got colder as dusk fell. Through the gloom, the corpse of a middle-aged woman floated towards them. Sima Ding climbed down, caught hold of the body and, without a second thought, stripped the clothes from it and let it drift back into the current.

They were good quality clothes and might prompt one to recall the saying 'Losing your boat to the river but finding a crock of gold'. Certainly, in those circumstances, the clothes were worth a crock of gold to Ah Xiang. Sima Ding clambered back up, handed them to her and then turned his back. Ah Xiang swiftly changed into them, but not without a superstitious shudder when she thought of where they had come from. She put Sima Ding's jacket down beside her nest and said: "Here. Take it."

He did so and then made his way back to his own nest.

Night fell, and all they could hear was the water gurgling past them below. They did not know how much time had passed when they saw a dot of red on the horizon. It was a flame, and the flame was moving – it must be a boat! They called out, at first taking it in turns, but finally both shouting together: "Hey!... Hey!... Over here…"

They shouted until they broke out into a sweat and their voices cracked, but the red dot gradually disappeared, and all they could see was the icy darkness again.

It had begun to rain and there was thunder in the air. The rain fell incessantly, pattering on the leaves of the tree. Lightning flashed starkly across the sky, giving glimpses of the surface of the water, pock-marked by the raindrops. The level seemed to be rising, and Ah Xiang's spirits plummeted. In that awful, endless darkness, if it hadn't been for the comforting presence of that patient and considerate young man, she thought that she might not have made it through to the morning.

When the rain finally stopped and the first glimmers of light showed in the east, dawn broke to show the whole scene enveloped in a thick mist.

The water had risen to within a *chi* of their nests, the sky was overcast and no sunshine broke through. Nonetheless, the coming of day brought with it some hope. The wind had blown their clothes dry, but there was still no sign of any boat. Occasionally, some waterfowl would fly up and rest for a while in the tree and then fly away, calling mournfully.

A day and a night without any food had left their stomachs knotted with hunger, and they were in desperate need of water. Perching on the branches nearest the surface of the river, they could reach down and touch the water. So, holding hands for fear of falling, they took it in turns to drink. The touch of the young man's hands made Ah Xiang's heart pound and brought a blush to her cheeks, but there was no help for it. Fate had put them in that tree. If they wanted to live, they had to drink, so there was no avoiding it.

They spent the whole day looking for a boat, but none came. As the second night approached, the rain had stopped and the waters had begun to recede a little, although the wind still blew.

"It's quite safe for you to go to sleep," Sima Ding said.

And sleep she did. Hungry and exhausted as she was, she covered herself with some more leaves he had collected for her. She slept through half the night until she suddenly woke up and began crying out shrilly – an army of ants had marched into her nest and then into her clothes, and they were crawling all over her body, biting her. There was no escaping them. Sima Ding, who had been resting in his own nest, came clambering over quickly as soon as he heard her screams.

"What is it? What is it?" he asked.

"Aaaaah!... Aaaaah!" her blood-curdling screams were coming out in great gasps and she couldn't speak. Sima Ding climbed over beside her and she scrambled out of her nest. But as she did so, she lost her footing, and almost fell into the water. Sima Ding grabbed her to haul her back up, but as he did so, some of the ants crawled across onto his hand. As they bit him viciously, the situation became clear to him. These were a type of ant found in the south of China, and a swarm of them could quickly reduce a large snake to a pile of bones. He pulled her away, shouting at her: "Take off your clothes! Take off your clothes!"

It wasn't entirely clear whether she did it by herself, or whether he helped her, but in no time at all in the darkness, her clothes were in a pile beside her. From this time on, Ah Xiang realised Sima Ding was now her only family.

Another dawn came, and once again awoke hope in them. They could see that the water level had dropped by about a *chi*, but Ah Xiang was ill; her body was burning up, her lips were parched and her throat was on fire. She drank the water he got for her by dipping his jacket into the receding water and then wringing it out for her.

The sun started to burst from the sky, through the trembling foliage of the tree and fell on their bodies, bringing back a warmth that seemed to have been missing for centuries. But in the end, another day went by with only the passing waterfowl and no sign of a boat.

That evening, she was lying in his arms when she felt his body begin to shiver. They clutched each other more tightly. When the next day dawned, bright and clear again, the water had dropped some more, but not enough for them to leave the tree. Some time later, she heard him cry out joyfully: "A boat! A boat!"

Uplifted, she looked all round, but nowhere, even on the distant horizon, was there any sign of a boat. She realised that he had also become sick and was hallucinating.

They did their best to comfort each other, but the combined effect of hunger, cold, fatigue and illness descended on them like a net of despair, tangling them in its folds… but then, at last, a boat, a real boat. A large boat of the type used for transporting fragrant plants used for making incense. They were rescued! On board was an important incense merchant called Chi Gan. When he heard that Sima Ding was a failed candidate in the civil service examinations, he decided to take him home to work as private tutor to his son.

The danger was finally passed, and the two survivors could begin to set up home. Sima Ding took up the post as tutor to the merchant's son, and from that time on, Ah Xiang stayed with him.

In ordinary affairs, Sima Ding was always very affable, but as tutor he was extremely strict. The merchant's son was very naughty and ill-behaved, and had already seen off a number of previous tutors with his temper. Out of gratitude and indebtedness to his rescuer, Sima Ding remained patient and conscientious with his lessons. Until, one day, the young mischief-maker defecated on his tutor's chair. Sima Ding exploded with anger and beat the young lad most severely. This was too much for the boy's mother, and she confronted her husband, shouting and screaming, demanding Sima Ding be dismissed.

That evening, the boy crept into Sima Ding's bedroom and hit him over the head with a rock, making him bleed profusely. Just like all the other tutors, Sima Ding could take no more, and left.

That same day, the boy also went missing.

Two days later, a fisherman brought up a child's body in his nets. It was the merchant's son. The merchant's wife suspected Sima Ding of killing her son and dumping his body in the river, so she went to lay a complaint with the magistrate and had him arrested. At his trial, Sima Ding had a confession tortured out of him, and he was sentenced to death.

At home, Ah Xiang wept bitterly. When she thought of the terrible disaster wreaked by the flood, and how considerate Sima Ding had been towards her, she could not bring herself to believe that he was a murderer. Without hesitation, she went to the *yamen* to complain of the miscarriage of justice. To her astonishment, she was herself arrested as an accessory and sent to prison – which was how she came to be in Guangzhou. After Sima Ding was executed, she lost all hope, and just wished to die herself. Then she developed an incessant pain in her abdomen and went into premature labour. The cries of her new-born baby brought her back from the brink. If she died, he would be left all alone, so she stayed alive, and that was how matters now stood...

The lamps in the interrogation room were giving off a bright-red glow, and the only sound was of the woman prisoner weeping. After her story had come tumbling out, she could hold back no longer, and abandoned herself to her grief. No one moved to comfort her, and the jailer's wife stayed silent. Song Ci sat murmuring to himself for a while and then asked: "Do you have any evidence to prove that your husband was not the killer?"

The woman shook her head weakly and said: "I just know he couldn't have done it."

Song Ci asked no more questions but just ordered the jailer's wife to take the prisoner back to her cell. After the two women had gone, Song Ci suddenly turned to Tong Gong and said: "You go, and take that sickly child back home."

Song left the jail down the cold stone staircase. Whether it was the woman's story that had left a lasting impression on him, or whether it was the fact that she had given birth to a child while in jail, he could not get her case out of his head. Although he had not been able to get a firm grasp on any of the other cases he had examined, with this woman prisoner he thought he could see a way through to a resolution of the matter.

When the party returned and Mistress Song saw the little three-year old boy, she was astonished, and her heart went out to the little creature.

"Qiu Juan, bring some hot water."

As she spoke, Mistress Song rolled up her sleeves and took out a washbasin. Qiu Juan soon came back with the hot water, and the two of them carefully gave the little child, whose body was covered in prison sores, a thorough and soothing wash.

When they had finished, one of the kitchen maids brought a set of children's clothes to change him into, and his appearance was transformed. Although his face was emaciated, his features were delicately formed, and his eyes large and limpid. Mistress Song ordered some food to be brought and watched as Qiu Juan fed him, and he guzzled what was given him until he was well and truly full.

From the time of his birth, never had he had such a soothing bath, nor worn such soft clothes, nor eaten such delicious food, nor slept on such a comfortable bed. As he stared in wonder at the large red lanterns, the like of which he had never seen before, the still nameless little boy drifted off into dreamland.

Very quietly, Song Ci told the maid, Ting'er, how to give him some medicine if he woke up, and only then did he return to their bedroom with Mistress Song. As he sat on the edge of the bed, Song Ci felt weary but did not want to sleep. Mistress Song urged him to get undressed.

"Husband, you should get some sleep."

Song Ci stretched out his arms so that she could take off his coat and said: "I want to visit every part of Guangdong Province."

His wife stopped what she was doing and fixed him with a stare.

"You have only just got here from Fujian."

Song Ci took her by the hand and said: "With so many suspect cases piled up, I have two starting points: one is cases that stem from malpractice or neglect of duty, and the second is cases caused by official corruption. If I want to bring them to court now, there will be a lot of resistance, and if I don't personally investigate wherever is necessary across the province, it will be very difficult to bring them to any kind of resolution."

His wife did not reply.

"What is more, everywhere throughout the land there are too many judicial officials with too little experience, and the slightest fault gets magnified a thousand times. And here I am, wielding the power of life and death in my court. Suppose I wrongly sentence someone to death – what comfort can there be for the soul of the unjustly executed?"

His wife sighed deeply – what could she say? Did she still not know him after all these years? Could she stop him once he was set on something? She took off his gown and settled him to sleep, then lay down beside him.

"Husband," she said, having been quiet for a while, "these are all old cases and any bodies will have rotted away long ago. What are you going to examine?"

Song Ci turned to look at his wife, thinking that this was, indeed, the crux of the matter.

"I will examine the bones."

3

# THE COTTON TREE FLOWERS BLOOM

The next morning, Song Ci gathered all the court recorders for a meeting. He knew that he could not handle such a huge body of unresolved cases by himself. The multitude of secretaries filed in, one by one, densely packing the main hall. Huo Xiong also brought the prison warden, who had been absent the night before, and when the man heard that the matter concerned the judicial commissioner's inspection of his jail that night, and he saw Song Ci before him, he fell to his knees to pay his respects.

"Where were you last night?" Song Ci asked.

The warden's heart skipped a beat at the question, and, thrown into confusion, he hesitated before answering: "Some friends invited me to watch a performance at the Boluo Temple fair."

There was a foreign enclave by the Boluo Temple where foreign businessmen lived, and at night it was brightly lit with lanterns and packed with noisy revellers. Merchants and dealers of all kinds could be found there. Song Ci didn't pause to ascertain whether the warden was telling the truth or not.

"Stand up!" Song Ci motioned to him to withdraw.

The warden hastily did so and joined the throng of other officials.

Song Ci looked at the assembled recorders for a long time, until the hall fell completely silent. Then, finally, he said: "Han Feizi[1] once said that, if the law is in disarray, then the country will be in disarray too. You are all beneficiaries of the public purse, and you should know that, if the prison system is not in order, then disorder among the people will ensue. And if the hearts of the people are lost, what state will the country be in? I give you all notice that I will show no mercy to anyone who fails in their duty, and trust that you will all do your utmost to live up to your office."

The hall stayed silent as they listened to Song Ci, who sat at his desk leafing through the register of names. They had all heard that the new commissioner had spent the previous day reading the case records, and the previous night visiting the jail, and none of them dared say a word in reply.

They received their new orders: from today, everyone was to set to work sorting through the caseload. Those responsible for a particular prefecture or district would take responsibility for that area's cases, and the work was to be clearly defined and apportioned. The officials all looked at one another, and although no one spoke, they were all clearly taken aback by the speed with which this new commissioner was moving.

Song Ci finished by saying: "Now, all of you sort yourselves out and get to work."

As one, they turned and left the hall.

Song Ci wanted to inspect the records of the case of Sima Ding's murder of the young boy in Dongguan County, and the recorders quickly hunted them out from the great pile in the storehouse.

As he was reading another scroll of court proceedings, his eye fell on the words 'The Four-Pearl Girl'.

'The Four-Pearl Girl'? A memory stirred in Song Ci of his prison visit the night before, and the man called Jiang Qing, who had said that the sister-in-law he was looking for had an extra nipple on each breast, making four in total. He read the case file carefully. It was a murder by affray that had taken place in that very city. Two customers in a brothel had been arguing over who should go with a girl known as 'The Four-Pearl Girl', and they had come to blows. Each had been injured, and it wasn't a particularly serious affair, except that, a few days later, one of them had suddenly died, and the other was arrested. There was insufficient evidence to proceed, and the case was left hanging.

Song Ci immediately sent for the prisoner in question and ascertained that 'The Four-Pearl Girl' did indeed have four nipples.

I wonder if it could be Jiang Qing's sister-in-law, Song Ci thought. He enquired about the location of the brothel, which was in a building on Guangta Street, and immediately sent Tong Gong and Huo Xiong there to find 'The Four-Pearl Girl'.

When the two of them reached the building and went in, a number of jasmine-garlanded girls appeared out of nowhere. The two men clapped their hands and called for the madam, who arrived magnificently dressed in dazzling silk brocade.

"I did have such a girl," she told them, "but her contract was bought out by someone who wanted her as his concubine."

How could they tell if she was telling the truth? The building had several floors, each divided into ten or more small bedrooms, with an equal number of girls on each floor. It was not an easy place to search.

Huo Xiong asked the madam for the name and address of the customer who had bought the girl, and Tong Gong fixed her with a glare and thundered: "Take us there!"

The madam led them to the customer's house, which turned out to be the establishment of a trader in pearls and precious stones. And there they did, indeed, find 'The Four-Pearl Girl'. Tong Gong and Hou Xiong flashed their badges of office at the merchant, who didn't dare obstruct them. They took 'The Four-Pearl Girl' back to the commissioner's office, where Song Ci summoned Jiang Qing to make the identification.

"Sister-in-law," he cried, "you have brought a whole load of worry down on my brother."

And, quite unexpectedly, that was how the case was eventually broken wide open.

After making enquiries, they soon tracked down the real killer of the girl from the wealthy family. On the day in question, the girl had also taken shelter from the rain in the ramshackle old temple, but because she had been alone, no one knew she had gone there. The culprit was a man who had made a business out of preying on pretty young women, and he was actually already in the city jail after being arrested the previous year on another charge. The man had forced Jiang Qing's sister-in-law to change clothes with the murdered woman and then taken her off to Guangzhou where he had sold her into prostitution. As a result, she was too ashamed even to think of trying to return home.

Thus, Jiang Qing became the first prisoner freed under Song Ci's rule as judicial commissioner. And after this, Song Ci's review of the remaining cases became even more detailed and even more scrupulous.

By the end of spring in the third year of the Jiaxi period, Song Ci had reviewed all of the outstanding cases and taken statements from all the prisoners. Among them he discovered some remand prisoners whose cases had not even been filed. After making careful enquiries, he immediately set free those against whom he was sure there was no case to be made, thereby releasing eighty or more prisoners at a stroke and consequently greatly improving prison conditions.

With regard to established cases where the suit was uncertain, along with those that were proving otherwise problematic, Song Ci either instructed the original officer to reinvestigate, or chose another officer to take over. For all of these cases he set a deadline by which they had to be resolved. And throughout this time, every day, express messengers were carrying Song's official rulings to all the prefectures.

When it was all done, Song Ci decided it was time to leave Guangzhou and make a tour of inspection of the interior. At the age of fifty-three, taking Tong Gong, Huo Xiong and a troop of men and horses with him, and with some of the heavier case files loaded onto a wagon, Song Ci took to the road.

After leaving the city by the south gate, Song Ci lodged that first night in Zhuangtou in the southern outskirts of Guangzhou. There was a hillside in the village known as Jasmine Flower Slope. The name dated from the time of the secession of the Southern Han dynasty (917-971 CE), when all the court ladies had worn garlands of jasmine flowers. When they died, many of them were buried on the hillside by Zhuangtou, and, by royal order, a veritable forest of jasmine was planted all around the area, which is how the hillside got its name. And after that, the farmers of the village began to grow jasmine for a living: 'Picked by lamplight, on sale the next morning' was how they described their produce in the city. On the first day of his tour, Song Ci resolved two puzzling cases, one of which involved a girl who sold jasmine flowers.

The party left the village and headed southeast towards Dongguan County.

Along the roadsides they travelled that late spring, the cotton trees were still in bloom, their branches full of red flowers like points of fire. Song Ci sat on the wagon looking at the tall, slender trees pushing up into the sky, always vying with the other trees to be the tallest, and found it a most heart-warming sight.

They travelled fast and light, and, within a day, Dongguan County appeared before them. When they arrived, Song Ci did not visit the county *yamen*, but went straight to the compound of a merchant of Dongguan by the name of Chi Gan.

"Master! Master!" The old gatekeeper ran into the compound, shouting as he went. "The judicial commissioner has arrived... he is at the gates."

Chi Gan, a man of forty-something, was in his inner courtyard, watering flowers, when he heard the gatekeeper's cries. Not sure whether he had heard aright, he put down his watering can and came out to ask: "What are you shouting about?"

"The judicial commissioner is about to enter the great court."

"Whose great court?"

"Our great court!"

Chi Gan was a well-connected man, but never before had the judicial commissioner himself come visiting, so he hurried out to welcome him.

"You are Landlord Chi?" Song Ci asked.

"I am indeed. Your Honour has had a long journey, and I apologise for my lack of manners in not knowing of your coming."

Landlord Chi clasped his hands in greeting and led Song Ci into the guest hall.

Song Ci seated himself in the hall, and, without waiting for orders, the household staff brought him some of the very best quality pressed Dragon Wind tea, and platters of seasonal fresh fruit and delicate pastries. Song Ci looked at the teapots and cups and saw that they were black-and-white glazed ware from the Jizhou kiln in Jiangxi. The platters contained lychees, honey and ginger beans, 'long-life turtle' buns, tangerines, milk-white pears and other rare delicacies that a normal household would not be able to produce at such short notice. He realised that this was a merchant's household such as might seldom be found in the south of China in these troubled times.

"Landlord Chi," Song Ci went straight to the point, "I understand that, in the first year of the Duanping period, your son died."

"Ah!" Landlord Chi stopped smiling when he heard these words, and the rims of his eyes seemed a little red. "That was a long time ago!"

"It was five years ago," Song Ci said. "Do you still remember the circumstances surrounding the case?"

"I do."

"Please explain them carefully to me."

"It happened this way. Sima Ding originally..." Landlord Chi's face was now full of pain and sorrow, and he was puzzled as to why the judicial commissioner should suddenly be raising these old events now. There must be something unusual going on. His merchant's prudence asserted itself as he spoke.

"Slow down." Song Ci heard the faintest rustling noise behind a screen and caught a glimpse of women's skirts. He realised Landlord Chi's womenfolk must be listening there, and he gestured at the merchant. "Your wife must also remember these events very clearly, so please ask her to come out and help us get to the bottom of them."

"She..."

"I'm sure you can't remember every detail. She will be able to fill in the gaps."

"Ah! Very well," said Landlord Chi, as he turned to one of his old retainers. "Go and fetch my wife."

The retainer was quick-witted and knew that his mistress was behind the screen, but he set off in an entirely different direction towards the inner courtyard. Song Ci also maintained this fiction and, as he asked the merchant to continue, listened for any differences between what the man said and what the women prisoner had told him. After a while, the old retainer reappeared from behind the screen with the merchant's wife. She was a woman of more than thirty, wearing pearls, jade and other precious stones. When she saw Song Ci, she bowed and greeted him formally.

"Please sit down and listen," Song Ci said.

Landlord Chi continued his careful account, and Song Ci occasionally interrupted with a question for him and his wife. When he had asked all that needed to be asked, he stood up and said: "Take me to see the stretch of river at the bottom of your back garden."

"As you request, Your Honour," Landlord Chi replied.

He led them through the residence to the rear garden, which was full of exotic flowers and grasses, beautiful to behold and delightfully scented. A green-tiled building stood hidden from view among the reds and greens of the plants. Over its door hung a sign that read 'The Hall of a Hundred Recitations'.

"Is that a place for reading?" Song Ci asked.

"It is. It's also where Sima Ding and his wife used to live."

When they went out of the garden gate they came to the river, which could be reached by a small path of dark green stones. Some drops of water were visible on the path, as though someone had just passed by carrying a bucket. It was no more than a hundred paces down to the river bank. The river was quite wide at this point, and the water by the banks was a greenish-yellow colour, rippling and eddying into miniature whirlpools. The banks themselves were thick with unidentifiable southern bushes and shrubs, as well as a twining mass of vines, kudzu and other creepers. There were also several willow trees, their twisted branches spilling over the surface of the river. Fine river grasses grew out of the water along the banks, lying flat along the surface as they were taken by the current. All this vegetation shaded the waters, making it a rather gloomy spot, with just enough light to see that the river flowed quite swiftly at this point, neither deep nor shallow; the yellow sand of the river bed was just visible too. Some sets of steps led down to the water, where there were rocks used for washing clothes, and this was clearly the laundry spot for the manservants and maidservants of the household. Descending the steps, Song Ci could see that, close by, up and down the river banks, there were similar washing stones that would have made it a popular spot for others to fetch water to do their own laundry. Song Ci took all this in and was about to speak, when the merchant's wife got in first: "Your Honour, you can see that any body thrown in the water here would soon get swept away."

"And that is why there is no eyewitness testimony in the case?" Song Ci turned to look at the merchant's wife.

"Why would a murderer let himself be seen?" she rejoined quickly.

"And, in any case, Sima Ding confessed in court," the merchant added.

"Nevertheless, this is a place where people come every day to fetch water for their laundry. How is it that you had no suspicion that Sima Ding might have tricked your son into coming down here and then pushed him into the river to drown?" Song Ci asked.

"It wasn't possible," the merchant replied.

"What do you mean, not possible?"

"After his tutor beat him, my son ran away whenever he saw him. And then, in addition, he got his own back, and hit the tutor over the head with a rock. After that, it's not possible that the tutor could have lured him down here."

"Is that what you think too?" Song Ci asked the merchant's wife.

"I think that must be so," she replied.

"In that case, was there anything stuck in your son's throat when he was brought out of the river in the fisherman's nets?"

"No, there wasn't," the merchant said.

"A dead person can't swallow, so the throat would be clear," the merchant's wife added.

"Could Sima Ding have covered your son's mouth before throwing him, alive, into the water?"

The merchant thought about this, then shook his head: "Teacher Sima wasn't a fool. My son disappeared before noon, and if he had been pushed into the river alive in the morning, and by some chance survived and been rescued, then Teacher Sima couldn't have avoided being implicated."

Song Ci listened and nodded. He remained by the river inspecting the scene and asked some more questions, until at last he turned to the merchant and his wife and said: "Very good. The two of you come with me now to the county *yamen*."

The merchant and his wife were greatly alarmed, and the woman blurted out: "Your Honour, why do you want us to go there?"

Song Ci didn't reply and was already on his way along the stone path towards the gate of the merchant's rear courtyard. The merchant and his wife didn't dare ask again, and they just hurried after him, close behind.

# 4

# THE EXHUMATION AND INSPECTION OF BONES

The carriage and horses halted outside the county *yamen*, and the porter went flying inside to report their arrival. The Dongguan county magistrate came hurrying out in a state of some alarm.

"I did not know Your Honour was in Dongguan – otherwise I would have welcomed you properly."

"Are you Lu Teng?"

"I am, Your Honour."

Lu Teng was the presiding judge at Sima Ding's trial earlier in the year. On entering the *yamen*, Song Ci instructed Chi Gan and his wife to wait at the bottom of the steps, while he and Magistrate Lu went into the main hall.

After they had sat down, Song Ci asked: "Last month, I rejected your assessment of the case you tried concerning Sima Ding's murder of the young boy and his dumping the body in the river. If you were to review it now, what would be your conclusion?"

"Your Honour, I have already reviewed it."

"Is it in the records?"

"It is," said Lu Teng, who then turned to his secretary and ordered him go and get the records.

The secretary quickly fetched the relevant scrolls and handed them to Song Ci, who took them and fell silent. He read… and read… and read… and then threw them down in disgust.

"This is just a copy of the case records. Where is the review?"

Lu Teng was stunned. He had assumed that the new judicial commissioner's review of cases was just a formality, going through the motions. He had never expected that Song Ci would thoroughly inspect the original case records.

"When you prepare a case record, you must carefully sort through and record the details, be precise on the nature of the accusation being levelled and ensure the testimony is consistent. Only then can a proper verdict be reached. Tell me how it is that the findings about the boy's body in the autopsy record are so vague and imprecise?"

"When the boy's body was dredged up from the river, it was already swollen and decomposing. There was no way to carry out an autopsy."

"What do you mean, no way to carry out an autopsy? No matter how decomposed a body is, the fingernails are still there, and so is the hair."

Magistrate Lu stared at him wordlessly. He couldn't comprehend what hair and fingernails could have to do with this case.

"Since you had 'no way of carrying out an autopsy', how were you able to determine that Sima Ding strangled the boy before putting the body into the river?"

"There were no knife wounds or cudgel marks on the body, so I thought it must... it must be that he was strangled."

"Must be?"

"The accused also confessed to it."

Song Ci was very perturbed that the case could have been decided like this. He continued: "Now, the best thing we can do is go and examine the corpse."

"Now?" Magistrate Lu was even more at a loss.


In late spring in the south, the midday sun is scorching hot and so fierce it makes the land steam. With the merchant and his wife leading the way, Song Ci took Magistrate Lu, the current coroner and the fisherman in whose nets the body had been brought up, out of the south gate towards the ancestral tombs of the merchant's family.

Landlord Chi and his wife were in a state of considerable mental turmoil as they went along. His eyes were red-rimmed, and his wife was actually weeping. When they heard that the judicial commissioner wanted to exhume their son and examine his bones, they had knelt in front of Song Ci and pleaded: "Your Honour, the dead find peace in the ground. My insignificant son has been buried for a number of years now, and if his bones are disinterred now, it would grieve me as a father to disturb his repose."

"Re-opening a coffin to determine the cause of death is a heavy responsibility for the living," Song Ci said severely. "Sima Ding is dead and his wife has been falsely implicated in the case. How could we not exhume your son to determine the cause of death?"

Chi Gan and his wife did not dare say anything in reply, but set about gathering fruit and other sweetmeats, incense sticks and wine with which to make the necessary offerings. Then they led the way to the graves.

The Chi family tombs were situated on a ridge called Turtle Hill in the eastern suburbs, surrounded by lush vegetation. When the party reached the site, the gravekeeper hurried off to boil water for tea, and soldiers began to dig up the grave. Huo Xiong lit a pewter brazier beside the mound. The breeze blowing through the grove of trees helped the flames take quickly, and he set a bowl of vinegar to heat on the brazier and added salted dried plums. The liquid soon came to the boil. Vinegar fumes filled the air and were carried on the breeze, making all the bystanders nauseous.

Quite soon, the grave was opened to reveal a shiny wooden coffin made of *nanmu*.[1] Because the coffin had been painted with nine layers of the finest southern lacquer, the tree roots had been deflected from it, and it was still completely intact. Huo Xiong inspected the coffin nails closely. They, too, had been coated with lacquer and were bright and shiny, without a scratch. It was evident they had not been tampered with. He swept the earth off the coffin lid, levered up the nails and carefully opened the coffin. A puff of white vapour rose from the interior. Huo Xiong filled his mouth with clear spirit and sprayed several mouthfuls over the coffin. Finally, he put a 'stench-dispelling pellet' in his mouth and began to examine the corpse.

The body was already rotted away but the skeleton was complete, When the boy's body had been placed in the coffin, he would have lain there with his fingernails clipped, his body bathed and his hair washed; but now, on this re-examination, only his bare bones were visible.

There was a powerful smell of decomposition, which made all the onlookers hold their noses and brought tears to the eyes of the merchant and his wife. His expression unchanged, Huo Xiong began to remove the skeleton, stopping occasionally to soak a piece of white gauze in the boiling vinegar mixture on the brazier and place it over the bones, wiping them clean. Continuing in this fashion, he placed the bones on a white porcelain platter and presented it to Song Ci, a perfectly white human skeleton, stripped of all fat and other residue.

Song Ci took the platter and put it on a large, dark-green rock beside the mound. Huo Xiong brought a slender-necked, round-bodied porcelain bottle, full of water, and handed it to his master. Song Ci took the bottle and then said to Magistrate Lu and Chi Gan and his wife: "Come over here, all of you."

None of them dared hesitate, and they hurried over.

"Look closely."

With these words, Song Ci took the porcelain bottle and began carefully to pour the water it contained into a small fissure at the acupuncture point on the forehead of the skull. The water began to trickle out of the seven apertures and it was at this moment that the truth of the case was revealed. As the water flowed out of the nasal cavities, little by little, it brought with it some fine grains of earth and sand, which showed up quite clearly against the white of the porcelain platter.

"Can you all see that?" Song Ci asked.

They stared dumbly, not knowing what to say.

Song Ci put down the slender-necked bottle and turned decisively to Magistrate Lu: "This child was most certainly not thrown in the river after he had been killed. Someone who has been put in the water after death would not exhibit sand and earth in their skull. Only if they were alive and descended to the riverbed, stirring up sediment, could they inhale these particles through their nose. Once they have been inhaled, there is no way of expelling them, and even after many years, when the brain matter and other contents of the skull have decomposed, the sand and earth will not be affected. Thus, it is completely impossible to maintain the verdict that Sima Ding strangled the boy and then dumped his body in the river."

Magistrate Lu was thrown into a state of consternation. Not just to have made a faulty judgment, but actually to have executed an innocent man. The consequences were quite plain to him. Chi Gan and his wife were equally devastated. He was too dumbfounded to speak, but she timidly asked: "Then... how did my son die?"

"Since your son was not killed by Sima Ding, and his body put in the river, nor could he have been pushed in by anyone else, there is only one possibility. After he left his tutor, with no one supervising him, he ran down to the river at the bottom of your garden to play in the water. He slipped and fell in, and drowned. It was an accident."

All the assembled aides, secretaries, soldiers and *yamen* staff, even the coroner and the fisherman, were holding their breath, listening in rapt attention. It was as though the heavens had opened and a divine voice had spoken. All of them were astounded by Song Ci's supernatural perspicacity. Within half a day of his arrival in Dongguan, in the space of a morning, Song Ci had revealed the truth of a case that had apparently been settled so many years before. And he had done it with apparent ease, without any fuss.

That night, Song Ci stayed in the Dongguan *yamen*. Once he had settled all the business before him, he sat, uneasy of mind, in the lamplight, with the draft of a document in his hand. He was recalling the great flood that had happened here all those years ago. He was thinking of a young man called Sima Ding, who had rescued a girl called Ah Xiang from the waters and looked after her day and night. He remembered that Sima Ding was a failed candidate in the imperial examinations, and he thought back to how he himself had twice failed in the same examinations... perhaps, given how young he was, Sima Ding might have persisted in his attempts to become an official, and perhaps the day might have come when he could have done great service to the nation and its people. But he was dead, an innocent man executed.

He thought of the prison: its manacles and leg irons, and its foul smell. He remembered the cobweb-covered lampstand with its three lamps, and thought of the young girl who had ripped her dress while kneeling in front of him, and how she had covered her exposed shoulder with her hand. He thought of her son, barely three years old, who had spent all his short life locked up in prison and was only just able to walk. Then he thought of the next day, when he would send this document he held, by express messenger, to the judicial commissioner's office, with the order it contained for his aides to go immediately and release that young girl. And he thought of the two of them, mother and son, stepping out into the sunshine to start a new life... a glow of satisfaction began to spread through him.

He got up and went to stand by the window. It was a beautiful night outside, the stars twinkling in the sky, and a half-moon just beginning to rise over the flying eaves of a building in the front courtyard, illuminating the lush plants and vibrant flowers of the garden. Guangdong was a province of many flowers, and he breathed in the windborne scents of jasmine, bay, white orchid and Chinese perfume plant, all mixed together into an indescribable fragrance. For a long time, he stood there gazing into the limitless night sky. From somewhere, a nightingale began to sing softly among the flowers, as if out of a desire to be not found wanting on such a beautiful night. As he listened to its song, clear and repetitive, suddenly he found himself thinking of his own daughter, Qi'er...

"Qi'er..." he called out softly to himself. He remembered the night she had died, just such a beautiful night as this. He remembered how she seemed to have been able to understand the conversations of the insects and to catch the subtle breathing of the flowers. He remembered every little detail of that night. And no matter where he was, he would always remember his daughter's interpretation of that line of Su Dongpo's: "Life is like a dream." It was true – human life is soon over, and human life is very sad. The next day, they were going to be on their way, and the journey was long. But there were so many things he was determined to accomplish. The wheels of his carriage would wear ruts in all the roads of the south. He had so many things to attend to…

The moon had risen and thunder rumbled in the distance. As the wind got up, Song Ci felt sick at heart, but he had no desire to sleep.

"Master, you should get some rest."

It was Tong Gong who spoke. A while ago, Tong Gong and Huo Xiong had finished their martial arts practice, bathed and then come inside. On every journey they made, they always slept in the same room as Song Ci.

"You go to bed first."

Neither man moved.

# CHAPTER XIV

## WHEEL TRACKS (1239)

The prisoners of Guangzhou came from all over the province, and Song Ci did not simply stay in the judicial commissioner's office handling their cases; history records his tour of inspection to the interior, or, as it is also described, 'his wheel tracks stopped wherever there was injustice'. He saw the scope of his responsibilities as extending to the most hazardous places and the poorest of villages, and he carried out inspections in every one. This is not some fiction added for dramatic effect. There is no record of such a high-ranking official acting in this way in the thirteenth century in any other country, so he may truly be called a model judge for all mankind, and the grandfather of forensic medicine. History also records that he settled many hundreds of long-delayed and troublesome cases. In doing this, he did not rely wholly on his investigative skills. He believed that one of the causes of the problem was the way officials would simply arrest the first person on whom suspicion fell. He therefore insisted that, if no firm proof of guilt could be found against a suspect, then that suspect should be released forthwith. In this way, he established the golden principle of the presumption of innocence.

# 1

## THE TOMB IN THE WELL

Song Ci left Dongguan and continued on his travels.

The vivid red flowers of the poinciana trees took over from the cottonwoods, announcing the arrival of summer in Guangdong. The long leaves of the boat orchids, and the broad leaves of the crepe myrtle flirted with the summer breeze. The temperature rose with the sun, and the cartwheels threw up dust devils on the road.

They visited noisy cities and bustling towns, shady lanes and secluded alleys, thatched cottages and woodcutter's hovels. They visited ancient cantons and huge counties, and passed through many remote and desolate places. Wherever they stopped, Song Ci instituted far-reaching enquiries and re-examined cases on the spot; those that couldn't be decided without further examination were minutely investigated; and in cases where the body had rotted away, they painstakingly exhumed the bones to look for conclusive proof. On the road, they braved wind and rain, and lodged in Confucian temples. They cracked many cases and arrived at many truths. All the time, Song Ci continued to send a record of the innocent men he released back to Guangzhou and ordered the local officials to send any guilty prisoners, under guard, to the prison at Guangzhou.

As Guangzhou sank further into the distance, they stopped travelling east and turned towards the north.

One day, they set out for Zhenyang to re-examine the case of a woman who had been murdered there. On the night when Song Ci had been inspecting the prison in Guangzhou, one man had cried out: "I only had a row with my wife. I didn't kill her…"

It was this case that Song Ci was going to re-examine.

Before he left Guangzhou, Song Ci had made a careful study of this case, reading and re-reading the records. From them it was clear to him that not only were there several areas of uncertainty, but also that the magistrates in Zhenyang and Yingde were men of firm opinions. The district magistrate in Zhenyang had recorded that he found a precedent in a case noted by the distinguished official of the Northern Song, Shen Kuo, in his work *Dream Pool Essays*. This particularly piqued Song Ci's interest.

A fork in the road lay ahead, and the horses and carriages headed towards the main road where there stood a boundary stone marked 'Zhenyang'. Inside his carriage, Song Ci once again took out the record of the case, even though, by now, he was familiar with every detail.

The woman had died in a well in front of her house. Another person had already died in the same well, so it was no longer used, and its mouth had been covered with a stone slab. One day, a neighbour noticed that the slab was sitting beside the well, and when he poked his head in to have a look, he was startled to see a woman's shoe, floating on the surface of the water at the bottom. He raised the alarm, and the woman's husband came running out. In consternation, he cried out that it belonged to his wife. They dredged the well and did indeed bring up a body, which, in turn, proved to be that of the man's wife.

"The shoe was not remarkable in any way, being of a kind worn by many women of the area. So how did the husband know it was his wife's body, before he had even seen it?"

That was the opinion of the district magistrate in Zhenyang. But Song Ci felt that the magistrate had not fully considered all possibilities. The husband, presumably, already knew his wife was missing, so when he heard there was a body in the well and saw a woman's shoe, he could quite easily have drawn this conclusion.

Of course, this was not all that the magistrate had relied on to reach his verdict of guilty of murder. When the body was brought up from the well, it was seen that there was a knife wound on its forehead, on which blood was still evident. In addition, the couple had a tempestuous relationship, and the woman's father strongly suspected the husband of killing his wife and throwing her down the well. He made a report to this effect to the authorities. The official examiner discovered another wound on the head where a blade had hacked right down to the bone, which he deemed sufficient evidence to pronounce that this was indeed a murder. Under interrogation in court, the prisoner confessed.

But when the case was referred up to the authorities in Yingde, the man retracted his confession, which he said had been beaten out of him.

"Since it is quite clear a knife was used to kill her, as the wound is there to be seen, and since she was then put down the well, once the body was brought up, if he was guilty, why did he not confess voluntarily and avoid torture? If he had wanted to make it look like suicide, why use a knife? He could simply have pushed her down the well alive and been done with it." This was the opinion of the county magistrate at Yingde, and, on this basis, he referred the case back down for retrial.

Thereafter, the magistrate at Zhenyang took no heed of his superior's doubts and changed his own opinion. He now said: "It was a disused well, covered by a stone slab and no one usually went there, so it would have been difficult to catch her unawares. If he used force, and his victim was still alive, she would have struggled and called out. Moreover, the accused had to remove the stone slab, which would have been no easy feat. It is unlikely that the accused would have considered such a course of action. The wounds to the top of the head and forehead must have been made when she was put down the well after death. There can be no other explanation."

The Zhenyang magistrate was blunt in his written opinion, and with it, he sent the case back to the superior court.

The county magistrate at Yingde wrote a fresh opinion: "If she was gagged and bound, and then taken to the well, then it most surely would have been possible. Thus, the greater likelihood is that she was not dead before she was put in the well."

However, this did not explain the bloody wounds on the head. Moreover, in the case report sent up by the Zhenyang magistrate, he referred to a similar case recorded by Shen Kuo and recommended that it be consulted. The magistrate at Yingde considered all this from every angle, without being able to come to a final decision.

Song Ci's eye fell on the case recorded by Shen Kuo. When the Tang dynasty prime minister, Zhang Jiuling, was magistrate at Runzhou, there was a woman whose husband had left home and not come back for several days. News came that a body had been found in a well on the local tea plantation, and the woman went to look, wailing: "It's my husband." Thereupon, the local official was summoned. The court staff gathered together some of the woman's neighbours and took them to the well to find out whether or not it was her husband. They all said the well was too deep to tell who it was without bringing up the body.

Zhang wrote: "If none of the others were able to identify him, how did the woman alone know it was her husband?"

In fact, when the woman was arrested and handed over to the relevant authorities to be taken into custody, it was revealed that it was her lover who had murdered her husband, and that she herself had been party to the plot.

After he had read the case, Song Ci sighed deeply. He thought to himself that the Zhenyang magistrate must be a very well-read man for him to make reference to this case. The pity was that, in taking his lead from it, he had been prevented from examining all the other possibilities. Of course, the main problem was that the autopsy was cursory and the search incomplete.

"At the very least, they should have dragged the bottom of the well."

At the time, the senior magistrate at Yingde considered the case too problematic, and he had not dared reach a verdict. Instead, he had sent the whole matter up to the provincial authorities in Guangzhou. Song Ci's predecessor as judicial commissioner had withheld judgment too, so, by this time, the case had been left hanging for four years. If it was to be settled now, the most reliable evidence was going to come from examining the skeletal remains.

They continued on their way to Zhenyang. Song Ci was in no rush to resolve the case. The most important thing he wanted to do now was to carry out the autopsy to obtain some evidence. Both the district magistrate at Zhenyang, and the county magistrate at Yingde, had already moved on to other posts, so, on reaching Zhenyang, Song Ci ordered the current incumbent and his assistants to join him in the defendant's village to inspect the well. However, it turned out that it was no longer disused, as, several years previously, the villagers had cleaned it out and begun drawing water from it again. This meant there was now no point in dredging it for evidence. Song Ci turned to the local representative and asked him about the circumstances of the cleaning of the well. Then he went to the woman's grave. At the same time as exhuming the body, he ordered that a pit be dug beside the grave, five *chi* long, three *chi* across and two *chi* deep, and a charcoal fire be laid in it. It wasn't long before the grave was opened and the coffin brought up.

As soon as Huo Xiong opened the coffin, he said: "Master, both the dead woman's hands are curled into fists."

"Ha!" said Song Ci, taking a look for himself. "Thread the bones back together."

This was very painstaking work. Tong Gong cut down a medium-sized bamboo stick and broke it down into splinters the thickness of wire. Huo Xiong washed the bones in diluted wine and then threaded each one in turn with the bamboo splinters, finally assembling them on a reed mat. By this time, the charcoal pit was glowing red, and Song Ci ordered it to be extinguished. Then he poured two catties of good wine and five catties of vinegar onto the embers and placed the bones into the pit amid the steam. He covered the pit with a straw mattress. This is a process known as 'steaming the bones'. The whole morning passed before Song Ci ordered Huo Xiong to remove the mattress and, with Tong Gong's help, to remove the bones and lay them out flat. All was now ready for the autopsy.

On inspection, the most noticeable feature was a hole in the skull in the shape of a truncated arc. But what implement could have caused it?

"It can't have been a knife," said the local magistrate.

"Could it have been a woodsman's hatchet with a curved head?" asked the county deputy.

Song Ci didn't reply but just said to Huo Xiong: "Get the umbrella."

Huo Xiong took out a red oil-paper umbrella specially brought for the autopsy, and held it over the bones. The sun was hanging large in the sky and Song Ci looked up at it through the umbrella. He held up all the bones in turn and examined them closely. It was at this point that the cause of death was revealed to him. He stood up and said to the magistrate and the county deputy: "Come over here, you two, and take a look."

The two men approached the bones and inspected them. Other than examining the arc-shaped hole in the skull, they didn't seem to see anything else of note. They looked at each other questioningly, not knowing what it was Song Ci wanted them to see.

"There are very faint traces of blood along the edges of the wound. Can you see?" Song Ci said.

The two men looked again, and there, indeed, were the faint traces of blood. But what did it mean? They were baffled, and said, one after the other: "Yes, there are traces of blood."

"There are, indeed."

"They are *very faint* traces," Song Ci said, with emphasis.

The two men still didn't say anything. Song Ci thought for a moment and then patiently explained the findings of the autopsy.

"In all judicial proceedings, there is nothing more serious than the crime of murder, and in dealing with this crime, the most important thing is to establish the circumstances at the very beginning of the affair. In doing this, nothing is more crucial than detailed examination. This requires what is known as 'profound consideration and clear differentiation'. Initially, careful examination revealed the arc-shaped wound but could not distinguish it from a knife cut. Now we have the skeleton out of the well, and since we know that it was put in there head first, when it comes to determining the cause of the cut on the face, we should examine the well itself, to see if there is broken pottery in it. There is nothing surprising in this – if someone falls down a well while still alive, in their struggles they could quite easily cut themselves on a shard of pottery or a sharp stone. Alternatively, they might simply have banged their head against a brick.

"In this case we know that the woman was not killed first and then put down the well, because if an injury to the skull occurs when the victim is still alive, evidence of blood-flow will show in the interior surfaces of the bone either side of the wound. These traces of blood were rendered faint by the action of the water, but their existence show that the victim was alive when she went down the well. She banged her head on something sharp, injuring her head and making it bleed. Although the blood was considerably diluted by the water, the traces are still there. The neighbours have told us that the well is very deep, and when it was being cleaned and dredged to be put back into use, they brought up a lot of broken pottery. Thus, there can only be one conclusion in this case – after quarrelling with her husband, the woman threw herself down the well."

When Song Ci finished speaking, the magistrate and the others just stood there dumbly, except for the young county deputy, who had a lively intellect. After a brief hesitation, he asked: "Can we exclude the possibility that she was killed indoors and then put down the well?"

"That is a good question," Song Ci said, looking attentively at the deputy. "But what you don't know is that blood congeals after death, so if a dead body is put down a well, and bangs its head against something sharp, it will still cause a wound, but there will be no traces of blood."

"In that case, can we also exclude the possibility that she was dragged by force to the side of the well and then thrown down it alive?" the deputy asked again.

"If she was dragged to the well," Song Ci replied, "she would surely have struggled violently, and the blood vessels would have left a web of red lines on the bones, especially on the arms. With this skeleton, the torso and four limbs are all intact, and there are no such marks. Moreover, in general, if someone is pushed down a well alive, their eyes and their hands remain open. If they throw themselves in, then their eyes and hands clench shut. Of course, we have not been able to examine the eyes in this case, but you can clearly see from the skeleton that she died with her hands bunched into fists."

2

# THE TECHNOLOGY OF MURDER

Time passed smoothly, and the chrysanthemums, peach trees and cotton rose hibiscus burst into bud. Summer was almost over and autumn would soon be upon them. Song Ci had journeyed the length of the northern road and now turned westwards.

Although Song Ci was constantly on the move, and busy every day, he had been away from home for so long that, inevitably, his thoughts turned to his wife, particularly as he slaved over his work until his bones ached on those long, hot days. He knew that his wife, too, would be thinking of him, worrying over his safety. It occurred to him that Yulan had not had many easy days in their time together as man and wife, and that, especially since Qi'er's passing, she seemed to have aged greatly.

Whether travelling along the main roads and highways, or making excursions into wilder country, Song Ci's tour of inspection had not been easy. They had resolved old cases, taken on new ones, arrested the real offenders in some, tracked down fugitives in others, and sometimes even had to deal with desperate criminals who resisted arrest. On the border between Wuzhou and Fengzhou in the area of Yuanjushan, they had taken shelter from the rain and spent the night in an old temple. There, they were attacked by a criminal gang they had been on their way to apprehend. In the course of that rain-sodden fight, two of their soldiers were killed. And if it had not been for Song Ci's own small skill in martial arts, and the combined protection of Tong Gong and Huo Xiong, the bandits might well have achieved their primary aim of, if not killing him, at least wounding him badly. As it was, however, he escaped unscathed and was able to bring the case against the bandits to a successful conclusion. Subsequently, he arranged the transfer of all the district's patrolmen, and all its soldiers, officers and men alike. Yet there were still more long-standing cases to be resolved and still more skeletons to be autopsied.

"Master, we previously knew that the bones of poisoned people turn greenish-black."

"But we now also know that, if a body is buried wearing green clothes, as it rots, its bones may turn the same colour."

"But in that case, the colour is only on the surface, and it doesn't show on the interior if the bone is cut."

No matter who raised the subject and who interjected, Song Ci, Tong Gong and Huo Xiong all delighted in discussing every minute detail of a new piece of knowledge.

They discovered that bones that had been boiled in vinegar should be kept away from tin, since, once they came into contact with that metal, they turned black and this made any wounds on them hard to distinguish. They also discovered that, in cases of death by beating, if there was no trauma to the bone, the flesh would stick to the bones; it could not be washed off with water, but only scraped off with a fingernail. Equally, if a body showed no outward sign of injury, but, on examination, trauma to the bone was evident, in such cases the bones often exhibited fine hairline cracks that were only visible under careful examination.

In Zhaoqing Prefecture, they met an old coroner from whom they learned a new, simple way of examining bones.

"The trick is to grind up some good quality ink and smear it on the bone," the old man explained. "Once it is dry, wash it off. If there is no trauma to the bone, the ink won't penetrate and will be completely washed away. If there is any trauma, the ink will get into it, and it won't be washed off but will stay behind, marking the wound site."

This information was invaluable to Song Ci, and he rewarded the man with a generous gift of silver.

"If you inspect a broken bone closely," the old man went on, "you will find that there are little bony spikes. Moreover, on one side of the break they face inwards, and on the other, outwards. The inward-pointing spikes mark the point of impact."

They encountered another case in which the body had been stolen and some of the bones substituted. They had to learn how to distinguish male bones from female, and even from animal ones, and they were able to accurately assemble a complete skeleton from any mixed-up pile of bones, whether broken or intact.

"When it comes to the dark bruising that appears on bones, if it is elongated in shape, it was caused by an object. If it is round, it was a fist – a big lump is caused by a head-butt, and a smaller one by a kick." This conclusion was drawn by Song Ci from the study of many examples...

"Own up now," Song Ci said to a prisoner who had been locked up after resisting arrest. "What did you use to dye the bone so cunningly that it could almost be taken for a real wound?"

The prisoner did not even open his eyes.

"Speak up!"

"..."

"Speak!"

The man's lips trembled and then he spoke: "I'm going to die soon anyway, and I won't tell you."

One of the man's co-defendants had admitted staining the bones just before he died, but that man, unfortunately, was now dead, and if the current prisoner also died without telling, then Song Ci might never discover the technique they used. So he took hold of the man, whose body was a mass of bleeding wounds, with both hands and said: "I will treat your injuries and save your life if you speak."

"Are you telling the truth?" said the prisoner, opening his eyes.

"I have never gone back on my word!"

"We used a poisonous plant."

"Which poisonous plant?"

"It's called *jiancao*."

"You are familiar with it?"

"I am."

"Will you teach me?"

"Only if you keep your word."

"Untie him, and fetch medicines for his wounds."

Song Ci did indeed keep his word, even though the prisoner had been convicted of a capital offence. Thus, not only did he learn about the use of *jiancao*, he also discovered a means of making the tricky differentiation between real and faked injuries to bones. This involved using some fresh cotton wadding to wipe over the bone: if there was genuine trauma, then fine strands of the cotton would get snagged on it; if not, even if there was black marking to the bone, you could be sure there was no actual trauma. Yet another method was to pour oil onto the bone and watch carefully how it behaved. If there was any damage to the bone, the flow of the oil would be stopped by it; if it flowed cleanly, without obstruction, then there was no trauma.

"Hah! The ancients concentrated much of their research into bones on identifying whether poison was present or not. I have extended knowledge in this field considerably!"

Song Ci took no little pride in this thought. It was true, moreover, that, over time, he had extended his research into deaths by assassination, illness, immolation, drowning, scalding, falling, crushing, smothering, lightning strike, snake-bite, trampling by horses, hanging... there was nothing he could not investigate.

Throughout history, the most difficult cases to resolve had been those that had been left pending over periods of years. The most intractable problem with such cases was the challenge of examining bodies that had rotted away. But for Song Ci, this was no longer an obstacle. So were there, in fact, any common types of case that could still nonplus him?

These three months on the road have been worth ten years of reading records, Song Ci thought to himself.

For a man such as Song Ci, the unresolved cases of Guangzhou had truly opened up a new world: a veritable wonderland. And as he galloped, imperturbably, across this fine new landscape, Song Ci often found himself entering fields of knowledge into which the ancients had never ventured.

To see things that have never been seen before and to do things that have never been done before! To travel the highways preventing cruelty, and righting injustice! What a noble achievement that is.

Guangzhou was getting nearer, and their tour of inspection was fast drawing to a close. Song Ci was sitting in his sedan chair and he ordered the bearer to lift the curtain so that he could take a look around. He thought to himself that this time, on his return, he must make sure to tell his wife all the extraordinary things he had seen and heard.

3

# THE BRUSH AND INK LADY

"Husband, be quiet a moment. There's something I want to tell you."

After Song Ci had bathed, his wife had laid out a fresh gown for him and was helping him into it, as she tried to halt the words that had been tumbling out of him ever since his arrival.

"What is it?"

"It's something I really should have got your approval for first."

"So, what is it?"

"You won't be cross with me?"

"Just tell me what it is."

"Not yet. I want to show you something first. Come with me."

As they were talking, Song Ci had put on the gown, and his wife tied the belt for him and led him out of the bedroom. They came to a room in one of the wings of the house, pushed the door open and went in. All was revealed to Song Ci: he saw a bed in the middle of the room, along with a dressing table and a writing desk. On the writing desk were the ink stone, ink sticks and brushes that Qi'er had always used. By the window was a *zitan* wood flower stand with a potted autumn orchid, whose flowers were fully open, bright and beautifully scented. But what surprised him most of all were the paintings hanging in the room.

As Song Ci looked around, he saw, hanging on one wall, a painting he recognised named after the following couplet: "*A river in the wilderness where no one crosses, / But still, all day, the lonely ferry plies its oars*".[1] This couplet had been the test subject for selection of the top students when Emperor Huizong was recruiting artists from across the empire for the painting academy he was establishing. At the time, what most candidates painted when confronted with the couplet was a single small boat, moored at the river bank, perhaps with a heron spreading its wings beside it, or with a crow perched on its mast. Only one candidate chose differently: he did not focus on the absence of people suggested by the couplet, but boldly depicted a boatman lying across the thwarts of the boat, playing a flute to himself. His reasoning was that there had to be a boatman, but, without passengers, he would have nothing to do but rest and entertain himself. Because of its deep appreciation of the subject and its unusual approach, this painting became a model of excellence for artists of the time and was passed on as an exemplar for future generations.

Next to that painting was a hanging, two-character calligraphy scroll, which read "六榕"(Six Banyans). This dated from the time when Su Dongpo was demoted to a post in Huizhou and was passing through Guangzhou. At the request of Daozong, abbot of the Jinghui Temple, he created this masterpiece. More recently, the Jinghui Temple had become known as the Six Banyan Temple, and these same two characters were carved into a plaque that hung over the temple gate – a sight that Song Ci had seen for himself.

Elsewhere in the room was a flower painting entitled *The Sound of Spring*. It depicted a Chinese new year plant. The plant's flowers are very similar in colour to peach blossom, and it also blooms before the leaves grow. In the painting, the trunk was in shade, with its branches emerging from the dark. It just showed a small section of the tree, and it was impossible to make out where the branches were sprouting from. Nor was there any sign of birds singing in its branches. But none of this mattered, as the brilliant red flowers hung upside down like burnished gold bells, full of seasonal joy. It was as though a throng of young maidens had decorated the tree with those bells, and were dancing and singing in honour of the coming of spring.

Song Ci had never seen the painting before, but he found himself saying: "This is by Ma Yijiao."

"It is!" his wife replied.

Ma Yijiao was the great Southern Song painter Ma Yuan, who, along with Li Tang, Liu Songnian and Xia Gui, was one of the 'Four masters of the Southern Song'.

"But this isn't an original painting," Song Ci said.

"I know it's not. It doesn't have Ma Yijiao's seal, so as not to try to deceive you."

"So where did it come from?"

"What do you think of the brushwork?"

"You could almost take it for the real thing."

"They are all the work of that poor woman prisoner!"

"Which woman prisoner?"

"Ah Xiang."

"Ah Xiang? How can that be?"

"Husband, you had better sit down." Song Ci allowed himself to be pushed gently to a chair, while his wife began to tell the whole story.

"You mustn't be cross with me – this kind of thing doesn't happen every day. Do you remember how, when you reached Dongguan, you sent back three warrants ordering the release of three innocent prisoners? Those three were all set free on the same day. Two of them were from the southern suburbs, and their relatives had all come to the prison to meet them on their release. On the day the three of them came out of the prison, the old couple who sell congee by the south gate immediately recognised their son. And the man from the suburbs who grows flowers on Suxin Hill recognised his wife. The first man's parents had brought his little son and daughter. The parents ran to their son in tears, and the children ran wailing to their father. At the same time, the wife ran bawling to her husband. It was a scene to bring tears to anyone's eyes.

"At the same time, I had taken the young boy to the prison too. I wanted to reunite him with his mother. You will remember that he was born in prison. He was malnourished and hardly got any exercise, so he was very unsteady on his feet. But as soon as he saw his mother, he stretched out his hands and tried to run to her. And as soon as Qiu Juan let him go, he really did run. But after a few steps he tripped and fell, and she had to help him up. At the same time, the mother had come running forward, but at the sight of her son, she stopped for a moment, as if she didn't recognise him. But then she took the young lad who had grown up so much, from Qiu Juan, and mother and son burst into tears together."

"What happened next?"

"Qiu Juan told her that I was Mistress Song, and, at that, the whole lot of them knelt down in front of me offering thanks. I didn't know what to do with myself. After that, the two prisoners and their relatives all left, leaving only Ah Xiang and her son outside the prison. They didn't have any family and had nowhere to go. I told Ting'er to give them two pieces of silver and some clothes I had brought along specially so they could make their way back to their home village. Ah Xiang looked at the silver and began to cry, but she didn't take it. Instead she knelt in front of me again, and said: 'Mistress, I can never repay the kindness you and Lord Song have shown me, so please take me in to your household as a maid.' I felt sorry for them both and couldn't bear to think of them just going away like that, so I agreed."

"So, how did you find out she could paint?"

"One day, an aide visiting the office of the judicial commissioner gave me an old painting, saying he had heard that you were a keen collector, and he wanted to present it to you. I didn't dare accept, so I told him to keep it and give it to you himself on your return. Ah Xiang happened to see the painting. She waited until the aide had gone and then told me: 'Mistress, that painting isn't genuine.'

"I asked her how she knew, and she said: 'The painting is called *Tree Peonies at Noon* – it shows a cluster of peonies and a cat. The cat's eyes are too narrow and elongated, so you can tell it's a rather clumsy copy.'

"'How can you tell?' I asked her.

"She explained that the tree peonies were the main subject of the painting and that the cat had only been added in by the artist as a display of virtuosity: 'A cat's eyes are normally round as a ball, but sometimes they narrow when the sun is strong in the sky, and at noon they can be just slits. In the original painting, the cat's eyes are just slits, so you can see considerable thought has gone into it – and it's that thought that makes it such a masterpiece. It struck me that, in the original painting, the cat's eyes must have been damaged, or just become blurred with age, so that, if the copyist hadn't properly understood the original thought behind the painting, it would be natural for him to give the cat narrow, elongated eyes, and paint it and the peonies together, on the assumption that it is looking at the flowers. This kind of thing happens quite often with old paintings.'

"I was completely taken aback that she could have this kind of expertise. Ah Xiang saw me looking at her and she said, with an embarrassed smile: 'Mistress, I am just talking nonsense. Don't take any notice. When the master comes back, he can explain it to you properly.'"

"It's certainly not nonsense," Song Ci said. "This painting is described by Shen Kuo in his *Dream Pool Essays*, and the cat does, indeed, have slits for eyes."

"I didn't know anything about her family background at the time. That night when you came back from inspecting the prison, you told me a lot about her adventures during the flood, but you didn't say anything about where she came from."

"She comes from a family of picture-mounters."

"Indeed. I thought at the time that there was something out of the ordinary in her speech and bearing, and supposed she must have come from a good family. When I asked her, she told me: 'I'm just the daughter of a picture-mounter.' But when I inquired more closely, I discovered that her father and grandfather had been experts in the identification of old paintings. By the time she lost her milk teeth, her grandfather said she had a natural gift that shouldn't be wasted just on mounting pictures. He encouraged her to study painting and invited great masters to instruct her. But when she was fifteen, both her grandfather and mother died. Her father remarried, and the family's fortunes began to decline. Her father had her work on the finest paintings that came in for mounting, but her heart wasn't in it. She particularly loved to study the paintings that were brought in, and so, as the years passed, she didn't gain any great mastery of the craft of picture-mounting, but she was able to make expert copies for people of the calligraphy and paintings. When her father saw that she was selling some of the paintings she had done herself and was also increasing the number of customers coming into the shop, he left her to carry on.

"I really wanted to see some of her work for myself, so I said to her: 'Ah Xiang, bring some of your paintings to show me.'

"She hesitated for a moment and said: 'I can't really say they're my paintings, but if Mistress would like, I can do a copy of a painting by one of the old masters. You might find it entertaining.'

"I immediately ordered Qiu Juan to fetch paper and brushes, and Ah Xiang proceeded to make this copy of Ma Yijiao's *The Sound of Spring*. 'Now write some characters for me,' I told her. She wrote a page of characters in elegant *kaishu* script, and before she had even finished one column, I started in amazement. The firmness and suppleness of her elegant *kaishu* was so like Qi'er's. I looked at Qiu Juan, and she was in tears.

"That night, I couldn't go to sleep for a long, long time. As dawn was about to break, I had a dream. In it, Qi'er was going, by herself, to the painting and calligraphy gallery in the Hanlin Academy in Lin'an to buy some paintings. She was suddenly attacked by a highwayman but a woman rescued her and took her into the gallery. That woman was Ah Xiang! I'm not clear about exactly what happened next, but Qi'er ended up bringing Ah Xiang home, saying that she had sworn sisterhood with her. Then I began hazily to become aware that this wasn't real, and as my head cleared I realised it was just a dream. I couldn't go back to sleep after that.

"From then on, I often asked Ah Xiang to do some calligraphy for me, and every time I saw her characters, looked at her, heard her voice, I thought of Qi'er. She is the same age as Qi'er, you know, and looks quite like her. In fact, she seemed to resemble her more and more. I lost my appetite, couldn't sleep and began to get ill. Qiu Juan, Ah Xiang and Ting'er looked after me constantly, day and night. At the time, I thought to myself, that if I let my mind wander as I slipped into my confused sleep, I could well think I was calling for Qi'er, not Ah Xiang. But I managed to keep my head clear. One night later on, when I was alone with Ah Xiang, I said to her: 'Ah Xiang, your family's name is also Song…'"

Mistress Song stopped there, thinking perhaps it was better not to go on. She looked at her husband, waiting for him to say something in reply.

Song Ci sat in silence. Before his wife was half way through her story, he had already guessed where she was leading. He also realised that, during the whole day since his return, he had not seen Ah Xiang and her son, and that must be because his wife was keeping them out of the way until she had had a chance to raise the matter with him. Only then would she summon them to greet him. But this had all come upon him very suddenly, and he needed to think.

After a long time, he said: "Tell them to come out now."

"I will go and get them."

Mistress Song left the room, calling out for the maid, Ting'er. When Ting'er answered, she ordered her to summon Ah Xiang and her son, and then came back into the room. It wasn't long before Ting'er reappeared, leading the mother and son.

Fine clothes and jewellery were never proof for anyone against Song Ci's piercing and perceptive eyes, which could see straight through to a person's true character. It seemed to him now, as he looked at Ah Xiang, that she was very different from when he had seen her in the prison. She was wearing a jade-green outfit, and her skin had lost its prison pallor and roughness. Her limpid eyes sparkled, and her lips were gently pursed, with a hint of a smile at the corners of her mouth. Even so, when she saw Song Ci, she still could not look at him directly. She seemed, if anything, even more cautious and reserved than when she had been in the prison. Holding her son by the hand, she immediately stepped forward and knelt in front of Song Ci, but she remained silent, presumably unsure of what best to say.

"So, you know Ma Yijiao?" It was Song Ci who broke the silence.

"I heard my grandfather talk about him," Ah Xiang replied.

"And do you also know his family history?"

"I only know that he was born into a family of artists. Over five generations, the family produced seven painters who were masters of the Painting Academy, but it is his compositions that are considered the most exceptional."

"How so?"

"In his ink paintings, he would show towering peaks but never reveal their summits. Or plummeting cliffs where you never saw the bottom. Or he might have the mountains in the foreground with their peaks touching the sky and the mountains in the distance beneath them. The majority of his landscapes only show partial views of the whole scene."

"And do you like his paintings?"

"Hmm! No!" Ah Xiang went on to correct herself, as she looked up briefly at Song Ci, then dropped her gaze again. "The unique nature of Ma Yijiao's composition is primarily what attracts people to his paintings. My own brushwork is weak and immature, but when I make a copy of Ma Yijiao's work, I can at least imitate his composition. Other great artists' paintings may not have the same strength and vividness, but they are full of charm and romance. If you don't have true spirit in your brush, you cannot reproduce such paintings, which is why I do not try to copy other artists."

Song Ci was moved by Ah Xiang's candour and asked: "Do you think the same applies to the painting *A River in the Wilderness Where No One Crosses; But Still, All Day, the Lonely Ferry Plies its Oars*?"

"Yes, I do," Ah Xiang nodded. "The brushwork is certainly bold and well-formed, but it is the composition that truly makes the painting."

"There were other similar paintings used in the test for the academy, such as *Ancient Temple Deep in the Mountains, The Fragrance of Flowers Released Under Horses' Hooves* and *Wine Shop by a Bamboo Bridge*. Have you copied those too?"

Song Ci's interest had been aroused, and he threw out the names of some other paintings.

"I have copied *Ancient Temple Deep in the Mountains*, not from the original, but from earlier copies. But those copies were all done by masters of the Painting Academy in the capital, and the brushwork often surpasses the original. The other two paintings, I have heard of, but never seen."

That Ah Xiang found she could speak so freely and naturally in front of such an erudite, albeit benevolent, scholar so many years her senior, was perhaps because she had shed her self-restraint in her enthusiasm. Or perhaps she was simply unconcerned whether Song Ci would agree to take her as an adoptive daughter. Just to be able to talk so freely about painting and calligraphy with Song Ci and his wife, as though they were her real father and mother, gave her much pleasure; and that pleasure allowed her to return to the innocence of her youth.

Mistress Song was sitting to one side listening, and as she watched the conversation between the young woman and the older man, she felt a warm glow inside.

I was right, she thought. He's going to agree.

"I did copy another of the examination paintings," Ah Xiang said.

"Which one?" Song Ci asked.

"*A Single Point of Red on a Tender Green Branch; What More is Needed to Stir Thoughts of Spring*?"

"Excellent! Excellent!" Song Ci stood up, and addressed his wife, clearly wanting to draw her attention to the deeper meaning of the title: "That painting is a most excellent subject. Mistress, this is how I see the situation: Ah Xiang is a childhood name, and from now on, we shall call her... Qi'er!"

At these words, his wife's eyes filled with tears. The little boy was still too young to understand what was going on, but Ah Xiang also found her eyes welling up. She too had been a spirited youth. There is an old saying: 'Thirteen is the age of beautiful bearing and graceful mien; like a cardamom flower in bud at the start of spring.' Up until her thirteenth birthday, she had been spoiled and indulged by her grandfather, but later, as misfortune came into her life, the passion left her face. Later still, when she came to copy the painting *The Sound of Spring*, she retained the passion bottled up deep inside, but let some of it spill out through her brush. But now, Master Song was showing her such honour and respect, young as she was, that not only was he taking her as his adoptive daughter, he was even giving her the name of his beloved real daughter. In the light of such love, how could she keep her feelings bottled up any more? As all the passion of her youth flooded back into her face, she looked even more spirited and vivacious than she had as a child. For the moment, she seemed to forget that she was already the mother of her own child, and she flung herself into Mistress Song's embrace, weeping without restraint…

4

## A BOLT FROM THE BLUE

Neither Song Ci nor his wife slept that night. Their thoughts were with the Qi'er who had departed, and their love was with the Qi'er who just been given to them. They lay side by side, talking through the night.

Finally, Mistress Song said: "Qi'er is ill. You must treat her."

"What's wrong with her?"

"Abnormal discharge."

"What kind of discharge?"

"Black discharge."

"Black discharge?" Song Ci knew there were five colours of abnormal discharge that afflicted women: white, yellow, red, green and black. Black was the most difficult to treat. Its principal causative agent was damp, so it was most likely Qi'er had contracted the condition in prison.

"She has had it for some years," his wife explained. "She gave birth in prison and breast-fed the child there too, and that's when she must have contracted it. After she was released, I had doctors examine her, and they gave her lots of medicines. It has improved, but it hasn't gone away."

"What other symptoms does she have?"

"Apart from severe discharge, her lower abdomen sometimes gets swollen and painful. She has urinary urgency, but passes only a little red-tinged water. And she gets severe itching. Can you help her?"

"I will examine and treat her tomorrow. There are quite a few examples of this kind of thing in Dr Haiting's book."

Talk of this reminded Song Ci that there were still many cases in the prison waiting to be re-examined – prisoners who could be released without any lengthy questioning, most of whom had also contracted prison illnesses. There was no time for any more delay, and he would have to set to work tomorrow.

Song Ci got up just as dawn was beginning to show outside the window, and he went into the central courtyard to practise a set of his internal qigong exercises. As he passed Qi'er's window, he heard the faint sound of movement inside and realised that Qi'er must be up already too. He called to her through the window.

"Eh?" There was a soft exclamation of surprise in response, then the door opened and Qi'er appeared in the doorway.

"Father!" She greeted Song Ci, when she saw who it was.

"Have you been awake all night too?" Song Ci asked her, seeing her bloodshot eyes

"I couldn't get to sleep."

Song Ci went into the room and saw Xiao Bao fast asleep. Xiao Bao was the name Mistress Song had suddenly come up with for the young boy.

Song Ci looked down at him as he lay in bed and then said to Qi'er: "Come, I will take your pulses."

Qi'er pulled up her sleeve. Mistress Song had told her that her husband would be able to treat her condition when he returned.

"Put your hand on this." Song Ci took down a thick volume of stone rubbings from the bookshelf.

She stretched out her hand, palm upwards, so that it naturally lay flat on the book. Song Ci began to feel for her pulses. He took his middle finger and pressed gently down on the point where the bone protruded at the back of Q'er's palm, at the *guan* point. He then let his index and fourth fingers fall naturally on the *cun* and *chi* regions, but he couldn't feel the pulses. He turned her hand palm downwards and felt again for a pulse, this time on the *cunkou* point. His heart leapt, and he said to her: "Your pulses are exactly the same as Qi'er's!"

She looked up at him, realising he was referring to his natural daughter: "How can that be?"

"You have reversed pulses. It's a very rare phenomenon. Your elder sister Qi had the same on both hands. Give me your other hand, so I can examine that too."

She held out her other hand for Song Ci to feel, and after a moment he cried out: "You are the same – reverse pulses on both hands!"

"What an extraordinary coincidence," she said with a smile, as a warm feeling of exceptional auspiciousness filled her heart.

"The ancients believed in predestined relationships, and quite clearly this is why we have taken you as our daughter now!" Song Ci said.

Qi'er didn't know what to say, so she just smiled as she revelled in the warm glow in her heart.

Song Ci carefully probed her pulses and felt them coming and going, above and below. They felt round, like a pearl, fluid and regular – what is called a 'slippery pulse'. This is caused by an excess of *yang* energy, but also indicates a deficiency in base *qi* and an inability properly to control the fire element of the liver and kidneys. This causes the blood to overheat, which here resulted in the pathology Qi'er was exhibiting through her 'slippery pulse'. Such a pulse in the *guan* region is mostly seen in conditions where there is a formation of internal contusions. Song Ci went on to discover that Qi'er's pulse was weak in the *chi* region, and strong in the *guan*, when her proper state should have been just the reverse. When he had finished with her hands, he inspected her tongue; it had a thick, muddy-yellow coating, and was red at the tip and along the sides. This indicated that Qi'er's stomach pains were a result of malfunction and imbalance in the stomach and spleen. It meant that her treatment should involve not just reduction of heat and increase of fluid, but should also focus on rectifying the spleen. Finally, Song Ci had nothing more to ask, and he took a sheet of paper and a brush from the bookshelf and wrote the following prescription:

*Stir-fried large-headed atractolydes rhizome: 5 qian*
*Prepared black atractolydes rhizome: 3 qian*
*Huai River yam: 5 qian*
*Guangdong dried orange peel: 1 qian*
*Plantain seed: 4 qian*
*Burnt schizonepeta: 1.5 qian*
*Hangzhou peony root: 3 qian*
*Honewort: 1.5 qian*
*Raw liquorice root: 1.5 qian*
*Silver-flower rattan: 1 liang*
*Dandelion: 8 qian*
*Tree of Heaven bark: 5 qian*

When he had finished writing, Song Ci said to Qi'er: "In addition, you can take some Dryopteris fern, peel off the outer layer of the leafstalk, chop up the remainder, boil it in white vinegar, dry it and pound it to a powder. Then you should take a dose of three *qian* twice a day, morning and evening. This is a separate prescription that I will make up for you. Now, take this other one to your mother, and the two of you can go and buy the ingredients yourselves."

As he was about to leave the room, Song Ci added: "This evening I will get your mother to make up a steaming hot *sitz* bath that you can take before you go to sleep. You mustn't worry, we will get you better in no time."

"Ah!" Qi'er grunted in reply, a blush spreading across her cheeks. She thought about thanking her father but, in the end, said nothing.

Song Ci busied himself with the re-examination of the cases of those prisoners set for release, and after ten days or more of continuous work, he had clarified every point that needed clarification. He took the decision to release all the prisoners on the same day.

The day of release arrived, and Song Ci got up and made his way to the prison just as the sound of the dawn bell was shimmering through the early morning light.

The sun rises quickly in the south. As dawn broke with brilliant red clouds colour-washing the city roofs, the 300 and more prisoners due for release had already been ordered out of the prison buildings and were gathered in the main courtyard. The prison guards were standing to attention, but clearly in high spirits, either on top of the ramparts, or around all sides of the yard.

At a command from Song Ci, the prisoners all filed out of the prison gates. Waiting for them outside was a crowd of more than a thousand, made up of friends and family members of local worthies, and relatives of the prisoners themselves, all mingling and milling around together. It was a very moving sight.

Without prompting, one of the prisoners turned back and knelt in the direction of the prison, calling out: "Our thanks to Lord Song, the judicial commissioner."

On the instant, everyone else fell to their knees. What a sight it was as they all turned back, knelt and stayed kneeling for a long, long time without getting up and leaving. The cry of thanks to Lord Song shook the city walls. Truly a moment of extraordinary emotion!

Mistress Song, however, was secretly worried, and she said to her husband: "Might not releasing so many prisoners at once cause some problems?"

"What problems?" Song replied. "Not releasing them would have caused problems. By releasing them I have addressed the open grievances of the nation and stopped them becoming more serious."

If you stop to analyse the body of longstanding cases that Song Ci examined in Guangdong, it is evident that the majority of them were ones where there was clear evidence of innocence on the part of the accused, and so injustices could be righted and the prisoners released. Nevertheless, there were still many cases where no such clear evidence could be produced, and which as a result had dragged on and on. What was to be done with them? Should the accused remain in prison? Song Ci was torn: how could he, as an official, reconcile his duty to maintain the order of the nation with his desire to free the people from their unjust burdens?

During his time in Guangdong, and in the course of his efforts to find proof of innocence for those prisoners, it is clear to see the development of the principle of 'the presumption of innocence' in his thinking. This was in marked contrast to many other judges who clearly worked on 'the presumption of guilt'. Song Ci's approach should be seen as the first step in one of the most important advances in the Chinese criminal justice system.

There were countless prisoners all across the empire, languishing in jail with their cases unheard. Apart from those in cases that had simply been consigned to oblivion from the start, or were of too extreme a nature, most of them had been arrested on suspicion of the crime and had been unable to produce any clear proof of their innocence. The result was their immediate incarceration by the courts. Song Ci regarded this as a dangerous approach.

"Locking up a prisoner because the chief investigating officer cannot produce any clear evidence can only be seen as punishing the accused for the incompetence of the official," Song Ci said. "And how much longer can we continue with the practice of settling a case by extracting a confession under torture, when, again, no evidence is produced by the examining officer?"

These words of Song Ci were only spoken in private to Tong Gong, Huo Xiong, Mistress Song, Qiu Juan and Qi'er. There was nowhere he could speak so freely in open, and they only took formal shape much later in his writings.

It must be said that, as judicial commissioner in Guangdong in charge of the penal system, he was wide-ranging and vigorous in his efforts and achieved a remarkable degree of success. This was not just because of his extraordinary talent for investigation, but also because of the judicial principles he established: the first was that, if there was no indisputable evidence of guilt, then there should be a verdict of not guilty; the second was that, if a verdict was to be given on the basis of a verbal confession alone, without any other corroborating evidence, then that confession should be ruled inadmissible. These two principles were the foundations on which he built his legal crusade to right injustices and free those wrongly imprisoned.

In fact, Song Ci did not have to fully re-examine every single case for reliable evidence; if an inspection of the original case records showed there was insufficient evidence, a verdict of not guilty was recorded, and the prisoner was set free.

The release of the prisoners in Guangzhou had freed up a lot of space in the jail, but there still remained 200 or more inmates. Most of these were resigned to their fate, whatever it might be, and their guilt was clearly established. Song Ci decided that their trials should be conducted immediately.

Among the 200, some were guilty of common theft, and they were sentenced to a beating, then released. Another group of more than 100 had effectively already served their sentences while on remand, and a day was fixed for their release.

A group remained who were clearly guilty of murder, and they were sentenced to death.

The day of execution arrived. The sky was clear and bright in autumnal Guangzhou, with not a cloud in sight. At the base of Zhuhuwa Ridge in the western foothills of Mount Yuexiu, what had formerly been a drill ground for thousands of troops during the Southern Han dynasty had been turned into the execution ground. Flags were flying, and soldiers were keeping the place under heavy guard. A great crowd had come to watch the executions with glee, since many of the condemned were local despots and petty gentry.

Song Ci's carriage arrived at the execution ground to be greeted by a tumult of shouting and cheering.

He stepped up onto the inspection platform and surveyed the scene. He remembered all his searches and struggles, and thought of the 200 and more dawns he had seen, and the eight months of trials and hardships he had endured since coming to Guangdong from Fujian. He could almost hear the pattering of raindrops and see himself and his guards in the steady drizzle, pushing his carriage as it got stuck in the mud of the rain-sodden roads. He could see the wind chimes swaying under the eaves of the broken-down old temple and the fire they had lit inside to burn through the night. He could see himself and the guards, naked round the fire, as they dried their clothes. He saw those two soldiers who fell in the fight that rainy night, never to get up again… he felt the tears pricking his eyelids.

Song Ci's renown continued to spread through the highways and byways, through city lanes and village alleys, across mountains and valleys. Tyrants and despots, hoodlums and corrupt officials all heard his reputation and quaked with fear. And countless ordinary folk told tales that grew in the telling of his amazing deeds in righting wrongs and preventing injustice…

The autumn flowers were in bloom, orchids and chrysanthemums, scholar trees and hibiscus, all vying with each other.

It was a clear morning like many others, the darkness just giving way to light, and the cocks beginning to crow inside the judicial commissioner's compound. Suddenly, apparently out of nowhere, a whistle-arrow[1] came flying in and landed neatly on the window frame of Song Ci's living quarters. It had a letter tied to its shaft.

Tong Gong, who had just come into the courtyard to do his martial arts practice, heard the sound of the arrow. It startled him into watchfulness, but when he looked around, there was no one to be seen. By this time, Song Ci had also come out of his room, and when he saw the arrow, he took it down from the window and inspected it. Written on the letter were the two characters "Top Secret". It also read: "For the eyes only of Inspector of Prisons and Judicial Commissioner Song Ci".

He took the envelope from the arrow and tried to open it, but it was stuck down very firmly. He prised up a corner, and then one edge, and extracted a sheet of paper. As he unfolded the paper, a lock of hair fell out. He inspected the soft, gold-tinged hair carefully and his first thought was: "This is a young girl's hair."

Mistress Song came outside too, and when she saw her husband looking at the letter, she asked: "What has happened?"

"This is a letter of denunciation."

"Who wrote it?"

"It's anonymous."

"Who does it accuse?"

"The current military and civil commissioner."

Mistress Song was astounded. The military and civil commissioner held overall authority over both the military and political establishments of Guangzhou. He was the most senior official in the province and Song Ci's direct superior.

"What does it accuse him of?" Mistress Song asked.

Song Ci didn't reply.

"Are you going to investigate it?"

Song Ci looked at the lock of hair in his hand and said: "Yes."

# CHAPTER XV

## A BOOK BORN OF ANGER (1239-1248)

Sima Qian, the grand historian of China, records that King Wen of Zhou adhered strictly to the guidance of the *Yi Jing* (*Book of Changes*). When in difficulty, Confucius turned to the *Spring and Autumn Annals*; when Qu Yuan was sent into exile, he wrote *Sorrow at Parting*; when Zuo Qiuming lost his sight, he wrote *Discourses of the States*... Song Ci only held the office of judicial commissioner in Guangdong for less than a year before he was re-posted to the same office in Jiangxi, which he also held for less than a year. After that he was appointed county magistrate in Changzhou in Jiangsu Province, where five years passed in the blink of an eye as he arrived at his sixtieth birthday. As he considered all the miscarriages of justice across the nation, he felt that his own contribution to redressing them had been very small. He fervently desired to wash away all the wrongs for the people of the empire, but he could not, especially now he was languishing as a lowly county magistrate. If only the emperor would promote him to judicial commissioner again, how much more effective he could be. It was this thought that planted in him the desire to start writing...

# 1

## ON REACHING SIXTY YEARS

One spring night in the fifth year of the Chunyou period (1245), the festivities that had been going on all day in the county *yamen* of Changzhou had ended and the place was quiet. Bold and striking in the middle of the great hall of the *yamen* was a large calligraphy banner with the character '壽' (long life) written in gold, and the four walls of the room were hung with lucky couplets:

'Virtue spreads everywhere like life-giving rain'
'Long life like the eternal spring of evergreen pine'
'Sixty years come round again like mountains in a range'
'Passing seasons do not age great virtue'.

It was the beginning of Song Ci's sixtieth year – in olden days, people calculated age from the beginning of the first solar term of the year. The couplets had all been presented to Song by the military and civil officials of the county, along with all the local merchants, gentry, scholars and other worthies; some had even come from officials in neighbouring districts. But on the eve of his birthday, Song Ci was unsettled and prey to some nameless disquiet.

The celebrations had lasted throughout the day, but all the guests had now gone. The last one Song Ci had seen off was Shan Zilin. When Song had taken up his first post as official registrar in Xinfeng County, Shan had been his immediate superior. He had now retired from public life and, several years ago, returned to his home town to run the 'Thousand Mu[1] Snowfield' silk brocade factory his father had left him. This was the most famous brocade factory in Changzhou.

After Shan Zilin had departed, Song Ci felt a strange emptiness inside; a feeling that soon changed to anxiety and then to extreme agitation. This feeling of distress seemed to press in on him from all sides and took root deep inside him. It surely couldn't have been occasioned by Shan Zilin's departure? Of course not, so what was it? Song Ci himself struggled to work it out.

He had originally been delighted at the arrangements his wife had made to mark his birthday. He himself had sent out invitations to Shan Zilin and to the father and son pharmacists from the 'Precious Plant' pharmacy in town. He had also invited the owner of the 'Thousand Rows of Brocade' engravers, and a few others, but somehow word had got out, and, from ten days before, all the local officials, high and low, had made great show of sending him presents. Since none of them had actually been invited, he had had no option but to sit down and write them all letters of acknowledgement, and to instruct his servants to return every one of the gifts.

On the day of his celebration, he had tied an apron round his waist and, with his own hands, slaughtered a specially fattened pig in the back yard. With Qi'er as assistant, he flayed, plucked and boned the carcass. Very pleased with himself, he had asked Qi'er: "So what do you think of your father's butchery skills?"

"Well, given your experience on the autopsy table, it rather goes without saying," Qi'er had replied playfully.

At that moment, the sound of celebratory drumming was heard from outside the main gates, and Huo Xiong came rushing into the rear courtyard.

"Master, it's not just this city's officials and important families. Officials from every neighbouring district are also out there, all with presents for you."

"How can this have happened?" Song Ci exclaimed in annoyance, throwing down the butcher's knife that he had in his hand. It stuck, quivering, in the pig-cradle.

"Grandpa! Grandpa!" Little Geng'er had come running into the yard with Xiao Bao and Xuan'er in tow. "There are lots and lots of people here!"

Geng'er was five, two years older than Xuan'er. Geng'er was Tong Gong and Qiu Juan's little boy, and Xuan'er was Huo Xiong and Qi'er's daughter. Five years ago, in this very county *yamen*, Song Ci and his wife had given permission for Qi'er to marry Huo Xiong. When their daughter was born, she was given the family name Song and the given name Xuan, which meant that she would carry on the Song family name.

Mistress Song came hurrying into the rear courtyard, saying: "Husband, everybody is here. How can you keep them waiting outside!"

So, reluctantly, Song Ci had to give in, and he went out to greet his guests.

But was it this that was making Song Ci so unsettled that evening? Apparently not.

"Husband, you are very tired. Go and get some sleep," said Mistress Song when they got back to their apartments after seeing off the last of the guests. She had not yet realised the change that had come over her husband's mood.

Song Ci had not gone to his bedroom, but to his study instead. He did not think he was tired.

He sat back in his rattan chair and half-closed his eyes. Unbidden, the compliments and congratulations voiced by all the officials he had met that day began to echo in his ears:

"My Lord is merciful in dispensing awesome power, his love and might go hand in hand…"

"My Lord's virtue benefits the world, his long life brings him honour…"

"My Lord's talents and wisdom are the glory of the age…"

"My Lord…"

"My Lord…"

Song Ci couldn't help groaning loudly, as if in an attempt to scatter the voices in his head. He took no pleasure in these flowery compliments. His ever-analytical brain had spent the time during the festivities categorising them. Mostly they fell into one of three types: the first were genuine and heartfelt; the second were simple courtesy; the third were pure sycophancy.

The moon was up and its bright rays were filtering into the room through the leaves of the old cassia tree at the corner of the building. The scattered light seemed to disturb him, and he couldn't collect his thoughts. Finally, unable to sit still any longer, he stood up to go out into the courtyard.

"'Beautiful flowers and a full moon, the new year star bright in the sky. The fragrance of cassia lends lustre to the nobleman's house' – that is well written!" Qi'er's voice carried across the courtyard. Looking through the window lattice, Song Ci could see Qi'er, her mother and some others admiring the birthday couplets. He could also see that they were all full of happiness. He didn't disturb them, but stepped down from the ledge and into the courtyard. The flowers, plants, trees and rocks in the courtyard were bathed in moonlight, and Song Ci let it wash over him too.

As he stood there, gazing raptly at his long, thin shadow in the moonlight, he suddenly heard his wife's voice from a few days ago, talking to him as he tried on some new clothes: "Husband, you've grown old over these last few years."

"Old?"

At the time, he hadn't agreed, but today, during the festivities, when he looked at all those merely competent officials who were actually older than him, but appeared much younger, he did indeed feel that he had aged considerably.

"Grandpa, Grandma says we're going to celebrate your birthday," Qi'er said.

"My birthday?"

"Yes, you're going to be sixty in a few days."

"I'm going to be sixty?"

"Look at you – you don't even remember your own birthday!"

This conversation took place a few days earlier.

"Ah! Sixty, yes... what are we going to do?"

Thinking about growing old calmed Song Ci, and he began to consider his life with the same degree of rigour that he had brought to all the cases he had examined over the years.

He remembered the bitter years of study of his youth, when his father and his teachers only had one demand of him: to devote himself to gruelling study in order to enter imperial service. He had not disagreed with them; except that, for him, entering imperial service was the stepping stone to allow him to devote his knowledge and ability to bringing the welfare of the people to the attention of his superiors. He had worked hard and passed the exams. So, he could justly say that he had no regrets about his life before entering imperial service. After passing the exams, he had stayed at home to observe the mourning period for his father and had no achievements to boast of then. Afterwards, he had continued his studies and done the best he could in the circumstances. But what about after he took up office?

Thinking about that began to stir his emotions. When he took up his first post as registrar in Xinfeng, although it was only a minor position in which he could not really spread his wings and show his true worth, it did at least seem to be the first step along his predestined path. He progressed from county registrar to county magistrate to senior magistrate to judicial commissioner... and as judicial commissioner for Guangdong he had travelled to every remote corner of the province, settled the majority of those troublesome cases, corrected many miscarriages of justice and righted grievous wrongs wherever he went. As he thought about all this, he saw again all the lonely, desolate places and heard the drumming of his horse's galloping hooves. He entered an almost trance-like state, which was interrupted by voices that seemed to be drifting in from a great distance.

"Husband, are you going to investigate it?"

"It is a great responsibility."

"Does the military and civil commissioner know you are investigating him?"

"His eyes and ears are everywhere. How could he not know?"

"Then…"

"Thorough investigation will reveal the truth."

Five years before, when he had decided he could not ignore the anonymous denunciation tied to that whistle-arrow and had been determined to get to the heart of the matter, that determination had landed him in a very difficult situation. He had been sitting by himself, one day, in the assembly room of the judicial commissioner's office in Guangzhou reading through examination records, when Tong Gong came hurrying in.

"Master, an imperial edict has arrived!"

"An imperial edict?" He couldn't help being alarmed.

Outside the gates, a convoy of men and horses escorting a yellow-covered carriage had arrived. He could even remember the rustling sound of the court eunuch unrolling the edict. He knelt in front of the hall and listened to the high-pitched voice of the eunuch.

"The emperor says," began the eunuch, "if regard for the law is strong, then the nation is strong. If regard for the law is weak, then the nation is weak. We have heard that, since Song Ci received our imperial order to rectify the penal system in Guangdong, the scope of his investigations has been extraordinary, he has righted grievous wrongs and prevented savage injustice, restoring peace across the province. This is both pleasing to us and commendable. Now, by this imperial command, we transfer Song Ci to the joint posts of judicial commissioner for Jiangxi and prefectural magistrate at Ganzhou. He is to proceed to Jiangxi immediately on receipt of this edict. This is our imperial command."

As Song Ci remained kneeling, he himself couldn't tell whether he was moved, distrustful, surprised or worried.

"Song Ci must receive the imperial edict," the eunuch said.

Song Ci scrambled to his feet and received the order.

It was late autumn in the third year of the Jiaxi period (1239). From the perspective of his official career, he had received a promotion, but there was still that one major case he was in the process of investigating, and he was afraid that, if it was left unsettled, his assistants might run into difficulties in the days following his departure. He considered submitting it to the emperor, but he still did not have all the evidence he needed. Would not submitting a case with insufficient evidence, or with errors in it, be tantamount to holding the emperor in contempt? Besides, he dared not delay in carrying out the emperor's orders, so he had no choice but to abandon the case and leave to take up office in Jiangxi.

And what was it like in Jiangxi? Day in and day out, month after month, he quartered the province, hearing countless cases, both new ones and those of long-standing. In no time, a year had passed and the autumn flowers were once again opening along the banks of the Gan River, when, one fine morning, some fishermen pulled an unknown female corpse out of the river. It was the body of a young woman, a girl even, no more than sixteen. Her hair was loose, black, with tinges of gold. Her body was well-proportioned and her skin white and smooth as mutton fat. There was evidence of a blow to her head, and in her mouth and nose there were traces of bloodstains that had been partly washed away by the water. She was wearing a thin, crimson-coloured jacket and skirt, already tattered, and her body was tight and swollen from immersion in the river. Although someone had tried to straighten her clothing, her breasts and belly were still exposed. A crowd of people had gathered round sighing, expressing their sorrow and generally discussing the affair, not able to tear themselves away from the sight. But none of them could identify the girl.

When Song Ci reached the riverbank, he took in the corpse's disordered hair, her pale hands, the shoes on her feet, her swelling abdomen and barely covered nipples... he knew straight away that her fate hadn't been as reported to him by the locals. Whether she had died at that spot or somewhere further upriver, someone had put her in the water after her death. Song Ci could see all this without difficulty.

Although the bloodstains in her mouth and nose, which had been partly washed away by the water, could be taken as evidence of drowning, the fact that there was no mud or silt in her hair, her fingernails or the uppers of her shoes, was enough to show that she had not been alive when she had been put in the river. The comparatively healthy appearance of the plump body and glossy skin was an indication that she had not died of some illness and then been put there. There were dark purple patches on her white face that were where her blood and *qi* had flowed back on themselves. There was evidence of a blow to her head, and finger-marks on her legs and feet. This poor girl had been killed by being put head first into a water jar. Her swollen belly was not because of any water she had swallowed, but because she was pregnant.

How extraordinary that this should be the second death of this kind that he had encountered. Song Ci instituted an investigation immediately.

With some difficulty, he was eventually able to establish that the girl had been a servant in the household of an old general downriver, once celebrated for his glorious contribution to the establishment of the empire, but now no longer active in military service. Just at that point, to his astonishment, he received another imperial command, appointing him to the prefectural magistracy in Changzhou.

His despondency increased. Incense sticks burned on the table in the reception room, and he put the imperial edict down, before wandering aimlessly back in front of the table. Qi'er, Tong Gong and Huo Xiong were all silently lurking outside the window, and Mistress Song was standing beside the offering table.

After a long pause, she said to Song Ci: "Husband, don't get angry."

He stopped his pacing and said, almost to himself: "When fate is against you, there's no point in getting angry."

He had held office in Guangdong for less than a year, and it had been just when he was investigating the case against the province's military and civil commissioner that he had suddenly been transferred. He had also been judicial commissioner in Jiangxi for less than a year, and this time he was investigating the household of a former general… this general had been living at home in retirement, but he had five sons all holding posts at court, and one of them was an official in the Ministry of Appointments, albeit a minor one. How was it that, out of the blue each time in these circumstances, he should receive an imperial edict?

2

# GREEN SHOOTS FROM ADVERSITY

Song Ci had been in post in Changzhou for five years, and it was only now that he had finally begun to appreciate his old friend Liu Kezhuang's views on devotion to duty in office. He also remembered how Liu had lost his post because of his poem *Falling Plum Blossom*. Now, as he thought about it, he could see that Qianfu wasn't just unconventional, he was also a man who followed his own ideals and his own feelings. He had a deep understanding of the failings of bureaucracy, but he himself was not willing to try to curry favour. In the first year of the Duanping period (1234), when he had re-entered court life as secretary to the Privy Council and deputy director of the Ministry of Personal Affairs, it was not long after he had received the imperial edict in Nanjianzhou recalling him to court, that for a second time people sought his impeachment and removal from office. Then, later on, when he was magistrate at Yuanzhou, the same thing had happened for a third time. But none of these events had seemed to concern Qianfu. The years went by, and he continued always to be the same honest and upright official, and the same open-hearted and generous individual. It could truly be said of him that 'the passing of his years in office flowed majestically like a mighty river'.

On reflection, Song Ci felt that in many ways he seemed childish and immature in comparison with Qianfu, but that, even if he had no hope of emulating his individuality, so far, at least, he had avoided being dismissed from office.

"But even that's not really true!" Song Ci felt that his own life had been dedicated to the examination of bodies and the solving of cases, and now that he had been removed from the post of judicial commissioner, and returned to being a simple prefectural magistrate, that was little different from being removed from office completely.

Thinking of being removed from office reminded him of Shan Zilin.

"Brother Huifu, who would have thought we would meet again like this," Shan Zilin had said to him when he came unexpectedly to visit not long after Song Ci's arrival in Changzhou.

He remembered then that Shan was a native of the place. When he saw him wearing a new suit of merchant's clothing, he couldn't help asking: "Brother Zilin, why are you dressed like that?"

"I run a silk brocade shop now," Shan Zilin replied.

"But..."

"I came back home here quite some years ago."

"Why?"

"When I was in office in Bin County in Hunan, I mishandled a case that came before me, and after that I came home."

"You were dismissed?"

"Not so much that, I just had to come home." Shan Zilin hesitated for a moment, and then went on. "When I was young, my father said I was the cleverest of the family, and out of all my brothers I was the one who should seek public office. He also said that having an official in the family would be good for business. At the time, I thought it was a good idea too. Later on, however, I came to realise that I was ill-suited for public life."

"Why do you say that?"

"It's true. After I'd been in office for a few years, and particularly around the time I met you, I saw that, in this world, you need two particular qualities to make an official."

"What are they?"

"One is that you must be cunning, know how to curry favour and be deceitful. The other is that you must have the qualities that you possess, my brother, and have real ability and learning so that nothing perplexes you. I have neither quality. I was not cut out to be an official, so I came home to run the family business."

Song Ci looked at Shan Zilin's glowing red face and his easy manner as he talked, and thought that he really had a lot more spirit and vitality than before. Remembering Shan's wife, who had been such an excellent cook, he asked: "And how is your wife?"

"She's back at home," Shan replied with a laugh. "She has given me three sons and two daughters, and four of them already have children of their own. But..." At this point, he suddenly stopped smiling.

"What is it?"

"My eldest daughter married out as a concubine and then fell ill with some disease. Within two years, she had fallen pregnant and then died."

This had all happened in the first year after Song Ci had arrived in Changzhou, and now, as he remembered it all, he didn't quite know what to think. Over his five years so far in Changzhou, he was vexed that, unlike his previous two years in office, he had not been able to cut a swathe through the load of cases, strange and difficult alike. Over these five years, he often found himself thinking: Guangxi, Jiangxi, throughout the empire… how many injustices are there unrighted? He used to say to his wife, rather boastfully, that if he hadn't been a mere magistrate, but was still judicial commissioner, using his skill in investigation, he could resolve cases wherever he went and achieve his youthful ambition of washing away wrongs. Then he could report to the emperor that the people were truly content. But now his rank was too lowly, and his authority too limited, and all he could do was dream.

Song Ci heaved a long sigh. Over the years, he had been so full of self-belief, that, listening to him, his wife sometimes had to reprimand him, saying: "A little modesty wouldn't go amiss sometimes." But, although the world might view modesty as a great virtue, he couldn't bring himself to use phrases such as 'Truth be told, I do not have any exceptional talent and learning'. Most of the time, however, he was able to conceal the haughty look that had characterised Liu Kezhuang. He used a veil of modesty to hide his exasperation with the incompetent bureaucrats he encountered. He believed that there should be no restrictions in life on the opportunities to use one's talents and strengths, as long as it was all done for the benefit of the state and the people. Even as a child, he had been neither reticent nor lacking in self-belief, and he could see no reason why he should be. He could easily memorise a long piece of prose that defeated other children his age. If he was faced with an unfamiliar field of activity, he would recognise his own deficiency in that area and confidently set about rectifying it. And when, after a short time he had mastered that challenge, he would feel a great sense of pride and satisfaction, because he was able to achieve what few others could.

But now, he couldn't help feeling that his fields of activity had narrowed considerably, and there were things that he could not achieve through his own efforts alone. He suddenly became aware of his own feelings of insignificance and self-pity. His low spirits that day were because, even though he had fought through to the age of sixty, he still felt the same inability to attain his goals that he had felt during those years as a young man living in straitened circumstances. He was sixty already, an old man, and what had he actually achieved that was particularly worthy of praise? And what chance was there now of him doing so? In his eyes, nothing could be worse than this failure, and this shaking of his previously resolute self-belief...

"Aah, aah..." Song Ci could not help remembering the old saying that reaching sixty is the end of happiness and the beginning of grief. He stared up at the sky. The sight of the moon still travelling, calm and unruffled, across the great vault of the sky, only served to increase the feeling of emptiness inside him. Now he felt tired as he climbed the steps in front of the hall.

"Look, Mother, this is a birthday couplet for women. 'Clad in brightly-coloured clothes, resplendent in the moonlight, we dance before the hall, in honour of our venerable mother's first sixty years.' They brought the wrong one!"

Qi'er's laughter rang out through the reception hall. Song Ci frowned and made his way, without a word, along the covered walkway to his study, where he stretched out in his rattan chair. He was disturbed by the sound of footsteps coming along the walkway, which seemed to him unnaturally loud.

It was Tong Gong bringing tea, and without quite knowing why, Song Ci slapped his hand down on the arm of the chair and shouted: "Go away!"

Tong Gong put the tea down on the desk in the study, and withdrew, in amazement. As he listened to Tong Gong's silent retreat, Song Ci let his eyes drift vacantly for a long moment, and then he was suddenly struck by the absurdity of the way he had shouted at the man. Still vexed and ill-at-ease, he stood up and began to pace the room. More footsteps sounded along the walkway, and this time it was his wife. Behind her was Qi'er. Their footsteps stopped outside the study door, and Mistress Song came in alone.

"You mustn't get yourself into a state, Husband. I've already given orders for all the presents to be returned tomorrow."

Song Ci stopped pacing but didn't reply.

"Are you still angry?"

Song Ci went back over to the bookshelves and stood there, stroking the many volumes. Understanding came to Mistress Song.

"There were many wise and able men in the past who did not achieve their ambitions. Marquis Wu tried seven times to leave Mount Qi and lead his armies into the central plain to unify the empire. In the end, he never succeeded, but no one would question his worth."

"Marquis Wu fought to his dying breath and perished in the attempt. But I am still alive, still alive..." Song Ci moaned in torment.

Mistress Song was greatly alarmed by this outburst, but she collected herself and said: "Marquis Wu was given a heavy burden of responsibility by his ruler, but you..." She stopped, not daring to go on. She knew this was at the heart of her husband's despair. He wanted to be judicial commissioner, but the emperor had made him a prefectural magistrate, and he could do nothing about it.

For the last five years, nothing she could say had brought any peace to her husband. She stood there dumbly for a while and then said: "You should get some rest."

With that, she withdrew from the study.

In the moonlight outside, Qiu Juan and Tong Gong, Qi'er and Huo Xiong all stood with their children in the courtyard in front of the study. They had heard Song Ci's despairing words, and when they saw Mistress Song emerge from the room, they hurried over to her.

"Mother!" Qi'er exclaimed.

Mistress Song took Qi'er by the hand and realised how cold her own hand felt.

"I really thought that celebrating your father's birthday would make him happy. How could I have known…"

"Grandma, what's the matter with Grandpa?" little Geng'er asked.

"It's nothing," Mistress Song said, patting the child on the head.

Then she turned to the adults: "Take the children off to bed."

The moon was setting in the west as Qiu Juan and Qi'er returned to the courtyard in front of the study, after settling the children down for the rest of the night. Mistress Song, Tong Gong and Huo Xiong were still there waiting for them. On the lattice of the study window, they could see Song Ci's flickering shadow as he paced restlessly up and down the room.

A cool wind had sprung up, and Mistress Song felt its chill on her body.

"If my husband is not going to go to sleep, I had better put on some more clothes," she thought, before calling softly to Qi'er.

"Yes, Mother?"

"You go and see if you can calm down your father."

"Me?" Qi'er frowned.

"He listens to you sometimes."

"But what shall I say?"

In the past, when Song Ci was upset, Qi'er had sometimes been able to soothe him. But of late, she seemed to have lost the right words, so what should she say now?

"Take him some more clothes and make him put them on. Then just say whatever comes into your head," Mistress Song told her.

"Very well." Qi'er turned and left.

After a while, just as Qi'er returned with some clothes she had fetched from her father's bedroom, Song Ci's voice was heard from inside the study: "Yulan! Yulan!"

"Yes?" Mistress Song hurriedly replied.

Over the last few years, Song Ci had only called his wife by her given name when they were alone together, so what could it be that had made him call it out now? Mistress Song and Qi'er hurried over towards the library. As they went in, Song Ci's first words were: "A book! I can write a book!"

"Write a book?" his wife asked.

"Yes," Song Ci's eyes were alight. "I know myself very well. I have travelled across the empire and handled countless cases. I know I have exceptional abilities, but how many more can I still deal with? Besides, I am getting old, and even the sun has its set course. When you consider all the injustices in this world, although there may be many different causes, a large proportion of them are the result of inadequate investigation by officers of the law. If I can collect into one book all the difficult cases I have either encountered or heard about in my life, as an example for my fellow officials and for future generations, then…"

Mistress Song and Qi'er smiled in heartfelt relief. They knew that, if Song Ci was absorbed in a worthy task, he would stop fretting at his inactivity.

Song Ci also smiled out of pure pleasure. This had turned into a birthday more worthy of celebrating than any that had preceded it.

3

# THE JUDICIAL COMMISSIONER IN HUNAN PUBLISHES HIS FIRST EDITION

So Song Ci began his book, and case after case flowed from his brush. By day, when he had no official business, he could be found hunched over his desk, writing. In the evenings, with the pomegranate trees in bloom outside his widow, he would sit in his study, deep into the night, silhouetted by candlelight as he thought and wrote, wrote and thought. It wasn't long, however, before this began to take a toll on his health. Most troublingly, he began to suffer frequent dizzy spells and headaches that affected his ability to think clearly. Often, his wife would tell him to stop writing, and she even forbade him from working at night, because once he had his brush in his hand he would forget about sleep entirely.

Initially, Song Ci resisted these restrictions, but he found that the following day his head ached intolerably. In the end he had no option but to fall in with his wife's rules.

Every day, Mistress Song would come to the study to read over what he had written that day, and make some suggestions of her own, as her husband had asked her to do. Indeed, if she didn't make any comments, he would get angry with her, for, as people age, their temper does become more unpredictable. Of course, most of the points she raised and questions she asked were ones that Song Ci was quite able to answer. But some of them did challenge his previous thinking, especially as her memory was excellent, and she remembered very clearly all the cases that he had discussed with her in the past.

During this time, Qi'er was also kept busy helping. She transcribed all Song Ci's manuscripts into her elegant kaishu script. No matter how illegible the original, she always managed to produce a fair copy as neat as if it had been printed, and the pile of pages on the old pine writing desk grew higher and higher.

Outside, snow was falling, dusting the roof tiles with a fine white powder. As it thawed, it dripped steadily down from the eaves. Flowers were in bloom, filling the courtyard with their gentle fragrance. Everywhere the foliage was lush and green, punctuated by the flaming red of maple leaves. After a year of hard work in the fields, it was now time for the harvest. Song Ci thought he had remembered and recorded almost every unusual case that was worth transcribing, and he felt it was time to turn his thoughts to publishing. Not just Song Ci, but Mistress Song and Qi'er too, felt as though they had completed some epic journey, and collectively they heaved a deep sigh of relief.

One day, Huo Xiong brought the manager and the owner of Changzhou's Thousand Rows of Brocade block-carving house to the commissioner's offices. Mistress Song was delighted, and when she realised that her husband wasn't yet aware of the visitors, she quickly said to Huo Xiong: "Go to the study and tell the Master who is here."

"Yes, Mistress," Huo Xiong replied.

In a short while, he returned to report: "Master is sitting in the study in a daze. He says the book can't be made."

"Can't be made?" Mistress Song stood up from her chair, frowning deeply. After a moment's thought, she turned to the two men from the block-carving house: "Please wait here for a short while."

She made her way over to Song Ci's study. Inside, Song Ci was indeed sitting at his desk, staring blankly at the manuscript.

"Husband," she said cautiously.

Song Ci seemed not to have heard her.

"This morning, didn't you yourself summon the owner of the block-carving house?" she said.

"That was this morning. Now..."

"Now what?"

"How do you think this collection of unusual cases is any different from all the other such anthologies compiled in the past?"

Mistress Song heard him out and then looked at him in a puzzled fashion.

"You must be aware," he said, taking down a copy each of Sunzi's *Art of War* and Zhang Zhongjing's *Treatise on Cold Injury* from among the treasures in the bookcase, "that when Sunzi wrote *The Art of War* he didn't just cite examples of battles, and Zhang Zhongjing didn't simply give case histories. Why am I not writing a specialist guide to autopsy and crime scene investigation?"

"A specialist guide?"

"Exactly! It has never been done before. I can collate all the expertise and experience of previous generations, index and organise it, and put it all into one volume as a gift to posterity."

"But... do you mean to start again from the beginning?" Mistress Song thought of all the hard work that had gone into the last year or more, and didn't know whether to laugh or cry.

"I must write!" Song Ci exclaimed.

The stars continued their journey across the sky, and the leaves fell and flowers closed. In no time, another year had passed. By now, Song Ci's hair was almost completely white, but finally, his new manuscript was complete. The work covered everything, from the stages of investigation to the differentiation of corpses, from the four stages of decomposition to analysis of the cause of death; how to identify murder, suicide by cutting the throat, self-hanging, poisoning, immolation, drowning and many more; how to determine when death occurred, and how to tell if injuries were real or faked. He included every aspect of knowledge about internal and external medicine, gynaecology, paediatrics, trauma and orthopaedics. Nor did he stop there – he incorporated every detail of the study of physiology, pathology, pharmacology, diagnosis, emergency treatment and dissection. Even he was amazed by the book's scope and profundity. After constant revisions and corrections, he was finally ready to send it to the printers.

It was during this same year that the prison system in the province of Hunan fell into irredeemable chaos. The people began openly to voice their discontent, and at court, even the imperial concubines were discussing the situation. A year before, the sixth year of the Chunyou period (1246), in recognition of Liu Kezhuang's outstanding talents as an author and historian, Emperor Lizong had conferred on him a special honour equivalent to the top rank in the imperial service. Against all expectation, Liu returned to court from retirement in the post of head of the Secretariat of Inspection. As a result of his friend's appointment, Song Ci was raised to the rank of judicial commissioner, and posted to Hunan. Packing up his household once again, Song Ci was torn between feelings of excitement and regret as he mounted his carriage. Following the same road that had brought him to Changzhou six years before, he hurried off to take up office in Hunan. While on the road, he kept his manuscript safe by his side every minute of the journey. It represented, after all, the greatest achievement of his time in Changzhou.

"Father, let me look after it for you," Qi'er said. "Why should you have to carry it with you all the time?"

"No. You have two children to look after. Much better that I take charge of it."

He would not have been comfortable seeing it in the hands of anyone else, not even Qi'er, that most conscientious and painstaking of women. He kept it with him in the carriage, and put it down beside his bed. Only if he could see it and touch it at all times, was he happy. His greatest fear was that it might get left behind and lost on the journey.

If it were to be lost, would he be able to recreate it? He very much doubted it.

Once installed in Hunan, he dedicated himself to reforming the penal system. But before completing the task, he turned his mind to the question of getting the woodblocks cut. Although he had not yet finished the preface, nor had he settled on a title for the book, he felt that he had no time to lose and that he needed to get the blocks cut as soon as possible. He was afraid that he might die before he could see it published. So the very first thing he did on his first day in Tanzhou (modern day Changsha), was to send Huo Xiong out to issue an invitation to the owner of the city's woodblock factory.

When the owner of the factory arrived, Song Ci handed the manuscript over to him with a thousand words of warning and exhortations to take care. In speech and manner, he was far removed from the calm and decisive Song Ci most people were used to seeing; he seemed more like a worrisome and annoying old man. That night, after the factory owner had taken the manuscript away, Song Ci could not sleep. As dawn broke, he got out of bed and summoned Tong Gong and Huo Xiong.

"The two of you go and get the manuscript back."

"Why?" Tong Gong asked.

"Just go, and bring the factory owner back with you."

The two men left.

Qi'er had overheard this exchange, and she came to stand beside Song Ci: "Do you have some changes you want to make, Father?"

"No."

"Then what are you doing?"

"Suppose the factory catches fire, or something else happens? What would I do then?"

Song Ci looked at his daughter, and then, laughing at himself, said: "I expect you think your father is getting old, and worrying too much."

"But how are the blocks going to get carved? Surely you are not thinking of having the craftsmen brought over to do the work here?"

"That's exactly what I am thinking. I'm too old for anything to happen to this book."

The factory owner arrived and listened to what Song Ci had to say.

Twenty or thirty craftsmen came over from the factory, and Song Ci instructed them to cut the blocks as quickly and accurately as possible. For the first and only time, a temporary woodblock factory was set up in the judicial commissioner's office.

It was ten days before the new year in 1247, and Song Ci was in the library carefully putting the finishing touches to his preface. He was taking great pains over the writing of it as he considered the preface the 'eyes' of the book. He had finished it once but felt there was still something lacking, so he added a few more sentences, and he kept adding until it had changed out of recognition. Then he wrote it all over again. He wrote and wrote, and then decided it was too long. He dithered over it for a while and then discarded it again. He really hadn't thought it was going to take ten or more attempts to get it right. This time, however, he seemed happy with it. He counted 343 characters in total, not too many. He also felt that he had managed to say what he wanted to say, so finally he put down his brush.

He sighed deeply, as though he had reached his destination after a long journey. He felt inexpressibly content.

He went to stand by the window, and his eye was caught by the sunlight reflecting off the clear waters of the Xiang River at the top of Tangerine Island. He felt as content as that time, so long ago, when he had first entered the imperial service and gone to visit the Six Harmonies Pagoda beside the Qiantang River in Lin'an.

After a while, Mistress Song and Qi'er came into the study. Song Ci turned when he heard their voices, and he asked them: "Have you come up with a name for the book, then?"

Qi'er's face was wreathed in smiles, and when she glanced at her mother, her mother smiled back, indicating that her daughter should be the one to speak: "Mother and I think that, since Father's book will help all the law officers of the empire to investigate and solve cases, and to implement the law, it could be called 'An Overview of Judicial Investigation'."

"'An Overview of Judicial Investigation'?" Song Ci thought for a moment. "Yes, that would do."

"Don't you like it?" Qi'er asked.

"It's fine. Let's call it that."

Song Ci loaded his brush with ink and poised it over the title page, but then he stopped just before the tip made contact with the paper.

"What's the matter? Is that title no good?" Qi'er asked anxiously.

Song Ci lowered his brush to the paper, and what he wrote was: 'An Overview of Righting Injustice'.

Mistress Song looked at the characters and raised her eyebrows.

"What do you think of it?" Song Ci asked.

"It won't do," his wife said firmly.

"What do you mean, it won't do?"

"Have you thought what is meant by a 'miscarriage of justice'? It refers to a case that has been wrongly adjudged by the courts. Grievances and injustices felt by the people, but which have not yet come before the courts, are not referred to in this way. As a highly esteemed imperial official, you can't just choose any title for a book you write. Just think what it would mean if you were to use the expression 'righting injustice'. It would be like you standing in front of the emperor and saying the reason you wrote the book was because there were so many miscarriages of justice taking place in his name!"

"But surely the emperor would earnestly wish his officials to avoid such miscarriages?" Song Ci said.

"Listen to you! Have you forgotten how that great man, Liu Kezhuang, wrote his poem *Falling Plum Blossom* that fell foul of the censor, resulting in his impeachment and removal from office? If this book of yours seems openly to be accusing the emperor of presiding over too many miscarriages of justice, do you think you can avoid the same fate?"

"But there are too many such miscarriages taking place in the empire. I think 'Righting Injustice' is the proper title."

"I agree with you. But the main point of your book is to talk about the science of investigation in order to help the nation's officials in the proper implementation of the law, so surely it would be better simply to call it 'An Overview of Judicial Investigation'. Think about it – when Sunzi wrote about the art of war, he called his book *The Art of War*. Your book is aimed at helping officials to investigate cases properly, so why not just call it what it is, and use the title we suggest? The worst that people will say is that you think rather highly of yourself, and you won't stir up all the trouble that will come if you insist on using the words 'righting injustice'."

"Since you feel so strongly about this, I will think it over."

4

# INSPECTOR AT LARGE

With the title of the book still undecided, Song Ci sent the manuscript copy of the preface to the woodblock factory that had been set up in the judicial commissioner's office. The same afternoon, Mistress Song had persuaded her husband to get some sleep. With nothing else to do, Song Ci had stretched out on his bed, but, when Mistress Song came back after leaving him for a while, he was nowhere to be seen.

"Where has he gone now?"

Mistress Song hurried over to the study to look for him, and sure enough, there he was. As she went into the room, Song Ci was standing by the window, lost in thought. She walked over to the desk where she saw a fresh sheet of writing paper, with the words 'Guiding Principles' written on it.

"Husband! What's all this about?" she blurted out.

Song Ci turned to her and said: "I have been thinking – this book is designed to instruct officials in the science of investigation, but suppose some of them decide to use it fraudulently for their own benefit."

"Well, what can you do about it?"

"I thought I would start the book with some 'guiding principles'."

"What do you mean?"

"They would set out some basic rules that all court officers have to abide by. For example, nobody with any connection to the accused or who might have reason to hinder the case should be appointed to an investigation. In any case referred down or handed over by a senior official, if the appointed junior official does not show sufficient concern for human life, or appears to be afraid of offending his superior, or skimps on the investigation or covers up an offence because of the status and wealth of the accused, then the originally appointed official will be held responsible."

"You really have given this a lot of thought. But will it actually have any effect?" Mistress Song couldn't help voicing her doubts. "All this isn't backed up by imperial law."

"You know quite well that the emperor's decrees and civil law work in tandem, and the one influences the other. Officers of the law take imperial decrees very seriously. I think that when this book is published it will have a profound effect in halting corrupt practices, reinforcing the rule of law and bringing stability to the nation. If the emperor reads it and approves, then he could issue an edict promulgating its adoption. Would that not have the same effect as it being taken into the civil law?"

Mistress Song's eyes fell on the title page of the manuscript, which now read 'Collected Cases of Injustice Righted'. "Is this your new title?" she asked.

"It is."

"Why did you settle on that?"

"You were right when you said people might consider I thought rather too much of myself. So, to avoid sounding arrogant, I got rid of the word 'overview'. The material for this book does not just come from my own knowledge and experience in legal affairs – it draws on historical cases from the Spring and Autumn period onwards, and some of its information came from the mouths of villagers and woodsmen. So I have called it 'Collected Cases'. As for the 'Injustice Righted' part, I thought long and hard, and decided I simply could not do away with it. Do you remember how Prime Minister Li Zongmian recommended me to the emperor for the post of judicial commissioner in Guangzhou? Well, I firmly believe that when the emperor reads this book, he will approve of it too."

"And if he doesn't?"

"Once the book has been published, it is out there for the world. No matter what happens, I will have no regrets."

Having spent most of a lifetime married to Song Ci, no one knew him better than Yulan. Having heard him out, she said: "In that case, 'Collected Cases of Injustice Righted' it shall be."

In the seventh year of the Chunyou period (1247) the world's first specialist work on the science of criminal investigation, *Collected Cases of Injustice Righted*, was published from the office of the judicial commissioner in Changzhou, Hunan Province. It was a brilliant summary of China's ancient knowledge in the field of judicial investigation, and a crystallisation of a lifetime of Song Ci's hard-won knowledge and experience.

Liu Kezhuang was the first to receive a copy, sent by special messenger, and he was so excited that he read it at a single sitting. He understood completely: throughout history, there had been people who had laboured for peace and prosperity, and there had also been those whose mission was to destroy that peace and prosperity. This book of Song Ci's had been written to support the rule of law in the empire, to oppose wrongdoing and to redress injustice. But at the same time as approving the use of the words 'Injustice Righted' in the title, he was well aware of their dangers and was worried for Song Ci. The more he thought about it, the more he felt that the book should be withheld from the censors until after the emperor had seen it. If the emperor could be shown that the words 'Injustice Righted' reflected to his own credit, it could be taken for granted that he would also appreciate the book's consummate scholarship, and so imperial approval was more than likely.

It is not clear exactly how Liu Kezhuang contrived it. The fact is that, that winter, *Collected Cases of Injustice Righted* did indeed meet with Emperor Lizong's approval, and it was officially recognised as authoritative by imperial decree. It became required reading for all legal officials throughout the empire.

Song Ci's extraordinary scholarship affected all levels of society from emperor to peasant.

At the end of the same year, Song Ci received a summons to the capital for an audience with the emperor. Of course, he could not ignore it, so he set out taking Tong Gong and Huo Xiong with him. It was the first month of spring, the following year, before they reached Lin'an, and Song Ci was sixty-two years old.

"It is surely true that time waits for no man." It was thirty-one years since Song Ci had first so illustriously entered imperial service, and then returned home to observe the mourning period for his father. Those thirty-one years had passed in a flash, but the city he had not seen for so long was still the same flourishing hive of activity, whereas he was a white-haired old man. This saddened him.

Song Ci had arrived too soon. It was the first month of the new year, and the court was on holiday. The emperor was hearing no business of state except for the most urgent and was spending his time with his concubines, admiring the lights of the lantern festival and watching plays. Song Ci's audience was not considered urgent business, and he was not admitted to the palace. He had no alternative but to stay with Liu Kezhuang. Even this meeting of old friends in the capital was something of an undertaking, since Liu had grown old as well, although his hair was not as white as Song Ci's. The two friends spent their time visiting old haunts together.

"This must be the busiest and most flourishing city in the world," Liu Kezhuang said. "And that's not my opinion, it's what all the foreigners say."

It might well have been true. The city is backed by the Tianmu mountain range, and in front of it are the mist-covered expanses of the Qiantang River flowing eastwards to the ocean. The city marked the beginning of the ocean-going Silk Route, and the multi-decked merchant ships congregated there like ants, their captains gathering on Yu Street to trade in all manner of precious and exotic cloths and jewellery.

Yu Street[1] was like few other streets in the empire. As an imperial street it was paved with huge stone slabs to allow the passage of the emperor, and it was flanked on either side by brick-lined imperial canals. The canals themselves were planted with lotuses, and their banks with peach and plum trees. The trees were enclosed by a black lacquer-painted fence that barred access from outside. On the other side of the fences was the hustle and bustle of Yu Street.

In the busy capital, Lin'an, Yu Street was the busiest place of all. It was a veritable forest of government offices, shops, inns and other buildings, all crammed together, public and private alike, in a tangle of lanes and alleys. All kinds of objects were available for sale: jewellery and precious stones, rare medicines, exotic plants and flowers, and various goods imported from foreign lands. The only problem was that the lacquer-painted fences prevented people on the eastern side from trading with people on the western side; all they could do was look. This division of the district was reminiscent of the division into north and south of the Song dynasty itself.

"What has caught your eye?" Liu Kezhuang asked.

Song Ci was looking across the street at the painting and calligraphy shop of the Hanlin Gallery, and remembering how his daughter had longed to come to the capital to visit it, but had never been able to.

"Shall we go to the North Quarter?" Liu Kezhuang asked.

"Yes, let's go."

The North Quarter was about one *li* away. These 'quarters' first developed in the Northern Song capital of Bianjing, and were commercial entertainment districts unique to the capital. A few years after Emperor Gaozong moved the capital south to Lin'an, the same 'quarters' began to flourish there as well. By this time there were more than twelve of them in the city, of which the North

Quarter was the largest. When the two men arrived there, they were attracted by the sound of drums and gongs coming from one of the brothels. A man was shouting out the names of the girls: Miss Xiaosan, Sister Heisi. When they looked up, they saw two women come out onto the catwalk, one wearing a red cloak and the other a black one.

"They are going to wrestle," Liu Kezhuang said.

The words were hardly spoken when, up on the platform, the two women clasped their hands and bowed to each other, just like male wrestlers. They took off their cloaks and, as they did so, the drums and gongs increased in volume. They were both strongly-built, one with skin as white as snow, and the other several shades darker; one was wearing a red silk backless halter on her top half, and the other, a black one; both wore silk trunks, and their arms and legs were bare. They assumed their opening fighting stances and set to. Song Ci was reminded of an essay written in the Northern Song by Sima Guang, entitled *An Essay on Women Wrestlers During the Lantern Festival*, suggesting that such improper entertainment be banned. He was about to mention this to Liu Kezhuang, but before he could open his mouth, the cheering of the densely-packed spectators reached a crescendo, the drums and gongs sounded three times and the bout came to an end with the two women saluting each other and retiring back into the tent they had emerged from. The crowd gradually dispersed, and Liu Kezhuang and Song Ci followed them out of the brothel.

Once outside, they were carried by the crowd to the front of another establishment. The North Quarter provided numerous different entertainments: musical comedy, shadow puppets, song and dance, puppet shows, acrobats and storytelling. There were even riddle competitions, talking birds, performing ants, comic monologues, animal and bird imitators, dressing-up booths and all manner of other wonders. Among the spectators were many court officials sitting in private boxes with their arms round a girl; but even more numerous were the soldiers and officers who had been lured into the brothels by garlanded and heavily made-up girls who leaned provocatively on the railings. What with the wine and tea vendors, and the knick-knack booths, all linked together, the whole place was crammed to bursting, a seething mass of humanity without an inch of elbow room. Altogether, the quarter was like a cauldron of boiling soup, bubbling noisily, in constant motion and giving off rich and tempting aromas.

Wanting to leave but finding it hard to tear themselves away, Liu Kezhuang and Song Ci saw a crowd making its way towards another stage. Liu tugged at Song Ci's sleeve, and they joined the throng. An imposing sign in front of the stage announced the subject of the musical storytelling to be 'Huo Qubing Goes to War West of the Yellow River', and up on the platform a blind man was telling the tale of the Han dynasty cavalry general Huo Qubing's war against the Xiongnu. A large but orderly crowd was listening quietly with rapt attention. Watching the scene, Song Ci felt his spirits rise and then fall. He stood with Liu Kezhuang, listening for a while, but they soon decided that the storyteller was stretching the truth too much, and they turned and left the quarter.

At Liu Kezhuang's suggestion, while waiting for the emperor to return to court, Song Ci took Tong Gong and Huo Xiong to visit the tomb and new memorial hall of General Yue Fei in the Xixia Mountains. The old memorial hall, which Song Ci had visited in the past, was in the Xianming Temple on West Lake. The new one had been built in the fourteenth year of the Jiading period (1221), five years after Song Ci left the capital, on the orders of Emperor Ningzong. It was situated in the Zhiguo Temple in the hills to the north, and this was the first time Song Ci had seen it. They also visited the Lingyin Temple and saw the Cuiwei Pavilion that Han Shizhong had built on the Feilai Peak at the temple site, and the inscription that Shizhong's son, Han Yanzhi, had carved in the cliff face.

West Lake was just as beautiful as ever, with the reflections of the various towers and pavilions rippling across its waters. Reflected there, too, were the peach and willow trees, swaying gently in the breeze on the shore, and the stone bridges and the painted pleasure boats, turning the surface of the lake into a piece of fine silk embroidery. As Song Ci listened to the sounds, carried to him on the wind, of the gaily dressed young men and women playing flutes, singing and joking with each other on the pleasure boats in the distance, he felt an indefinable sense of melancholy. There were even more of these revellers than in the past, and from the merchants who had their wares laid out on the ground around the lake shores, they could use their money to buy tour guides and tour maps. The paths were also lined with hawkers selling sticks of candied haws that looked like sugar-coated maces.

Song Ci and his companions hailed one of the horse-drawn carriages that were for plying for hire, and, with West Lake on their right and the walls of the ancient Five Dynasties capital on their left, once again ascended Yuelun Hill to the Six Harmonies Pagoda. But after that, Song Ci did not feel like visiting anywhere else.

After several more weeks had passed without the emperor returning, Liu Kezhuang heard some news from the court. The emperor had caught a chill and fallen ill after playing polo in the snow with his concubines. The whole of spring passed, and still the emperor did not return.

After staying with Liu Kezhuang another two months, Song Ci began to become ill-tempered and restless. Part of him still hoped to see the emperor as soon as possible, but part of him was also missing his family back in Hunan. Then, at last, the day of his audience at court arrived.

The imperial palace was situated in the eastern foothills of Phoenix Mountain; to the north were the endless pine forests of Ten Thousand Pine Ridge, sighing in the wind; behind it were the rippling waters of West Lake, its reflections silhouetted by the morning sun, and looking like a phoenix spreading its wings in readiness for flight. Song Ci did not know exactly how large the palace was, but he was familiar with its layout and its four gates at each of the cardinal points of the compass. The eastern and western gates were called the Donghua Gate and the Xihua Gate respectively; the northern gate was the Hening Gate, and the southern gate, which was the principal gate of the palace, was called the Lizheng Gate. That morning, Song Ci was conducted by two imperial censors through a side gate of the Lizheng Gate, and into the palace. Inside and out, the palace gates were guarded by countless infantrymen of the imperial bodyguard and crack cavalry soldiers, to left and right, their arms and armour glinting magnificently in the spring sunshine. Song Ci made his way through the three-passage side gate, and in front of him beheld the majestic sight of gold-studded vermilion doors, and painted and carved beams and rafters. As he walked, he remembered the day he had taken the imperial examinations, when Emperor Ningzong was on the throne, and how he had hurried on his way to the examination hall, not taking in all the magnificence of the palace buildings. He was just the same today, hurrying on his way, and not stopping or looking at his surroundings.

When Song Ci finally reached the imperial presence, Emperor Lizong was seated under a dragon and phoenix fan, wearing a vermilion dragon robe. He remembered that, all those years ago, he had not had more than a glimpse of Emperor Ningzong, before sitting the examination and leaving the palace straight after. And it was just the same today; before Song Ci had time to take a proper look, or collect his thoughts, it was over and he was left in a state of some agitation. For, this time, after the audience, the emperor had bestowed an imperial gift upon him in the form of a book box, intricately carved with a dragon and phoenix design. Inside the box, bearing the imprint of the emperor's jade seal, was a copy of *Collected Cases of Injustice Righted*, and a letter of appointment as a Scholar of the Zizheng Hall.[2] This gave him direct access to the emperor, and the opportunity to use his knowledge and talents to help shape imperial policy. As this had been the ambition he had first formed thirty years ago, it was hardly surprising that Song Ci was in a state of emotional turmoil. But that turmoil soon gradually began to change into careful and dispassionate contemplation. That night he told Liu Kezhuang the results of that contemplation, since, in a matter of such importance, he felt it essential to seek the advice of his old friend.

Their faces glowing red in the light of the brazier in Liu Kezhuang's study, the two men discussed the matter intently.

"Your decision may well be the right one," said Liu Kezhuang.

"Do you really think so?"

"Indeed." Liu hesitated for a moment, and then went on. "For an imperial secretary such as myself, direct access to the emperor is the ultimate aim. My first thought was that I should once again recommend you for high office in the Grand Court of Revision. But then, when I considered more carefully, and thought of all the intricacies of court life, I felt maybe this might not be the best course for you. Your proposal is a wise one, and I think the emperor may well approve it."

"Do you really think he might?"

"The emperor has appointed you Scholar of the Zizheng Hall, demonstrating to the world how much he values your ability and desires to use it. Your proposal can achieve the same effect and satisfy the emperor's wishes."

"So, it is decided?"

"It is decided."

The two friends talked until dawn. During the night, they carefully considered every word, as Song Ci wrote out a petition to the emperor. If, thirty years ago, it had been Song Ci's one ambition to gain direct access to the emperor, and the opportunity to use his knowledge and talents to help shape imperial policy, now, thirty years later, he was troubled by all those unresolved cases he had left in Guangdong and Jiangxi. Before his arrival in the capital this time, he had heard that the military and civil commissioner in Jiangxi had been assassinated, and he immediately thought of the whistle arrow and its denunciation. He had also heard that more than thirty people had been arrested on suspicion of involvement, and promptly executed. On the other hand, he had heard no more news about the drowned girl in Jiangxi, which presumably meant that the old general was still carrying on unconcerned. There were countless other cases across the empire that also still preoccupied him. So now, his greatest desire was to travel the country again, righting injustice wherever it occurred.

The two friends went back to court together. Unhurriedly, Song Ci walked through the palace, looking at the smoke rising from the huge, ancient bronze incense burners in front of the halls, and listening to the lively music coming from the drum and bell towers that flanked the inner palace. And, in the late spring of that year, the eighth year of the Chunyou period, Emperor Lizong did indeed approve his petition. At the age of sixty-two, Song Ci was appointed to the Baomo Pavilion and commissioned to oversee unresolved cases across the Four Highways[3] as inspector general of prisons.

Song Ci offered his humble thanks to the emperor and took leave of his old friend. With Tong Gong and Huo Xiong, he hurried back to Hunan. He told his family the joyous news, and set out on his final expedition across the empire, preventing outrage and righting injustice. As his carriage sped along the highway between Hunan and Zhejiang, the sound of the horse hooves startled some birds roosting in the trees beside the road, which spread their wings and flew up into the sky in alarm…

# CHAPTER XVI

## ABSORBING WITHOUT LIMIT (1248-1249)

In 1248 Song Ci was inspector of highways with responsibility for the prison system, and he travelled around righting wrongs and preventing outrages wherever he went. This was what he had longed to do his whole life, to the utmost of his ability. History said of him that he was: 'Orderly in the hearing of litigation and firm in his decisions; revered by the good, and feared by the bad. He brought fear to corrupt officials, bullies and petty tyrants wherever he went, and felt deep kinship with the poor people of the lanes and alleys and the mountains and valleys.' However, within a year, when he was back in Guangdong once again, he fell ill. Just at that time, a bizarre and extraordinary murder case arose, in which the method employed surpassed anything recorded in Song Ci's book.

1

## A TRANQUIL MORNING

It was the year 1249 in the Chunyou period of Emperor Lizong's reign.

Early one bright spring day, the morning bell of the Six Banyan Tree Temple in Guangdong was sounding faintly through the mist, signalling the nearby provincial secretariat to open its heavy wooden gates.

This was the highest military and civil agency in Guangdong. Inside the gates, the stone-paved pathway ran straight as an arrow, flanked by ancient, twisted cedars where swallows twittered and tweeted. Grass spread in a green carpet across the open spaces, which were studded with steles mounted on the backs of stone turtles, and statues of fantastic beasts. Flowers of every colour and kind released their perfumes under the gentle touch of the morning sun.

The sound of vigorous combat interrupted the quiet. It was Tong Gong and Huo Xiong at their martial arts practice. Over the years, under Tong Gong's tutelage, Huo Xiong's fighting skills had improved considerably. He particularly favoured the use of a fine-linked steel chain that he had frequently employed in the capture of fugitives and those criminals who resisted arrest.

"Ah, how welcoming the compound looks." It was Song Ci's voice coming from the other end of the path.

"That's because you're not used to seeing it," said Qi'er.

The two of them were strolling along the path, and it was the first time Song Ci had been outside for quite a while. He had set out the previous spring, under imperial orders, to inspect the state of the penal system across the empire. He had expected to spend several years travelling the southern provinces, but unfortunately, that winter, after arriving in Guangzhou, he had fallen ill with dizzy spells and headaches.

He knew that the headaches were the result of an imbalance in his inner organs being reflected in his head: his lucid *yang* and turbid *yin*, and the blood and *qi* of his five viscera and six bowels, had all risen to his head, causing the headaches. Dr Haiting had been wont to say that headaches could be classified in two types: those caused by exterior disturbance, and those resulting from interior trauma. The chronic nature of these headaches precluded exterior disturbance as the cause. But headaches caused by interior trauma were usually the result of pathology of the liver, spleen and stomach, or of a chronic deficiency of blood and *qi*. Song Ci did not believe there was anything fundamentally wrong with his liver, spleen or stomach. The headaches were continuous throughout the day, getting worse when he was up and about, and abating somewhat when he lay down. This indicated a deficiency of blood and *qi* reaching the region that nourishes the head, probably caused by over-use of the cognitive function damaging the heart and spleen.

But for Song Ci to stop thinking was no easy task. Based on his self-diagnosis, he decided that all he needed was a few days' rest. To his and everyone's surprise, the few days' rest turned into two weeks, two weeks into a month and a month into six weeks. In the end, he had no alternative but to send a messenger to the emperor to report his illness. When Emperor Lizong heard the news, he gave Song Ci a new double appointment as military and civil commissioner for the province of Guangdong, and prefectural magistrate for Guangzhou. This was how he came to be staying in Guangzhou.

More than three months had passed, and his health was gradually improving to the extent that he was able to get up and walk around. This particular morning, as he was strolling in the courtyard with Qi'er, he felt in very good spirits.

"Come on, let's climb the Flower Pagoda at the Six Banyan Tree Temple."

Song Ci had been contemplating the burgeoning flowers and grasses in the courtyard, and the lofty pagoda nearby, and he had conceived a desire to view the countryside from up high.

"Climb the Flower Pagoda?" Qi'er echoed.

"Yes, you can see the whole city from up there."

Qi'er hesitated, wondering whether to dissuade her father, but in the end she said nothing and, somewhat unwillingly, nodded her head.

"Will you go and have a word with Tong Gong and Huo Xiong?"

"No need. I'll go by myself," Song Ci said, setting off as he spoke. Father in front and daughter behind, the two of them left the office compound and soon came to the Six Banyan Tree Temple not far away.

The temple was built during the Northern and Southern dynasties, in the time of Emperor Wu of Liang (464-569 CE), when it was called the Baozhuangyan Temple, the Temple of Stately Treasure. In the Southern Han dynasty, it became the Longevity Temple, and in the Northern Song, the Pure Thought Temple. Its current name, the Six Banyan Tree Temple, was taken from Su Dongpo's writings, which in turn had been inspired by the elegance of the six ancient, densely-foliaged banyan trees that grew in the temple grounds. Soon, Song Ci and Qi'er were standing in the shade of the six banyans.

Under the trees a young monk was doing his morning chores, sweeping the ground, and he greeted the visitors. Song Ci and Qi'er threaded their way through the trees and emerged in front of the Flower Pagoda. The pagoda was famous as the repository for a tooth of the Buddha that had been brought from the Kingdom of Zhenla (modern-day Cambodia). It was called the Flower Pagoda because the eaves of the octagonal, nine-storey building stretched out into the air like petals opening on a flower, and the finial on top looked like the stamen. The finial itself was topped by a pearl in a precious metal mount, which glinted in the morning sun.

"Father, I have heard that in the early Tang dynasty, the poet Wang Bo, who wrote the *Preface to the Prince of Teng's Pavilion*, came here, and that he also wrote a long inscription called *On the Monument at the Reliquary Pagoda of the Baozhuangyan Temple*. What a shame that the original carving was lost in the Southern Han, because I am sure you would have appreciated it, Father."

Song Ci looked at Qi'er with paternal admiration. Both his daughters shared a love of calligraphy that was quite out of the ordinary.

Viewed from the outside, the Flower Pagoda had nine storeys, rising about seventeen *zhang* from the ground. Inside, however, it actually had seventeen floors. When the two of them reached its base, Qi'er hesitated, fearing the climb to the top might make her father dizzy. In the end, she said: "Father, we can still... let's not climb it!"

"It won't be a problem," Song Ci said, setting off up the stairs.

With father in front, once again, and daughter behind, the pair climbed the winding staircase that connected the balconies of the pagoda, right to the topmost storey.

"See, Qi'er, your old father is still up to it," Song Ci said, as though that morning's ascent had, in fact, been a test of the strength of his recovery.

"Ha! Yes, not too bad!" Qi'er replied, thinking to herself that her father's health really had improved. He might be a bit out of breath, but wasn't she the same? And wasn't the sweat pouring down her own back from the exertion?

The cool of the spring morning in Guangzhou does not last long, and by the time they had reached the top of the pagoda, the sun was fully up. As they leaned on the parapet looking out, the huge disc of the sun turned the birds flying across the sky into golden silhouettes, and tinged Song Ci's silver hair with gold. Looking around, the whole city was spread out before them, and Qi'er felt herself relax. To the south, she noticed another ancient tower, rising into the sky. It was not, in fact, another pagoda, but the Guangta minaret of the Huaisheng Mosque, built long ago by the Muslim clerics and Arab traders who had come to China in the Tang dynasty. It differed from the pagoda in that it was cylindrical in shape, some tens of *zhang* high, and the staircase leading to the top was on the inside, not the exterior. Its outside walls were smooth and rounded. Two stone collars encircled the topmost portion of the tower where it was narrower than the main body, and at its very top was a gold weathervane in the shape of a bird.

Song Ci looked at it with narrowed eyes, and thought to himself: "What does this building resemble?"

"Father," Qi'er suddenly called out. "It looks like a huge writing brush, thrusting up into the sky. Isn't it fine?"

"Yes, yes. That's just what it looks like. But a writing brush with a gold weathervane at its tip!"

"Can't you imagine that the brush has just drawn the weathervane?"

"Yes, absolutely."

Father and daughter were very content that fine morning. Perhaps because of his improving health after a long illness, Song Ci found himself particularly appreciating the spring weather, and his spirits were high. Starting with the Huaisheng Mosque where the Guangta minaret stood, and moving on to the Qilin Mosque in Quanzhou and the Fenghuang Mosque in Lin'an, he told Qi'er about the three great coastal mosques of the Song dynasty. Standing on top of the Flower Pagoda in the Six Banyan Tree Temple, looking at the Pearl River in the distance beyond the Guangta minaret, he thought of the Qiantang River, and that prompted him to talk about the Six Harmonies Pagoda, and the libraries and painting galleries in the capital, Lin'an, and all its other marvellous sights. Qi'er listened, entranced, as the rest of the morning slipped by unnoticed. While they were passing the time in happy conversation, Tong Gong, having received directions from the young monk, also climbed the winding staircase up to the top floor of the pagoda. He, too, was concerned for Song Ci's safety.

"What has brought you up here, Master?"

"The spring light is so beautiful, I wanted to admire it."

"But did you have to climb all the way up here to do so?"

Song Ci drummed on his forehead with his fingers, a gesture that used to be an indication of the start of a headache, and he shrugged his shoulders.

"The college at Panyu is holding a new term ceremony today," Tong Gong continued. "Who do you want to send to represent you?"

"A college festival?" Song Ci repeated. "No need to send anyone – I'll go myself."

"Go yourself?" Qi'er said. "You can't do that."

"You really should send someone else," Tong Gong said.

"According to custom, the most important local representative should attend such a significant event. How can I not go?"

"You can't. Mother will never agree," Qi'er said.

"Oh, you are both too much! For the last few months I have relied on you for everything. Now, a college is opening, which is a cause for general rejoicing, and if I go, it can only do me good. Look, haven't I just climbed this great tall pagoda without any ill effects?"

Qi'er looked at her father and didn't know what to say. After a while she mumbled, so quietly that only she could hear: "Ha... it's not as though you're going to court to judge a case."

"Tong Gong, prepare a horse for me."

Song Ci got ready to descend the pagoda. Tong Gong didn't move.

"If you're not going to do it," Song Ci said, setting off, "I'll do it myself."

2

# THE SOUND OF HORSES' HOOVES

Mistress Song couldn't dissuade him either, and she contented herself with saying: "If you are going, take a sedan chair."

But Song Ci had never liked sedan chairs, and he didn't take one this time. He got into a carriage, driven by Huo Xiong, with Tong Gong following behind on horseback and a solemn troupe of armed guards surrounding the whole party as it proceeded along the highway. The clopping of the horses' hooves and the tinkling of the carriage bells filled the air, delighting Song Ci, who had not heard these once familiar sounds for quite some time.

He was averse to riding in sedan chairs not just because he didn't like being carried, but mainly because it was so slow. Over the years, both experience and inclination had told him that if something was to be done, it should be done quickly. Quite often it had been the case that delay could mean an investigation slipped through his fingers. He still regretted that he had not acted quickly enough in the case of the whistle arrow, when he had been judicial commissioner in Guangdong a decade or so before. Prompter action might have borne fruit, and neither the assassination of the civil and military commissioner, nor the execution on suspicion of involvement of thirty or more people, would have taken place.

His tour of inspection the year before had been carried out at quite a pace – otherwise he would not have been able to visit so many places. While hastening towards Jiangxi, he had arrived at a village where he came across two young married women fighting each other. One of them was pregnant and, mid-combat, she was assailed by a crippling pain in her abdomen and began to bleed copiously. She fell to the ground as if dead, unable to draw breath. Song Ci hurried over and propped her up in a sitting position, so she looked as though she was meditating. After ordering Huo Xiong to lift her head up slightly, he used a fresh stem of crow-dipper to blow into her nostril to make her sneeze. After a moment she did so, and it brought her back to her senses. Because crow-dipper itself is poisonous, Song Ci used the juice of some stewed ginger to draw out the poison, and thus was able to save the pregnant woman's life.

Unfortunately, the other woman did not realise her opponent had survived and she fled in shock and terror, to hang herself from a roof-beam. So Song Ci had to save her life as well. When he got to her and felt her chest, her heart was still warm. He ordered her to be gently taken down from the beam and then laid out supine on the ground. There was no time to lose, and no place for modesty. Song Ci himself loosened her upper garments, and ordered Tong Gong to kneel firmly on her shoulders and pull back her hair to expose her neck. He massaged her larynx and, at the same time, pressed down on her chest and abdomen. He also ordered Huo Xiong to rip open her lower garments, and to pump her legs up and down, bending them at the knees. They did this for some time until, finally, a rush of air came out of her mouth, and she started breathing again. Song Ci poured a little cinnamon tea down her throat and finally blew down a tube into both ears, bringing her fully back to life.

Thus, his swift actions saved the two women, and three lives in total. If he hadn't made such haste on the road to Ganzhou that day, then that young woman, just entering the flower of her youth, would have suffered a heart-rending death.

All this time, Song Ci's thoughts had been preoccupied by the unresolved case from his time in office in Jiangxi, and he was determined to get a result. So, on arrival in Ganzhou, he hurried downriver to the hometown of the retired general. He was unaware that the general in question had recently been murdered. Another assassination – who was responsible this time? A maidservant, apparently yet another maidservant!

Upon investigation, Song Ci discovered that the general had died while stark naked on top of the young girl. On hearing this, Song Ci immediately went to inspect the body and discovered that, even in death, the general was still in a state of sexual arousal. All was immediately clear. This was no murder – overwhelmed by lust, the old man had exhausted his vital energies and expired on top of the girl. Further careful investigation also shed light on the other case from the same year. It turned out that the old general had been trying to find ways to make himself live longer, and someone had told him that, if an old man had sex with young girls, he could draw on their flourishing *yin* to augment his failing *yang*. Thereupon, the general had bought as many young maids as he could, and had sex with them as often as possible. The maid in question had been particularly beautiful and the general was greatly enamoured of her. In the end, she fell pregnant. This roused the extreme jealousy of the general's wives and concubines, and she was stuffed headfirst into a water butt, where she choked to death. After that, her body was loaded onto a cargo vessel bound for Ganzhou, and thrown into the river further upstream.

Having arrived at these solutions to the two cases, Song Ci made all speed to find the girl who had been taken into custody. The case against her for murdering the old general had been conducted with exceptional speed. A confession had been extracted, and she had been sentenced to death by a thousand cuts. She had been put into a 'standing cage' and sent to the marketplace for public execution. Song Ci had galloped post-haste to the marketplace where he had found a huge crowd gathered, looking on at the girl, stripped naked and bound, with her hair pulled up into an iron hoop, waiting for the first of the thousand cuts.

This case left an indelible impression on Song Ci. For many days after, he only had to shut his eyes and he could still see the pitiful sight of the naked young girl. What parent's heart would not go out to such a girl, not yet out of maidenhood, trapped in such dire circumstances? Song Ci berated himself for arriving too late – if only he had made a little more speed, he could have spared the girl this shameful exposure in the marketplace. From then on, whatever Song Ci did, he did at top speed, brooking no delay. Having been unavoidably delayed by illness, and forced to lay up in Guangzhou for three months, now he had decided he was better, nothing and no one was going to hold him up.


The sound of the horses' hooves on the city streets, and the tinkling of the carriage bells, rhythmic and harmonious, were music to Song Ci's ears.

The Panyu Academy is located inside the main East Gate of Panyu City, with Yushan Hill to the east. Song Ci's carriage passed along Guangta Street and then turned east. Many military and civil officials would be attending the college festival that day, so it would be a good opportunity to meet some of the more important figures in Guangzhou society. Song Ci considered this as he rode along in his carriage. This was the first time he had gone out in his official capacity since he had taken on the joint roles of civil commissioner for Guangdong and provincial magistrate in Guangzhou; it would be an excellent way of getting to know his subordinates in the department. The sounds of an excited drum orchestra and the explosions of firecrackers could be heard outside. He had arrived at the college.

Outside its gates, two rows of cotton trees were bursting into their vivid red blossom, as though offering thousands of tiny red lanterns to the heavens. The perimeter walls were also red, and above the main gate there was a large stone tablet inscribed with the words 'Panyu College'. A crowd of civil and military officials was gathered beneath the tablet, all wearing their hats and caps of office.

Once again, the sound of hoofbeats rang through the city streets: the festival was over, and Song Ci had not forgotten his wife's exhortation: "You simply must not stay on for the banquet."

She was afraid that his body wouldn't be able to take the rich food and, especially, the wine that would be served. So at the end of the ceremony itself, he stood up to leave.

In the Spring and Autumn period, the new term ceremony was held to mark the first day of school for the children of the nobility, and that tradition persisted in the Southern Song dynasty. This was the first time that Song Ci had presided over such a ceremony, and he was greatly excited by it. Previous ceremonies that he had attended had been as a student at the imperial academy in Lin'an, and he and his classmates had all been the sons of government officials. At this ceremony at Panyu College, the students were by no means all the sons of officials, but that didn't stop Song Ci seeing his own past self in them. He remembered the words of Mr Zhen Dexiu at one such ceremony, which had left a lasting impression on him, and now he fervently repeated them to the students at Panyu. Such words of wisdom as: "If you devote yourselves wholeheartedly to your studies, and work hard at them, many among you will become pillars of the nation…" And so on. He truly believed these were not just empty words, since he himself had held them close to his heart for so many years. After seeing Song Ci back to his carriage, the last member of staff to turn to go back into the college was a lecturer in his middle years. It was, in fact, one of the prisoners Song Ci had released all those years ago, but Song Ci did not recognise him initially.

"My Lord, you don't remember me. My name is Hai Wentai."

The ceremony was over and Song Ci was scanning the college grounds, when one of the lecturers appeared in front of him, greeting him with great reverence. Song Ci had indeed forgotten him – he had heard so many cases in his career, and seen so many prisoners, why should he remember this one in particular?

"Ten years ago, My Lord, when you were in Guangzhou, you released a batch of prisoners whose cases had not yet been filed," Hai Wentai went on.

"Ah!" said Song Ci, remembering. "You are that fellow who failed the civil service exams in Guangzhou. You were staying in an inn and were arrested for the murder of a foreign girl in the establishment next door…"

"That's right, My Lord."

Song Ci looked at the lecturer, now so changed in appearance, and asked him some more about what had happened to him since his release from prison. He discovered that the man had returned to the capital to re-sit the imperial examinations, but once again had failed them. Even so, Panyu College had taken him onto its staff. Song Ci was delighted, and he recalled to himself his own thinking at the time: "Why would a murderer hide the blood-stained murder weapon under his own pillow?"

Given this element of doubt, in addition to the fact that the case had not yet been officially filed, he had taken the decision to release him.

The carriage continued on its way and soon reached the bustle of Guangta Street. Dressed in his hat and belt of office, Song Ci was feeling particularly comfortable with the way the day had turned out, as he drove around looking at the sights.

Suddenly, the carriage slowed down, confronted by some kind of disturbance up ahead. The sound of galloping hooves approached and a young nobleman wearing mourning clothes rode up, followed by two mounted bodyguards with swords at their belts. Seeing what was going on, Huo Xiong stopped the carriage, and Tong Gong mounted his horse and stationed himself in front. At the same time, Song Ci's own mounted guards on either side ahead of the carriage gave a great shout and raised their halberds, blocking the way.

The three men approaching reined in their horses, rolled from their saddles and knelt on the ground, kowtowing. The noisy street suddenly seemed to go quiet, and the passers-by silently lined the street on either side, waiting to see what was going on.

"Who are you?" Tong Gong asked.

"I am Xu Hong, son of Xu Tiju, the customs inspector."

"Why are you blocking our way?"

"My father was killed in his study last night."

"Then you need to make a report to the justice department right away," said Tong Gong. His master was only just recovering from illness, and he couldn't possibly let anyone accost him in the street to plead their case.

But Xu Hong remained kneeling and wailed: "I have already reported it, and someone was sent to investigate. They ruled that he had hanged himself. My father was an official all his life. He never gave family and friends preferential treatment, and he never neglected his duty to the emperor. Why should he suddenly hang himself? Besides, I've heard it said that when someone hangs himself, his tongue sticks out of his mouth, and my father's tongue was not sticking out. I am convinced there has been a miscarriage of justice. My mother ordered me to come and beg Your Lordship to investigate."

Song Ci had been listening carefully from inside the carriage. He knew that the emperor had appointed customs inspectors in Guangzhou, Quanzhou and Mingzhou (modern day Ningbo in Zhejiang Province). Their job was to inspect the shipping as it entered and left the harbour, to collect taxes and duty, and to supervise the office that dealt with foreign merchants. Customs Inspector Xu Tiju was a senior official appointed by the emperor, so how did he come to be murdered? The affair had to be investigated.

"In that case..." Tong Gong was about to go on, but Song Ci had considered long enough. He parted the curtain of the carriage and interrupted Tong Gong.

"Straight to the customs office," he ordered.

Tong Gong hesitated for a moment and turned to look at Song Ci.

"But, Master, you..."

"Straight to the customs office," Song Ci repeated, closing the carriage curtain.

"Thank you, My Lord." Xu Hong kowtowed and stood up. He and his two bodyguards quickly remounted their horses.

Huo Xiong considered trying to dissuade Song Ci, but he could see his master's mind was made up and thought better of it. The sound of horses' hooves and carriage bells was heard once again, as they made their way to the customs office on South Street.

3

# INVESTIGATION AT THE CUSTOMS OFFICE

It was dusk, and the red evening sun had disappeared into layers of cloud, painting the sky in vivid colours. A pale purple mist was rising over the vast Southern Ocean.

In the secretariat to the south of Mount Yuexiu, Mistress Song was standing by the tracery window of a pavilion in the inner courtyard, looking at the clouds lit by the evening sun as they drifted across the sky. She was becoming more and more uneasy. Her husband had gone to preside over the new term ceremony at the college, but he had been gone all day now. Why wasn't he home yet? She had given him plenty of advice when he set out.

"If you meet lots of people while you are out, you could easily spend half the day without noticing it."

That was her initial thought, but, as time passed and morning became afternoon, she said to herself: "Tong Gong and Huo Xiong are with him. I just hope they haven't let him drink any wine."

But now it was dusk, and he had still not returned, so she began to wonder what could have happened to him.

Outside, she could hear the evening bell of the Six Banyan Tree Temple, sounding rather eerie in the solemn dusk of the government offices. The fronds of the willow trees in the courtyard stirred as the evening breeze got up, and Mistress Song felt a slight chill run through her. The multi-coloured layers of clouds in the evening sky were gradually darkening.

Finally, Mistress Song called out: "Qi'er!"

"Yes."

Qi'er had been at her mother's side since early evening, and as she had watched her in a state of agitation – standing up, sitting down and then standing up again to go over to the window – she knew just how worried she was. She had thought of advising her mother to send out a messenger to look for Song Ci, but then decided it might just increase her anxiety, so she had said nothing. Now, when her mother called for her, she replied immediately, knowing full well what her mother was going to say.

As expected, Mistress Song said: "Do you think we should send someone out to look for him?"

Qi'er was, in fact, quite worried herself, and regretting that she hadn't insisted on accompanying her father that morning. But she fought to maintain an appearance of calm.

"Tong Gong and Huo Xiong are with him," she said. "No harm can have happened. Still, there's nothing to stop us sending someone, and if Father has decided to stay on for the banquet after the ceremony, they can tell Tong Gong to persuade him to come straight home."

"Very well. Send someone, and tell them to be quick about it."

"Yes, Mother," Qi'er replied, turning to leave the room and give the instructions.

As she left, she heard the sound of horses' hooves and carriage bells outside the compound gates. Startled, she hurried off in their direction. The two women had been concerned for Song Ci, but something way outside anything they had imagined had taken place…

Stretched out on the couch, looking at the flickering candlelight being reflected in the glaze of the Jingdezhen[1] porcelain vase on the bookshelf opposite, Song Ci thought the flame looked as though it were writhing in pain. It also seemed to him that countless tongues of flame were leaping all around him. He really wanted to sleep – just for a while. He had always felt better after a nap. But now his head was muzzy, and it ached. He felt dizzy, as though his head was being whirled through the clouds.

Song Ci decided he would sleep, and he shut his eyes.

But the sound of horses' hooves and carriage bells filled his ears. He seemed still to be in the carriage, endlessly travelling onwards. He wanted it to stop, but it wouldn't… finally, it did come to a halt. A horse whinnied and the carriage stopped – yes, it really had stopped. There was no sound from the horses' hooves, the bells were quiet and the carriage wasn't moving. What was going on? Through his daze, he remembered: they had reached the customs office.

Then came the sound of Mistress Xu's voice, thick, hoarse and still full of tears. He couldn't clearly make out what she was saying. Something about how she had sent her son to find Lord Song and ask him to attend; and how she had been waiting outside the office gate for a long time. She had invited them into the compound and led the way across the courtyard to Xu Tiju's study in a nearby building. On the way, Mistress Xu's tears had choked off most of her explanation, and the only sentence that was clear was: Xu Tiju had not hanged himself. Well, whether it was suicide or not was a matter to be determined by the investigation. Song Ci had handled many cases of suspected suicide. For him, whether the cause was suicide by hanging or murder by hanging; whether death had been caused by some foreign object and then faked to look like suicide; all this was clearly 'written' on the neck of the victim, and Song Ci could read the signs as easily as reading a book. He was quite confident that a close inspection would reveal the truth.

A large group of soldiers were gathered outside Xu Tiju's study.

"No one has entered the study since it happened last night, except for the investigator sent by the judicial commissioner, and the coroner," Mistress Xu said.

The door to the study was closed and Tong Gong stepped up, pushed it open and went in. Song Ci followed him, with Huo Xiong bringing up the rear – wherever they went during all those years together, they always followed the same procedure for entering the room of a crime scene.

Inside the study, incense smoke was rising from the desk, and the thick smell of sandalwood filled their nostrils. This was unfortunate as it masked the smell from any foreign substance on Xu Tiju's body that might have contributed to his death. Song Ci immediately instructed that the incense be extinguished, and Mistress Xu ordered one of her servants to do so.

On one side of the room a silk noose hung from a crossbeam, and under it there stood an x-frame chair. When Song Ci looked, he could see several sets of footprints from the same individual, overlaid on the cushion on the chair. They indicated that the deceased, in a state of mental agitation, had climbed up onto the chair and then got down, before climbing up again. In what were evidently the top-most of the overlaid footprints, the toe-end was more heavily indented than the heel. This suggested the man was standing on tiptoe just before he died. Song Ci saw all this before he had even stopped in front of the chair. He didn't give it another look, before saying to Tong Gong and Huo Xiong: "Let's examine the body."

In one corner of the room, curtained off by a purple gauze hanging, they could just make out the shape of a body lying on a couch, covered with a white shroud. Song Ci went over to the couch, Tong Gong lifted the shroud, Huo Xiong fished out a ruler and some other instruments, and the autopsy began.

Crown of the head, tips of the hair, nape of the neck, neck, forehead, eyes, ears, mouth, teeth, tongue, fingernails, toenails; Song Ci inspected the whole body before frowning slightly. He had come to the same conclusion as the investigating officer – it was suicide by hanging.

"My Lord, my husband must have been murdered. He would never have committed suicide," said Mistress Xu, who was standing to one side.

Song Ci didn't reply. He too was thinking: why would a high-ranking imperial official suddenly kill himself?

After a moment, he asked Mistress Xu: "Who was the first to find him?"

"I was," she replied.

"How did you find him?"

Mistress Xu's voice choked and she started sobbing. Song Ci listened for a while, and he finally made out what she was trying to say. Her husband had been feeling rather unwell recently, and by the third drum of the previous night, he still hadn't retired to bed, so Mistress Xu had gone to fetch him. Normally, when he was working alone in his study, he hated to be disturbed, and even his wife and son would not go in without a specific reason. That evening, Mistress Xu stood by the study window, from where she could see that the lamp was still lit inside. She called quietly to her husband, but there was no reply. She called again with the same result. Only then did she push the door open and go in. Not seeing her husband, she called again, but still there was no reply. All was quiet in the room, and the lamp was almost out, its light flickering across the desk and casting long shadows. Suddenly Mistress Xu was afraid, and she called out again: "Husband, come out now and stop scaring me!"

Still no one replied. Now she was really frightened, and she decided to go and summon her son. But, just as she turned to go, she saw her husband's body hanging from a beam near the door...

"Who cut the body down, and was he still alive?" Song Ci asked.

Mistress Xu broke down and couldn't answer. Her son spoke for her: "My Lord, it was I and some of the servants who cut him down. He wasn't breathing and there was no hope of reviving him."

As Xu Hong was speaking, Huo Xiong had removed Xu Tiju's shoes and was comparing them to the shoeprints on the chair under the beam. Half-listening to Xu Hong, Song Ci made his way over to the chair. The soles of the shoes were an exact match to the prints on the chair. Huo Xiong also measured the distance from the seat of the chair to the silk rope, and it tallied with Xu Tiju's height.

"My Lord, the murderer must have faked it. It can't be true! It simply can't be true!" Xu Hong said, seeing what was going on.

Song Ci didn't reply, and his face gave nothing away.

"My Lord, the dust on the beam has been disturbed," Tong Gong reported from the rafters where he had climbed.

Only Song Ci and Tong Gong understood the significance of what Tong Gong said. If the dust on the rafter was undisturbed, then they could be sure it wasn't suicide, but the body had been hung there when it was already dead. The disturbance of the dust indicated the death struggles of a suicide.

Could the murderer have faked it? Song Ci asked himself.

Of course, the evidence could have been manufactured, but the evidence in the room and the state of the body all tallied with a verdict of suicide. So, was that, that?

"We should examine the body again," Song Ci thought.

This time the examination was even more detailed, looking into every wrinkle and crease on the body, but the verdict was still written just as clearly on Xu Tiju's corpse – the face was purple and the bruises on the neck from the rope were black, converging from either side, but not crossing. This was different from the marks left if someone had strangled the victim first and then faked suicide; in that case the marks from the rope would have crossed. Nor was it consistent with the body having been suspended after death, in which case the marks around the neck would have been white, not dark and livid. On top of that, Xu Tiju's hair was not disordered, his hands were not outstretched, and his arms and legs were hanging straight down. Nor were there any signs of other injuries. As for what Xu Hong had said about the tongue sticking out on corpses that had hanged themselves, that only happened if the rope was round the throat below the larynx, and two times out of three, the mouth was forced open and the tongue protruded through the teeth. In addition, there would be evidence of saliva at the corners of the mouth and on the chest. But in Xu Tiju's case, the tongue had stayed in the mouth because the rope was above the larynx, keeping the mouth shut and the teeth clenched, so the tongue could not stick out. There was also urine and faeces on Xu's trousers, something often seen in suicide by hanging. All of this was clear evidence that Xu Tiju had hanged himself.

"Lord Song, my father can't have killed himself, he simply can't," Xu Hong insisted.

Song Ci still did not reply. If he told the family that it was suicide, they might then find out the reason behind it. The implications of this were not something to be taken lightly.

He questioned the household about Xu Tiju's everyday routine, and what he usually ate and drank. He interrogated not just Mistress Xu and her son and daughter, but any guests, aides and other minor officials, the office guards and servant girls, but none of them suggested any reason for their master's suicide. Song Ci's frown grew deeper.

He wondered whether he could still reach a verdict of suicide without finding a reason for it.

Tong Gong and Huo Xiong searched high and low, inside and outside, turning the place upside down in the hunt for any trace of anything hidden away, but everywhere the dust was undisturbed, and they found nothing suspicious.

Before they noticed, the sun had begun to set, the light was fading and dusk falling. Mistress Xu and her son were terrified that Song Ci would give his verdict of suicide and leave, so they kept repeating:

"My father cannot have killed himself."

"My husband cannot have killed himself."

Song Ci still said nothing, and felt he cut rather a sorry figure for not being willing to commit himself. Why can I not even decide if it is suicide or murder? he thought to himself.

Just at that moment, however, he felt a sudden hot flush across his forehead. A blinding light flashed in front of his eyes and the roof beams seemed to be spinning round above his head. He was unable to remain standing, and he toppled over…

Ah, there it was again: the sound of horses' hooves in his ear, and it was as though every step resonated through his whole body. The wheels of the carriage seemed to be whirling through his head, making him dizzier and dizzier, and his head ached terribly.

"Husband!… Husband!…"

Song Ci could hear his wife calling him, her voice full of anxiety, and he felt a hand gently probing the greater *yang* meridian on his temple.

"Father, you need to relax. You mustn't think about it any more!"

Song Ci heard the tears in his daughter's voice, even though she was speaking very quietly.

"Yes, you're right… mustn't think about it… must sleep for a while… sleep for a while…"

4

# STRANGULATION THROUGH A FOREIGN OBJECT

Outside the room, Qiu Juan was tearfully fanning the flames of a portable stove on which she was brewing some medicine. The flickering flames of the stove were casting a red light across the gloomy evening, and the pot was emitting a gentle burbling noise. A fine column of steam was rising and dispersing through the air.

Qi'er came out and stood beside Qiu Juan, taking the palm-leaf fan from her hand. Qiu Juan was about to tell Qi'er there was no need until she looked up and saw the tears flowing freely from Qi'er's eyes. She handed the fan over without a word.

Qi'er had been with her step-parents for ten years, together morning and evening, never parted. She had shared in all the difficulties and dangers of her stepfather's trials and investigations, and felt every moment of her stepmother's worries and concerns. She thought about how much better her father had been, as he recovered from his illness, and how he had welcomed the new spring. Standing on top of the pagoda at the Six Banyan Tree Temple, looking out over the Pearl River, he had spoken of how the Tongyou River in his home town only flowed during the high waters of the spring flood.

"I must take you to my old home, Qi'er," he had said. "You've never seen Jianyang."

She also thought about how talkative her father had been that morning, about all the rich food he had eaten at the banquet, and she regretted that she hadn't stopped him from going out on the investigation.

"I'm so stupid," she upbraided herself, as though she should have anticipated what happened, as if her father being stopped in the street and being asked to investigate a case was an everyday occurrence.

And she thought about what her mother had just whispered, as she gently wiped a tear from the corner of her daughter's eye with her finger: "Don't take it so hard, Qi'er. You know that, once your father decides to do something, no one can stop him."

But all that these comforting words had served to accomplish was to make her eyes fill with tears again, and send her running here. And now she stood fanning the stove, thinking, and wiping her tears. She really wanted to stop crying and go back to her mother's side, but the tears just wouldn't stop.

"Let me by, and I'll strain the medicine," Qiu Juan said.

It was only then that Qi'er noticed that the medicine had already come to the boil, and, in fact, was boiling over. She looked for a cloth to protect her hands so she could lift the pot off the heat, but Qiu Juan was ahead of her and had used a headscarf to pick the pot up by its handles and put it down on the table. The flames of the stove reflected off Qi'er's tears and made her face glow red.

"You take it in," Qiu Juan said.

It was the first watch of the night, and the office compound was immersed in darkness. Even the sturdy Tong Gong was feeling the cold from the night wind. He was standing by the window, outside Song Ci's room, looking distractedly at the distant stars, lost in his own thoughts. He wanted to go in and see his master, but he didn't dare disturb him.

When they had got back, and he had rushed Song Ci to his room and into bed, Song Ci had revived briefly, and when he recognised Tong Gong, the first thing he said was: "Go... go back..."

Tong Gong understood. His master wanted him to get to the bottom of the matter. That in itself was not unusual, but with that day's case, Song Ci himself had undertaken an exhaustive investigation and found nothing to indicate murder. What would he, Tong Gong, be able to achieve?

He wracked his brains, thinking of all the cases of unusual death they had handled in the past, but he found no inspiration. Finally, one man presented himself to his thoughts: Shu Gengshi. Shu Gengshi who had been local magistrate in Jianyang, then prefectural magistrate in Nanjianzhou and now a senior provincial government official in Guangdong.

When they had arrived at the college that morning, amid all the drum rolls and fanfares, Song Ci had been surrounded by all the invited officials.

"Long life and good health to you, Lord Song!"

"The college thanks you, My Lord, for gracing this trivial affair with your presence."

"My Lord, your attendance brings great honour to the college."

"My Lord…"

Amid the noise, Song Ci had advanced towards the college gates, acknowledging the greetings of the crowd. Tong Gong and Huo Xiong followed behind. They noticed that, among all the assembled officials, only one was absent from those surging forward, and had actually turned away. Seeing it too, Song Ci headed towards him, asking: "Who is that?"

"Good health to Your Lordship!"

As Song Ci reached the man's side, he turned and made a reverence.

Then, they all saw who it was. Song Ci nodded his head and was about to speak, when one of the attendant officials appeared at his side saying: "This is the judicial commissioner, Lord Shu."

"It's Shu Gengshi, isn't it?" Song Ci said, smiling.

"Yes, My Lord, it is," Shu said, also smiling.

This meeting was quite unexpected. As was only natural with the passage of time, Shu Gengshi's eyes had narrowed somewhat, with crows-feet at their corners, and his face had reddened rather.

"It's been ten years, but you still look like a young man," Song Ci said.

"Thank you, thank you," Shu Gengshi replied, addressing Song Ci, but with half an eye on Tong Gong and Huo Xiong behind him.

Although many years had passed, just the sight of Shu Gengshi upset Tong Gong. Meanwhile, the other officials were staring at the two men, greatly intrigued that Lord Song should know Commissioner Shu. Song Ci gestured to them all, saying: "Come on, come on. Let us go into the college."

So, was there anything significant in this incident? Tong Gong considered it and found himself shaking his head. Probably the only reason he had thought of Shu Gengshi was because of the resentment he was still harbouring from that business thirty years ago. What could the death of Xu Tiju possibly have to do with Shu Gengshi? It was hard to see any connection. And although Song Ci had ordered an investigation into the supposed suicide, they hadn't found any indication that it might have been murder.

"Well, Master!" Tong Gong looked up at the night sky and found himself thinking that, of all the puzzling cases they had investigated in the past, not one had been been resolved without Song Ci's personal direction…

Under the shimmering starlight, the buildings, plants and trees were fuzzy and indistinct, as though seen through a silk screen. Huo Xiong was unable to keep still as he waited outside Song Ci's room. He wandered between the buildings, sometimes standing in Song Ci's doorway, then moving to the colonnade outside, or into the shadows of the trees that grew in the courtyard. He desperately wanted to do something for his master, but didn't know what. He turned that day's case over in his mind, and thought back to his grandfather's stories, long, long ago of all the strange cases he had seen. But no matter how hard he thought, nothing helpful came to him.

Just for a moment, as he looked up at the stars, he found himself staring into a boundless ocean and he seemed to hear the sound of waves crashing against the shoals, and the strange babbling of foreign tongues. Then he found himself looking at the mouth of the Pearl River outside Humen, where armed soldiers were inspecting the shipping coming in and out of the harbour. He could see the Haishan Inn,[1] where a host of foreign merchants, in their outlandish clothes, were raising their wine cups in a toast to a man dressed in the garb of an imperial Song official. That official was the chief inspector of customs, Xu Tiju!

He remembered that Mistress Xu had said that, some days before, a number of exotically dressed foreigners had invited Xu Tiju to a banquet. Her husband hadn't gone because he was ill, but he had said something to them in a strange language and sent them on their way. Could this case involve those foreigners?

He knew that Xu Tiju had overseen foreign trade and often had dealings with foreigners. It was more than probable, also, that he handled contraband smuggled in by those foreigners. If that was the origin of this case, then it might be just the start of something much bigger. But would the foreigners dare to take such a huge risk? And for them to slip unnoticed into Xu Tiju's study, and not leave any trace, would have been no easy task. Besides, there was nothing particularly unusual, given his involvement with foreign trade, for Xu Tiju to have been their guest…

"Aaaah!" Huo Xiong looked up and heaved a deep sigh. His thoughts had taken him round in a circle, and he was back where he started. Above him, all he could see was the boundless night sky.

Clouds floated across that sky, obscuring the stars, and a cold wind rustled the leaves of the trees in the courtyard. The darkness deepened. A faint whinnying came from the stables where Song Ci's chestnut horse was stalled. Horses and humans pick up on each others' emotions, and the whinnying did nothing to calm the mood.

The sound of footsteps came from inside the room, and Qi'er emerged through the door. Tong Gong hurried over to her and asked: "The Master?"

"He's sleeping."

Only then did Huo Xiong and Tong Gong go into the bedroom.

A doctor was keeping watch beside the bed. As Tong Gong and Huo

Xiong joined them, they relaxed a little when they saw the faint frown on their master's face as he slept. They thought he looked as though he was mulling over some problem.

The candles in the silver candleholder were gradually going out, and Qi'er brought some new ones, brightening the room considerably. When she turned around, she saw her mother drawing a hand across her brow, as though exhausted.

"You must go and get some rest, Mother," she urged.

Mistress Song dropped her hand and replied: "Qi'er, you're the one who should go and rest. If little Xuan'er wakes up, he will be wanting you."

"There's no need. Qiu Juan is looking after that." Qi'er sat down and huddled up to her mother.

Mistress Song put an arm round her daughter, and she was suddenly overwhelmed by sadness. A shudder ran through her as she clutched Qi'er's hand, and her tears fell freely onto the back of it. Always sensitive to such things, Qi'er realised her mother was thinking of her birth daughter. She wanted to comfort her mother, but simply didn't know how. She was also worried that she might just increase her mother's distress, so she just put her own hand on her mother's and pressed it gently.

Tong Gong and Huo Xiong looked at this scene but said nothing and just sat down in silence.

The wind was blowing, and Song Ci heard a thud as a shutter was blown open by the wind, and a gust blew in. He felt the slight chill and opened his eyes, expecting to tell Qi'er to close the window. But there was no one beside the bed and the room was empty.

"What time is it, and where have they all gone?"

Another gust of cold air blew in, leaving only a single candle alight in the candleholder, flickering gently, on the point of going out. Black shadows appeared at the window, and two men climbed into the room, two masked men carrying short knives.

"Aah! This time I won't escape the assassin's knife!" The thought flashed through Song Ci's head.

But after flourishing their blades, the two killers put them away. One of them suddenly took a length of rope from inside his jacket, and the two of them advanced, step by step, on the bed where Song Ci lay… I'll wait for them to get close, he thought to himself, then catch them unawares with a double-fisted strike and lay them out! But they were already upon him, and he felt his hands being tied so he couldn't move. He tried to cry out, but could not. A pair of hands lifted his head, and someone snatched away his neck pillow,[2] and put it on his throat, with the cushion on top. They were about to strangle him…

Aah! He could feel them pressing down…

"Husband! Husband! What's the matter?" Mistress Song cried out, seeing the sweat beading on Song Ci's brow and hearing his breathing coarsen.

Song Ci woke up and opened his eyes with an effort. Through his blurred vision, he could see the figure sitting next to him was his wife, with Qi'er, Tong Gong, Huo Xiong and the doctor standing behind her. After a moment, he frowned and half-closed his eyes again, as though grasping for a forgotten dream. Another long pause, and suddenly his eyes were open again, glittering with the kind of gleam that, in the past, had meant that the pieces of a puzzling case had suddenly fallen into place.

"Go… go quickly…" Song Ci was looking at Tong Gong and Huo Xiong, and although his voice was weak, every word was clear. "Xu Tiju's body… go… and re-examine it… I think it's possible… he was strangled… but they put something between the rope and his neck."[3]

When Tong Gong and Huo Xiong heard this, their eyes lit up and the blood started coursing through their veins. Tong Gong put his mouth beside Song Ci's ear and whispered: "We understand. We'll go immediately and get to the bottom of this."

The two of them left. Soon, as he lay on his bed, Song Ci heard the sound of horses outside the window, and he heaved a great sigh of relief.

A little while later he thought of something else, and he turned to his wife, looking both at her and at the huge collection of precious volumes on his bookshelves.

"Do you have to look at it now?" Mistress Song knew what her husband was thinking, and she stared hard at him.

"I have to see it," Song Ci said firmly.

Mistress Song sighed and turned to Qi'er: "Go and get it!"

Also realising what it was her father wanted to look at, Song Qi went over to the bookshelves. She took down the beautiful book box the emperor had given her father, opened it and took out the two volumes it contained. She carried them over to her mother.

Mistress Song took the copy of *Collected Cases of Injustice Righted*, quickly flipped through to the section in the third scroll entitled 'Suicide by hanging', unrolled it, and put it on Song Ci's chest where he could read it.

That was, of course, precisely the chapter Song Ci wanted to consult. Propping himself up on the pillow Qi'er put behind him, Song Ci took the volume in both hands and began to read, carefully. When he came to the end of a page, he looked up, and Qi'er helped him turn to the next one. He read the section on suicide by hanging, and the one on how strangling could be made to look like suicide. Both were clearly and concisely written, but there was no recorded case of strangulation through a foreign object, since this was something he had never encountered.

Song Ci closed his eyes and called up the image of Xu Tiju's corpse. He remembered that the head had shown nothing to indicate murder, and if it really had been strangulation made to look like suicide, then the perpetrator was no ordinary assassin.

But could the murderer have possessed such a high degree of expertise? Song Ci asked himself.

Yes, yes, it was quite possible if he knew about the use of a foreign object as a buffer. Quite possible, he answered himself.

Then a thought struck him that pierced his heart like a knife. He had written his book to help the empire's law officers deal properly with the cases that came before them. But supposing a criminal got hold of a copy, could it not help him to conceal a crime more efficiently?

"Books can help the nation prosper, or they can throw it into disorder. If men with evil intentions study them, and apply the knowledge in false judgments, the country will be thrown into chaos."

In the midst of his consternation, he heard the words, so many years before, of the proprietor of the Hall of Ten Thousand Scrolls, Yu Renzhong.

Pain filled his head. The copy of the book he was cradling on his chest began to sway in front of his eyes, and then disappeared in a blinding white light...

"Husband, what have you just thought of?" Mistress Song asked quietly but urgently, taking the book from him as she spoke. "You mustn't tax yourself any more. Let's put the book away, shall we?"

"Father," Qi'er said, gently wiping the sweat from his forehead, "wait until you are better, and then read it."

"You mustn't read it again, you really must not," ordered the old doctor.

Song Ci nodded his head. He felt very strange and wondered why he couldn't put the book down. Gradually he relaxed the hands that held it.

5

## A LIFE OR DEATH STRUGGLE

Tong Gong and Huo Xiong reached the customs office before the third watch.

Back in Xu Tiju's study, they carried out a through re-examination of the whole body, and after taking careful measurements, Huo Xiong re-covered it with the shroud, and he and Tong Gong left through the curtained doorway.

"We can now say with certainty that Lord Xu did not commit suicide," Huo Xiong said.

Mistress Xu and his son and daughter had maintained all along that a third party was involved, but even so, this pronouncement startled them.

"So... it was murder?" asked Mistress Xu.

"In this very residence," Tong Gong replied.

"Ha!" Mistress Xu exclaimed, as she felt the hairs rise on the back of her neck, as though there was an insect crawling up it.

"You must understand," Huo Xiong said, "that there are no traces left behind in the room. Up in the beams and rafters, and anywhere at all a person could have hidden, the dust is undisturbed. The murderer must have walked right up to Lord Xu, and, with only the minimum of exertion, strangled him through some foreign object. If it wasn't someone from the household, how could they have got so close, so easily. I remember you saying, Mistress Xu, that whenever your husband was alone in his study, even you and your children would not disturb him. So, who else could it have been?"

"I suppose it could have been Wu Cheng," Xu Hong blurted out.

"Who is Wu Cheng?"

"My father's personal secretary."

"On what basis do you suspect him?"

"He could go in and out freely when my father was reading in his study."

"Is there anyone else who had that kind of access?"

"Nobody."

Thus, Wu Cheng became the prime suspect.

Initially, Mistress Xu found this hard to believe, as Wu Cheng was her husband's most trusted member of staff. But she turned to her son and instructed him to summon the guard.

"Best not to involve anyone else just yet," Tong Gong urged. "This crime couldn't have been committed by just one man. There must have been an accomplice, but we don't know who. The two of us and your son will go to his lodgings to interrogate him, and then we can see where we go from there."

"That is definitely the best way, Mistress Xu," Huo Xiong agreed.

"Very well. You go, but be careful."

With Xu Hong leading the way, and all of them armed, the three men made their way to Wu Cheng's lodgings, which were in a side courtyard. It was quiet and secluded in there, deeply shadowed by trees and strewn with fallen blossom; it hummed with the noise of insects hidden in its shady recesses. There was an open space in front, across which a narrow path led to a tiled building with a hallway and a wooden lean-to. Behind this building was a tile-capped perimeter wall, on the inside of which grew a row of tall banana palms. Outside the wall, some tall cottonwood trees stretched their blossom-laden branches over the ridge tiles into the courtyard.

The three men followed the dark brick path to Wu Cheng's quarters, where they found the door closed, but a light showing from inside. It was abnormally still. Tong Gong mounted the threshold and thrust the door open violently. They were dumbfounded by the scene before them. Wu Cheng's body was lying in a pool of blood, a sword lying across his chest, dripping with fresh blood. The three men all gasped as they stood in the doorway.

Around them all was quiet as the grave.

"He has cut his own throat," Xu Hong said.

He then made to go into the room, but just at that moment, a thought flashed into Tong Gong's head. With knitted brows, he reached out and silently grabbed hold of Xu Hong, pulled off his jacket and threw it into the room.

There was a clashing noise, and two flashes of light, as two steel knives hacked down from behind the door, slashing the jacket into pieces, which then fell to the floor.

Xu Hong broke into a cold sweat, unable to take in what had just happened; he just heard a hissing noise and felt a cold draught flash across his face. There was a clatter of blade on blade as Tong Gong stretched out his knife to parry the two others that came streaking out from behind the door. Xu Hong and Huo Xiong drew their own weapons, and a hand-to-hand fight broke out in the courtyard.

Two masked men flourishing knives attacked ferociously, like bolts of white lightning. One of them engaged Tong Gong, and the other took on Xu Hong and Huo Xiong. This second man seemed to have enormously long arms, and was untroubled by the unequal odds. His steel knife flashing with cold light, he pressed home his attack, following his blade in, so that man and knife became one – left, right, up, down he whirled, changing his point of attack with lightning speed. There was a clatter as Xu Hong's knife dropped to the ground, blood dripping from a slash to his wrist. It was all up with him, and he tumbled out of the fight.

Huo Xiong himself had been taken by surprise, as the long-armed man's blade came flashing and whistling towards him, pressing him close. The fight hadn't lasted long before he began to think he was in trouble; he needed to find a counter. He felt the cold draught of his opponent's blade as it sliced down past his own raised knife towards his belly. He couldn't defend against the blow, so, quick as a flash, using a move taught to him by Tong Gong, he twisted his body and dropped, so that the blade caught in his belt and slid past harmlessly, not even scratching him. But before he could right himself, the knife came flashing in again, and when he raised his own blade to parry, he felt his arm go numb and he dropped his knife. In the same breath, he twisted and hurled himself, cat-like, out of range. As he did so, he unwrapped the length of fine-link chain from around his waist, and flicked it out at his opponent's wrist. He heard a confused clatter of metal as the chain wrapped itself, like a silver snake, around the man's knife. The barbs on the links at the end of the chain prevented the man from catching hold of it, and in the blink of an eye, his knife had gone flying.

This time it was Huo Xiong's turn to prevent his long-armed opponent from catching his breath. Making the chain dance and sing, he went on the attack. Even disarmed and empty-handed, the man showed no fear. Twisting like a swimming dragon and turning like a dancing snake as Huo Xiong's barbed chain whipped past him, front and back, he somehow managed to prevent it from catching hold. Huo Xiong soon realised his chain was not going to be effective. Moreover, he was finding it increasingly difficult to defend against the two long arms that came whirling at him, apparently from all directions at once. Just as he registered this thought, his opponent seized hold of the chain, and used it to launch himself through the air, aiming his boot in a side-kick at Huo Xiong. He tried to use the chain to defend, but one of his opponent's feet pinned the chain to the ground, while the other shot out and struck Huo Xiong on the arm. He felt a shooting pain run through his limb, as he dropped the chain and stumbled. He immediately righted himself, but before he could properly steady himself, he saw the two long arms, outspread like an eagle's wings, smashing down towards him. Even though the man was some distance away, Huo Xiong felt the wind from his long, whirling arms. Unable to lift one of his own arms, Huo Xiong knew he was in real trouble, and shouted out for Tong Gong. At the same time, he tried to use his good arm to ward off the blow, but to no avail. The double-handed strike landed flush on his chest, knocking all the wind out of him, and making his ears ring. He was sent hurtling backwards into a banana palm. He fell to the ground, blood coming from his mouth, and unable to move.

All this had taken only moments. Tong Gong was still engaged in an evenly matched battle with the other masked man, when he heard Huo Xiong's cry for help. He knew it was ominous and, as he turned to look, saw the last stage of the fight. Not knowing whether Huo Xiong was dead or alive after that final blow, he feinted, and thrust aside his onrushing opponent, fearful that the other masked man was about to finish off Huo Xiong. Before he could get there, he saw Xu Hong, scrambling up from the ground, and picking up the sword that lay fallen a few paces from him. But the masked man had also picked up his own sword, and had leapt in front of Xu Hong, slashing down at him. Xu Hong dodged left and right, but as he did so, he landed on some rotting leaves, and his back leg slipped from under him, sending him tumbling to the ground. As his life flashed before his eyes, he heard a clanging noise and saw sparks fly as Tong Gong's knife intercepted the other man's blow, and saved his life. Tong Gong felt the weight of the other man's strike, and regretted that he had not been able to settle him once and for all. Now, with the odds stacked against him two to one, he was in extreme danger.

As he faced off against the two men, he shouted to Xu Hong: "Quick, go and get help!"

Xu Hong did not want to go, but when he went to pick up the fallen sword, he saw his hand was covered in blood and realised he didn't have the strength to wield the blade. When he looked at Tong Gong again, he saw him whirling his sword in a protective circle, up, down and around, leaping nimbly, ceaselessly on the move. He watched through blurry eyes, and thought to himself that if he didn't go for help now, Tong Gong would certainly get hurt. It went against the grain to leave, but there was no time to lose.

After Xu Hong had gone, the two masked men pressed Tong Gong even harder, but he exerted his skills to the utmost. He dodged every attack and seized every opportunity to advance, nimble as a monkey and lithe as a swallow. His two opponents couldn't touch him. After a while, the sound of shouting came from outside the courtyard's moon gate. Fearing for Tong Gong's safety, Xu Hong had ordered the soldiers he had fetched to make as much noise as possible as they advanced so as to reassure Tong Gong. When the two masked men heard the commotion, and realised there was no immediate prospect of overcoming Tong Gong, they signalled to each other and, without warning, hurled their knives straight at Tong Gong.

"Clang! Clang!" Tong Gong dodged the two blades, and when he looked up, he saw the two men leap up and scale the perimeter wall, one after the other. There was a clattering noise as the tiles they dislodged from the top of the wall fell to the ground.

"Don't let them get away!" Tong Gong picked up the knives and threw them, flashing across the yard. He heard a sharp cry as one of the knives hit the trailing leg of the slower of the two men, and he fell back from the wall with a thud, as the other man twisted himself over the wall and dropped to the other side.

Tong Gong raced to the base of the wall, and hurled himself up and over it in pursuit. What he had not anticipated was that, waiting on the other side, there was a man, dressed in black, astride one horse and leading two others. Without a word, the masked man who had made it over the wall grabbed the reins of one of the horses, mounted and rode away.

It all happened so quickly, the man in black didn't have time to take in what was happening, as Tong Gong rushed in front of him. When he realised something had gone wrong, he tried to flee with the other empty horse, but Tong Gong had hurled himself onto it, snatched the reins, shoved away the man in black and galloped off in pursuit of the masked man.

With the masked man in front, Tong Gong behind him and the man in black bringing up the rear, the three horses raced away. After about two *li*, Tong Gong realised he was gaining on the masked man, and he took from his belt his own length of fine-link steel chain, which he sent snaking out at his quarry. The man heard it hiss through the air, and put up his hand to ward it off. The chain wrapped itself around his arm, and with an almighty heave, Tong Gong pulled him from the saddle. But he had not accounted for the man's extraordinarily long arms, which reached out as he fell, and caught hold of Tong Gong, so the two of them both tumbled from their horses, which galloped off into the distance.

On the ground, Tong Gong and the masked man attacked each other again. This time, Tong Gong's first aim was to snatch off the man's mask. He was well-practised in this, having developed a particular technique. This was because his old martial arts master, Song Xie, had instructed him: "Whenever you are pursuing a masked criminal, if you can unmask him, it puts you at a psychological advantage. Besides, if you don't manage to arrest him then, at least you can recognise him later, and that is almost as good."

After several exchanges, Tong Gong eventually got hold of the man's mask. When he tore it off, it seemed to him that the face it revealed, with long wavy hair and moustaches like a young dragon, was very familiar. As he was puzzling over this, the black-clad man on the other horse arrived on the scene and drew his sword with a hissing noise, forcing Tong Gong to leap out of the way.

"Well, old man, this time I'll not let you get away," said the unmasked man through clenched teeth. Now Tong Gong recognised him: it was the captain of police from the prefectural *yamen* at Jianyang, Liang E.

Without warning, Liang E drew a glittering short knife from inside his clothes. The pair of them, Liang E and the man in black, one on horseback, one on foot, advanced together on Tong Gong, who drew his own short knife from his leggings. Another fierce battle ensued, with Liang E and his accomplice determined to kill Tong Gong. But once again, as they slashed left and right, they still could not touch him.

They heard the sound of galloping horses approaching from a distance. It was Xu Hong and his men in hot pursuit. Liang E, who had been fighting lustily up to that point, saw that the momentum was shifting, so he shoved Tong Gong away and suddenly aimed a blow at the man in black. Taken by surprise, he fell from his saddle with a yell, and almost simultaneously, Liang E sprang onto the horse, clamped his legs around it, and galloped off.

In far less time than it takes to tell, Tong Gong hurled his knife after the horse and rider. It flashed through the air and struck the horse in the rump. The horse whinnied in shock and reared on its hind legs. It seemed that Liang E was going to be thrown, but he managed to grip the reins even tighter, and remained in the saddle. Maddened by the pain of the knife wound, the horse bolted, with Liang E still on its back, and rapidly disappeared from sight.

Left behind were Tong Gong and the man in black, who stood watching as Liang E rode into the distance. Then they turned to face each other. The sound of the horses bringing Xu Hong and his men was very close now, and Tong Gong yelled at the other man: "Who are you?"

The man didn't reply, but his eyes gleamed with a strange light, and the whole of his face seemed to shudder. Suddenly he raised his knife crosswise in front of him, looking like a cornered animal about to fight for its life. His body coiled, and he leapt into the attack with knife and feet, limbs whirling, launching a golden eagle throat strike at the empty-handed Tong Gong. Tong Gong saw the move coming and threw himself back and down so he ended up flat on the ground. The man went flying over the top of him and Tong Gong thought about delivering an upwards head strike with his feet. But he held back because he really needed to take the man alive. He simply watched the man fly past. Even so, the man lay motionless where he landed.

Tong Gong hurried over and lifted the man by his jacket, demanding: "Who sent you?"

The man's head lolled to one side, and he didn't reply. Tong Gong looked more closely and saw that he was, in fact, already dead. Sticking out from his back was the handle of a short sword. Tong Gong hadn't seen it happen, but Liang E had thrust the sword into the man when he struck him. Xu Hong and his men arrived. Without a word, Tong Gong took one of their horses and slung the black-clad body over its back. He then mounted the horse himself, and rode back with Xu Hong to the customs office.

Back at the office, the other assassin, who had fallen back down from the wall, was standing tied to a pillar. Tong Gong took the body of the black-clad man and tossed it down with a shout in front of his associate. He took the short sword that was now strapped to his back, and held it to the assassin's chest.

"Speak! Who sent you?"

"I'll… I'll tell you."

6

## BEFORE DAWN

The stars were almost gone, and the night mist had thickened.

Back at the secretariat, Mistress Song, Qi'er, Qiu Juan and the others were waiting anxiously for news of Tong Gong. Little Song Geng had woken up and wanted his mother. Xiao Bao had brought him to his grandfather's room, and he was now standing, wide awake, beside the bed.

The doors and windows looking out onto the courtyard were all tightly fastened, sealing out any draught. Even so, Mistress Song still found herself shivering from time to time.

In the middle of the third watch, Song Ci suddenly developed a blinding headache. He couldn't swallow his medicine, so Qiu Juan fed it to him spoonful by spoonful. At first, he choked on it, but eventually it slipped past his parched mouth and down his throat, and finally put him into a drugged sleep. It was only by pinching his nostrils that the faintest of breaths could be felt. Mistress Song and her daughters were gripped by overwhelming fear and sadness, sure that Song Ci was about to slip away from them. They didn't dare close their eyes for an instant. Occasionally, Song Ci's lips moved, as though he was about to wake up, but he didn't.

How Mistress Song wished Tong Gong and the others would return. If they brought back good news, they would be able to tell Song Ci when he woke up… and just as she thought of this, she lifted her head and turned to listen. Sure enough, she could hear the sound of horses fast approaching.

"I can hear two horses," Qi'er said.

Suddenly, Mistress Song was alert, and she turned to Qi'er and Qiu Juan. They were looking back at her.

"They've come back," Qiu Juan said.

Mistress Song hurriedly stood up and went out of the room and then of the building, to meet the arrivals. After a little while, she saw two unfamiliar soldiers. The one in front was carrying the bloodied form of Huo Xiong, with the other soldier supporting him from behind. They quickly crossed the threshold.

Qi'er came running past the startled Mistress Song, to throw her arms around her husband. As she helped him inside, she asked, in a broken voice: "What have they done to you?"

Qiu Juan hurried up with a chair for Huo Xiong to sit on, and Mistress Song asked: "What about Tong Gong?"

"He's gone to break into the commissioner's office," Huo Xiong said.

"Why?" Mistress Song and Qiu Juan asked together in alarm.

"It's all become clear... the ringleader is... Commissioner Shu Gengshi."

Mistress Song jumped in amazement.

It turned out that the inspectors in Nanenzhou had been colluding with pirates, and there had been many cases of both smuggling and plundering of merchant shipping. When these were brought before Commissioner Shu Gengshi, not only did he decline to prosecute, he actively collaborated with the perpetrators and shared in the profits. When Superintendent of Customs Xu Tiju found out what was going on, he wrote a letter exposing the crime, intending to make a report to Chief Provincial Administrator Song Ci. He had been unable to do so, as Song Ci was already ill and confined to bed. It was such a significant affair that, in order to keep it secret, Xu Tiju did not breathe a word of it even to his wife and son. Little did he think that his most trusted secretary had long ago been bribed by Shu Gengshi to keep him informed of any threats to his business.

When Shu Gengshi heard what was going on, he was greatly alarmed and immediately sent his acolyte of many years, Liang E, and an experienced investigator called Wu Zuo to confer with Xu Tiju's secretary. And because he was scared of Song Ci's uncanny abilities, he thought hard for a plan to cover his tracks.

When, on that day, Shu Gengshi learned that Song Ci was already at the customs office investigating the case, he had a premonition that things were not going to turn out well. He sent Liang E to keep an eye on the situation, under cover of darkness, with the instructions: "If it looks like all is discovered, spare no efforts to assassinate Song Ci and his party. If Wu Cheng is found out, then kill him likewise."

Then Song Ci succumbed to his old illness before he had had a chance to uncover any clues, and he returned to the secretariat. Even when Shu Gengshi heard this, he didn't dare relax, and ordered the surveillance to be maintained. That night, Liang E and the others discovered that Tong Gong and Huo Xiong were returning to the customs office; he realised there must have been some kind of development, so he followed them. He led his men to Wu Cheng's quarters in the side courtyard, and when the secretary came back and reported on his eavesdropping of the new investigation, Liang E drew his sword and cut Wu Cheng's throat. Then he waited quietly for Tong Gong and the others to come...

The reason Tong Gong had gone back to break into Shu Gengshi's offices was to recover Xu Tiju's handwritten letter of denunciation. The masked man who had been hit by Tong Gong's knife and fallen back from the top of the wall, was also a long-time follower and confidant of Shu Gengshi. He had told Tong Gong that Shu was in possession of the letter, and Tong Gong determined to retrieve it.

Mistress Xu did her best to dissuade him: "The murderer has already confessed. Why put your head back in the lion's mouth just to get that letter?"

Tong Gong didn't agree: "Throughout his career, Lord Song has always valued solid evidence. A spoken confession is not reliable enough. If this letter implicates the inspectors and the pirates in this affair, then we have got to have it."

Xu Hong joined in his mother's urgings. "The judicial commissioner's office at Panshan is heavily guarded," he said, "and you don't know where the letter is hidden. It won't be easy to find. Why not go back and make your report to Lord Song, and then make a proper plan in the morning?"

"It can't wait until tomorrow," Tong Gong replied. "When Liang E goes back and tells Shu Gengshi what has happened, an old fox like Shu will certainly act tonight. If he destroys the letter, then our case will be in all kinds of trouble."

Tong Gong took his short knife, thrust it down the side of his leggings and was about to leave.

"You can't go," Mistress Xu insisted. "I can't bear to see you put yourself in danger like this."

"Honoured Sir, please listen to a young man," Xu Hong chimed in, falling to his knees in front of Tong Gong. "I have already seen that you are tremendously skilled in martial arts, and are both brave and cunning. But if you go to the commissioner's office tonight, you will be stirring up a hornet's nest. Shu Gengshi is both cunning and resourceful. Everything points to disaster. And if some misfortune does befall you, how will Lord Song cope without you?"

Xu Hong recalled how his father had been killed by his most trusted secretary, and he fell to silent weeping.

"Get up, and stop this nonsense!" said Tong Gong, lifting Xu Hong to his feet. "Lord Song never lets go of an unfinished case – he hangs onto it like a coiling snake, like an avenging demon. Now he has been laid low by his old illness, I have undertaken to uncover the truth of this case. My master will not be able to relax until I have found solid evidence. And he won't get better until he can relax."

These stirring words, spoken with such heartfelt emotion, deeply moved Mistress Xu, her son and all the soldiers who were also gathered there. Tong Gong ordered Huo Xiong, who had suffered a broken right arm and serious internal injuries, to return to the secretariat to make a report, while he set out to put his head firmly in the lion's mouth.

Huo Xiong's hurried explanation of the situation caused consternation all around. "We must send reinforcements to Tong Gong immediately," Qiu Juan said to her mother.

"Go and tell the aides to send troops to the Commissioner's office. They are to act as the situation demands," Mistress Song replied.

"I'll go," Huo Xiong said, rising from his chair, but he only managed a couple of steps before he stumbled and fell.

Qi'er hurried to help him up.

"You must let me set your arm and see to your injuries this instant," said the doctor.

Qiu Juan left the room to pass on Mistress Song's orders. Huo Xiong contented himself with giving Mistress Song a detailed description of the new autopsy results.

The secretariat burst into life, and the neighing of horses could be heard through the window. As the sound of hoofbeats receded into the distance, Song Ci's eyelids flickered, as though startled by the sound. He was waking up.


"Husband! Husband!" Mistress Song cried out.

Song Ci's eyelids flickered again and then opened with an effort. He saw Qi'er, and his face twitched in what might have been a smile. Then he looked at his wife, and their eyes met. His parched lips moved and he said in a faint voice: "Tong Gong... Huo Xiong..."

Mistress Song wiped away her tears, and with the same faint smile as of old, whispered gently in Song Ci's ear: "You were right. They did indeed use a foreign object when they strangled him. Huo Xiong has returned. He says when they re-examined the body, they found faint marks on the back of the neck. When they measured the circumference of the purple bruising on the neck, it wasn't consistent with suicide. And on either side they found white marks that indicated post-mortem suspension, standing out from the purple bruising. It was clear that a wooden strip, wider than the neck, had been used as a spacer."

When Song Ci heard this, his eyes remained motionless, but his wife could tell he was considering the evidence.

"Husband," she continued, "do you remember when Old Man Huo told you about the Indian madder. The murderers used Indian madder juice to fake the injuries. Huo Xiong and Tong Gong used dried madder juice to wash it off, and they revealed faint knife marks in several places. It was clear that Xu Tiju had put up a fight, and there was probably more than one assailant…"

Song Ci's eyes remained still as he listened, but when his wife stopped abruptly, he raised them to look at her and asked: "What happened next?"

She shook her head and said: "Still… still at the customs office."

Song Ci frowned slightly and asked: "Who is still at the customs office?"

Mistress Song decided she had to keep the truth from her husband, so she smiled hurriedly and lied: "Why… Tong Gong and the others."

But as she spoke, tears filled her eyes. She was thinking that, in all their lifetime together, she had never before kept anything from Song Ci. So why now was she keeping this vital information from him?

"Yulan, you mustn't try to deceive me." Song Ci spoke after a moment's silence. Moreover, he used Yulan's name in front of Qi'er and Qiu Juan. Yulan felt as though her heart was on fire. She thought of the time when Song Ci had composed the chapter on 'Guiding Principles of Investigation' at the front of *Collected Cases of Injustice Righted*, and of his hope that the book would be endorsed by the emperor and become the gold standard for law enforcement officials throughout the empire. And later, when *Collected Cases* did indeed receive imperial approval, how, because of it, Song Ci was appointed inspector of the four highways. Now, right across the empire, every official knew the work by heart, and even the most self-important, most influential people in the land did not dare break the law. From then on, and after a lifetime of effort, Song Ci was deeply content to have produced something to make his ancestors proud, and in which he himself could take pleasure. But now, the ringleader in this case was part of the legal establishment in Guangdong, the highest legislative and investigative official. If she told him the truth, would it upset him? Just at the moment, she did not wish to cause her husband the least distress.

Moreover, Song Ci and Tong Gong had been as close as the wind and the rain for more than twenty years, and they had experienced many hardships together. Song Ci treated Tong Gong like a son, had taught him all the arts of criminal investigation and had tried to protect him from danger. But now, if her husband knew the situation Tong Gong found himself in... Mistress Song did not know what to do for the best.

"Yulan, since we know that... they used a foreign object... the case is now straightforward," Song Ci said.

Yulan was in turmoil. Even when ill, her husband was no easy man to deceive. Supposing she failed; doubt was written all over her face, and her eyes were full of tears – how could she hope to fool this man who had known her innermost thoughts for so many years? She tried to stem her tears, but to no avail.

"Yulan, are Tong Gong and the others in some kind of..."

She saw her husband's eyes gradually fill with apprehension. She felt as though her heart was being split with a knife. If he suspected that Tong Gong was in danger, then the distress would surely break him. But even as she had this thought, her determination to deceive her husband crumbled away. As a wife she had to be completely truthful with her husband. As she spoke, she took his hand and stroked it gently, and tears fell like rain from her eyes. To her surprise, after she had told him everything, her husband stayed extraordinarily calm.

It was as if he had arrived at some important new understanding. Even though his 'General Principles of Investigation' had been endorsed by the emperor, that was still not enough to stop officers of the law consciously going against it. The usefulness of his book *Collected Cases of Injustice Righted* to future generations, the book into which he had put every drop of his life's blood, might actually be limited.

The appearance of a case of 'strangulation through a foreign object' was a perfect illustration of man's ingenuity. Each generation surpassed the previous one in cunning, but each generation also went further than its predecessors in the skills it brought to solving cases. So all scholarship had limits to its value, and would be replaced by new discoveries – his own book was no exception. Thus the most important thing was to emulate Mr Zhen Dexiu's aspiration when he returned to his home town to open a school: to ensure that the empire had a constant supply of fresh blood dedicated to strengthening the state and protecting the people.

This then reminded him of his old friend, Liu Kezhuang, who, last summer, had displeased the prime minister Shi Songzhi, and been removed from office for the fourth time. At the time, Song Ci had been on a tour of inspection of the Jiangnan Eastern Highway. It was the same route that Liu Kezhuang took on his way home, and the two old friends met when he caught up with Song Ci in Xinzhou in the north-west of Jiangxi Province's Shangrao Prefecture. Song Ci had never seen Liu Kezhuang in tears before, but his old friend had sighed and wept as he spoke with him at length.

"The nation has not been without men of talent," Liu had said. "Even looking no further back than the empire's retreat to the south, as civilian officials we have seen Li Gang, Zhu Xi, Zhen Dexiu. Those who combined military and civil office included Yue Fei, Zong Ze and Xin Qiji. But did the court ever use them and value them properly? Whatever good each one of them achieved at court was opposed by the toadies and the flatterers, and belittled by the ranks of the dull-witted and ill-informed.

"Nor did the nation fall short in its people. Take the Two Rivers[1] Eight-Character Army[2] for example, and how deeply it moved people. In the Northern Song, the faces of soldiers were tattooed to prevent them deserting, a tactic strongly opposed by Sima Guang. But after the retreat south, the members of the Two Rivers Eight-Character Army voluntarily had the eight characters '赤心报国，誓杀金贼'[3] tattooed on their foreheads.

"The ancients said: 'Cook the dog after it has caught the rabbit. Put away your bow when the birds are gone. Discharge your ministers when the enemy has been defeated.' But recently, the court has been cooking the dog before it had caught the rabbit, hiding its bow before the birds had been shot and dismissing its ministers before the enemy had been defeated. If that is the case, how can the nation restore its glory, and how can the people find security? However you look at it, the line Du Fu wrote in his later years – 'For thieves and robbers, look among the emperor's ministers' – still stands as a stark warning through the generations.

"Ah, Brother Huifu, the ancients also said that a great mansion on the verge of collapse cannot be propped up with a single tree trunk. And that a vast dam about to burst cannot be plugged with a single stone. This perfectly illustrates my country's current state."

Liu Kezhuang then fell to weeping in silence. Song Ci was deeply moved, as it was quite unlike his old friend to be so pessimistic. He, himself, believed that the nation would always need people to govern, and the people would always wish for security. Recently, he had felt very keenly that you cannot build a great mansion with a single tree trunk, and nor is one stone enough to construct a mighty dam. The righting of wrongs, the preventing of outrages and keeping the common people content through honest reporting – these noble aims did indeed require a host of dedicated and well-educated scholars.

"Yulan, don't be sad..." In a faint voice, Song Ci tried to comfort his wife. He gave a slight nod. She realised that he wanted her to bring her head a little closer, so she leaned forward. He stretched out a withered hand and gently wiped the tears from her face. But however many he wiped away, more kept coming. He scrutinised his wife, her lined face covered in tears and the buxom charms of her youth all but vanished. Suddenly he remembered that his wife was entering her sixtieth year, and that her birthday was next month.

He recalled how, at his own celebrations, someone had mistakenly sent him a congratulatory couplet meant for a woman. He thought about telling her he was planning a big celebration for her too, but said nothing in case it distressed her even more. Her whole life, his wife had broken her heart with worry over him, so what could he do to offer her some comfort now? Finally he said: "Yulan, the book... the book..."

Of course, she knew immediately which book he meant, handing him the copy of *Collected Cases of Injustice Righted*.

He stroked it with a trembling hand. It was only after he had reached sixty that he had begun to write the book. If he had been content with his lot, and had no further agenda to pursue, then life would have gone on as usual, and there would have been no book. But that is not how it had been, and he had struggled through any obstacle to make it happen. He thought to himself that, if someone has a true passion that he stubbornly pursues through joy and disaster, then he can find joy even in that disaster, and rejoice in the task. Despite what he had originally hoped, his book's benefits to future generations would be limited, just as life inevitably ends in death. But this book was new-born and still had all its life ahead of it. He had given it its life, and his own life was contained within it, as well of the lives of his wife and his daughters. Its life represented the continuation of their own.

"Yulan... in the end... this book is our heritage."

With trembling hands, he tried to open the cover of the book. His wife helped him turn the pages to the frontispiece containing Song Ci's handwritten preface. Song Ci's eye fell on two rows of small characters at the end of the preface. He stroked them with his fingers: "Honoured scholars and officials who read this book, you may notice that there are some areas of investigation and examination that are not touched upon. In particular, these may be areas of which you have your own expert knowledge. I would ask you, please, to write such knowledge down and send it to me, so that I may rectify the omissions in future reprints of this book. Song Ci respectfully thanks you."

"Do you remember, Yulan?" Song Ci asked, his voice sounding as it had a lifetime ago.

"I remember... this is from before the book was printed. You went to the block-carving factory and added this in at the last moment." Mistress Song's hand trembled slightly in her husband's, and her voice was thin and tearful.

"Write an entry on 'strangulation through a foreign object' and add it to the section on 'making assault and strangulation look like suicide' at the end of chapter twenty in scroll three. Then reprint..."

As he spoke, Song Ci turned over on his side, with a huge effort, and gripped his wife's hand.

"Yes," she nodded, and said, through renewed sobs: "Husband, you are going to get better."

"Qi'er…"

"I'm here," Qi'er replied, putting her hand on her father's, and feeling how cold it was.

"Qi'er," he said, gripping her delicate hand. "I once said… I would take you back… to Jianyang…"

"Father." Qi'er was about to say they would go together once he was recovered, but the words wouldn't come and tears coursed down her cheeks.

"Qi'er… this is a really important case… no matter… how it turns out… you must write it up yourself… and find a way… to lay it before the emperor."

"Yes, Father. Now put it out of your mind."

"Don't worry about it now, Husband."

"Qiu Juan…" Song Ci looked for her.

"I'm here," Qiu Juan said, coming closer.

Song Ci's head moved slightly. His wife understood that he wanted Qiu Juan to come even closer, so she pushed her gently towards him. Song Ci moved his hand, and Qi'er released her own from her father's grip.

"Qiu Juan…" Song Ci opened his hand and looked at her.

Qiu Juan put one of her hands in his, and he gripped it tight. Her tears fell like rain. Qiu Juan and Mistress Song suddenly remembered the time when Mistress Song wanted Song Ci to take Qiu Juan as his concubine. Qiu Juan had the greatest respect for the way Mistress Song had treated her, and had thought of their relationship more as sisters than as mother and daughter. But then Song Ci had made the match between her and Tong Gong. She had given birth to Geng'er, and given him the Song family name. He had treated Geng'er as if he were his own grandson. Now, Song Ci was squeezing her hand tightly, and her own tears were flowing freely. She wept as she felt Song Ci's hand tremble, and she thought of how she had arrived in the Song household when she was only ten years old, and now she was forty-seven. Tears fell down her elegant face like raindrops on white marble. Song Ci raised his hand shakily towards Qiu Juan's face, but he wasn't strong enough. Qiu Juan leaned forward and put her face on his hand. He wiped away her tears, but that just made her cry harder. Song Ci's voice seemed to regain some of its old clarity as, still wiping her tears, he said: "Don't cry, Qiu Juan. Don't cry."

But as he spoke, his own tears began to flow. In all the years, neither Qiu Juan nor Mistress Song had ever seen him weep like this.

Qiu Juan, in her turn, wiped away his tears and said: "Father, you will get better… you will…"

"I'm fine." As he spoke, his face smoothed out, with no sign of pain or worry. His own tears continued to flow freely, and he stopped wiping away Qiu Juan's tears and placed his hand over Qiu Juan's, which had been doing the same for him, as if to say: "There's no need to wipe them away, just let them flow."

His hands began to tremble again as he took both of Qiu Juan's in them and grasped them firmly. Song Ci had always cherished her over many years, but never before had he held her hands. After Ah Xiang became the new Qi'er, Song Ci had often held her hand while they spoke, but never had he done so with Qiu Juan. Qiu Juan felt a strange heat in Song Ci's hands, and she seemed to draw strength from their grip.

"Qiu Juan," Song Ci said, looking straight into her eyes. "We never taught you to read and write, but I have always said that you are a woman among women, and quite extraordinary."

Qiu Juan gripped him even more tightly as her tears flooded down on both their hands together.

"Where is Geng'er?" Song Ci asked.

"He's here..." Qiu Juan embraced the nine-year-old Geng'er.

"Study!" Song Ci said, taking the boy's chubby little hand. "And when you grow up... work hard and become an official."

All around was the stillness just before dawn, and in it, Song Ci thought he could hear the sound of hoofbeats growing louder as they approached...

With the world still shrouded in darkness, along the wooded road to the secretariat, urgent hoofbeats could indeed be heard.

Several horses came flying along the road, the foremost one carrying the blood-stained figure of a man – Tong Gong. He was slumped motionless on his horse, just letting himself be carried along by it. Finally, he forced himself to raise his head and look... why was it so dark? He couldn't see a thing. Instinct told him he must be almost at the gates, but the road appeared to have got longer. His high-strung mount seemed to be alarmed by the quiet of the dawn, and as it sped along, the noise of its hooves shattered the still of the sleeping world...

# ENDNOTES

## 1. STORMY WEATHER

1. In ancient times, on reaching the age of twenty, a Chinese man of a certain standing, along with married women, would be addressed by an additional name as a mark of respect. This additional name was similar to the given name and conveyed aspirational virtues

## 1. THE MAID QIU JUAN

1. A *yamen* was the administrative office and/or residence of a local bureaucrat or mandarin in imperial China. A *yamen* can also be any governmental office or body headed by a mandarin, at any level of government: the offices of one of the Six Ministries is a *yamen*, but so is a prefectural magistracy

## 2. THE STRANGE GRIEVANCE OF THE TONG FAMILY

1. Five Li River, so named because it was situated about five *li* outside the city. A *li* is a traditional measure of distance equivalent to about 500 yards

## 2. ANOTHER HUMAN LIFE

1. 1131-1162

## 3. A WIFE HAS HER SAY

1. This zither still exists and was exhibited in 2016 at the Tianjin Museum. The name 'Ice in the Jade Ewer' refers to a phrase used in several poems of the Tang dynasty
2. Zhuge Liang was a chancellor and regent of the state of Shu Han during the Three Kingdoms period, when China was divided between the states of Wei, Shu and Wu. He was an important military strategist and statesman, as well as being an accomplished scholar and inventor

## 4. THE HALL OF TEN THOUSAND SCROLLS

1. The Five Dynasties cover the period between the fall of the Tang dynasty in 907 CE and the founding of the Song dynasty in 960 CE, when five aspiring dynasties followed one another in quick succession in north China
2. During the Song dynasty, the Hall of 10,000 Scrolls was owned by the Yu family, and the block-carving business had been passed down through the generations. Its reputation for the finest craftsmanship remained unrivalled over the 600 years from the Northern Song dynasty to the end of the Ming

### 5. THE LIANYUAN RUSHI TEMPLE

1. A martial arts weapon comprising a wooden fighting staff, one half painted red, the other white, one end rounded, the other slightly flattened

### 7. A SURPRISE ACQUISITION IN A CELLAR

1. The Jingkang Incident occurred in 1172 during the Jin-Song Wars when the forces of the Jurchen-led dynasty besieged Bianjing (Kaifeng). They captured the Song ruler, Emperor Qinzong and his father, Emperor Huizong, along with many of their family members and court officials. The event marked the end of the Northern Song dynasty

## CHAPTER V

1. In Chinese history, the Spring and Autumn period lasted from approximately 771 to 476 BCE, which corresponds roughly to the first half of the Eastern Zhou period, when China was beginning to fragment under the waning power of the ruling Zhou dynasty

### 1. THE ASTONISHMENT OF LIU KEZHUANG

1. In the third year of the Shaoxi period (1192), Zhu Xi built a lecture hall outside the west gate of Jianyang. Originally called the Bamboo Grove House, it later became known as Cangzhou House. Forty-four years after Zhu Xi's death, Emperor Lizong, as a mark of his deep respect for Zhu Xi, issued an imperial edict renaming it as the Examination Hall Institute

### 2. THE STRANGE CASE OF THE HARE'S FUR CUP

1. Originally, tea in China was drunk by whisking powdered leaves in the tea bowl, much as it still done in a Japanese tea ceremony. The Ming dynasty's founding emperor, Hongwu, however, preferred loose leaf tea, and from that time on this became the preferred method
2. Dōgen Zenji (1200-1253) was a Japanese Buddhist priest, writer, poet, philosopher and founder of the Sōtō school of Zen in Japan. Originally ordained as a monk in Kyoto, he was ultimately dissatisfied with its teaching and travelled to China to seek out what he believed to be a more authentic Buddhism
3. A unit of measurement, equivalent to a little over one pound in weight
4. An instrument of punishment formerly used in some Asian countries for petty criminals. It consists of a heavy wooden collar enclosing the neck and arms

### 4. THE ZHU XI MEMORIAL

1. A mythical creature that symbolises good luck or prosperity
2. This barbarous act is known as 'the faction prohibition of the Qingyuan era'

### 5. WHITE TIGER JOINT DISEASE

1. These were templates for the recording of autopsy examinations printed under the authority of the Ministry of Justice in the Southern Song dynasty
2. In Western medicine, serious joint pains such as acute arthritis, multiple arthralgia, or severe and migratory arthralgia

## 6. PLUM BLOSSOM FALLING IN THE WIND AND SNOW

1. Lu You (1125-1210), widely regarded as the greatest of the Southern Song poets

## 1. SMOKE FROM AN INCENSE BURNER

1. Located at the highest point of the muscle when thumb and index fingers are held together
2. From the space between the bottom of the thumb and forefinger to the crook of the elbow

## 2. ONE NIGHT

1. 画蛇添足 'Painting legs on the snake' is a Chinese saying that came originally from the ancient text *Strategies of the Warring States*. It tells the story of an artist who spoiled his painting of a snake by adding legs to it in order to show off his skill and speed. The meaning is the same as the English phrase 'over-egging the pudding', to spoil something by going too far

## 5. TAKING RESPONSIBILITY

1. An acupuncture point located at the top of the chest, under the throat

## 3. ANOTHER MURDER

1. Lateral to the fifth lumbar vertebra
2. *Qian* literally means 'copper coin' but here is used as a unit of weight. The standard unit of weight in ancient China was the 斤 jin or 'catty', equivalent to just over one pound. One *jin* subdivided into ten *liang* and 100 *qian*, so one *qian* was about one-eighth of an ounce

## 1. THEFT OF A CATTY OF SALT

1. The trigrams and hexagrams of the Book of Changes are ordered in conjunction with the Ten Heavenly Stems and Twelve Earthly Branches of the traditional sixty-year temporal cycle. All of them also coordinate with the five elements (earth, metal, wood, fire and water) and five directions (north, east, south, west and centre). The southerly flow of the river aligned it with the Celestial Stem 丁 (dīng) so it was originally called 丁水 (dīng shuǐ – Ding River/Water). Over time, the two characters merged, with 水 assuming its shortened form 氵, in the character 汀, pronounced Tīng
2. Hua Tuo (c. 140-208 CE) was a Chinese physician who lived in the late Eastern Han dynasty. The historical texts *Records of the Three Kingdoms* and *Book of the Later Han* record Hua as the first person in China to use anaesthesia during surgery

## 3. GRANDFATHER AND GRANDSON OF THE HUO FAMILY

1. Fu Rong, courtesy name Boxiu, formally Duke Ai of Yangping, was an official and general of the Di state of Former Qin. He was a younger brother of Fu Jiān, the third emperor of the state
2. One of the Wudang styles of Chinese martial arts. The name translates approximately as

'form-intention fist', or 'shape-will fist'. Internal form indicates that Song Ci is concerned with concentrating his internal energy, or *qi*

## 4. THE CASE OF THE WORMWOOD IMAGE

1. The seat of the body's energy, or *qi*. It is situated internally about three finger widths below the navel
2. Wang Shenzhi (862-925 CE), formally Prince Zhongyi of Min and later posthumously honoured as Emperor Taizu of Min, was the founder of the kingdom of Min on the southeast coast of China during the Five Dynasties and Ten Kingdoms period

## 5. THE CASE OF THE SWIM ACROSS THE LAKE

1. An ancient Chinese ball game recognised as being the earliest form of football. It was essentially a form of 'keepy-uppy', in which the use of the hands was not permitted, and the object was to kick a ball through an opening into a net

## 4. THE LIFE OF QIU JUAN

1. Liu Bei (161-223 CE) was a warlord in the late Eastern Han dynasty who founded the state of Shu Han in the Three Kingdoms period and became its first ruler. Despite early failings and lacking both the material resources and social status of his rivals, he gathered support among disheartened Han loyalists and led a popular movement to restore the Han dynasty

## 1. FAMINE IN A DROUGHT-STRICKEN LAND

1. An old Chinese measure of length, equal to about twelve feet

## 2. THE DU FAMILY COMPOUND

1. One *dou* is made up of ten *jin* and therefore equivalent to about ten pounds in weight

## 4. ON-THE-SPOT INVESTIGATION

1. 走马灯, literally a 'running horse lantern, is a device first recorded in the Qin dynasty (221-206 BCE) in which a carousel of horses or other figures mounted inside a lantern, rotate under the convection of heat from a candle or lamp, and appear as moving images on the 'screens' of the lantern's sides

## 2. THE FIVE-BLADED STEEL CLAW

1. Before the widespread use of clocks, time was sometimes measured in terms of how long it took to burn a standard-length incense stick. One stick took about thirty minutes, so 'half a stick of time' was around fifteen minutes

### 3. MIRACULOUS COLLECTION OF EVIDENCE

1. Liang Hongyu (1102-1135) was a general of the Song dynasty who became famous during the Jin-Song wars. She was the wife of Han Shizhong, a Song general also famous for his resistance against the Jin alongside Yue Fei and others. Her deeds passed into legend, and are celebrated in poetry, painting and opera. Along with Mulan, she is one of the most celebrated female warriors in Chinese history

### 6. PURE OF HEART

1. The 10,000 Generations Bridge
2. Bao Zheng (999-1062 CE), more commonly known as Bao Gong, was a government official under Emperor Renzong of the Northern Song dynasty. He was famous for his extreme honesty and uprightness, in which he showed no fear of offending his superiors, and no favour to family. He impeached an uncle of the emperor's favourite concubine, and imprisoned his own uncle. He became, and remains, a symbol of incorruptible justice in China

### 3. THE COTTON TREE FLOWERS BLOOM

1. A famous political philosopher of the Warring States period (475-221 BCE). He was the greatest representative of the Legalist school of thought that was particularly espoused, in opposition to Confucianism, by Qin Shi Huang, the first emperor

### 4. THE EXHUMATION AND INSPECTION OF BONES

1. One of the most prized of the southern hardwoods. It has no English name, but is a member of the Lauraceae family. It was the principal wood used in the construction of the Forbidden City

### 3. THE BRUSH AND INK LADY

1. A line from a poem by the Song dynasty official Kou Zhun, who was, in turn, borrowing from a poem by the Tang dynasty poet Wei Yingwu

### 4. A BOLT FROM THE BLUE

1. A type of arrow with a blunt metal or pottery whistle instead of an arrow head, which was used by the military for signalling

### 1. ON REACHING SIXTY YEARS

1. An ancient unit of area equivalent to 0.06 of a hectare

### 4. INSPECTOR AT LARGE

1. Although described a 'street', Yu Street was essentially an enclosed commercial district. Visitors to modern Chengdu can get a feel for what it was like in the reconstructed Jinli 'shopping street'

2. The name of an official post in the imperial service. During the Song dynasty, Scholars of the Zizheng Hall, the Guanwen Hall, the Longtu Pavilion and the Tianzhang Pavilion were equivalent in senior official rank to Scholars of the Imperial Academy
3. The four great trunk roads that connected the provinces south of the Yangtze in the Song dynasty

## 3. INVESTIGATION AT THE CUSTOMS OFFICE

1. A city in northeastern Jiangxi Province, Jingdezhen may have been producing pottery since as early as the sixth century CE. By the 14th century it had become the largest centre of production of Chinese porcelain. From the Ming period onwards, official kilns in Jingdezhen were controlled by the emperor, making imperial porcelain for the court and the emperor to give as gifts. It is still a centre of porcelain production today

## 4. STRANGULATION THROUGH A FOREIGN OBJECT

1. One of the first establishments in Guangzhou to cater for foreign merchants, the inn hosted many banquets and receptions
2. In the Tang and Song dynasties, people slept with elaborately moulded porcelain neck rests as pillows. The porcelain was supposed to have cooling properties, and the pillows were often decorated with auspicious designs to ward off evil spirits and bring good dreams
3. Strangulation through a foreign object to fake suicide is first recorded in Song Ci's *Collected Cases of Injustice Righted*. Highly respected forensic experts in China have said that, even hundreds of years after Song Ci's death, very few authors of forensic medical textbooks from any other country have recorded such a case

## 6. BEFORE DAWN

1. This refers to the two rivers of the Taihang Mountain region in northern China where the army was founded
2. The Eight-Character Army started out with 700 men but later swelled to several hundred thousand. It was established by the Song general Wang Yan and in 1140 it inflicted a crushing defeat on the main army of Jin Wuzhu in Anhui
3. Protect the nation with our hearts' blood – death to the Jin bandits

# ABOUT THE AUTHOR

**Wang Hongjia** is a celebrated scholar and cultural historian from Jianyang in Fujian province. He is vice-chairman of the Reportage Committee of the Chinese Authors' Association and deputy chairman of the Chinese Reportage Society. He has won a number of awards including the Chinese Book Prize, the Best Works Award, the Lu Xun Literary Prize, the Xu Chi Reportage Prize and the Bing Xin Essay Prize. He is considered the founder of a new style of documentary literature in the information age. His books *Information Revolution* and *The New Education Crisis* have had a profound influence on the development of contemporary education. Starting in 1979 he has reintroduced the almost forgotten figure of Song Ci to China and the rest of the world, through his writings, his lectures and through television dramas. He has visited South Korea, France and Russia to deliver lectures at international literary symposia.